breaking dawn

STEPHENIE MEYER

Megan Tingley Books

LITTLE, BROWN AND COMPANY

New York   Boston

Little, Brown and Company

Hachette Book Group
237 Park Avenue, New York, NY 10017
Visit our website at www.lb-teens.com

Little, Brown and Company is a division of Hachette Book Group, Inc.
The Little, Brown name and logo are trademarks of Hachette Book Group, Inc.

First Hardcover Edition: August 2008
First Special Edition: August 2009

ISBN 978-0-316-04461-5

Library of Congress Control Number: 2008928027

10 9 8 7 6 5 4 3 2 1

RRD-C

Printed in the United States of America

This book is dedicated to my ninja/agent, Jodi Reamer.
Thank you for keeping me off the ledge.

And thanks also to my favorite band,
the very aptly named Muse,
for providing a saga's worth of inspiration.

⤙ ⤚

BOOK ONE

⊰ ⊱

bella

CONTENTS

❖❖ ❖❖

PREFACE   1

1. ENGAGED   3

2. LONG NIGHT   23

3. BIG DAY   38

4. GESTURE   51

5. ISLE ESME   75

6. DISTRACTIONS   99

7. UNEXPECTED   118

Childhood is not from birth to a certain age and at a certain age
The child is grown, and puts away childish things.
Childhood is the kingdom where nobody dies.

Edna St. Vincent Millay

PREFACE

I'D HAD MORE THAN MY FAIR SHARE OF NEAR-DEATH
experiences; it wasn't something you ever really got used to.

It seemed oddly inevitable, though, facing death again.
Like I really *was* marked for disaster. I'd escaped time and
time again, but it kept coming back for me.

Still, this time was so different from the others.

You could run from someone you feared, you could
try to fight someone you hated. All my reactions were
geared toward those kinds of killers—the monsters, the
enemies.

When you loved the one who was killing you, it left you
no options. How could you run, how could you fight, when

doing so would hurt that beloved one? If your life was all you had to give your beloved, how could you not give it?

If it was someone you truly loved?

1. ENGAGED

NO ONE IS STARING AT YOU, I PROMISED MYSELF. *NO ONE IS staring at you. No one is staring at you.*

But, because I couldn't lie convincingly even to myself, I had to check.

As I sat waiting for one of the three traffic lights in town to turn green, I peeked to the right—in her minivan, Mrs. Weber had turned her whole torso in my direction. Her eyes bored into mine, and I flinched back, wondering why she didn't drop her gaze or look ashamed. It was still considered rude to stare at people, wasn't it? Didn't that apply to me anymore?

Then I remembered that these windows were so darkly tinted that she probably had no idea if it was even me in here, let alone that I'd caught her looking. I tried to take some comfort in the fact that she wasn't really staring at me, just the car.

My car. Sigh.

I glanced to the left and groaned. Two pedestrians were frozen on the sidewalk, missing their chance to cross as they stared. Behind them, Mr. Marshall was gawking through the plate-glass window of his little souvenir shop. At least he didn't have his nose pressed up against the glass. Yet.

The light turned green and, in my hurry to escape, I stomped on the gas pedal without thinking—the normal way I would have punched it to get my ancient Chevy truck moving.

Engine snarling like a hunting panther, the car jolted forward so fast that my body slammed into the black leather seat and my stomach flattened against my spine.

"Arg!" I gasped as I fumbled for the brake. Keeping my head, I merely tapped the pedal. The car lurched to an absolute standstill anyway.

I couldn't bear to look around at the reaction. If there had been any doubt as to who was driving this car before, it was gone now. With the toe of my shoe, I gently nudged the gas pedal down one half millimeter, and the car shot forward again.

I managed to reach my goal, the gas station. If I hadn't been running on vapors, I wouldn't have come into town at all. I was going without a lot of things these days, like Pop-Tarts and shoelaces, to avoid spending time in public.

Moving as if I were in a race, I got the hatch open, the cap off, the card scanned, and the nozzle in the tank within seconds. Of course, there was nothing I could do to make the numbers on the gauge pick up the pace. They ticked by sluggishly, almost as if they were doing it just to annoy me.

It wasn't bright out—a typical drizzly day in Forks, Washington—but I still felt like a spotlight was trained on me, drawing attention to the delicate ring on my left hand. At times like this, sensing the eyes on my back, it felt as if the ring were pulsing like a neon sign: *Look at me, look at me.*

It was stupid to be so self-conscious, and I knew that. Besides my dad and mom, did it really matter what people were saying about my engagement? About my new car? About my mysterious acceptance into an Ivy League college? About the shiny black credit card that felt red-hot in my back pocket right now?

"Yeah, who cares what they think," I muttered under my breath.

"Um, miss?" a man's voice called.

I turned, and then wished I hadn't.

Two men stood beside a fancy SUV with brand-new kayaks tied to the top. Neither of them was looking at me; they both were staring at the car.

Personally, I didn't get it. But then, I was just proud I could distinguish between the symbols for Toyota, Ford, and Chevy. This car was glossy black, sleek, and pretty, but it was still just a car to me.

"I'm sorry to bother you, but could you tell me what kind of car you're driving?" the tall one asked.

"Um, a Mercedes, right?"

"Yes," the man said politely while his shorter friend rolled his eyes at my answer. "I know. But I was wondering, is that . . . are you driving a Mercedes *Guardian*?" The man said the name with reverence. I had a feeling this guy would get along well with Edward Cullen, my . . . my fiancé (there really was no getting around that truth with the wedding just days away). "They aren't supposed to be available in Europe yet," the man went on, "let alone here."

While his eyes traced the contours of my car—it didn't look much different from any other Mercedes sedan to me, but what did I know?—I briefly contemplated my issues with words like *fiancé*, *wedding*, *husband*, etc.

I just couldn't put it together in my head.

On the one hand, I had been raised to cringe at the very thought of poofy white dresses and bouquets. But more than that, I just couldn't reconcile a staid, respectable, dull concept like *husband* with my concept of *Edward*. It was like casting an archangel as an accountant; I couldn't visualize him in any commonplace role.

Like always, as soon as I started thinking about Edward I was caught up in a dizzy spin of fantasies. The stranger had to clear his throat to get my attention; he was still waiting for an answer about the car's make and model.

"I don't know," I told him honestly.

"Do you mind if I take a picture with it?"

It took me a second to process that. "Really? You want to take a picture with the car?"

"Sure—nobody is going to believe me if I don't get proof."

"Um. Okay. Fine."

I swiftly put away the nozzle and crept into the front seat to hide while the enthusiast dug a huge professional-looking camera out of his backpack. He and his friend took turns posing by the hood, and then they went to take pictures at the back end.

"I miss my truck," I whimpered to myself.

Very, very convenient—too convenient—that my truck would wheeze its last wheeze just weeks after Edward and I had agreed to our lopsided compromise, one detail of which was that he be allowed to replace my truck when it passed on. Edward swore it was only to be expected; my truck had lived a long, full life and then expired of natural causes. According to him. And, of course, I had no way to verify his story or to try to raise my truck from the dead on my own. My favorite mechanic—

I stopped that thought cold, refusing to let it come to a conclusion. Instead, I listened to the men's voices outside, muted by the car walls.

". . . went at it with a flamethrower in the online video. Didn't even pucker the paint."

"Of course not. You could roll a tank over this baby. Not much of a market for one over here. Designed for Middle East diplomats, arms dealers, and drug lords mostly."

"Think *she's* something?" the short one asked in a softer voice. I ducked my head, cheeks flaming.

"Huh," the tall one said. "Maybe. Can't imagine what you'd need missile-proof glass and four thousand pounds of body armor for around here. Must be headed somewhere more hazardous."

Body armor. *Four thousand pounds* of body armor. And *missile*-proof glass? Nice. What had happened to good old-fashioned bulletproof?

Well, at least this made some sense—if you had a twisted sense of humor.

It wasn't like I hadn't expected Edward to take advantage of our deal, to weight it on his side so that he could give so much more than he would receive. I'd agreed that he could replace my truck when it needed replacing, not expecting that moment to come quite so soon, of course. When I'd been forced to admit that the truck had become no more than a still-life tribute to classic Chevys on my curb, I knew his idea of a replacement was probably going to embarrass me. Make me the focus of stares and whispers. I'd been right about that part. But even in my darkest imaginings I had not foreseen that he would get me *two* cars.

The "before" car and the "after" car, he'd explained when I'd flipped out.

This was just the "before" car. He'd told me it was a loaner and promised that he was returning it after the wedding. It all had made absolutely no sense to me. Until now.

Ha ha. Because I was so fragilely human, so accident-prone, so much a victim to my own dangerous bad luck, apparently I needed a tank-resistant car to keep me safe. Hilarious. I was sure he and his brothers had enjoyed the joke quite a bit behind my back.

Or maybe, just maybe, a small voice whispered in my head, *it's not a joke, silly. Maybe he's really that worried about you. This wouldn't be the first time he's gone a little overboard trying to protect you.*

I sighed.

I hadn't seen the "after" car yet. It was hidden under a sheet in the deepest corner of the Cullens' garage. I knew most people would have peeked by now, but I really didn't want to know.

Probably no body armor on that car—because I wouldn't need it after the honeymoon. Virtual indestructibility was just one of the many perks I was looking forward to. The best parts about being a Cullen were not expensive cars and impressive credit cards.

"Hey," the tall man called, cupping his hands to the glass in an effort to peer in. "We're done now. Thanks a lot!"

"You're welcome," I called back, and then tensed as I started the engine and eased the pedal—ever so gently—down. . . .

No matter how many times I drove down the familiar road home, I still couldn't make the rain-faded flyers fade into the background. Each one of them, stapled to telephone poles and taped to street signs, was like a fresh slap in the face. A well-deserved slap in the face. My mind was sucked back into the thought I'd interrupted so immediately before. I couldn't avoid it on this road. Not with pictures of *my favorite mechanic* flashing past me at regular intervals.

My best friend. My Jacob.

The HAVE YOU SEEN THIS BOY? posters were not Jacob's father's idea. It had been *my* father, Charlie, who'd printed up the flyers and spread them all over town. And not just Forks, but Port Angeles and Sequim and Hoquiam and Aberdeen and every other town in the Olympic Peninsula. He'd made sure that all the police stations in the state of Washington had the same flyer hanging on the wall, too. His own station had a whole corkboard dedicated to finding Jacob. A corkboard that was mostly empty, much to his disappointment and frustration.

My dad was disappointed with more than the lack of response. He was most disappointed with Billy, Jacob's father—and Charlie's closest friend.

For Billy's not being more involved with the search for his sixteen-year-old "runaway." For Billy's refusing to put up the flyers in La Push, the reservation on the coast that was Jacob's home. For his seeming resigned to Jacob's disappearance, as if there was nothing he could do. For his saying, "Jacob's grown up now. He'll come home if he wants to."

And he was frustrated with me, for taking Billy's side.

I wouldn't put up posters, either. Because both Billy and I knew where Jacob was, roughly speaking, and we also knew that no one had seen this *boy*.

The flyers put the usual big, fat lump in my throat, the usual stinging tears in my eyes, and I was glad Edward was out hunting this Saturday. If Edward saw my reaction, it would only make him feel terrible, too.

Of course, there were drawbacks to it being Saturday. As I turned slowly and carefully onto my street, I could see my dad's police cruiser in the driveway of our home. He'd skipped fishing again today. Still sulking about the wedding.

So I wouldn't be able to use the phone inside. But I *had* to call. . . .

I parked on the curb behind the Chevy sculpture and pulled the cell phone Edward had given me for emergencies out of the glove compartment. I dialed, keeping my finger on the "end" button as the phone rang. Just in case.

"Hello?" Seth Clearwater answered, and I sighed in relief. I was way too chicken to speak to his older sister, Leah. The phrase "bite my head off" was not entirely a figure of speech when it came to Leah.

"Hey, Seth, it's Bella."

"Oh, hiya, Bella! How are you?"

Choked up. Desperate for reassurance. "Fine."

"Calling for an update?"

"You're psychic."

"Not hardly. I'm no Alice—you're just predictable," he joked. Among the Quileute pack down at La Push, only Seth was comfortable even mentioning the Cullens by name, let alone joking about things like my nearly omniscient sister-in-law-to-be.

"I know I am." I hesitated for a minute. "How is he?"

Seth sighed. "Same as ever. He won't talk, though we know he hears us. He's trying not to think *human*, you know. Just going with his instincts."

"Do you know where he is now?"

"Somewhere in northern Canada. I can't tell you which province. He doesn't pay much attention to state lines."

"Any hint that he might . . ."

"He's not coming home, Bella. Sorry."

I swallowed. "S'okay, Seth. I knew before I asked. I just can't help wishing."

"Yeah. We all feel the same way."

"Thanks for putting up with me, Seth. I know the others must give you a hard time."

"They're not your hugest fans," he agreed cheerfully. "Kind of lame, I think. Jacob made his choices, you made yours. Jake doesn't like their attitude about it. 'Course, he isn't super thrilled that you're checking up on him, either."

I gasped. "I thought he wasn't talking to you?"

"He can't hide everything from us, hard as he's trying."

So Jacob knew I was worried. I wasn't sure how I felt about that. Well, at least he knew I hadn't skipped off into the sunset and forgotten him completely. He might have imagined me capable of that.

"I guess I'll see you at the . . . wedding," I said, forcing the word out through my teeth.

"Yeah, me and my mom will be there. It was cool of you to ask us."

I smiled at the enthusiasm in his voice. Though inviting the Clearwaters had been Edward's idea, I was glad he'd thought of it. Having Seth there would be nice—a link, however tenuous, to my missing best man. "It wouldn't be the same without you."

"Tell Edward I said hi, 'kay?"

"Sure thing."

I shook my head. The friendship that had sprung up between Edward and Seth was something that still boggled my mind. It was proof, though, that things didn't have to be this way. That vampires and werewolves could get along just fine, thank you very much, if they were of a mind to.

Not everybody liked this idea.

"Ah," Seth said, his voice cracking up an octave. "Er, Leah's home."

"Oh! Bye!"

The phone went dead. I left it on the seat and prepared myself mentally to go inside the house, where Charlie would be waiting.

My poor dad had so much to deal with right now. Jacob-the-runaway was just *one* of the straws on his overburdened back. He was almost as worried about me, his barely-a-legal-adult daughter who was about to become a Mrs. in just a few days' time.

I walked slowly through the light rain, remembering the night we'd told him. . . .

*   *   *

As the sound of Charlie's cruiser announced his return, the ring suddenly weighed a hundred pounds on my finger. I wanted to shove my left hand in a pocket, or maybe sit on it, but Edward's cool, firm grasp kept it front and center.

"Stop fidgeting, Bella. Please try to remember that you're not confessing to a murder here."

"Easy for you to say."

I listened to the ominous sound of my father's boots clomping up the sidewalk. The key rattled in the already open door. The sound reminded me of that part of the horror movie when the victim realizes she's forgotten to lock her deadbolt.

"Calm down, Bella," Edward whispered, listening to the acceleration of my heart.

The door slammed against the wall, and I flinched like I'd been Tasered.

"Hey, Charlie," Edward called, entirely relaxed.

"No!" I protested under my breath.

"What?" Edward whispered back.

"Wait till he hangs his gun up!"

Edward chuckled and ran his free hand through his tousled bronze hair.

Charlie came around the corner, still in his uniform, still armed, and tried not to make a face when he spied us sitting together on the loveseat. Lately, he'd been putting forth a lot of effort to like Edward more. Of course, this revelation was sure to end that effort immediately.

"Hey, kids. What's up?"

"We'd like to talk to you," Edward said, so serene. "We have some good news."

Charlie's expression went from strained friendliness to black suspicion in a second.

"Good news?" Charlie growled, looking straight at me.

"Have a seat, Dad."

He raised one eyebrow, stared at me for five seconds, then stomped to the recliner and sat down on the very edge, his back ramrod straight.

"Don't get worked up, Dad," I said after a moment of loaded silence. "Everything's okay."

Edward grimaced, and I knew it was in objection to the word *okay*. He probably would have used something more like *wonderful* or *perfect* or *glorious*.

"Sure it is, Bella, sure it is. If everything is so great, then why are you sweating bullets?"

"I'm not sweating," I lied.

I leaned away from his fierce scowl, cringing into Edward, and instinctively wiped the back of my right hand across my forehead to remove the evidence.

"You're pregnant!" Charlie exploded. "You're pregnant, aren't you?"

Though the question was clearly meant for me, he was glaring at Edward now, and I could have sworn I saw his hand twitch toward the gun.

"No! Of course I'm not!" I wanted to elbow Edward in the ribs, but I knew that move would only give me a bruise. I'd *told* Edward that people would immediately jump to this conclusion! What other possible reason would sane people have for getting married at eighteen? (His answer then had made me roll my eyes. *Love*. Right.)

Charlie's glower lightened a shade. It was usually pretty clear on my face when I was telling the truth, and he believed me now. "Oh. Sorry."

"Apology accepted."

There was a long pause. After a moment, I realized everyone was waiting for *me* to say something. I looked up at Edward, panic-stricken. There was no way I was going to get the words out.

He smiled at me and then squared his shoulders and turned to my father.

"Charlie, I realize that I've gone about this out of order. Traditionally, I should have asked you first. I mean no disrespect, but since Bella has already said yes and I don't want to diminish her choice in the matter, instead of asking you for her hand, I'm asking you for your blessing. We're getting married, Charlie. I love her more than anything in the world, more than my own life, and—by some miracle—she loves me that way, too. Will you give us your blessing?"

He sounded so sure, so calm. For just an instant, listening to the absolute confidence in his voice, I experienced a rare moment of insight. I could see, fleetingly, the way the world looked to him. For the length of one heartbeat, this news made perfect sense.

And then I caught sight of the expression on Charlie's face, his eyes now locked on the ring.

I held my breath while his skin changed colors—fair to red, red to purple, purple to blue. I started to get up—I'm not sure what I planned to do; maybe use the Heimlich maneuver to make sure he wasn't choking—but Edward squeezed my hand and murmured "Give him a minute" so low that only I could hear.

The silence was much longer this time. Then, gradually, shade by shade, Charlie's color returned to normal. His lips pursed, and his eyebrows furrowed; I recognized his "deep in thought" expression. He studied the two of us for a long moment, and I felt Edward relax at my side.

"Guess I'm not that surprised," Charlie grumbled. "Knew I'd have to deal with something like this soon enough."

I exhaled.

"You sure about this?" Charlie demanded, glaring at me.

"I'm one hundred percent sure about Edward," I told him without missing a beat.

"Getting married, though? What's the rush?" He eyed me suspiciously again.

The rush was due to the fact that I was getting closer to nineteen every stinking day, while Edward stayed frozen in all his seventeen-year-old perfection, as he had for over ninety years. Not that this fact necessitated *marriage* in my book, but the wedding was required due to the delicate and tangled compromise Edward and I had made to finally get to this point, the brink of my transformation from mortal to immortal.

These weren't things I could explain to Charlie.

"We're going away to Dartmouth together in the fall, Charlie," Edward reminded him. "I'd like to do that, well, the right way. It's how I was raised." He shrugged.

He wasn't exaggerating; they'd been big on old-fashioned morals during World War I.

Charlie's mouth twisted to the side. Looking for an angle to argue from. But what could he say? *I'd prefer you live in sin first?* He was a dad; his hands were tied.

"Knew this was coming," he muttered to himself, frowning. Then, suddenly, his face went perfectly smooth and blank.

"Dad?" I asked anxiously. I glanced at Edward, but I couldn't read his face, either, as he watched Charlie.

"Ha!" Charlie exploded. I jumped in my seat. "Ha, ha, ha!"

I stared incredulously as Charlie doubled over in laughter; his whole body shook with it.

I looked at Edward for a translation, but Edward had his lips pressed tightly together, like he was trying to hold back laughter himself.

"Okay, fine," Charlie choked out. "Get married." Another roll of laughter shook through him. "But . . ."

"But what?" I demanded.

"But *you* have to tell your mom! I'm not saying one word to Renée! That's all yours!" He busted into loud guffaws.

* * *

I paused with my hand on the doorknob, smiling. Sure, at the time, Charlie's words had terrified me. The ultimate doom: telling Renée. Early marriage was higher up on her blacklist than boiling live puppies.

Who could have foreseen her response? Not me. Certainly not Charlie. Maybe Alice, but I hadn't thought to ask her.

"Well, Bella," Renée had said after I'd choked and stuttered out the impossible words: *Mom, I'm marrying Edward.* "I'm a little miffed that you waited so long to tell me. Plane tickets only get more expensive. Oooh," she'd fretted. "Do you think Phil's cast will be off by then? It will spoil the pictures if he's not in a tux—"

"Back up a second, Mom." I'd gasped. "What do you mean, waited so long? I just got en-en . . ."—I'd been unable to force out the word *engaged*—"things settled, you know, today."

"Today? Really? That *is* a surprise. I assumed . . ."

"What did you assume? *When* did you assume?"

"Well, when you came to visit me in April, it looked like things were pretty much sewn up, if you know what I mean. You're not very hard to read, sweetie. But I didn't say anything because I knew it wouldn't do any good. You're exactly like Charlie." She'd sighed, resigned. "Once you make up your mind, there is no reasoning with you. Of course, exactly like Charlie, you stick by your decisions, too."

And then she'd said the last thing that I'd ever expected to hear from my mother.

"You're not making my mistakes, Bella. You sound like you're scared silly, and I'm guessing it's because you're afraid of *me*." She'd giggled. "Of what I'm going to think. And I know I've said a lot of things about marriage and stupidity—and I'm not taking them back—but you need to realize that those things specifically applied to *me*. You're a completely different person than I am. You make your own kinds of mistakes, and I'm sure you'll have your share of regrets in life. But commitment was never your problem, sweetie. You have a better chance of making this work than most forty-year-olds I know." Renée had laughed again. "My little middle-aged child. Luckily, you seem to have found another old soul."

"You're not . . . mad? You don't think I'm making a humongous mistake?"

"Well, sure, I wish you'd wait a few more years. I mean, do I look old enough to be a mother-in-law to you? Don't answer that. But this isn't about me. This is about you. Are you happy?"

"I don't know. I'm having an out-of-body experience right now."

Renée had chuckled. "Does he make you happy, Bella?"

"Yes, but—"

"Are you ever going to want anyone else?"

"No, but—"

"But what?"

"But aren't you going to say that I sound exactly like every other infatuated teenager since the dawn of time?"

"You've never been a teenager, sweetie. You know what's best for *you*."

For the last few weeks, Renée had unexpectedly immersed herself in wedding plans. She'd spent hours every day on the phone with Edward's mother, Esme—no worries about the in-laws getting along. Renée *adored* Esme, but then, I doubted anyone could help responding that way to my lovable almost-mother-in-law.

It let me right off the hook. Edward's family and my family were taking care of the nuptials together without my having to do or know or think too hard about any of it.

Charlie was furious, of course, but the sweet part was that he wasn't furious at *me*. Renée was the traitor. He'd counted on her to play the heavy. What could he do now, when his ultimate threat—telling Mom—had turned out to be utterly empty? He had nothing, and he knew it. So he moped around the house, muttering things about not being able to trust anyone in this world. . . .

"Dad?" I called as I pushed open the front door. "I'm home."

"Hold on, Bells, stay right there."

"Huh?" I asked, pausing automatically.

"Gimme a second. Ouch, you got me, Alice."

Alice?

"Sorry, Charlie," Alice's trilling voice responded. "How's that?"

"I'm bleeding on it."

"You're fine. Didn't break the skin—trust me."

"What's going on?" I demanded, hesitating in the doorway.

"Thirty seconds, please, Bella," Alice told me. "Your patience will be rewarded."

"Humph," Charlie added.

I tapped my foot, counting each beat. Before I got to thirty, Alice said, "Okay, Bella, come in!"

Moving with caution, I rounded the little corner into our living room.

"Oh," I huffed. "Aw. Dad. Don't you look—"

"Silly?" Charlie interrupted.

"I was thinking more like *debonair*."

Charlie blushed. Alice took his elbow and tugged him around into a slow spin to showcase the pale gray tux.

"Now cut that out, Alice. I look like an idiot."

"No one dressed by me *ever* looks like an idiot."

"She's right, Dad. You look fabulous! What's the occasion?"

Alice rolled her eyes. "It's the final check on the fit. For both of you."

I peeled my gaze off the unusually elegant Charlie for the first time and saw the dreaded white garment bag laid carefully across the sofa.

"Aaah."

"Go to your happy place, Bella. It won't take long."

I sucked in a deep breath and closed my eyes. Keeping them shut, I stumbled my way up the stairs to my room. I stripped down to my underwear and held my arms straight out.

"You'd think I was shoving bamboo splinters under your nails," Alice muttered to herself as she followed me in.

I paid no attention to her. I was in my happy place.

In my happy place, the whole wedding mess was over and done. Behind me. Already repressed and forgotten.

We were alone, just Edward and me. The setting was fuzzy and constantly in flux—it morphed from misty forest to cloud-covered city to arctic night—because Edward was keeping the location of our honeymoon a secret to surprise me. But I wasn't especially concerned about the *where* part.

Edward and I were together, and I'd fulfilled my side of our compromise perfectly. I'd married him. That was the big one. But I'd also accepted all his outrageous gifts and was registered, however futilely, to attend Dartmouth College in the fall. Now it was his turn.

Before he turned me into a vampire—his big compromise—he had one other stipulation to make good on.

Edward had an obsessive sort of concern over the human things that I would be giving up, the experiences he didn't want me to miss. Most of them—like the prom, for example—seemed silly to me. There was only one human experience I worried about missing. Of course it would be the one he wished I would forget completely.

Here was the thing, though. I knew a little about what I was going to be like when I wasn't human anymore. I'd seen newborn vampires firsthand, and I'd heard all my family-to-be's stories about those wild early days. For several years, my biggest personality trait was going to be *thirsty*. It would take some time before I could be *me* again. And even when I was in control of myself, I would never feel exactly the way I felt now.

Human . . . and passionately in love.

I wanted the complete experience before I traded in my warm, breakable, pheromone-riddled body for something beautiful, strong . . . and unknown. I wanted a *real* honeymoon with Edward. And, despite the danger he feared this would put me in, he'd agreed to try.

I was only vaguely aware of Alice and the slip and slide of satin over my skin. I didn't care, for the moment, that the whole town was talking about me. I didn't think about the spectacle I would have to star in much too soon. I didn't worry about tripping on my train or giggling at the wrong moment or being too young or the staring audience or even the empty seat where my best friend should be.

I was with Edward in my happy place.

2. LONG NIGHT

"I MISS YOU ALREADY."

"I don't need to leave. I can stay. . . ."

"Mmm."

It was quiet for a long moment, just the thud of my heart hammering, the broken rhythm of our ragged breathing, and the whisper of our lips moving in synchronization.

Sometimes it was so easy to forget that I was kissing a vampire. Not because he seemed ordinary or human—I could never for a second forget that I was holding someone more angel than man in my arms—but because he made it seem like nothing at all to have his lips against my lips, my face, my throat. He claimed he was long past the temptation my blood used to be for him, that the idea of losing me had cured him of any desire for it. But I knew the smell of my blood still caused him pain—still burned his throat like he was inhaling flames.

I opened my eyes and found his open, too, staring at my face. It made no sense when he looked at me that way. Like I was the prize rather than the outrageously lucky winner.

Our gazes locked for a moment; his golden eyes were so deep that I imagined I could see all the way into his soul. It seemed silly that this fact—the existence of his soul—had ever been in question, even if he *was* a vampire. He had the most beautiful soul, more beautiful than his brilliant mind or his incomparable face or his glorious body.

He looked back at me as if he could see my soul, too, and as if he liked what he saw.

He couldn't see into my mind, though, the way he saw into everyone else's. Who knew why—some strange glitch in my brain that made it immune to all the extraordinary and frightening things some immortals could do. (Only my mind was immune; my body was still subject to vampires with abilities that worked in ways other than Edward's.) But I was seriously grateful to whatever malfunction it was that kept my thoughts a secret. It was just too embarrassing to consider the alternative.

I pulled his face to mine again.

"Definitely staying," he murmured a moment later.

"No, no. It's your bachelor party. You have to go."

I said the words, but the fingers of my right hand locked into his bronze hair, my left pressed tighter against the small of his back. His cool hands stroked my face.

"Bachelor parties are designed for those who are sad to

see the passing of their single days. I couldn't be more eager to have mine behind me. So there's really no point."

"True." I breathed against the winter-cold skin of his throat.

This was pretty close to my happy place. Charlie slept obliviously in his room, which was almost as good as being alone. We were curled up on my small bed, intertwined as much as it was possible, considering the thick afghan I was swathed in like a cocoon. I hated the necessity of the blanket, but it sort of ruined the romance when my teeth started chattering. Charlie would notice if I turned the heat on in August. . . .

At least, if *I* had to be bundled up, Edward's shirt was on the floor. I never got over the shock of how perfect his body was—white, cool, and polished as marble. I ran my hand down his stone chest now, tracing across the flat planes of his stomach, just marveling. A light shudder rippled through him, and his mouth found mine again. Carefully, I let the tip of my tongue press against his glass-smooth lip, and he sighed. His sweet breath washed—cold and delicious—over my face.

He started to pull away—that was his automatic response whenever he decided things had gone too far, his reflex reaction whenever he most wanted to keep going. Edward had spent most of his life rejecting any kind of physical gratification. I knew it was terrifying to him trying to change those habits now.

"Wait," I said, gripping his shoulders and hugging myself close to him. I kicked one leg free and wrapped it around his waist. "Practice makes perfect."

He chuckled. "Well, we should be fairly close to perfection

by this point, then, shouldn't we? Have you slept at all in the last month?"

"But this is the dress rehearsal," I reminded him, "and we've only practiced certain scenes. It's no time for playing safe."

I thought he would laugh, but he didn't answer, and his body was motionless with sudden stress. The gold in his eyes seemed to harden from a liquid to a solid.

I thought over my words, realized what he would have heard in them.

"Bella . . . ," he whispered.

"Don't start this again," I said. "A deal's a deal."

"I don't know. It's too hard to concentrate when you're with me like this. I—I can't think straight. I won't be able to control myself. You'll get hurt."

"I'll be fine."

"Bella . . ."

"Shh!" I pressed my lips to his to stop his panic attack. I'd heard it before. He wasn't getting out of this deal. Not after insisting I marry him first.

He kissed me back for a moment, but I could tell he wasn't as into it as before. Worrying, always worrying. How different it would be when he didn't need to worry about me anymore. What would he do with all his free time? He'd have to get a new hobby.

"How are your feet?" he asked.

Knowing he didn't mean that literally, I answered, "Toasty warm."

"Really? No second thoughts? It's not too late to change your mind."

"Are you trying to ditch me?"

He chuckled. "Just making sure. I don't want you to do anything you're not sure about."

"I'm sure about you. The rest I can live through."

He hesitated, and I wondered if I'd put my foot in my mouth again.

"Can you?" he asked quietly. "I don't mean the wedding—which I am positive you will survive despite your qualms—but afterward . . . what about Renée, what about Charlie?"

I sighed. "I'll miss them." Worse, that they would miss me, but I didn't want to give him any fuel.

"Angela and Ben and Jessica and Mike."

"I'll miss my friends, too." I smiled in the darkness. "Especially Mike. Oh, Mike! How will I go on?"

He growled.

I laughed but then was serious. "Edward, we've been through this and through this. I know it will be hard, but this is what I want. I want you, and I want you forever. One lifetime is simply not enough for me."

"Frozen forever at eighteen," he whispered.

"Every woman's dream come true," I teased.

"Never changing . . . never moving forward."

"What does that mean?"

He answered slowly. "Do you remember when we told Charlie we were getting married? And he thought you were . . . pregnant?"

"And he thought about shooting you," I guessed with a laugh. "Admit it—for one second, he honestly considered it."

He didn't answer.

"What, Edward?"

"I just wish . . . well, I wish that he'd been right."

"Gah," I gasped.

"More that there was some way he *could* have been. That we had that kind of potential. I *hate* taking that away from you, too."

It took me a minute. "I know what I'm doing."

"How could you know that, Bella? Look at my mother, look at my sister. It's not as easy a sacrifice as you imagine."

"Esme and Rosalie get by just fine. If it's a problem later, we can do what Esme did—we'll adopt."

He sighed, and then his voice was fierce. "It's not *right*! I don't want you to have to make sacrifices for me. I want to give you things, not take things away from you. I don't want to steal your future. If I were human—"

I put my hand over his lips. "*You* are my future. Now stop. No moping, or I'm calling your brothers to come and get you. Maybe you *need* a bachelor party."

"I'm sorry. I am moping, aren't I? Must be the nerves."

"Are *your* feet cold?"

"Not in that sense. I've been waiting a century to marry you, Miss Swan. The wedding ceremony is the one thing I can't wait—" He broke off mid-thought. "Oh, for the love of all that's holy!"

"What's wrong?"

He gritted his teeth. "You don't have to call my brothers. Apparently Emmett and Jasper are not going to let me bow out tonight."

I clutched him closer for one second and then released him. I didn't have a prayer of winning a tug-of-war with Emmett. "Have fun."

There was a squeal against the window—someone

deliberately scraping their steel nails across the glass to make a horrible, cover-your-ears, goose-bumps-down-your-spine noise. I shuddered.

"If you don't send Edward out," Emmett—still invisible in the night—hissed menacingly, "we're coming in after him!"

"Go," I laughed. "*Before* they break my house."

Edward rolled his eyes, but he got to his feet in one fluid movement and had his shirt back on in another. He leaned down and kissed my forehead.

"Get to sleep. You've got a big day tomorrow."

"Thanks! That's sure to help me wind down."

"I'll meet you at the altar."

"I'll be the one in white." I smiled at how perfectly blasé I sounded.

He chuckled, said, "Very convincing," and then suddenly sank into a crouch, his muscles coiled like a spring. He vanished—launching himself out my window too swiftly for my eyes to follow.

Outside, there was a muted thud, and I heard Emmett curse.

"You'd better not make him late," I murmured, knowing they could hear.

And then Jasper's face was peering in my window, his honey hair silver in the weak moonlight that worked through the clouds.

"Don't worry, Bella. We'll get him home in plenty of time."

I was suddenly very calm, and my qualms all seemed unimportant. Jasper was, in his own way, just as talented as Alice with her uncannily accurate predictions. Jasper's medium was moods rather than the future, and it was impossible to resist feeling the way he wanted you to feel.

I sat up awkwardly, still tangled in my blanket. "Jasper? What do vampires do for bachelor parties? You're not taking him to a strip club, are you?"

"Don't tell her anything!" Emmett growled from below. There was another thud, and Edward laughed quietly.

"Relax," Jasper told me—and I did. "We Cullens have our own version. Just a few mountain lions, a couple of grizzly bears. Pretty much an ordinary night out."

I wondered if I would ever be able to sound so cavalier about the "vegetarian" vampire diet.

"Thanks, Jasper."

He winked and dropped from sight.

It was completely silent outside. Charlie's muffled snores droned through the walls.

I lay back against my pillow, sleepy now. I stared at the walls of my little room, bleached pale in the moonlight, from under heavy lids.

My last night in my room. My last night as Isabella Swan. Tomorrow night, I would be Bella Cullen. Though the whole marriage ordeal was a thorn in my side, I had to admit that I liked the sound of that.

I let my mind wander idly for a moment, expecting sleep to take me. But, after a few minutes, I found myself more alert, anxiety creeping back into my stomach, twisting it into uncomfortable positions. The bed seemed too soft, too warm without Edward in it. Jasper was far away, and all the peaceful, relaxed feelings were gone with him.

It was going to be a very long day tomorrow.

I was aware that most of my fears were stupid—I just had to get over myself. Attention was an inevitable part of life. I couldn't always blend in with the scenery. However, I did have a few specific worries that were completely valid.

First there was the wedding dress's train. Alice clearly had let her artistic sense overpower practicalities on that one. Maneuvering the Cullens' staircase in heels and a train sounded impossible. I should have practiced.

Then there was the guest list.

Tanya's family, the Denali clan, would be arriving sometime before the ceremony.

It would be touchy to have Tanya's family in the same room with our guests from the Quileute reservation, Jacob's father and the Clearwaters. The Denalis were no fans of the werewolves. In fact, Tanya's sister Irina was not coming to the wedding at all. She still nursed a vendetta against the werewolves for killing her friend Laurent (just as he was about to kill me). Thanks to that grudge, the Denalis had abandoned Edward's family in their worst hour of need. It had been the unlikely alliance with the Quileute wolves that had saved all our lives when the horde of newborn vampires had attacked. . . .

Edward had promised me it wouldn't be dangerous to have the Denalis near the Quileutes. Tanya and all her family—besides Irina—felt horribly guilty for that defection. A truce with the werewolves was a small price to make up some of that debt, a price they were prepared to pay.

That was the big problem, but there was a small problem, too: my fragile self-esteem.

I'd never seen Tanya before, but I was sure that meeting

her wouldn't be a pleasant experience for my ego. Once upon a time, before I was born probably, she'd made her play for Edward—not that I blamed her or anyone else for wanting him. Still, she would be beautiful at the very least and magnificent at best. Though Edward clearly—if inconceivably—preferred me, I wouldn't be able to help making comparisons.

I had grumbled a little until Edward, who knew my weaknesses, made me feel guilty.

"We're the closest thing they have to family, Bella," he'd reminded me. "They still feel like orphans, you know, even after all this time."

So I'd conceded, hiding my frown.

Tanya had a big family now, almost as big as the Cullens. There were five of them; Tanya, Kate, and Irina had been joined by Carmen and Eleazar much the same way the Cullens had been joined by Alice and Jasper, all of them bonded by their desire to live more compassionately than normal vampires did.

For all the company, though, Tanya and her sisters were still alone in one way. Still in mourning. Because a very long time ago, they'd had a mother, too.

I could imagine the hole that loss would leave, even after a thousand years; I tried to visualize the Cullen family without their creator, their center, and their guide—their father, Carlisle. I couldn't see it.

Carlisle had explained Tanya's history during one of the many nights I'd stayed late at the Cullens' home, learning as much as I could, preparing as much as was possible for the future I'd chosen. Tanya's mother's story was one among many, a cautionary tale illustrating just one of the rules

I would need to be aware of when I joined the immortal world. Only one rule, actually—one law that broke down into a thousand different facets: *Keep the secret.*

Keeping the secret meant a lot of things—living inconspicuously like the Cullens, moving on before humans could suspect they weren't aging. Or keeping clear of humans altogether—except at mealtime—the way nomads like James and Victoria had lived; the way Jasper's friends, Peter and Charlotte, still lived. It meant keeping control of whatever new vampires you created, like Jasper had done when he'd lived with Maria. Like Victoria had failed to do with her newborns.

And it meant not creating some things in the first place, because some creations were uncontrollable.

"I don't know Tanya's mother's name," Carlisle had admitted, his golden eyes, almost the exact shade of his fair hair, sad with remembering Tanya's pain. "They never speak of her if they can avoid it, never think of her willingly.

"The woman who created Tanya, Kate, and Irina—who loved them, I believe—lived many years before I was born, during a time of plague in our world, the plague of the immortal children.

"What they were thinking, those ancient ones, I can't begin to understand. They created vampires out of humans who were barely more than infants."

I'd had to swallow back the bile that rose in my throat as I'd pictured what he was describing.

"They were very beautiful," Carlisle had explained quickly, seeing my reaction. "So endearing, so enchanting, you can't imagine. You had but to be near them to love them; it was an automatic thing.

"However, they could not be taught. They were frozen at whatever level of development they'd achieved before being bitten. Adorable two-year-olds with dimples and lisps that could destroy half a village in one of their tantrums. If they hungered, they fed, and no words of warning could restrain them. Humans saw them, stories circulated, fear spread like fire in dry brush. . . .

"Tanya's mother created such a child. As with the other ancients, I cannot fathom her reasons." He'd taken a deep, steadying breath. "The Volturi became involved, of course."

I'd flinched as I always did at that name, but of course the legion of Italian vampires—royalty in their own estimation—was central to this story. There couldn't be a law if there was no punishment; there couldn't be a punishment if there was no one to deliver it. The ancients Aro, Caius, and Marcus ruled the Volturi forces; I'd only met them once, but in that brief encounter, it seemed to me that Aro, with his powerful mind-reading gift—one touch, and he knew every thought a mind had ever held—was the true leader.

"The Volturi studied the immortal children, at home in Volterra and all around the world. Caius decided the young ones were incapable of protecting our secret. And so they had to be destroyed.

"I told you they were loveable. Well, covens fought to the last man—were utterly decimated—to protect them. The carnage was not as widespread as the southern wars on this continent, but more devastating in its own way. Long-established covens, old traditions, friends . . . Much was lost. In the end, the practice was completely eliminated. The immortal children became unmentionable, a taboo.

"When I lived with the Volturi, I met two immortal children, so I know firsthand the appeal they had. Aro studied the little ones for many years after the catastrophe they'd caused was over. You know his inquisitive disposition; he was hopeful that they could be tamed. But in the end, the decision was unanimous: the immortal children could not be allowed to exist."

I'd all but forgotten the Denali sisters' mother when the story returned to her.

"It is unclear precisely what happened with Tanya's mother," Carlisle had said. "Tanya, Kate, and Irina were entirely oblivious until the day the Volturi came for them, their mother and her illegal creation already their prisoners. It was ignorance that saved Tanya's and her sisters' lives. Aro touched them and saw their total innocence, so they were not punished with their mother.

"None of them had ever seen the boy before, or dreamed of his existence, until the day they watched him burn in their mother's arms. I can only guess that their mother had kept her secret to protect them from this exact outcome. But why had she created him in the first place? Who was he, and what had he meant to her that would cause her to cross this most uncrossable of lines? Tanya and the others never received an answer to any of these questions. But they could not doubt their mother's guilt, and I don't think they've ever truly forgiven her.

"Even with Aro's perfect assurance that Tanya, Kate, and Irina were innocent, Caius wanted them to burn. Guilty by association. They were lucky that Aro felt like being merciful that day. Tanya and her sisters were pardoned, but left with unhealing hearts and a very healthy respect for the law. . . ."

I'm not sure where exactly the memory turned into a dream. One moment it seemed that I was listening to Carlisle in my memory, looking at his face, and then a moment later I was looking at a gray, barren field and smelling the thick scent of burning incense in the air. I was not alone there.

The huddle of figures in the center of the field, all shrouded in ashy cloaks, should have terrified me—they could only be Volturi, and I was, against what they'd decreed at our last meeting, still human. But I knew, as I sometimes did in dreams, that I was invisible to them.

Scattered all around me were smoking heaps. I recognized the sweetness in the air and did not examine the mounds too closely. I had no desire to see the faces of the vampires they had executed, half afraid that I might recognize someone in the smoldering pyres.

The Volturi soldiers stood in a circle around something or someone, and I heard their whispery voices raised in agitation. I edged closer to the cloaks, compelled by the dream to see whatever thing or person they were examining with such intensity. Creeping carefully between two of the tall hissing shrouds, I finally saw the object of their debate, raised up on a little hillock above them.

He was beautiful, adorable, just as Carlisle had described. The boy was a toddler still, maybe two years of age. Light brown curls framed his cherubic face with its round cheeks and full lips. And he was trembling, his eyes closed as if he was too frightened to watch death coming closer every second.

I was struck with such a powerful need to save the lovely, terrified child that the Volturi, despite all their devastating menace, no longer mattered to me. I shoved past them, not caring if they realized my presence. Breaking free of them altogether, I sprinted toward the boy.

Only to stagger to a halt as I got a clear view of the hillock that he sat upon. It was not earth and rock, but a pile of human bodies, drained and lifeless. Too late not to see these faces. I knew them all—Angela, Ben, Jessica, Mike. . . . And directly beneath the adorable boy were the bodies of my father and my mother.

The child opened his bright, bloodred eyes.

3. BIG DAY

MY OWN EYES FLEW OPEN.

I lay shivering and gasping in my warm bed for several minutes, trying to break free of the dream. The sky outside my window turned gray and then pale pink while I waited for my heart to slow.

When I was fully back to the reality of my messy, familiar room, I was a little annoyed with myself. What a dream to have the night before my wedding! That's what I got for obsessing over disturbing stories in the middle of the night.

Eager to shake off the nightmare, I got dressed and headed down to the kitchen long before I needed to. First I cleaned the already tidy rooms, and then when Charlie was up I made him pancakes. I was much too keyed up to have any interest in eating breakfast myself—I sat bouncing in my seat while he ate.

"You're picking up Mr. Weber at three o'clock," I reminded him.

"I don't have that much to do today besides bring the minister, Bells. I'm not likely to forget my only job." Charlie had taken the entire day off for the wedding, and he was definitely at loose ends. Now and then, his eyes flickered furtively to the closet under the stairs, where he kept his fishing gear.

"That's not your only job. You also have to be dressed and presentable."

He scowled into his cereal bowl and muttered the words "monkey suit" under his breath.

There was a brisk tapping on the front door.

"You think you have it bad," I said, grimacing as I rose. "Alice will be working on me all day long."

Charlie nodded thoughtfully, conceding that he did have the lesser ordeal. I ducked in to kiss the top of his head as I passed—he blushed and *harrumph*ed—and then continued on to get the door for my best girlfriend and soon-to-be sister.

Alice's short black hair was not in its usual spiky do—it was smoothed into sleek pin curls around her pixie face, which wore a contrastingly businesslike expression. She dragged me from the house with barely a "Hey, Charlie" called over her shoulder.

Alice appraised me as I got into her Porsche.

"Oh, hell, look at your eyes!" She *tsk*ed in reproach. "What did you *do*? Stay up all night?"

"Almost."

She glowered. "I've only allotted so much time to make you stunning, Bella—you might have taken better care of my raw material."

"No one expects me to be stunning. I think the bigger problem is that I might fall asleep during the ceremony and not be able to say 'I do' at the right part, and then Edward will make his escape."

She laughed. "I'll throw my bouquet at you when it gets close."

"Thanks."

"At least you'll have plenty of time to sleep on the plane tomorrow."

I raised one eyebrow. *Tomorrow*, I mused. If we were heading out tonight after the reception, and we would still be on a plane tomorrow . . . well, we weren't going to Boise, Idaho. Edward hadn't dropped a single hint. I wasn't too stressed about the mystery, but it *was* strange not knowing where I would be sleeping tomorrow night. Or hopefully *not* sleeping . . .

Alice realized that she'd given something away, and she frowned.

"You're all packed and ready," she said to distract me.

It worked. "Alice, I wish you would let me pack my own things!"

"It would have given too much away."

"And denied you an opportunity to shop."

"You'll be my sister officially in ten short hours . . . it's about time to get over this aversion to new clothes."

I glowered groggily out the windshield until we were almost to the house.

"Is he back yet?" I asked.

"Don't worry, he'll be there before the music starts. But you don't get to see him, no matter when he gets back. We're doing this the traditional way."

I snorted. "Traditional!"

"Okay, aside from the bride and groom."

"You know he's already peeked."

"Oh no—that's why I'm the only one who's seen you in the dress. I've been very careful to not think about it when he's around."

"Well," I said as we turned into the drive, "I see you got to reuse your graduation decorations." Three miles of drive were once again wrapped in hundreds of thousands of twinkle lights. This time, she'd added white satin bows.

"Waste not, want not. Enjoy this, because you don't get to see the inside decorations until it's time." She pulled into the cavernous garage north of the main house; Emmett's big Jeep was still gone.

"Since when is the bride not allowed to see the decorations?" I protested.

"Since she put me in charge. I want you to get the full impact coming down the stairs."

She clapped her hand over my eyes before she let me inside the kitchen. I was immediately assailed by the scent.

"What is *that*?" I wondered as she guided me into the house.

"Is it too much?" Alice's voice was abruptly worried. "You're the first human in here; I hope I got it right."

"It smells wonderful!" I assured her—almost intoxicating,

but not at all overwhelming, the balance of the different fragrances was subtle and flawless. "Orange blossoms . . . lilac . . . and something else—am I right?"

"Very good, Bella. You only missed the freesia and the roses."

She didn't uncover my eyes until we were in her oversized bathroom. I stared at the long counter, covered in all the paraphernalia of a beauty salon, and began to feel my sleepless night.

"Is this really necessary? I'm going to look plain next to him no matter what."

She pushed me down into a low pink chair. "No one will dare to call you plain when I'm through with you."

"Only because they're afraid you'll suck their blood," I muttered. I leaned back in the chair and closed my eyes, hoping I'd be able to nap through it. I did drift in and out a little bit while she masked, buffed, and polished every surface of my body.

It was after lunchtime when Rosalie glided past the bathroom door in a shimmery silver gown with her golden hair piled up in a soft crown on top of her head. She was so beautiful it made me want to cry. What was even the point of dressing up with Rosalie around?

"They're back," Rosalie said, and immediately my childish fit of despair passed. Edward was home.

"Keep him out of here!"

"He won't cross you today," Rosalie reassured her. "He values his life too much. Esme's got them finishing things up out back. Do you want some help? I could do her hair."

My jaw fell open. I floundered around in my head, trying to remember how to close it.

I had never been Rosalie's favorite person in the world. Then, making things even more strained between us, she was personally offended by the choice I was making now. Though she had her impossible beauty, her loving family, and her soul mate in Emmett, she would have traded it all to be human. And here I was, callously throwing away everything she wanted in life like it was garbage. It didn't exactly warm her to me.

"Sure," Alice said easily. "You can start braiding. I want it intricate. The veil goes here, underneath." Her hands started combing through my hair, hefting it, twisting it, illustrating in detail what she wanted. When she was done, Rosalie's hands replaced hers, shaping my hair with a feather-light touch. Alice moved back to my face.

Once Rosalie received Alice's commendation on my hair, she was sent off to retrieve my dress and then to locate Jasper, who had been dispatched to pick up my mother and her husband, Phil, from their hotel. Downstairs, I could faintly hear the door opening and closing over and over. Voices began to float up to us.

Alice made me stand so that she could ease the dress over my hair and makeup. My knees shook so badly as she fastened the long line of pearl buttons up my back that the satin quivered in little wavelets down to the floor.

"Deep breaths, Bella," Alice said. "And try to lower your heart rate. You're going to sweat off your new face."

I gave her the best sarcastic expression I could manage. "I'll get right on that."

"I have to get dressed now. Can you hold yourself together for two minutes?"

"Um . . . maybe?"

She rolled her eyes and darted out the door.

I concentrated on my breathing, counting each movement of my lungs, and stared at the patterns that the bathroom light made on the shiny fabric of my skirt. I was afraid to look in the mirror—afraid the image of myself in the wedding dress would send me over the edge into a full-scale panic attack.

Alice was back before I had taken two hundred breaths, in a dress that flowed down her slender body like a silvery waterfall.

"Alice—wow."

"It's nothing. No one will be looking at me today. Not while you're in the room."

"Har har."

"Now, are you in control of yourself, or do I have to bring Jasper up here?"

"They're back? Is my mom here?"

"She just walked in the door. She's on her way up."

Renée had flown in two days ago, and I'd spent every minute I could with her—every minute that I could pry her away from Esme and the decorations, in other words. As far as I could tell, she was having more fun with this than a kid locked inside Disneyland overnight. In a way, I felt almost as cheated as Charlie. All that wasted terror over her reaction . . .

"Oh, Bella!" she squealed now, gushing before she was all the way through the door. "Oh, honey, you're so beautiful! Oh, I'm going to cry! Alice, you're amazing! You and Esme should go into business as wedding planners. Where did you find this dress? It's gorgeous! So graceful, so elegant. Bella, you look like you just stepped out of an Austen movie." My mother's voice sounded a little distance away, and everything in the room was slightly blurry. "Such a creative idea, designing the theme around Bella's ring. So romantic! To think it's been in Edward's family since the eighteen hundreds!"

Alice and I exchanged a brief conspiratorial look. My mom was off on the dress style by more than a hundred years. The wedding wasn't actually centered around the ring, but around Edward himself.

There was a loud, gruff throat-clearing in the doorway.

"Renée, Esme said it's time you got settled down there," Charlie said.

"Well, Charlie, don't you look dashing!" Renée said in a tone that was almost shocked. That might have explained the crustiness of Charlie's answer.

"Alice got to me."

"Is it really time already?" Renée said to herself, sounding almost as nervous as I felt. "This has all gone so fast. I feel dizzy."

That made two of us.

"Give me a hug before I go down," Renée insisted. "Carefully now, don't tear anything."

My mother squeezed me gently around the waist, then wheeled for the door, only to complete the spin and face me again.

"Oh goodness, I almost forgot! Charlie, where's the box?"

My dad rummaged in his pockets for a minute and then produced a small white box, which he handed to Renée. Renée lifted the lid and held it out to me.

"Something blue," she said.

"Something old, too. They were your Grandma Swan's," Charlie added. "We had a jeweler replace the paste stones with sapphires."

Inside the box were two heavy silver hair combs. Dark blue sapphires were clustered into intricate floral shapes atop the teeth.

My throat got all thick. "Mom, Dad . . . you shouldn't have."

"Alice wouldn't let us do anything else," Renée said. "Every time we tried, she all but ripped our throats out."

A hysterical giggle burst through my lips.

Alice stepped up and quickly slid both combs into my hair under the edge of the thick braids. "That's something old and something blue," Alice mused, taking a few steps back to admire me. "And your dress is new . . . so here—"

She flicked something at me. I held my hands out automatically, and the filmy white garter landed in my palms.

"That's mine and I want it back," Alice told me.

I blushed.

"There," Alice said with satisfaction. "A little color— that's all you needed. You are officially perfect." With a little self-congratulatory smile, she turned to my parents. "Renée, you need to get downstairs."

"Yes, ma'am." Renée blew me a kiss and hurried out the door.

"Charlie, would you grab the flowers, please?"

While Charlie was out of the room, Alice hooked the garter out of my hands and then ducked under my skirt. I gasped and tottered as her cold hand caught my ankle; she yanked the garter into place.

She was back on her feet before Charlie returned with the

two frothy white bouquets. The scent of roses and orange blossom and freesia enveloped me in a soft mist.

Rosalie—the best musician in the family next to Edward—began playing the piano downstairs. Pachelbel's Canon. I began hyperventilating.

"Easy, Bells," Charlie said. He turned to Alice nervously. "She looks a little sick. Do you think she's going to make it?"

His voice sounded far away. I couldn't feel my legs.

"She'd better."

Alice stood right in front of me, on her tiptoes to better stare me in the eye, and gripped my wrists in her hard hands.

"Focus, Bella. Edward is waiting for you down there."

I took a deep breath, willing myself into composure.

The music slowly morphed into a new song. Charlie nudged me. "Bells, we're up to bat."

"Bella?" Alice asked, still holding my gaze.

"Yes," I squeaked. "Edward. Okay." I let her pull me from the room, with Charlie tagging along at my elbow.

The music was louder in the hall. It floated up the stairs along with the fragrance of a million flowers. I concentrated on the idea of Edward waiting below to get my feet to shuffle forward.

The music was familiar, Wagner's traditional march surrounded by a flood of embellishments.

"It's my turn," Alice chimed. "Count to five and follow me." She began a slow, graceful dance down the staircase. I should have realized that having Alice as my only bridesmaid was a mistake. I would look that much more uncoordinated coming behind her.

A sudden fanfare trilled through the soaring music. I recognized my cue.

"Don't let me fall, Dad," I whispered. Charlie pulled my hand through his arm and then grasped it tightly.

One step at a time, I told myself as we began to descend to the slow tempo of the march. I didn't lift my eyes until my feet were safely on the flat ground, though I could hear the murmurs and rustling of the audience as I came into view. Blood flooded my cheeks at the sound; of course I could be counted on to be the blushing bride.

As soon as my feet were past the treacherous stairs, I was looking for him. For a brief second, I was distracted by the profusion of white blossoms that hung in garlands from everything in the room that wasn't alive, dripping with long lines of white gossamer ribbons. But I tore my eyes from the bowery canopy and searched across the rows of satin-draped chairs—blushing more deeply as I took in the crowd of faces all focused on me—until I found him at last, standing before an arch overflowing with more flowers, more gossamer.

I was barely conscious that Carlisle stood by his side, and Angela's father behind them both. I didn't see my mother where she must have been sitting in the front row, or my new family, or any of the guests—they would have to wait till later.

All I really saw was Edward's face; it filled my vision and overwhelmed my mind. His eyes were a buttery, burning gold; his perfect face was almost severe with the depth of his emotion. And then, as he met my awed gaze, he broke into a breathtaking smile of exultation.

Suddenly, it was only the pressure of Charlie's hand

on mine that kept me from sprinting headlong down the aisle.

The march was too slow as I struggled to pace my steps to its rhythm. Mercifully, the aisle was very short. And then, at last, at last, I was there. Edward held out his hand. Charlie took my hand and, in a symbol as old as the world, placed it in Edward's. I touched the cool miracle of his skin, and I was home.

Our vows were the simple, traditional words that had been spoken a million times, though never by a couple quite like us. We'd asked Mr. Weber to make only one small change. He obligingly traded the line "till death do us part" for the more appropriate "as long as we both shall live."

In that moment, as the minister said his part, my world, which had been upside down for so long now, seemed to settle into its proper position. I saw just how silly I'd been for fearing this—as if it were an unwanted birthday gift or an embarrassing exhibition, like the prom. I looked into Edward's shining, triumphant eyes and knew that I was winning, too. Because nothing else mattered but that I could stay with him.

I didn't realize I was crying until it was time to say the binding words.

"I do," I managed to choke out in a nearly unintelligible whisper, blinking my eyes clear so I could see his face.

When it was his turn to speak, the words rang clear and victorious.

"I do," he vowed.

Mr. Weber declared us husband and wife, and then Edward's hands reached up to cradle my face, carefully, as if it were as delicate as the white petals swaying above our heads. I tried to comprehend, through the film of tears blinding me, the surreal fact that this amazing person was *mine*. His golden eyes looked as if they would have tears, too, if such a thing were not impossible. He bent his head toward mine, and I stretched up on the tips of my toes, throwing my arms—bouquet and all—around his neck.

He kissed me tenderly, adoringly; I forgot the crowd, the place, the time, the reason . . . only remembering that he loved me, that he wanted me, that I was his.

He began the kiss, and he had to end it; I clung to him, ignoring the titters and the throat-clearing in the audience. Finally, his hands restrained my face and he pulled back— too soon—to look at me. On the surface his sudden smile was amused, almost a smirk. But underneath his momentary entertainment at my public exhibition was a deep joy that echoed my own.

The crowd erupted into applause, and he turned our bodies to face our friends and family. I couldn't look away from his face to see them.

My mother's arms were the first to find me, her tear-streaked face the first thing I saw when I finally tore my eyes unwillingly from Edward. And then I was handed through the crowd, passed from embrace to embrace, only vaguely aware of who held me, my attention centered on Edward's hand clutched tightly in my own. I did recognize the difference between the soft, warm hugs of my human friends and the gentle, cool embraces of my new family.

One scorching hug stood out from all the others—Seth Clearwater had braved the throng of vampires to stand in for my lost werewolf friend.

4. GESTURE

The wedding flowed into the reception party smoothly—proof of Alice's flawless planning. It was just twilight over the river; the ceremony had lasted exactly the right amount of time, allowing the sun to set behind the trees. The lights in the trees glimmered as Edward led me through the glass back doors, making the white flowers glow. There were another ten thousand flowers out here, serving as a fragrant, airy tent over the dance floor set up on the grass under two of the ancient cedars.

Things slowed down, relaxed as the mellow August evening surrounded us. The little crowd spread out under the soft shine of the twinkle lights, and we were greeted again by the friends we'd just embraced. There was time to talk now, to laugh.

"Congrats, guys," Seth Clearwater told us, ducking his head under the edge of a flower garland. His mother, Sue, was tight by his side, eyeing the guests with wary intensity. Her face was thin and fierce, an expression that was accented by her short, severe hairstyle; it was as short as her daughter Leah's—I wondered if she'd cut it the same way in a show of solidarity. Billy Black, on Seth's other side, was not as tense as Sue.

When I looked at Jacob's father, I always felt like I was seeing two people rather than just one. There was the old man in the wheelchair with the lined face and the white smile that everyone else saw. And then there was the direct descendant of a long line of powerful, magical chieftains, cloaked in the authority he'd been born with. Though the magic had—in the absence of a catalyst—skipped his generation, Billy was still a part of the power and the legend. It flowed straight through him. It flowed to his son, the heir to the magic, who had turned his back on it. That left Sam Uley to act as the chief of legends and magic now. . . .

Billy seemed oddly at ease considering the company and the event—his black eyes sparkled like he'd just gotten some good news. I was impressed by his composure. This wedding must have seemed a very bad thing, the worst thing that could happen to his best friend's daughter, in Billy's eyes.

I knew it wasn't easy for him to restrain his feelings, considering the challenge this event foreshadowed to the ancient treaty between the Cullens and the Quileutes— the treaty that prohibited the Cullens from ever creating another vampire. The wolves knew a breach was coming, but the Cullens had no idea how they would react. Before the alliance, it would have meant an immediate attack. A war. But now that they knew each other better, would there be forgiveness instead?

As if in response to that thought, Seth leaned toward Edward, arms extended. Edward returned the hug with his free arm.

I saw Sue shudder delicately.

"It's good to see things work out for you, man," Seth said. "I'm happy for you."

"Thank you, Seth. That means a lot to me." Edward pulled away from Seth and looked at Sue and Billy. "Thank you, as well. For letting Seth come. For supporting Bella today."

"You're welcome," Billy said in his deep, gravelly voice, and I was surprised at the optimism in his tone. Perhaps a stronger truce was on the horizon.

A bit of a line was forming, so Seth waved goodbye and wheeled Billy toward the food. Sue kept one hand on each of them.

Angela and Ben were the next to claim us, followed by Angela's parents and then Mike and Jessica—who were, to my surprise, holding hands. I hadn't heard that they were together again. That was nice.

Behind my human friends were my new cousins-in-law, the Denali vampire clan. I realized I was holding my breath as the vampire in front—Tanya, I assumed from the strawberry tint in her blond curls—reached out to embrace Edward. Next to her, three other vampires with golden eyes stared at me with open curiosity. One woman had long, pale blond hair, straight as corn silk. The other woman and the man beside her were both black-haired, with a hint of an olive tone to their chalky complexions.

And they were all four so beautiful that it made my stomach hurt.

Tanya was still holding Edward.

"Ah, Edward," she said. "I've missed you."

Edward chuckled and deftly maneuvered out of the hug, placing his hand lightly on her shoulder and stepping back, as if to get a better look at her. "It's been too long, Tanya. You look well."

"So do you."

"Let me introduce you to my wife." It was the first time Edward had said that word since it was officially true; he seemed like he would explode with satisfaction saying it now. The Denalis all laughed lightly in response. "Tanya, this is my Bella."

Tanya was every bit as lovely as my worst nightmares had predicted. She eyed me with a look that was much more speculative than it was resigned, and then reached out to take my hand.

"Welcome to the family, Bella." She smiled, a little rueful. "We consider ourselves Carlisle's extended family, and I *am* sorry about the, er, recent incident when we did not behave as such. We should have met you sooner. Can you forgive us?"

"Of course," I said breathlessly. "It's so nice to meet you."

"The Cullens are all evened up in numbers now. Perhaps it will be our turn next, eh, Kate?" She grinned at the blonde.

"Keep the dream alive," Kate said with a roll of her

golden eyes. She took my hand from Tanya's and squeezed it gently. "Welcome, Bella."

The dark-haired woman put her hand on top of Kate's. "I'm Carmen, this is Eleazar. We're all so very pleased to finally meet you."

"M-me, too," I stuttered.

Tanya glanced at the people waiting behind her— Charlie's deputy, Mark, and his wife. Their eyes were huge as they took in the Denali clan.

"We'll get to know each other later. We'll have *eons* of time for that!" Tanya laughed as she and her family moved on.

All the standard traditions were kept. I was blinded by flashbulbs as we held the knife over a spectacular cake—too grand, I thought, for our relatively intimate group of friends and family. We took turns shoving cake in each other's faces; Edward manfully swallowed his portion as I watched in disbelief. I threw my bouquet with atypical skill, right into Angela's surprised hands. Emmett and Jasper howled with laughter at my blush while Edward removed my borrowed garter—which I'd shimmied down nearly to my ankle— *very* carefully with his teeth. With a quick wink at me, he shot it straight into Mike Newton's face.

And when the music started, Edward pulled me into his arms for the customary first dance; I went willingly, despite my fear of dancing—especially dancing in front of an audience—just happy to have him holding me. He did all the work, and I twirled effortlessly under the glow of a canopy of lights and the bright flashes from the cameras.

"Enjoying the party, Mrs. Cullen?" he whispered in my ear.

I laughed. "That will take a while to get used to."

"We have a while," he reminded me, his voice exultant, and he leaned down to kiss me while we danced. Cameras clicked feverishly.

The music changed, and Charlie tapped on Edward's shoulder.

It wasn't nearly as easy to dance with Charlie. He was no better at it than I was, so we moved safely from side to side in a tiny square formation. Edward and Esme spun around us like Fred Astaire and Ginger Rogers.

"I'm going to miss you at home, Bella. I'm already lonely."

I spoke through a tight throat, trying to make a joke of it. "I feel just horrible, leaving you to cook for yourself—it's practically criminal negligence. You could arrest me."

He grinned. "I suppose I'll survive the food. Just call me whenever you can."

"I promise."

It seemed like I danced with everyone. It was good to see all my old friends, but I really wanted to be with Edward more than anything else. I was happy when he finally cut in, just half a minute after a new dance started.

"Still not that fond of Mike, eh?" I commented as Edward whirled me away from him.

"Not when I have to listen to his thoughts. He's lucky I didn't kick him out. Or worse."

"Yeah, right."

"Have you had a chance to look at yourself?"

"Um. No, I guess not. Why?"

"Then I suppose you don't realize how utterly, heart-breakingly beautiful you are tonight. I'm not surprised

Mike's having difficulty with improper thoughts about a married woman. I *am* disappointed that Alice didn't make sure you were forced to look in a mirror."

"You are very biased, you know."

He sighed and then paused and turned me around to face the house. The wall of glass reflected the party back like a long mirror. Edward pointed to the couple in the mirror directly across from us.

"Biased, am I?"

I caught just a glimpse of Edward's reflection—a perfect duplicate of his perfect face—with a dark-haired beauty at his side. Her skin was cream and roses, her eyes were huge with excitement and framed with thick lashes. The narrow sheath of the shimmering white dress flared out subtly at the train almost like an inverted calla lily, cut so skillfully that her body looked elegant and graceful—while it was motionless, at least.

Before I could blink and make the beauty turn back into me, Edward suddenly stiffened and turned automatically in the other direction, as if someone had called his name.

"Oh!" he said. His brow furrowed for an instant and then smoothed out just as quickly.

Suddenly, he was smiling a brilliant smile.

"What is it?" I asked.

"A surprise wedding gift."

"Huh?"

He didn't answer; he just started dancing again, spinning me the opposite way we'd been headed before, away from the lights and then into the deep swath of night that ringed the luminous dance floor.

He didn't pause until we reached the dark side of one

of the huge cedars. Then Edward looked straight into the blackest shadow.

"Thank you," Edward said to the darkness. "This is very . . . kind of you."

"Kind is my middle name," a husky familiar voice answered from the black night. "Can I cut in?"

My hand flew up to my throat, and if Edward hadn't been holding me I would have collapsed.

"Jacob!" I choked as soon as I could breathe. "Jacob!"

"Hey there, Bells."

I stumbled toward the sound of his voice. Edward kept his grip under my elbow until another set of strong hands caught me in the darkness. The heat from Jacob's skin burned right through the thin satin dress as he pulled me close. He made no effort to dance; he just hugged me while I buried my face in his chest. He leaned down to press his cheek to the top of my head.

"Rosalie won't forgive me if she doesn't get her official turn on the dance floor," Edward murmured, and I knew he was leaving us, giving me a gift of his own—this moment with Jacob.

"Oh, Jacob." I was crying now; I couldn't get the words out clearly. "Thank you."

"Stop blubbering, Bella. You'll ruin your dress. It's just me."

"Just? Oh, Jake! Everything is perfect now."

He snorted. "Yeah—the party can start. The best man finally made it."

"Now *everyone* I love is here."

I felt his lips brush my hair. "Sorry I'm late, honey."

"I'm just so happy you came!"

"That was the idea."

I glanced toward the guests, but I couldn't see through the dancers to the spot where I'd last seen Jacob's father. I didn't know if he'd stayed. "Does Billy know you're here?" As soon as I asked, I knew that he must have—it was the only way to explain his uplifted expression before.

"I'm sure Sam's told him. I'll go see him when . . . when the party's over."

"He'll be so glad you're home."

Jacob pulled back a little bit and straightened up. He left one hand on the small of my back and grabbed my right hand with the other. He cradled our hands to his chest; I could feel his heart beat under my palm, and I guessed that he hadn't placed my hand there accidentally.

"I don't know if I get more than just this one dance," he said, and he began pulling me around in a slow circle that didn't match the tempo of the music coming from behind us. "I'd better make the best of it."

We moved to the rhythm of his heart under my hand.

"I'm glad I came," Jacob said quietly after a moment. "I didn't think I would be. But it's good to see you . . . one more time. Not as sad as I'd thought it would be."

"I don't want you to feel sad."

"I know that. And I didn't come tonight to make you feel guilty."

"No—it makes me very happy that you came. It's the best gift you could have given me."

He laughed. "That's good, because I didn't have time to stop for a real present."

My eyes were adjusting, and I could see his face now, higher up than I expected. Was it possible that he was still growing? He had to be closer to seven feet than to six. It was a relief to see his familiar features again after all this time—his deep-set eyes shadowed under his shaggy black brows, his high cheekbones, his full lips stretched over his bright teeth in the sarcastic smile that matched his tone. His eyes were tight around the edges—careful; I could see that he was being *very* careful tonight. He was doing all he could to make me happy, to not slip and show how much this cost him.

I'd never done anything good enough to deserve a friend like Jacob.

"When did you decide to come back?"

"Consciously or subconsciously?" He took a deep breath before he answered his own question. "I don't really know. I guess I've been wandering back this direction for a while, and maybe it's because I was headed here. But it wasn't until this morning that I really started *running*. I didn't know if I could make it." He laughed. "You wouldn't believe how weird this feels—walking around on two legs again. And clothes! And then it's more bizarre *because* it feels weird. I didn't expect that. I'm out of practice with the whole human thing."

We revolved steadily.

"It would have been a shame to miss seeing you like this, though. That's worth the trip right there. You look unbelievable, Bella. So beautiful."

"Alice invested a lot of time in me today. The dark helps, too."

"It's not so dark for me, you know."

"Right." Werewolf senses. It was easy to forget all the

things he could do, he seemed so human. Especially right now.

"You cut your hair," I noted.

"Yeah. Easier, you know. Thought I'd better take advantage of the hands."

"It looks good," I lied.

He snorted. "Right. I did it myself, with rusty kitchen shears." He grinned widely for a moment, and then his smile faded. His expression turned serious. "Are you happy, Bella?"

"Yes."

"Okay." I felt his shoulders shrug. "That's the main thing, I guess."

"How are you, Jacob? Really?"

"I'm fine, Bella, really. You don't need to worry about me anymore. You can stop bugging Seth."

"I'm not just bugging him because of you. I *like* Seth."

"He's a good kid. Better company than some. I tell you, if I could get rid of the voices in my head, being a wolf would be about perfect."

I laughed at the way it sounded. "Yeah, I can't get mine to shut up, either."

"In your case, that would mean you're insane. Of course, I already knew that you were insane," he teased.

"Thanks."

"Insanity is probably easier than sharing a pack mind. Crazy people's voices don't send babysitters to watch them."

"Huh?"

"Sam's out there. And some of the others. Just in case, you know."

"In case of what?"

"In case I can't keep it together, something like that. In case I decide to trash the party." He flashed a quick smile at what was probably an appealing thought to him. "But I'm not here to ruin your wedding, Bella. I'm here to . . ." He trailed off.

"To make it perfect."

"That's a tall order."

"Good thing you're so tall."

He groaned at my bad joke and then sighed. "I'm just here to be your friend. Your best friend, one last time."

"Sam should give you more credit."

"Well, maybe I'm being oversensitive. Maybe they'd be here anyway, to keep an eye on Seth. There are a *lot* of vampires here. Seth doesn't take that as seriously as he should."

"Seth knows that he's not in any danger. He understands the Cullens better than Sam does."

"Sure, sure," Jacob said, making peace before it could turn into a fight.

It was strange to have him being the diplomat.

"Sorry about those voices," I said. "Wish I could make it better." In so many ways.

"It's not that bad. I'm just whining a little."

"You're . . . happy?"

"Close enough. But enough about me. You're the star today." He chuckled. "I bet you're just *loving* that. Center of attention."

"Yeah. Can't get enough attention."

He laughed and then stared over my head. With pursed lips, he studied the shimmering glow of the reception party, the graceful whirl of the dancers, the fluttering petals falling from the garlands; I looked with him. It all seemed very distant from this black, quiet space. Almost like watching the white flurries swirling inside a snow globe.

"I'll give them this much," he said. "They know how to throw a party."

"Alice is an unstoppable force of nature."

He sighed. "Song's over. Do you think I get another one? Or is that asking too much?"

I tightened my hand around his. "You can have as many dances as you want."

He laughed. "That would be interesting. I think I'd better stick with two, though. Don't want to start talk."

We turned in another circle.

"You'd think I'd be used to telling you goodbye by now," he murmured.

I tried to swallow the lump in my throat, but I couldn't force it down.

Jacob looked at me and frowned. He wiped his fingers across my cheek, catching the tears there.

"You're not supposed to be the one crying, Bella."

"Everyone cries at weddings," I said thickly.

"This is what you want, right?"

"Right."

"Then smile."

I tried. He laughed at my grimace.

"I'm going to try to remember you like this. Pretend that . . ."

"That what? That I died?"

He clenched his teeth. He was struggling with himself— with his decision to make his presence here a gift and not a judgment. I could guess what he wanted to say.

"No," he finally answered. "But I'll see you this way in my head. Pink cheeks. Heartbeat. Two left feet. All of that."

I deliberately stomped on his foot as hard as I could.

He smiled. "That's my girl."

He started to say something else and then snapped his mouth closed. Struggling again, teeth gritted against the words he didn't want to say.

My relationship with Jacob used to be so easy. Natural as breathing. But since Edward had come back into my life, it was a constant strain. Because—in Jacob's eyes—by choosing Edward, I was choosing a fate that was worse than death, or at least equivalent to it.

"What is it, Jake? Just tell me. You can tell me anything."

"I—I . . . I don't have anything to tell you."

"Oh please. Spit it out."

"It's true. It's not . . . it's—it's a question. It's something I want *you* to tell *me*."

"Ask me."

He struggled for another minute and then exhaled. "I shouldn't. It doesn't matter. I'm just morbidly curious."

Because I knew him so well, I understood.

"It's not tonight, Jacob," I whispered.

Jacob was even more obsessed with my humanity than Edward. He treasured every one of my heartbeats, knowing that they were numbered.

"Oh," he said, trying to smother his relief. "Oh."

A new song started playing, but he didn't notice the change this time.

"When?" he whispered.

"I don't know for sure. A week or two, maybe."

His voice changed, took on a defensive, mocking edge. "What's the holdup?"

"I just didn't want to spend my honeymoon writhing in pain."

"You'd rather spend it how? Playing checkers? Ha ha."

"Very funny."

"Kidding, Bells. But, honestly, I don't see the point. You can't have a real honeymoon with your vampire, so why go through the motions? Call a spade a spade. This isn't the first time you've put this off. That's a *good* thing, though," he said, suddenly earnest. "Don't be embarrassed about it."

"I'm not putting anything off," I snapped. "And *yes I can* have a real honeymoon! I can do anything I want! Butt out!"

He stopped our slow circling abruptly. For a moment, I wondered if he'd finally noticed the music change, and I scrambled in my head for a way to patch up our little tiff before he said goodbye to me. We shouldn't part on this note.

And then his eyes bulged wide with a strange kind of confused horror.

"What?" he gasped. "What did you say?"

"About what . . . ? Jake? What's wrong?"

"What do you mean? Have a real honeymoon? While you're still *human*? Are you kidding? That's a sick joke, Bella!"

I glared at him. "I said butt out, Jake. This is *so* not your business. I shouldn't have . . . we shouldn't even be talking about this. It's private—"

His enormous hands gripped the tops of my arms, wrapping all the way around, fingers overlapping.

"Ow, Jake! Let go!"

He shook me.

"Bella! Have you lost your mind? You can't be that stupid! Tell me you're joking!"

He shook me again. His hands, tight as tourniquets, were quivering, sending vibrations deep into my bones.

"Jake—stop!"

The darkness was suddenly very crowded.

"Take your hands off her!" Edward's voice was cold as ice, sharp as razors.

Behind Jacob, there was a low snarl from the black night, and then another, overlapping the first.

"Jake, bro, back away," I heard Seth Clearwater urge. "You're losing it."

Jacob seemed frozen as he was, his horrified eyes wide and staring.

"You'll hurt her," Seth whispered. "Let her go."

"Now!" Edward snarled.

Jacob's hands dropped to his sides, and the sudden gush of blood through my waiting veins was almost painful. Before I could register more than that, cold hands replaced the hot ones, and the air was suddenly whooshing past me.

I blinked, and I was on my feet a half dozen feet away from where I'd been standing. Edward was tensed in front of me. There were two enormous wolves braced between him and Jacob, but they did not seem aggressive to me. More like they were trying to prevent the fight.

And Seth—gangly, fifteen-year-old Seth—had his long arms around Jacob's shaking body, and he was tugging him away. If Jacob phased with Seth so close . . .

"C'mon, Jake. Let's go."

"I'll kill you," Jacob said, his voice so choked with rage that it was low as a whisper. His eyes, focused on Edward, burned with fury. "I'll kill you myself! I'll do it now!" He shuddered convulsively.

The biggest wolf, the black one, growled sharply.

"Seth, get out of the way," Edward hissed.

Seth tugged on Jacob again. Jacob was so bewildered with rage that Seth was able to yank him a few feet farther back. "Don't do it, Jake. Walk away. C'mon."

Sam—the bigger wolf, the black one—joined Seth then. He put his massive head against Jacob's chest and shoved.

The three of them—Seth towing, Jake trembling, Sam pushing—disappeared swiftly into the darkness.

The other wolf stared after them. I wasn't sure, in the weak light, about the color of his fur—chocolate brown, maybe? Was it Quil, then?

"I'm sorry," I whispered to the wolf.

"It's all right now, Bella," Edward murmured.

The wolf looked at Edward. His gaze was not friendly. Edward gave him one cold nod. The wolf huffed and then turned to follow the others, vanishing as they had.

"All right," Edward said to himself, and then he looked at me. "Let's get back."

"But Jake—"

"Sam has him in hand. He's gone."

"Edward, I'm so sorry. I was stupid—"

"You did nothing wrong—"

"I have such a big mouth! Why would I . . . I shouldn't have let him get to me like that. What was I thinking?"

"Don't worry." He touched my face. "We need to get back to the reception before someone notices our absence."

I shook my head, trying to reorient myself. Before someone noticed? Had anyone *missed* that?

Then, as I thought about it, I realized the confrontation that had seemed so catastrophic to me had, in reality, been very quiet and short here in the shadows.

"Give me two seconds," I pleaded.

My insides were chaotic with panic and grief, but that didn't matter—only the outside mattered right now. Putting on a good show was something I knew I had to master.

"My dress?"

"You look fine. Not a hair out of place."

I took two deep breaths. "Okay. Let's go."

He put his arms around me and led me back to the light. When we passed under the twinkle lights, he spun me gently onto the dance floor. We melted in with the other dancers as if our dance had never been interrupted.

I glanced around at the guests, but no one seemed shocked or frightened. Only the very palest faces there showed any signs of stress, and they hid it well. Jasper and Emmett were on the edge of the floor, close together, and I guessed that they had been nearby during the confrontation.

"Are you—"

"I'm fine," I promised. "I can't believe I did that. What's wrong with me?"

"Nothing is wrong with *you*."

I'd been so glad to see Jacob here. I knew the sacrifice it had taken him. And then I'd ruined it, turned his gift into a disaster. I should be quarantined.

But my idiocy would not ruin anything else tonight. I would put this away, shove it in a drawer and lock it up to deal with later. There would be plenty of time to flagellate myself for this, and nothing I could do now would help.

"It's over," I said. "Let's not think of it again tonight."

I expected a quick agreement from Edward, but he was silent.

"Edward?"

He closed his eyes and touched his forehead to mine. "Jacob is right," he whispered. "What *am* I thinking?"

"He is not." I tried to keep my face smooth for the watching crowd of friends. "Jacob is way too prejudiced to see anything clearly."

He mumbled something low that sounded almost like "*should* let him kill me for even thinking . . ."

"Stop it," I said fiercely. I grabbed his face in my hands and waited until he opened his eyes. "You and me. That's the only thing that matters. The only thing you're allowed to think about now. Do you hear me?"

"Yes," he sighed.

"Forget Jacob came." I could do that. I *would* do that. "For me. Promise that you'll let this go."

He stared into my eyes for a moment before answering. "I promise."

"Thank you. Edward, I'm not afraid."

"I am," he whispered.

"Don't be." I took a deep breath and smiled. "By the way, I love you."

He smiled just a little in return. "That's why we're here."

"You're monopolizing the bride," Emmett said, coming up behind Edward's shoulder. "Let me dance with my little sister. This could be my last chance to make her blush."

He laughed loudly, as unaffected as he usually was by any serious atmosphere.

It turned out there were actually lots of people I hadn't danced with yet, and that gave me a chance to truly compose and resolve myself. When Edward claimed me again, I found that the Jacob-drawer was shut nice and tight. As he wrapped his arms around me, I was able to unearth my earlier sense of joy, my certainty that everything in my life was in the right place tonight. I smiled and laid my head against his chest. His arms tightened.

"I could get used to this," I said.

"Don't tell me you've gotten over your dancing issues?"

"Dancing isn't so bad—with you. But I was thinking more of this,"—and I pressed myself to him even tighter— "of never having to let you go."

"Never," he promised, and he leaned down to kiss me.

It was a serious kind of kiss—intense, slow but building. . . .

I'd pretty much forgotten where I was when I heard Alice call, "Bella! It's time!"

I felt a brief flicker of irritation with my new sister for the interruption.

Edward ignored her; his lips were hard against mine, more urgent than before. My heart broke into a sprint and my palms were slick against his marble neck.

"Do you want to miss your plane?" Alice demanded, right next to me now. "I'm sure you'll have a lovely honeymoon camped out in the airport waiting for another flight."

Edward turned his face slightly to murmur, "Go away, Alice," and then pressed his lips to mine again.

"Bella, do you want to wear that dress on the airplane?" she demanded.

I wasn't really paying much attention. At the moment, I simply didn't care.

Alice growled quietly. "I'll tell her where you're taking her, Edward. So help me, I will."

He froze. Then he lifted his face from mine and glared at his favorite sister. "You're awfully small to be so hugely irritating."

"I didn't pick out the perfect going-away dress to have it wasted," she snapped back, taking my hand. "Come with me, Bella."

I tugged against her hold, stretching up on my toes to kiss him one more time. She jerked my arm impatiently, hauling me away from him. There were a few chuckles from the watching guests. I gave up then and let her lead me into the empty house.

She looked annoyed.

"Sorry, Alice," I apologized.

"I don't blame you, Bella." She sighed. "You don't seem to be able to help yourself."

I giggled at her martyred expression, and she scowled.

"Thank you, Alice. It was the most beautiful wedding anyone ever had," I told her earnestly. "Everything was exactly right. You're the best, smartest, most talented sister in the whole world."

That thawed her out; she smiled a huge smile. "I'm glad you liked it."

Renée and Esme were waiting upstairs. The three of them quickly had me out of my dress and into Alice's deep blue going-away ensemble. I was grateful when someone pulled the pins out of my hair and let it fall loose down my back, wavy from the braids, saving me from a hairpin headache later. My mother's tears streamed without a break the entire time.

"I'll call you when I know where I'm going," I promised as I hugged her goodbye. I knew the honeymoon secret was probably driving her crazy; my mother hated secrets, unless she was in on them.

"I'll tell you as soon as she's safely away," Alice outdid me, smirking at my wounded expression. How unfair, for me to be the last to know.

"You have to visit me and Phil very, very soon. It's your turn to go south—see the sun for once," Renée said.

"It didn't rain today," I reminded her, avoiding her request.

"A miracle."

"Everything's ready," Alice said. "Your suitcases are in the car—Jasper's bringing it around." She pulled me back toward the stairs with Renée following, still halfway embracing me.

"I love you, Mom," I whispered as we descended. "I'm so glad you have Phil. Take care of each other."

"I love you, too, Bella, honey."

"Goodbye, Mom. I love you," I said again, my throat thick.

Edward was waiting at the bottom of the stairs. I took his outstretched hand but leaned away, scanning the little crowd that was waiting to see us off.

"Dad?" I asked, my eyes searching.

"Over here," Edward murmured. He pulled me through

the guests; they made a pathway for us. We found Charlie leaning awkwardly against the wall behind everyone else, looking a little like he was hiding. The red rims around his eyes explained why.

"Oh, Dad!"

I hugged him around the waist, tears streaming again—I was crying so much tonight. He patted my back.

"There, now. You don't want to miss your plane."

It was hard to talk about love with Charlie—we were so much alike, always reverting to trivial things to avoid embarrassing emotional displays. But this was no time for being self-conscious.

"I love you forever, Dad," I told him. "Don't forget that."

"You, too, Bells. Always have, always will."

I kissed his cheek at the same time that he kissed mine.

"Call me," he said.

"Soon," I promised, knowing this was *all* I could promise. Just a phone call. My father and my mother could not be allowed to see me again; I would be too different, and much, much too dangerous.

"Go on, then," he said gruffly. "Don't want to be late."

The guests made another aisle for us. Edward pulled me close to his side as we made our escape.

"Are you ready?" he asked.

"I am," I said, and I knew that it was true.

Everyone applauded when Edward kissed me on the doorstep. Then he rushed me to the car as the rice storm began. Most of it went wide, but someone, probably Emmett, threw with uncanny precision, and I caught a lot of the ricochets off Edward's back.

The car was decorated with more flowers that trailed in streamers along its length, and long gossamer ribbons that were tied to a dozen shoes—designer shoes that looked brand-new—dangling behind the bumper.

Edward shielded me from the rice while I climbed in, and then he was in and we were speeding away as I waved out the window and called "I love you" to the porch, where my families waved back.

The last image I registered was one of my parents. Phil had both arms wrapped tenderly around Renée. She had one arm tight around his waist but had her free hand reached out to hold Charlie's. So many different kinds of love, harmonious in this one moment. It seemed a very hopeful picture to me.

Edward squeezed my hand.

"I love you," he said.

I leaned my head against his arm. "That's why we're here," I quoted him.

He kissed my hair.

As we turned onto the black highway and Edward really hit the accelerator, I heard a noise over the purr of the engine, coming from the forest behind us. If I could hear it, then he certainly could. But he said nothing as the sound slowly faded in the distance. I said nothing, either.

The piercing, heartbroken howling grew fainter and then disappeared entirely.

5. ISLE ESME

"HOUSTON?" I ASKED, RAISING MY EYEBROWS WHEN WE reached the gate in Seattle.

"Just a stop along the way," Edward assured me with a grin.

It felt like I'd barely fallen asleep when he woke me. I was groggy as he pulled me through the terminals, struggling to remember how to open my eyes after every blink. It took me a few minutes to catch up with what was going on when we stopped at the international counter to check in for our next flight.

"Rio de Janeiro?" I asked with slightly more trepidation.

"Another stop," he told me.

The flight to South America was long but comfortable in the wide first-class seat, with Edward's arms cradled around me. I slept myself out and awoke unusually alert as we circled toward the airport with the light of the setting sun slanting through the plane's windows.

We didn't stay in the airport to connect with another flight as I'd expected. Instead we took a taxi through the dark, teeming, living streets of Rio. Unable to understand a word of Edward's Portuguese instructions to the driver, I guessed that we were off to find a hotel before the next leg of our journey. A sharp twinge of something very close to stage fright twisted in the pit of my stomach as I considered that. The taxi continued through the swarming crowds until they thinned somewhat, and we appeared to be nearing the extreme western edge of the city, heading into the ocean.

We stopped at the docks.

Edward led the way down the long line of white yachts moored in the night-blackened water. The boat he stopped at was smaller than the others, sleeker, obviously built for speed instead of space. Still luxurious, though, and more graceful than the rest. He leaped in lightly, despite the heavy bags he carried. He dropped those on the deck and turned to help me carefully over the edge.

I watched in silence while he prepared the boat for departure, surprised at how skilled and comfortable he seemed, because he'd never mentioned an interest in boating before. But then again, he was good at just about everything.

As we headed due east into the open ocean, I reviewed basic geography in my head. As far as I could remember, there wasn't much east of Brazil . . . until you got to Africa.

But Edward sped forward while the lights of Rio faded and ultimately disappeared behind us. On his face was a familiar exhilarated smile, the one produced by any form of speed. The boat plunged through the waves and I was showered with sea spray.

Finally the curiosity I'd suppressed so long got the best of me.

"Are we going much farther?" I asked.

It wasn't like him to forget that I was human, but I wondered if he planned for us to live on this small craft for any length of time.

"About another half hour." His eyes took in my hands, clenched on the seat, and he grinned.

Oh well, I thought to myself. He was a vampire, after all. Maybe we were going to Atlantis.

Twenty minutes later, he called my name over the roar of the engine.

"Bella, look there." He pointed straight ahead.

I saw only blackness at first, and the moon's white trail across the water. But I searched the space where he pointed until I found a low black shape breaking into the sheen of moonlight on the waves. As I squinted into the darkness, the silhouette became more detailed. The shape grew into a squat, irregular triangle, with one side trailing longer than the other before sinking into the waves. We drew closer, and I could see the outline was feathery, swaying to the light breeze.

And then my eyes refocused and the pieces all made sense: a small island rose out of the water ahead of us, waving with palm fronds, a beach glowing pale in the light of the moon.

"Where are we?" I murmured in wonder while he shifted course, heading around to the north end of the island.

He heard me, despite the noise of the engine, and smiled a wide smile that gleamed in the moonlight.

"This is Isle Esme."

The boat slowed dramatically, drawing with precision into position against a short dock constructed of wooden planks, bleached into whiteness by the moon. The engine cut off, and the silence that followed was profound. There was nothing but the waves, slapping lightly against the boat, and the rustle of the breeze in the palms. The air was warm, moist, and fragrant—like the steam left behind after a hot shower.

"Isle *Esme?*" My voice was low, but it still sounded too loud as it broke into the quiet night.

"A gift from Carlisle—Esme offered to let us borrow it."

A gift. Who gives an island as a gift? I frowned. I hadn't realized that Edward's extreme generosity was a learned behavior.

He placed the suitcases on the dock and then turned back, smiling his perfect smile as he reached for me. Instead of taking my hand, he pulled me right up into his arms.

"Aren't you supposed to wait for the threshold?" I asked, breathless, as he sprung lightly out of the boat.

He grinned. "I'm nothing if not thorough."

Gripping the handles of both huge steamer trunks in one hand and cradling me in the other arm, he carried me up the dock and onto a pale sand pathway through the dark vegetation.

For a short while it was pitch black in the jungle-like growth, and then I could see a warm light ahead. It was about at the point when I realized the light was a house—the two bright, perfect squares were wide windows framing a front door—that the stage fright attacked again, more forcefully than before, worse than when I'd thought we were headed for a hotel.

My heart thudded audibly against my ribs, and my breath seemed to get stuck in my throat. I felt Edward's eyes on my face, but I refused to meet his gaze. I stared straight ahead, seeing nothing.

He didn't ask what I was thinking, which was out of character for him. I guessed that meant that he was just as nervous as I suddenly was.

He set the suitcases on the deep porch to open the doors—they were unlocked.

Edward looked down at me, waiting until I met his gaze before he stepped through the threshold.

He carried me through the house, both of us very quiet, flipping on lights as he went. My vague impression of the house was that it was quite large for a tiny island, and oddly familiar. I'd gotten used to the pale-on-pale color scheme preferred by the Cullens; it felt like home. I couldn't focus on any specifics, though. The violent pulse beating behind my ears made everything a little blurry.

Then Edward stopped and turned on the last light.

The room was big and white, and the far wall was mostly glass—standard décor for my vampires. Outside, the moon was bright on white sand and, just a few yards away from the house, glistening waves. But I barely noted that part. I was more focused on the absolutely *huge* white bed in the center of the room, hung with billowy clouds of mosquito netting.

Edward set me on my feet.

"I'll . . . go get the luggage."

The room was too warm, stuffier than the tropical night outside. A bead of sweat dewed up on the nape of my neck. I walked slowly forward until I could reach out and touch the foamy netting. For some reason I felt the need to make sure everything was real.

I didn't hear Edward return. Suddenly, his wintry finger caressed the back of my neck, wiping away the drop of perspiration.

"It's a little hot here," he said apologetically. "I thought . . . that would be best."

"Thorough," I murmured under my breath, and he chuckled. It was a nervous sound, rare for Edward.

"I tried to think of everything that would make this . . . easier," he admitted.

I swallowed loudly, still facing away from him. Had there ever been a honeymoon like this before?

I knew the answer to that. No. There had not.

"I was wondering," Edward said slowly, "if . . . first . . . maybe you'd like to take a midnight swim with me?" He took a deep breath, and his voice was more at ease when he spoke again. "The water will be very warm. This is the kind of beach you approve of."

"Sounds nice." My voice broke.

"I'm sure you'd like a human minute or two. . . . It was a long journey."

I nodded woodenly. I felt barely human; maybe a few minutes alone would help.

His lips brushed against my throat, just below my ear. He chuckled once and his cool breath tickled my overheated skin. "Don't take *too* long, Mrs. Cullen."

I jumped a little at the sound of my new name.

His lips brushed down my neck to the tip of my shoulder. "I'll wait for you in the water."

He walked past me to the French door that opened right onto the beach sand. On the way, he shrugged out of his shirt, dropping it on the floor, and then slipped through the door into the moonlit night. The sultry, salty air swirled into the room behind him.

Did my skin burst into flames? I had to look down to check. Nope, nothing was burning. At least, not visibly.

I reminded myself to breathe, and then I stumbled toward the giant suitcase that Edward had opened on top of a low white dresser. It must be mine, because my familiar bag of toiletries was right on top, and there was a lot of pink in there, but I didn't recognize even one article of clothing. As I pawed through the neatly folded piles—looking for something familiar and comfortable, a pair of old sweats maybe—it came to my attention that there was an awful lot of sheer lace and skimpy satin in my hands. Lingerie. Very lingerie-ish lingerie, with French tags.

I didn't know how or when, but someday, Alice was going to pay for this.

Giving up, I went to the bathroom and peeked out

through the long windows that opened to the same beach as the French doors. I couldn't see him; I guessed he was there in the water, not bothering to come up for air. In the sky above, the moon was lopsided, almost full, and the sand was bright white under its shine. A small movement caught my eye—draped over a bend in one of the palm trees that fringed the beach, the rest of his clothes were swaying in the light breeze.

A rush of heat flashed across my skin again.

I took a couple of deep breaths and then went to the mirrors above the long stretch of counters. I looked exactly like I'd been sleeping on a plane all day. I found my brush and yanked it harshly through the snarls on the back of my neck until they were smoothed out and the bristles were full of hair. I brushed my teeth meticulously, twice. Then I washed my face and splashed water on the back of my neck, which was feeling feverish. That felt so good that I washed my arms as well, and finally I decided to just give up and take the shower. I knew it was ridiculous to shower before swimming, but I needed to calm down, and hot water was one reliable way to do that.

Also, shaving my legs again seemed like a pretty good idea.

When I was done, I grabbed a huge white towel off the counter and wrapped it under my arms.

Then I was faced with a dilemma I hadn't considered. What was I supposed to put on? Not a swimsuit, obviously. But it seemed silly to put my clothes back on, too. I didn't even want to think about the things Alice had packed for me.

My breathing started to accelerate again and my hands

trembled—so much for the calming effects of the shower. I started to feel a little dizzy, apparently a full-scale panic attack on the way. I sat down on the cool tile floor in my big towel and put my head between my knees. I prayed he wouldn't decide to come look for me before I could pull myself together. I could imagine what he would think if he saw me going to pieces this way. It wouldn't be hard for him to convince himself that we were making a mistake.

And I wasn't freaking out because I thought we were making a mistake. Not at all. I was freaking out because I had no idea how to do this, and I was afraid to walk out of this room and face the unknown. Especially in French lingerie. I knew I wasn't ready for *that* yet.

This felt exactly like having to walk out in front of a theater full of thousands with no idea what my lines were.

How did people do this—swallow all their fears and trust someone else so implicitly with every imperfection and fear they had—with less than the absolute commitment Edward had given me? If it weren't Edward out there, if I didn't know in every cell of my body that he loved me as much as I loved him—unconditionally and irrevocably and, to be honest, irrationally—I'd never be able to get up off this floor.

But it *was* Edward out there, so I whispered the words "Don't be a coward" under my breath and scrambled to my feet. I hitched the towel tighter under my arms and marched determinedly from the bathroom. Past the suitcase full of lace and the big bed without looking at either. Out the open glass door onto the powder-fine sand.

Everything was black-and-white, leached colorless by the moon. I walked slowly across the warm powder, pausing beside the curved tree where he had left his clothes. I laid my hand against the rough bark and checked my breathing to make sure it was even. Or even enough.

I looked across the low ripples, black in the darkness, searching for him.

He wasn't hard to find. He stood, his back to me, waist deep in the midnight water, staring up at the oval moon. The pallid light of the moon turned his skin a perfect white, like the sand, like the moon itself, and made his wet hair black as the ocean. He was motionless, his hands resting palms down against the water; the low waves broke around him as if he were a stone. I stared at the smooth lines of his back, his shoulders, his arms, his neck, the flawless shape of him. . . .

The fire was no longer a flash burn across my skin—it was slow and deep now; it smoldered away all my awkwardness, my shy uncertainty. I slipped the towel off without hesitation, leaving it on the tree with his clothes, and walked out into the white light; it made me pale as the snowy sand, too.

I couldn't hear the sound of my footsteps as I walked to the water's edge, but I guessed that he could. Edward did not turn. I let the gentle swells break over my toes, and found that he'd been right about the temperature—it was very warm, like bath water. I stepped in, walking carefully across the invisible ocean floor, but my care was unnecessary; the sand continued perfectly smooth, sloping gently toward Edward. I waded through the weightless current till I was at his side, and then I placed my hand lightly over his cool hand lying on the water.

"Beautiful," I said, looking up at the moon, too.

"It's all right," he answered, unimpressed. He turned slowly to face me; little waves rolled away from his movement and broke against my skin. His eyes looked silver in his ice-colored face. He twisted his hand up so that he could twine our fingers beneath the surface of the water. It was warm enough that his cool skin did not raise goose bumps on mine.

"But I wouldn't use the word *beautiful*," he continued. "Not with you standing here in comparison."

I half-smiled, then raised my free hand—it didn't tremble now—and placed it over his heart. White on white; we matched, for once. He shuddered the tiniest bit at my warm touch. His breath came rougher now.

"I promised we would *try*," he whispered, suddenly tense. "If . . . if I do something wrong, if I hurt you, you must tell me at once."

I nodded solemnly, keeping my eyes on his. I took another step through the waves and leaned my head against his chest.

"Don't be afraid," I murmured. "We belong together."

I was abruptly overwhelmed by the truth of my own words. This moment was so perfect, so right, there was no way to doubt it.

His arms wrapped around me, holding me against him, summer and winter. It felt like every nerve ending in my body was a live wire.

"Forever," he agreed, and then pulled us gently into deeper water.

The sun, hot on the bare skin of my back, woke me in the morning. Late morning, maybe afternoon, I wasn't sure.

Everything besides the time was clear, though; I knew exactly where I was—the bright room with the big white bed, brilliant sunlight streaming through the open doors. The clouds of netting would soften the shine.

I didn't open my eyes. I was too happy to change anything, no matter how small. The only sounds were the waves outside, our breathing, my heartbeat. . . .

I was comfortable, even with the baking sun. His cool skin was the perfect antidote to the heat. Lying across his wintry chest, his arms wound around me, felt very easy and natural. I wondered idly what I'd been so panicky about last night. My fears all seemed silly now.

His fingers softly trailed down the contours of my spine, and I knew that he knew I was awake. I kept my eyes shut and tightened my arms around his neck, holding myself closer to him.

He didn't speak; his fingers moved up and down my back, barely touching it as he lightly traced patterns on my skin.

I would have been happy to lie here forever, to never disturb this moment, but my body had other ideas. I laughed at my impatient stomach. It seemed sort of prosaic to be hungry after all that had passed last night. Like being brought back down to earth from some great height.

"What's funny?" he murmured, still stroking my back. The sound of his voice, serious and husky, brought with it a deluge of memories from the night, and I felt a blush color my face and neck.

To answer his question, my stomach growled. I laughed again. "You just can't escape being human for very long."

I waited, but he did not laugh with me. Slowly, sinking

through the many layers of bliss that clouded my head, came the realization of a different atmosphere outside my own glowing sphere of happiness.

I opened my eyes; the first thing I saw was the pale, almost silvery skin of his throat, the arc of his chin above my face. His jaw was taut. I propped myself up on my elbow so I could see his face.

He was staring at the frothy canopy above us, and he didn't look at me as I studied his grave features. His expression was a shock—it sent a physical jolt through my body.

"Edward," I said, a strange little catch in my throat, "what is it? What's wrong?"

"You have to ask?" His voice was hard, cynical.

My first instinct, the product of a lifetime of insecurities, was to wonder what I had done wrong. I thought through everything that had happened, but I couldn't find any sour note in the memory. It had all been simpler than I'd expected; we'd fit together like corresponding pieces, made to match up. This had given me a secret satisfaction—we were compatible physically, as well as all the other ways. Fire and ice, somehow existing together without destroying each other. More proof that I belonged with him.

I couldn't think of any part that would make him look like this—so severe and cold. What had I missed?

His finger smoothed the worried lines on my forehead.

"What are you thinking?" he whispered.

"You're upset. I don't understand. Did I . . . ?" I couldn't finish.

His eyes tightened. "How badly are you hurt, Bella? The truth—don't try to downplay it."

"Hurt?" I repeated; my voice came out higher than usual because the word took me so by surprise.

He raised one eyebrow, his lips a tight line.

I made a quick assessment, stretching my body automatically, tensing and flexing my muscles. There was stiffness, and a lot of soreness, too, it was true, but mostly there was the odd sensation that my bones all had become unhinged at the joints, and I had changed halfway into the consistency of a jellyfish. It was not an unpleasant feeling.

And then I was a little angry, because he was darkening this most perfect of all mornings with his pessimistic assumptions.

"Why would you jump to that conclusion? I've never been better than I am now."

His eyes closed. "Stop that."

"Stop *what*?"

"Stop acting like I'm not a monster for having agreed to this."

"Edward!" I whispered, really upset now. He was pulling my bright memory through the darkness, staining it. "Don't ever say that."

He didn't open his eyes; it was like he didn't want to see me.

"Look at yourself, Bella. Then tell me I'm not a monster."

Wounded, shocked, I followed his instruction unthinkingly and then gasped.

What had happened to me? I couldn't make sense of the fluffy white snow that clung to my skin. I shook my head, and a cascade of white drifted out of my hair.

I pinched one soft white bit between my fingers. It was a piece of down.

"Why am I covered in feathers?" I asked, confused.

He exhaled impatiently. "I bit a pillow. Or two. That's not what I'm talking about."

"You . . . bit a pillow? *Why?*"

"Look, Bella!" he almost growled. He took my hand— very gingerly—and stretched my arm out. "Look at *that.*"

This time, I saw what he meant.

Under the dusting of feathers, large purplish bruises were beginning to blossom across the pale skin of my arm. My eyes followed the trail they made up to my shoulder, and then down across my ribs. I pulled my hand free to poke at a discoloration on my left forearm, watching it fade where I touched and then reappear. It throbbed a little.

So lightly that he was barely touching me, Edward placed his hand against the bruises on my arm, one at a time, matching his long fingers to the patterns.

"Oh," I said.

I tried to remember this—to remember pain—but I couldn't. I couldn't recall a moment when his hold had been too tight, his hands too hard against me. I only remembered wanting him to hold me tighter, and being pleased when he did. . . .

"I'm . . . so sorry, Bella," he whispered while I stared at the bruises. "I knew better than this. I should not have—" He made a low, revolted sound in the back of his throat. "I am more sorry than I can tell you."

He threw his arm over his face and became perfectly still.

I sat for one long moment in total astonishment, trying

to come to terms—now that I understood it—with his misery. It was so contrary to the way that I felt that it was difficult to process.

The shock wore off slowly, leaving nothing in its absence. Emptiness. My mind was blank. I couldn't think of what to say. How could I explain it to him in the right way? How could I make him as happy as I was—or as I *had* been, a moment ago?

I touched his arm, and he didn't respond. I wrapped my fingers around his wrist and tried to pry his arm off his face, but I could have been yanking on a sculpture for all the good it did me.

"Edward."

He didn't move.

"Edward?"

Nothing. So, this would be a monologue, then.

"*I'm* not sorry, Edward. I'm . . . I can't even tell you. I'm *so* happy. That doesn't cover it. Don't be angry. Don't. I'm really f—"

"Do not say the word *fine*." His voice was ice cold. "If you value my sanity, do not say that you are fine."

"But I *am*," I whispered.

"Bella," he almost moaned. "Don't."

"No. *You* don't, Edward."

He moved his arm; his gold eyes watched me warily.

"Don't ruin this," I told him. "I. Am. Happy."

"I've already ruined this," he whispered.

"Cut it out," I snapped.

I heard his teeth grind together.

"Ugh!" I groaned. "Why can't you just read my mind already? It's so *inconvenient* to be a mental mute!"

His eyes widened a little bit, distracted in spite of himself.

"That's a new one. You love that I can't read your mind."

"Not today."

He stared at me. "Why?"

I threw my hands up in frustration, feeling an ache in my shoulder that I ignored. My palms fell back against his chest with a sharp smack. "Because all this angst would be completely unnecessary if you could see how I feel right now! Or five minutes ago, anyway. I *was* perfectly happy. Totally and completely blissed out. Now—well, I'm sort of pissed, actually."

"You *should* be angry at me."

"Well, I am. Does that make you feel better?"

He sighed. "No. I don't think anything could make me feel better now."

"*That*," I snapped. "That right there is why I'm angry. You are *killing my buzz*, Edward."

He rolled his eyes and shook his head.

I took a deep breath. I was feeling more of the soreness now, but it wasn't that bad. Sort of like the day after lifting weights. I'd done that with Renée during one of her fitness obsessions. Sixty-five lunges with ten pounds in each hand. I couldn't walk the next day. This was not as painful as that had been by half.

I swallowed my irritation and tried to make my voice soothing. "We knew this was going to be tricky. I thought that was assumed. And then—well, it was a lot easier than I thought it would be. And this is really nothing." I brushed my fingers along my arm. "I think for a first time, not knowing what to expect, we did amazing. With a little practice——"

His expression was suddenly so livid that I broke off mid-sentence.

"Assumed? Did you *expect* this, Bella? Were you anticipating that I would hurt you? Were you thinking it would be worse? Do you consider the experiment a success because you can walk away from it? No broken bones—that equals a victory?"

I waited, letting him get it all out. Then I waited some more while his breathing went back to normal. When his eyes were calm, I answered, speaking with slow precision.

"I didn't know what to expect—but I definitely did not expect how . . . how . . . just wonderful and perfect it was." My voice dropped to a whisper, my eyes slipped from his face down to my hands. "I mean, I don't know how it was for you, but it was like that for me."

A cool finger pulled my chin back up.

"Is that what you're worried about?" he said through his teeth. "That I didn't *enjoy* myself?"

My eyes stayed down. "I know it's not the same. You're not human. I just was trying to explain that, for a human, well, I can't imagine that life gets any better than that."

He was quiet for so long that, finally, I had to look up. His face was softer now, thoughtful.

"It seems that I have more to apologize for." He frowned. "I didn't dream that you would construe the way I feel about what I did to you to mean that last night wasn't . . . well, the best night of my existence. But I don't want to think of it that way, not when you were . . ."

My lips curved up a little at the edges. "Really? The best ever?" I asked in a small voice.

He took my face between his hands, still introspective. "I spoke to Carlisle after you and I made our bargain, hoping he could help me. Of course he warned me that this would be very dangerous for you." A shadow crossed his expression. "He had faith in me, though—faith I didn't deserve."

I started to protest, and he put two fingers over my lips before I could comment.

"I also asked him what *I* should expect. I didn't know what it would be for me . . . what with my being a vampire." He smiled halfheartedly. "Carlisle told me it was a very powerful thing, like nothing else. He told me physical love was something I should not treat lightly. With our rarely changing temperaments, strong emotions can alter us in permanent ways. But he said I did not need to worry about that part—you had already altered me so completely." This time his smile was more genuine.

"I spoke to my brothers, too. They told me it was a very great pleasure. Second only to drinking human blood." A line creased his brow. "But I've tasted your blood, and there could be no blood more potent than *that*. . . . I don't think they were wrong, really. Just that it was different for us. Something more."

"It *was* more. It was everything."

"That doesn't change the fact that it was wrong. Even if it were possible that you really did feel that way."

"What does *that* mean? Do you think I'm making this up? Why?"

"To ease my guilt. I can't ignore the evidence, Bella. Or

your history of trying to let me off the hook when I make mistakes."

I grabbed his chin and leaned forward so that our faces were inches apart. "You listen to me, Edward Cullen. I am not pretending anything for your sake, okay? I didn't even know there was a reason to make you feel better until you started being all miserable. *I've* never been so happy in all my life—I wasn't this happy when you decided that you loved me more than you wanted to kill me, or the first morning I woke up and you were there waiting for me. . . . Not when I heard your voice in the ballet studio"— he flinched at the old memory of my close call with a hunting vampire, but I didn't pause—"or when you said 'I do' and I realized that, somehow, I get to keep you forever. Those are the happiest memories I have, and this is better than any of it. So just deal with it."

He touched the frown line between my eyebrows. "I'm making you unhappy now. I don't want to do that."

"Then don't *you* be unhappy. That's the only thing that's wrong here."

His eyes tightened, then he took a deep breath and nodded. "You're right. The past is past and I can't do anything to change it. There's no sense in letting my mood sour this time for you. I'll do whatever I can to make you happy now."

I examined his face suspiciously, and he gave me a serene smile.

"Whatever makes me happy?"

My stomach growled at the same time that I asked.

"You're hungry," he said quickly. He was swiftly out of

the bed, stirring up a cloud of feathers. Which reminded me.

"So, why exactly did you decide to ruin Esme's pillows?" I asked, sitting up and shaking more down from my hair.

He had already pulled on a pair of loose khaki pants, and he stood by the door, rumpling his hair, dislodging a few feathers of his own.

"I don't know if I *decided* to do anything last night," he muttered. "We're just lucky it was the pillows and not you." He inhaled deeply and then shook his head, as if shaking off the dark thought. A very authentic-looking smile spread across his face, but I guessed it took a lot of work to put it there.

I slid carefully off the high bed and stretched again, more aware, now, of the aches and sore spots. I heard him gasp. He turned away from me, and his hands balled up, knuckles white.

"Do I look that hideous?" I asked, working to keep my tone light. His breath caught, but he didn't turn, probably to hide his expression from me. I walked to the bathroom to check for myself.

I stared at my naked body in the full-length mirror behind the door.

I'd definitely had worse. There was a faint shadow across one of my cheekbones, and my lips were a little swollen, but other than that, my face was fine. The rest of me was decorated with patches of blue and purple. I concentrated on the bruises that would be the hardest to hide—my arms and my shoulders. They weren't so bad. My skin marked up easily. By the time a bruise showed I'd usually forgotten how I'd come by it. Of course, these were just developing. I'd look even worse tomorrow. That would not make things any easier.

I looked at my hair, then, and groaned.

"Bella?" He was right there behind me as soon as I'd made a sound.

"I'll *never* get this all out of my hair!" I pointed to my head, where it looked like a chicken was nesting. I started picking at the feathers.

"You *would* be worried about your hair," he mumbled, but he came to stand behind me, pulling out the feathers much more quickly.

"How did you keep from laughing at this? I look ridiculous."

He didn't answer; he just kept plucking. And I knew the answer anyway—there was nothing that would be funny to him in this mood.

"This isn't going to work," I sighed after a minute. "It's all dried in. I'm going to have to try to wash it out." I turned around, wrapping my arms around his cool waist. "Do you want to help me?"

"I'd better find some food for you," he said in a quiet voice, and he gently unwound my arms. I sighed as he disappeared, moving too fast.

It looked like my honeymoon was over. The thought put a big lump in my throat.

When I was mostly feather-free and dressed in an unfamiliar white cotton dress that concealed the worst of the violet blotches, I padded off barefoot to where the smell of eggs and bacon and cheddar cheese was coming from.

Edward stood in front of the stainless steel stove, sliding an omelet onto the light blue plate waiting on the counter. The scent of the food overwhelmed me. I felt like I could eat the plate and the frying pan, too; my stomach snarled.

"Here," he said. He turned with a smile on his face and set the plate on a small tiled table.

I sat in one of the two metal chairs and started snarfing down the hot eggs. They burned my throat, but I didn't care.

He sat down across from me. "I'm not feeding you often enough."

I swallowed and then reminded him, "I was asleep. This is really good, by the way. Impressive for someone who doesn't eat."

"Food Network," he said, flashing my favorite crooked smile.

I was happy to see it, happy that he seemed more like his normal self.

"Where did the eggs come from?"

"I asked the cleaning crew to stock the kitchen. A first, for this place. I'll have to ask them to deal with the feathers. . . ." He trailed off, his gaze fixed on a space above my head. I didn't respond, trying to avoid saying anything that would upset him again.

I ate everything, though he'd made enough for two.

"Thank you," I told him. I leaned across the table to kiss him. He kissed me back automatically, and then suddenly stiffened and leaned away.

I gritted my teeth, and the question I meant to ask came out sounding like an accusation. "You aren't going to touch me again while we're here, are you?"

He hesitated, then half-smiled and raised his hand to stroke my cheek. His fingers lingered softly on my skin, and I couldn't help leaning my face into his palm.

"You know that's not what I meant."

He sighed and dropped his hand. "I know. And you're right." He paused, lifting his chin slightly. And then he spoke again with firm conviction. "I will not make love with you until you've been changed. I will never hurt you again."

6. DISTRACTIONS

MY ENTERTAINMENT BECAME THE NUMBER-ONE PRIOR-
ity on Isle Esme. We snorkeled (well, I snorkeled while he
flaunted his ability to go without oxygen indefinitely). We
explored the small jungle that ringed the rocky little peak.
We visited the parrots that lived in the canopy on the south
end of the island. We watched the sunset from the rocky
western cove. We swam with the porpoises that played in
the warm, shallow waters there. Or at least I did; when
Edward was in the water, the porpoises disappeared as if a
shark was near.

I knew what was going on. He was trying to keep
me busy, distracted, so that I wouldn't continue badger-
ing him about the sex thing. Whenever I tried to talk him

into taking it easy with one of the million DVDs under the big-screen plasma TV, he would lure me out of the house with magic words like *coral reefs* and *submerged caves* and *sea turtles*. We were going, going, going all day, so that I found myself completely famished and exhausted when the sun eventually set.

I drooped over my plate after I finished dinner every night; once I'd actually fallen asleep right at the table and he'd had to carry me to bed. Part of it was that Edward always made too much food for one, but I was so *hungry* after swimming and climbing all day that I ate most of it. Then, full and worn out, I could barely keep my eyes open. All part of the plan, no doubt.

Exhaustion didn't help much with my attempts at persuasion. But I didn't give up. I tried reasoning, pleading, and grouching, all to no avail. I was usually unconscious before I could really press my case far. And then my dreams felt so real—nightmares mostly, made more vivid, I guessed, by the too-bright colors of the island—that I woke up tired no matter how long I slept.

About a week or so after we'd gotten to the island, I decided to try compromise. It had worked for us in the past.

I was sleeping in the blue room now. The cleaning crew wasn't due until the next day, and so the white room still had a snowy blanket of down. The blue room was smaller, the bed more reasonably proportioned. The walls were dark, paneled in teak, and the fittings were all luxurious blue silk.

I'd taken to wearing some of Alice's lingerie collection to sleep in at night—which weren't so revealing compared to the scanty bikinis she'd packed for me when it came right down to it. I wondered if she'd seen a vision of why I would want such things, and then shuddered, embarrassed by that thought.

I'd started out slow with innocent ivory satins, worried that revealing more of my skin would be the opposite of helpful, but ready to try anything. Edward seemed to notice nothing, as if I were wearing the same ratty old sweats I wore at home.

The bruises were much better now—yellowing in some places and disappearing altogether in others—so tonight I pulled out one of the scarier pieces as I got ready in the paneled bathroom. It was black, lacy, and embarrassing to look at even when it wasn't on. I was careful not to look in the mirror before I went back to the bedroom. I didn't want to lose my nerve.

I had the satisfaction of watching his eyes pop open wide for just a second before he controlled his expression.

"What do you think?" I asked, pirouetting so that he could see every angle.

He cleared his throat. "You look beautiful. You always do."

"Thanks," I said a bit sourly.

I was too tired to resist climbing quickly into the soft bed. He put his arms around me and pulled me against his chest, but this was routine—it was too hot to sleep without his cool body close.

"I'll make you a deal," I said sleepily.

"I will not make any deals with you," he answered.

"You haven't even heard what I'm offering."

"It doesn't matter."

I sighed. "Dang it. And I really wanted . . . Oh well."

He rolled his eyes.

I closed mine and let the bait sit there. I yawned.

It took only a minute—not long enough for me to zonk out.

"All right. What is it you want?"

I gritted my teeth for a second, fighting a smile. If there was one thing he couldn't resist, it was an opportunity to give me something.

"Well, I was thinking . . . I know that the whole Dartmouth thing was just supposed to be a cover story, but honestly, one semester of college probably wouldn't kill me," I said, echoing his words from long ago, when he'd tried to persuade me to put off becoming a vampire. "Charlie would get a thrill out of Dartmouth stories, I bet. Sure, it might be embarrassing if I can't keep up with all the brainiacs. Still . . . eighteen, nineteen. It's really not such a big difference. It's not like I'm going to get crow's feet in the next year."

He was silent for a long moment. Then, in a low voice, he said, "You would wait. You would stay human."

I held my tongue, letting the offer sink in.

"Why are you *doing* this to me?" he said through his teeth, his tone suddenly angry. "Isn't it hard enough without all of this?" He grabbed a handful of lace that was ruffled on my thigh. For a moment, I thought he was going to rip it from the seam. Then his hand relaxed. "It doesn't matter. I won't make any deals with you."

"I want to go to college."

"No, you don't. And there is nothing that is worth risking your life again. That's worth hurting you."

"But I *do* want to go. Well, it's not college as much as it's that I want—I want to be human a little while longer."

He closed his eyes and exhaled through his nose. "You are making me insane, Bella. Haven't we had this argument a million times, you always begging to be a vampire without delay?"

"Yes, but . . . well, I have a reason to be human that I didn't have before."

"What's that?"

"Guess," I said, and I dragged myself off the pillows to kiss him.

He kissed me back, but not in a way that made me think I was winning. It was more like he was being careful not to hurt my feelings; he was completely, maddeningly in control of himself. Gently, he pulled me away after a moment and cradled me against his chest.

"You are *so* human, Bella. Ruled by your hormones." He chuckled.

"That's the whole point, Edward. I *like* this part of being human. I don't want to give it up yet. I don't want to wait through years of being a blood-crazed newborn for some part of this to come back to me."

I yawned, and he smiled.

"You're tired. Sleep, love." He started humming the lullaby he'd composed for me when we first met.

"I wonder why I'm so tired," I muttered sarcastically. "That couldn't be part of your scheme or anything."

He just chuckled once and went back to humming.

"For as tired as I've been, you'd think I'd sleep better."

The song broke off. "You've been sleeping like the dead,

Bella. You haven't said a word in your sleep since we got here. If it weren't for the snoring, I'd worry you were slipping into a coma."

I ignored the snoring jibe; I didn't snore. "I haven't been tossing? That's weird. Usually I'm all over the bed when I'm having nightmares. And shouting."

"You've been having nightmares?"

"Vivid ones. They make me so tired." I yawned. "I can't believe I haven't been babbling about them all night."

"What are they about?"

"Different things—but the same, you know, because of the colors."

"Colors?"

"It's all so bright and real. Usually, when I'm dreaming, I know that I am. With these, I don't know I'm asleep. It makes them scarier."

He sounded disturbed when he spoke again. "What is frightening you?"

I shuddered slightly. "Mostly . . ." I hesitated.

"Mostly?" he prompted.

I wasn't sure why, but I didn't want to tell him about the child in my recurring nightmare; there was something private about that particular horror. So, instead of giving him the full description, I gave him just one element. Certainly enough to frighten me or anyone else.

"The Volturi," I whispered.

He hugged me tighter. "They aren't going to bother us anymore. You'll be immortal soon, and they'll have no reason."

I let him comfort me, feeling a little guilty that he'd misunderstood. The nightmares weren't like that, exactly.

It wasn't that I was afraid for myself—I was afraid for the boy.

He wasn't the same boy as that first dream—the vampire child with the bloodred eyes who sat on a pile of dead people I loved. This boy I'd dreamed of four times in the last week was definitely human; his cheeks were flushed and his wide eyes were a soft green. But just like the other child, he shook with fear and desperation as the Volturi closed in on us.

In this dream that was both new and old, I simply *had* to protect the unknown child. There was no other option. At the same time, I knew that I would fail.

He saw the desolation on my face. "What can I do to help?"

I shook it off. "They're just dreams, Edward."

"Do you want me to sing to you? I'll sing all night if it will keep the bad dreams away."

"They're not all bad. Some are nice. So . . . colorful. Underwater, with the fish and the coral. It all seems like it's really happening—I don't know that I'm dreaming. Maybe this island is the problem. It's really *bright* here."

"Do you want to go home?"

"No. No, not yet. Can't we stay awhile longer?"

"We can stay as long as you want, Bella," he promised me.

"When does the semester start? I wasn't paying attention before."

He sighed. He may have started humming again, too, but I was under before I could be sure.

Later, when I awoke in the dark, it was with shock. The dream had been so very real . . . so vivid, so sensory. . . .

I gasped aloud, now, disoriented by the dark room. Only a second ago, it seemed, I had been under the brilliant sun.

"Bella?" Edward whispered, his arms tight around me, shaking me gently. "Are you all right, sweetheart?"

"Oh," I gasped again. Just a dream. Not real. To my utter astonishment, tears overflowed from my eyes without warning, gushing down my face.

"Bella!" he said—louder, alarmed now. "What's wrong?" He wiped the tears from my hot cheeks with cold, frantic fingers, but others followed.

"It was only a dream." I couldn't contain the low sob that broke in my voice. The senseless tears were disturbing, but I couldn't get control of the staggering grief that gripped me. I wanted so badly for the dream to be real.

"It's okay, love, you're fine. I'm here." He rocked me back and forth, a little too fast to soothe. "Did you have another nightmare? It wasn't real, it wasn't real."

"Not a nightmare." I shook my head, scrubbing the back of my hand against my eyes. "It was a *good* dream." My voice broke again.

"Then why are you crying?" he asked, bewildered.

"Because I woke up," I wailed, wrapping my arms around his neck in a chokehold and sobbing into his throat.

He laughed once at my logic, but the sound was tense with concern.

"Everything's all right, Bella. Take deep breaths."

"It was so real," I cried. "I *wanted* it to be real."

"Tell me about it," he urged. "Maybe that will help."

"We were on the beach. . . ." I trailed off, pulling back to look with tear-filled eyes at his anxious angel's face, dim in the darkness. I stared at him broodingly as the unreasonable grief began to ebb.

"And?" he finally prompted.

I blinked the tears out of my eyes, torn. "Oh, Edward . . ."

"Tell me, Bella," he pleaded, eyes wild with worry at the pain in my voice.

But I couldn't. Instead I clutched my arms around his neck again and locked my mouth with his feverishly. It wasn't desire at all—it was need, acute to the point of pain. His response was instant but quickly followed by his rebuff.

He struggled with me as gently as he could in his surprise, holding me away, grasping my shoulders.

"No, Bella," he insisted, looking at me as if he was worried that I'd lost my mind.

My arms dropped, defeated, the bizarre tears spilling in a fresh torrent down my face, a new sob rising in my throat. He was right—I must be crazy.

He stared at me with confused, anguished eyes.

"I'm s-s-s-orry," I mumbled.

But he pulled me to him then, hugging me tightly to his marble chest.

"I can't, Bella, I can't!" His moan was agonized.

"Please," I said, my plea muffled against his skin. "Please, Edward?"

I couldn't tell if he was moved by the tears trembling in my voice, or if he was unprepared to deal with the suddenness of my attack, or if his need was simply as unbearable in that moment as my own. But whatever the reason, he pulled my lips back to his, surrendering with a groan.

And we began where my dream had left off.

I stayed very still when I woke up in the morning and tried to keep my breathing even. I was afraid to open my eyes.

I was lying across Edward's chest, but he was very still and his arms were not wrapped around me. That was a bad sign. I was afraid to admit I was awake and face his anger— no matter whom it was directed at today.

Carefully, I peeked through my eyelashes. He was staring up at the dark ceiling, his arms behind his head. I pulled myself up on my elbow so that I could see his face better. It was smooth, expressionless.

"How much trouble am I in?" I asked in a small voice.

"Heaps," he said, but turned his head and smirked at me.

I breathed a sigh of relief. "I *am* sorry," I said. "I didn't mean . . . Well, I don't know exactly what that *was* last night." I shook my head at the memory of the irrational tears, the crushing grief.

"You never did tell me what your dream was about."

"I guess I didn't—but I sort of *showed* you what it was about." I laughed nervously.

"Oh," he said. His eyes widened, and then he blinked. "Interesting."

"It was a very good dream," I murmured. He didn't comment, so a few seconds later I asked, "Am I forgiven?"

"I'm thinking about it."

I sat up, planning to examine myself—there didn't seem to be any feathers, at least. But as I moved, an odd wave of vertigo hit. I swayed and fell back against the pillows.

"Whoa . . . head rush."

His arms were around me then. "You slept for a long time. Twelve hours."

"*Twelve?*" How strange.

I gave myself a quick once-over while I spoke, trying to be inconspicuous about it. I looked fine. The bruises on my arms were still a week old, yellowing. I stretched experimentally. I felt fine, too. Well, better than fine, actually.

"Is the inventory complete?"

I nodded sheepishly. "The pillows all appear to have survived."

"Unfortunately, I can't say the same for your, er, nightgown." He nodded toward the foot of the bed, where several scraps of black lace were strewn across the silk sheets.

"That's too bad," I said. "I liked that one."

"I did, too."

"Were there any other casualties?" I asked timidly.

"I'll have to buy Esme a new bed frame," he confessed, glancing over his shoulder. I followed his gaze and was shocked to see that large chunks of wood had apparently been gouged from the left side of the headboard.

"Hmm." I frowned. "You'd think I would have heard that."

"You seem to be extraordinarily unobservant when your attention is otherwise involved."

"I was a bit absorbed," I admitted, blushing a deep red.

He touched my burning cheek and sighed. "I'm really going to miss that."

I stared at his face, searching for any signs of the anger or remorse I feared. He gazed back at me evenly, his expression calm but otherwise unreadable.

"How are *you* feeling?"

He laughed.

"What?" I demanded.

"You look so guilty—like you've committed a crime."

"I *feel* guilty," I muttered.

"So you seduced your all-too-willing husband. That's not a capital offense."

He seemed to be teasing.

My cheeks got hotter. "The word *seduced* implies a certain amount of premeditation."

"Maybe that was the wrong word," he allowed.

"You're not angry?"

He smiled ruefully. "I'm not angry."

"Why not?"

"Well . . ." He paused. "I didn't hurt you, for one thing. It was easier this time, to control myself, to channel the excesses." His eyes flickered to the damaged frame again. "Maybe because I had a better idea of what to expect."

A hopeful smile started to spread across my face. "I *told* you that it was all about practice."

He rolled his eyes.

My stomach growled, and he laughed. "Breakfast time for the human?" he asked.

"Please," I said, hopping out of bed. I moved too quickly, though, and had to stagger drunkenly to regain my balance. He caught me before I could stumble into the dresser.

"Are you all right?"

"If I don't have a better sense of equilibrium in my next life, I'm demanding a refund."

I cooked this morning, frying up some eggs—too hungry

to do anything more elaborate. Impatient, I flipped them onto a plate after just a few minutes.

"Since when do you eat eggs sunny-side up?" he asked.

"Since now."

"Do you know how many eggs you've gone through in the last week?" He pulled the trash bin out from under the sink—it was full of empty blue cartons.

"Weird," I said after swallowing a scorching bite. "This place is messing with my appetite." And my dreams, and my already dubious balance. "But I like it here. We'll probably have to leave soon, though, won't we, to make it to Dartmouth in time? Wow, I guess we need to find a place to live and stuff, too."

He sat down next to me. "You can give up the college pretense now—you've gotten what you wanted. And we didn't agree to a deal, so there are no strings attached."

I snorted. "It wasn't a pretense, Edward. I don't spend *my* free time plotting like some people do. *What can we do to wear Bella out today?*" I said in a poor impression of his voice. He laughed, unashamed. "I really do want a little more time being human." I leaned over to run my hand across his bare chest. "I have not had enough."

He gave me a dubious look. "For *this*?" he asked, catching my hand as it moved down his stomach. "Sex was the key all along?" He rolled his eyes. "Why didn't I think of that?" he muttered sarcastically. "I could have saved myself a lot of arguments."

I laughed. "Yeah, probably."

"You are *so* human," he said again.

"I know."

A hint of a smile pulled at his lips. "We're going to Dartmouth? Really?"

"I'll probably fail out in one semester."

"I'll tutor you." The smile was wide now. "You're going to love college."

"Do you think we can find an apartment this late?"

He grimaced, looking guilty. "Well, we sort of already have a house there. You know, just in case."

"You bought a house?"

"Real estate is a good investment."

I raised one eyebrow and then let it go. "So we're ready, then."

"I'll have to see if we can keep your 'before' car for a little longer. . . ."

"Yes, heaven forbid I not be protected from tanks."

He grinned.

"How much longer can we stay?" I asked.

"We're fine on time. A few more weeks, if you want. And then we can visit Charlie before we go to New Hampshire. We could spend Christmas with Renée. . . ."

His words painted a very happy immediate future, one free of pain for everyone involved. The Jacob-drawer, all but forgotten, rattled, and I amended the thought—for *almost* everyone.

This wasn't getting any easier. Now that I'd discovered *exactly* how good being human could be, it was tempting to let my plans drift. Eighteen or nineteen, nineteen or twenty . . . Did it really matter? I wouldn't change so much in a year. And being human with Edward . . . The choice got trickier every day.

"A few weeks," I agreed. And then, because there never

seemed to be enough time, I added, "So I was thinking—you know what I was saying about practice before?"

He laughed. "Can you hold on to that thought? I hear a boat. The cleaning crew must be here."

He wanted me to hold on to that thought. So did that mean he was not going to give me any more trouble about practicing? I smiled.

"Let me explain the mess in the white room to Gustavo, and then we can go out. There's a place in the jungle on the south—"

"I don't want to go out. I am not hiking all over the island today. I want to stay here and watch a movie."

He pursed his lips, trying not to laugh at my disgruntled tone. "All right, whatever you'd like. Why don't you pick one out while I get the door?"

"I didn't hear a knock."

He cocked his head to the side, listening. A half second later, a faint, timid rap on the door sounded. He grinned and turned for the hallway.

I wandered over to the shelves under the big TV and started scanning through the titles. It was hard to decide where to begin. They had more DVDs than a rental store.

I could hear Edward's low, velvet voice as he came back down the hall, conversing fluidly in what I assumed was perfect Portuguese. Another, harsher, human voice answered in the same tongue.

Edward led them into the room, pointing toward the kitchen on his way. The two Brazilians looked incredibly short and dark next to him. One was a round man, the other a slight female, both their faces creased with lines. Edward gestured to me with a proud smile, and I heard my name mixed in with a flurry of unfamiliar words. I flushed a little as I thought of the downy mess in the white room, which they would soon encounter. The little man smiled at me politely.

But the tiny coffee-skinned woman didn't smile. She stared at me with a mixture of shock, worry, and most of all, wide-eyed *fear*. Before I could react, Edward motioned for them to follow him toward the chicken coop, and they were gone.

When he reappeared, he was alone. He walked swiftly to my side and wrapped his arms around me.

"What's with her?" I whispered urgently, remembering her panicked expression.

He shrugged, unperturbed. "Kaure's part Ticuna Indian. She was raised to be more superstitious—or you could call it more aware—than those who live in the modern world. She suspects what I am, or close enough." He still didn't sound worried. "They have their own legends here. The *Libishomen*—a blood-drinking demon who preys exclusively on beautiful women." He leered at me.

Beautiful women only? Well, that was kind of flattering.

"She looked terrified," I said.

"She is—but mostly she's worried about you."

"Me?"

"She's afraid of why I have you here, all alone." He chuckled darkly and then looked toward the wall of movies. "Oh well, why don't you choose something for us to watch? That's an acceptably human thing to do."

"Yes, I'm sure a movie will convince her that you're human." I laughed and clasped my arms securely around his neck, stretching up on my tiptoes. He leaned down so that I could kiss him, and then his arms tightened around me, lifting me off the floor so he didn't have to bend.

"Movie, schmovie," I muttered as his lips moved down my throat, twisting my fingers in his bronze hair.

Then I heard a gasp, and he put me down abruptly. Kaure stood frozen in the hallway, feathers in her black hair, a large sack of more feathers in her arms, an expression of horror on her face. She stared at me, her eyes bugging out, as I blushed and looked down. Then she recovered herself and murmured something that, even in an unfamiliar language, was clearly an apology. Edward smiled and answered in a friendly tone. She turned her dark eyes away and continued down the hall.

"She was thinking what I think she was thinking, wasn't she?" I muttered.

He laughed at my convoluted sentence. "Yes."

"Here," I said, reaching out at random and grabbing a movie. "Put this on and we can pretend to watch it."

It was an old musical with smiling faces and fluffy dresses on the front.

"Very honeymoonish," Edward approved.

While actors on the screen danced their way through a perky introduction song, I lolled on the sofa, snuggled into Edward's arms.

"Will we move back into the white room now?" I wondered idly.

"I don't know. . . . I've already mangled the headboard in the other room beyond repair—maybe if we limit the destruction to one area of the house, Esme might invite us back someday."

I smiled widely. "So there will be more destruction?"

He laughed at my expression. "I think it might be safer if it's premeditated, rather than if I wait for you to assault me again."

"It would only be a matter of time," I agreed casually, but my pulse was racing in my veins.

"Is there something the matter with your heart?"

"Nope. Healthy as a horse." I paused. "Did you want to go survey the demolition zone now?"

"Maybe it would be more polite to wait until we're alone. *You* may not notice me tearing the furniture apart, but it would probably scare them."

In truth, I'd already forgotten the people in the other room. "Right. Drat."

Gustavo and Kaure moved quietly through the house while I waited impatiently for them to finish and tried to pay attention to the happily-ever-after on the screen. I was starting to get sleepy—though, according to Edward, I'd slept half the day—when a rough voice startled me. Edward sat up, keeping me cradled against him, and answered Gustavo in flowing Portuguese. Gustavo nodded and walked quietly toward the front door.

"They're finished," Edward told me.

"So that would mean that we're alone now?"

"How about lunch first?" he suggested.

I bit my lip, torn by the dilemma. I *was* pretty hungry.

With a smile, he took my hand and led me to the kitchen. He knew my face so well, it didn't matter that he couldn't read my mind.

"This is getting out of hand," I complained when I finally felt full.

"Do you want to swim with the dolphins this afternoon—burn off the calories?" he asked.

"Maybe later. I had another idea for burning calories."

"And what was that?"

"Well, there's an awful lot of headboard left—"

But I didn't finish. He'd already swept me up into his arms, and his lips silenced mine as he carried me with inhuman speed to the blue room.

7. UNEXPECTED

THE LINE OF BLACK ADVANCED ON ME THROUGH THE shroud-like mist. I could see their dark ruby eyes glinting with desire, lusting for the kill. Their lips pulled back over their sharp, wet teeth—some to snarl, some to smile.

I heard the child behind me whimper, but I couldn't turn to look at him. Though I was desperate to be sure that he was safe, I could not afford any lapse in focus now.

They ghosted closer, their black robes billowing slightly with the movement. I saw their hands curl into bone-colored claws. They started to drift apart, angling to come at us from all sides. We were surrounded. We were going to die.

And then, like a burst of light from a flash, the whole

scene was different. Yet nothing changed—the Volturi still stalked toward us, poised to kill. All that really changed was how the picture looked to me. Suddenly, I was hungry for it. I *wanted* them to charge. The panic changed to bloodlust as I crouched forward, a smile on my face, and a growl ripped through my bared teeth.

I jolted upright, shocked out of the dream.

The room was black. It was also steamy hot. Sweat matted my hair at the temples and rolled down my throat.

I groped the warm sheets and found them empty.

"Edward?"

Just then, my fingers encountered something smooth and flat and stiff. One sheet of paper, folded in half. I took the note with me and felt my way across the room to the light switch.

The outside of the note was addressed to Mrs. Cullen.

I'm hoping you won't wake and notice my absence, but, if you should, I'll be back very soon. I've just gone to the mainland to hunt. Go back to sleep and I'll be here when you wake again. I love you.

I sighed. We'd been here about two weeks now, so I should have been expecting that he would have to leave, but I hadn't been thinking about time. We seemed to exist outside of time here, just drifting along in a perfect state.

I wiped the sweat off my forehead. I felt absolutely wide awake, though the clock on the dresser said it was after one. I knew I would never be able to sleep as hot and sticky as

I felt. Not to mention the fact that if I shut off the light and closed my eyes, I was sure to see those prowling black figures in my head.

I got up and wandered aimlessly through the dark house, flipping on lights. It felt so big and empty without Edward there. Different.

I ended up in the kitchen and decided that maybe comfort food was what I needed.

I poked around in the fridge until I found all the ingredients for fried chicken. The popping and sizzling of the chicken in the pan was a nice, homey sound; I felt less nervous while it filled the silence.

It smelled so good that I started eating it right out of the pan, burning my tongue in the process. By the fifth or sixth bite, though, it had cooled enough for me to taste it. My chewing slowed. Was there something off about the flavor? I checked the meat, and it was white all the way through, but I wondered if it was completely done. I took another experimental bite; I chewed twice. Ugh—definitely bad. I jumped up to spit it into the sink. Suddenly, the chicken-and-oil smell was revolting. I took the whole plate and shook it into the garbage, then opened the windows to chase away the scent. A coolish breeze had picked up outside. It felt good on my skin.

I was abruptly exhausted, but I didn't want to go back to the hot room. So I opened more windows in the TV room and lay on the couch right beneath them. I turned on the same movie we'd watched the other day and quickly fell asleep to the bright opening song.

When I opened my eyes again, the sun was halfway up the sky, but it was not the light that woke me. Cool arms were around me, pulling me against him. At the same time, a sudden pain twisted in my stomach, almost like the aftershock of catching a punch in the gut.

"I'm sorry," Edward was murmuring as he wiped a wintry hand across my clammy forehead. "So much for thoroughness. I didn't think about how hot you would be with me gone. I'll have an air conditioner installed before I leave again."

I couldn't concentrate on what he was saying. "Excuse me!" I gasped, struggling to get free of his arms.

He dropped his hold automatically. "Bella?"

I streaked for the bathroom with my hand clamped over my mouth. I felt so horrible that I didn't even care—at first—that he was with me while I crouched over the toilet and was violently sick.

"Bella? What's wrong?"

I couldn't answer yet. He held me anxiously, keeping my hair out of my face, waiting till I could breathe again.

"Damn rancid chicken," I moaned.

"Are you all right?" His voice was strained.

"Fine," I panted. "It's just food poisoning. You don't need to see this. Go away."

"Not likely, Bella."

"Go away," I moaned again, struggling to get up so I could rinse my mouth out. He helped me gently, ignoring the weak shoves I aimed at him.

After my mouth was clean, he carried me to the bed and sat me down carefully, supporting me with his arms.

"Food poisoning?"

"Yeah," I croaked. "I made some chicken last night. It tasted off, so I threw it out. But I ate a few bites first."

He put a cold hand on my forehead. It felt nice. "How do you feel now?"

I thought about that for a moment. The nausea had passed as suddenly as it had come, and I felt like I did any other morning. "Pretty normal. A little hungry, actually."

He made me wait an hour and keep down a big glass of water before he fried me some eggs. I felt perfectly normal, just a little tired from being up in the middle of the night. He put on CNN—we'd been so out of touch, world war three could have broken out and we wouldn't have known—and I lounged drowsily across his lap.

I got bored with the news and twisted around to kiss him. Just like this morning, a sharp pain hit my stomach when I moved. I lurched away from him, my hand tight over my mouth. I knew I'd never make it to the bathroom this time, so I ran to the kitchen sink.

He held my hair again.

"Maybe we should go back to Rio, see a doctor," he suggested anxiously when I was rinsing my mouth afterward.

I shook my head and edged toward the hallway. Doctors meant needles. "I'll be fine right after I brush my teeth."

When my mouth tasted better, I searched through my suitcase for the little first-aid kit Alice had packed for me, full of human things like bandages and painkillers and—my object now—Pepto-Bismol. Maybe I could settle my stomach and calm Edward down.

But before I found the Pepto, I happened across something else that Alice had packed for me. I picked up the small blue box and stared at it in my hand for a long moment, forgetting everything else.

Then I started counting in my head. Once. Twice. Again.

The knock startled me; the little box fell back into the suitcase.

"Are you well?" Edward asked through the door. "Did you get sick again?"

"Yes and no," I said, but my voice sounded strangled.

"Bella? Can I please come in?" Worriedly now.

"O . . . kay?"

He came in and appraised my position, sitting cross-legged on the floor by the suitcase, and my expression, blank and staring. He sat next to me, his hand going to my forehead at once.

"What's wrong?"

"How many days has it been since the wedding?" I whispered.

"Seventeen," he answered automatically. "Bella, what is it?"

I was counting again. I held up a finger, cautioning him to wait, and mouthed the numbers to myself. I'd been wrong about the days before. We'd been here longer than I'd thought. I started over again.

"Bella!" he whispered urgently. "I'm losing my mind over here."

I tried to swallow. It didn't work. So I reached into the suitcase and fumbled around until I found the little blue box of tampons again. I held them up silently.

He stared at me in confusion. "What? Are you trying to pass this illness off as PMS?"

"No," I managed to choke out. "No, Edward. I'm trying to tell you that my period is five days late."

His facial expression didn't change. It was like I hadn't spoken.

"I don't think I have food poisoning," I added.

He didn't respond. He had turned into a sculpture.

"The dreams," I mumbled to myself in a flat voice. "Sleeping so much. The crying. All that food. Oh. Oh. *Oh*."

Edward's stare seemed glassy, as if he couldn't see me anymore.

Reflexively, almost involuntarily, my hand dropped to my stomach.

"Oh!" I squeaked again.

I lurched to my feet, slipping out of Edward's unmoving hands. I'd never changed out of the little silk shorts and camisole I'd worn to bed. I yanked the blue fabric out of the way and stared at my stomach.

"Impossible," I whispered.

I had absolutely no experience with pregnancy or babies or any part of that world, but I wasn't an idiot. I'd seen enough movies and TV shows to know that this wasn't how it worked. I was only five days late. If I *was* pregnant, my body wouldn't even have registered that fact. I would not have morning sickness. I would not have changed my eating or sleeping habits.

And I most definitely would not have a small but defined bump sticking out between my hips.

I twisted my torso back and forth, examining it from every angle, as if it would disappear in exactly the right light. I ran my fingers over the subtle bulge, surprised by how rock hard it felt under my skin.

"Impossible," I said again, because, bulge or no bulge,

period or no period (and there was definitely no period, though I'd never been late a day in my life), there was no way I could be *pregnant*. The only person I'd ever had sex with was a vampire, for crying out loud.

A vampire who was still frozen on the floor with no sign of ever moving again.

So there had to be some other explanation, then. Something wrong with me. A strange South American disease with all the signs of pregnancy, only accelerated . . .

And then I remembered something—a morning of internet research that seemed a lifetime ago now. Sitting at the old desk in my room at Charlie's house with gray light glowing dully through the window, staring at my ancient, wheezing computer, reading avidly through a website called "Vampires A–Z." It had been less than twenty-four hours since Jacob Black, trying to entertain me with the Quileute legends he didn't believe in yet, had told me that Edward was a vampire. I'd scanned anxiously through the first entries on the site, which was dedicated to vampire myths around the world. The Filipino *Danag*, the Hebrew *Estrie*, the Romanian *Varacolaci*, the Italian *Stregoni benefici* (a legend actually based on my new father-in-law's early exploits with the Volturi, not that I'd known anything about that at the time) . . . I'd paid less and less attention as the stories had grown more and more implausible. I only remembered vague bits of the later entries. They mostly seemed like excuses dreamed up to explain things like infant mortality rates—and infidelity. *No, honey, I'm not having an affair! That sexy woman you saw sneaking out of the house was an evil succubus. I'm lucky I escaped with my life!* (Of course, with what I knew now about Tanya and her sisters, I suspected that some of those excuses had been nothing but fact.) There had been one for the ladies, too. *How can you accuse me of cheating on you—just because you've come home from a two-year sea voyage and I'm pregnant? It was the incubus. He hypnotized me with his mystical vampire powers. . . .*

That had been part of the definition of the incubus—the ability to father children with his hapless prey.

I shook my head, dazed. But . . .

I thought of Esme and especially Rosalie. Vampires couldn't have children. If it were possible, Rosalie would have found a way by now. The incubus myth was nothing but a fable.

Except that . . . well, there *was* a difference. Of course Rosalie could not conceive a child, because she was frozen in the state in which she passed from human to inhuman. Totally unchanging. And human women's bodies had to *change* to bear children. The constant change of a monthly cycle for one thing, and then the bigger changes needed to accommodate a growing child. Rosalie's body couldn't change.

But mine could. Mine did. I touched the bump on my stomach that had not been there yesterday.

And human men—well, they pretty much stayed the same from puberty to death. I remembered a random bit of trivia, gleaned from who knows where: Charlie Chaplin was in his seventies when he fathered his youngest child. Men had no such thing as child-bearing years or cycles of fertility.

Of course, how would anyone know if vampire men could father children, when their partners were not able? What vampire on earth would have the restraint necessary to test the theory with a human woman? Or the inclination?

I could think of only one.

Part of my head was sorting through fact and memory and speculation, while the other half—the part that controlled the ability to move even the smallest muscles—was stunned beyond the capacity for normal operations. I couldn't move my lips to speak, though I wanted to ask Edward to *please* explain to me what was going on. I needed to go back to where he sat, to touch him, but my body wouldn't follow instructions. I could only stare at my shocked eyes in the mirror, my fingers gingerly pressed against the swelling on my torso.

And then, like in my vivid nightmare last night, the scene abruptly transformed. Everything I saw in the mirror looked completely different, though nothing actually *was* different.

What happened to change everything was that a soft little nudge bumped my hand—from inside my body.

In the same moment, Edward's phone rang, shrill and demanding. Neither of us moved. It rang again and again. I tried to tune it out while I pressed my fingers to my stomach, waiting. In the mirror my expression was no longer bewildered—it was wondering now. I barely noticed when the strange, silent tears started streaming down my cheeks.

The phone kept ringing. I wished Edward would answer it—I was having a moment. Possibly the biggest of my life.

Ring! Ring! Ring!

Finally, the annoyance broke through everything else. I got down on my knees next to Edward—I found myself moving more carefully, a thousand times more aware of the way each motion felt—and patted his pockets until I found the phone. I half-expected him to thaw out and answer it himself, but he was perfectly still.

I recognized the number, and I could easily guess why she was calling.

"Hi, Alice," I said. My voice wasn't much better than before. I cleared my throat.

"Bella? Bella, are you okay?"

"Yeah. Um. Is Carlisle there?"

"He is. What's the problem?"

"I'm not . . . one hundred percent . . . sure. . . ."

"Is Edward all right?" she asked warily. She called Carlisle's name away from the phone and then demanded, "Why didn't he pick up the phone?" before I could answer her first question.

"I'm not sure."

"Bella, what's going on? I just saw—"

"What did you see?"

There was a silence. "Here's Carlisle," she finally said.

It felt like ice water had been injected in my veins. If Alice had seen a vision of me with a green-eyed, angel-faced child in my arms, she would have answered me, wouldn't she?

While I waited through the split second it took for Carlisle to speak, the vision I'd imagined for Alice danced behind my lids. A tiny, beautiful little baby, even more beautiful than the boy in my dream—a tiny Edward in my arms. Warmth shot through my veins, chasing the ice away.

"Bella, it's Carlisle. What's going on?"

"I—" I wasn't sure how to answer. Would he laugh at my

conclusions, tell me I was crazy? Was I just having another colorful dream? "I'm a little worried about Edward. . . . Can vampires go into shock?"

"Has he been harmed?" Carlisle's voice was suddenly urgent.

"No, no," I assured him. "Just . . . taken by surprise."

"I don't understand, Bella."

"I think . . . well, I think that . . . maybe . . . I might be . . ." I took a deep breath. "Pregnant."

As if to back me up, there was another tiny nudge in my abdomen. My hand flew to my stomach.

After a long pause, Carlisle's medical training kicked in. "When was the first day of your last menstrual cycle?"

"Sixteen days before the wedding." I'd done the mental math thoroughly enough just before to be able to answer with certainty.

"How do you feel?"

"Weird," I told him, and my voice broke. Another trickle of tears dribbled down my cheeks. "This is going to sound crazy—look, I know it's way too early for any of this. Maybe I *am* crazy. But I'm having bizarre dreams and eating all the time and crying and throwing up and . . . and . . . I swear something *moved* inside me just now."

Edward's head snapped up.

I sighed in relief.

Edward held his hand out for the phone, his face white and hard.

"Um, I think Edward wants to talk to you."

"Put him on," Carlisle said in a strained voice.

Not entirely sure that Edward *could* talk, I put the phone in his outstretched hand.

He pressed it to his ear. "Is it possible?" he whispered.

He listened for a long time, staring blankly at nothing.

"And Bella?" he asked. His arm wrapped around me as he spoke, pulling me close into his side.

He listened for what seemed like a long time and then said, "Yes. Yes, I will."

He pulled the phone away from his ear and pressed the "end" button. Right away, he dialed a new number.

"What did Carlisle say?" I asked impatiently.

Edward answered in a lifeless voice. "He thinks you're pregnant."

The words sent a warm shiver down my spine. The little nudger fluttered inside me.

"Who are you calling now?" I asked as he put the phone back to his ear.

"The airport. We're going home."

Edward was on the phone for more than an hour without a break. I guessed that he was arranging our flight home, but I couldn't be sure because he wasn't speaking English. It sounded like he was arguing; he spoke through his teeth a lot.

While he argued, he packed. He whirled around the room like an angry tornado, leaving order rather than destruction in his path. He threw a set of my clothes on the bed without looking at them, so I assumed it was time for me to get dressed. He continued with his argument while I changed, gesturing with sudden, agitated movements.

When I could no longer bear the violent energy radiating out of him, I quietly left the room. His manic concentration made me sick to my stomach—not like the morning sickness, just uncomfortable. I would wait somewhere else for his mood to pass. I couldn't talk to this icy, focused Edward who honestly frightened me a little.

Once again, I ended up in the kitchen. There was a bag of pretzels in the cupboard. I started chewing on them absently, staring out the window at the sand and rocks and trees and ocean, everything glittering in the sun.

Someone nudged me.

"I know," I said. "I don't want to go, either."

I stared out the window for a moment, but the nudger didn't respond.

"I don't understand," I whispered. "What is *wrong* here?"

Surprising, absolutely. Astonishing, even. But *wrong*? No.

So why was Edward so *furious*? He was the one who had actually wished out loud for a shotgun wedding.

I tried to reason through it.

Maybe it wasn't so confusing that Edward wanted us to go home right away. He'd want Carlisle to check me out, make sure my assumption was right—though there was absolutely no doubt in my head at this point. Probably they'd want to figure out why I was already *so* pregnant, with the bump and the nudging and all of that. That wasn't normal.

Once I thought of this, I was sure I had it. He must be so worried about the baby. I hadn't gotten around to freaking out yet. My brain worked slower than his—it was still stuck marveling over the picture it had conjured up before: the tiny child with Edward's eyes—green, as his had been when he was human—lying fair and beautiful in my arms. I hoped he would have Edward's face exactly, with no interference from mine.

It was funny how abruptly and entirely necessary this vision had become. From that first little touch, the whole world had shifted. Where before there was just one thing I could not live without, now there were two. There was no division—my love was not split between them now; it wasn't like that. It was more like my heart had grown, swollen up to twice its size in that moment. All that extra space, already filled. The increase was almost dizzying.

I'd never really understood Rosalie's pain and resentment before. I'd never imagined myself a mother, never wanted that. It had been a piece of cake to promise Edward that I didn't care about giving up children for him, because I truly didn't. Children, in the abstract, had never appealed to me. They seemed to be loud creatures, often dripping some form of goo. I'd never had much to do with them. When I'd dreamed of Renée providing me with a brother, I'd always imagined an *older* brother. Someone to take care of me, rather than the other way around.

This child, Edward's child, was a whole different story.

I wanted him like I wanted air to breathe. Not a choice—a necessity.

Maybe I just had a really bad imagination. Maybe that was why I'd been unable to imagine that I would *like* being married until after I already was—unable to see that I would want a baby until after one was already coming. . . .

As I put my hand on my stomach, waiting for the next nudge, tears streaked down my cheeks again.

"Bella?"

I turned, made wary by the tone of his voice. It was too cold, too careful. His face matched his voice, empty and hard.

And then he saw that I was crying.

"Bella!" He crossed the room in a flash and put his hands on my face. "Are you in pain?"

"No, no—"

He pulled me against his chest. "Don't be afraid. We'll be home in sixteen hours. You'll be fine. Carlisle will be ready when we get there. We'll take care of this, and you'll be fine, you'll be fine."

"Take care of this? What do you mean?"

He leaned away and looked me in the eye. "We're going to get that thing out before it can hurt any part of you. Don't be scared. I *won't* let it hurt you."

"That *thing*?" I gasped.

He looked sharply away from me, toward the front door. "Dammit! I forgot Gustavo was due today. I'll get rid of him and be right back." He darted out of the room.

I clutched the counter for support. My knees were wobbly.

Edward had just called my little nudger a *thing*. He said Carlisle would get it out.

"No," I whispered.

I'd gotten it wrong before. He didn't care about the baby at all. He wanted to *hurt* him. The beautiful picture in my head shifted abruptly, changed into something dark. My pretty baby crying, my weak arms not enough to protect him. . . .

What could I do? Would I be able to reason with them?

What if I couldn't? Did this explain Alice's strange silence on the phone? Is that what she'd seen? Edward and Carlisle killing that pale, perfect child before he could live?

"No," I whispered again, my voice stronger. That could *not* be. I would not allow it.

I heard Edward speaking Portuguese again. Arguing again. His voice got closer, and I heard him grunt in exasperation. Then I heard another voice, low and timid. A woman's voice.

He came into the kitchen ahead of her and went straight to me. He wiped the tears from my cheeks and murmured in my ear through the thin, hard line of his lips.

"She's insisting on leaving the food she brought—she made us dinner." If he had been less tense, less furious, I knew he would have rolled his eyes. "It's an excuse—she wants to make sure I haven't killed you yet." His voice went ice cold at the end.

Kaure edged nervously around the corner with a covered dish in her hands. I wished I could speak Portuguese, or that my Spanish was less rudimentary, so that I could try to thank this woman who had dared to anger a vampire just to check on me.

Her eyes flickered between the two of us. I saw her measuring the color in my face, the moisture in my eyes. Mumbling something I didn't understand, she put the dish on the counter.

Edward snapped something at her; I'd never heard him be so impolite before. She turned to go, and the whirling motion of her long skirt wafted the smell of the food into my face. It was strong—onions and fish. I gagged and whirled for the sink. I felt Edward's hands on my forehead and heard his soothing murmur through the roaring in my ears. His hands disappeared for a second, and I heard the refrigerator slam shut. Mercifully, the smell disappeared with the sound, and Edward's hands were cooling my clammy face again. It was over quickly.

I rinsed my mouth in the tap while he caressed the side of my face.

There was a tentative little nudge in my womb.

It's okay. We're okay, I thought toward the bump.

Edward turned me around, pulling me into his arms. I rested my head on his shoulder. My hands, instinctively, folded over my stomach.

I heard a little gasp and I looked up.

The woman was still there, hesitating in the doorway with her hands half-outstretched as if she had been looking for some way to help. Her eyes were locked on my hands, popping wide with shock. Her mouth hung open.

Then Edward gasped, too, and he suddenly turned to face the woman, pushing me slightly behind his body. His arm wrapped across my torso, like he was holding me back.

Suddenly, Kaure was shouting at him—loudly, furiously, her unintelligible words flying across the room like knives. She raised her tiny fist in the air and took two steps forward, shaking it at him. Despite her ferocity, it was easy to see the terror in her eyes.

Edward stepped toward her, too, and I clutched at his arm, frightened for the woman. But when he interrupted her tirade, his voice took me by surprise, especially considering how sharp he'd been with her when she *wasn't* screeching at him. It was low now; it was pleading. Not only that, but the sound was different, more guttural, the cadence off. I didn't think he was speaking Portuguese anymore.

For a moment, the woman stared at him in wonder, and then her eyes narrowed as she barked out a long question in the same alien tongue.

I watched as his face grew sad and serious, and he nodded once. She took a quick step back and crossed herself.

He reached out to her, gesturing toward me and then resting his hand against my cheek. She replied angrily again, waving her hands accusingly toward him, and then gestured to him. When she finished, he pleaded again with the same low, urgent voice.

Her expression changed—she stared at him with doubt plain on her face as he spoke, her eyes repeatedly flashing to my confused face. He stopped speaking, and she seemed to be deliberating something. She looked back and forth between the two of us, and then, unconsciously it seemed, took a step forward.

She made a motion with her hands, miming a shape like a balloon jutting out from her stomach. I started—did her legends of the predatory blood-drinker include *this*? Could she possibly know something about what was growing inside me?

She walked a few steps forward deliberately this time and asked a few brief questions, which he responded to tensely. Then he became the questioner—one quick query. She hesitated and then slowly shook her head. When he spoke again, his voice was so agonized that I looked up at him in shock. His face was drawn with pain.

In answer, she walked slowly forward until she was

close enough to lay her small hand on top of mine, over my stomach. She spoke one word in Portuguese.

"*Morte*," she sighed quietly. Then she turned, her shoulders bent as if the conversation had aged her, and left the room.

I knew enough Spanish for that one.

Edward was frozen again, staring after her with the tortured expression fixed on his face. A few moments later, I heard a boat's engine putter to life and then fade into the distance.

Edward did not move until I started for the bathroom. Then his hand caught my shoulder.

"Where are you going?" His voice was a whisper of pain.

"To brush my teeth again."

"Don't worry about what she said. It's nothing but legends, old lies for the sake of entertainment."

"I didn't understand anything," I told him, though it wasn't entirely true. As if I could discount something because it was a legend. My life was circled by legend on every side. They were all true.

"I packed your toothbrush. I'll get it for you."

He walked ahead of me to the bedroom.

"Are we leaving soon?" I called after him.

"As soon as you're done."

He waited for my toothbrush to repack it, pacing silently around the bedroom. I handed it to him when I was finished.

"I'll get the bags into the boat."

"Edward—"

He turned back. "Yes?"

I hesitated, trying to think of some way to get a few seconds alone. "Could you . . . pack some of the food? You know, in case I get hungry again."

"Of course," he said, his eyes suddenly soft. "Don't worry about anything. We'll get to Carlisle in just a few hours, really. This will all be over soon."

I nodded, not trusting my voice.

He turned and left the room, one big suitcase in each hand.

I whirled and scooped up the phone he'd left on the counter. It was very unlike him to forget things—to forget that Gustavo was coming, to leave his phone lying here. He was so stressed he was barely himself.

I flipped it open and scrolled through the preprogrammed numbers. I was glad he had the sound turned off, afraid that he would catch me. Would he be at the boat now? Or back already? Would he hear me from the kitchen if I whispered?

I found the number I wanted, one I had never called before in my life. I pressed the "send" button and crossed my fingers.

"Hello?" the voice like golden wind chimes answered.

"Rosalie?" I whispered. "It's Bella. Please. You have to help me."

BOOK TWO

✦ ✦

jacob

*A*nd yet, to say the truth,
reason and love keep little company together nowadays.

William Shakespeare
A Midsummer Night's Dream
Act III, Scene i

PREFACE

Life sucks, and then you die.

Yeah, I should be so lucky.

8. WAITING FOR THE DAMN FIGHT TO START ALREADY

"JEEZ, PAUL, DON'T YOU FREAKING HAVE A HOME OF YOUR *own*?"

Paul, lounging across *my* whole couch, watching some stupid baseball game on *my* crappy TV, just grinned at me and then—real slow—he lifted one Dorito from the bag in his lap and wedged it into his mouth in one piece.

"You better've brought those with you."

Crunch. "Nope," he said while chewing. "Your sister said to go ahead and help myself to anything I wanted."

I tried to make my voice sound like I wasn't about to punch him. "Is Rachel here now?"

It didn't work. He heard where I was going and shoved

the bag behind his back. The bag crackled as he smashed it into the cushion. The chips crunched into pieces. Paul's hands came up in fists, close to his face like a boxer.

"Bring it, kid. I don't need Rachel to protect me."

I snorted. "Right. Like you wouldn't go crying to her first chance."

He laughed and relaxed into the sofa, dropping his hands. "I'm not going to go tattle to a girl. If you got in a lucky hit, that would be just between the two of us. And vice versa, right?"

Nice of him to give me an invitation. I made my body slump like I'd given up. "Right."

His eyes shifted to the TV.

I lunged.

His nose made a very satisfying crunching sound of its own when my fist connected. He tried to grab me, but I danced out of the way before he could find a hold, the ruined bag of Doritos in my left hand.

"You broke my nose, idiot."

"Just between us, right, Paul?"

I went to put the chips away. When I turned around, Paul was repositioning his nose before it could set crooked. The blood had already stopped; it looked like it had no source as it trickled down his lips and off his chin. He cussed, wincing as he pulled at the cartilage.

"You are such a pain, Jacob. I swear, I'd rather hang out with Leah."

"Ouch. Wow, I bet Leah's really going to love to hear that you want to spend some quality time with her. It'll just warm the cockles of her heart."

"You're going to forget I said that."

"Of course. I'm sure it won't slip out."

"Ugh," he grunted, and then settled back into the couch, wiping the leftover blood on the collar of his t-shirt. "You're fast, kid. I'll give you that." He turned his attention back to the fuzzy game.

I stood there for a second, and then I stalked off to my room, muttering about alien abductions.

Back in the day, you could count on Paul for a fight pretty much whenever. You didn't have to hit him then—any mild insult would do. It didn't take a lot to flip him out of control. Now, of course, when I really *wanted* a good snarling, ripping, break-the-trees-down match, he had to be all mellow.

Wasn't it bad enough that yet another member of the pack had imprinted—because, really, that made four of ten now! When would it stop? Stupid myth was supposed to be *rare,* for crying out loud! All this mandatory love-at-first-sight was completely sickening!

Did it have to be *my* sister? Did it have to be *Paul*?

When Rachel'd come home from Washington State at the end of the summer semester—graduated early, the nerd—my biggest worry'd been that it would be hard keeping the secret around her. I wasn't used to covering things up in my own home. It made me real sympathetic to kids like Embry and Collin, whose parents didn't know they were werewolves. Embry's mom thought he was going through some kind of rebellious stage. He was permanently grounded for constantly sneaking out, but, of course, there wasn't much he could do about that. She'd check his room every night, and every night it would be empty again. She'd yell and he'd take it in silence, and then go through it all again the next day. We'd tried to talk Sam into giving Embry a break and letting his mom in on the gig, but Embry'd said he didn't mind. The secret was too important.

So I'd been all geared up to be keeping that secret. And then, two days after Rachel got home, Paul ran into her on the beach. Bada bing, bada boom—true love! No secrets necessary when you found your other half, and all that imprinting werewolf garbage.

Rachel got the whole story. And I got Paul as a brother-in-law someday. I knew Billy wasn't much thrilled about it, either. But he handled it better than I did. 'Course, he did escape to the Clearwaters' more often than usual these days. I didn't see where that was so much better. No Paul, but plenty of Leah.

I wondered—would a bullet through my temple actually kill me or just leave a really big mess for me to clean up?

I threw myself down on the bed. I was tired—hadn't slept since my last patrol—but I knew I wasn't going to sleep. My head was too crazy. The thoughts bounced around inside my skull like a disoriented swarm of bees. Noisy. Now and then they stung. Must be hornets, not bees. Bees died after one sting. And the same thoughts were stinging me again and again.

This waiting was driving me insane. It had been almost four weeks. I'd expected, one way or another, the news would have come by now. I'd sat up nights imagining what form it would take.

Charlie sobbing on the phone—Bella and her husband lost in an accident. A plane crash? That would be hard to fake. Unless the leeches didn't mind killing a bunch of bystanders to authenticate it, and why would they? Maybe a small plane instead. They probably had one of those to spare.

Or would the murderer come home alone, unsuccessful in his attempt to make her one of them? Or not even getting that far. Maybe he'd smashed her like a bag of chips in his drive to get some? Because her life was less important to him than his own pleasure . . .

The story would be so tragic—Bella lost in a horrible accident. Victim of a mugging gone wrong. Choking to death at dinner. A car accident, like my mom. So common. Happened all the time.

Would he bring her home? Bury her here for Charlie? Closed-casket ceremony, of course. My mom's coffin had been nailed shut. . . .

I could only hope that he'd come back here, within my reach.

Maybe there would be no story at all. Maybe Charlie would call to ask my dad if he'd heard anything from Dr. Cullen, who just didn't show up to work one day. The house abandoned. No answer on any of the Cullens' phones. The mystery picked up by some second-rate news program, foul play suspected . . .

Maybe the big white house would burn to the ground, everyone trapped inside. Of course, they'd need bodies for that one. Eight humans of roughly the right size. Burned beyond recognition—beyond the help of dental records.

Either of those would be tricky—for me, that is. It would be hard to find them if they didn't want to be found. Of course, I had forever to look. If you had forever, you could check out every single piece of straw in the haystack, one by one, to see if it was the needle.

Right now, I wouldn't mind dismantling a haystack. At least that would be something to *do*. I hated knowing that I could be losing my chance. Giving the bloodsuckers the time to escape, if that was their plan.

We could go tonight. We could kill every one of them that we could find.

I liked that plan because I knew Edward well enough to know that, if I killed any one of his coven, I would get my chance at him, too. He'd come for revenge. And I'd give it to him—I wouldn't let my brothers take him down as a pack. It would be just him and me. May the better man win.

But Sam wouldn't hear of it. *We're not going to break the treaty. Let them make the breach.* Just because we had no proof that the Cullens had done anything wrong. Yet. You had to add the yet, because we all knew it was inevitable. Bella was either coming back one of them, or not coming back. Either way, a human life had been lost. And that meant game on.

In the other room, Paul brayed like a mule. Maybe he'd switched to a comedy. Maybe the commercial was funny. Whatever. It grated on my nerves.

I thought about breaking his nose again. But it wasn't Paul I wanted to fight with. Not really.

I tried to listen to other sounds, the wind in the trees. It wasn't the same, not through human ears. There were a million voices in the wind that I couldn't hear in this body.

But these ears were sensitive enough. I could hear past the trees, to the road, the sounds of the cars coming around that last bend where you could finally see the beach—the vista of the islands and the rocks and the big blue ocean stretching to the horizon. The La Push cops liked to hang out right around there. Tourists never noticed the reduced speed limit sign on the other side of the road.

I could hear the voices outside the souvenir shop on the beach. I could hear the cowbell clanging as the door opened and closed. I could hear Embry's mom at the cash register, printing out a receipt.

I could hear the tide raking across the beach rocks. I could hear the kids squeal as the icy water rushed in too fast for them to get out of the way. I could hear the moms complain about the wet clothes. And I could hear a familiar voice. . . .

I was listening so hard that the sudden burst of Paul's donkey laugh made me jump half off the bed.

"Get out of my house," I grumbled. Knowing he wouldn't pay any attention, I followed my own advice. I wrenched open my window and climbed out the back way so that I wouldn't see Paul again. It would be too tempting. I knew I would hit him again, and Rachel was going to be pissed enough already. She'd see the blood on his shirt, and she'd blame me right away without waiting for proof. Of course, she'd be right, but still.

I paced down to the shore, my fists in my pockets. Nobody looked at me twice when I went through the dirt lot by First Beach. That was one nice thing about summer—no one cared if you wore nothing but shorts.

I followed the familiar voice I'd heard and found Quil easy enough. He was on the south end of the crescent, avoiding the bigger part of the tourist crowd. He kept up a constant stream of warnings.

"Keep out of the water, Claire. C'mon. No, don't. Oh! *Nice*, kid. Seriously, do you want Emily to yell at me? I'm not bringing you back to the beach again if you don't—Oh yeah? Don't—ugh. You think that's funny, do you? Hah! Who's laughing now, huh?"

He had the giggling toddler by the ankle when I reached them. She had a bucket in one hand, and her jeans were drenched. He had a huge wet mark down the front of his t-shirt.

"Five bucks on the baby girl," I said.

"Hey, Jake."

Claire squealed and threw her bucket at Quil's knees. "Down, down!"

He set her carefully on her feet and she ran to me. She wrapped her arms around my leg.

"Unca Jay!"

"How's it going, Claire?"

She giggled. "Qwil *aaaaawl* wet now."

"I can see that. Where's your mama?"

"Gone, gone, gone," Claire sang, "Cwaire pway wid Qwil *aaaawl* day. Cwaire nebber gowin home." She let go of me and ran to Quil. He scooped her up and slung her onto his shoulders.

"Sounds like somebody's hit the terrible twos."

"Threes actually," Quil corrected. "You missed the party. Princess theme. She made me wear a crown, and then Emily suggested they all try out her new play makeup on me."

"Wow, I'm *really* sorry I wasn't around to see that."

"Don't worry, Emily has pictures. Actually, I look pretty hot."

"You're such a patsy."

Quil shrugged. "Claire had a great time. That was the point."

I rolled my eyes. It was hard being around imprinted people. No matter what stage they were in—about to tie the knot like Sam or just a much-abused nanny like Quil— the peace and certainty they always radiated was downright puke-inducing.

Claire squealed on his shoulders and pointed at the ground. "Pity wock, Qwil! For me, for me!"

"Which one, kiddo? The red one?"

"No wed!"

Quil dropped to his knees—Claire screamed and pulled his hair like a horse's reigns.

"This blue one?"

"No, no, no . . . ," the little girl sang, thrilled with her new game.

The weird part was, Quil was having just as much fun as she was. He didn't have that face on that so many of the tourist dads and moms were wearing—the when-is-nap-time? face. You never saw a real parent so jazzed to play whatever stupid kiddie sport their rugrat could think up. I'd seen Quil play peekaboo for an hour straight without getting bored.

And I couldn't even make fun of him for it—I envied him too much.

Though I did think it sucked that he had a good fourteen years of monk-i-tude ahead of him until Claire was his age—for Quil, at least, it was a good thing werewolves didn't get older. But even all that time didn't seem to bother him much.

"Quil, you ever think about dating?" I asked.

"Huh?"

"No, no yewwo!" Claire crowed.

"You know. A real girl. I mean, just for now, right? On your nights off babysitting duty."

Quil stared at me, his mouth hanging open.

"Pity wock! Pity wock!" Claire screamed when he didn't offer her another choice. She smacked him on the head with her little fist.

"Sorry, Claire-bear. How about this pretty purple one?"

"No," she giggled. "No poopoh."

"Give me a clue. I'm begging, kid."

Claire thought it over. "Gween," she finally said.

Quil stared at the rocks, studying them. He picked four rocks in different shades of green, and offered them to her.

"Did I get it?"

"Yay!"

"Which one?"

"*Aaaaawl* ob dem!!"

She cupped her hands and he poured the small rocks into them. She laughed and immediately clunked him on the head with them. He winced theatrically and then got to his feet and started walking back up toward the parking lot. Probably worried about her getting cold in her wet clothes. He was worse than any paranoid, overprotective mother.

"Sorry if I was being pushy before, man, about the girl thing," I said.

"Naw, that's cool," Quil said. "It kind of took me by surprise is all. I hadn't thought about it."

"I bet she'd understand. You know, when she's grown up. She wouldn't get mad that you had a life while she was in diapers."

"No, I know. I'm sure she'd understand that."

He didn't say anything else.

"But you won't do that, will you?" I guessed.

"I can't see it," he said in a low voice. "I can't imagine. I just don't . . . see anyone that way. I don't notice girls anymore, you know. I don't see their faces."

"Put that together with the tiara and makeup, and maybe Claire will have a different kind of competition to worry about."

Quil laughed and made kissing noises at me. "You available this Friday, Jacob?"

"You wish," I said, and then I made a face. "Yeah, guess I am, though."

He hesitated a second and then said, "You ever think about dating?"

I sighed. Guess I'd opened myself up for that one.

"You know, Jake, maybe you should think about getting a life."

He didn't say it like a joke. His voice was sympathetic. That made it worse.

"I don't see them, either, Quil. I don't see their faces."

Quil sighed, too.

Far away, too low for anyone but just us two to hear it over the waves, a howl rose out of the forest.

"Dang, that's Sam," Quil said. His hands flew up to touch Claire, as if making sure she was still there. "I don't know where her mom's at!"

"I'll see what it is. If we need you, I'll let you know." I raced through the words. They came out all slurred together. "Hey, why don't you take her up to the Clearwaters'? Sue and Billy can keep an eye on her if they need to. They might know what's going on, anyway."

"Okay—get outta here, Jake!"

I took off running, not for the dirt path through the weedy hedge, but in the shortest line toward the forest. I hurdled the first line of driftwood and then ripped my way through the briars, still running. I felt the little tears as the thorns cut into my skin, but I ignored them. Their sting would be healed before I made the trees.

I cut behind the store and darted across the highway. Somebody honked at me. Once in the safety of the trees, I ran faster, taking longer strides. People would stare if I was out in the open. Normal people couldn't run like this. Sometimes I thought it might be fun to enter a race—you know, like the Olympic trials or something. It would be cool to watch the expressions on those star athletes' faces when I blew by them. Only I was pretty sure the testing they did to make sure you weren't on steroids would probably turn up some really freaky crap in my blood.

As soon as I was in the true forest, unbound by roads or houses, I skidded to a stop and kicked my shorts off. With quick, practiced moves, I rolled them up and tied them to the leather cord around my ankle. As I was still pulling the ends tight, I started shifting. The fire trembled down my spine, throwing tight spasms out along my arms and legs. It only took a second. The heat flooded through me, and I felt the silent shimmer that made me something else. I threw my heavy paws against the matted earth and stretched my back in one long, rolling extension.

Phasing was very easy when I was centered like this. I didn't have issues with my temper anymore. Except when it got in the way.

For one half second, I remembered the awful moment at that unspeakable joke of a wedding. I'd been so insane with fury that I couldn't make my body work right. I'd been trapped, shaking and burning, unable to make the change and kill the monster just a few feet away from me. It had been so confusing. Dying to kill him. Afraid to hurt her. My friends in the way. And then, when I was finally able to take the form I wanted, the order from my leader. The edict from the Alpha. If it had been just Embry and Quil there that night without Sam . . . would I have been able to kill the murderer, then?

I hated it when Sam laid down the law like that. I hated the feeling of having no choice. Of having to obey.

And then I was conscious of an audience. I was not alone in my thoughts.

So self-absorbed all the time, Leah thought.

Yeah, no hypocrisy there, Leah, I thought back.

Can it, guys, Sam told us.

We fell silent, and I felt Leah's wince at the word *guys.* Touchy, like always.

Sam pretended not to notice. *Where's Quil and Jared?*

Quil's got Claire. He's taking her to the Clearwaters'.

Good. Sue will take her.

Jared was going to Kim's, Embry thought. *Good chance he didn't hear you.*

There was a low grumble through the pack. I moaned along with them. When Jared finally showed up, no doubt he'd still be thinking about Kim. And nobody wanted a replay of what they were up to right now.

Sam sat back on his haunches and let another howl rip into the air. It was a signal and an order in one.

The pack was gathered a few miles east of where I was. I loped through the thick forest toward them. Leah,

Embry, and Paul all were working in toward them, too. Leah was close—soon I could hear her footfalls not far into the woods. We continued in a parallel line, choosing not to run together.

Well, we're not waiting all day for him. He'll just have to catch up later.

'Sup, boss? Paul wanted to know.

We need to talk. Something's happened.

I felt Sam's thoughts flicker to me—and not just Sam's, but Seth's and Collin's and Brady's as well. Collin and Brady—the new kids—had been running patrol with Sam today, so they would know whatever he knew. I didn't know why Seth was already out here, and in the know. It wasn't his turn.

Seth, tell them what you heard.

I sped up, wanting to be there. I heard Leah move faster, too. She hated being outrun. Being the fastest was the only edge she claimed.

Claim this, moron, she hissed, and then she really kicked it into gear. I dug my nails into the loam and shot myself forward.

Sam didn't seem in the mood to put up with our usual crap. *Jake, Leah, give it a rest.*

Neither of us slowed.

Sam growled, but let it go. *Seth?*

Charlie called around till he found Billy at my house.

Yeah, I talked to him, Paul added.

I felt a jolt go through me as Seth thought Charlie's name. This was it. The waiting was over. I ran faster, forcing myself to breathe, though my lungs felt kinda stiff all of a sudden.

Which story would it be?

So he's all flipped out. Guess Edward and Bella got home last week, and . . .

My chest eased up.

She was alive. Or she wasn't *dead* dead, at least.

I hadn't realized how much difference it would make to me. I'd been thinking of her as dead this whole time, and I only saw that now. I saw that I'd never believed that he would bring her back alive. It shouldn't matter, because I knew what was coming next.

Yeah, bro, and here's the bad news. Charlie talked to her, said she sounded bad. She told him she's sick. Carlisle got on and told Charlie that Bella picked up some rare disease in South America. Said she's quarantined. Charlie's going crazy, 'cause even he's not allowed to see her. He says he doesn't care if he gets sick, but Carlisle wouldn't bend. No visitors. Told Charlie it was pretty serious, but that he's doing everything he can. Charlie's been stewing about it for days, but he only called Billy now. He said she sounded worse today.

The mental silence when Seth finished was profound. We all understood.

So she would die of this disease, as far as Charlie knew. Would they let him view the corpse? The pale, perfectly still, unbreathing white body? They couldn't let him touch the cold skin—he might notice how hard it was. They'd have to wait until she could hold still, could keep from killing Charlie and the other mourners. How long would that take?

Would they bury her? Would she dig herself out, or would the bloodsuckers come for her?

The others listened to my speculating in silence. I'd put a lot more thought into this than any of them.

Leah and I entered the clearing at nearly the same time. She was sure her nose led the way, though. She dropped onto her haunches beside her brother while I trotted forward to stand at Sam's right hand. Paul circled and made room for me in my place.

Beatcha again, Leah thought, but I barely heard her.

I wondered why I was the only one on my feet. My fur stood up on my shoulders, bristling with impatience.

Well, what are we waiting for? I asked.

No one said anything, but I heard their feelings of hesitation.

Oh, come on! The treaty's broken!

We have no proof—maybe she is sick. . . .

OH, PLEASE!

Okay, so the circumstantial evidence is pretty strong. Still . . . Jacob. Sam's thought came slow, hesitant. *Are you sure this is what you want? Is it really the right thing? We all know what she wanted.*

The treaty doesn't mention anything about victim preferences, Sam!

Is she really a victim? Would you label her that way?

Yes!

Jake, Seth thought, *they aren't our enemies.*

Shut up, kid! Just 'cause you've got some kind of sick hero worship thing going on with that bloodsucker, it doesn't change the law. They are our enemies. They are in our territory. We take them out. I don't care if you had fun fighting alongside Edward Cullen once upon a time.

So what are you going to do when Bella fights with them, Jacob? Huh? Seth demanded.

She's not Bella anymore.

You gonna be the one to take her down?

I couldn't stop myself from wincing.

No, you're not. So, what? You gonna make one of us do it? And then hold a grudge against whoever it is forever?

I wouldn't. . . .

Sure you won't. You're not ready for this fight, Jacob.

Instinct took over and I crouched forward, snarling at the gangly sand-colored wolf across the circle.

Jacob! Sam cautioned. *Seth, shut up for a second.*

Seth nodded his big head.

Dang, what'd I miss? Quil thought. He was running for the gathering place full-out. *Heard about Charlie's call. . . .*

We're getting ready to go, I told him. *Why don't you swing by Kim's and drag Jared out with your teeth? We're going to need everyone.*

Come straight here, Quil, Sam ordered. *We've decided nothing yet.*

I growled.

Jacob, I have to think about what's best for this pack. I have to choose the course that protects you all best. Times have changed since our ancestors made that treaty. I . . . well, I don't honestly believe that the Cullens are a danger to us. And we know that they will not be here much longer. Surely once they've told their story, they will disappear. Our lives can return to normal.

Normal?

If we challenge them, Jacob, they will defend themselves well. Are you afraid?

Are you so ready to lose a brother? He paused. *Or a sister?* he tacked on as an afterthought.

I'm not afraid to die.

I know that, Jacob. It's one reason I question your judgment on this.

I stared into his black eyes. *Do you intend to honor our fathers' treaty or not?*

I honor my pack. I do what's best for them.

Coward.

His muzzle tensed, pulling back over his teeth.

Enough, Jacob. You're overruled. Sam's mental voice changed, took on that strange double timbre that we could not disobey. The voice of the Alpha. He met the gaze of every wolf in the circle.

The pack is not attacking the Cullens without provocation. The spirit of the treaty remains. They are not a danger to our people, nor are they a danger to the people of Forks. Bella Swan made an informed choice, and we are not going to punish our former allies for her choice.

Hear, hear, Seth thought enthusiastically.

I thought I told you to shut it, Seth.

Oops. Sorry, Sam.

Jacob, where do you think you're going?

I left the circle, moving toward the west so that I could turn my back on him. *I'm going to tell my father goodbye. Apparently there was no purpose in me sticking around this long.*

Aw, Jake—don't do that again!

Shut up, Seth, several voices thought together.

We don't want you to leave, Sam told me, his thought softer than before.

So force me to stay, Sam. Take away my will. Make me a slave.

You know I won't do that.

Then there's nothing more to say.

I ran away from them, trying very hard not to think about what was next. Instead, I concentrated on my memories of the long wolf months, of letting the humanity bleed out of me until I was more animal than man. Living in the moment, eating when hungry, sleeping when tired, drinking when thirsty, and running—running just to run. Simple desires, simple answers to those desires. Pain came in easily managed forms. The pain of hunger. The pain of cold ice under your paws. The pain of cutting claws when dinner got feisty. Each pain had a simple answer, a clear action to end that pain.

Not like being human.

Yet, as soon as I was in jogging distance of my house, I shifted back into my human body. I needed to be able to think in privacy.

I untied my shorts and yanked them on, already running for the house.

I'd done it. I'd hidden what I was thinking and now it was too late for Sam to stop me. He couldn't hear me now.

Sam had made a very clear ruling. The pack would not attack the Cullens. Okay.

He hadn't mentioned an individual acting alone.

Nope, the pack wasn't attacking anyone today.

But I was.

9. SURE AS HELL DIDN'T SEE THAT ONE COMING

I DIDN'T REALLY PLAN TO SAY GOODBYE TO MY FATHER.

After all, one quick call to Sam and the game would be up. They'd cut me off and push me back. Probably try to make me angry, or even hurt me—somehow force me to phase so that Sam could lay down a new law.

But Billy was expecting me, knowing I'd be in some kind of state. He was in the yard, just sitting there in his wheelchair with his eyes right on the spot where I came through the trees. I saw him judge my direction—headed straight past the house to my homemade garage.

"Got a minute, Jake?"

I skidded to a stop. I looked at him and then toward the garage.

"C'mon kid. At least help me inside."

I gritted my teeth but decided that he'd be more likely to cause trouble with Sam if I didn't lie to him for a few minutes.

"Since when do you need help, old man?"

He laughed his rumbling laugh. "My arms are tired. I pushed myself all the way here from Sue's."

"It's downhill. You coasted the whole way."

I rolled his chair up the little ramp I'd made for him and into the living room.

"Caught me. Think I got up to about thirty miles per hour. It was great."

"You're gonna wreck that chair, you know. And then you'll be dragging yourself around by your elbows."

"Not a chance. It'll be your job to carry me."

"You won't be going many places."

Billy put his hands on the wheels and steered himself to the fridge. "Any food left?"

"You got me. Paul was here all day, though, so probably not."

Billy sighed. "Have to start hiding the groceries if we're gonna avoid starvation."

"Tell Rachel to go stay at his place."

Billy's joking tone vanished, and his eyes got soft. "We've only had her home a few weeks. First time she's been here in a long time. It's hard—the girls were older than you when your mom passed. They have more trouble being in this house."

"I know."

Rebecca hadn't been home once since she got married, though she did have a good excuse. Plane tickets from Hawaii were pretty pricey. Washington State was close enough that Rachel didn't have the same defense. She'd taken classes straight through the summer semesters, working double shifts over the holidays at some café on campus. If it hadn't been for Paul, she probably would have taken off again real quick. Maybe that was why Billy wouldn't kick him out.

"Well, I'm going to go work on some stuff. . . ." I started for the back door.

"Wait up, Jake. Aren't you going to tell me what happened? Do I have to call Sam for an update?"

I stood with my back to him, hiding my face.

"Nothing happened. Sam's giving them a bye. Guess we're all just a bunch of leech lovers now."

"Jake . . ."

"I don't want to talk about it."

"Are you leaving, son?"

The room was quiet for a long time while I decided how to say it.

"Rachel can have her room back. I know she hates that air mattress."

"She'd rather sleep on the floor than lose you. So would I."

I snorted.

"Jacob, please. If you need . . . a break. Well, take it. But not so long again. Come back."

"Maybe. Maybe my gig will be weddings. Make a cameo at Sam's, then Rachel's. Jared and Kim might come first, though. Probably ought to have a suit or something."

"Jake, look at me."

I turned around slowly. "What?"

He stared into my eyes for a long minute. "Where are you going?"

"I don't really have a specific place in mind."

He cocked his head to the side, and his eyes narrowed. "Don't you?"

We stared each other down. The seconds ticked by.

"Jacob," he said. His voice was strained. "Jacob, don't. It's not worth it."

"I don't know what you're talking about."

"Leave Bella and the Cullens be. Sam is right."

I stared at him for a second, and then I crossed the room in two long strides. I grabbed the phone and disconnected the cable from the box and the jack. I wadded the gray cord up in the palm of my hand.

"Bye, Dad."

"Jake, wait—," he called after me, but I was out the door, running.

The motorcycle wasn't as fast as running, but it was more discreet. I wondered how long it would take Billy to wheel himself down to the store and then get someone on the phone who could get a message to Sam. I'd bet Sam was still in his wolf form. The problem would be if Paul came back to our place anytime soon. He could phase in a second and let Sam know what I was doing. . . .

I wasn't going to worry about it. I would go as fast as I could, and if they caught me, I'd deal with that when I had to.

I kicked the bike to life and then I was racing down the muddy lane. I didn't look behind me as I passed the house.

The highway was busy with tourist traffic; I wove in and

out of the cars, earning a bunch of honks and a few fingers. I took the turn onto the 101 at seventy, not bothering to look. I had to ride the line for a minute to avoid getting smeared by a minivan. Not that it would have killed me, but it would have slowed me down. Broken bones—the big ones, at least—took *days* to heal completely, as I had good cause to know.

The freeway cleared up a little, and I pushed the bike to eighty. I didn't touch the brake until I was close to the narrow drive; I figured I was in the clear then. Sam wouldn't come this far to stop me. It was too late.

It wasn't until that moment—when I was sure that I'd made it—that I started to think about what exactly I was going to do now. I slowed down to twenty, taking the twists through the trees more carefully than I needed to.

I knew they would hear me coming, bike or no bike, so surprise was out. There was no way to disguise my intentions. Edward would hear my plan as soon as I was close enough. Maybe he already could. But I thought this would still work out, because I had his ego on my side. He'd *want* to fight me alone.

So I'd just walk in, see Sam's precious evidence for myself, and then challenge Edward to a duel.

I snorted. The parasite'd probably get a kick out of the theatrics of it.

When I finished with him, I'd take as many of the rest of them as I could before they got me. Huh—I wondered if Sam would consider my death *provocation*. Probably say I got what I deserved. Wouldn't want to offend his bloodsucker BFFs.

The drive opened up into the meadow, and the smell hit

me like a rotten tomato to the face. Ugh. Reeking vampires. My stomach started churning. The stench would be hard to take this way—undiluted by the scent of humans as it had been the other time I'd come here—though not as bad as smelling it through my wolf nose.

I wasn't sure what to expect, but there was no sign of life around the big white crypt. Of course they knew I was here.

I cut the engine and listened to the quiet. Now I could hear tense, angry murmurs from just the other side of the wide double doors. Someone was home. I heard my name and I smiled, happy to think I was causing them a little stress.

I took one big gulp of air—it would only be worse inside—and leaped up the porch stairs in one bound.

The door opened before my fist touched it, and the doctor stood in the frame, his eyes grave.

"Hello, Jacob," he said, calmer than I would have expected. "How are you?"

I took a deep breath through my mouth. The reek pouring through the door was overpowering.

I was disappointed that it was Carlisle who answered. I'd rather Edward had come through the door, fangs out. Carlisle was so . . . just *human* or something. Maybe it was the house calls he made last spring when I got busted up. But it made me uncomfortable to look into his face and know that I was planning to kill him if I could.

"I heard Bella made it back alive," I said.

"Er, Jacob, it's not really the best time." The doctor seemed uncomfortable, too, but not in the way I expected. "Could we do this later?"

I stared at him, dumbfounded. Was he asking to postpone the death match for a more convenient time?

And then I heard Bella's voice, cracked and rough, and I couldn't think about anything else.

"Why not?" she asked someone. "Are we keeping secrets from Jacob, too? What's the point?"

Her voice was not what I was expecting. I tried to remember the voices of the young vampires we'd fought in the spring, but all I'd registered was snarling. Maybe those newborns hadn't had the piercing, ringing sound of the older ones, either. Maybe all new vampires sounded hoarse.

"Come in, please, Jacob," Bella croaked more loudly.

Carlisle's eyes tightened.

I wondered if Bella was thirsty. My eyes narrowed, too.

"Excuse me," I said to the doctor as I stepped around him. It was hard—it went against all my instincts to turn my back to one of them. Not impossible, though. If there was such a thing as a safe vampire, it was the strangely gentle leader.

I would stay away from Carlisle when the fight started. There were enough of them to kill without including him.

I sidestepped into the house, keeping my back to the wall. My eyes swept the room—it was unfamiliar. The last time I'd been in here it had been all done up for a party. Everything was bright and pale now. Including the six vampires standing in a group by the white sofa.

They were all here, all together, but that was not what froze me where I stood and had my jaw dropping to the floor.

It was Edward. It was the expression on his face.

I'd seen him angry, and I'd seen him arrogant, and once I'd seen him in pain. But this—this was beyond agony. His eyes were half-crazed. He didn't look up to glare at me. He stared down at the couch beside him with an expression like someone had lit him on fire. His hands were rigid claws at his side.

I couldn't even enjoy his anguish. I could only think of one thing that would make him look like that, and my eyes followed his.

I saw her at the same moment that I caught her scent. Her warm, clean, human scent.

Bella was half-hidden behind the arm of the sofa, curled up in a loose fetal position, her arms wrapped around her knees. For a long second I could see nothing except that she was still the Bella that I loved, her skin still a soft, pale peach, her eyes still the same chocolate brown. My heart thudded a strange, broken meter, and I wondered if this was just some lying dream that I was about to wake up from.

Then I really saw her.

There were deep circles under her eyes, dark circles that jumped out because her face was all haggard. Was she thinner? Her skin seemed tight—like her cheekbones might break right through it. Most of her dark hair was pulled away from her face into a messy knot, but a few strands stuck limply to her forehead and neck, to the sheen of sweat that covered her skin. There was something about her fingers and wrists that looked so fragile it was scary.

She *was* sick. Very sick.

Not a lie. The story Charlie'd told Billy was not a story. While I stared, eyes bugging, her skin turned light green.

The blond bloodsucker—the showy one, Rosalie—bent over her, cutting into my view, hovering in a strange, protective way.

This was wrong. I knew how Bella felt about almost everything—her thoughts were so obvious; sometimes it was like they were printed on her forehead. So she didn't have to tell me every detail of a situation for me to get it. I knew that Bella didn't like Rosalie. I'd seen it in the set of her lips when she talked about her. Not just that she didn't like her. She was *afraid* of Rosalie. Or she had been.

There was no fear as Bella glanced up at her now. Her expression was . . . apologetic or something. Then Rosalie snatched a basin from the floor and held it under Bella's chin just in time for Bella to throw up noisily into it.

Edward fell to his knees by Bella's side—his eyes all tortured-looking—and Rosalie held out her hand, warning him to keep back.

None of it made sense.

When she could raise her head, Bella smiled weakly at me, sort of embarrassed. "Sorry about that," she whispered to me.

Edward moaned real quiet. His head slumped against Bella's knees. She put one of her hands against his cheek. Like she was comforting *him*.

I didn't realize my legs had carried me forward until Rosalie hissed at me, suddenly appearing between me and the couch. She was like a person on a TV screen. I didn't care she was there. She didn't seem real.

"Rose, don't," Bella whispered. "It's fine."

Blondie moved out of my way, though I could tell she hated to do it. Scowling at me, she crouched by Bella's head, tensed to spring. She was easier to ignore than I ever would have dreamed.

"Bella, what's wrong?" I whispered. Without thinking about it, I found myself on my knees, too, leaning over the back of the couch across from her . . . husband. He didn't seem to notice me, and I barely glanced at him. I reached out for her free hand, taking it in both of mine. Her skin was icy. "Are you all right?"

It was a stupid question. She didn't answer it.

"I'm so glad you came to see me today, Jacob," she said.

Even though I knew Edward couldn't hear her thoughts, he seemed to hear some meaning I didn't. He moaned again, into the blanket that covered her, and she stroked his cheek.

"What is it, Bella?" I insisted, wrapping my hands tight around her cold, fragile fingers.

Instead of answering, she glanced around the room like she was searching for something, both a plea and a warning in her look. Six pairs of anxious yellow eyes stared back at her. Finally, she turned to Rosalie.

"Help me up, Rose?" she asked.

Rosalie's lips pulled back over her teeth, and she glared up at me like she wanted to rip my throat out. I was sure that was exactly the case.

"Please, Rose."

The blonde made a face, but leaned over her again, next to Edward, who didn't move an inch. She put her arm carefully behind Bella's shoulders.

"No," I whispered. "Don't get up. . . ." She looked so weak.

"I'm answering your question," she snapped, sounding a little bit more like the way she usually talked to me.

Rosalie pulled Bella off the couch. Edward stayed where he was, sagging forward till his face was buried in the cushions. The blanket fell to the ground at Bella's feet.

Bella's body was swollen, her torso ballooning out in a strange, sick way. It strained against the faded gray sweatshirt that was way too big for her shoulders and arms. The rest of her seemed thinner, like the big bulge had grown out of what it had sucked from her. It took me a second to realize what the deformed part was—I didn't understand until she folded her hands tenderly around her bloated stomach, one above and one below. Like she was cradling it.

I saw it then, but I still couldn't believe it. I'd seen her just a month ago. There was no way she could be pregnant. Not *that* pregnant.

Except that she was.

I didn't want to see this, didn't want to think about this. I didn't want to imagine him inside her. I didn't want to know that something I hated so much had taken root in the body I loved. My stomach heaved, and I had to swallow back vomit.

But it was worse than that, so much worse. Her distorted body, the bones jabbing against the skin of her face. I could only guess that she looked like this—so pregnant, so sick—because whatever was inside her was taking her life to feed its own. . . .

Because it was a monster. Just like its father.

I always knew he would kill her.

His head snapped up as he heard the words inside mine. One second we were both on our knees, and then he was on his feet, towering over me. His eyes were flat black, the circles under them dark purple.

"Outside, Jacob," he snarled.

I was on my feet, too. Looking down on him now. This was why I was here.

"Let's do this," I agreed.

The big one, Emmett, pushed forward on Edward's other side, with the hungry-looking one, Jasper, right behind him. I really didn't care. Maybe my pack would clean up the scraps when they finished me off. Maybe not. It didn't matter.

For the tiniest part of a second my eyes touched on the two standing in the back. Esme. Alice. Small and distractingly feminine. Well, I was sure the others would kill me before I had to do anything about them. I didn't want to kill girls . . . even vampire girls.

Though I might make an exception for that blonde.

"No," Bella gasped, and she stumbled forward, out of balance, to clutch at Edward's arm. Rosalie moved with her, like there was a chain locking them to each other.

"I just need to talk to him, Bella," Edward said in a low voice, talking only to her. He reached up to touch her face, to stroke it. This made the room turn red, made me see fire—that, after all he'd done to her, he was still allowed to touch her that way. "Don't strain yourself," he went on, pleading. "Please rest. We'll both be back in just a few minutes."

She stared at his face, reading it carefully. Then she nodded and drooped toward the couch. Rosalie helped lower her back onto the cushions. Bella stared at me, trying to hold my eyes.

"Behave," she insisted. "And then come back."

I didn't answer. I wasn't making any promises today. I looked away and then followed Edward out the front door.

A random, disjointed voice in my head noted that separating him from the coven hadn't been so difficult, had it?

He kept walking, never checking to see if I was about to spring at his unprotected back. I supposed he didn't need to check. He would know when I decided to attack. Which meant I'd have to make that decision very quickly.

"I'm not ready for you to kill me yet, Jacob Black," he whispered as he paced quickly away from the house. "You'll have to have a little patience."

Like I cared about his schedule. I growled under my breath. "Patience isn't my specialty."

He kept walking, maybe a couple hundred yards down the drive away from the house, with me right on his heels. I was all hot, my fingers trembling. On the edge, ready and waiting.

He stopped without warning and pivoted to face me. His expression froze me again.

For a second I was just a kid—a kid who had lived all of his life in the same tiny town. Just a child. Because I knew I would have to live a lot more, suffer a lot more, to ever understand the searing agony in Edward's eyes.

He raised a hand as if to wipe sweat from his forehead, but his fingers scraped against his face like they were going to rip his granite skin right off. His black eyes burned in their sockets, out of focus, or seeing things that weren't there. His mouth opened like he was going to scream, but nothing came out.

This was the face a man would have if he were burning at the stake.

For a moment I couldn't speak. It was too real, this face—I'd seen a shadow of it in the house, seen it in her eyes and his, but this made it final. The last nail in her coffin.

"It's killing her, right? She's dying." And I knew when I said it that my face was a watered-down echo of his. Weaker, different, because I was still in shock. I hadn't wrapped my head around it yet—it was happening too fast. He'd had time to get to this point. And it was different because I'd already lost her so many times, so many ways, in my head. And different because she was never really mine to lose.

And different because this wasn't my fault.

"My fault," Edward whispered, and his knees gave out. He crumpled in front of me, vulnerable, the easiest target you could imagine.

But I felt cold as snow—there was no fire in me.

"Yes," he groaned into the dirt, like he was confessing to the ground. "Yes, it's killing her."

His broken helplessness irritated me. I wanted a fight, not an execution. Where was his smug superiority now?

"So why hasn't Carlisle done anything?" I growled. "He's a doctor, right? Get it out of her."

He looked up then and answered me in a tired voice. Like he was explaining this to a kindergartener for the tenth time. "She won't let us."

It took a minute for the words to sink in. Jeez, she was running true to form. Of course, die for the monster spawn. It was so *Bella*.

"You know her well," he whispered. "How quickly you see. . . . I didn't see. Not in time. She wouldn't talk to me on the way home, not really. I thought she was frightened—that would be natural. I thought she was angry with me for putting her through this, for endangering her life. Again. I never imagined what she was really thinking, what she was *resolving*. Not until my family met us at the airport and she ran right into Rosalie's arms. Rosalie's! And then I heard what Rosalie was thinking. I didn't understand until I heard that. Yet *you* understand after one second. . . ." He half-sighed, half-groaned.

"Just back up a second. She won't *let* you." The sarcasm was acid on my tongue. "Did you ever notice that she's exactly as strong as a normal hundred-and-ten-pound human girl? How stupid are you vamps? Hold her down and knock her out with drugs."

"I wanted to," he whispered. "Carlisle would have. . . ."

What, too noble were they?

"No. Not noble. Her bodyguard complicated things."

Oh. His story hadn't made much sense before, but it fit together now. So that's what Blondie was up to. What was in it for her, though? Did the beauty queen want Bella to die so bad?

"Maybe," he said. "Rosalie doesn't look at it quite that way."

"So take the blonde out first. Your kind can be put back together, right? Turn her into a jigsaw and take care of Bella."

"Emmett and Esme are backing her up. Emmett would never let us . . . and Carlisle won't help me with Esme against it. . . ." He trailed off, his voice disappearing.

"You should have left Bella with me."

"Yes."

It was a bit late for that, though. Maybe he should have thought about all this *before* he knocked her up with the life-sucking monster.

He stared up at me from inside his own personal hell, and I could see that he agreed with me.

"We didn't know," he said, the words as quiet as a breath. "I never dreamed. There's never been anything like Bella and I before. How could we know that a human was able to conceive a child with one of us—"

"When the human should get ripped to shreds in the process?"

"Yes," he agreed in a tense whisper. "They're out there, the sadistic ones, the incubus, the succubus. They exist. But the seduction is merely a prelude to the feast. No one *survives*." He shook his head like the idea revolted him. Like he was any different.

"I didn't realize they had a special name for what you are," I spit.

He stared up at me with a face that looked a thousand years old.

"Even you, Jacob Black, cannot hate me as much as I hate myself."

Wrong, I thought, too enraged to speak.

"Killing me now doesn't save her," he said quietly.

"So what does?"

"Jacob, you have to do something for me."

"The *hell* I do, parasite!"

He kept staring at me with those half-tired, half-crazy eyes. "For her?"

I clenched my teeth together hard. "I did everything I could to keep her away from you. Every single thing. It's too late."

"You know her, Jacob. You connect to her on a level that I don't even understand. You are part of her, and she is part of you. She won't listen to me, because she thinks I'm underestimating her. She thinks she's strong enough for this. . . ." He choked and then swallowed. "She might listen to you."

"Why would she?"

He lurched to his feet, his eyes burning brighter than before, wilder. I wondered if he was really going crazy. Could vampires lose their minds?

"Maybe," he answered my thought. "I don't know. It feels like it." He shook his head. "I have to try to hide this in front of her, because stress makes her more ill. She can't keep anything down as it is. I have to be composed; I can't make it harder. But that doesn't matter now. She has to listen to you!"

"I can't tell her anything you haven't. What do you want me to do? Tell her she's stupid? She probably already knows that. Tell her she's going to die? I bet she knows that, too."

"You can offer her what she wants."

He wasn't making any sense. Part of the crazy?

"I don't care about anything but keeping her alive," he said, suddenly focused now. "If it's a child she wants, she can have it. She can have half a dozen babies. Anything she wants." He paused for one beat. "She can have puppies, if that's what it takes."

He met my stare for a moment and his face was frenzied under the thin layer of control. My hard scowl crumbled as I processed his words, and I felt my mouth pop open in shock.

"But not this way!" he hissed before I could recover. "Not this *thing* that's sucking the life from her while I stand there helpless! Watching her sicken and waste away. Seeing it *hurting* her." He sucked in a fast breath like someone had punched him in the gut. "You *have* to make her see reason, Jacob. She won't listen to me anymore. Rosalie's always there, feeding her insanity—encouraging her. Protecting her. No, protecting *it*. Bella's life means nothing to her."

The noise coming from my throat sounded like I was choking.

What was he saying? That Bella should, what? Have a baby? With *me*? What? How? Was he giving her up? Or did he think she wouldn't mind being shared?

"Whichever. Whatever keeps her alive."

"That's the craziest thing you've said yet," I mumbled.

"She loves you."

"Not enough."

"She's ready to die to have a child. Maybe she'd accept something less extreme."

"Don't you know her at all?"

"I know, I know. It's going to take a lot of convincing. That's why I need you. You know how she thinks. Make her see sense."

I couldn't think about what he was suggesting. It was too much. Impossible. Wrong. Sick. Borrowing Bella for the weekends and then returning her Monday morning like a rental movie? So messed up.

So tempting.

I didn't want to consider, didn't want to imagine, but

the images came anyway. I'd fantasized about Bella that way too many times, back when there was still a possibility of *us*, and then long after it was clear that the fantasies would only leave festering sores because there was no possibility, none at all. I hadn't been able to help myself then. I couldn't stop myself now. Bella in *my* arms, Bella sighing *my* name . . .

Worse still, this new image I'd never had before, one that by all rights shouldn't have existed for me. Not yet. An image I knew I wouldn't've suffered over for *years* if he hadn't shoved it in my head now. But it stuck there, winding threads through my brain like a weed—poisonous and unkillable. Bella, healthy and glowing, so different than now, but something the same: her body, not distorted, changed in a more natural way. Round with *my* child.

I tried to escape the venomous weed in my mind. "Make *Bella* see sense? What universe do you live in?"

"At least try."

I shook my head fast. He waited, ignoring the negative answer because he could hear the conflict in my thoughts.

"Where is this psycho crap coming from? Are you making this up as you go?"

"I've been thinking of nothing but ways to save her since I realized what she was planning to do. What she would die to do. But I didn't know how to contact you. I knew you wouldn't listen if I called. I would have come to find you soon, if you hadn't come today. But it's hard to leave her, even for a few minutes. Her condition . . . it changes so fast. The thing is . . . growing. Swiftly. I can't be away from her now."

"What *is* it?"

"None of us have any idea. But it is stronger than she is. Already."

I could suddenly see it then—see the swelling monster in my head, breaking her from the inside out.

"Help me stop it," he whispered. "Help me stop this from happening."

"*How?* By offering my stud services?" He didn't even flinch when I said that, but I did. "You're really sick. She'll never listen to this."

"Try. There's nothing to lose now. How will it hurt?"

It would hurt me. Hadn't I taken enough rejection from Bella without this?

"A little pain to save her? Is it such a high cost?"

"But it won't work."

"Maybe not. Maybe it will confuse her, though. Maybe she'll falter in her resolve. One moment of doubt is all I need."

"And then you pull the rug out from under the offer? 'Just kidding, Bella'?"

"If she wants a child, that's what she gets. I won't rescind."

I couldn't believe I was even thinking about this. Bella would punch me—not that I cared about that, but it would probably break her hand again. I shouldn't let him talk to me, mess with my head. I should just kill him now.

"Not now," he whispered. "Not yet. Right or wrong, it would destroy her, and you know it. No need to be hasty. If she won't listen to you, you'll get your chance. The moment Bella's heart stops beating, I will be begging for you to kill me."

"You won't have to beg long."

The hint of a worn smile tugged at the corner of his mouth. "I'm very much counting on that."

"Then we have a deal."

He nodded and held out his cold stone hand.

Swallowing my disgust, I reached out to take his hand. My fingers closed around the rock, and I shook it once.

"We have a deal," he agreed.

10. WHY DIDN'T I JUST WALK AWAY? OH RIGHT, BECAUSE I'M AN IDIOT.

I FELT LIKE—LIKE I DON'T KNOW WHAT. LIKE THIS WASN'T real. Like I was in some Goth version of a bad sitcom. Instead of being the A/V dweeb about to ask the head cheerleader to the prom, I was the finished-second-place werewolf about to ask the vampire's wife to shack up and procreate. Nice.

No, I wouldn't do it. It was twisted and wrong. I was going to forget all about what he'd said.

But I would talk to her. I'd try to make her listen to me.

And she wouldn't. Just like always.

Edward didn't answer or comment on my thoughts as he led the way back to the house. I wondered about the place that he'd chosen to stop. Was it far enough from the house that the others couldn't hear his whispers? Was that the point?

Maybe. When we walked through the door, the other Cullens' eyes were suspicious and confused. No one looked disgusted or outraged. So they must not have heard either favor Edward had asked me for.

I hesitated in the open doorway, not sure what to do now. It was better right there, with a little bit of breathable air blowing in from outside.

Edward walked into the middle of the huddle, shoulders stiff. Bella watched him anxiously, and then her eyes flickered to me for a second. Then she was watching him again.

Her face turned a grayish pale, and I could see what he meant about the stress making her feel worse.

"We're going to let Jacob and Bella speak privately," Edward said. There was no inflection at all in his voice. Robotic.

"Over my pile of ashes," Rosalie hissed at him. She was still hovering by Bella's head, one of her cold hands placed possessively on Bella's sallow cheek.

Edward didn't look at her. "Bella," he said in that same empty tone. "Jacob wants to talk to you. Are you afraid to be alone with him?"

Bella looked at me, confused. Then she looked at Rosalie.

"Rose, it's fine. Jake's not going to hurt us. Go with Edward."

"It might be a trick," the blonde warned.

"I don't see how," Bella said.

"Carlisle and I will always be in your sight, Rosalie,"

Edward said. The emotionless voice was cracking, showing the anger through it. "We're the ones she's afraid of."

"No," Bella whispered. Her eyes were glistening, her lashes wet. "No, Edward. I'm not. . . ."

He shook his head, smiling a little. The smile was painful to look at. "I didn't mean it that way, Bella. I'm fine. Don't worry about me."

Sickening. He was right—she was beating herself up about hurting his feelings. The girl was a classic martyr. She'd totally been born in the wrong century. She should have lived back when she could have gotten herself fed to some lions for a good cause.

"Everyone," Edward said, his hand stiffly motioning toward the door. "Please."

The composure he was trying to keep up for Bella was shaky. I could see how close he was to that burning man he'd been outside. The others saw it, too. Silently, they moved out the door while I shifted out of the way. They moved fast; my heart beat twice, and the room was cleared except for Rosalie, hesitating in the middle of the floor, and Edward, still waiting by the door.

"Rose," Bella said quietly. "I want you to go."

The blonde glared at Edward and then gestured for him to go first. He disappeared out the door. She gave me a long warning glower, and then she disappeared, too.

Once we were alone, I crossed the room and sat on the floor next to Bella. I took both her cold hands in mine, rubbing them carefully.

"Thanks, Jake. That feels good."

"I'm not going to lie, Bells. You're hideous."

"I know," she sighed. "I'm scary-looking."

"Thing-from-the-swamp scary," I agreed.

She laughed. "It's so good having you here. It feels nice to smile. I don't know how much more drama I can stand."

I rolled my eyes.

"Okay, okay," she agreed. "I bring it on myself."

"Yeah, you do. What're you thinking, Bells? Seriously!"

"Did he ask you to yell at me?"

"Sort of. Though I can't figure why he thinks you'd listen to me. You never have before."

She sighed.

"I told you——," I started to say.

"Did you know that '*I told you so*' has a brother, Jacob?" she asked, cutting me off. "His name is '*Shut the hell up.*'"

"Good one."

She grinned at me. Her skin stretched tight over the bones. "I can't take credit—I got it off a rerun of *The Simpsons.*"

"Missed that one."

"It was funny."

We didn't talk for a minute. Her hands were starting to warm up a little.

"Did he really ask you to talk to me?"

I nodded. "To talk some sense into you. *There's* a battle that's lost before it starts."

"So why did you agree?"

I didn't answer. I wasn't sure I knew.

I did know this—every second I spent with her was only going to add to the pain I would have to suffer later. Like a junkie with a limited supply, the day of reckoning was coming for me. The more hits I took now, the harder it would be when my supply ran out.

"It'll work out, you know," she said after a quiet minute. "I believe that."

That made me see red again. "Is dementia one of your symptoms?" I snapped.

She laughed, though my anger was so real that my hands were shaking around hers.

"Maybe," she said. "I'm not saying things will work out *easily*, Jake. But how could I have lived through all that I've lived through and not believe in magic by this point?"

"Magic?"

"Especially for you," she said. She was smiling. She pulled one of her hands away from mine and pressed it against my cheek. Warmer than before, but it felt cool against my skin, like most things did. "More than anyone else, you've got some magic waiting to make things right for you."

"What are you babbling about?"

Still smiling. "Edward told me once what it was like—your imprinting thing. He said it was like *A Midsummer Night's Dream*, like magic. You'll find who you're really looking for, Jacob, and maybe then all of this will make sense."

If she hadn't looked so fragile I would've been screaming.

As it was, I *did* growl at her.

"If you think that imprinting could ever make sense of this *insanity* . . ." I struggled for words. "Do you really think that just because I might someday imprint on some stranger it would make this right?" I jabbed a finger toward her swollen body. "Tell me what the point was then,

Bella! What was the point of me loving you? What was the point of *you* loving *him*? When you die"—the words were a snarl—"how is that ever right again? What's the point to all the pain? Mine, yours, his! You'll kill him, too, not that I care about that." She flinched, but I kept going. "So what was the point of your twisted love story, in the end? If there is *any* sense, please show me, Bella, because I don't see it."

She sighed. "I don't know yet, Jake. But I just . . . feel . . . that this is all going somewhere good, hard to see as it is now. I guess you could call it *faith*."

"You're dying for *nothing*, Bella! Nothing!"

Her hand dropped from my face to her bloated stomach, caressed it. She didn't have to say the words for me to know what she was thinking. She was dying for *it*.

"I'm not going to die," she said through her teeth, and I could tell she was repeating things she'd said before. "I *will* keep my heart beating. I'm strong enough for that."

"That's a load of crap, Bella. You've been trying to keep up with the supernatural for too long. No normal person can do it. You're *not* strong enough." I took her face in my hand. I didn't have to remind myself to be gentle. Everything about her screamed *breakable*.

"I can do this. I can do this," she muttered, sounding a lot like that kids' book about the little engine that could.

"Doesn't look like it to me. So what's your plan? I hope you have one."

She nodded, not meeting my eyes. "Did you know Esme jumped off a cliff? When she was human, I mean."

"So?"

"So she was close enough to dead that they didn't even

bother taking her to the emergency room—they took her right around to the morgue. Her heart was still beating, though, when Carlisle found her. . . ."

That's what she'd meant before, about keeping her heart beating.

"You're not planning on surviving this human," I stated dully.

"No. I'm not stupid." She met my stare then. "I guess you probably have your own opinion on that point, though."

"Emergency vampirization," I mumbled.

"It worked for Esme. And Emmett, and Rosalie, and even Edward. None of them were in such great shape. Carlisle only changed them because it was that or death. He doesn't end lives, he saves them."

I felt a sudden twinge of guilt about the good vampire doctor, like before. I shoved the thought away and started in on the begging.

"Listen to me, Bells. Don't do it that way." Like before, when the call from Charlie had come, I could see how much difference it really made to me. I realized I needed her to stay alive, in some form. In any form. I took a deep breath. "Don't wait until it's too late, Bella. Not that way. Live. Okay? Just live. Don't do this to me. Don't do it to him." My voice got harder, louder. "You know what he's going to do when you die. You've seen it before. You want him to go back to those Italian killers?" She cringed into the sofa.

I left out the part about how that wouldn't be necessary this time.

Struggling to make my voice softer, I asked, "Remember when I got mangled up by those newborns? What did you tell me?"

I waited, but she wouldn't answer. She pressed her lips together.

"You told me to be good and listen to Carlisle," I reminded her. "And what did I do? I listened to the vampire. For you."

"You listened because it was the right thing to do."

"Okay—pick either reason."

She took a deep breath. "It's not the right thing now." Her gaze touched her big round stomach and she whispered under her breath, "I won't kill him."

My hands shook again. "Oh, I hadn't heard the great news. A bouncing baby boy, huh? Shoulda brought some blue balloons."

Her face turned pink. The color was so beautiful—it twisted in my stomach like a knife. A serrated knife, rusty and ragged.

I was going to lose this. Again.

"I don't know he's a boy," she admitted, a little sheepish. "The ultrasound wouldn't work. The membrane around the baby is too hard—like their skin. So he's a little mystery. But I always see a boy in my head."

"It's not some pretty baby in there, Bella."

"We'll see," she said. Almost smug.

"*You* won't," I snarled.

"You're very pessimistic, Jacob. There is definitely a chance that I might walk away from this."

I couldn't answer. I looked down and breathed deep and slow, trying to get a grip on my fury.

"Jake," she said, and she patted my hair, stroked my cheek. "It's going to be okay. Shh. It's okay."

I didn't look up. "No. It will not be okay."

She wiped something wet from my cheek. "Shh."

"What's the deal, Bella?" I stared at the pale carpet. My bare feet were dirty, leaving smudges. Good. "I thought the whole point was that you wanted your vampire more than anything. And now you're just giving him up? That doesn't make any sense. Since when are you desperate to be a mom? If you wanted that so much, why did you marry a vampire?"

I was dangerously close to that offer he wanted me to make. I could see the words taking me that way, but I couldn't change their direction.

She sighed. "It's not like that. I didn't really care about having a baby. I didn't even think about it. It's not just having a baby. It's . . . well . . . *this* baby."

"It's a killer, Bella. Look at yourself."

"He's not. It's me. I'm just weak and human. But I can tough this out, Jake, I can—"

"Aw, *come on!* Shut up, Bella. You can spout this crap to your bloodsucker, but you're not fooling me. You know you're not going to make it."

She glared at me. "I do not *know* that. I'm worried about it, sure."

"*Worried* about it," I repeated through my teeth.

She gasped then and clutched at her stomach. My fury vanished like a light switch being turned off.

"I'm fine," she panted. "It's nothing."

But I didn't hear; her hands had pulled her sweatshirt to the side, and I stared, horrified, at the skin it exposed. Her stomach looked like it was stained with big splotches of purple-black ink.

She saw my stare, and she yanked the fabric back in place.

"He's strong, that's all," she said defensively.

The ink spots were bruises.

I almost gagged, and I understood what he'd said, about watching it hurt her. Suddenly, I felt a little crazy myself.

"Bella," I said.

She heard the change in my voice. She looked up, still breathing heavy, her eyes confused.

"Bella, don't do this."

"Jake—"

"Listen to me. Don't get your back up yet. Okay? Just listen. What if . . . ?"

"What if what?"

"What if this wasn't a one-shot deal? What if it wasn't all or nothing? What if you just listened to Carlisle like a good girl, and kept yourself alive?"

"I won't—"

"I'm not done yet. So you stay alive. Then you can start over. This didn't work out. Try again."

She frowned. She raised one hand and touched the place where my eyebrows were mashing together. Her fingers smoothed my forehead for a moment while she tried to make sense of it.

"I don't understand. . . . What do you mean, try again? You can't think Edward would let me . . . ? And what difference would it make? I'm sure any baby—"

"Yes," I snapped. "Any kid *of his* would be the same."

Her tired face just got more confused. "What?"

But I couldn't say any more. There was no point. I would never be able to save her from herself. I'd never been able to do that.

Then she blinked, and I could see she got it.

"Oh. Ugh. *Please*, Jacob. You think I should kill my baby and replace it with some generic substitute? Artificial insemination?" She was mad now. "Why would I want to have some stranger's baby? I suppose it just doesn't make a difference? Any baby will do?"

"I didn't mean that," I muttered. "Not a stranger."

She leaned forward. "Then what are you saying?"

"Nothing. I'm saying nothing. Same as ever."

"Where did that come from?"

"Forget it, Bella."

She frowned, suspicious. "Did *he* tell you to say that?"

I hesitated, surprised that she'd made that leap so quick. "No."

"He did, didn't he?"

"No, really. He didn't say anything about artificial whatever."

Her face softened then, and she sank back against the pillows, looking exhausted. She stared off to the side when she spoke, not talking to me at all. "He would do anything for me. And I'm hurting him so much. . . . But what is he thinking? That I would trade this"—her hand traced across her belly—"for some stranger's . . ." She mumbled the last part, and then her voice trailed off. Her eyes were wet.

"You don't have to hurt him," I whispered. It burned like poison in my mouth to beg for him, but I knew this angle was probably my best bet for keeping her alive. Still a thousand-to-one odds. "You could make him happy again, Bella. And I really think he's losing it. Honestly, I do."

She didn't seem to be listening; her hand made small circles on her battered stomach while she chewed on her lip.

It was quiet for a long time. I wondered if the Cullens were very far away. Were they listening to my pathetic attempts to reason with her?

"Not a stranger?" she murmured to herself. I flinched. "What exactly did Edward say to you?" she asked in a low voice.

"Nothing. He just thought you might listen to me."

"Not that. About trying again."

Her eyes locked on mine, and I could see that I'd already given too much away.

"Nothing."

Her mouth fell open a little. "Wow."

It was silent for a few heartbeats. I looked down at my feet again, unable to meet her stare.

"He really would do *anything*, wouldn't he?" she whispered.

"I told you he was going crazy. Literally, Bells."

"I'm surprised you didn't tell on him right away. Get him in trouble."

When I looked up, she was grinning.

"Thought about it." I tried to grin back, but I could feel the smile mangle on my face.

She knew what I was offering, and she wasn't going to think twice about it. I'd known that she wouldn't. But it still stung.

"There isn't much you wouldn't do for me, either, is there?" she whispered. "I really don't know why you bother. I don't deserve either of you."

"It makes no difference, though, does it?"

"Not this time." She sighed. "I wish I could explain it to you right so that you would understand. I can't hurt him"—she pointed to her stomach—"any more than I could pick up a gun and shoot you. I love him."

"Why do you always have to love the wrong things, Bella?"

"I don't think I do."

I cleared the lump out of my throat so that I could make my voice hard like I wanted it. "Trust me."

I started to get to my feet.

"Where are you going?"

"I'm not doing any good here."

She held out her thin hand, pleading. "Don't go."

I could feel the addiction sucking at me, trying to keep me near her.

"I don't belong here. I've got to get back."

"Why did you come today?" she asked, still reaching limply.

"Just to see if you were really alive. I didn't believe you were sick like Charlie said."

I couldn't tell from her face whether she bought that or not.

"Will you come back again? Before . . ."

"I'm not going to hang around and watch you die, Bella."

She flinched. "You're right, you're right. You *should* go."

I headed for the door.

"Bye," she whispered behind me. "Love you, Jake."

I almost went back. I almost turned around and fell down on my knees and started begging again. But I knew that I had to quit Bella, quit her cold turkey, before she killed me, like she was going to kill him.

"Sure, sure," I mumbled on my way out.

I didn't see any of the vampires. I ignored my bike, standing all alone in the middle of the meadow. It wasn't fast enough for me now. My dad would be freaked out—Sam, too. What would the pack make of the fact that they hadn't heard me phase? Would they think the Cullens got me before I'd had the chance? I stripped down, not caring who might be watching, and started running. I blurred into wolf mid-stride.

They were waiting. Of course they were.

Jacob, Jake, eight voices chorused in relief.

Come home now, the Alpha voice ordered. Sam was furious.

I felt Paul fade out, and I knew Billy and Rachel were waiting to hear what had happened to me. Paul was too anxious to give them the good news that I wasn't vampire chow to listen to the whole story.

I didn't have to tell the pack I was on my way—they could see the forest blurring past me as I sprinted for home. I didn't have to tell them that I was half-past crazy, either. The sickness in my head was obvious.

They saw all the horror—Bella's mottled stomach; her raspy voice: *he's strong, that's all*; the burning man in Edward's face: *watching her sicken and waste away . . . seeing it hurting her*; Rosalie crouched over Bella's limp body: *Bella's life means nothing to her*—and for once, no one had anything to say.

Their shock was just a silent shout in my head. Wordless.

!!!!

I was halfway home before anyone recovered. Then they all started running to meet me.

It was almost dark—the clouds covered the sunset completely. I risked darting across the freeway and made it without being seen.

We met up about ten miles out of La Push, in a clearing left by the loggers. It was out of the way, wedged between two spurs of the mountain, where no one would see us. Paul found them when I did, so the pack was complete.

The babble in my head was total chaos. Everyone shouting at once.

Sam's hackles were sticking straight up, and he was growling in an unbroken stream as he paced back and forth around the top of the ring. Paul and Jared moved like shadows behind him, their ears flat against the sides of their head. The whole circle was agitated, on their feet and snarling in low bursts.

At first their anger was undefined, and I thought I was in for it. I was too messed up to care about that. They could do whatever they wanted to me for circumventing orders.

And then the unfocused confusion of thoughts began to move together.

How can this be? What does it mean? What will it be?
Not safe. Not right. Dangerous.
Unnatural. Monstrous. An abomination.
We can't allow it.

The pack was pacing in synchronization now, thinking in synchronization, all but myself and one other. I sat beside whichever brother it was, too dazed to look over with either my eyes or my mind and see who was next to me, while the pack circled around us.

The treaty does not cover this.
This puts everyone in danger.

I tried to understand the spiraling voices, tried to follow the curling pathway the thoughts made to see where they were leading, but it wasn't making sense. The pictures in the center of their thoughts were *my* pictures—the very worst of them. Bella's bruises, Edward's face as he burned.

They fear it, too.

But they won't do anything about it.

Protecting Bella Swan.

We can't let that influence us.

The safety of our families, of everyone here, is more important than one human.

If they won't kill it, we have to.

Protect the tribe.

Protect our families.

We have to kill it before it's too late.

Another of my memories, Edward's words this time: *The thing is growing. Swiftly.*

I struggled to focus, to pick out individual voices.

No time to waste, Jared thought.

It will mean a fight, Embry cautioned. *A bad one.*

We're ready, Paul insisted.

We'll need surprise on our side, Sam thought.

If we catch them divided, we can take them down separately. It will increase our chances of victory, Jared thought, starting to strategize now.

I shook my head, rising slowly to my feet. I felt unsteady there—like the circling wolves were making me dizzy. The wolf beside me got up, too. His shoulder pushed against mine, propping me up.

Wait, I thought.

The circling paused for one beat, and then they were pacing again.

There's little time, Sam said.

But—what are you thinking? You wouldn't attack them for breaking the treaty this afternoon. Now you're planning an ambush, when the treaty is still intact?

This is not something our treaty anticipated, Sam said. *This is a danger to every human in the area. We don't know what kind of creature the Cullens have bred, but we know that it is strong and fast-growing. And it will be too young to follow any treaty. Remember the newborn vampires we fought? Wild, violent, beyond the reach of reason or restraint. Imagine one like that, but protected by the Cullens.*

We don't know— I tried to interrupt.

We don't know, he agreed. *And we can't take chances with the unknown in this case. We can only allow the Cullens to exist while we're absolutely sure that they can be trusted not to cause harm. This . . . thing cannot be trusted.*

They don't like it any more than we do.

Sam pulled Rosalie's face, her protective crouch, from my mind and put it on display for everyone.

Some are ready to fight for it, no matter what it is.

It's just a baby, *for crying out loud.*

Not for long, Leah whispered.

Jake, buddy, this is a big problem, Quil said. *We can't just ignore it.*

You're making it into something bigger than it is, I argued. *The only one who's in danger here is Bella.*

Again by her own choice, Sam said. *But this time her choice affects us all.*

I don't think so.

We can't take that chance. We won't allow a blood drinker to hunt on our lands.

Then tell them to leave, the wolf who was still supporting me said. It was Seth. Of course.

And inflict the menace on others? When blood drinkers cross our land, we destroy them, no matter where they plan to hunt. We protect everyone we can.

This is crazy, I said. *This afternoon you were afraid to put the pack in danger.*

This afternoon I didn't know our families were at risk.

I can't believe this! How're you going to kill this creature without killing Bella?

There were no words, but the silence was full of meaning.

I howled. *She's human, too! Doesn't our protection apply to her?*

She's dying anyway, Leah thought. *We'll just shorten the process.*

That did it. I leaped away from Seth, toward his sister, with my teeth bared. I was about to catch her left hind leg when I felt Sam's teeth cut into my flank, dragging me back.

I howled in pain and fury and turned on him.

Stop! he ordered in the double timbre of the Alpha.

My legs seemed to buckle under me. I jerked to a halt, only managing to keep on my feet by sheer willpower.

He turned his gaze away from me. *You will not be cruel to him, Leah,* he commanded her. *Bella's sacrifice is a heavy price, and we will all recognize that. It is against everything we stand for to take a human life. Making an exception to that code is a bleak thing. We will all mourn for what we do tonight.*

Tonight? Seth repeated, shocked. *Sam—I think we should*

talk about this some more. Consult with the Elders, at least. You can't seriously mean for us to—

We can't afford your tolerance for the Cullens now. There is no time for debate. You will *do as you are told, Seth.*

Seth's front knees folded, and his head fell forward under the weight of the Alpha's command.

Sam paced in a tight circle around the two of us.

We need the whole pack for this. Jacob, you are our strongest fighter. You will *fight with us tonight. I understand that this is hard for you, so you will concentrate on their fighters—Emmett and Jasper Cullen. You don't have to be involved with the . . . other part. Quil and Embry will fight with you.*

My knees trembled; I struggled to hold myself upright while the voice of the Alpha lashed at my will.

Paul, Jared, and I will take on Edward and Rosalie. I think, from the information Jacob has brought us, they will be the ones guarding Bella. Carlisle and Alice will also be close, possibly Esme. Brady, Collin, Seth, and Leah will concentrate on them. Whoever has a clear line on—we all heard him mentally stutter over Bella's name—*the creature will take it. Destroying the creature is our first priority.*

The pack rumbled in nervous agreement. The tension had everyone's fur standing on end. The pacing was quicker, and the sound of the paws against the brackish floor was sharper, toenails tearing into the soil.

Only Seth and I were still, the eye in the center of a storm of bared teeth and flattened ears. Seth's nose was almost touching the ground, bowed under Sam's commands. I felt his pain at the coming disloyalty. For him this was a betrayal—during that one day of alliance, fighting beside Edward Cullen, Seth had truly become the vampire's friend.

There was no resistance in him, however. He would obey no matter how much it hurt him. He had no other choice.

And what choice did I have? When the Alpha spoke, the pack followed.

Sam had never pushed his authority this far before; I knew he honestly hated to see Seth kneeling before him like a slave at the foot of his master. He wouldn't force this if he didn't believe that he had no other choice. He couldn't lie to us when we were linked mind to mind like this. He really believed it was our duty to destroy Bella and the monster she carried. He really believed we had no time to waste. He believed it enough to die for it.

I saw that he would face Edward himself; Edward's ability to read our thoughts made him the greatest threat in Sam's mind. Sam would not let someone else take on that danger.

He saw Jasper as the second-greatest opponent, which is why he'd given him to me. He knew that I had the best chance of any of the pack to win that fight. He'd left the easiest targets for the younger wolves and Leah. Little Alice was no danger without her future vision to guide her, and we knew from our time of alliance that Esme was not a fighter. Carlisle would be more of a challenge, but his hatred of violence would hinder him.

I felt sicker than Seth as I watched Sam plan it out, trying to work the angles to give each member of the pack the best chance of survival.

Everything was inside out. This afternoon, I'd been chomping at the bit to attack them. But Seth had been right—it wasn't a fight I'd been ready for. I'd blinded myself with that hate. I hadn't let myself look at it carefully, because I must have known what I would see if I did.

Carlisle Cullen. Looking at him without that hate clouding my eyes, I couldn't deny that killing him was murder. He was good. Good as any human we protected. Maybe better. The others, too, I supposed, but I didn't feel as strongly about them. I didn't know them as well. It was Carlisle who would hate fighting back, even to save his own life. That's why we would be able to kill him—because he wouldn't want *us*, his enemies, to die.

This was wrong.

And it wasn't just because killing Bella felt like killing *me*, like suicide.

Pull it together, Jacob, Sam ordered. *The tribe comes first.*

I was wrong today, Sam.

Your reasons were wrong then. But now we have a duty to fulfill.

I braced myself. *No.*

Sam snarled and stopped pacing in front of me. He stared into my eyes and a deep growl slid between his teeth.

Yes, the Alpha decreed, his double voice blistering with the heat of his authority. *There are no loopholes tonight. You, Jacob, are going to fight the Cullens with us. You, with Quil and Embry, will take care of Jasper and Emmett. You are obligated to protect the tribe. That is why you exist. You* will *perform this obligation.*

My shoulders hunched as the edict crushed me. My legs collapsed, and I was on my belly under him.

No member of the pack could refuse the Alpha.

11. THE TWO THINGS AT THE VERY TOP OF MY THINGS-I-NEVER-WANT-TO-DO LIST

SAM STARTED MOVING THE OTHERS INTO FORMATION while I was still on the ground. Embry and Quil were at my sides, waiting for me to recover and take the point.

I could feel the drive, the need, to get on my feet and lead them. The compulsion grew, and I fought it uselessly, cringing on the ground where I was.

Embry whined quietly in my ear. He didn't want to think the words, afraid that he would bring me to Sam's attention again. I felt his wordless plea for me to get up, for me to get this over with and be done with it.

There was fear in the pack, not so much for self but for the whole. We couldn't imagine that we would all make it out alive tonight. Which brothers would we lose? Which minds would leave us forever? Which grieving families would we be consoling in the morning?

My mind began to work with theirs, to think in unison, as we dealt with these fears. Automatically, I pushed up from the ground and shook out my coat.

Embry and Quil huffed in relief. Quil touched his nose to my side once.

Their minds were filled with our challenge, our assignment. We remembered together the nights we'd watched the Cullens practicing for the fight with the newborns. Emmett Cullen was strongest, but Jasper would be the bigger problem. He moved like a lightning strike—power and speed and death rolled into one. How many centuries' experience did he have? Enough that all the other Cullens looked to him for guidance.

I'll take point, if you want flank, Quil offered. There was more excitement in his mind than most of the others. When Quil had watched Jasper's instruction those nights, he'd been dying to test his skill against the vampire's. For him, this would be a contest. Even knowing it was his life on the line, he saw it that way. Paul was like that, too, and the kids who had never been in battle, Collin and Brady. Seth probably would've been the same—if the opponents were not his friends.

Jake? Quil nudged me. *How do you want to roll?*

I just shook my head. I couldn't concentrate—the compulsion to follow orders felt like puppet strings hooked into all of my muscles. One foot forward, now another.

Seth was dragging behind Collin and Brady—Leah had assumed point there. She ignored Seth while planning with the others, and I could see that she'd rather leave him out of the fight. There was a maternal edge to her feelings for her younger brother. She wished Sam would send him home. Seth didn't register Leah's doubts. He was adjusting to the puppet strings, too.

Maybe if you stopped resisting . . . , Embry whispered.

Just focus on our part. The big ones. We can take them down. We own them! Quil was working himself up—like a pep talk before a big game.

I could see how easy it would be—to think about nothing more than my part. It wasn't hard to imagine attacking Jasper and Emmett. We'd been close to that before. I'd thought of them as enemies for a very long time. I could do that now again.

I just had to forget that they were protecting the same thing I would protect. I had to forget the reason why I might want them to win. . . .

Jake, Embry warned. *Keep your head in the game.*

My feet moved sluggishly, pulling against the drag of the strings.

There's no point fighting it, Embry whispered again.

He was right. I would end up doing what Sam wanted, if he was willing to push it. And he was. Obviously.

There was a good reason for the Alpha's authority. Even a pack as strong as ours wasn't much of a force without a leader. We had to move together, to think together, in order to be effective. And that required the body to have a head.

So what if Sam was wrong now? There was nothing anyone could do. No one could dispute his decision.

Except.

And there it was—a thought I'd never, never wanted to have. But now, with my legs all tied up in strings, I recognized the exception with relief—more than relief, with a fierce joy.

No one could dispute the Alpha's decision—except for *me*.

I hadn't earned anything. But there were things that had been born in me, things that I'd left unclaimed.

I'd never wanted to lead the pack. I didn't want to do it now. I didn't want the responsibility for all our fates resting on my shoulders. Sam was better at that than I would ever be.

But he was wrong tonight.

And I had not been born to kneel to him.

The bonds fell off my body the second that I embraced my birthright.

I could feel it gathering in me, both a freedom and also a strange, hollow power. Hollow because an Alpha's power came from his pack, and I had no pack. For a second, loneliness overwhelmed me.

I had no pack now.

But I was straight and strong as I walked to where Sam stood, planning with Paul and Jared. He turned at the sound of my advance, and his black eyes narrowed.

No, I told him again.

He heard it right away, heard the choice that I'd made in the sound of the Alpha voice in my thoughts.

He jumped back a half step with a shocked yelp.

Jacob? What have you done?

I won't follow you, Sam. Not for something so wrong.

He stared at me, stunned. *You would . . . you would choose your enemies over your family?*

They aren't—I shook my head, clearing it—*they aren't*

our enemies. They never have been. Until I really thought about destroying them, thought it through, I didn't see that.

This isn't about them, he snarled at me. *This is about Bella. She has never been the one for you, she has never chosen you, but you continue to destroy your life for her!*

They were hard words, but true words. I sucked in a big gulp of air, breathing them in.

Maybe you're right. But you're going to destroy the pack over her, Sam. No matter how many of them survive tonight, they will always have murder on their hands.

We have to protect our families!

I know what you've decided, Sam. But you don't decide for me, not anymore.

Jacob—you can't turn your back on the tribe.

I heard the double echo of his Alpha command, but it was weightless this time. It no longer applied to me. He clenched his jaw, trying to *force* me to respond to his words.

I stared into his furious eyes. *Ephraim Black's son was not born to follow Levi Uley's.*

Is this it, then, Jacob Black? His hackles rose and his muzzle pulled back from his teeth. Paul and Jared snarled and bristled at his sides. *Even if you can defeat me, the pack will never follow you!*

Now *I* jerked back, a surprised whine escaping my throat.

Defeat you? I'm not going to fight you, Sam.

Then what's your plan? I'm not stepping aside so that you can protect the vampire spawn at the tribe's expense.

I'm not telling you to step aside.

If you order them to follow you—

I'll never *take anyone's will away from him.*

His tail whipped back and forth as he recoiled from the judgment in my words. Then he took a step forward so that we were toe to toe, his exposed teeth inches from mine. I hadn't noticed till this moment that I'd grown taller than him.

There cannot be more than one Alpha. The pack has chosen me. Will you rip us apart tonight? Will you turn on your brothers? Or will you end this insanity and join us again? Every word was layered with command, but it couldn't touch me. Alpha blood ran undiluted in my veins.

I could see why there was never more than one Alpha male in a pack. My body was responding to the challenge. I could feel the instinct to defend my claim rising in me. The primitive core of my wolf-self tensed for the battle of supremacy.

I focused all my energy to control that reaction. I would not fall into a pointless, destructive fight with Sam. He was my brother still, even though I was rejecting him.

There is only one Alpha for this pack. I'm not contesting that. I'm just choosing to go my own way.

Do you belong to a coven *now, Jacob?*

I flinched.

I don't know, Sam. But I do know this—

He shrunk back as he felt the weight of the Alpha in my tone. It affected him more than his touched me. Because I *had* been born to lead him.

I will stand between you and the Cullens. I won't just watch while the pack kills innocent—it was hard to apply that word to vampires, but it was true—*people. The pack is better than that. Lead them in the right direction, Sam.*

I turned my back on him, and a chorus of howls tore into the air around me.

Digging my nails into the earth, I raced away from the uproar I'd caused. I didn't have much time. At least Leah was the only one with a prayer of outrunning me, and I had a head start.

The howling faded with the distance, and I took comfort as the sound continued to rip apart the quiet night. They weren't after me yet.

I had to warn the Cullens before the pack could get it together and stop me. If the Cullens were prepared, it might give Sam a reason to rethink this before it was too late. I sprinted toward the white house I still hated, leaving my home behind me. Home didn't belong to me anymore. I'd turned my back on it.

Today had begun like any other day. Made it home from patrol with the rainy sunrise, breakfast with Billy and Rachel, bad TV, bickering with Paul . . . How did it change so completely, turn all surreal? How did everything get messed up and twisted so that I was here now, all alone, an unwilling Alpha, cut off from my brothers, choosing vampires over them?

The sound I'd been fearing interrupted my dazed thoughts—it was the soft impact of big paws against the ground, chasing after me. I threw myself forward, rocketing through the black forest. I just had to get close enough so that Edward could hear the warning in my head. Leah wouldn't be able to stop me alone.

And then I caught the mood of the thoughts behind me. Not anger, but enthusiasm. Not chasing . . . but following.

My stride broke. I staggered two steps before it evened out again.

Wait up. My legs aren't as long as yours.

SETH! What do you think you're DOING? GO HOME!

He didn't answer, but I could feel his excitement as he kept right on after me. I could see through his eyes as he could see through mine. The night scene was bleak for me—full of despair. For him, it was hopeful.

I hadn't realized I was slowing down, but suddenly he was on my flank, running in position beside me.

I am not joking, Seth! This is no place for you. Get out of here.

The gangly tan wolf snorted. *I've got your back, Jacob. I think you're right. And I'm not going to stand behind Sam when—*

Oh yes you are the hell going to stand behind Sam! Get your furry butt back to La Push and do what Sam tells you to do.

No.

Go, Seth!

Is that an order, *Jacob?*

His question brought me up short. I skidded to a halt, my nails gouging furrows in the mud.

I'm not ordering anyone to do anything. I'm just telling you what you already know.

He plopped down on his haunches beside me. *I'll tell you what I know—I know that it's awful quiet. Haven't you noticed?*

I blinked. My tail swished nervously as I realized what he was thinking underneath the words. It wasn't quiet in one sense. Howls still filled the air, far away in the west.

They haven't phased back, Seth said.

I knew that. The pack would be on red alert now. They would be using the mind link to see all sides clearly. But I couldn't hear what they were thinking. I could only hear Seth. No one else.

Looks to me like separate packs aren't linked. Huh. Guess there was no reason for our fathers to know that before. 'Cause there was no reason for separate packs before. Never enough wolves for two. Wow. It's really quiet. Sort of eerie. But also kinda nice, don't you think? I bet it was easier, like this, for Ephraim and Quil and Levi. Not such a babble with just three. Or just two.

Shut up, Seth.

Yes, sir.

Stop that! There are not two packs. There is THE pack, and then there is me. That's all. So you can go home now.

If there aren't two packs, then why can we hear each other and not the rest? I think that when you turned your back on Sam, that was a pretty significant move. A change. And when I followed you away, I think that was significant, too.

You've got a point, I conceded. *But what can change can change right back.*

He got up and started trotting toward the east. *No time to argue about it now. We should be moving right along before Sam . . .*

He was right about that part. There was no time for this argument. I fell into a run again, not pushing myself quite as hard. Seth stayed on my heels, holding the Second's traditional place on my right flank.

I can run somewhere else, he thought, his nose dipping a little. *I didn't follow you because I was after a promotion.*

Run wherever you want. Makes no difference to me.

There was no sound of pursuit, but we both stepped it

up a little at the same time. I was worried now. If I couldn't tap into the pack's mind, it was going to make this more difficult. I'd have no more advance warning of attack than the Cullens.

We'll run patrols, Seth suggested.

And what do we do if the pack challenges us? My eyes tightened. *Attack our brothers? Your sister?*

No—we sound the alarm and fall back.

Good answer. But then what? I don't think . . .

I know, he agreed. Less confident now. *I don't think I can fight them, either. But they won't be any happier with the idea of attacking us than we are with attacking them. That might be enough to stop them right there. Plus, there're only eight of them now.*

Stop being so . . . Took me a minute to decide on the right word. *Optimistic. It's getting on my nerves.*

No problem. You want me to be all doom and gloom, or just shut up?

Just shut up.

Can do.

Really? Doesn't seem like it.

He was finally quiet.

And then we were across the road and moving through the forest that ringed the Cullens' house. Could Edward hear us yet?

Maybe we should be thinking something like, "We come in peace."

Go for it.

Edward? He called the name tentatively. *Edward, you there? Okay, now I feel kinda stupid.*

You sound stupid, too.

Think he can hear us?

We were less than a mile out now. *I think so. Hey, Edward. If you can hear me—circle the wagons, bloodsucker. You've got a problem.*

We've *got a problem,* Seth corrected.

Then we broke through the trees into the big lawn. The house was dark, but not empty. Edward stood on the porch between Emmett and Jasper. They were snow white in the pale light.

"Jacob? Seth? What's going on?"

I slowed and then paced back a few steps. The smell was so sharp through this nose that it felt like it was honestly burning me. Seth whined quietly, hesitating, and then he fell back behind me.

To answer Edward's question, I let my mind run over the confrontation with Sam, moving through it backward. Seth thought with me, filling in the gaps, showing the scene from another angle. We stopped when we got to the part about the "abomination," because Edward hissed furiously and leaped off the porch.

"They want to kill Bella?" he snarled flatly.

Emmett and Jasper, not having heard the first part of the conversation, took his inflectionless question for a statement. They were right next to him in a flash, teeth exposed as they moved on us.

Hey, now, Seth thought, backing away.

"Em, Jazz—not *them*! The others. The pack is coming."

Emmett and Jasper rocked back on their heels; Emmett turned to Edward while Jasper kept his eyes locked on us.

"What's *their* problem?" Emmett demanded.

"The same one as mine," Edward hissed. "But they have their own plan to handle it. Get the others. Call Carlisle! He and Esme have to get back here now."

I whined uneasily. They *were* separated.

"They aren't far," Edward said in the same dead voice as before.

I'm going to go take a look, Seth said. *Run the western perimeter.*

"Will you be in danger, Seth?" Edward asked.

Seth and I exchanged a glance.

Don't think so, we thought together. And then I added, *But maybe I should go. Just in case . . .*

They'll be less likely to challenge me, Seth pointed out. *I'm just a kid to them.*

You're just a kid to me, kid.

I'm outta here. You need to coordinate with the Cullens.

He wheeled and darted into the darkness. I wasn't going to order Seth around, so I let him go.

Edward and I stood facing each other in the dark meadow. I could hear Emmett muttering into his phone. Jasper was watching the place where Seth had vanished into the woods. Alice appeared on the porch and then, after staring at me with anxious eyes for a long moment, she flitted to Jasper's side. I guessed that Rosalie was inside with Bella. Still guarding her—from the wrong dangers.

"This isn't the first time I've owed you my gratitude, Jacob," Edward whispered. "I would never have asked for this from you."

I thought of what he'd asked me for earlier today. When it came to Bella, there were no lines he wouldn't cross. *Yeah, you would.*

He thought about it and then nodded. "I suppose you're right about that."

I sighed heavily. *Well, this isn't the first time that I didn't do it for you.*

"Right," he murmured.

Sorry I didn't do any good today. Told you she wouldn't listen to me.

"I know. I never really believed she would. But . . ."

You had to try. I get it. She any better?

His voice and eyes went hollow. "Worse," he breathed.

I didn't want to let that word sink in. I was grateful when Alice spoke.

"Jacob, would you mind switching forms?" Alice asked. "I want to know what's going on."

I shook my head at the same time Edward answered.

"He needs to stay linked to Seth."

"Well, then would *you* be so kind as to tell me what's happening?"

He explained in clipped, emotionless sentences. "The pack thinks Bella's become a problem. They foresee potential danger from the . . . from what she's carrying. They feel it's their duty to remove that danger. Jacob and Seth disbanded from the pack to warn us. The rest are planning to attack tonight."

Alice hissed, leaning away from me. Emmett and Jasper exchanged a glance, and then their eyes ranged across the trees.

Nobody out here, Seth reported. *All's quiet on the western front.*

They may go around.

I'll make a loop.

"Carlisle and Esme are on their way," Emmett said. "Twenty minutes, tops."

"We should take up a defensive position," Jasper said.

Edward nodded. "Let's get inside."

I'll run perimeter with Seth. If I get too far for you to hear my head, listen for my howl.

"I will."

They backed into the house, eyes flickering everywhere. Before they were inside, I turned and ran toward the west.

I'm still not finding much, Seth told me.

I'll take half the circle. Move fast—we don't want them to have a chance to sneak past us.

Seth lurched forward in a sudden burst of speed.

We ran in silence, and the minutes passed. I listened to the noises around him, double-checking his judgment.

Hey—something coming up fast! he warned me after fifteen minutes of silence.

On my way!

Hold your position—I don't think it's the pack. It sounds different.

Seth—

But he caught the approaching scent on the breeze, and I read it in his mind.

Vampire. Bet it's Carlisle.

Seth, fall back. It might be someone else.

No, it's them. I recognize the scent. Hold up, I'm going to phase to explain it to them.

Seth, I don't think—

But he was gone.

Anxiously, I raced along the western border. Wouldn't it be just peachy if I couldn't take care of Seth for one freaking night? What if something happened to him on my watch? Leah would shred me into kibble.

At least the kid kept it short. It wasn't two minutes later when I felt him in my head again.

Yep, Carlisle and Esme. Boy, were they surprised to see me! They're probably inside by now. Carlisle said thanks.

He's a good guy.

Yeah. That's one of the reasons why we're right about this.

Hope so.

Why're you so down, Jake? I'll bet Sam won't bring the pack tonight. He's not going to launch a suicide mission.

I sighed. It didn't seem to matter, either way.

Oh. This isn't about Sam so much, is it?

I made the turn at the end of my patrol. I caught Seth's scent where he'd turned last. We weren't leaving any gaps.

You think Bella's going to die anyway, Seth whispered.

Yeah, she is.

Poor Edward. He must be crazy.

Literally.

Edward's name brought other memories boiling to the surface. Seth read them in astonishment.

And then he was howling. *Oh, man! No way! You did not! That just plain ol' sucks rocks, Jacob! And you know it, too! I can't believe you said you'd kill him. What is that? You have to tell him no.*

Shut up, shut up, you idiot! They're going to think the pack is coming!

Oops! He cut off mid-howl.

I wheeled and started loping in toward the house. *Just keep out of this, Seth. Take the whole circle for now.*

Seth seethed and I ignored him.

False alarm, false alarm, I thought as I ran closer in. *Sorry. Seth is young. He forgets things. No one's attacking. False alarm.*

When I got to the meadow, I could see Edward staring out of a dark window. I ran in, wanting to be sure he got the message.

There's nothing out there—you got that?

He nodded once.

This would be a lot easier if the communication wasn't one way. Then again, I was kinda glad I wasn't in *his* head.

He looked over his shoulder, back into the house, and I saw a shudder run through his whole frame. He waved me away without looking in my direction again and then moved out of my view.

What's going on?

Like I was going to get an answer.

I sat very still in the meadow and listened. With these ears, I could almost hear Seth's soft footfalls, miles out into the forest. It was easy to hear every sound inside the dark house.

"It was a false alarm," Edward was explaining in that dead voice, just repeating what I'd told him. "Seth was upset about something else, and he forgot we were listening for a signal. He's very young."

"Nice to have toddlers guarding the fort," a deeper voice grumbled. Emmett, I thought.

"They've done us a great service tonight, Emmett," Carlisle said. "At great personal sacrifice."

"Yeah, I know. I'm just jealous. Wish I was out there."

"Seth doesn't think Sam will attack now," Edward said mechanically. "Not with us forewarned, and lacking two members of the pack."

"What does Jacob think?" Carlisle asked.

"He's not as optimistic."

No one spoke. There was a quiet dripping sound that I couldn't place. I heard their low breathing—and I could separate Bella's from the rest. It was harsher, labored. It hitched and broke in strange rhythms. I could hear her heart. It seemed . . . too fast. I paced it against my own heartbeat, but I wasn't sure if that was any measure. It wasn't like I was normal.

"Don't touch her! You'll wake her up," Rosalie whispered.

Someone sighed.

"Rosalie," Carlisle murmured.

"Don't start with me, Carlisle. We let you have your way earlier, but that's all we're allowing."

It seemed like Rosalie and Bella were both talking in plurals now. Like they'd formed a pack of their own.

I paced quietly in front of the house. Each pass brought me a little closer. The dark windows were like a TV set running in some dull waiting room—it was impossible to keep my eyes off them for long.

A few more minutes, a few more passes, and my fur was brushing the side of the porch as I paced.

I could see up through the windows—see the top of the walls and the ceiling, the unlit chandelier that hung there. I was tall enough that all I would have to do was stretch my neck a little . . . and maybe one paw up on the edge of the porch. . . .

I peeked into the big, open front room, expecting to see something very similar to the scene this afternoon. But it had changed so much that I was confused at first. For a second I thought I'd gotten the wrong room.

The glass wall was gone—it looked like metal now. And the furniture was all dragged out of the way, with Bella curled up awkwardly on a narrow bed in the center of the open space. Not a normal bed—one with rails like in a hospital. Also like a hospital were the monitors strapped to her body, the tubes stuck into her skin. The lights on the monitors flashed, but there was no sound. The dripping noise was from the IV plugged into her arm—some fluid that was thick and white, not clear.

She choked a little in her uneasy sleep, and both Edward and Rosalie moved in to hover over her. Her body jerked, and she whimpered. Rosalie smoothed her hand across Bella's forehead. Edward's body stiffened—his back was to me, but his expression must have been something to see, because Emmett wrenched himself between them before there was time to blink. He held his hands up to Edward.

"Not tonight, Edward. We've got other things to worry about."

Edward turned away from them, and he was the burning man again. His eyes met mine for one moment, and then I dropped back to all fours.

I ran back into the dark forest, running to join Seth, running away from what was behind me.

Worse. Yes, she was worse.

12. SOME PEOPLE JUST DON'T GRASP THE CONCEPT OF "UNWELCOME"

I WAS RIGHT ON THE EDGE OF SLEEP.

The sun had risen behind the clouds an hour ago—the forest was gray now instead of black. Seth'd curled up and passed out around one, and I'd woken him at dawn to trade off. Even after running all night, I was having a hard time making my brain shut up long enough to fall asleep, but Seth's rhythmic run was helping. One, two-three, four, one, two-three, four—*dum dum-dum dum*—dull paw thuds against the damp earth, over and over as he made the wide circuit surrounding the Cullens' land. We were already wearing a trail into the ground. Seth's thoughts were empty, just a blur of green and gray as the woods flew past him.

It was restful. It helped to fill my head with what he saw rather than letting my own images take center stage.

And then Seth's piercing howl broke the early morning quiet.

I lurched up from the ground, my front legs pulling toward a sprint before my hind legs were off the ground. I raced toward the place where Seth had frozen, listening with him to the tread of paws running in our direction.

Morning, boys.

A shocked whine broke through Seth's teeth. And then we both snarled as we read deeper into the new thoughts.

Oh, man! Go away, Leah! Seth groaned.

I stopped when I got to Seth, head thrown back, ready to howl again—this time to complain.

Cut the noise, Seth.

Right. Ugh! Ugh! Ugh! He whimpered and pawed at the ground, scratching deep furrows in the dirt.

Leah trotted into view, her small gray body weaving through the underbrush.

Stop whining, Seth. You're such a baby.

I growled at her, my ears flattening against my skull. She skipped back a step automatically.

What do you think you're doing, Leah?

She huffed a heavy sigh. *It's pretty obvious, isn't it? I'm joining your crappy little renegade pack. The vampires' guard dogs.* She barked out a low, sarcastic laugh.

No, you're not. Turn around before I rip out one of your hamstrings.

Like you could catch me. She grinned and coiled her body for launch. *Wanna race, O fearless leader?*

I took a deep breath, filling my lungs until my sides bulged. Then, when I was sure I wasn't going to scream, I exhaled in a gust.

Seth, go let the Cullens know that it's just your stupid sister— I thought the words as harshly as possible. *I'll deal with this.*

On it! Seth was only too happy to leave. He vanished toward the house.

Leah whined, and she leaned after him, the fur on her shoulders rising. *You're just going to let him run off to the vampires alone?*

I'm pretty sure he'd rather they took him out than spend another minute with you.

Shut up, Jacob. Oops, I'm sorry—I meant, shut up, most high Alpha.

Why the hell *are you here?*

You think I'm just going to sit home while my little brother volunteers as a vampire chew toy?

Seth doesn't want or need your protection. In fact, no one wants you here.

Oooh, ouch, that's gonna leave a huge *mark. Ha,* she barked. *Tell me who* does *want me around, and I'm outta here.*

So this isn't about Seth at all, is it?

Of course it is. I'm just pointing out that being unwanted is not a first for me. Not really a motivating factor, if you know what I mean.

I gritted my teeth and tried to get my head straight.
Did Sam send you?

If I was here on Sam's errand, you wouldn't be able to hear me. My allegiance is no longer with him.

I listened carefully to the thoughts mixed in with the

words. If this was a diversion or a ploy, I had to be alert enough to see through it. But there was nothing. Her declaration was nothing but the truth. Unwilling, almost despairing truth.

You're loyal to me now? I asked with deep sarcasm. *Uh-huh. Right.*

My choices are limited. I'm working with the options I've got. Trust me, I'm not enjoying this any more than you are.

That wasn't true. There was an edgy kind of excitement in her mind. She was unhappy about this, but she was also riding some weird high. I searched her mind, trying to understand.

She bristled, resenting the intrusion. I usually tried to tune Leah out—I'd never tried to make sense of her before.

We were interrupted by Seth, thinking his explanation at Edward. Leah whined anxiously. Edward's face, framed in the same window as last night, showed no reaction to the news. It was a blank face, dead.

Wow, he looks bad, Seth muttered to himself. The vampire showed no reaction to that thought, either. He disappeared into the house. Seth pivoted and headed back out to us. Leah relaxed a little.

What's going on? Leah asked. *Catch me up to speed.*

There's no point. You're not staying.

Actually, Mr. Alpha, I am. Because since apparently I have to belong to someone—and don't think I haven't tried breaking off on my own, you know yourself how well that *doesn't work— I choose you.*

Leah, you don't like me. I don't like you.

Thank you, Captain Obvious. That doesn't matter to me. I'm staying with Seth.

You don't like vampires. Don't you think that's a little conflict of interest right there?

You don't like vampires either.

But I am *committed to this alliance. You aren't.*

I'll keep my distance from them. I can run patrols out here, just like Seth.

And I'm supposed to trust you with that?

She stretched her neck, leaning up on her toes, trying to be as tall as me as she stared into my eyes. *I will not betray my pack.*

I wanted to throw my head back and howl, like Seth had before. *This isn't your pack! This isn't even a pack. This is just me, going off on my own! What is it with you Clearwaters? Why can't you leave me alone?*

Seth, just coming up behind us now, whined; I'd offended him. Great.

I've been helpful, haven't I, Jake?

You haven't made too much a nuisance of yourself, kid, but if you and Leah are a package deal—if the only way to get rid of her is for you to go home. . . . Well, can you blame me for wanting you gone?

Ugh, Leah, you ruin everything!

Yeah, I know, she told him, and the thought was loaded with the heaviness of her despair.

I felt the pain in the three little words, and it was more than I would've guessed. I didn't want to feel that. I didn't want to feel bad for her. Sure, the pack was rough on her, but she brought it all on herself with the bitterness that tainted her every thought and made being in her head a nightmare.

Seth was feeling guilty, too. *Jake . . . You're not really*

*gonna send me away, are you? Leah's not so bad. Really. I mean,
with her here, we can push the perimeter out farther. And this puts
Sam down to seven. There's no way he's going to mount an attack
that outnumbered. It's probably a good thing. . . .*

You know I don't want to lead a pack, Seth.

So don't lead us, Leah offered.

I snorted. *Sounds perfect to me. Run along home now.*

Jake, Seth thought. *I belong here. I do like vampires. Cullens,
anyway. They're people to me, and I'm going to protect them, 'cause
that's what we're supposed to do.*

*Maybe you belong, kid, but your sister doesn't. And she's going
to go wherever you are—*

I stopped short, because I saw something when I said
that. Something Leah had been trying not to think.

Leah wasn't going anywhere.

Thought this was about Seth, I thought sourly.

She flinched. *Of course I'm here for Seth.*

And to get away from Sam.

Her jaw clenched. *I don't have to explain myself to you. I just
have to do what I'm told. I belong to your pack, Jacob. The end.*

I paced away from her, growling.

Crap. I was never going to get rid of her. As much as she
disliked me, as much as she loathed the Cullens, as happy as
she'd be to go kill all the vampires right now, as much as it
pissed her off to have to protect them instead—none of that
was *anything* compared to what she felt being free of Sam.

Leah didn't like me, so it wasn't such a chore having me
wish she would disappear.

She loved Sam. Still. And having *him* wish she would
disappear was more pain than she was willing to live with,
now that she had a choice. She would have taken any other

option. Even if it meant moving in with the Cullens as their lapdog.

I don't know if I'd go that far, she thought. She tried to make the words tough, aggressive, but there were big cracks in her show. *I'm sure I'd give killing myself a few good tries first.*

Look, Leah . . .

No, you look, *Jacob. Stop arguing with me, because it's not going to do any good. I'll stay out of your way, okay? I'll do anything you want. Except go back to Sam's pack and be the pathetic ex-girlfriend he can't get away from. If you want me to leave—* she sat back on her haunches and stared straight into my eyes—*you're going to have to* make *me.*

I snarled for a long, angry minute. I was beginning to feel some sympathy for Sam, despite what he had done to me, to Seth. No wonder he was always ordering the pack around. How else would you ever get anything done?

Seth, are you gonna get mad at me if I kill your sister?

He pretended to think about it for a minute. *Well . . . yeah, probably.*

I sighed.

Okay, then, Ms. Do-Anything-I-Want. Why don't you make yourself useful by telling us what you know? What happened after we left last night?

Lots of howling. But you probably heard that part. It was so loud that it took us a while to figure out that we couldn't hear either of you anymore. Sam was . . . Words failed her, but we could see it in our head. Both Seth and I cringed. *After that, it was clear pretty quick that we were going to have to rethink things. Sam was planning to talk to the other Elders first thing this morning. We were supposed to meet up and figure out a game plan. I could tell he wasn't going to mount another attack right away, though. Suicide at this point, with you and Seth AWOL and the bloodsuckers forewarned. I'm not sure what they'll do, but I wouldn't be wandering the forest alone if I was a leech. It's open season on vamps now.*

You decided to skip the meeting this morning? I asked.

When we split up for patrols last night, I asked permission to go home, to tell my mother what had happened—

Crap! You told Mom? Seth growled.

Seth, hold off on the sibling stuff for a sec. Go on, Leah.

So once I was human, I took a minute to think things through. Well, actually, I took all night. I bet the others think I fell asleep. But the whole two-separate-packs, two-separate-pack-minds thing gave me a lot to sift through. In the end, I weighed Seth's safety and the, er, other benefits against the idea of turning traitor and sniffing vampire stink for who knows how long. You know what I decided. I left a note for my mom. I expect we'll hear it when Sam finds out. . . .

Leah cocked an ear to the west.

Yeah, I expect we will, I agreed.

So that's everything. What do we do now? she asked.

She and Seth both looked at me expectantly.

This was exactly the kind of thing I didn't want to have to do.

I guess we just keep an eye out for now. That's all we can do. You should probably take a nap, Leah.

You've had as much sleep as I have.

Thought you were going to do what you were told?

Right. That's going to get old, she grumbled, and then she yawned. *Well, whatever. I don't care.*

I'll run the border, Jake. I'm not tired at all. Seth was so glad I hadn't forced them home, he was all but prancing with excitement.

Sure, sure. I'm going to go check in with the Cullens.

Seth took off along the new path worn into the damp earth. Leah looked after him thoughtfully.

Maybe a round or two before I crash. . . . Hey Seth, wanna see how many times I can lap you?

NO!

Barking out a low chuckle, Leah lunged into the woods after him.

I growled uselessly. So much for peace and quiet.

Leah was trying—for Leah. She kept her jibes to a minimum as she raced around the circuit, but it was impossible not to be aware of her smug mood. I thought of the whole "two's company" saying. It didn't really apply, because *one* was plenty to my mind. But if there *had* to be three of us, it was hard to think of anyone that I wouldn't trade her for.

Paul? she suggested.

Maybe, I allowed.

She laughed to herself, too jittery and hyper to get offended. I wondered how long the buzz from dodging Sam's pity would last.

That will be my goal, then—to be less annoying than Paul.

Yeah, work on that.

I changed into my other form when I was a few yards from the lawn. I hadn't been planning to spend much time human here. But I hadn't been planning to have Leah in my head, either. I pulled on my ragged shorts and started across the lawn.

The door opened before I got to the steps, and I was surprised to see Carlisle rather than Edward step outside to meet me—his face looked exhausted and defeated. For a second, my heart froze. I faltered to a stop, unable to speak.

"Are you all right, Jacob?" Carlisle asked.

"Is Bella?" I choked out.

"She's . . . much the same as last night. Did I startle you? I'm sorry. Edward said you were coming in your human form, and I came out to greet you, as he didn't want to leave her. She's awake."

And Edward didn't want to lose any time with her, because he didn't have much time left. Carlisle didn't say the words out loud, but he might as well have.

It had been a while since I'd slept—since before my last patrol. I could really feel that now. I took a step forward, sat down on the porch steps, and slumped against the railing.

Moving whisper-quiet as only a vampire could, Carlisle took a seat on the same step, against the other railing.

"I didn't get a chance to thank you last night, Jacob. You don't know how much I appreciate your . . . compassion. I know your goal was to protect Bella, but I owe you the safety of the rest of my family as well. Edward told me what you had to do. . . ."

"Don't mention it," I muttered.

"If you prefer."

We sat in silence. I could hear the others in the house. Emmett, Alice, and Jasper, speaking in low, serious voices upstairs. Esme humming tunelessly in another room. Rosalie and Edward breathing close by—I couldn't tell which was which, but I could hear the difference in

Bella's labored panting. I could hear her heart, too. It seemed . . . uneven.

It was like fate was out to make me do everything I'd ever sworn I wouldn't in the course of twenty-four hours. Here I was, hanging around, waiting for her to die.

I didn't want to listen anymore. Talking was better than listening.

"She's family to you?" I asked Carlisle. It had caught my notice before, when he'd said I'd helped the *rest* of his family, too.

"Yes. Bella is already a daughter to me. A beloved daughter."

"But you're going to let her die."

He was quiet long enough that I looked up. His face was very, very tired. I knew how he felt.

"I can imagine what you think of me for that," he finally said. "But I can't ignore her will. It wouldn't be right to make such a choice for her, to force her."

I wanted to be angry with him, but he was making it hard. It was like he was throwing my own words back at me, just scrambled up. They'd sounded right before, but they couldn't be right now. Not with Bella dying. Still . . . I remembered how it felt to be broken on the ground under Sam—to have no choice but be involved in the murder of someone I loved. It wasn't the same, though. Sam was wrong. And Bella loved things she shouldn't.

"Do you think there's any chance she'll make it? I mean, as a vampire and all that. She told me about . . . about Esme."

"I'd say there's an even chance at this point," he answered quietly. "I've seen vampire venom work miracles, but there are conditions that even venom cannot overcome. Her heart is working too hard now; if it should fail . . . there won't be anything for me to do."

Bella's heartbeat throbbed and faltered, giving an agonizing emphasis to his words.

Maybe the planet had started turning backward. Maybe that would explain how everything was the opposite of what it had been yesterday—how I could be hoping for what had once seemed like the very worst thing in the world.

"What is that thing doing to her?" I whispered. "She was so much worse last night. I saw . . . the tubes and all that. Through the window."

"The fetus isn't compatible with her body. Too strong, for one thing, but she could probably endure that for a while. The bigger problem is that it won't allow her to get the sustenance she needs. Her body is rejecting every form of nutrition. I'm trying to feed her intravenously, but she's just not absorbing it. Everything about her condition is accelerated. I'm watching her—and not just her, but the fetus as well—starve to death by the hour. I can't stop it and I can't slow it down. I can't figure out what it *wants*." His weary voice broke at the end.

I felt the same way I had yesterday, when I'd seen the black stains across her stomach—furious, and a little crazy.

I clenched my hands into fists to control the shaking. I hated the thing that was hurting her. It wasn't enough for the monster to beat her from the inside out. No, it was starving her, too. Probably just looking for something to sink its teeth into—a throat to suck dry. Since it wasn't big enough to kill anyone else yet, it settled for sucking Bella's life from her.

I could tell them exactly what it wanted: death and blood, blood and death.

My skin was all hot and prickly. I breathed slowly in and out, focusing on that to calm myself.

"I wish I could get a better idea of what exactly it is," Carlisle murmured. "The fetus is well protected. I haven't been able to produce an ultrasonic image. I doubt there is any way to get a needle through the amniotic sac, but Rosalie won't agree to let me try, in any case."

"A needle?" I mumbled. "What good would that do?"

"The more I know about the fetus, the better I can estimate what it will be capable of. What I wouldn't give for even a little amniotic fluid. If I knew even the chromosomal count . . ."

"You're losing me, Doc. Can you dumb it down?"

He chuckled once—even his laugh sounded exhausted. "Okay. How much biology have you taken? Did you study chromosomal pairs?"

"Think so. We have twenty-three, right?"

"Humans do."

I blinked. "How many do you have?"

"Twenty-five."

I frowned at my fists for a second. "What does that mean?"

"I thought it meant that our species were almost completely different. Less related than a lion and a house cat. But this new life—well, it suggests that we're more genetically compatible than I'd thought." He sighed sadly. "I didn't know to warn them."

I sighed, too. It had been easy to hate Edward for the same ignorance. I still hated him for it. It was just hard to feel the same way about Carlisle. Maybe because I wasn't ten shades of jealous in Carlisle's case.

"It might help to know what the count was—whether the fetus was closer to us or to her. To know what to expect." Then he shrugged. "And maybe it wouldn't help anything. I guess I just wish I had something to study, anything to do."

"Wonder what my chromosomes are like," I muttered randomly. I thought of those Olympic steroids tests again. Did they run DNA scans?

Carlisle coughed self-consciously. "You have twenty-four pairs, Jacob."

I turned slowly to stare at him, raising my eyebrows.

He looked embarrassed. "I was . . . curious. I took the liberty when I was treating you last June."

I thought about it for a second. "I guess that should piss me off. But I don't really care."

"I'm sorry. I should have asked."

"S'okay, Doc. You didn't mean any harm."

"No, I promise you that I did *not* mean you any harm. It's just that . . . I find your species fascinating. I suppose that the elements of vampiric nature have come to seem commonplace to me over the centuries. Your family's divergence from humanity is much more interesting. Magical, almost."

"Bibbidi-Bobbidi-Boo," I mumbled. He was just like Bella with all the magic garbage.

Carlisle laughed another weary laugh.

Then we heard Edward's voice inside the house, and we both paused to listen.

"I'll be right back, Bella. I want to speak with Carlisle for a moment. Actually, Rosalie, would you mind accompanying me?" Edward sounded different. There was a little life in his dead voice. A spark of something. Not hope exactly, but maybe the *desire* to hope.

"What is it, Edward?" Bella asked hoarsely.

"Nothing you need to worry about, love. It will just take a second. Please, Rose?"

"Esme?" Rosalie called. "Can you mind Bella for me?"

I heard the whisper of wind as Esme flitted down the stairs.

"Of course," she said.

Carlisle shifted, twisting to look expectantly at the door. Edward was through the door first, with Rosalie right on his heels. His face was, like his voice, no longer dead. He seemed intensely focused. Rosalie looked suspicious.

Edward shut the door behind her.

"Carlisle," he murmured.

"What is it, Edward?"

"Perhaps we've been going about this the wrong way. I was listening to you and Jacob just now, and when you were speaking of what the . . . fetus wants, Jacob had an interesting thought."

Me? What had *I* thought? Besides my obvious hatred for the thing? At least I wasn't alone in that. I could tell that Edward had a difficult time using a term as mild as *fetus.*

"We haven't actually addressed *that* angle," Edward went on. "We've been trying to get Bella what she needs. And her body is accepting it about as well as one of ours would. Perhaps we should address the needs of the . . . fetus first.

Maybe if we can satisfy it, we'll be able to help her more effectively."

"I'm not following you, Edward," Carlisle said.

"Think about it, Carlisle. If that creature is more vampire than human, can't you guess what it craves—what it's not getting? Jacob did."

I did? I ran through the conversation, trying to remember what thoughts I'd kept to myself. I remembered at the same time that Carlisle understood.

"Oh," he said in a surprised tone. "You think it is . . . thirsty?"

Rosalie hissed under her breath. She wasn't suspicious anymore. Her revoltingly perfect face was all lit up, her eyes wide with excitement. "Of course," she muttered. "Carlisle, we have all that type O negative laid aside for Bella. It's a good idea," she added, not looking at me.

"Hmm." Carlisle put his hand to his chin, lost in thought. "I wonder . . . And then, what would be the best way to administer. . . ."

Rosalie shook her head. "We don't have time to be creative. I'd say we should start with the traditional way."

"Wait a minute," I whispered. "Just hold on. Are you— are you talking about making Bella drink *blood*?"

"It was your idea, dog," Rosalie said, scowling at me without ever quite looking at me.

I ignored her and watched Carlisle. That same ghost of hope that had been in Edward's face was now in the doctor's eyes. He pursed his lips, speculating.

"That's just . . ." I couldn't find the right word.

"Monstrous?" Edward suggested. "Repulsive?"

"Pretty much."

"But what if it helps her?" he whispered.

I shook my head angrily. "What are you gonna do, shove a tube down her throat?"

"I plan to ask her what she thinks. I just wanted to run it past Carlisle first."

Rosalie nodded. "If you tell her it might help the baby, she'll be willing to do anything. Even if we do have to feed them through a tube."

I realized then—when I heard how her voice got all lovey-dovey as she said the word *baby*—that Blondie would be in line with anything that helped the little life-sucking monster. Was that what was going on, the mystery factor that was bonding the two of them? Was Rosalie after the kid?

From the corner of my eye, I saw Edward nod once, absently, not looking in my direction. But I knew he was answering my questions.

Huh. I wouldn't have thought the ice-cold Barbie would have a maternal side. So much for protecting Bella—Rosalie'd probably jam the tube down Bella's throat herself.

Edward's mouth mashed into a hard line, and I knew I was right again.

"Well, we don't have time to sit around discussing this," Rosalie said impatiently. "What do you think, Carlisle? Can we try?"

Carlisle took a deep breath, and then he was on his feet. "We'll ask Bella."

Blondie smiled smugly—sure that, if it was up to Bella, she would get her way.

I dragged myself up from the stairs and followed after

them as they disappeared into the house. I wasn't sure why. Just morbid curiosity, maybe. It was like a horror movie. Monsters and blood all over the place.

Maybe I just couldn't resist another hit of my dwindling drug supply.

Bella lay flat on the hospital bed, her belly a mountain under the sheet. She looked like wax—colorless and sort of see-through. You'd think she was already dead, except for the tiny movement of her chest, her shallow breathing. And then her eyes, following the four of us with exhausted suspicion.

The others were at her side already, flitting across the room with sudden darting motions. It was creepy to watch. I ambled along at a slow walk.

"What's going on?" Bella demanded in a scratchy whisper. Her waxy hand twitched up—like she was trying to protect her balloon-shaped stomach.

"Jacob had an idea that might help you," Carlisle said. I wished he would leave me out of it. I hadn't suggested anything. Give the credit to her bloodsucking husband, where it belonged. "It won't be . . . pleasant, but—"

"But it will help the baby," Rosalie interrupted eagerly. "We've thought of a better way to feed him. Maybe."

Bella's eyelids fluttered. Then she coughed out a weak chuckle. "Not pleasant?" she whispered. "Gosh, that'll be such a change." She eyed the tube stuck into her arm and coughed again.

Blondie laughed with her.

The girl looked like she only had hours left, and she had to be in pain, but she was making jokes. So Bella. Trying to ease the tension, make it better for everyone else.

Edward stepped around Rosalie, no humor touching his intense expression. I was glad for that. It helped, just a little bit, that he was suffering worse than me. He took her hand, not the one that was still protecting her swollen belly.

"Bella, love, we're going to ask you to do something monstrous," he said, using the same adjectives he'd offered me. "Repulsive."

Well, at least he was giving it to her straight.

She took a shallow, fluttery breath. "How bad?"

Carlisle answered. "We think the fetus might have an appetite closer to ours than to yours. We think it's thirsty."

She blinked. "Oh. *Oh.*"

"Your condition—both of your conditions—are deteriorating rapidly. We don't have time to waste, to come up with more palatable ways to do this. The fastest way to test the theory—"

"I've got to drink it," she whispered. She nodded slightly —barely enough energy for a little head bob. "I can do that. Practice for the future, right?" Her colorless lips stretched into a faint grin as she looked at Edward. He didn't smile back.

Rosalie started tapping her toe impatiently. The sound was really irritating. I wondered what she would do if I threw her through a wall right now.

"So, who's going to catch me a grizzly bear?" Bella whispered.

Carlisle and Edward exchanged a quick glance. Rosalie stopped tapping.

"What?" Bella asked.

"It will be a more effective test if we don't cut corners, Bella," Carlisle said.

"*If* the fetus is craving blood," Edward explained, "it's not craving animal blood."

"It won't make a difference to you, Bella. Don't think about it," Rosalie encouraged.

Bella's eyes widened. "Who?" she breathed, and her gaze flickered to me.

"I'm not here as a donor, Bells," I grumbled. "'Sides, it's human blood that thing's after, and I don't think mine applies—"

"We have blood on hand," Rosalie told her, talking over me before I'd finished, like I wasn't there. "For you—just in case. Don't worry about anything at all. It's going to be fine. I have a good feeling about this, Bella. I think the baby will be so much better."

Bella's hand ran across her stomach.

"Well," she rasped, barely audible. "*I'm* starving, so I'll bet he is, too." Trying to make another joke. "Let's go for it. My first vampire act."

13. GOOD THING I'VE GOT A STRONG STOMACH

CARLISLE AND ROSALIE WERE OFF IN A FLASH, DARTING upstairs. I could hear them debating whether they should warm it up for her. Ugh. I wondered what all house-of-horrors stuff they kept around here. Fridge full of blood, check. What else? Torture chamber? Coffin room?

Edward stayed, holding Bella's hand. His face was dead again. He didn't seem to have the energy to keep up even that little hint of hope he'd had before. They stared into each other's eyes, but not in a gooey way. It was like they were having a conversation. Kind of reminded me of Sam and Emily.

No, it wasn't gooey, but that only made it harder to watch.

I knew what it was like for Leah, having to see that all the time. Having to hear it in Sam's head. Of course we all felt bad for her, we weren't monsters—in that sense, anyway. But I guess we'd blamed her for how she handled it. Lashing out at everyone, trying to make us all as miserable as she was.

I would never blame her again. How could anyone help spreading this kind of misery around? How could anyone *not* try to ease some of the burden by shoving a little piece of it off on someone else?

And if it meant that I had to have a pack, how could I blame her for taking my freedom? I would do the same. If there was a way to escape this pain, I'd take it, too.

Rosalie darted downstairs after a second, flying through the room like a sharp breeze, stirring up the burning smell. She stopped inside the kitchen, and I heard the creak of a cupboard door.

"Not *clear*, Rosalie," Edward murmured. He rolled his eyes.

Bella looked curious, but Edward just shook his head at her.

Rosalie blew back through the room and disappeared again.

"This was your idea?" Bella whispered, her voice rough as she strained to make it loud enough for me to hear. Forgetting that I could hear just fine. I kind of liked how, a lot of the time, she seemed to forget that I wasn't completely human. I moved closer, so that she wouldn't have to work so hard.

"Don't blame me for this one. Your vampire was just picking snide comments out of my head."

She smiled a little. "I didn't expect to see you again."

"Yeah, me, either," I said.

It felt weird just standing here, but the vampires had shoved all the furniture out of the way for the medical setup. I imagined that it didn't bother them—sitting or standing didn't make much difference when you were stone. Wouldn't bother me much, either, except that I was so exhausted.

"Edward told me what you had to do. I'm sorry."

"S'okay. It was probably only a matter of time till I snapped over something Sam wanted me to do," I lied.

"And Seth," she whispered.

"He's actually happy to help."

"I hate causing you trouble."

I laughed once—more a bark than a laugh.

She breathed a faint sigh. "I guess that's nothing new, is it?"

"No, not really."

"You don't have to stay and watch this," she said, barely mouthing the words.

I could leave. It was probably a good idea. But if I did, with the way she looked right now, I could be missing the last fifteen minutes of her life.

"I don't really have anywhere else to go," I told her, trying to keep the emotion out of my voice. "The wolf thing is a lot less appealing since Leah joined up."

"Leah?" she gasped.

"You didn't tell her?" I asked Edward.

He just shrugged without moving his eyes from her face. I could see it wasn't very exciting news to him, not something worth sharing with the more important events that were going down.

Bella didn't take it so lightly. It looked like it was bad news to her.

"Why?" she breathed.

I didn't want to get into the whole novel-length version. "To keep an eye on Seth."

"But Leah hates us," she whispered.

Us. Nice. I could see that she was afraid, though.

"Leah's not going to bug anyone." But me. "She's in my pack"—I grimaced at the words—"so she follows my lead." Ugh.

Bella didn't look convinced.

"You're scared of *Leah*, but you're best buds with the psychopath blonde?"

There was a low hiss from the second floor. Cool, she'd heard me.

Bella frowned at me. "Don't. Rose . . . understands."

"Yeah," I grunted. "She understands that you're gonna die and she doesn't care, s'long as she gets her mutant spawn out of the deal."

"Stop being a jerk, Jacob," she whispered.

She looked too weak to get mad at. I tried to smile instead. "You say that like it's possible."

Bella tried not to smile back for a second, but she couldn't help it in the end; her chalky lips pulled up at the corners.

And then Carlisle and the psycho in question were there. Carlisle had a white plastic cup in his hand—the kind with a lid and a bendy straw. Oh—*not clear*; now I got it. Edward didn't want Bella to have to think about what she was doing any more than necessary. You couldn't see what was in the cup at all. But I could smell it.

Carlisle hesitated, the hand with the cup half-extended. Bella eyed it, looking scared again.

"We could try another method," Carlisle said quietly.

"No," Bella whispered. "No, I'll try this first. We don't have time. . . ."

At first I thought she'd finally gotten a clue and was worried about herself, but then her hand fluttered feebly against her stomach.

Bella reached out and took the cup from him. Her hand shook a little, and I could hear the sloshing from inside. She tried to prop herself up on one elbow, but she could barely lift her head. A whisper of heat brushed down my spine as I saw how frail she'd gotten in less than a day.

Rosalie put her arm under Bella's shoulders, supporting her head, too, like you did with a newborn. Blondie was all about the babies.

"Thanks," Bella whispered. Her eyes flickered around at us. Still aware enough to feel self-conscious. If she wasn't so drained, I'd bet she'd've blushed.

"Don't mind them," Rosalie murmured.

It made me feel awkward. I should've left when Bella'd offered the chance. I didn't belong here, being part of this. I thought about ducking out, but then I realized a move like that would only make this worse for Bella—make it harder for her to go through with it. She'd figure I was too disgusted to stay. Which was almost true.

Still. While I wasn't going to claim responsibility for this idea, I didn't want to jinx it, either.

Bella lifted the cup to her face and sniffed at the end of the straw. She flinched, and then made a face.

"Bella, sweetheart, we can find an easier way," Edward said, holding his hand out for the cup.

"Plug your nose," Rosalie suggested. She glared at Edward's hand like she might take a snap at it. I wished she would. I bet Edward wouldn't take *that* sitting down, and I'd love to see Blondie lose a limb.

"No, that's not it. It's just that it—" Bella sucked in a deep breath. "It smells good," she admitted in a tiny voice.

I swallowed hard, fighting to keep the disgust off my face.

"That's a good thing," Rosalie told Bella eagerly. "That means we're on the right track. Give it a try." Given Blondie's new expression, I was surprised she didn't break into a touchdown dance.

Bella shoved the straw between her lips, squeezed her eyes shut, and wrinkled her nose. I could hear the blood slopping around in the cup again as her hand shook. She sipped at it for a second, and then moaned quietly with her eyes still closed.

Edward and I stepped forward at the same time. He touched her face. I clenched my hands behind my back.

"Bella, love—"

"I'm okay," she whispered. She opened her eyes and stared up at him. Her expression was . . . apologetic. Pleading. Scared. "It *tastes* good, too."

Acid churned in my stomach, threatening to overflow. I ground my teeth together.

"That's good," Blondie repeated, still jazzed. "A good sign."

Edward just pressed his hand to her cheek, curling his fingers around the shape of her fragile bones.

Bella sighed and put her lips to the straw again. She took a real pull this time. The action wasn't as weak as everything else about her. Like some instinct was taking over.

"How's your stomach? Do you feel nauseated?" Carlisle asked.

Bella shook her head. "No, I don't feel sick," she whispered. "There's a first, eh?"

Rosalie beamed. "Excellent."

"I think it's a bit early for that, Rose," Carlisle murmured.

Bella gulped another mouthful of blood. Then she flashed a look at Edward. "Does this screw my total?" she whispered. "Or do we start counting *after* I'm a vampire?"

"No one is counting, Bella. In any case, no one died for this." He smiled a lifeless smile. "Your record is still clean."

They'd lost me.

"I'll explain later," Edward said, so low the words were just a breath.

"What?" Bella whispered.

"Just talking to myself," he lied smoothly.

If he succeeded with this, if Bella lived, Edward wasn't going to be able to get away with so much when her senses were as sharp as his. He'd have to work on the honesty thing.

Edward's lips twitched, fighting a smile.

Bella chugged a few more ounces, staring past us toward the window. Probably pretending we weren't here. Or maybe just me. No one else in this group would be disgusted by what she was doing. Just the opposite—they were probably having a tough time not ripping the cup away from her.

Edward rolled his eyes.

Jeez, how did anyone stand living with him? It was really too bad he couldn't hear Bella's thoughts. Then he'd annoy the crap out of her, too, and she'd get tired of him.

Edward chuckled once. Bella's eyes flicked to him immediately, and she half-smiled at the humor in his face. I would guess that wasn't something she'd seen in a while.

"Something funny?" she breathed.

"Jacob," he answered.

She looked over with another weary smile for me. "Jake's a crack-up," she agreed.

Great, now I was the court jester. "Bada *bing*," I mumbled in weak rim-shot impression.

She smiled again, and then took another swig from the cup. I flinched when the straw pulled at empty air, making a loud sucking sound.

"I did it," she said, sounding pleased. Her voice was clearer—rough, but not a whisper for the first time today. "If I keep this down, Carlisle, will you take the needles out of me?"

"As soon as possible," he promised. "Honestly, they aren't doing that much good where they are."

Rosalie patted Bella's forehead, and they exchanged a hopeful glance.

And anyone could see it—the cup full of human blood had made an immediate difference. Her color was returning—there was a tiny hint of pink in her waxy cheeks. Already she didn't seem to need Rosalie's support so much anymore. Her breathing was easier, and I would swear her heartbeat was stronger, more even.

Everything accelerated.

That ghost of hope in Edward's eyes had turned into the real thing.

"Would you like more?" Rosalie pressed.

Bella's shoulders slumped.

Edward flashed a glare at Rosalie before he spoke to Bella. "You don't have to drink more right away."

"Yeah, I know. But . . . I *want* to," she admitted glumly.

Rosalie pulled her thin, sharp fingers through Bella's lank hair. "You don't need to be embarrassed about that, Bella. Your body has cravings. We all understand that." Her tone was soothing at first, but then she added harshly, "Anyone who doesn't understand shouldn't be here."

Meant for me, obviously, but I wasn't going to let Blondie get to me. I was glad Bella felt better. So what if the means grossed me out? It wasn't like I'd said anything.

Carlisle took the cup from Bella's hand. "I'll be right back."

Bella stared at me while he disappeared.

"Jake, you look awful," she croaked.

"Look who's talking."

"Seriously—when's the last time you slept?"

I thought about that for a second. "Huh. I'm not actually sure."

"Aw, Jake. Now I'm messing with your health, too. Don't be stupid."

I gritted my teeth. She was allowed to kill herself for a monster, but I wasn't allowed to miss a few nights' sleep to watch her do it?

"Get some rest, please," she went on. "There're a few beds upstairs—you're welcome to any of them."

The look on Rosalie's face made it clear that I wasn't welcome to one of them. It made me wonder what Sleepless Beauty needed a bed for anyway. Was she that possessive of her props?

"Thanks, Bells, but I'd rather sleep on the ground. Away from the stench, you know."

She grimaced. "Right."

Carlisle was back then, and Bella reached out for the blood, absentminded, like she was thinking of something else. With the same distracted expression, she started sucking it down.

She really was looking better. She pulled herself forward, being careful of the tubes, and scooted into a sitting position. Rosalie hovered, her hands ready to catch Bella if she sagged. But Bella didn't need her. Taking deep breaths in between swallows, Bella finished the second cup quickly.

"How do you feel now?" Carlisle asked.

"Not sick. Sort of hungry . . . only I'm not sure if I'm hungry or *thirsty*, you know?"

"Carlisle, just look at her," Rosalie murmured, so smug she should have canary feathers on her lips. "This is obviously what her body wants. She should drink more."

"She's still human, Rosalie. She needs food, too. Let's give her a little while to see how this affects her, and then maybe we can try some food again. Does anything sound particularly good to you, Bella?"

"Eggs," she said immediately, and then she exchanged a look and a smile with Edward. His smile was brittle, but there was more life on his face than before.

I blinked then, and almost forgot how to open my eyes again.

"Jacob," Edward murmured. "You really should sleep. As Bella said, you're certainly welcome to the accommodations here, though you'd probably be more comfortable outside. Don't worry about anything—I promise I'll find you if there's a need."

"Sure, sure," I mumbled. Now that it appeared Bella had a few more hours, I could escape. Go curl up under a tree somewhere. . . . Far enough away that the smell couldn't reach me. The bloodsucker would wake me up if something went wrong. He owed me.

"I do," Edward agreed.

I nodded and then put my hand on Bella's. Hers was icy cold.

"Feel better," I said.

"Thanks, Jacob." She turned her hand over and squeezed mine. I felt the thin band of her wedding ring riding loose on her skinny finger.

"Get her a blanket or something," I muttered as I turned for the door.

Before I made it, two howls pierced the still morning air. There was no mistaking the urgency of the tone. No misunderstanding this time.

"Dammit," I snarled, and I threw myself through the door. I hurled my body off the porch, letting the fire rip me apart midair. There was a sharp tearing sound as my shorts shredded. *Crap.* Those were the only clothes I had. Didn't matter now. I landed on paws and took off toward the west.

What is it? I shouted in my head.

Incoming, Seth answered. *At least three.*

Did they split up?

I'm running the line back to Seth at the speed of light, Leah promised. I could feel the air huffing through her lungs as she pushed herself to an incredible velocity. The forest whipped around her. *So far, no other point of attack.*

Seth, do not *challenge them. Wait for me.*

They're slowing. Ugh—it's so off *not being able to hear them. I think . . .*

What?

I think they've stopped.

Waiting for the rest of the pack?

Shh. Feel that?

I absorbed his impressions. The faint, soundless shimmer in the air.

Someone's phasing?

Feels like it, Seth agreed.

Leah flew into the small open space where Seth waited. She raked her claws into the dirt, spinning out like a race car.

Got your back, bro.

They're coming, Seth said nervously. *Slow. Walking.*

Almost there, I told them. I tried to fly like Leah. It felt horrible being separated from Seth and Leah with potential danger closer to their end than mine. Wrong. I should be with them, between them and whatever was coming.

Look who's getting all paternal, Leah thought wryly.

Head in the game, Leah.

Four, Seth decided. Kid had good ears. *Three wolves, one man.*

I made the little clearing then, moving immediately to the point. Seth sighed with relief and then straightened up, already in place at my right shoulder. Leah fell in on my left with a little less enthusiasm.

So now I rank under Seth, she grumbled to herself.

First come, first served, Seth thought smugly. *'Sides, you were never an Alpha's Third before. Still an upgrade.*

Under my baby brother is not an upgrade.

Shh! I complained. *I don't care where you stand. Shut up and get ready.*

They came into view a few seconds later, walking, as Seth had thought. Jared in the front, human, hands up. Paul and Quil and Collin on four legs behind him. There was no aggression in their postures. They hung back behind Jared, ears up, alert but calm.

But . . . it was weird that Sam would send Collin rather than Embry. That wasn't what I would do if I were sending a diplomacy party into enemy territory. I wouldn't send a kid. I'd send the experienced fighter.

A diversion? Leah thought.

Were Sam, Embry, and Brady making a move alone? That didn't seem likely.

Want me to check? I can run the line and be back in two minutes.

Should I warn the Cullens? Seth wondered.

What if the point was to divide us? I asked. *The Cullens know something's up. They're ready.*

Sam wouldn't be so stupid . . . , Leah whispered, fear jagged in her mind. She was imagining Sam attacking the Cullens with only the two others beside him.

No, he wouldn't, I assured her, though I felt a little sick at the image in her head, too.

All the while, Jared and the three wolves stared at us,

waiting. It was eerie not to hear what Quil and Paul and Collin were saying to one another. Their expressions were blank—unreadable.

Jared cleared his throat, and then he nodded to me. "White flag of truce, Jake. We're here to talk."

Think it's true? Seth asked.

Makes sense, but . . .

Yeah, Leah agreed. *But.*

We didn't relax.

Jared frowned. "It would be easier to talk if I could hear you, too."

I stared him down. I wasn't going to phase back until I felt better about this situation. Until it made sense. Why Collin? That was the part that had me most worried.

"Okay. I guess I'll just talk, then," Jared said. "Jake, we want you to come back."

Quil let out a soft whine behind him. Seconding the statement.

"You've torn our family apart. It's not meant to be this way."

I wasn't exactly in disagreement with that, but it was hardly the point. There were a few unresolved differences of opinion between me and Sam at the moment.

"We know that you feel . . . strongly about the situation with the Cullens. We know that's a problem. But this is an overreaction."

Seth growled. *Overreaction? And attacking our allies without warning isn't?*

Seth, you ever heard of a poker face? Cool it.

Sorry.

Jared's eyes flickered to Seth and back to me. "Sam is

willing to take this slowly, Jacob. He's calmed down, talked to the other Elders. They've decided that immediate action is in no one's best interest at this point."

Translation: They've already lost the element of surprise, Leah thought.

It was weird how distinct our joint thinking was. The pack was already Sam's pack, was already "them" to us. Something outside and other. It was especially weird to have Leah thinking that way—to have her be a solid part of the "us."

"Billy and Sue agree with you, Jacob, that we can wait for Bella . . . to be separated from the problem. Killing her is not something any of us feel comfortable with."

Though I'd just given Seth crap for it, I couldn't hold back a small snarl of my own. So they didn't quite *feel comfortable* with murder, huh?

Jared raised his hands again. "Easy, Jake. You know what I mean. The point is, we're going to wait and reassess the situation. Decide later if there's a problem with the . . . thing."

Ha, Leah thought. *What a load.*

You don't buy it?

I know what they're thinking, Jake. What Sam's thinking. They're betting on Bella dying anyway. And then they figure you'll be so mad . . .

That I'll lead the attack myself. My ears pressed against my skull. What Leah was guessing sounded pretty spot-on. And very possible, too. When . . . if that thing killed Bella, it was going to be easy to forget how I felt about Carlisle's family right now. They would probably look like enemies—like no more than bloodsucking leeches—to me all over again.

I'll remind you, Seth whispered.

I know you will, kid. Question is whether I'll listen to you.

"Jake?" Jared asked.

I huffed a sigh.

Leah, make a circuit—just to be sure. I'm going to have to talk to him, and I want to be positive there isn't anything else going on while I'm phased.

Give me a break, Jacob. You can phase in front of me. Despite my best efforts, I've seen you naked before—doesn't do much for me, so no worries.

I'm not trying to protect the innocence of your eyes, I'm trying to protect our backs. Get out of here.

Leah snorted once and then launched herself into the forest. I could hear her claws cutting into the soil, pushing her faster.

Nudity was an inconvenient but unavoidable part of pack life. We'd all thought nothing of it before Leah came along. Then it got awkward. Leah had average control when it came to her temper—it took her the usual length of time to stop exploding out of her clothes every time she got pissed. We'd all caught a glimpse. And it wasn't like she wasn't worth looking at; it was just that it was so *not* worth it when she caught you thinking about it later.

Jared and the others were staring at the place where she'd disappeared into the brush with wary expressions.

"Where's she going?" Jared asked.

I ignored him, closing my eyes and pulling myself together again. It felt like the air was trembling around me, shaking out from me in small waves. I lifted myself up on my hind legs, catching the moment just right so that I was fully upright as I shimmered down into my human self.

"Oh," Jared said. "Hey, Jake."

"Hey, Jared."

"Thanks for talking to me."

"Yeah."

"We want you to come back, man."

Quil whined again.

"I don't know if it's that easy, Jared."

"Come home," he said, leaning forward. Pleading. "We can sort this out. You don't belong here. Let Seth and Leah come home, too."

I laughed. "Right. Like I haven't been begging them to do that from hour one."

Seth snorted behind me.

Jared assessed that, his eyes cautious again. "So, what now, then?"

I thought that over for a minute while he waited.

"I don't know. But I'm not sure things could just go back to normal anyway, Jared. I don't know how it works—it doesn't feel like I can just turn this Alpha thing off and on as the mood strikes. It feels sort of permanent."

"You still belong with us."

I raised my eyebrows. "Two Alphas can't belong in the same place, Jared. Remember how close it got last night? The instinct is too competitive."

"So are you all just going to hang out with the parasites for the rest of your lives?" he demanded. "You don't have a home here. You're already out of clothes," he pointed out.

"You gonna stay wolf all the time? You know Leah doesn't like eating that way."

"Leah can do whatever she wants when she gets hungry. She's here by her own choice. *I'm* not telling anyone what to do."

Jared sighed. "Sam is sorry about what he did to you."

I nodded. "I'm not angry anymore."

"But?"

"But I'm not coming back, not now. We're going to wait and see how it plays out, too. And we're going to watch out for the Cullens for as long as that seems necessary. Because, despite what you think, this isn't just about Bella. We're protecting those who should be protected. And that applies to the Cullens, too." At least a fair number of them, anyway.

Seth yelped softly in agreement.

Jared frowned. "I guess there's nothing I can say to you, then."

"Not now. We'll see how things go."

Jared turned to face Seth, concentrating on him now, separate from me. "Sue asked me to tell you—no, to *beg* you—to come home. She's brokenhearted, Seth. All alone. I don't know how you and Leah can do this to her. Abandon her this way, when your dad just barely died—"

Seth whimpered.

"Ease up, Jared," I warned.

"Just letting him know how it is."

I snorted. "Right." Sue was tougher than anyone I knew. Tougher than my dad, tougher than me. Tough enough to play on her kids' sympathies if that's what it took to get them home. But it wasn't fair to work Seth that way. "Sue's known about this for how many hours now? And most of that time spent with Billy and Old Quil and Sam? Yeah, I'm sure she's just perishing of loneliness. 'Course you're free to go if you want, Seth. You know that."

Seth sniffed.

Then, a second later, he cocked an ear to the north. Leah must be close. Jeez, she was fast. Two beats, and Leah skidded to a stop in the brush a few yards away. She trotted in, taking the point in front of Seth. She kept her nose in the air, very obviously not looking in my direction.

I appreciated that.

"Leah?" Jared asked.

She met his gaze, her muzzle pulling back a little over her teeth.

Jared didn't seem surprised by her hostility. "Leah, you *know* you don't want to be here."

She snarled at him. I gave her a warning glance she didn't see. Seth whined and nudged her with his shoulder.

"Sorry," Jared said. "Guess I shouldn't assume. But you don't have any ties to the bloodsuckers."

Leah very deliberately looked at her brother and then at me.

"So you want to watch out for Seth, I get that," Jared said. His eyes touched my face and then went back to hers. Probably wondering about that second look—just like I was. "But Jake's not going to let anything happen to him, and he's not afraid to be here." Jared made a face. "Anyway, *please*, Leah. We want you back. Sam wants you back."

Leah's tail twitched.

"Sam told me to beg. He told me to literally get down

on my knees if I have to. He wants you home, Lee-lee, where you belong."

I saw Leah flinch when Jared used Sam's old nickname for her. And then, when he added those last three words, her hackles rose and she was yowling a long stream of snarls through her teeth. I didn't have to be in her head to hear the cussing-out she was giving him, and neither did he. You could almost hear the exact words she was using.

I waited till she was done. "I'm going to go out on a limb here and say that Leah belongs wherever she wants to be."

Leah growled, but, as she was glaring at Jared, I figured it was in agreement.

"Look, Jared, we're still family, okay? We'll get past the feud, but, until we do, you probably ought to stick to your land. Just so there aren't misunderstandings. Nobody wants a family brawl, right? Sam doesn't want that, either, does he?"

"Of course, not," Jared snapped. "We'll stick to our land. But where is *your* land, Jacob? Is it vampire land?"

"No, Jared. Homeless at the moment. But don't worry—this isn't going to last forever." I had to take a breath. "There's not that much time . . . left. Okay? Then the Cullens will probably go, and Seth and Leah will come home."

Leah and Seth whined together, their noses turning my direction in synchronization.

"And what about you, Jake?"

"Back to the forest, I think. I can't really stick around La Push. Two Alphas means too much tension. 'Sides, I was headed that way anyway. Before this mess."

"What if we need to talk?" Jared asked.

"Howl—but watch the line, 'kay? We'll come to you.

And Sam doesn't need to send so many. We aren't looking for a fight."

Jared scowled, but nodded. He didn't like me setting conditions for Sam. "See you around, Jake. Or not." He waved halfheartedly.

"Wait, Jared. Is Embry okay?"

Surprise crossed his face. "Embry? Sure, he's fine. Why?"

"Just wondering why Sam sent Collin."

I watched his reaction, still suspicious that something was going on. I saw knowledge flash in his eyes, but it didn't look like the kind I was expecting.

"That's not really your business anymore, Jake."

"Guess not. Just curious."

I saw a twitch from the corner of my eye, but I didn't acknowledge it, because I didn't want to give Quil away. He was reacting to the subject.

"I'll let Sam know about your . . . instructions. Goodbye, Jacob."

I sighed. "Yeah. Bye, Jared. Hey, tell my dad that I'm okay, will you? And that I'm sorry, and that I love him."

"I'll pass that along."

"Thanks."

"C'mon, guys," Jared said. He turned away from us, heading out of sight to phase because Leah was here. Paul and Collin were right on his heels, but Quil hesitated. He yelped softly, and I took a step toward him.

"Yeah, I miss you, too, bro."

Quil jogged over to me, his head hanging down morosely. I patted his shoulder.

"It'll be okay."

He whined.

"Tell Embry I miss having you two on my flanks."

He nodded and then pressed his nose to my forehead. Leah snorted. Quil looked up, but not at her. He looked back over his shoulder at where the others had gone.

"Yeah, go home," I told him.

Quil yelped again and then took off after the others. I'd bet Jared wasn't waiting super-patiently. As soon as he was gone, I pulled the warmth from the center of my body and let it surge through my limbs. In a flash of heat, I was on four legs again.

Thought you were going to make out with him, Leah snickered.

I ignored her.

Was that okay? I asked them. It worried me, speaking *for* them that way, when I couldn't hear exactly what they were thinking. I didn't want to assume anything. I didn't want to be like Jared that way. *Did I say anything you didn't want me to? Did I not say something I should have?*

You did great, Jake! Seth encouraged.

You could have hit Jared, Leah thought. *I wouldn't have minded that.*

I guess we know why Embry wasn't allowed to come, Seth thought.

I didn't understand. *Not allowed?*

Jake, didya see Quil? He's pretty torn up, right? I'd put ten to one that Embry's even more upset. And Embry doesn't have a Claire. There's no way Quil can just pick up and walk away from La Push. Embry might. So Sam's not going to take any chances on him getting convinced to jump ship. He doesn't want our pack any bigger than it is now.

Really? You think? I doubt Embry would mind shredding some Cullens.

But he's your best friend, Jake. He and Quil would rather stand behind you than face you in a fight.

Well, I'm glad Sam kept him home, then. This pack is big enough. I sighed. *Okay, then. So we're good, for now. Seth, you mind keeping an eye on things for a while? Leah and I both need to crash. This felt on the level, but who knows? Maybe it was a distraction.*

I wasn't always so paranoid, but I remembered the feel of Sam's commitment. The total one-track focus on destroying the danger he saw. Would he take advantage of the fact that he could lie to us now?

No problem! Seth was only too eager to do whatever he could. *You want me to explain to the Cullens? They're probably still kinda tense.*

I got it. I want to check things out anyway.

They caught the whir of images from my fried brain.

Seth whimpered in surprise. *Ew.*

Leah whipped her head back and forth like she was trying to shake the image out of her mind. *That is easily the freakin' grossest thing I've heard in my life. Yuck. If there was anything in my stomach, it would be coming back.*

They are *vampires, I guess,* Seth allowed after a minute, compensating for Leah's reaction. *I mean, it makes sense. And if it helps Bella, it's a good thing, right?*

Both Leah and I stared at him.

What?

Mom dropped him a lot when he was a baby, Leah told me. *On his head, apparently.*

He used to gnaw on the crib bars, too.

Lead paint?

Looks like it, she thought.

Seth snorted. *Funny. Why don't you two shut up and sleep?*

14. YOU KNOW THINGS ARE BAD WHEN YOU FEEL GUILTY FOR BEING RUDE TO VAMPIRES

WHEN I GOT BACK TO THE HOUSE, THERE WAS NO ONE waiting outside for my report. Still on alert?

Everything's cool, I thought tiredly.

My eyes quickly caught a small change in the now-familiar scene. There was a stack of light-colored fabric on the bottom step of the porch. I loped over to investigate. Holding my breath, because the vampire smell stuck to the fabric like you wouldn't believe, I nudged the stack with my nose.

Someone had laid out clothes. Huh. Edward must have caught my moment of irritation as I'd bolted out the door. Well. That was . . . nice. And weird.

I took the clothes gingerly between my teeth—ugh—

and carried them back to the trees. Just in case this was some joke by the blond psychopath and I had a bunch of girls' stuff here. Bet she'd love to see the look on my human face as I stood there naked, holding a sundress.

In the cover of the trees, I dropped the stinking pile and shifted back to human. I shook the clothes out, snapping them against a tree to beat some of the smell from them. They were definitely guy's clothes—tan pants and a white button-down shirt. Neither of them long enough, but they looked like they'd fit around me. Must be Emmett's. I rolled the cuffs up on the shirtsleeves, but there wasn't much I could do about the pants. Oh well.

I had to admit, I felt better with some clothes to my name, even stinky ones that didn't quite fit. It was hard not being able to just jet back home and grab another pair of old sweatpants when I needed them. The homeless thing again—not having anyplace to go *back* to. No possessions, either, which wasn't bothering me too bad now, but would probably get annoying soon.

Exhausted, I walked slowly up the Cullens' porch steps in my fancy new secondhand clothes but hesitated when I got to the door. Did I knock? Stupid, when they knew I was here. I wondered why no one acknowledged that—told me either to *come in* or *get lost*. Whatever. I shrugged and let myself in.

More changes. The room had shifted back to normal—almost—in the last twenty minutes. The big flat-screen was on, low volume, showing some chick flick that no one seemed to be watching. Carlisle and Esme stood by the back windows, which were open to the river again. Alice, Jasper, and Emmett were out of sight, but I heard them murmuring upstairs. Bella was on the couch like yesterday, with just one tube still hooked into her, and an IV hanging behind the back of the sofa. She was wrapped up like a burrito in a couple of thick quilts, so at least they'd listened to me before. Rosalie was cross-legged on the ground by her head. Edward sat at the other end of the couch with Bella's burrito'ed feet in his lap. He looked up when I came in and smiled at me—just a little twitch of his mouth—like something pleased him.

Bella didn't hear me. She only glanced up when he did, and then she smiled, too. With real energy, her whole face lighting up. I couldn't remember the last time she'd looked so excited to see me.

What was *with* her? For crying out loud, she was *married*! Happily married, too—there was no question that she was in love with her vampire past the boundaries of sanity. And hugely pregnant, to top it off.

So why did she have to be so damn thrilled to see me? Like I'd made her whole freakin' day by walking through the door.

If she would just not care . . . Or more than that—really not want me around. It would be so much easier to stay away.

Edward seemed to be in agreement with my thoughts— we were on the same wavelength so much lately it was crazy. He was frowning now, reading her face while she beamed at me.

"They just wanted to talk," I mumbled, my voice dragging with exhaustion. "No attack on the horizon."

"Yes," Edward answered. "I heard most of it."

That woke me up a little. We'd been a good three miles out. "How?"

"I'm hearing you more clearly—it's a matter of familiarity and concentration. Also, your thoughts are slightly easier to pick up when you're in your human form. So I caught most of what passed out there."

"Oh." It bugged me a little, but for no good reason, so I shrugged it off. "Good. I hate repeating myself."

"I'd tell you to go get some sleep," Bella said, "but my guess is that you're going to pass out on the floor in about six seconds, so there's probably no point."

It was amazing how much better she sounded, how much stronger she looked. I smelled fresh blood and saw that the cup was in her hands again. How much blood would it take to keep her going? At some point, would they start trotting in the neighbors?

I headed for the door, counting off the seconds for her as I walked. "One Mississippi . . . two Mississippi . . ."

"Where's the flood, mutt?" Rosalie muttered.

"You know how you drown a blonde, Rosalie?" I asked without stopping or turning to look at her. "Glue a mirror to the bottom of a pool."

I heard Edward chuckle as I pulled the door shut. His mood seemed to improve in exact correlation to Bella's health.

"I've already heard that one," Rosalie called after me.

I trudged down the steps, my only goal to drag myself far enough into the trees that the air would be pure again. I planned to ditch the clothes a convenient distance from the house for future use rather than tying them to my leg, so I wouldn't be smelling them, either. As I fumbled with the buttons on the new shirt, I thought randomly about how buttons would never be in style for werewolves.

I heard the voices while I slogged across the lawn.

"Where are you going?" Bella asked.

"There was something I forgot to say to him."

"Let Jacob sleep—it can wait."

Yes, *please*, let Jacob sleep.

"It will only take a moment."

I turned slowly. Edward was already out the door. He had an apology in his expression as he approached me.

"Jeez, what *now*?"

"I'm sorry," he said, and then he hesitated, like he didn't know how to phrase what he was thinking.

What's on your mind, mind reader?

"When you were speaking to Sam's delegates earlier," he murmured, "I was giving a play-by-play for Carlisle and Esme and the rest. They were concerned—"

"Look, we're not dropping our guard. You don't have to believe Sam like we do. We're keeping our eyes open regardless."

"No, no, Jacob. Not about that. We trust your judgment. Rather, Esme was troubled by the hardships this is putting your pack through. She asked me to speak to you privately about it."

That took me off guard. "Hardships?"

"The *homeless* part, particularly. She's very upset that you are all so . . . bereft."

I snorted. Vampire mother hen—bizarre. "We're tough. Tell her not to worry."

"She'd still like to do what she can. I got the impression that Leah prefers not to eat in her wolf form?"

"And?" I demanded.

"Well, we do have normal human food here, Jacob. Keeping up appearances, and, of course, for Bella. Leah is welcome to anything she'd like. All of you are."

"I'll pass that along."

"Leah hates us."

"So?"

"So try to pass it along in such a way as to make her consider it, if you don't mind."

"I'll do what I can."

"And then there's the matter of clothes."

I glanced down at the ones I was wearing. "Oh yeah. Thanks." It probably wouldn't be good manners to mention how bad they reeked.

He smiled, just a little. "Well, we're easily able to help out with any needs there. Alice rarely allows us to wear the same thing twice. We've got piles of brand-new clothes that are destined for Goodwill, and I'd imagine that Leah is fairly close to Esme's size. . . ."

"Not sure how she'll feel about bloodsucker castoffs. She's not as practical as I am."

"I trust that you can present the offer in the best possible light. As well as the offer for any other physical object you might need, or transportation, or anything else at all. And showers, too, since you prefer to sleep outdoors. Please . . . don't consider yourselves without the benefits of a home."

He said the last line softly—not trying to keep quiet this time, but with some kind of real emotion.

I stared at him for a second, blinking sleepily. "That's, er, nice of you. Tell Esme we appreciate the, uh, thought. But the perimeter cuts through the river in a few places, so we stay pretty clean, thanks."

"If you would pass the offer on, regardless."

"Sure, sure."

"Thank you."

I turned away from him, only to stop cold when I heard the low, pained cry from inside the house. By the time I looked back, he was already gone.

What *now*?

I followed after him, shuffling like a zombie. Using about the same number of brain cells, too. It didn't feel like I had a choice. Something was wrong. I would go see what it was. There would be nothing I could do. And I would feel worse.

It seemed inevitable.

I let myself in again. Bella was panting, curled over the bulge in the center of her body. Rosalie held her while Edward, Carlisle, and Esme all hovered. A flicker of motion caught my eye; Alice was at the top of the stairs, staring down into the room with her hands pressed to her temples. It was weird—like she was barred from entering somehow.

"Give me a second, Carlisle," Bella panted.

"Bella," the doctor said anxiously, "I heard something crack. I need to take a look."

"Pretty sure"—pant—"it was a rib. Ow. Yep. Right here." She pointed to her left side, careful not to touch.

It was breaking her *bones* now.

"I need to take an X-ray. There might be splinters. We don't want it to puncture anything."

Bella took a deep breath. "Okay."

Rosalie lifted Bella carefully. Edward seemed like he

was going to argue, but Rosalie bared her teeth at him and growled, "I've already got her."

So Bella was stronger now, but the thing was, too. You couldn't starve one without starving the other, and healing worked just the same. No way to win.

Blondie carried Bella swiftly up the big staircase with Carlisle and Edward right on her heels, none of them taking any notice of me standing dumbstruck in the doorway.

So they had a blood bank *and* an X-ray machine? Guess the doc brought his work home with him.

I was too tired to follow them, too tired to move. I leaned back against the wall and then slid to the ground. The door was still open, and I pointed my nose toward it, grateful for the clean breeze blowing in. I leaned my head against the jamb and listened.

I could hear the sound of the X-ray machinery upstairs. Or maybe I just assumed that's what it was. And then the lightest of footsteps coming down the stairs. I didn't look to see which vampire it was.

"Do you want a pillow?" Alice asked me.

"No," I mumbled. What was with the pushy hospitality? It was creeping me out.

"That doesn't look comfortable," she observed.

"S'not."

"Why don't you move, then?"

"Tired. Why aren't you upstairs with the rest of them?" I shot back.

"Headache," she answered.

I rolled my head around to look at her.

Alice was a tiny little thing. 'Bout the size of one of my

arms. She looked even smaller now, sort of hunched in on herself. Her small face was pinched.

"Vampires get headaches?"

"Not the normal ones."

I snorted. Normal vampires.

"So how come you're never with Bella anymore?" I asked, making the question an accusation. It hadn't occurred to me before, because my head had been full of other crap, but it was weird that Alice was never around Bella, not since I'd been here. Maybe if Alice were by her side, Rosalie *wouldn't* be. "Thought you two were like this." I twisted two of my fingers together.

"Like I said"—she curled up on the tile a few feet from me, wrapping her skinny arms around her skinny knees—"headache."

"Bella's giving you a headache?"

"Yes."

I frowned. Pretty sure I was too tired for riddles. I let my head roll back around toward the fresh air and closed my eyes.

"Not Bella, really," she amended. "The . . . fetus."

Ah, someone else who felt like I did. It was pretty easy to recognize. She said the word grudgingly, the way Edward did.

"I can't see it," she told me, though she might have been talking to herself. For all she knew, I was already gone. "I can't see anything about it. Just like you."

I flinched, and then my teeth ground together. I didn't like being compared to the creature.

"Bella gets in the way. She's all wrapped around it, so she's . . . blurry. Like bad reception on a TV—like trying to focus your eyes on those fuzzy people jerking around on the screen. It's killing my head to watch her. And I can't see more than a few minutes ahead, anyway. The . . . fetus is too much a part of her future. When she first decided . . . when she knew she wanted it, she blurred right out of my sight. Scared me to death."

She was quiet for a second, and then she added, "I have to admit, it's a relief having you close by—in spite of the wet-dog smell. Everything goes away. Like having my eyes closed. It numbs the headache."

"Happy to be of service, ma'am," I mumbled.

"I wonder what it has in common with you . . . why you're the same that way."

Sudden heat flashed in the center of my bones. I clenched my fists to hold off the tremors.

"I have nothing in common with that life-sucker," I said through my teeth.

"Well, there's *something* there."

I didn't answer. The heat was already burning away. I was too dead tired to stay furious.

"You don't mind if I sit here by you, do you?" she asked.

"Guess not. Stinks anyway."

"Thanks," she said. "This is the best thing for it, I guess, since I can't take aspirin."

"Could you keep it down? Sleeping, here."

She didn't respond, immediately lapsing into silence. I was out in seconds.

I was dreaming that I was really thirsty. And there was a big glass of water in front of me—all cold, you could see the condensation running down the sides. I grabbed the cup and took a huge gulp, only to find out pretty quick that it wasn't water—it was straight bleach. I choked it back out, spewing it everywhere, and a bunch of it blew out of my nose. It burned. My nose was on fire. . . .

The pain in my nose woke me up enough to remember where I'd fallen asleep. The smell was pretty fierce, considering that my nose wasn't actually inside the house. Ugh. And it was noisy. Someone was laughing too loud. A familiar laugh, but one that didn't go with the smell. Didn't belong.

I groaned and opened my eyes. The skies were dull gray—it was daytime, but no clue as to when. Maybe close to sunset—it was pretty dark.

"About time," Blondie mumbled from not too far away. "The chainsaw impersonation was getting a little tired."

I rolled over and wrenched myself into a sitting position. In the process, I figured out where the smell was coming from. Someone had stuffed a wide feather pillow under my face. Probably *trying* to be nice, I'd guess. Unless it'd been Rosalie.

Once my face was out of the stinking feathers, I caught other scents. Like bacon and cinnamon, all mixed up with the vampire smell.

I blinked, taking in the room.

Things hadn't changed too much, except that now Bella was sitting up in the middle of the sofa, and the IV was gone. Blondie sat at her feet, her head resting against Bella's knees. Still gave me chills to see how casually they touched her, though I guess that was pretty brain-dead, all things considered. Edward was on one side of her, holding her hand. Alice was on the floor, too, like Rosalie. Her face wasn't pinched up now. And it was easy to see why—she'd found another painkiller.

"Hey, Jake's coming around!" Seth crowed.

He was sitting on Bella's other side, his arm slung carelessly over her shoulders, an overflowing plate of food on his lap.

What the hell?

"He came to find you," Edward said while I got to my feet. "And Esme convinced him to stay for breakfast."

Seth took in my expression, and he hurried to explain. "Yeah, Jake—I was just checking to see if you were okay 'cause you didn't ever phase back. Leah got worried. I *told* her you probably just crashed human, but you know how she is. Anyway, they had all this food and, dang,"—he turned to Edward—"man, you can *cook*."

"Thank you," Edward murmured.

I inhaled slowly, trying to unclench my teeth. I couldn't take my eyes off Seth's arm.

"Bella got cold," Edward said quietly.

Right. None of my business, anyway. She didn't belong to me.

Seth heard Edward's comment, looked at my face, and suddenly he needed both hands to eat with. He took his arm off Bella and dug in. I walked over to stand a few feet from the couch, still trying to get my bearings.

"Leah running patrol?" I asked Seth. My voice was still thick with sleep.

"Yeah," he said as he chewed. Seth had new clothes on, too. They fit him better than mine fit me. "She's on it. No worries. She'll howl if there's anything. We traded off around midnight. I ran twelve hours." He was proud of that, and it showed in his tone.

"Midnight? Wait a minute—what time is it now?"

"'Bout dawn." He glanced toward the window, checking.

Well, *damn*. I'd slept through the rest of the day and the whole night—dropped the ball. "Crap. Sorry about that, Seth. Really. You shoulda kicked me awake."

"Naw, man, you needed some serious sleep. You haven't taken a break since when? Night before your last patrol for Sam? Like forty hours? Fifty? You're not a machine, Jake. 'Sides, you didn't miss anything at all."

Nothing at all? I glanced quickly at Bella. Her color was back to the way I remembered it. Pale, but with the rose undertone. Her lips were pink again. Even her hair looked better—shinier. She saw me appraising and gave me a grin.

"How's the rib?" I asked.

"Taped up nice and tight. I don't even feel it."

I rolled my eyes. I heard Edward grind his teeth together, and I figured her blow-it-off attitude bugged him as much at it bugged me.

"What's for breakfast?" I asked, a little sarcastic. "O negative or AB positive?"

She stuck her tongue out at me. Totally herself again. "Omelets," she said, but her eyes darted down, and I saw that her cup of blood was wedged between her leg and Edward's.

"Go get some breakfast, Jake," Seth said. "There's a bunch in the kitchen. You've got to be empty."

I examined the food in his lap. Looked like half a cheese

omelet and the last fourth of a Frisbee-sized cinnamon roll. My stomach growled, but I ignored it.

"What's Leah having for breakfast?" I asked Seth critically.

"Hey, I took food to her before I ate *anything*," he defended himself. "She said she'd rather eat roadkill, but I bet she caves. These cinnamon rolls . . . " He seemed at a loss for words.

"I'll go hunt with her, then."

Seth sighed as I turned to leave.

"A moment, Jacob?"

It was Carlisle asking, so when I turned around again, my face was probably less disrespectful than it would have been if anyone else had stopped me.

"Yeah?"

Carlisle approached me while Esme drifted off toward the other room. He stopped a few feet away, just a little bit farther away than the normal space between two humans having a conversation. I appreciated him giving me my space.

"Speaking of hunting," he began in a somber tone. "That's going to be an issue for my family. I understand that our previous truce is inoperative at the moment, so I wanted your advice. Will Sam be hunting for us outside of the perimeter you've created? We don't want to take a chance with hurting any of your family—or losing any of ours. If you were in our shoes, how would you proceed?"

I leaned away, a little surprised, when he threw it back at me like that. What would I know about being in a bloodsucker's expensive shoes? But, then again, I did know Sam.

"It's a risk," I said, trying to ignore the other eyes I felt on me and to talk only to him. "Sam's calmed down some, but I'm pretty sure that in his head, the treaty is void. As long as he thinks the tribe, or any other human, is in real danger, he's not going to ask questions first, if you know what I mean. But, with all that, his priority is going to be La Push. There really aren't enough of them to keep a decent watch on the people while putting out hunting parties big enough to do much damage. I'd bet he's keeping it close to home."

Carlisle nodded thoughtfully.

"So I guess I'd say, go out together, just in case. And probably you should go in the day, 'cause we'd be expecting night. Traditional vampire stuff. You're fast—go over the mountains and hunt far enough away that there's no chance he'd send anyone that far from home."

"And leave Bella behind, unprotected?"

I snorted. "What are we, chopped liver?"

Carlisle laughed, and then his face was serious again. "Jacob, you can't fight against your brothers."

My eyes tightened. "I'm not saying it wouldn't be hard, but if they were really coming to kill her—I would be able to stop them."

Carlisle shook his head, anxious. "No, I didn't mean that you would be . . . incapable. But that it would be very wrong. I can't have that on my conscience."

"It wouldn't be on yours, Doc. It would be on mine. And I can take it."

"No, Jacob. We will make sure that our actions don't make that a necessity." He frowned thoughtfully "We'll go three at a time," he decided after a second. "That's probably the best we can do."

"I don't know, Doc. Dividing down the middle isn't the best strategy."

"We've got some extra abilities that will even it up. If Edward is one of the three, he'll be able to give us a few miles' radius of safety."

We both glanced at Edward. His expression had Carlisle backtracking quickly.

"I'm sure there are other ways, too," Carlisle said. Clearly, there was no physical need strong enough to get Edward away from Bella now. "Alice, I would imagine you could see which routes would be a mistake?"

"The ones that disappear," Alice said, nodding. "Easy."

Edward, who had gone all tense with Carlisle's first plan, loosened up. Bella was staring unhappily at Alice, that little crease between her eyes that she got when she was stressed out.

"Okay, then," I said. "That's settled. I'll just be on my way. Seth, I'll expect you back on at dusk, so get a nap in there somewhere, all right?"

"Sure, Jake. I'll phase back soon as I'm done. Unless . . ." he hesitated, looking at Bella. "Do you need me?"

"She's got blankets," I snapped at him.

"I'm fine, Seth, thanks," Bella said quickly.

And then Esme flitted back in the room, a big covered dish in her hands. She stopped hesitantly just behind Carlisle's elbow, her wide, dark gold eyes on my face. She held the dish out and took a shy step closer.

"Jacob," she said quietly. Her voice wasn't quite so piercing as the others'. "I know it's . . . unappetizing to you, the idea of eating here, where it smells so unpleasant. But I would feel much better if you would take some food with you when you go. I know you can't go home, and that's because of us. Please—ease some of my remorse. Take something to eat." She held the food out to me, her face all soft and pleading. I don't know how she did it, because she didn't look older than her mid-twenties, and she was bone pale, too, but something about her expression suddenly reminded me of my mom.

Jeez.

"Uh, sure, sure," I mumbled. "I guess. Maybe Leah's still hungry or something."

I reached out and took the food with one hand, holding it away, at arm's length. I'd go dump it under a tree or something. I didn't want her to feel bad.

Then I remembered Edward.

Don't you say anything to her! Let her think I ate it.

I didn't look at him to see if he was in agreement. He'd *better* be in agreement. Bloodsucker owed me.

"Thank you, Jacob," Esme said, smiling at me. How did a stone face have *dimples*, for crying out loud?

"Um, thank you," I said. My face felt hot—hotter than usual.

This was the problem with hanging out with vampires—you got used to them. They started messing up the way you saw the world. They started feeling like friends.

"Will you come back later, Jake?" Bella asked as I tried to make a run for it.

"Uh, I don't know."

She pressed her lips together, like she was trying not to smile. "Please? I might get cold."

I inhaled deeply through my nose, and then realized, too late, that that was not a good idea. I winced. "Maybe."

"Jacob?" Esme asked. I backed toward the door as she continued; she took a few steps after me. "I left a basket of clothes on the porch. They're for Leah. They're freshly washed—I tried to touch them as little as possible." She frowned. "Do you mind taking them to her?"

"On it," I muttered, and then I ducked out the door before anyone could guilt me into anything else.

15. TICK TOCK TICK TOCK TICK TOCK

H*EY,* J*AKE,* THOUGHT YOU SAID YOU WANTED ME AT DUSK. *How come you didn't have Leah wake me up before she crashed?*

'Cause I didn't need you. I'm still good.

He was already picking up the north half of the circle. *Anything?*

Nope. Nothing but nothing.

You did some scouting?

He'd caught the edge of one of my side trips. He headed up the new trail.

Yeah—I ran a few spokes. You know, just checking. If the Cullens are going to make a hunting trip . . .

Good call.

Seth looped back toward the main perimeter.

It was easier to run with him than it was to do the same with Leah. Though she was trying—trying hard—there was always an edge to her thoughts. She didn't want to be here. She didn't want to feel the softening toward the vampires that was going on in my head. She didn't want to deal with Seth's cozy friendship with them, a friendship that was only getting stronger.

Funny, though, I'd've thought her biggest issue would just be *me*. We'd always gotten on each other's nerves when we were in Sam's pack. But there was no antagonism toward me now at all, just the Cullens and Bella. I wondered why. Maybe it was simply gratitude that I wasn't forcing her to leave. Maybe it was because I understood her hostility better now. Whichever, running with Leah wasn't nearly as bad as I'd expected.

Of course, she hadn't eased up *that* much. The food and clothes Esme had sent for her were all taking a trip down-river right now. Even after I'd eaten my share—not because it smelled nearly irresistible away from the vampire burn, but to set a good example of self-sacrificing tolerance for Leah— she'd refused. The small elk she'd taken down around noon had not totally satisfied her appetite. Did make her mood worse, though. Leah hated eating raw.

Maybe we should run a sweep east? Seth suggested. *Go deep, see if they're out there waiting.*

I was thinking about that, I agreed. *But let's do it when we're all awake. I don't want to let down our guard. We should do it before the Cullens give it a try, though. Soon.*

Right.

That got me thinking.

If the Cullens were able to get out of the immediate area

safely, they really ought to keep on going. They probably should have taken off the second we'd come to warn them. They had to be able to afford other digs. And they had friends up north, right? Take Bella and run. It seemed like an obvious answer to their problems.

I probably ought to suggest that, but I was afraid they would listen to me. And I didn't want to have Bella disappear—to never know whether she'd made it or not.

No, that was stupid. I would tell them to go. It made no sense for them to stay, and it would be better—not less painful, but healthier—for me if Bella left.

Easy to say now, when Bella wasn't right there, looking all thrilled to see me and also clinging to life by her fingernails at the same time . . .

Oh, I already asked Edward about that, Seth thought.

What?

I asked him why they hadn't taken off yet. Gone up to Tanya's place or something. Somewhere too far for Sam to come after them.

I had to remind myself that I'd just decided to give the Cullens that exact advice. That it was best. So I shouldn't be mad at Seth for taking the chore out of my hands. Not mad at all.

So what did he say? Are they waiting for a window?

No. They're not leaving.

And that shouldn't sound like good news.

Why not? That's just stupid.

Not really, Seth said, defensive now. *It takes some time to build up the kind of medical access that Carlisle has here. He's got all the stuff he needs to take care of Bella, and the credentials to get more. That's one of the reasons they want to make a hunting run. Carlisle thinks they're going to need more blood for Bella soon.*

She's using up all the O negative they stored for her. He doesn't like depleting the stockpile. He's going to buy some more. Did you know you can buy *blood? If you're a doctor.*

I wasn't ready to be logical yet. *Still seems stupid. They could bring most of it with them, right? And steal what they need wherever they go. Who cares about legal crap when you're the undead?*

Edward doesn't want to take any risks moving her.

She's better than she was.

Seriously, Seth agreed. In his head, he was comparing my memories of Bella hooked up to the tubes with the last time he'd seen her as he'd left the house. She'd smiled at him and waved. *But she can't move around much, you know. That thing is kicking the hell out of her.*

I swallowed back the stomach acid in my throat. *Yeah, I know.*

Broke another of her ribs, he told me somberly.

My stride faltered, and I staggered a step before I regained my rhythm.

Carlisle taped her up again. Just another crack, he said. *Then Rosalie said something about how even normal human babies have been known to crack ribs. Edward looked like he was gonna rip her head off.*

Too bad he didn't.

Seth was in full report mode now—knowing it was all vitally interesting to me, though I'd never've asked to hear it. *Bella's been running a fever off and on today. Just low grade—sweats and then chills. Carlisle's not sure what to make of it—she might* just *be sick. Her immune system can't be in peak form right now.*

Yeah, I'm sure it's just a coincidence.

She's in a good mood, though. She was chatting with Charlie, laughing and all—

Charlie! What?! *What do you mean, she was talking to Charlie?!*

Now Seth's pace stuttered; my fury surprised him. *Guess he calls every day to talk to her. Sometimes her mom calls, too. Bella sounds so much better now, so she was reassuring him that she was on the mend—*

On the mend? *What the* hell *are they thinking?! Get Charlie's hopes up just so that he can be destroyed even worse when she dies? I thought they were getting him ready for that! Trying to prepare him! Why would she set him up like this?*

She might not die, Seth thought quietly.

I took a deep breath, trying to calm myself. *Seth. Even if she pulls through this, she's not doing it human. She knows that, and so do the rest of them. If she doesn't die, she's going to have to do a pretty convincing impersonation of a corpse, kid. Either that, or disappear. I thought they were trying to make this easier on Charlie. Why . . . ?*

Think it's Bella's idea. No one said anything, but Edward's face kinda went right along with what you're thinking now.

On the same wavelength with the bloodsucker yet again.

We ran in silence for a few minutes. I started off along a new line, probing south.

Don't get too far.

Why?

Bella asked me to ask you to stop by.

My teeth locked together.

Alice wants you, too. She says she's tired of hanging out in the attic like the vampire bat in the belfry. Seth snorted a laugh.

I was switching off with Edward before. Trying to keep Bella's temperature stable. Cold to hot, as needed. I guess, if you don't want to do it, I could go back—

No. I got it, I snapped.

Okay. Seth didn't make any more comments. He concentrated very hard on the empty forest.

I kept my southern course, searching for anything new. I turned around when I got close to the first signs of habitation. Not near the town yet, but I didn't want to get any wolf rumors going again. We'd been nice and invisible for a long while now.

I passed right through the perimeter on my way back, heading for the house. As much as I knew it was a stupid thing to do, I couldn't stop myself. I must be some kind of masochist.

There's nothing wrong with you, Jake. This isn't the most normal situation.

Shut up, please, Seth.

Shutting.

I didn't hesitate at the door this time; I just walked through like I owned the place. I figured that would piss Rosalie off, but it was a wasted effort. Neither Rosalie or Bella were anywhere in sight. I looked around wildly, hoping I'd missed them somewhere, my heart squeezing against my ribs in a weird, uncomfortable way.

"She's all right," Edward whispered. "Or, the same, I should say."

Edward was on the couch with his face in his hands; he hadn't looked up to speak. Esme was next to him, her arm wrapped tight around his shoulders.

"Hello, Jacob," she said. "I'm so glad you came back."

"Me, too," Alice said with a deep sigh. She came prancing down the stairs, making a face. Like I was late for an appointment.

"Uh, hey," I said. It felt weird to try to be polite.

"Where's Bella?"

"Bathroom," Alice told me. "Mostly fluid diet, you know. Plus, the whole pregnancy thing does that to you, I hear."

"Ah."

I stood there awkwardly, rocking back and forth on my heels.

"Oh, wonderful," Rosalie grumbled. I whipped my head around and saw her coming from a hall half-hidden behind the stairway. She had Bella cradled gently in her arms, a harsh sneer on her face for me. "I knew I smelled something nasty."

And, just like before, Bella's face lit up like a kid's on Christmas morning. Like I'd brought her the greatest gift ever.

It was so unfair.

"Jacob," she breathed. "You came."

"Hi, Bells."

Esme and Edward both got up. I watched how carefully Rosalie laid Bella out on the couch. I watched how, despite that, Bella turned white and held her breath—like she was set on not making any noise no matter how much it hurt.

Edward brushed his hand across her forehead and then along her neck. He tried to make it look as if he was just sweeping her hair back, but it looked like a doctor's examination to me.

"Are you cold?" he murmured.

"I'm fine."

"Bella, you know what Carlisle told you," Rosalie said. "Don't downplay *anything*. It doesn't help us take care of either of you."

"Okay, I'm a little cold. Edward, can you hand me that blanket?"

I rolled my eyes. "Isn't that sort of the point of me being here?"

"You just walked in," Bella said. "After running all day, I'd bet. Put your feet up for a minute. I'll probably warm up again in no time."

I ignored her, going to sit on the floor next the sofa while she was still telling me what to do. At that point, though, I wasn't sure how. . . . She looked pretty brittle, and I was afraid to move her, even to put my arms around her. So I just leaned carefully against her side, letting my arm rest along the length of hers, and held her hand. Then I put my other hand against her face. It was hard to tell if she felt colder than usual.

"Thanks, Jake," she said, and I felt her shiver once.

"Yeah," I said.

Edward sat on the arm of the sofa by Bella's feet, his eyes always on her face.

It was too much to hope, with all the super-hearing in the room, that no one would notice my stomach rumbling.

"Rosalie, why don't you get Jacob something from the kitchen?" Alice said. She was invisible now, sitting quietly behind the back of the sofa.

Rosalie stared at the place Alice's voice had come from in disbelief.

"Thanks, anyway, Alice, but I don't think I'd want to

eat something Blondie's spit in. I'd bet my system wouldn't take too kindly to venom."

"Rosalie would never embarrass Esme by displaying such a lack of hospitality."

"Of *course* not," Blondie said in a sugar-sweet voice that I immediately distrusted. She got up and breezed out of the room.

Edward sighed.

"You'd tell me if she poisoned it, right?" I asked.

"Yes," Edward promised.

And for some reason I believed him.

There was a lot of banging in the kitchen, and—weirdly—the sound of metal protesting as it was abused. Edward sighed again, but smiled just a little, too. Then Rosalie was back before I could think much more about it. With a pleased smirk, she set a silver bowl on the floor next to me.

"Enjoy, mongrel."

It had once probably been a big mixing bowl, but she'd bent the bowl back in on itself until it was shaped almost exactly like a dog dish. I had to be impressed with her quick craftsmanship. And her attention to detail. She'd scratched the word *Fido* into the side. Excellent handwriting.

Because the food looked pretty good—steak, no less, and a big baked potato with all the fixings—I told her, "Thanks, Blondie."

She snorted.

"Hey, do you know what you call a blonde with a brain?" I asked, and then continued on the same breath, "a golden retriever."

"I've heard that one, too," she said, no longer smiling.

"I'll keep trying," I promised, and then I dug in.

She made a disgusted face and rolled her eyes. Then she sat in one of the armchairs and started flicking through channels on the big TV so fast that there was no way she could really be surfing for something to watch.

The food was good, even with the vampire stink in the air. I was getting really used to that. Huh. Not something I'd been wanting to do, exactly . . .

When I was finished—though I was considering licking the bowl, just to give Rosalie something to complain about—I felt Bella's cold fingers pulling softly through my hair. She patted it down against the back of my neck.

"Time for a haircut, huh?"

"You're getting a little shaggy," she said. "Maybe—"

"Let me guess, someone around here used to cut hair in a salon in Paris?"

She chuckled. "Probably."

"No thanks," I said before she could really offer. "I'm good for a few more weeks."

Which made me wonder how long *she* was good for. I tried to think of a polite way to ask.

"So . . . um . . . what's the, er, date? You know, the due date for the little monster."

She smacked the back of my head with about as much force as a drifting feather, but didn't answer.

"I'm serious," I told her. "I want to know how long I'm gonna have to be here." *How long* you're *gonna be here*, I added in my head. I turned to look at her then. Her eyes were thoughtful; the stress line was there between her brows again.

"I don't know," she murmured. "Not exactly. Obviously, we're not going with the nine-month model here, and we can't get an ultrasound, so Carlisle is guesstimating from how big I am. Normal people are supposed to be about forty centimeters here"—she ran her finger right down the middle of her bulging stomach—"when the baby is fully grown. One centimeter for every week. I was thirty this morning, and I've been gaining about two centimeters a day, sometimes more. . . ."

Two weeks to a day, the days flying by. Her life speeding by in fast-forward. How many days did that give her, if she was counting to forty? Four? It took me a minute to figure out how to swallow.

"You okay?" she asked.

I nodded, not really sure how my voice would come out.

Edward's face was turned away from us as he listened to my thoughts, but I could see his reflection in the glass wall. He was the burning man again.

Funny how having a deadline made it harder to think about leaving, or having her leave. I was glad Seth'd brought that up, so I knew they were staying here. It would be intolerable, wondering if they were about to go, to take away one or two or three of those four days. My four days.

Also funny how, even knowing that it was almost over, the hold she had on me only got harder to break. Almost like it was related to her expanding belly—as if by getting bigger, she was gaining gravitational force.

For a minute I tried to look at her from a distance, to separate myself from the pull. I knew it wasn't my imagination that my need for her was stronger than ever. Why was that? Because she was dying? Or knowing that even if she didn't, still—best case scenario—she'd be changing into something else that I wouldn't know or understand?

She ran her finger across my cheekbone, and my skin was wet where she touched it.

"It's going to be okay," she sort of crooned. It didn't matter that the words meant nothing. She said it the way people sang those senseless nursery rhymes to kids. Rock-a-bye, baby.

"Right," I muttered.

She curled against my arm, resting her head on my shoulder. "I didn't think you would come. Seth said you would, and so did Edward, but I didn't believe them."

"Why not?" I asked gruffly.

"You're not happy here. But you came anyway."

"You wanted me here."

"I know. But you didn't have to come, because it's not fair for me to want you here. I would have understood."

It was quiet for a minute. Edward'd put his face back together. He looked at the TV as Rosalie went on flipping through the channels. She was into the six hundreds. I wondered how long it would take to get back to the beginning.

"Thank you for coming," Bella whispered.

"Can I ask you something?" I asked.

"Of course."

Edward didn't look like he was paying attention to us at all, but he knew what I was about to ask, so he didn't fool me.

"Why *do* you want me here? Seth could keep you warm, and he's probably easier to be around, happy little punk. But when *I* walk in the door, you smile like I'm your favorite person in the world."

"You're one of them."

"That sucks, you know."

"Yeah." She sighed. "Sorry."

"Why, though? You didn't answer that."

Edward was looking away again, like he was staring out the windows. His face was blank in the reflection.

"It feels . . . *complete* when you're here, Jacob. Like all my family is together. I mean, I guess that's what it's like—I've never had a big family before now. It's nice." She smiled for half a second. "But it's just not whole unless you're here."

"I'll never be part of your family, Bella."

I could have been. I would have been good there. But that was just a distant future that died long before it had a chance to live.

"You've always been a part of my family," she disagreed.

My teeth made a grinding sound. "That's a crap answer."

"What's a good one?"

"How about, 'Jacob, I get a kick out of your pain.'"

I felt her flinch.

"You'd like that better?" she whispered.

"It's easier, at least. I could wrap my head around it. I could deal with it."

I looked back down at her face then, so close to mine. Her eyes were shut and she was frowning. "We got off track, Jake. Out of balance. You're supposed to be part of my life—I can feel that, and so can you." She paused for a second without opening her eyes—like she was waiting for me to deny it. When I didn't say anything, she went on.

"But not like this. We did something wrong. No. I did. I did something wrong, and we got off track. . . ."

Her voice trailed off, and the frown on her face relaxed until it was just a little pucker at the corner of her lips. I waited for her to pour some more lemon juice into my paper cuts, but then a soft snore came from the back of her throat.

"She's exhausted," Edward murmured. "It's been a long day. A hard day. I think she would have gone to sleep earlier, but she was waiting for you."

I didn't look at him.

"Seth said it broke another of her ribs."

"Yes. It's making it hard for her to breathe."

"Great."

"Let me know when she gets hot again."

"Yeah."

She still had goose bumps on the arm that wasn't touching mine. I'd barely raised my head to look for a blanket when Edward snagged one draped over the arm of the sofa and flung it out so that it settled over her.

Occasionally, the mind-reading thing saved time. For example, maybe I wouldn't have to make a big production out of the accusation about what was going on with Charlie. That mess. Edward would just *hear* exactly how furious—

"Yes," he agreed. "It's not a good idea."

"Then why?" Why was Bella telling her father she was *on the mend* when it would only make him more miserable?

"She can't bear his anxiety."

"So it's better—"

"No. It's *not* better. But I'm not going to force her to do anything that makes her unhappy now. Whatever happens, this makes her feel better. I'll deal with the rest afterward."

That didn't sound right. Bella wouldn't just shuffle Charlie's pain off to some later date, for someone else to face. Even dying. That wasn't her. If I knew Bella, she had to have some other plan.

"She's very sure she's going to live," Edward said.

"But not human," I protested.

"No, not human. But she hopes to see Charlie again, anyway."

Oh, this just got better and better.

"See. Charlie." I finally looked at him, my eyes bugging. "Afterwards. See Charlie when she's all sparkly white with the bright red eyes. I'm not a bloodsucker, so maybe I'm missing something, but *Charlie* seems like kind of a strange choice for her first meal."

Edward sighed. "She knows she won't be able to be near him for at least a year. She thinks she can stall. Tell Charlie she has to go to a special hospital on the other side of the world. Keep in contact through phone calls. . . ."

"That's insane."

"Yes."

"Charlie's not stupid. Even if she doesn't kill him, he's going to notice a difference."

"She's sort of banking on that."

I continued to stare, waiting for him to explain.

"She wouldn't be aging, of course, so that would set a time limit, even if Charlie accepted whatever excuse she comes up with for the changes." He smiled faintly. "Do you remember when you tried to tell her about your transformation? How you made her guess?"

My free hand flexed into a fist. "She told you about that?"

"Yes. She was explaining her . . . idea. You see, she's not allowed to tell Charlie the truth—it would be very dangerous for him. But he's a smart, practical man. She thinks he'll come up with his own explanation. She assumes he'll get it wrong." Edward snorted. "After all, we hardly adhere to vampire canon. He'll make some wrong assumption about us, like she did in the beginning, and we'll go along with it. She thinks she'll be able to see him . . . from time to time."

"Insane," I repeated.

"Yes," he agreed again.

It was weak of him to let her get her way on this, just to keep her happy now. It wouldn't turn out well.

Which made me think that he probably wasn't expecting her to live to try out her crazy plan. Placating her, so that she could be happy for a little while longer.

Like four more days.

"I'll deal with whatever comes," he whispered, and he turned his face down and away so that I couldn't even read his reflection. "I won't cause her pain now."

"Four days?" I asked.

He didn't look up. "Approximately."

"Then what?"

"What do you mean, exactly?"

I thought about what Bella had said. About the thing being wrapped up nice and tight in something strong, something like vampire skin. So how did that work? How did it get out?

"From what little research we've been able to do, it

would appear the creatures use their own teeth to escape the womb," he whispered.

I had to pause to swallow back the bile.

"Research?" I asked weakly.

"That's why you haven't seen Jasper and Emmett around. That's what Carlisle is doing now. Trying to decipher ancient stories and myths, as much as we can with what we have to work with here, looking for anything that might help us predict the creature's behavior."

Stories? If there were myths, then . . .

"Then is this thing not the first of its kind?" Edward asked, anticipating my question. "Maybe. It's all very sketchy. The myths could easily be the products of fear and imagination. Though . . ."—he hesitated—"your myths are true, are they not? Perhaps these are, too. They do seem to be localized, linked. . . ."

"How did you find . . . ?"

"There was a woman we encountered in South America. She'd been raised in the traditions of her people. She'd heard warnings about such creatures, old stories that had been passed down."

"What were the warnings?" I whispered.

"That the creature must be killed immediately. Before it could gain too much strength."

Just like Sam thought. Was he right?

"Of course, their legends say the same of us. That we must be destroyed. That we are soulless murderers."

Two for two.

Edward laughed one hard chuckle.

"What did their stories say about the . . . mothers?"

Agony ripped across his face, and, as I flinched away

from his pain, I knew he wasn't going to give me an answer. I doubted he could talk.

It was Rosalie—who'd been so still and quiet since Bella'd fallen asleep that I'd nearly forgotten her—who answered.

She made a scornful noise in the back of her throat. "Of course there were no survivors," she said. *No survivors*, blunt and uncaring. "Giving birth in the middle of a disease-infested swamp with a medicine man smearing sloth spit across your face to drive out the evil spirits was never the safest method. Even the normal births went badly half the time. None of them had what this baby has—caregivers with an idea of what the baby needs, who try to meet those needs. A doctor with a totally unique knowledge of vampire nature. A plan in place to deliver the baby as safely as possible. Venom that will repair anything that goes wrong. The baby will be fine. And those other mothers would probably have survived if they'd had that—if they even existed in the first place. Something I am not convinced of." She sniffed disdainfully.

The baby, the baby. Like that was all that mattered. Bella's life was a minor detail to her—easy to blow off.

Edward's face went white as snow. His hands curved into claws. Totally egotistical and indifferent, Rosalie twisted in her chair so that her back was to him. He leaned forward, shifting into a crouch.

Allow me, I suggested.

He paused, raising one eyebrow.

Silently, I lifted my doggy bowl off the floor. Then, with a quick, powerful flip of my wrist, I threw it into the back of Blondie's head so hard that—with an earsplitting *bang*—it smashed flat before it ricocheted across the room and snapped the round top piece off the thick newel post at the foot of the stairs.

Bella twitched but didn't wake up.

"Dumb blonde," I muttered.

Rosalie turned her head slowly, and her eyes were blazing.

"You. Got. Food. In. My. Hair."

That did it.

I busted up. I pulled away from Bella so that I wouldn't shake her, and laughed so hard that tears ran down my face. From behind the couch, I heard Alice's tinkling laugh join in.

I wondered why Rosalie didn't spring. I sort of expected it. But then I realized that my laughing had woken Bella up, though she'd slept right through the real noise.

"What's so funny?" she mumbled.

"I got food in her hair," I told her, chortling again.

"I'm not going to forget this, dog," Rosalie hissed.

"S'not so hard to erase a blonde's memory," I countered. "Just blow in her ear."

"Get some new jokes," she snapped.

"C'mon, Jake. Leave Rose alo—" Bella broke off mid-sentence and sucked in a sharp breath. In the same second, Edward was leaning over the top of me, ripping the blanket out of the way. She seemed to convulse, her back arching off the sofa.

"He's just," she panted, "stretching."

Her lips were white, and she had her teeth locked together like she was trying to hold back a scream.

Edward put both hands on either side of her face.

"Carlisle?" he called in a tense, low voice.

"Right here," the doctor said. I hadn't heard him come in.

"Okay," Bella said, still breathing hard and shallow. "Think it's over. Poor kid doesn't have enough room, that's all. He's getting so big."

It was really hard to take, that adoring tone she used to describe the thing that was tearing her up. Especially after Rosalie's callousness. Made me wish I could throw something at Bella, too.

She didn't pick up on my mood. "You know, he reminds me of you, Jake," she said—affectionate tone—still gasping.

"Do *not* compare me to that thing," I spit out through my teeth.

"I just meant your growth spurt," she said, looking like I'd hurt her feelings. Good. "You shot right up. I could watch you getting taller by the minute. He's like that, too. Growing so fast."

I bit my tongue to keep from saying what I wanted to say—hard enough that I tasted blood in my mouth. Of course, it would heal before I could swallow. That's what Bella needed. To be strong like me, to be able to heal. . . .

She took an easier breath and then relaxed back into the sofa, her body going limp.

"Hmm," Carlisle murmured. I looked up, and his eyes were on me.

"What?" I demanded.

Edward's head leaned to one side as he reflected on whatever was in Carlisle's head.

"You know that I was wondering about the fetus's genetic makeup, Jacob. About his chromosomes."

"What of it?"

"Well, taking your similarities into consideration—"

"Similari*ties?*" I growled, not appreciating the plural.

"The accelerated growth, and the fact that Alice cannot see either of you."

I felt my face go blank. I'd forgotten about that other one.

"Well, I wonder if that means that we have an answer. If the similarities are gene-deep."

"Twenty-four pairs," Edward muttered under his breath.

"You don't know that."

"No. But it's interesting to speculate," Carlisle said in a soothing voice.

"Yeah. Just *fascinating.*"

Bella's light snore started up again, accenting my sarcasm nicely.

They got into it then, quickly taking the genetics conversation to a point where the only words I could understand were the *the*'s and the *and*'s. And my own name, of course. Alice joined in, commenting now and then in her chirpy bird voice.

Even though they were talking about me, I didn't try to figure out the conclusions they were drawing. I had other things on my mind, a few facts I was trying to reconcile.

Fact one, Bella'd said that the creature was protected by something as strong as vampire skin, something that was too impenetrable for ultrasounds, too tough for needles. Fact two, Rosalie'd said they had a plan to deliver the creature safely. Fact three, Edward'd said that—in myths—other monsters like this one would chew their way out of their own mothers.

I shuddered.

And that made a sick kind of sense, because, fact four, not many things could cut through something as strong as vampire skin. The half-creature's teeth—according to myth—were strong enough. My teeth were strong enough.

And vampire teeth were strong enough.

It was hard to miss the obvious, but I sure wished I could. Because I had a pretty good idea exactly how Rosalie planned to get that thing "safely" out.

16. TOO-MUCH-INFORMATION ALERT

I TOOK OFF EARLY, LONG BEFORE SUNRISE WAS DUE. I'd gotten just a little bit of uneasy sleep leaning against the side of the sofa. Edward woke me when Bella's face was flushed, and he took my spot to cool her back down. I stretched and decided I was rested enough to get some work done.

"Thank you," Edward said quietly, seeing my plans. "If the route is clear, they'll go today."

"I'll let you know."

It felt good to get back to my animal self. I was stiff from sitting still for so long. I extended my stride, working out the kinks.

Morning, Jacob, Leah greeted me.

Good, you're up. How long's Seth been out?

Not out yet, Seth thought sleepily. *Almost there. What do you need?*

You think you got another hour in you?

Sure thing. No problem. Seth got to his feet right away, shaking out his fur.

Let's make the deep run, I told Leah. *Seth, take the perimeter.*

Gotcha. Seth broke into an easy jog.

Off on another vampire errand, Leah grumbled.

You got a problem with that?

Of course *not. I just* love *to coddle those darling leeches.*

Good. Let's see how fast we can run.

Okay, I'm definitely up for that*!*

Leah was on the far western rim of the perimeter. Rather than cut close to the Cullens' house, she stuck to the circle as she raced around to meet me. I sprinted off straight east, knowing that even with the head start, she'd be passing me soon if I took it easy for even a second.

Nose to the ground, Leah. This isn't a race, it's a reconnaissance mission.

I can do both and still kick your butt.

I gave her that one. *I know.*

She laughed.

We took a winding path through the eastern mountains. It was a familiar route. We'd run these mountains when the vampires had left a year ago, making it part of our patrol route to better protect the people here. Then we'd pulled back the lines when the Cullens returned. This was their treaty land.

But that fact would probably mean nothing to Sam now.

The treaty was dead. The question today was how thin he was willing to spread his force. Was he looking for stray Cullens to poach on their land or not? Had Jared spoken the truth or taken advantage of the silence between us?

We got deeper and deeper into the mountains without finding any trace of the pack. Fading vampire trails were everywhere, but the scents were familiar now. I was breathing them in all day long.

I found a heavy, somewhat recent concentration on one particular trail—all of them coming and going here except for Edward. Some reason for gathering that must have been forgotten when Edward brought his dying pregnant wife home. I gritted my teeth. Whatever it was, it had nothing to do with me.

Leah didn't push herself past me, though she could have now. I was paying more attention to each new scent than I was to the speed contest. She kept to my right side, running with me rather than racing against me.

We're getting pretty far out here, she commented.

Yeah. If Sam was hunting strays, we should have crossed his trail by now.

Makes more sense right now for him to bunker down in La Push, Leah thought. *He knows we're giving the bloodsuckers three extra sets of eyes and legs. He's not going to be able to surprise them.*

This was just a precaution, really.

Wouldn't want our precious parasites taking unnecessary chances.

Nope, I agreed, ignoring the sarcasm.

You've changed so much, Jacob. Talk about one-eighties.

You're not exactly the same Leah I've always known and loved, either.

True. Am I less annoying than Paul now?

Amazingly . . . yes.

Ah, sweet success.

Congrats.

We ran in silence again then. It was probably time to turn around, but neither of us wanted to. It felt nice to run like this. We'd been staring at the same small circle of a trail for too long. It felt good to stretch our muscles and take the rugged terrain. We weren't in a huge hurry, so I thought maybe we should hunt on the way back. Leah was pretty hungry.

Yum, yum, she thought sourly.

It's all in your head, I told her. *That's the way wolves eat. It's natural. It tastes fine. If you didn't think about it from a human perspective—*

Forget the pep talk, Jacob. I'll hunt. I don't have to like it.

Sure, sure, I agreed easily. It wasn't my business if she wanted to make things harder for herself.

She didn't add anything for a few minutes; I started thinking about turning back.

Thank you, Leah suddenly told me in a much different tone.

For?

For letting me be. For letting me stay. You've been nicer than I had any right to expect, Jacob.

Er, no problem. Actually, I mean that. I don't mind having you here like I thought I would.

She snorted, but it was a playful sound. *What a glowing commendation!*

Don't let it go to your head.

Okay—if you don't let this go to yours. She paused for a

second. *I think you make a good Alpha. Not in the same way Sam does, but in your own way. You're worth following, Jacob.*

My mind went blank with surprise. It took me a second to recover enough to respond.

Er, thanks. Not totally sure I'll be able to stop that one from going to my head, though. Where did that come from?

She didn't answer right away, and I followed the wordless direction of her thoughts. She was thinking about the future—about what I'd said to Jared the other morning. About how the time would be up soon, and then I'd go back to the forest. About how I'd promised that she and Seth would return to the pack when the Cullens were gone. . . .

I want to stay with you, she told me.

The shock shot through my legs, locking my joints. She blew past me and then put on the brakes. Slowly, she walked back to where I was frozen in place.

I won't be a pain, I swear. I won't follow you around. You can go wherever you want, and I'll go where I want. You'll only have to put up with me when we're both wolves. She paced back and forth in front of me, swishing her long gray tail nervously. *And, as I'm planning on quitting as soon as I can manage it . . . maybe that won't be so often.*

I didn't know what to say.

I'm happier now, as a part of your pack, than I have been in years.

I want to stay, too, Seth thought quietly. I hadn't realized he'd been paying much attention to us as he ran the perimeter. *I like this pack.*

Hey, now! Seth, this isn't going to be a pack much longer. I tried to put my thoughts together so they would convince him. *We've got a purpose now, but when . . . after that's over, I'm just going to go wolf. Seth, you need a purpose. You're a good kid. You're the kind of person who always has a crusade. And there's no way you're leaving La Push now. You're going to graduate from high school and do something with your life. You're going to take care of Sue. My issues are not going to mess up your future.*

But—

Jacob is right, Leah seconded.

You're agreeing with me?

Of course. But none of that applies to me. *I was on my way out, anyway. I'll get a job somewhere away from La Push. Maybe take some courses at a community college. Get into yoga and meditation to work on my temper issues. . . . And stay a part of this pack for the sake of my mental well-being. Jacob—you can see how that makes sense, right? I won't bother you, you won't bother me, everyone is happy.*

I turned back and started loping slowly toward the west.

This is a bit much to deal with, Leah. Let me think about it, 'kay?

Sure. Take your time.

It took us longer to make the run back. I wasn't trying for speed. I was just trying to concentrate enough that I wouldn't plow headfirst into a tree. Seth was grumbling a little bit in the back of my head, but I was able to ignore him. He knew I was right. He wasn't going to abandon his mom. He would go back to La Push and protect the tribe like he should.

But I couldn't see Leah doing that. And that was just plain scary.

A pack of the two of us? No matter the physical distance,

I couldn't imagine the . . . the *intimacy* of that situation. I wondered if she'd really thought it through, or if she was just desperate to stay free.

Leah didn't say anything as I chewed it over. It was like she was trying to prove how easy it would be if it was just us.

We ran into a herd of black-tailed deer just as the sun was coming up, brightening the clouds a little bit behind us. Leah sighed internally but didn't hesitate. Her lunge was clean and efficient—graceful, even. She took down the largest one, the buck, before the startled animal fully understood the danger.

Not to be outdone, I swooped down on the next largest deer, snapping her neck between my jaws quickly, so she wouldn't feel unnecessary pain. I could feel Leah's disgust warring with her hunger, and I tried to make it easier for her by letting the wolf in me have my head. I'd lived all-wolf for long enough that I knew how to be the animal completely, to see his way and think his way. I let the practical instincts take over, letting her feel that, too. She hesitated for a second, but then, tentatively, she seemed to reach out with her mind and try to see my way. It felt very strange—our minds were more closely linked than they had ever been before, because we both were *trying* to think together.

Strange, but it helped her. Her teeth cut through the fur and skin of her kill's shoulder, tearing away a thick slab of streaming flesh. Rather than wince away as her human thoughts wanted to, she let her wolf-self react instinctively. It was kind of a numbing thing, a thoughtless thing. It let her eat in peace.

It was easy for me to do the same. And I was glad I hadn't forgotten this. This would be my life again soon.

Was Leah going to be a part of that life? A week ago, I would've found that idea beyond horrifying. I wouldn't've been able to stand it. But I knew her better now. And, relieved from the constant pain, she wasn't the same wolf. Not the same girl.

We ate together until we both were full.

Thanks, she told me later as she was cleaning her muzzle and paws against the wet grass. I didn't bother; it had just started to drizzle and we had to swim the river again on our way back. I'd get clean enough. *That wasn't so bad, thinking your way.*

You're welcome.

Seth was dragging when we hit the perimeter. I told him to get some sleep; Leah and I would take over the patrol. Seth's mind faded into unconsciousness just seconds later.

You headed back to the bloodsuckers? Leah asked.

Maybe.

It's hard for you to be there, but hard to stay away, too. I know how that feels.

You know, Leah, you might want to think a little bit about the future, about what you really want to do. My head is not going to be the happiest place on earth. And you'll have to suffer right along with me.

She thought about how to answer me. *Wow, this is going to sound bad. But, honestly, it will be easier to deal with your pain than face mine.*

Fair enough.

I know it's going to be bad for you, Jacob. I understand that—maybe better than you think. I don't like her, but . . . she's your Sam. She's everything you want and everything you can't have.

I couldn't answer.

I know it's worse for you. At least Sam is happy. At least he's alive and well. I love him enough that I want that. I want him to have what's best for him. She sighed. *I just don't want to stick around to watch.*

Do we need to talk about this?

I think we do. Because I want you to know that I won't make it worse for you. Hell, maybe I'll even help. I wasn't born *a compassionless shrew. I used to be sort of nice, you know.*

My memory doesn't go that far back.

We both laughed once.

I'm sorry about this, Jacob. I'm sorry you're in pain. I'm sorry it's getting worse and not better.

Thanks, Leah.

She thought about the things that were worse, the black pictures in my head, while I tried to tune her out without much success. She was able to look at them with some distance, some perspective, and I had to admit that this was helpful. I could imagine that maybe I would be able to see it that way, too, in a few years.

She saw the funny side of the daily irritations that came from hanging out around vampires. She liked my ragging on Rosalie, chuckling internally and even running through a few blonde jokes in her mind that I might be able to work in. But then her thoughts turned serious, lingering on Rosalie's face in a way that confused me.

You know what's crazy? she asked.

Well, almost everything is crazy right now. But what do you mean?

That blond vampire you hate so much—I totally get her perspective.

For a second I thought she was making a joke that was in

very poor taste. And then, when I realized she was serious, the fury that ripped through me was hard to control. It was a good thing we'd spread out to run our watch. If she'd been within *biting* distance . . .

Hold up! Let me explain!

Don't want to hear it. I'm outta here.

Wait! Wait! she pleaded as I tried to calm myself enough to phase back. *C'mon, Jake!*

Leah, this isn't really the best way to convince me that I want to spend more time with you in the future.

Yeesh! What an overreaction. You don't even know what I'm talking about.

So what are *you talking about?*

And then she was suddenly the pain-hardened Leah from before. *I'm talking about being a genetic dead end, Jacob.*

The vicious edge to her words left me floundering. I hadn't expected to have my anger trumped.

I don't understand.

You would, *if you weren't just like the rest of them. If my "female stuff"*—she thought the words with a hard, sarcastic tone—*didn't send you running for cover just like any stupid male, so you could actually pay attention to what it all means.*

Oh.

Yeah, so none of us like to think about that stuff with her. Who would? Of course I remembered Leah's panic that first month after she joined the pack—and I remembered cringing away from it just like everyone else. Because she couldn't be *pregnant*—not unless there was some really freaky religious immaculate crap going on. She hadn't been with anyone since Sam. And then, when the weeks dragged on and nothing turned into more nothing, she'd realized that her body wasn't following the normal patterns anymore. The horror—what *was* she now? Had her body changed because she'd become a werewolf? Or had she become a werewolf because her body was *wrong*? The only female werewolf in the history of forever. Was that because she wasn't as female as she should be?

None of us had wanted to deal with that breakdown. Obviously, it wasn't like we could *empathize.*

You know why Sam thinks we imprint, she thought, calmer now.

Sure. To carry on the line.

Right. To make a bunch of new little werewolves. Survival of the species, genetic override. You're drawn to the person who gives you the best chance to pass on the wolf gene.

I waited for her to tell me where she was going with this.

If I was any good for that, Sam would have been drawn to me.

Her pain was enough that I broke stride under it.

But I'm not. There's something wrong with me. I don't have the ability to pass on the gene, apparently, despite my stellar bloodlines. So I become a freak—the girlie-wolf—good for nothing else. I'm a genetic dead end and we both know it.

We do not, I argued with her. *That's just Sam's theory. Imprinting happens, but we don't know why. Billy thinks it's something else.*

I know, I know. He thinks you're imprinting to make stronger *wolves. Because you and Sam are such humongous monsters—bigger than our fathers. But either way, I'm still not a candidate. I'm . . . I'm menopausal. I'm twenty years old and I'm menopausal.*

Ugh. I *so* didn't want to have this conversation. *You don't know that, Leah. It's probably just the whole frozen-in-time thing.*

When you quit your wolf and start getting older again, I'm sure things will . . . er . . . pick right back up.

I might *think that—except that no one's imprinting on* me, *notwithstanding my impressive pedigree. You know,* she added thoughtfully, *if you weren't around, Seth would probably have the best claim to being Alpha—through his blood, at least. Of course, no one would ever consider me. . . .*

You really want *to imprint, or be imprinted on, or whichever?* I demanded. *What's wrong with going out and falling in love like a normal person, Leah? Imprinting is just another way of getting your choices taken away from you.*

Sam, Jared, Paul, Quil . . . they don't seem to mind.

None of them have *a mind of their own.*

You don't want to imprint?

Hell, no!

That's just because you're already in love with her. *That would go away, you know, if you imprinted. You wouldn't have to hurt over her anymore.*

Do you want to forget the way you feel about Sam?

She deliberated for a moment. *I think I do.*

I sighed. She was in a healthier place than I was.

But back to my original point, Jacob. I understand why your blond vampire is so cold—in the figurative sense. She's focused. She's got her eyes on the prize, right? Because you always want the very most what you can never, ever have.

You *would act like Rosalie? You* would *murder someone— because that's what she's doing, making sure no one interferes with Bella's death—you would do that to have a baby? Since when are you a breeder?*

I just want the options I don't have, Jacob. Maybe, if there was nothing wrong with me, I would never give it a thought.

You would kill for that? I demanded, not letting her escape my question.

That's not what she's doing. I think it's more like she's living vicariously. And . . . if Bella asked me to help her with this . . . She paused, considering. *Even though I don't think too much of her, I'd probably do the same as the bloodsucker.*

A loud snarl ripped through my teeth.

Because, if it was turned around, I'd want Bella to do that for me. And so would Rosalie. We'd both do it her way.

Ugh! You're as bad as they are!

That's the funny thing about knowing you can't have something. It makes you desperate.

And . . . that's my limit. Right there. This conversation is over.

Fine.

It wasn't enough that she'd agreed to stop. I wanted a stronger termination than that.

I was only about a mile from where I'd left my clothes, so I phased back to human and walked. I didn't think about our conversation. Not because there wasn't anything to think about, but because I couldn't stand it. I would *not* see it that way—but it was harder to keep from doing that when Leah had put the thoughts and emotions straight into my head.

Yeah, I wasn't running with her when this was finished. She could go be miserable in La Push. One little Alpha command before I left for good wasn't going to kill anybody.

It was real early when I got to the house. Bella was probably still asleep. I figured I'd poke my head in, see what was going on, give 'em the green light to go hunting, and then find a patch of grass soft enough to sleep on while human. I wasn't phasing back until Leah was asleep.

But there was a lot of low mumbling going on inside the house, so maybe Bella wasn't sleeping. And then I heard the machinery sound from upstairs again—the X-ray? Great. It looked like day four on the countdown was starting off with a bang.

Alice opened the door for me before I could walk in.

She nodded. "Hey, wolf."

"Hey, shortie. What's going on upstairs?" The big room was empty—all the murmurs were on the second floor.

She shrugged her pointy little shoulders. "Maybe another break." She tried to say the words casually, but I could see the flames in the very back of her eyes. Edward and I weren't the only ones who were burning over this. Alice loved Bella, too.

"Another rib?" I asked hoarsely.

"No. Pelvis this time."

Funny how it kept hitting me, like each new thing was a surprise. When was I going to stop being surprised? Each new disaster seemed kinda obvious in hindsight.

Alice was staring at my hands, watching them tremble.

Then we were listening to Rosalie's voice upstairs.

"See, I *told* you I didn't hear a crack. You need your ears checked, Edward."

There was no answer.

Alice made a face. "Edward's going to end up ripping Rose into small pieces, I think. I'm surprised she doesn't see that. Or maybe she thinks Emmett will be able to stop him."

"I'll take Emmett," I offered. "You can help Edward with the ripping part."

Alice half-smiled.

The procession came down the stairs then—Edward had Bella this time. She was gripping her cup of blood in both hands, and her face was white. I could see that, though he compensated for every tiny movement of his body to keep from jostling her, she was hurting.

"Jake," she whispered, and she smiled through the pain.

I stared at her, saying nothing.

Edward placed Bella carefully on her couch and sat on the floor by her head. I wondered briefly why they didn't leave her upstairs, and then decided at once that it must be Bella's idea. She'd want to act like things were normal, avoid the hospital setup. And he was humoring her. Naturally.

Carlisle came down slowly, the last one, his face creased with worry. It made him look old enough to be a doctor for once.

"Carlisle," I said. "We went halfway to Seattle. There's no sign of the pack. You're good to go."

"Thank you, Jacob. This is good timing. There's much that we need." His black eyes flickered to the cup that Bella was holding so tight.

"Honestly, I think you're safe to take more than three. I'm pretty positive that Sam is concentrating on La Push."

Carlisle nodded in agreement. It surprised me how willingly he took my advice. "If you think so. Alice, Esme, Jasper, and I will go. Then Alice can take Emmett and Rosa—"

"Not a chance," Rosalie hissed. "Emmett can go with you now."

"You should hunt," Carlisle said in a gentle voice.

His tone didn't soften hers. "I'll hunt when *he* does," she growled, jerking her head toward Edward and then flipping her hair back.

Carlisle sighed.

Jasper and Emmett were down the stairs in a flash, and Alice joined them by the glass back door in the same second. Esme flitted to Alice's side.

Carlisle put his hand on my arm. The icy touch did not feel good, but I didn't jerk away. I held still, half in surprise, and half because I didn't want to hurt his feelings.

"Thank you," he said again, and then he darted out the door with the other four. My eyes followed them as they flew across the lawn and then disappeared before I took another breath. Their needs must have been more urgent than I'd imagined.

There was no sound for a minute. I could feel someone glaring at me, and I knew who it would be. I'd been planning to take off and get some Z's, but the chance to ruin Rosalie's morning seemed too good to pass up.

So I sauntered over to the armchair next to the one Rosalie had and settled in, sprawling out so that my head was tilted toward Bella and my left foot was near Rosalie's face.

"Ew. Someone put the dog out," she murmured, wrinkling her nose.

"Have you heard this one, Psycho? How do a blonde's brain cells die?"

She didn't say anything.

"Well?" I asked. "Do you know the punch line or not?"

She looked pointedly at the TV and ignored me.

"Has she heard it?" I asked Edward.

There was no humor on his tense face—he didn't move his eyes from Bella. But he said, "No."

"Awesome. So you'll enjoy this, bloodsucker—a blonde's brain cells die *alone*."

Rosalie still didn't look at me. "I have killed a hundred times more often than you have, you disgusting beast. Don't forget that."

"Someday, Beauty Queen, you're going to get tired of just threatening me. I'm really looking forward to that."

"Enough, Jacob," Bella said.

I looked down, and she was scowling at me. It looked like yesterday's good mood was long gone.

Well, I didn't want to bug her. "You want me to take off?" I offered.

Before I could hope—or fear—that she'd finally gotten tired of me, she blinked, and her frown disappeared. She seemed totally shocked that I would come to that conclusion. "No! Of course not."

I sighed, and I heard Edward sigh very quietly, too. I knew he wished she'd get over me, too. Too bad he'd never ask her to do anything that might make her unhappy.

"You look tired," Bella commented.

"Dead beat," I admitted.

"*I'd* like to beat you dead," Rosalie muttered, too low for Bella to hear.

I just slumped deeper into the chair, getting comfortable. My bare foot dangled closer to Rosalie, and she stiffened. After a few minutes Bella asked Rosalie for a refill. I felt the wind as Rosalie blew upstairs to get her some more blood. It was really quiet. Might as well take a nap, I figured.

And then Edward said, "Did you say something?" in a puzzled tone. Strange. Because no one *had* said anything, and because Edward's hearing was as good as mine, and he should have known that.

He was staring at Bella, and she was staring back. They both looked confused.

"Me?" she asked after a second. "I didn't say anything."

He moved onto his knees, leaning forward over her, his expression suddenly intense in a whole different way. His black eyes focused on her face.

"What are you thinking about right now?"

She stared at him blankly. "Nothing. What's going on?"

"What were you thinking about a minute ago?" he asked.

"Just . . . Esme's island. And feathers."

Sounded like total gibberish to me, but then she blushed, and I figured I was better off not knowing.

"Say something else," he whispered.

"Like what? Edward, what's going on?"

His face changed again, and he did something that made my mouth fall open with a pop. I heard a gasp behind me, and I knew that Rosalie was back, and just as flabbergasted as I was.

Edward, very lightly, put both of his hands against her huge, round stomach.

"The f—" He swallowed. "It . . . the baby likes the sound of your voice."

There was one short beat of total silence. I could not move a muscle, even to blink. Then—

"Holy crow, you can hear him!" Bella shouted. In the next second, she winced.

Edward's hand moved to the top peak of her belly and gently rubbed the spot where it must have kicked her.

"Shh," he murmured. "You startled it . . . him."

Her eyes got all wide and full of wonder. She patted the side of her stomach. "Sorry, baby."

Edward was listening hard, his head tilted toward the bulge.

"What's he thinking now?" she demanded eagerly.

"It . . . he or she, is . . ." He paused and looked up into her eyes. His eyes were filled with a similar awe—only his were more careful and grudging. "He's *happy*," Edward said in an incredulous voice.

Her breath caught, and it was impossible not to see the fanatical gleam in her eyes. The adoration and the devotion. Big, fat tears overflowed her eyes and ran silently down her face and over her smiling lips.

As he stared at her, his face was not frightened or angry or burning or any of the other expressions he'd worn since their return. He was marveling with her.

"Of course you're happy, pretty baby, of course you are," she crooned, rubbing her stomach while the tears washed her cheeks. "How could you not be, all safe and warm and loved? I love you so much, little EJ, of course you're happy."

"What did you call him?" Edward asked curiously.

She blushed again. "I sort of named him. I didn't think you would want . . . well, you know."

"EJ?"

"Your father's name was Edward, too."

"Yes, it was. What—?" He paused and then said, "Hmm."

"What?"

"He likes my voice, too."

"Of course he does." Her tone was almost gloating now. "You have the most beautiful voice in the universe. Who wouldn't love it?"

"Do you have a backup plan?" Rosalie asked then, leaning over the back of the sofa with the same wondering, gloating look on her face that was on Bella's. "What if he's a she?"

Bella wiped the back of her hand under her wet eyes. "I kicked a few things around. Playing with Renée and Esme. I was thinking . . . Ruh-*nez*-may."

"Ruhnezmay?"

"R-e-n-e-s-m-e-e. Too weird?"

"No, I like it," Rosalie assured her. Their heads were close together, gold and mahogany. "It's beautiful. And one of a kind, so *that* fits."

"I still think he's an Edward."

Edward was staring off into space, his face blank as he listened.

"What?" Bella asked, her face just glowing away. "What's he thinking now?"

At first he didn't answer, and then—shocking all the rest of us again, three distinct and separate gasps—he laid his ear tenderly against her belly.

"He loves you," Edward whispered, sounding dazed. "He absolutely *adores* you."

In that moment, I knew that I was alone. All alone.

I wanted to kick myself when I realized how much I'd been counting on that loathsome vampire. How stupid—as if you could ever trust a leech! Of course he would betray me in the end.

I'd counted on him to be on my side. I'd counted on him to suffer more than I suffered. And, most of all, I'd counted on him to hate that revolting thing killing Bella more than I hated it.

I'd trusted him with that.

Yet now they were together, the two of them bent over the budding, invisible monster with their eyes lit up like a happy family.

And I was all alone with my hatred and the pain that was so bad it was like being tortured. Like being dragged slowly across a bed of razor blades. Pain so bad you'd take death with a smile just to get away from it.

The heat unlocked my frozen muscles, and I was on my feet.

All three of their heads snapped up, and I watched my pain ripple across Edward's face as he trespassed in my head again.

"Ahh," he choked.

I didn't know what I was doing; I stood there, trembling, ready to bolt for the very first escape that I could think of.

Moving like the strike of a snake, Edward darted to a small end table and ripped something from the drawer there. He tossed it at me, and I caught the object reflexively.

"Go, Jacob. Get away from here." He didn't say it harshly—he threw the words at me like they were a life preserver. He was helping me find the escape I was dying for.

The object in my hand was a set of car keys.

17. WHAT DO I LOOK LIKE? THE WIZARD OF OZ? YOU NEED A BRAIN? YOU NEED A HEART? GO AHEAD. TAKE MINE. TAKE EVERYTHING I HAVE.

I SORT OF HAD A PLAN AS I RAN TO THE CULLENS' GARAGE. The second part of it was totaling the bloodsucker's car on my way back.

So I was at a loss when I mashed the button on the keyless remote, and it was not his Volvo that beeped and flashed its lights for me. It was another car—a standout even in the long line of vehicles that were mostly all drool-worthy in their own ways.

Did he actually *mean* to give me the keys to an Aston Martin Vanquish, or was that an accident?

I didn't pause to think about it, or if this would change that second part of my plan. I just threw myself into the silky leather seat and cranked the engine while my knees were still crunched up under the steering wheel. The sound of the motor's purr might have made me moan another day, but right now it was all I could do to concentrate enough to put it in drive.

I found the seat release and shoved myself back as my foot rammed the pedal down. The car felt almost airborne as it leaped forward.

It only took seconds to race through the tight, winding drive. The car responded to me like my thoughts were steering rather than my hands. As I blew out of the green tunnel and onto the highway, I caught a fleeting glimpse of Leah's gray face peering uneasily through the ferns.

For half a second, I wondered what she'd think, and then I realized that I didn't care.

I turned south, because I had no patience today for ferries or traffic or anything else that meant I might have to lift my foot off the pedal.

In a sick way, it was my lucky day. If by lucky you meant taking a well-traveled highway at two hundred without so much as seeing one cop, even in the thirty-mile-an-hour speed-trap towns. What a letdown. A little chase action might have been nice, not to mention that the license plate info would bring the heat down on the leech. Sure, he'd buy his way out of it, but it might have been just a *little* inconvenient for him.

The only sign of surveillance I came across was just a hint of dark brown fur flitting through the woods, running parallel to me for a few miles on the south side of Forks. Quil, it looked like. He must have seen me, too, because he disappeared after a minute without raising an alarm.

Again, I almost wondered what his story would be before I remembered that I didn't care.

I raced around the long U-shaped highway, heading for the biggest city I could find. That was the first part of my plan.

It seemed to take forever, probably because I was still on the razor blades, but it actually didn't even take two hours before I was driving north into the undefined sprawl that was part Tacoma and part Seattle. I slowed down then, because I really wasn't trying to kill any innocent bystanders.

This was a stupid plan. It wasn't going to work. But, as I'd searched my head for any way at all to get away from the pain, what Leah'd said today had popped in there.

That would go away, you know, if you imprinted. You wouldn't have to hurt over her anymore.

Seemed like maybe getting your choices taken away from you wasn't the very worst thing in the world. Maybe feeling like *this* was the very worst thing in the world.

But I'd seen all the girls in La Push and up on the Makah rez and in Forks. I needed a wider hunting range.

So how do you look for a random soul mate in a crowd? Well, first, I needed a crowd. So I tooled around, looking for a likely spot. I passed a couple of malls, which probably would've been pretty good places to find girls my age, but I couldn't make myself stop. Did I *want* to imprint on some girl who hung out in a mall all day?

I kept going north, and it got more and more crowded. Eventually, I found a big park full of kids and families and skateboards and bikes and kites and picnics and the whole bit. I hadn't noticed till now—it was a nice day. Sun and all that. People were out celebrating the blue sky.

I parked across two handicapped spots—just begging for a ticket—and joined the crowd.

I walked around for what felt like hours. Long enough that the sun changed sides in the sky. I stared into the face of every girl who passed anywhere near me, making myself really look, noticing who was pretty and who had blue eyes and who looked good in braces and who had way too much makeup on. I tried to find something interesting about each face, so that I would know for sure that I'd really tried. Things like: This one had a really straight nose; that one should pull her hair out of her eyes; this one could do lipstick ads if the rest of her face was as perfect as her mouth. . . .

Sometimes they stared back. Sometimes they looked scared—like they were thinking, *Who is this big freak glaring at me?* Sometimes I thought they looked kind of interested, but maybe that was just my ego running wild.

Either way, nothing. Even when I met the eyes of the girl who was—no contest—the hottest girl in the park and probably in the city, and she stared right back with a speculation that *looked* like interest, I felt nothing. Just the same desperate drive to find a way out of the pain.

As time went on, I started noticing all the wrong things. Bella things. This one's hair was the same color. That one's eyes were sort of shaped the same. This one's cheekbones cut across her face in just the same way. That one had the same little crease between her eyes—which made me wonder what she was worrying about. . . .

That was when I gave up. Because it was beyond stupid to think that I had picked exactly the right place and time and I was going to simply walk into my soul mate just because I was so desperate to.

It wouldn't make sense to find her here, anyway. If Sam was right, the best place to find my genetic match would be in La Push. And, clearly, no one there fit the bill. If Billy was right, then who knew? What made for a stronger wolf?

I wandered back to the car and then slumped against the hood and played with the keys.

Maybe I was what Leah thought she was. Some kind of dead end that shouldn't be passed on to another generation. Or maybe it was just that my life was a big, cruel joke, and there was no escape from the punch line.

"Hey, you okay? Hello? You there, with the stolen car."

It took me a second to realize that the voice was talking to me, and then another second to decide to raise my head.

A familiar-looking girl was staring at me, her expression kind of anxious. I knew why I recognized her face—I'd already catalogued this one. Light red-gold hair, fair skin, a few gold-colored freckles sprinkled across her cheeks and nose, and eyes the color of cinnamon.

"If you're feeling that remorseful over boosting the car," she said, smiling so that a dimple popped out in her chin, "you could always turn yourself in."

"It's borrowed, not stolen," I snapped. My voice sounded horrible—like I'd been crying or something. Embarrassing.

"Sure, *that*'ll hold up in court."

I glowered. "You need something?"

"Not really. I was kidding about the car, you know. It's just that . . . you look really upset about something. Oh, hey, I'm Lizzie." She held out her hand.

I looked at it until she let it fall.

"Anyway . . . ," she said awkwardly, "I was just wondering

if I could help. Seemed like you were looking for someone before." She gestured toward the park and shrugged.

"Yeah."

She waited.

I sighed. "I don't need any help. She's not here."

"Oh. Sorry."

"Me, too," I muttered.

I looked at the girl again. Lizzie. She was pretty. Nice enough to try to help a grouchy stranger who must seem nuts. Why couldn't she be the one? Why did everything have to be so freaking complicated? Nice girl, pretty, and sort of funny. Why not?

"This is a beautiful car," she said. "It's really a shame they're not making them anymore. I mean, the Vantage's body styling is gorgeous, too, but there's just something about the Vanquish. . . ."

Nice girl *who knew cars*. Wow. I stared at her face harder, wishing I knew how to make it work. *C'mon, Jake—imprint already.*

"How's it drive?" she asked.

"Like you wouldn't believe," I told her.

She grinned her one-dimple smile, clearly pleased to have dragged a halfway civil response out of me, and I gave her a reluctant smile back.

But her smile did nothing about the sharp, cutting blades that raked up and down my body. No matter how much I wanted it to, my life was not going to come together like that.

I wasn't in that healthier place where Leah was headed. I wasn't going to be able to fall in love like a normal person. Not when I was bleeding over someone else. Maybe—if it was ten years from now and Bella's heart was long dead and I'd hauled myself through the whole grieving process and come out in one piece again—maybe then I could offer Lizzie a ride in a fast car and talk makes and models and get to know something about her and see if I liked her as a person. But that wasn't going to happen now.

Magic wasn't going to save me. I was just going to have to take the torture like a man. Suck it up.

Lizzie waited, maybe hoping I was going to offer her that ride. Or maybe not.

"I'd better get this car back to the guy I borrowed it from," I muttered.

She smiled again. "Glad to hear you're going straight."

"Yeah, you convinced me."

She watched me get in the car, still sort of concerned. I probably looked like someone who was about to drive off a cliff. Which maybe I would've, if that kind of move'd work for a werewolf. She waved once, her eyes trailing after the car.

At first, I drove more sanely on the way back. I wasn't in a rush. I didn't want to go where I was going. Back to that house, back to that forest. Back to the pain I'd run from. Back to being absolutely alone with it.

Okay, that was melodramatic. I wouldn't be *all* alone, but that was a bad thing. Leah and Seth would have to suffer with me. I was glad Seth wouldn't have to suffer long. Kid didn't deserve to have his peace of mind ruined. Leah didn't, either, but at least it was something she understood. Nothing new about pain for Leah.

I sighed big as I thought about what Leah wanted from me, because I knew now that she was going to get it. I was still pissed at her, but I couldn't ignore the fact that I could make her life easier. And—now that I knew her better—I thought she would probably do this for me, if our positions were reversed.

It would be interesting, at the very least, and strange, too, to have Leah as a companion—as a friend. We were going to get under each other's skin a lot, that was for sure. She wouldn't be one to let me wallow, but I thought that was a good thing. I'd probably need someone to kick my butt now and then. But when it came right down to it, she was really the only friend who had any chance of understanding what I was going through now.

I thought of the hunt this morning, and how close our minds had been for that one moment in time. It hadn't been a bad thing. Different. A little scary, a little awkward. But also nice in a weird way.

I didn't have to be all alone.

And I knew Leah was strong enough to face with me the months that were coming. Months and years. It made me tired to think about it. I felt like I was staring out across an ocean that I was going to have to swim from shore to shore before I could rest again.

So much time coming, and then so *little* time before it started. Before I was flung into that ocean. Three and a half more days, and here I was, wasting that little bit of time I had.

I started driving too fast again.

I saw Sam and Jared, one on either side of the road like sentinels, as I raced up the road toward Forks. They were well hidden in the thick branches, but I was expecting them, and I knew what to look for. I nodded as I blew past them, not bothering to wonder what they made of my day trip.

I nodded to Leah and Seth, too, as I cruised up the Cullens' driveway. It was starting to get dark, and the clouds were thick on this side of the sound, but I saw their eyes glitter in the glow of the headlights. I would explain to them later. There'd be plenty of time for that.

It was a surprise to find Edward waiting for me in the garage. I hadn't seen him away from Bella in days. I could tell from his face that nothing bad had happened to her. In fact, he looked more peaceful than before. My stomach tightened as I remembered where that peace came from.

It was too bad that—with all my brooding—I'd forgotten to wreck the car. Oh well. I probably wouldn't have been able to stand hurting *this* car, anyway. Maybe he'd guessed as much, and that's why he'd lent it to me in the first place.

"A few things, Jacob," he said as soon as I cut the engine.

I took a deep breath and held it for a minute. Then, slowly, I got out of the car and threw the keys to him.

"Thanks for the loan," I said sourly. Apparently, it would have to be repaid. "What do you want *now*?"

"Firstly . . . I know how averse you are to using your authority with your pack, but . . ."

I blinked, astonished that he would even dream of starting in on this one. "What?"

"If you can't or won't control Leah, then I—"

"Leah?" I interrupted, speaking through my teeth. "What happened?"

Edward's face was hard. "She came up to see why you'd left so abruptly. I tried to explain. I suppose it might not have come out right."

"What did she do?"

"She phased to her human form and—"

"Really?" I interrupted again, shocked this time. I couldn't process that. Leah letting her guard down right in the mouth of the enemy's lair?

"She wanted to . . . *speak* to Bella."

"To *Bella*?"

Edward got all hissy then. "I won't let Bella be upset like that again. I don't care how justified Leah thinks she is! I didn't hurt her—of course I wouldn't—but I'll throw her out of the house if it happens again. I'll launch her right across the river—"

"Hold *on*. What did she *say*?" None of this was making any sense.

Edward took a deep breath, composing himself. "Leah was unnecessarily harsh. I'm not going to pretend that I understand why Bella is unable to let go of you, but I do know that she does not behave this way to hurt you. She suffers a great deal over the pain she's inflicting on you, and on me, by asking you to stay. What Leah said was uncalled for. Bella's been crying—"

"Wait—Leah was yelling at Bella about *me*?"

He nodded one sharp nod. "You were quite vehemently championed."

Whoa. "I didn't ask her to do that."

"I know."

I rolled my eyes. Of course he knew. He knew everything.

But that was really something about Leah. Who would have believed it? Leah walking into the bloodsuckers' place *human* to complain about how *I* was being treated.

"I can't promise to control Leah," I told him. "I won't do that. But I'll talk to her, okay? And I don't think there'll be a repeat. Leah's not one to hold back, so she probably got it all off her chest today."

"I would say so."

"Anyway, I'll talk to Bella about it, too. She doesn't need to feel bad. This one's on me."

"I already told her that."

"Of course you did. Is she okay?"

"She's sleeping now. Rose is with her."

So the psycho was "Rose" now. He'd completely crossed over to the dark side.

He ignored that thought, continuing with a more complete answer to my question. "She's . . . better in some ways. Aside from Leah's tirade and the resulting guilt."

Better. Because Edward was hearing the monster and everything was all lovey-dovey now. Fantastic.

"It's a bit more than that," he murmured. "Now that I can make out the child's thoughts, it's apparent that he or she has remarkably developed mental facilities. He can understand us, to an extent."

My mouth fell open. "Are you *serious*?"

"Yes. He seems to have a vague sense of what hurts her now. He's trying to avoid that, as much as possible. He . . . *loves* her. Already."

I stared at Edward, feeling sort of like my eyes might pop out of their sockets. Underneath that disbelief, I could see right away that this was the critical factor. This was what had changed Edward—that the monster had convinced him of this *love*. He couldn't hate what loved Bella. It was probably why he couldn't hate me, either. There was a big difference, though. I wasn't killing her.

Edward went on, acting like he hadn't heard all that. "The progress, I believe, is more than we'd judged. When Carlisle returns—"

"They're not back?" I cut in sharply. I thought of Sam and Jared, watching the road. Would they get curious as to what was going on?

"Alice and Jasper are. Carlisle sent all the blood he was able to acquire, but it wasn't as much as he was hoping for—Bella will use up this supply in another day the way her appetite has grown. Carlisle stayed to try another source. I don't think that's necessary now, but he wants to be covered for any eventuality."

"Why isn't it necessary? If she needs more?"

I could tell he was watching and listening to my reaction carefully as he explained. "I'm trying to persuade Carlisle to deliver the baby as soon as he is back."

"What?"

"The child seems to be attempting to avoid rough movements, but it's difficult. He's become too big. It's madness to wait, when he's clearly developed beyond what Carlisle had guessed. Bella's too fragile to delay."

I kept getting my legs knocked out from under me. First, counting on Edward's hatred of the thing so much. Now, I'd realized that I thought of those four days as a sure thing. I'd banked on them.

The endless ocean of grief that waited stretched out before me.

I tried to catch my breath.

Edward waited. I stared at his face while I recovered, recognizing another change there.

"You think she's going to make it," I whispered.

"Yes. That was the other thing I wanted to talk to you about."

I couldn't say anything. After a minute, he went on.

"Yes," he said again. "Waiting, as we have been, for the child to be ready, that was insanely dangerous. At any moment it could have been too late. But if we're proactive about this, if we act quickly, I see no reason why it should not go well. Knowing the child's mind is unbelievably helpful. Thankfully, Bella and Rose agree with me. Now that I've convinced them it's safe for the child if we proceed, there's nothing to keep this from working."

"When will Carlisle be back?" I asked, still whispering. I hadn't got my breath back yet.

"By noon tomorrow."

My knees buckled. I had to grab the car to hold myself up. Edward reached out like he was offering support, but then he thought better of it and dropped his hands.

"I'm sorry," he whispered. "I am truly sorry for the pain this causes you, Jacob. Though you hate me, I must admit that I don't feel the same about you. I think of you as a . . . a brother in many ways. A comrade in arms, at the very least. I regret your suffering more than you realize. But Bella *is* going to survive"—when he said that his voice was fierce, even violent—"and I know that's what really matters to you."

He was probably right. It was hard to tell. My head was spinning.

"So I hate to do this now, while you're already dealing with too much, but, clearly, there is little time. I have to ask you for something—to beg, if I must."

"I don't have anything left," I choked out.

He lifted his hand again, as if to put it on my shoulder, but then let it drop like before and sighed.

"I know how much you have given," he said quietly. "But this is something you *do* have, and only you. I'm asking this of the true Alpha, Jacob. I'm asking this of Ephraim's heir."

I was way past being able to respond.

"I want your permission to deviate from what we agreed to in our treaty with Ephraim. I want you to grant us an exception. I want your permission to save her life. You know I'll do it anyway, but I don't want to break faith with you if there is any way to avoid it. We never intended to go back on our word, and we don't do it lightly now. I want your understanding, Jacob, because you know exactly why we do this. I want the alliance between our families to survive when this is over."

I tried to swallow. *Sam*, I thought. *It's Sam you want.*

"No. Sam's authority is assumed. It belongs to you. You'll never take it from him, but no one can rightfully agree to what I'm asking except for *you*."

It's not my decision.

"It is, Jacob, and you know it. Your word on this will condemn us or absolve us. Only you can give this to me."

I can't think. I don't know.

"We don't have much time." He glanced back toward the house.

No, there was no time. My few days had become a few hours.

I don't know. Let me think. Just give me a minute here, okay?

"Yes."

I started walking to the house, and he followed. Crazy how easy it was, walking through the dark with a vampire right beside me. It didn't feel unsafe, or even uncomfortable, really. It felt like walking next to anybody. Well, anybody who smelled bad.

There was a movement in the brush at the edge of the big lawn, and then a low whimper. Seth shrugged through the ferns and loped over to us.

"Hey, kid," I muttered.

He dipped his head, and I patted his shoulder.

"S'all cool," I lied. "I'll tell you about it later. Sorry to take off on you like that."

He grinned at me.

"Hey, tell your sister to back off now, okay? Enough."

Seth nodded once.

I shoved against his shoulder this time. "Get back to work. I'll spell you in a bit."

Seth leaned against me, shoving back, and then he galloped into the trees.

"He has one of the purest, sincerest, *kindest* minds I've ever heard," Edward murmured when he was out of sight. "You're lucky to have his thoughts to share."

"I know that," I grunted.

We started toward the house, and both of our heads snapped up when we heard the sound of someone sucking through a straw. Edward was in a hurry then. He darted up the porch stairs and was gone.

"Bella, love, I thought you were sleeping," I heard him say. "I'm sorry, I wouldn't have left."

"Don't worry. I just got so thirsty—it woke me up. It's a good thing Carlisle is bringing more. This kid is going to need it when he gets out of me."

"True. That's a good point."

"I wonder if he'll want anything else," she mused.

"I suppose we'll find out."

I walked through the door.

Alice said, "Finally," and Bella's eyes flashed to me. That infuriating, irresistible smile broke across her face for one second. Then it faltered, and her face fell. Her lips puckered, like she was trying not to cry.

I wanted to punch Leah right in her stupid mouth.

"Hey, Bells," I said quickly. "How ya doing?"

"I'm fine," she said.

"Big day today, huh? Lots of new stuff."

"You don't have to do that, Jacob."

"Don't know what you're talking about," I said, going to sit on the arm of the sofa by her head. Edward had the floor there already.

She gave me a reproachful look. "I'm *so* s—" she started to say.

I pinched her lips together between my thumb and finger.

"Jake," she mumbled, trying to pull my hand away. Her attempt was so weak it was hard to believe that she was really trying.

I shook my head. "You can talk when you're not being stupid."

"Fine, I won't say it," it sounded like she mumbled.

I pulled my hand away.

"Sorry!" she finished quickly, and then grinned.

I rolled my eyes and then smiled back at her.

When I stared into her eyes, I saw everything that I'd been looking for in the park.

Tomorrow, she'd be someone else. But hopefully alive, and that was what counted, right? She'd look at me with the same eyes, sort of. Smile with the same lips, almost. She'd still know me better than anyone who didn't have full access to the inside of my head.

Leah might be an interesting companion, maybe even a true friend—someone who would stand up for me. But she wasn't my *best* friend the way that Bella was. Aside from the impossible love I felt for Bella, there was also that other bond, and it ran bone deep.

Tomorrow, she'd be my enemy. Or she'd be my ally. And, apparently, that distinction was up to me.

I sighed.

Fine! I thought, giving up the very last thing I had to give. It made me feel hollow. *Go ahead. Save her. As Ephraim's heir, you have my permission, my word, that this will not violate the treaty. The others will just have to blame me. You were right— they can't deny that it's my right to agree to this.*

"Thank you." Edward's whisper was low enough that Bella didn't hear anything. But the words were so fervent that, from the corner of my eye, I saw the other vampires turning to stare.

"So," Bella asked, working to be casual. "How was your day?"

"Great. Went for a drive. Hung out in the park."

"Sounds nice."

"Sure, sure."

Suddenly, she made a face. "Rose?" she asked.

I heard Blondie chuckle. "Again?"

"I think I've drunk two gallons in the last hour," Bella explained.

Edward and I both got out of the way while Rosalie came to lift Bella from the couch and take her to the bathroom.

"Can I walk?" Bella asked. "My legs are so stiff."

"Are you sure?" Edward asked.

"Rose'll catch me if I trip over my feet. Which could happen pretty easily, since I can't see them."

Rosalie set Bella carefully on her feet, keeping her hands right at Bella's shoulders. Bella stretched her arms out in front of her, wincing a little.

"That feels good," she sighed. "Ugh, but I'm huge."

She really was. Her stomach was its own continent.

"One more day," she said, and patted her stomach.

I couldn't help the pain that shot through me in a sudden, stabbing burst, but I tried to keep it off my face. I could hide it for one more day, right?

"All righty, then. Whoops—oh, no!"

The cup Bella had left on the sofa tumbled to one side, the dark red blood spilling out onto the pale fabric.

Automatically, though three other hands beat her there, Bella bent over, reaching out to catch it.

There was the strangest, muffled ripping sound from the center of her body.

"Oh!" she gasped.

And then she went totally limp, slumping toward the floor. Rosalie caught her in the same instant, before she could fall. Edward was there, too, hands out, the mess on the sofa forgotten.

"Bella?" he asked, and then his eyes unfocused, and panic shot across his features.

A half second later, Bella screamed.

It was not just a scream, it was a blood-curdling shriek of agony. The horrifying sound cut off with a gurgle, and her eyes rolled back into her head. Her body twitched, arched in Rosalie's arms, and then Bella vomited a fountain of blood.

18. THERE ARE NO WORDS FOR THIS.

BELLA'S BODY, STREAMING WITH RED, STARTED TO TWITCH, jerking around in Rosalie's arms like she was being electrocuted. All the while, her face was blank—unconscious. It was the wild thrashing from inside the center of her body that moved her. As she convulsed, sharp snaps and cracks kept time with the spasms.

Rosalie and Edward were frozen for the shortest half second, and then they broke. Rosalie whipped Bella's body into her arms, and, shouting so fast it was hard to separate the individual words, she and Edward shot up the staircase to the second floor.

I sprinted after them.

"Morphine!" Edward yelled at Rosalie.

"Alice—get Carlisle on the phone!" Rosalie screeched.

The room I followed them to looked like an emergency ward set up in the middle of a library. The lights were brilliant and white. Bella was on a table under the glare, skin ghostly in the spotlight. Her body flopped, a fish on the sand. Rosalie pinned Bella down, yanking and ripping her clothes out of the way, while Edward stabbed a syringe into her arm.

How many times had I imagined her naked? Now I couldn't look. I was afraid to have these memories in my head.

"What's *happening*, Edward?"

"He's suffocating!"

"The placenta must have detached!"

Somewhere in this, Bella came around. She responded to their words with a shriek that clawed at my eardrums.

"Get him OUT!" she screamed. "He can't BREATHE! Do it NOW!"

I saw the red spots pop out when her scream broke the blood vessels in her eyes.

"The morphine—," Edward growled.

"NO! NOW—!" Another gush of blood choked off what she was shrieking. He held her head up, desperately trying to clear her mouth so that she could breathe again.

Alice darted into the room and clipped a little blue earpiece under Rosalie's hair. Then Alice backed away, her gold eyes wide and burning, while Rosalie hissed frantically into the phone.

In the bright light, Bella's skin seemed more purple and

black than it was white. Deep red was seeping beneath the skin over the huge, shuddering bulge of her stomach. Rosalie's hand came up with a scalpel.

"Let the morphine spread!" Edward shouted at her.

"There's no time," Rosalie hissed. "He's dying!"

Her hand came down on Bella's stomach, and vivid red spouted out from where she pierced the skin. It was like a bucket being turned over, a faucet twisted to full. Bella jerked, but didn't scream. She was still choking.

And then Rosalie lost her focus. I saw the expression on her face shift, saw her lips pull back from her teeth and her black eyes glint with thirst.

"No, Rose!" Edward roared, but his hands were trapped, trying to prop Bella upright so she could breathe.

I launched myself at Rosalie, jumping across the table without bothering to phase. As I hit her stone body, knocking her toward the door, I felt the scalpel in her hand stab deep into my left arm. My right palm smashed against her face, locking her jaw and blocking her airways.

I used my grip on Rosalie's face to swing her body out so that I could land a solid kick in her gut; it was like kicking concrete. She flew into the door frame, buckling one side of it. The little speaker in her ear crackled into pieces. Then Alice was there, yanking her by the throat to get her into the hall.

And I had to give it to Blondie—she didn't put up an ounce of fight. She *wanted* us to win. She let me trash her like that, to save Bella. Well, to save the thing.

I ripped the blade out of my arm.

"Alice, get her out of here!" Edward shouted. "Take her to Jasper and *keep* her there! Jacob, I need you!"

I didn't watch Alice finish the job. I wheeled back to the operating table, where Bella was turning blue, her eyes wide and staring.

"CPR?" Edward growled at me, fast and demanding.

"Yes!"

I judged his face swiftly, looking for any sign that he was going to react like Rosalie. There was nothing but single-minded ferocity.

"Get her breathing! I've got to get him out before—"

Another shattering crack inside her body, the loudest yet, so loud that we both froze in shock waiting for her answering shriek. Nothing. Her legs, which had been curled up in agony, now went limp, sprawling out in an unnatural way.

"Her spine," he choked in horror.

"Get it *out* of her!" I snarled, flinging the scalpel at him. "She won't feel anything now!"

And then I bent over her head. Her mouth looked clear, so I pressed mine to hers and blew a lungful of air into it. I felt her twitching body expand, so there was nothing blocking her throat.

Her lips tasted like blood.

I could hear her heart, thumping unevenly. *Keep it going,* I thought fiercely at her, blowing another gust of air into her body. *You promised. Keep your heart beating.*

I heard the soft, wet sound of the scalpel across her stomach. More blood dripping to the floor.

The next sound jolted through me, unexpected, terrifying. Like metal being shredded apart. The sound brought back the fight in the clearing so many months ago, the tearing sound of the newborns being ripped apart. I glanced over to see Edward's face pressed against the bulge. Vampire teeth—a surefire way to cut through vampire skin.

I shuddered as I blew more air into Bella.

She coughed back at me, her eyes blinking, rolling blindly.

"You stay with *me* now, Bella!" I yelled at her. "Do you hear me? Stay! You're not leaving me. Keep your heart beating!"

Her eyes wheeled, looking for me, or him, but seeing nothing.

I stared into them anyway, keeping my gaze locked there.

And then her body was suddenly still under my hands, though her breathing picked up roughly and her heart continued to thud. I realized the stillness meant that it was over. The internal beating was over. It must be out of her.

It was.

Edward whispered, "Renesmee."

So Bella'd been wrong. It wasn't the boy she'd imagined. No big surprise there. What *hadn't* she been wrong about?

I didn't look away from her red-spotted eyes, but I felt her hands lift weakly.

"Let me . . . ," she croaked in a broken whisper. "Give her to me."

I guess I should have known that he would always give her what she wanted, no matter how stupid her request might be. But I didn't dream he would listen to her now. So I didn't think to stop him.

Something warm touched my arm. That right there should have caught my attention. Nothing felt warm to me.

But I couldn't look away from Bella's face. She blinked and then stared, finally seeing something. She moaned out a strange, weak croon.

"Renes . . . mee. So . . . beautiful."

And then she gasped—gasped in pain.

By the time I looked, it was too late. Edward had snatched the warm, bloody thing out of her limp arms. My eyes flickered across her skin. It was red with blood—the blood that had flowed from her mouth, the blood smeared all over the creature, and fresh blood welling out of a tiny double-crescent bite mark just over her left breast.

"No, Renesmee," Edward murmured, like he was teaching the monster manners.

I didn't look at him or it. I watched only Bella as her eyes rolled back into her head.

With a last dull *ga-lump*, her heart faltered and went silent.

She missed maybe half of one beat, and then my hands were on her chest, doing compressions. I counted in my head, trying to keep the rhythm steady. One. Two. Three. Four.

Breaking away for a second, I blew another lungful of air into her.

I couldn't see anymore. My eyes were wet and blurry. But I was hyperaware of the sounds in the room. The unwilling *glug-glug* of her heart under my demanding hands, the pounding of my own heart, and another—a fluttering beat that was too fast, too light. I couldn't place it.

I forced more air down Bella's throat.

"What are you waiting for?" I choked out breathlessly, pumping her heart again. One. Two. Three. Four.

"Take the baby," Edward said urgently.

"Throw it out the window." One. Two. Three. Four.

"Give her to me," a low voice chimed from the doorway.

Edward and I snarled at the same time.

One. Two. Three. Four.

"I've got it under control," Rosalie promised. "Give me the baby, Edward. I'll take care of her until Bella . . ."

I breathed for Bella again while the exchange took place. The fluttering *thumpa-thumpa-thumpa* faded away with distance.

"Move your hands, Jacob."

I looked up from Bella's white eyes, still pumping her heart for her. Edward had a syringe in his hand—all silver, like it was made from steel.

"What's that?"

His stone hand knocked mine out of the way. There was a tiny crunch as his blow broke my little finger. In the same second, he shoved the needle straight into her heart.

"My venom," he answered as he pushed the plunger down.

I heard the jolt in her heart, like he'd shocked her with paddles.

"Keep it moving," he ordered. His voice was ice, was dead. Fierce and unthinking. Like he was a machine.

I ignored the healing ache in my finger and started pumping her heart again. It was harder, as if her blood was congealing there—thicker and slower. While I pushed the now-viscous blood through her arteries, I watched what he was doing.

It was like he was kissing her, brushing his lips at her throat, at her wrists, into the crease at the inside of her arm.

But I could hear the lush tearing of her skin as his teeth bit through, again and again, forcing venom into her system at as many points as possible. I saw his pale tongue sweep along the bleeding gashes, but before this could make me either sick or angry, I realized what he was doing. Where his tongue washed the venom over her skin, it sealed shut. Holding the poison and the blood inside her body.

I blew more air into her mouth, but there was nothing there. Just the lifeless rise of her chest in response. I kept pumping her heart, counting, while he worked manically over her, trying to put her back together. All the king's horses and all the king's men . . .

But there was nothing there, just me, just him.

Working over a corpse.

Because that's all that was left of the girl we both loved. This broken, bled-out, mangled corpse. We couldn't put Bella together again.

I knew it was too late. I knew she was dead. I knew it for sure because the pull was gone. I didn't feel any reason to be here beside her. *She* wasn't here anymore. So this body had no more draw for me. The senseless need to be near her had vanished.

Or maybe *moved* was the better word. It seemed like I felt the pull from the opposite direction now. From down the stairs, out the door. The longing to get away from here and never, ever come back.

"Go, then," he snapped, and he hit my hands out of the way again, taking my place this time. Three fingers broken, it felt like.

I straightened them numbly, not minding the throb of pain.

He pushed her dead heart faster than I had.

"She's not dead," he growled. "She's going to be fine."

I wasn't sure he was talking to me anymore.

Turning away, leaving him with his dead, I walked slowly to the door. So slowly. I couldn't make my feet move faster.

This was it, then. The ocean of pain. The other shore so far away across the boiling water that I couldn't imagine it, much less see it.

I felt empty again, now that I'd lost my purpose. Saving Bella had been my fight for so long now. And she wouldn't be saved. She'd willingly sacrificed herself to be torn apart by that monster's young, and so the fight was lost. It was all over.

I shuddered at the sound coming from behind me as I plodded down the stairs—the sound of a dead heart being forced to thud.

I wanted to somehow pour bleach inside my head and let it fry my brain. To burn away the images left from Bella's final minutes. I'd take the brain damage if I could get rid of that—the screaming, the bleeding, the unbearable crunching and snapping as the newborn monster tore through her from the inside out. . . .

I wanted to sprint away, to take the stairs ten at a time and race out the door, but my feet were heavy as iron and my body was more tired than it had ever been before. I shuffled down the stairs like a crippled old man.

I rested at the bottom step, gathering my strength to get out the door.

Rosalie was on the clean end of the white sofa, her back

to me, cooing and murmuring to the blanket-wrapped thing in her arms. She must have heard me pause, but she ignored me, caught up in her moment of stolen motherhood. Maybe she would be happy now. Rosalie had what she wanted, and Bella would never come to take the creature from her. I wondered if that's what the poisonous blonde had been hoping for all along.

She held something dark in her hands, and there was a greedy sucking sound coming from the tiny murderer she held.

The scent of blood in the air. Human blood. Rosalie was feeding it. Of course it would want blood. What else would you feed the kind of monster that would brutally mutilate its own mother? It might as well have been drinking Bella's blood. Maybe it was.

My strength came back to me as I listened to the sound of the little executioner feeding.

Strength and hate and heat—red heat washing through my head, burning but erasing nothing. The images in my head were fuel, building up the inferno but refusing to be consumed. I felt the tremors rock me from head to toe, and I did not try to stop them.

Rosalie was totally absorbed in the creature, paying no attention to me at all. She wouldn't be quick enough to stop me, distracted as she was.

Sam had been right. The thing was an aberration—its existence went against nature. A black, soulless demon. Something that had no right to be.

Something that had to be destroyed.

It seemed like the pull had not been leading to the door

after all. I could feel it now, encouraging me, tugging me forward. Pushing me to finish this, to cleanse the world of this abomination.

Rosalie would try to kill me when the creature was dead, and I would fight back. I wasn't sure if I would have time to finish her before the others came to help. Maybe, maybe not. I didn't much care either way.

I didn't care if the wolves, either set, avenged me or called the Cullens' justice fair. None of that mattered. All I cared about was my own justice. *My* revenge. The thing that had killed Bella would not live another minute longer.

If Bella'd survived, she would have hated me for this. She would have wanted to kill me personally.

But I didn't care. She didn't care what she had done to me—letting herself be slaughtered like an animal. Why should I take her feelings into account?

And then there was Edward. He must be too busy now—too far gone in his insane denial, trying to reanimate a corpse—to listen to my plans.

So I wouldn't get the chance to keep my promise to him, unless—and it was not a wager *I'd* put money on—I managed to win the fight against Rosalie, Jasper, and Alice, three on one. But even if I did win, I didn't think I had it in me to kill Edward.

Because I didn't have enough compassion for that. Why should I let him get away from what he'd done? Wouldn't it be more fair—more satisfying—to let him live with nothing, nothing at all?

It made me almost smile, as filled with hate as I was, to imagine it. No Bella. No killer spawn. And also missing as many members of his family as I was able to take down. Of course, he could probably put those back together, since I wouldn't be around to burn them. Unlike Bella, who would never be whole again.

I wondered if the creature could be put back together. I doubted it. It was part Bella, too—so it must have inherited some of her vulnerability. I could hear that in the tiny, thrumming beat of its heart.

Its heart was beating. Hers wasn't.

Only a second had passed as I made these easy decisions.

The trembling was getting tighter and faster. I coiled myself, preparing to spring at the blond vampire and rip the murderous thing from her arms with my teeth.

Rosalie cooed at the creature again, setting the empty metal bottle-thing aside and lifting the creature into the air to nuzzle her face against its cheek.

Perfect. The new position was perfect for my strike. I leaned forward and felt the heat begin to change me while the pull toward the killer grew—it was stronger than I'd ever felt it before, so strong it reminded me of an Alpha's command, like it would crush me if I didn't obey.

This time I *wanted* to obey.

The murderer stared past Rosalie's shoulder at me, its gaze more focused than any newborn creature's gaze should be.

Warm brown eyes, the color of milk chocolate—the exact same color that Bella's had been.

My shaking jerked to a stop; heat flooded through me, stronger than before, but it was a new kind of heat—not a burning.

It was a glowing.

Everything inside me came undone as I stared at the tiny porcelain face of the half-vampire, half-human baby. All the lines that held me to my life were sliced apart in swift cuts, like clipping the strings to a bunch of balloons. Everything that made me who I was—my love for the dead girl upstairs, my love for my father, my loyalty to my new pack, the love for my other brothers, my hatred for my enemies, my home, my name, my *self*—disconnected from me in that second— *snip, snip, snip*—and floated up into space.

I was not left drifting. A new string held me where I was.

Not one string, but a million. Not strings, but steel cables. A million steel cables all tying me to one thing—to the very center of the universe.

I could see that now—how the universe swirled around this one point. I'd never seen the symmetry of the universe before, but now it was plain.

The gravity of the earth no longer tied me to the place where I stood.

It was the baby girl in the blond vampire's arms that held me here now.

Renesmee.

From upstairs, there was a new sound. The only sound that could touch me in this endless instant.

A frantic pounding, a racing beat . . .

A changing heart.

BOOK THREE

✦✦

bella

CONTENTS

⊰⊱

PREFACE   367

19. BURNING   369

20. NEW   387

21. FIRST HUNT   407

22. PROMISED   428

23. MEMORIES   452

24. SURPRISE   471

25. FAVOR   486

26. SHINY   512

27. TRAVEL PLANS   525

28. THE FUTURE   540

29. DEFECTION   554

30. IRRESISTIBLE   572

31. TALENTED   594

32. COMPANY   607

33. FORGERY   629

34. DECLARED   649

35. DEADLINE   665

36. BLOODLUST   679

37. CONTRIVANCES   701

38. POWER   725

39. THE HAPPILY EVER AFTER   742

Personal affection is a luxury you can have only after all your enemies are eliminated. Until then, everyone you love is a hostage, sapping your courage and corrupting your judgment.

Orson Scott Card
Empire

PREFACE

N<small>O LONGER JUST A NIGHTMARE, THE LINE OF BLACK</small> advanced on us through the icy mist stirred up by their feet.

We're going to die, I thought in panic. I was desperate for the precious one I guarded, but even to think of that was a lapse in attention I could not afford.

They ghosted closer, their dark robes billowing slightly with the movement. I saw their hands curl into bone-colored claws. They drifted apart, angling to come at us from all sides. We were outnumbered. It was over.

And then, like a burst of light from a flash, the whole scene was different. Yet nothing changed—the Volturi still stalked toward us, poised to kill. All that really changed was how the picture looked to me. Suddenly, I was hungry for it. I *wanted* them to charge. The panic changed to bloodlust as I crouched forward, a smile on my face, and a growl ripped through my bared teeth.

19. BURNING

THE PAIN WAS BEWILDERING.

Exactly that—I was bewildered. I couldn't understand, couldn't make sense of what was happening.

My body tried to reject the pain, and I was sucked again and again into a blackness that cut out whole seconds or maybe even minutes of the agony, making it that much harder to keep up with reality.

I tried to separate them.

Non-reality was black, and it didn't hurt so much.

Reality was red, and it felt like I was being sawed in half, hit by a bus, punched by a prize fighter, trampled by bulls, and submerged in acid, all at the same time.

Reality was feeling my body twist and flip when I couldn't possibly move because of the pain.

Reality was knowing there was something so much more important than all this torture, and not being able to remember what it was.

Reality had come on so fast.

One moment, everything was as it should have been. Surrounded by people I loved. Smiles. Somehow, unlikely as it was, it seemed like I was about to get everything I'd been fighting for.

And then one tiny, inconsequential thing had gone wrong.

I'd watched as my cup tilted, dark blood spilling out and staining the perfect white, and I'd lurched toward the accident reflexively. I'd seen the other, faster hands, but my body had continued to reach, to stretch. . . .

Inside me, something had yanked the opposite direction.

Ripping. Breaking. Agony.

The darkness had taken over, and then washed away to a wave of torture. I couldn't breathe—I had drowned once before, and this was different; it was too hot in my throat.

Pieces of me shattering, snapping, slicing apart. . . .

More blackness.

Voices, this time, shouting, as the pain came back.

"The placenta must have detached!"

Something sharper than knives ripped through me—the words, making sense in spite of the other tortures. *Detached placenta*—I knew what that meant. It meant that my baby was dying inside me.

"Get him out!" I screamed to Edward. Why hadn't he done it yet? "He can't breathe! Do it now!"

"The morphine—"

He wanted to wait, to give me painkillers, while our baby was dying?!

"No! Now—," I choked, unable to finish.

Black spots covered the light in the room as a cold point of new pain stabbed icily into my stomach. It felt wrong— I struggled automatically to protect my womb, my baby, my little Edward Jacob, but I was weak. My lungs ached, oxygen burned away.

The pain faded away again, though I clung to it now. My baby, my baby, dying. . . .

How long had passed? Seconds or minutes? The pain was gone. Numb. I couldn't feel. I still couldn't see, either, but I could hear. There was air in my lungs again, scraping in rough bubbles up and down my throat.

"You stay with *me* now, Bella! Do you hear me? Stay! You're not leaving me. Keep your heart beating!"

Jacob? Jacob, still here, still trying to save me.

Of course, I wanted to tell him. Of course I would keep my heart beating. Hadn't I promised them both?

I tried to feel my heart, to find it, but I was so lost inside my own body. I couldn't feel the things I should, and nothing felt in the right place. I blinked and I found my eyes. I could see the light. Not what I was looking for, but better than nothing.

As my eyes struggled to adjust, Edward whispered, "Renesmee."

Renesmee?

Not the pale and perfect son of my imagination? I felt a moment of shock. And then a flood of warmth.

Renesmee.

I willed my lips to move, willed the bubbles of air to turn into whispers on my tongue. I forced my numb hands to reach.

"Let me . . . Give her to me."

The light danced, shattering off Edward's crystal hands. The sparkles were tinged with red, with the blood that covered his skin. And more red in his hands. Something small and struggling, dripping with blood. He touched the warm body to my weak arms, almost like I was holding her. Her wet skin was hot—as hot as Jacob's.

My eyes focused; suddenly everything was absolutely clear.

Renesmee did not cry, but she breathed in quick, startled pants. Her eyes were open, her expression so shocked it was almost funny. The little, perfectly round head was covered in a thick layer of matted, bloody curls. Her irises were a familiar—but astonishing—chocolate brown. Under the blood, her skin looked pale, a creamy ivory. All besides her cheeks, which flamed with color.

Her tiny face was so absolutely perfect that it stunned me. She was even more beautiful than her father. Unbelievable. Impossible.

"Renesmee," I whispered. "So . . . beautiful."

The impossible face suddenly smiled—a wide, deliberate smile. Behind the shell-pink lips was a full complement of snowy milk teeth.

She leaned her head down, against my chest, burrowing

against the warmth. Her skin was warm and silky, but it didn't give the way mine did.

Then there was pain again—just one warm slash of it. I gasped.

And she was gone. My angel-faced baby was nowhere. I couldn't see or feel her.

No! I wanted to shout. *Give her back to me!*

But the weakness was too much. My arms felt like empty rubber hoses for a moment, and then they felt like nothing at all. I couldn't feel them. I couldn't feel *me*.

The blackness rushed over my eyes more solidly than before. Like a thick blindfold, firm and fast. Covering not just my eyes but also my *self* with a crushing weight. It was exhausting to push against it. I knew it would be so much easier to give in. To let the blackness push me down, down, down to a place where there was no pain and no weariness and no worry and no fear.

If it had only been for myself, I wouldn't have been able to struggle very long. I was only human, with no more than human strength. I'd been trying to keep up with the supernatural for too long, like Jacob had said.

But this wasn't just about me.

If I did the easy thing now, let the black nothingness erase me, I would hurt them.

Edward. Edward. My life and his were twisted into a single strand. Cut one, and you cut both. If he were gone, I would not be able to live through that. If I were gone, he wouldn't live through it, either. And a world without Edward seemed completely pointless. Edward *had* to exist.

Jacob—who'd said goodbye to me over and over but kept

coming back when I needed him. Jacob, who I'd wounded so many times it was criminal. Would I hurt him again, the worst way yet? He'd stayed for me, despite everything. Now all he asked was that I stay for him.

But it was so dark here that I couldn't see either of their faces. Nothing seemed real. That made it hard not to give up.

I kept pushing against the black, though, almost a reflex. I wasn't trying to lift it. I was just resisting. Not allowing it to crush me completely. I wasn't Atlas, and the black felt as heavy as a planet; I couldn't shoulder it. All I could do was not be entirely obliterated.

It was sort of the pattern to my life—I'd never been strong enough to deal with the things outside my control, to attack the enemies or outrun them. To avoid the pain. Always human and weak, the only thing I'd ever been able to do was keep going. Endure. Survive.

It had been enough up to this point. It would have to be enough today. I would endure this until help came.

I knew Edward would be doing everything he could. He would not give up. Neither would I.

I held the blackness of nonexistence at bay by inches.

It wasn't enough, though—that determination. As the time ground on and on and the darkness gained by tiny eighths and sixteenths of my inches, I needed something more to draw strength from.

I couldn't pull even Edward's face into view. Not Jacob's, not Alice's or Rosalie's or Charlie's or Renée's or Carlisle's or Esme's . . . Nothing. It terrified me, and I wondered if it was too late.

I felt myself slipping—there was nothing to hold on to.

No! I had to survive this. Edward was depending on me. Jacob. Charlie Alice Rosalie Carlisle Renée Esme . . .

Renesmee.

And then, though I still couldn't see anything, suddenly I could *feel* something. Like phantom limbs, I imagined I could feel my arms again. And in them, something small and hard and very, very warm.

My baby. My little nudger.

I had done it. Against the odds, I *had* been strong enough to survive Renesmee, to hold on to her until she was strong enough to live without me.

That spot of heat in my phantom arms felt so real. I clutched it closer. It was exactly where my heart should be. Holding tight the warm memory of my daughter, I knew that I would be able to fight the darkness as long as I needed to.

The warmth beside my heart got more and more real, warmer and warmer. Hotter. The heat was so real it was hard to believe that I was imagining it.

Hotter.

Uncomfortable now. Too hot. Much, much too hot.

Like grabbing the wrong end of a curling iron—my automatic response was to drop the scorching thing in my arms. But there was nothing in my arms. My arms were not curled to my chest. My arms were dead things lying somewhere at my side. The heat was inside me.

The burning grew—rose and peaked and rose again until it surpassed anything I'd ever felt.

I felt the pulse behind the fire raging now in my chest and realized that I'd found my heart again, just in time to wish I never had. To wish that I'd embraced the blackness while I'd still had the chance. I wanted to raise my arms and claw my chest open and rip the heart from it—anything to get rid of this torture. But I couldn't feel my arms, couldn't move one vanished finger.

James, snapping my leg under his foot. That was nothing. That was a soft place to rest on a feather bed. I'd take that now, a hundred times. A hundred snaps. I'd take it and be grateful.

The baby, kicking my ribs apart, breaking her way through me piece by piece. That was nothing. That was floating in a pool of cool water. I'd take it a thousand times. Take it and be grateful.

The fire blazed hotter and I wanted to scream. To beg for someone to kill me now, before I lived one more second in this pain. But I couldn't move my lips. The weight was still there, pressing on me.

I realized it wasn't the darkness holding me down; it was my body. So heavy. Burying me in the flames that were chewing their way out from my heart now, spreading with impossible pain through my shoulders and stomach, scalding their way up my throat, licking at my face.

Why couldn't I move? Why couldn't I scream? This wasn't part of the stories.

My mind was unbearably clear—sharpened by the fierce pain—and I saw the answer almost as soon as I could form the questions.

The morphine.

It seemed like a million deaths ago that we'd discussed it—Edward, Carlisle, and I. Edward and Carlisle had hoped that enough painkillers would help fight the pain of the venom. Carlisle had tried with Emmett, but the venom had burned ahead of the medicine, sealing his veins. There hadn't been time for it to spread.

I'd kept my face smooth and nodded and thanked my rarely lucky stars that Edward could not read my mind.

Because I'd had morphine and venom together in my system before, and I knew the truth. I knew the numbness of the medicine was completely irrelevant while the venom seared through my veins. But there'd been no way I was going to mention that fact. Nothing that would make him more unwilling to change me.

I hadn't guessed that the morphine would have this effect—that it would pin me down and gag me. Hold me paralyzed while I burned.

I knew all the stories. I knew that Carlisle had kept quiet enough to avoid discovery while he burned. I knew that, according to Rosalie, it did no good to scream. And I'd hoped that maybe I could be like Carlisle. That I would believe Rosalie's words and keep my mouth shut. Because I knew that every scream that escaped my lips would torment Edward.

Now it seemed like a hideous joke that I was getting my wish fulfilled.

If I couldn't scream, *how could I tell them to kill me?*

All I wanted was to die. To never have been born. The whole of my existence did not outweigh this pain. Wasn't worth living through it for one more heartbeat.

Let me die, let me die, let me die.

And, for a never-ending space, that was all there was. Just the fiery torture, and my soundless shrieks, pleading for death to come. Nothing else, not even time. So that made it infinite, with no beginning and no end. One infinite moment of pain.

The only change came when suddenly, impossibly, my pain was doubled. The lower half of my body, deadened since before the morphine, was suddenly on fire, too. Some broken connection had been healed—knitted together by the scorching fingers of the flame.

The endless burn raged on.

It could have been seconds or days, weeks or years, but, eventually, time came to mean something again.

Three things happened together, grew from each other so that I didn't know which came first: time restarted, the morphine's weight faded, and I got stronger.

I could feel the control of my body come back to me in increments, and those increments were my first markers of the time passing. I knew it when I was able to twitch my toes and twist my fingers into fists. I knew it, but I did not act on it.

Though the fire did not decrease one tiny degree—in fact, I began to develop a new capacity for experiencing it, a new sensitivity to appreciate, separately, each blistering tongue of flame that licked through my veins—I discovered that I could think around it.

I could remember *why* I shouldn't scream. I could remember the reason why I'd committed to enduring this unendurable agony. I could remember that, though it felt impossible now, there was something that might be worth the torture.

This happened just in time for me to hold on when

the weights left my body. To anyone watching me, there would be no change. But for me, as I struggled to keep the screams and thrashing locked up inside my body, where they couldn't hurt anyone else, it felt like I'd gone from being *tied* to the stake as I burned, to *gripping* that stake to hold myself in the fire.

I had just enough strength to lie there unmoving while I was charred alive.

My hearing got clearer and clearer, and I could count the frantic, pounding beats of my heart to mark the time.

I could count the shallow breaths that gasped through my teeth.

I could count the low, even breaths that came from somewhere close beside me. These moved slowest, so I concentrated on them. They meant the most time passing. More even than a clock's pendulum, those breaths pulled me through the burning seconds toward the end.

I continued to get stronger, my thoughts clearer. When new noises came, I could listen.

There were light footsteps, the whisper of air stirred by an opening door. The footsteps got closer, and I felt pressure against the inside of my wrist. I couldn't feel the coolness of the fingers. The fire blistered away every memory of cool.

"Still no change?"

"None."

The lightest pressure, breath against my scorched skin.

"There's no scent of the morphine left."

"I know."

"Bella? Can you hear me?"

I knew, beyond all doubt, that if I unlocked my teeth I would lose it—I would shriek and screech and writhe and thrash. If I opened my eyes, if I so much as twitched a finger—any change at all would be the end of my control.

"Bella? Bella, love? Can you open your eyes? Can you squeeze my hand?"

Pressure on my fingers. It was harder not to answer this voice, but I stayed paralyzed. I knew that the pain in his voice now was nothing compared to what it *could* be. Right now he only *feared* that I was suffering.

"Maybe . . . Carlisle, maybe I was too late." His voice was muffled; it broke on the word *late.*

My resolve wavered for a second.

"Listen to her heart, Edward. It's stronger than even Emmett's was. I've never heard anything so *vital.* She'll be perfect."

Yes, I was right to keep quiet. Carlisle would reassure him. He didn't need to suffer with me.

"And her—her spine?"

"Her injuries weren't so much worse than Esme's. The venom will heal her as it did Esme."

"But she's so still. I *must* have done something wrong."

"Or something right, Edward. Son, you did everything I could have and more. I'm not sure I would have had the persistence, the faith it took to save her. Stop berating yourself. Bella is going to be fine."

A broken whisper. "She must be in agony."

"We don't know that. She had so much morphine in her system. We don't know the effect that will have on her experience."

Faint pressure inside the crease of my elbow. Another whisper. "Bella, I love you. Bella, I'm sorry."

I wanted so much to answer him, but I wouldn't make his pain worse. Not while I had the strength to hold myself still.

Through all this, the racking fire went right on burning me. But there was so much space in my head now. Room to ponder their conversation, room to remember what had happened, room to look ahead to the future, with still endless room left over to suffer in.

Also room to worry.

Where was my baby? Why wasn't she here? Why weren't they talking about her?

"No, I'm staying right here," Edward whispered, answering an unspoken thought. "They'll sort it out."

"An interesting situation," Carlisle responded. "And I'd thought I'd seen just about everything."

"I'll deal with it later. *We'll* deal with it." Something pressed softly to my blistering palm.

"I'm sure, between the five of us, we can keep it from turning into bloodshed."

Edward sighed. "I don't know which side to take. I'd love to flog them both. Well, later."

"I wonder what Bella will think—whose side she'll take," Carlisle mused.

One low, strained chuckle. "I'm sure she'll surprise me. She always does."

Carlisle's footsteps faded away again, and I was frustrated that there was no further explanation. Were they talking so mysteriously just to annoy me?

I went back to counting Edward's breaths to mark the time.

Ten thousand, nine hundred forty-three breaths later, a

different set of footsteps whispered into the room. Lighter. More . . . rhythmic.

Strange that I could distinguish the minute differences between footsteps that I'd never been able to hear at all before today.

"How much longer?" Edward asked.

"It won't be long now," Alice told him. "See how clear she's becoming? I can see her so much better." She sighed.

"Still feeling a little bitter?"

"Yes, thanks so much for bringing it up," she grumbled. "You would be mortified, too, if you realized that you were handcuffed by your own nature. I see vampires best, because I am one; I see humans okay, because I was one. But I can't see these odd half-breeds at all because they're nothing I've experienced. Bah!"

"Focus, Alice."

"Right. Bella's almost too easy to see now."

There was a long moment of silence, and then Edward sighed. It was a new sound, happier.

"She's really going to be fine," he breathed.

"Of course she is."

"You weren't so sanguine two days ago."

"I couldn't *see* right two days ago. But now that she's free of all the blind spots, it's a piece of cake."

"Could you concentrate for me? On the clock—give me an estimate."

Alice sighed. "So impatient. Fine. Give me a sec—"

Quiet breathing.

"Thank you, Alice." His voice was brighter.

How long? Couldn't they at least say it aloud for me? Was that too much to ask? How many more seconds would

I burn? Ten thousand? Twenty? Another day—eighty-six thousand, four hundred? More than that?

"She's going to be dazzling."

Edward growled quietly. "She always has been."

Alice snorted. "You know what I mean. *Look* at her."

Edward didn't answer, but Alice's words gave me hope that maybe I didn't resemble the charcoal briquette I felt like. It seemed as if I *must* be just a pile of charred bones by now. Every cell in my body had been razed to ash.

I heard Alice breeze out of the room. I heard the swish of the fabric she moved, rubbing against itself. I heard the quiet buzz of the light hanging from the ceiling. I heard the faint wind brushing against the outside of the house. I could hear *everything*.

Downstairs, someone was watching a ball game. The Mariners were winning by two runs.

"It's my *turn*," I heard Rosalie snap at someone, and there was a low snarl in response.

"Hey, now," Emmett cautioned.

Someone hissed.

I listened for more, but there was nothing but the game. Baseball was not interesting enough to distract me from the pain, so I listened to Edward's breathing again, counting the seconds.

Twenty-one thousand, nine hundred seventeen and a half seconds later, the pain changed.

On the good-news side of things, it started to fade from my fingertips and toes. Fading *slowly*, but at least it was doing something new. This had to be it. The pain was on its way out. . . .

And then the bad news. The fire in my throat wasn't the

same as before. I wasn't only on fire, but I was now parched, too. Dry as bone. So thirsty. Burning fire, and burning thirst . . .

Also bad news: The fire inside my heart got hotter.

How was that *possible*?

My heartbeat, already too fast, picked up—the fire drove its rhythm to a new frantic pace.

"Carlisle," Edward called. His voice was low but clear. I knew that Carlisle would hear it, if he were in or near the house.

The fire retreated from my palms, leaving them blissfully pain-free and cool. But it retreated to my heart, which blazed hot as the sun and beat at a furious new speed.

Carlisle entered the room, Alice at his side. Their footsteps were so distinct, I could even tell that Carlisle was on the right, and a foot ahead of Alice.

"Listen," Edward told them.

The loudest sound in the room was my frenzied heart, pounding to the rhythm of the fire.

"Ah," Carlisle said. "It's almost over."

My relief at his words was overshadowed by the excruciating pain in my heart.

My wrists were free, though, and my ankles. The fire was totally extinguished there.

"Soon," Alice agreed eagerly. "I'll get the others. Should I have Rosalie . . . ?"

"Yes—keep the baby away."

What? No. *No!* What did he mean, keep my baby away? What was he thinking?

My fingers twitched—the irritation breaking through my perfect façade. The room went silent besides the jackhammering of my heart as they all stopped breathing for a second in response.

A hand squeezed my wayward fingers. "Bella? Bella, love?"

Could I answer him without screaming? I considered that for a moment, and then the fire ripped hotter still through my chest, draining in from my elbows and knees. Better not to chance it.

"I'll bring them right up," Alice said, an urgent edge to her tone, and I heard the swish of wind as she darted away.

And then—*oh!*

My heart took off, beating like helicopter blades, the sound almost a single sustained note; it felt like it would grind through my ribs. The fire flared up in the center of my chest, sucking the last remnants of the flames from the rest of my body to fuel the most scorching blaze yet. The pain was enough to stun me, to break through my iron grip on the stake. My back arched, bowed as if the fire was dragging me upward by my heart.

I allowed no other piece of my body to break rank as my torso slumped back to the table.

It became a battle inside me—my sprinting heart racing against the attacking fire. Both were losing. The fire was doomed, having consumed everything that was combustible; my heart galloped toward its last beat.

The fire constricted, concentrating inside that one remaining human organ with a final, unbearable surge. The surge was answered by a deep, hollow-sounding thud. My heart stuttered twice, and then thudded quietly again just once more.

There was no sound. No breathing. Not even mine.

For a moment, the absence of pain was all I could comprehend.

And then I opened my eyes and gazed above me in wonder.

20. NEW

Everything was so *clear*.

Sharp. Defined.

The brilliant light overhead was still blinding-bright, and yet I could plainly see the glowing strands of the filaments inside the bulb. I could see each color of the rainbow in the white light, and, at the very edge of the spectrum, an eighth color I had no name for.

Behind the light, I could distinguish the individual grains in the dark wood ceiling above. In front of it, I could see the dust motes in the air, the sides the light touched, and the dark sides, distinct and separate. They spun like little planets, moving around each other in a celestial dance.

The dust was so beautiful that I inhaled in shock; the

air whistled down my throat, swirling the motes into a vortex. The action felt wrong. I considered, and realized the problem was that there was no relief tied to the action. I didn't need the air. My lungs weren't waiting for it. They reacted indifferently to the influx.

I did not need the air, but I *liked* it. In it, I could taste the room around me—taste the lovely dust motes, the mix of the stagnant air mingling with the flow of slightly cooler air from the open door. Taste a lush whiff of silk. Taste a faint hint of something warm and desirable, something that should be moist, but wasn't. . . . That smell made my throat burn dryly, a faint echo of the venom burn, though the scent was tainted by the bite of chlorine and ammonia. And most of all, I could taste an almost-honey-lilac-and-sun-flavored scent that was the strongest thing, the closest thing to me.

I heard the sound of the others, breathing again now that I did. Their breath mixed with the scent that was something just off honey and lilac and sunshine, bringing new flavors. Cinnamon, hyacinth, pear, seawater, rising bread, pine, vanilla, leather, apple, moss, lavender, chocolate. . . . I traded a dozen different comparisons in my mind, but none of them fit exactly. So sweet and pleasant.

The TV downstairs had been muted, and I heard someone—Rosalie?—shift her weight on the first floor.

I also heard a faint, thudding rhythm, with a voice shouting angrily to the beat. Rap music? I was mystified for a moment, and then the sound faded away like a car passing by with the windows rolled down.

With a start, I realized that this could be exactly right. Could I hear all the way to the freeway?

I didn't realize someone was holding my hand until whoever it was squeezed it lightly. Like it had before to hide the pain, my body locked down again in surprise. This was not a touch I expected. The skin was perfectly smooth, but it was the wrong temperature. Not cold.

After that first frozen second of shock, my body responded to the unfamiliar touch in a way that shocked me even more.

Air hissed up my throat, spitting through my clenched teeth with a low, menacing sound like a swarm of bees. Before the sound was out, my muscles bunched and arched, twisting away from the unknown. I flipped off my back in a spin so fast it should have turned the room into an incomprehensible blur—but it did not. I saw every dust mote, every splinter in the wood-paneled walls, every loose thread in microscopic detail as my eyes whirled past them.

So by the time I found myself crouched against the wall defensively—about a sixteenth of a second later—I already understood what had startled me, and that I had overreacted.

Oh. Of course. Edward wouldn't feel cold to me. We were the same temperature now.

I held my pose for an eighth of a second longer, adjusting to the scene before me.

Edward was leaning across the operating table that had been my pyre, his hand reached out toward me, his expression anxious.

Edward's face was the most important thing, but my peripheral vision catalogued everything else, just in case. Some instinct to defend had been triggered, and I automatically searched for any sign of danger.

My vampire family waited cautiously against the far wall by the door, Emmett and Jasper in the front. Like there *was* danger. My nostrils flared, searching for the threat. I could smell nothing out of place. That faint scent of something delicious—but marred by harsh chemicals—tickled my throat again, setting it to aching and burning.

Alice was peeking around Jasper's elbow with a huge grin on her face; the light sparkled off her teeth, another eight-color rainbow.

That grin reassured me and then put the pieces together. Jasper and Emmett were in the front to protect the others, as I had assumed. What I hadn't grasped immediately was that *I* was the danger.

All this was a sideline. The greater part of my senses and my mind were still focused on Edward's face.

I had never seen it before this second.

How many times had I stared at Edward and marveled over his beauty? How many hours—days, weeks—of my life had I spent dreaming about what I then deemed to be perfection? I thought I'd known his face better than my own. I'd thought this was the one sure physical thing in my whole world: the flawlessness of Edward's face.

I may as well have been blind.

For the first time, with the dimming shadows and limiting weakness of humanity taken off my eyes, I saw his face. I gasped and then struggled with my vocabulary, unable to find the right words. I needed better words.

At this point, the other part of my attention had ascertained that there was no danger here besides myself, and I automatically straightened out of my crouch; almost a whole second had passed since I'd been on the table.

I was momentarily preoccupied by the way my body moved. The instant I'd considered standing erect, I was already straight. There was no brief fragment of time in which the action occurred; change was instantaneous, almost as if there was no movement at all.

I continued to stare at Edward's face, motionless again.

He moved slowly around the table—each step taking nearly half a second, each step flowing sinuously like river water weaving over smooth stones—his hand still outstretched.

I watched the grace of his advance, absorbing it with my new eyes.

"Bella?" he asked in a low, calming tone, but the worry in his voice layered my name with tension.

I could not answer immediately, lost as I was in the velvet folds of his voice. It was the most perfect symphony, a symphony in one instrument, an instrument more profound than any created by man. . . .

"Bella, love? I'm sorry, I know it's disorienting. But you're all right. Everything is fine."

Everything? My mind spun out, spiraling back to my last human hour. Already, the memory seemed dim, like I was watching through a thick, dark veil—because my human eyes had been half blind. Everything had been so blurred.

When he said everything was fine, did that include Renesmee? Where was she? With Rosalie? I tried to remember her face—I knew that she had been beautiful—but it was irritating to try to see through the human memories. Her face was shrouded in darkness, so poorly lit. . . .

What about Jacob? Was *he* fine? Did my long-suffering

best friend hate me now? Had he gone back to Sam's pack? Seth and Leah, too?

Were the Cullens safe, or had my transformation ignited the war with the pack? Did Edward's blanket assurance cover all of that? Or was he just trying to calm me?

And Charlie? What would I tell him now? He must have called while I was burning. What had they told him? What did he think had happened to me?

As I deliberated for one small piece of a second over which question to ask first, Edward reached out tentatively and stroked his fingertips across my cheek. Smooth as satin, soft as a feather, and now exactly matched to the temperature of my skin.

His touch seemed to sweep beneath the surface of my skin, right through the bones of my face. The feeling was tingly, electric—it jolted through my bones, down my spine, and trembled in my stomach.

Wait, I thought as the trembling blossomed into a warmth, a yearning. Wasn't I supposed to lose this? Wasn't giving up this feeling a part of the bargain?

I was a newborn vampire. The dry, scorching ache in my throat gave proof to that. And I knew what being a newborn entailed. Human emotions and longings would come back to me later in some form, but I'd accepted that I would not feel them in the beginning. Only thirst. That was the deal, the price. I'd agreed to pay it.

But as Edward's hand curled to the shape of my face like satin-covered steel, desire raced through my dried-out veins, singing from my scalp to my toes.

He arched one perfect eyebrow, waiting for me to speak.

I threw my arms around him.

Again, it was like there was no movement. One moment I stood straight and still as a statue; in the same instant, he was in my arms.

Warm—or at least, that was my perception. With the sweet, delicious scent that I'd never been able to really take in with my dull human senses, but that was one hundred percent Edward. I pressed my face into his smooth chest.

And then he shifted his weight uncomfortably. Leaned away from my embrace. I stared up at his face, confused and frightened by the rejection.

"Um . . . carefully, Bella. Ow."

I yanked my arms away, folding them behind my back as soon as I understood.

I was too strong.

"Oops," I mouthed.

He smiled the kind of smile that would have stopped my heart if it were still beating.

"Don't panic, love," he said, lifting his hand to touch my lips, parted in horror. "You're just a bit stronger than I am for the moment."

My eyebrows pushed together. I'd known this, too, but it felt more surreal than any other part of this ultimately surreal moment. I was stronger than Edward. I'd made him say *ow*.

His hand stroked my cheek again, and I all but forgot my distress as another wave of desire rippled through my motionless body.

These emotions were so much stronger than I was used to that it was hard to stick to one train of thought despite the extra room in my head. Each new sensation overwhelmed me. I remembered Edward saying once—his voice in my head a weak shadow compared to the crystal, musical clarity I was hearing now—that his kind, *our* kind, were easily distracted. I could see why.

I made a concerted effort to focus. There was something I needed to say. The most important thing.

Very carefully, so carefully that the movement was actually discernible, I brought my right arm out from behind my back and raised my hand to touch his cheek. I refused to let myself be sidetracked by the pearly color of my hand or by the smooth silk of his skin or by the charge that zinged in my fingertips.

I stared into his eyes and heard my own voice for the first time.

"I love you," I said, but it sounded like singing. My voice rang and shimmered like a bell.

His answering smile dazzled me more than it ever had when I was human; I could really see it now.

"As I love you," he told me.

He took my face between his hands and leaned his face to mine—slow enough to remind me to be careful. He kissed me, soft as a whisper at first, and then suddenly stronger, fiercer. I tried to remember to be gentle with him, but it was hard work to remember anything in the onslaught of sensation, hard to hold on to any coherent thoughts.

It was like he'd never kissed me—like this was our first kiss. And, in truth, he'd never kissed me *this* way before.

It almost made me feel guilty. Surely I was in breach of the contract. I couldn't be allowed to have this, too.

Though I didn't need oxygen, my breathing sped, raced

as fast as it had when I was burning. This was a different kind of fire.

Someone cleared his throat. Emmett. I recognized the deep sound at once, joking and annoyed at the same time.

I'd forgotten we weren't alone. And then I realized that the way I was curved around Edward now was not exactly polite for company.

Embarrassed, I half-stepped away in another instantaneous movement.

Edward chuckled and stepped with me, keeping his arms tight around my waist. His face was glowing—like a white flame burned from behind his diamond skin.

I took an unnecessary breath to settle myself.

How different this kissing was! I read his expression as I compared the indistinct human memories to this clear, intense feeling. He looked . . . a little smug.

"You've been holding out on me," I accused in my singing voice, my eyes narrowing a tiny bit.

He laughed, radiant with relief that it was all over—the fear, the pain, the uncertainties, the waiting, all of it behind us now. "It was sort of necessary at the time," he reminded me. "Now it's your turn to not break *me*." He laughed again.

I frowned as I considered that, and then Edward was not the only one laughing.

Carlisle stepped around Emmett and walked toward me swiftly; his eyes were only slightly wary, but Jasper shadowed his footsteps. I'd never seen Carlisle's face before either, not really. I had an odd urge to blink—like I was staring at the sun.

"How do you feel, Bella?" Carlisle asked.

I considered that for a sixty-fourth of a second.

"Overwhelmed. There's so *much*. . . ." I trailed off, listening to the bell-tone of my voice again.

"Yes, it can be quite confusing."

I nodded one fast, jerky bob. "But I feel like me. Sort of. I didn't expect that."

Edward's arms squeezed lightly around my waist. "I told you so," he whispered.

"You are quite controlled," Carlisle mused. "More so than *I* expected, even with the time you had to prepare yourself mentally for this."

I thought about the wild mood swings, the difficulty concentrating, and whispered, "I'm not sure about that."

He nodded seriously, and then his jeweled eyes glittered with interest. "It seems like we did something right with the morphine this time. Tell me, what do you remember of the transformation process?"

I hesitated, intensely aware of Edward's breath brushing against my cheek, sending whispers of electricity through my skin.

"Everything was . . . very dim before. I remember the baby couldn't breathe. . . ."

I looked at Edward, momentarily frightened by the memory.

"Renesmee is healthy and well," he promised, a gleam I'd never seen before in his eyes. He said her name with an understated fervor. A reverence. The way devout people talked about their gods. "What do you remember after that?"

I focused on my poker face. I'd never been much of a liar.

"It's hard to remember. It was so dark before. And then . . .
I opened my eyes and I could see *everything*."

"Amazing," Carlisle breathed, his eyes alight.

Chagrin washed through me, and I waited for the heat
to burn in my cheeks and give me away. And then I remembered that I would never blush again. Maybe that
would protect Edward from the truth.

I'd have to find a way to tip off Carlisle, though. Someday.
If he ever needed to create another vampire. That possibility
seemed very unlikely, which made me feel better about
lying.

"I want you to think—to tell me everything you
remember," Carlisle pressed excitedly, and I couldn't help
the grimace that flashed across my face. I didn't want to have
to keep lying, because I might slip up. And I didn't want
to think about the burning. Unlike the human memories,
that part was perfectly clear and I found I could remember
it with far too much precision.

"Oh, I'm so sorry, Bella," Carlisle apologized immediately.
"Of course your thirst must be very uncomfortable. This
conversation can wait."

Until he'd mentioned it, the thirst actually wasn't un-
manageable. There was so much room in my head. A separate part of my brain was keeping tabs on the burn in my
throat, almost like a reflex. The way my old brain had
handled breathing and blinking.

But Carlisle's assumption brought the burn to the
forefront of my mind. Suddenly, the dry ache was all I could
think about, and the more I thought about it, the more
it hurt. My hand flew up to cup my throat, like I could
smother the flames from the outside. The skin of my neck

was strange beneath my fingers. So smooth it was somehow soft, though it was hard as stone, too.

Edward dropped his arms and took my other hand, tugging gently. "Let's hunt, Bella."

My eyes opened wider and the pain of the thirst receded, shock taking its place.

Me? Hunt? With Edward? But . . . *how?* I didn't know what to do.

He read the alarm in my expression and smiled encouragingly. "It's quite easy, love. Instinctual. Don't worry, I'll show you." When I didn't move, he grinned his crooked smile and raised his eyebrows. "I was under the impression that you'd always *wanted* to see me hunt."

I laughed in a short burst of humor (part of me listened in wonder to the pealing bell sound) as his words reminded me of cloudy human conversations. And then I took a whole second to run quickly through those first days with Edward—the true beginning of my life—in my head so that I would never forget them. I did not expect that it would be so uncomfortable to remember. Like trying to squint through muddy water. I knew from Rosalie's experience that if I thought of my human memories *enough*, I would not lose them over time. I did not want to forget one minute I'd spent with Edward, even now, when eternity stretched in front of us. I would have to make sure those human memories were cemented into my infallible vampire mind.

"Shall we?" Edward asked. He reached up to take the hand that was still at my neck. His fingers smoothed down the column of my throat. "I don't want you to be hurting," he added in a low murmur. Something I would not have been able to hear before.

"I'm fine," I said out of lingering human habit. "Wait. First."

There was so much. I'd never gotten to my questions. There were more important things than the ache.

It was Carlisle who spoke now. "Yes?"

"I want to see her. Renesmee."

It was oddly difficult to say her name. *My daughter*; these words were even harder to think. It all seemed so distant. I tried to remember how I had felt three days ago, and automatically, my hands pulled free of Edward's and dropped to my stomach.

Flat. Empty. I clutched at the pale silk that covered my skin, panicking again, while an insignificant part of my mind noted that Alice must have dressed me.

I knew there was nothing left inside me, and I faintly remembered the bloody removal scene, but the physical proof was still hard to process. All I knew was loving my little nudger *inside* of me. Outside of me, she seemed like something I must have imagined. A fading dream—a dream that was half nightmare.

While I wrestled with my confusion, I saw Edward and Carlisle exchange a guarded glance.

"What?" I demanded.

"Bella," Edward said soothingly. "That's not really a good idea. She's half human, love. Her heart beats, and blood runs in her veins. Until your thirst is positively under control . . . You don't want to put her in danger, do you?"

I frowned. Of course I must not want that.

Was I out of control? Confused, yes. Easily unfocused, yes. But dangerous? To her? My daughter?

I couldn't be positive that the answer was no. So I

would have to be patient. That sounded difficult. Because until I saw her again, she wouldn't be real. Just a fading dream . . . of a stranger . . .

"Where is she?" I listened hard, and then I could hear the beating heart on the floor below me. I could hear more than one person breathing—quietly, like they were listening, too. There was also a fluttering sound, a thrumming, that I couldn't place. . . .

And the sound of the heartbeat was so moist and appealing, that my mouth started watering.

So I would definitely have to learn how to hunt before I saw her. My stranger baby.

"Is Rosalie with her?"

"Yes," Edward answered in a clipped tone, and I could see that something he'd thought of upset him. I'd thought he and Rose were over their differences. Had the animosity erupted again? Before I could ask, he pulled my hands away from my flat stomach, tugging gently again.

"Wait," I protested again, trying to focus. "What about Jacob? And Charlie? Tell me everything that I missed. How long was I . . . unconscious?"

Edward didn't seem to notice my hesitation over the last word. Instead, he was exchanging another wary glance with Carlisle.

"What's wrong?" I whispered.

"Nothing is *wrong*," Carlisle told me, emphasizing the last word in a strange way. "Nothing has changed much, actually—you were only unaware for just over two days. It was very fast, as these things go. Edward did an excellent job. Quite innovative—the venom injection straight to your heart was his idea." He paused to smile proudly at his son and then sighed. "Jacob is still here, and Charlie still believes that you are sick. He thinks you're in Atlanta right now, undergoing tests at the CDC. We gave him a bad number, and he's frustrated. He's been speaking to Esme."

"I should call him . . . ," I murmured to myself, but, listening to my own voice, I understood the new difficulties. He wouldn't recognize this voice. It wouldn't reassure him. And then the earlier surprise intruded. "Hold on—Jacob is *still here?*"

Another glance between them.

"Bella," Edward said quickly. "There's much to discuss, but we should take care of you first. You have to be in pain. . . ."

When he pointed that out, I remembered the burn in my throat and swallowed convulsively. "But Jacob—"

"We have all the time in the world for explanations, love," he reminded me gently.

Of course. I could wait a little longer for the answer; it would be easier to listen when the fierce pain of the fiery thirst was no longer scattering my concentration. "Okay."

"Wait, wait, wait," Alice trilled from the doorway. She danced across the room, dreamily graceful. As with Edward and Carlisle, I felt some shock as I really looked at her face for the first time. So lovely. "You promised I could be there the first time! What if you two run past something reflective?"

"Alice—," Edward protested.

"It will only take a second!" And with that, Alice darted from the room.

Edward sighed.

"What is she talking about?"

But Alice was already back, carrying the huge, gilt-framed mirror from Rosalie's room, which was nearly twice as tall as she was, and several times as wide.

Jasper had been so still and silent that I'd taken no notice of him since he'd followed behind Carlisle. Now he moved again, to hover over Alice, his eyes locked on my expression. Because I was the danger here.

I knew he would be tasting the mood around me, too, and so he must have felt my jolt of shock as I studied his face, looking at it closely for the first time.

Through my sightless human eyes, the scars left from his former life with the newborn armies in the South had been mostly invisible. Only with a bright light to throw their slightly raised shapes into definition could I even make out their existence.

Now that I could see, the scars were Jasper's most dominant feature. It was hard to take my eyes off his ravaged neck and jaw—hard to believe that even a vampire could have survived so many sets of teeth ripping into his throat.

Instinctively, I tensed to defend myself. Any vampire who saw Jasper would have had the same reaction. The scars were like a lighted billboard. *Dangerous*, they screamed. How many vampires had tried to kill Jasper? Hundreds? Thousands? The same number that had died in the attempt.

Jasper both saw and felt my assessment, my caution, and he smiled wryly.

"Edward gave me grief for not getting you to a mirror before the wedding," Alice said, pulling my attention away from her frightening lover. "I'm not going to be chewed out again."

"Chewed out?" Edward asked skeptically, one eyebrow curving upward.

"Maybe I'm overstating things," she murmured absently as she turned the mirror to face me.

"And maybe this has solely to do with your own voyeuristic gratification," he countered.

Alice winked at him.

I was only aware of this exchange with the lesser part of my concentration. The greater part was riveted on the person in the mirror.

My first reaction was an unthinking pleasure. The alien creature in the glass was indisputably beautiful, every bit as beautiful as Alice or Esme. She was fluid even in stillness, and her flawless face was pale as the moon against the frame of her dark, heavy hair. Her limbs were smooth and strong, skin glistening subtly, luminous as a pearl.

My second reaction was horror.

Who *was* she? At first glance, I couldn't find my face anywhere in the smooth, perfect planes of her features.

And her eyes! Though I'd known to expect them, her eyes still sent a thrill of terror through me.

All the while I studied and reacted, her face was perfectly composed, a carving of a goddess, showing nothing of the turmoil roiling inside me. And then her full lips moved.

"The eyes?" I whispered, unwilling to say *my eyes*. "How long?"

"They'll darken up in a few months," Edward said in a soft, comforting voice. "Animal blood dilutes the color more quickly than a diet of human blood. They'll turn amber first, then gold."

My eyes would blaze like vicious red flames for *months?*

"Months?" My voice was higher now, stressed. In the mirror, the perfect eyebrows lifted incredulously above her glowing crimson eyes—brighter than any I'd ever seen before.

Jasper took a step forward, alarmed by the intensity of my sudden anxiety. He knew young vampires only too well; did this emotion presage some misstep on my part?

No one answered my question. I looked away, to Edward and Alice. Both their eyes were slightly unfocused—reacting to Jasper's unease. Listening to its cause, looking ahead to the immediate future.

I took another deep, unnecessary breath.

"No, I'm fine," I promised them. My eyes flickered to the stranger in the mirror and back. "It's just . . . a lot to take in."

Jasper's brow furrowed, highlighting the two scars over his left eye.

"I don't know," Edward murmured.

The woman in the mirror frowned. "What question did I miss?"

Edward grinned. "Jasper wonders how you're doing it."

"Doing what?"

"Controlling your emotions, Bella," Jasper answered. "I've never seen a newborn do that—stop an emotion in its tracks that way. You were upset, but when you saw our concern, you reined it in, regained power over yourself. I was prepared to help, but you didn't need it."

"Is that wrong?" I asked. My body automatically froze as I waited for his verdict.

"No," he said, but his voice was unsure.

Edward stroked his hand down my arm, as if encouraging me to thaw. "It's very impressive, Bella, but we don't understand it. We don't know how long it can hold."

I considered that for a portion of a second. At any moment, would I snap? Turn into a monster?

I couldn't feel it coming on. . . . Maybe there was no way to anticipate such a thing.

"But what do you think?" Alice asked, a little impatient now, pointing to the mirror.

"I'm not sure," I hedged, not wanting to admit how frightened I really was.

I stared at the beautiful woman with the terrifying eyes, looking for pieces of me. There *was* something there in the shape of her lips—if you looked past the dizzying beauty, it was true that her upper lip was slightly out of balance, a bit too full to match the lower. Finding this familiar little flaw made me feel a tiny bit better. Maybe the rest of me was in there, too.

I raised my hand experimentally, and the woman in the mirror copied the movement, touching her face, too. Her crimson eyes watched me warily.

Edward sighed.

I turned away from her to look at him, raising one eyebrow.

"Disappointed?" I asked, my ringing voice impassive.

He laughed. "Yes," he admitted.

I felt the shock break through the composed mask on my face, followed instantly by the hurt.

Alice snarled. Jasper leaned forward again, waiting for me to snap.

But Edward ignored them and wrapped his arms tightly

around my newly frozen form, pressing his lips against my cheek. "I was rather hoping that I'd be able to hear your mind, now that it is more similar to my own," he murmured. "And here I am, as frustrated as ever, wondering what could possibly be going on inside your head."

I felt better at once.

"Oh well," I said lightly, relieved that my thoughts were still my own. "I guess my brain will never work right. At least I'm pretty."

It was becoming easier to joke with him as I adjusted, to think in straight lines. To be myself.

Edward growled in my ear. "Bella, you have *never* been merely pretty."

Then his face pulled away from mine, and he sighed. "All right, all right," he said to someone.

"What?" I asked.

"You're making Jasper more edgy by the second. He may relax a little when you've hunted."

I looked at Jasper's worried expression and nodded. I didn't want to snap here, if that was coming. Better to be surrounded by trees than family.

"Okay. Let's hunt," I agreed, a thrill of nerves and anticipation making my stomach quiver. I unwrapped Edward's arms from around me, keeping one of his hands, and turned my back on the strange and beautiful woman in the mirror.

21. FIRST HUNT

"THE WINDOW?" I ASKED, STARING TWO STORIES DOWN.

I'd never really been afraid of heights per se, but being able to see all the details with such clarity made the prospect less appealing. The angles of the rocks below were sharper than I would have imagined them.

Edward smiled. "It's the most convenient exit. If you're frightened, I can carry you."

"We have all eternity, and you're worried about the time it would take to walk to the back door?"

He frowned slightly. "Renesmee and Jacob are downstairs. . . ."

"Oh."

Right. I was the monster now. I had to keep away from scents that might trigger my wild side. From the people that I loved in particular. Even the ones I didn't really know yet.

"Is Renesmee . . . okay . . . with Jacob there?" I whispered. I realized belatedly that it must have been Jacob's heart I'd heard below. I listened hard again, but I could only hear the one steady pulse. "He doesn't like her much."

Edward's lips tightened in an odd way. "Trust me, she is perfectly safe. I know exactly what Jacob is thinking."

"Of course," I murmured, and looked at the ground again.

"Stalling?" he challenged.

"A little. I don't know how. . . ."

And I was very conscious of my family behind me, watching silently. Mostly silently. Emmett had already chuckled under his breath once. One mistake, and he'd be rolling on the floor. Then the jokes about the world's only clumsy vampire would start. . . .

Also, this dress—that Alice must have put me in sometime when I was too lost in the burning to notice— was not what I would have picked out for either jumping or hunting. Tightly fitted ice-blue silk? What did she think I would need it for? Was there a cocktail party later?

"Watch me," Edward said. And then, very casually, he stepped out of the tall, open window and fell.

I watched carefully, analyzing the angle at which he bent his knees to absorb the impact. The sound of his landing was very low—a muted thud that could have been a door softly closed, or a book gently laid on a table.

It didn't *look* hard.

Clenching my teeth as I concentrated, I tried to copy his casual step into empty air.

Ha! The ground seemed to move toward me so slowly that it was nothing at all to place my feet—what shoes had Alice put me in? Stilettos? She'd lost her mind—to place my silly shoes exactly right so that landing was no different than stepping one foot forward on a flat surface.

I absorbed the impact in the balls of my feet, not wanting to snap off the thin heels. My landing seemed just as quiet as his. I grinned at him.

"Right. Easy."

He smiled back. "Bella?"

"Yes?"

"That was quite graceful—even for a vampire."

I considered that for a moment, and then I beamed. If he'd just been saying that, then Emmett would have laughed. No one found his remark humorous, so it must have been true. It was the first time anyone had ever applied the word *graceful* to me in my entire life . . . or, well, existence anyway.

"*Thank* you," I told him.

And then I hooked the silver satin shoes off my feet one by one and lobbed them together back through the open window. A little too hard, maybe, but I heard someone catch them before they could damage the paneling.

Alice grumbled, "Her fashion sense hasn't improved as much as her balance."

Edward took my hand—I couldn't stop marveling at the smoothness, the comfortable temperature of his skin—and darted through the backyard to the edge of the river. I went along with him effortlessly.

Everything physical seemed very simple.

"Are we swimming?" I asked him when we stopped beside the water.

"And ruin your pretty dress? No. We're jumping."

I pursed my lips, considering. The river was about fifty yards wide here.

"You first," I said.

He touched my cheek, took two quick backward strides, and then ran back those two steps, launching himself from a flat stone firmly embedded in the riverbank. I studied the flash of movement as he arced over the water, finally turning a somersault just before he disappeared into the thick trees on the other side of the river.

"Show-off," I muttered, and heard his invisible laugh.

I backed up five paces, just in case, and took a deep breath.

Suddenly, I was anxious again. Not about falling or getting hurt—I was more worried about the forest getting hurt.

It had come on slowly, but I could feel it now—the raw, massive strength thrilling in my limbs. I was suddenly sure that if I wanted to tunnel *under* the river, to claw or beat my way straight through the bedrock, it wouldn't take me very long. The objects around me—the trees, the shrubs, the rocks . . . the house—had all begun to look very fragile.

Hoping very much that Esme was not particularly fond of any specific trees across the river, I began my first stride. And then stopped when the tight satin split six inches up my thigh. Alice!

Well, Alice always seemed to treat clothes as if they were disposable and meant for one-time usage, so she shouldn't mind this. I bent to carefully grasp the hem at the undamaged right seam between my fingers and, exerting the tiniest amount of pressure possible, I ripped the dress open to the top of my thigh. Then I fixed the other side to match.

Much better.

I could hear the muffled laughter in the house, and even the sound of someone gritting her teeth. The laughter came from upstairs and down, and I very easily recognized the much different, rough, throaty chuckle from the first floor.

So Jacob was watching, too? I couldn't imagine what he was thinking now, or what he was still doing here. I'd envisioned our reunion—if he could ever forgive me—taking place far in the future, when I was more stable, and time had healed the wounds I'd inflicted in his heart.

I didn't turn to look at him now, wary of my mood swings. It wouldn't be good to let any emotion take too strong a hold on my frame of mind. Jasper's fears had me on edge, too. I had to hunt before I dealt with anything else. I tried to forget everything else so I could *concentrate*.

"Bella?" Edward called from the woods, his voice moving closer. "Do you want to watch again?"

But I remembered everything perfectly, of course, and I didn't want to give Emmett a reason to find *more* humor in my education. This was physical—it should be instinctive. So I took a deep breath and ran for the river.

Unhindered by my skirt, it took only one long bound to reach the water's edge. Just an eighty-fourth of a second, and yet it was plenty of time—my eyes and my mind moved so quickly that one step was enough. It was simple to position my right foot just so against the flat stone and exert the adequate pressure to send my body wheeling up into the air. I was paying more attention to aim than force, and I erred on the amount of power necessary—but at least I didn't err on the side that would have gotten me wet. The fifty yard width was slightly *too* easy a distance. . . .

It was a strange, giddy, electrifying thing, but a short thing. An entire second had yet to pass, and I was across.

I was expecting the close-packed trees to be a problem, but they were surprisingly helpful. It was a simple matter to reach out with one sure hand as I fell back toward the earth again deep inside the forest and catch myself on a convenient branch; I swung lightly from the limb and landed on my toes, still fifteen feet from the ground on the wide bough of a Sitka spruce.

It was fabulous.

Over the sound of my peals of delighted laughter, I could hear Edward racing to find me. My jump had been twice as long as his. When he reached my tree, his eyes were wide. I leaped nimbly from the branch to his side, soundlessly landing again on the balls of my feet.

"Was that good?" I wondered, my breathing accelerated with excitement.

"Very good." He smiled approvingly, but his casual tone didn't match the surprised expression in his eyes.

"Can we do it again?"

"Focus, Bella—we're on a hunting trip."

"Oh, right." I nodded. "Hunting."

"Follow me . . . if you can." He grinned, his expression suddenly taunting, and broke into a run.

He was faster than me. I couldn't imagine how he moved his legs with such blinding speed, but it was beyond me.

However, I *was* stronger, and every stride of mine matched the length of three of his. And so I flew with him through the living green web, by his side, not following at all. As I ran, I couldn't help laughing quietly at the thrill of it; the laughter neither slowed me nor upset my focus.

I could finally understand why Edward never hit the trees when he ran—a question that had always been a mystery to me. It was a peculiar sensation, the balance between the speed and the clarity. For, while I rocketed over, under, and through the thick jade maze at a rate that should have reduced everything around me to a streaky green blur, I could plainly see each tiny leaf on all the small branches of every insignificant shrub that I passed.

The wind of my speed blew my hair and my torn dress out behind me, and, though I knew it shouldn't, it felt warm against my skin. Just as the rough forest floor shouldn't feel like velvet beneath my bare soles, and the limbs that whipped against my skin shouldn't feel like caressing feathers.

The forest was much more alive than I'd ever known— small creatures whose existence I'd never guessed at teemed in the leaves around me. They all grew silent after we passed, their breath quickening in fear. The animals had a much wiser reaction to our scent than humans seemed to. Certainly, it'd had the opposite effect on me.

I kept waiting to feel winded, but my breath came effortlessly. I waited for the burn to begin in my muscles, but my strength only seemed to increase as I grew accustomed to my stride. My leaping bounds stretched longer, and soon he was trying to keep up with me. I laughed again, exultant, when I heard him falling behind. My naked feet touched the ground so infrequently now it felt more like flying than running.

"Bella," he called dryly, his voice even, lazy. I could hear nothing else; he had stopped.

I briefly considered mutiny.

But, with a sigh, I whirled and skipped lightly to his side, some hundred yards back. I looked at him expectantly. He was smiling, with one eyebrow raised. He was so beautiful that I could only stare.

"Did you want to stay in the country?" he asked, amused. "Or were you planning to continue on to Canada this afternoon?"

"This is fine," I agreed, concentrating less on what he was saying and more on the mesmerizing way his lips moved when he spoke. It was hard not to become sidetracked with everything fresh in my strong new eyes. "What are we hunting?"

"Elk. I thought something easy for your first time . . ." He trailed off when my eyes narrowed at the word *easy*.

But I wasn't going to argue; I was too thirsty. As soon as I'd started to think about the dry burn in my throat, it was *all* I could think about. Definitely getting worse. My mouth felt like four o'clock on a June afternoon in Death Valley.

"Where?" I asked, scanning the trees impatiently. Now that I had given the thirst my attention, it seemed to taint every other thought in my head, leaking into the more pleasant thoughts of running and Edward's lips and kissing and . . . scorching thirst. I couldn't get away from it.

"Hold still for a minute," he said, putting his hands lightly on my shoulders. The urgency of my thirst receded momentarily at his touch.

"Now close your eyes," he murmured. When I obeyed, he raised his hands to my face, stroking my cheekbones. I felt my breathing speed and waited briefly again for the blush that wouldn't come.

"Listen," Edward instructed. "What do you hear?"

Everything, I could have said; his perfect voice, his breath, his lips brushing together as he spoke, the whisper of birds preening their feathers in the treetops, their fluttering heartbeats, the maple leaves scraping together, the faint clicking of ants following each other in a long line up the bark of the nearest tree. But I knew he meant something specific, so I let my ears range outward, seeking something different than the small hum of life that surrounded me. There was an open space near us—the wind had a different sound across the exposed grass—and a small creek, with a rocky bed. And there, near the noise of the water, was the splash of lapping tongues, the loud thudding of heavy hearts, pumping thick streams of blood. . . .

It felt like the sides of my throat had sucked closed.

"By the creek, to the northeast?" I asked, my eyes still shut.

"Yes." His tone was approving. "Now . . . wait for the breeze again and . . . what do you smell?"

Mostly him—his strange honey-lilac-and-sun perfume. But also the rich, earthy smell of rot and moss, the resin in the evergreens, the warm, almost nutty aroma of the small rodents cowering beneath the tree roots. And then, reaching out again, the clean smell of the water, which was surprisingly unappealing despite my thirst. I focused toward the water and found the scent that must have gone with the lapping noise and the pounding heart. Another warm smell, rich and tangy, stronger than the others. And yet nearly as unappealing as the brook. I wrinkled my nose.

He chuckled. "I know—it takes some getting used to."

"Three?" I guessed.

"Five. There are two more in the trees behind them."

"What do I do now?"

His voice sounded like he was smiling. "What do you feel like doing?"

I thought about that, my eyes still shut as I listened and breathed in the scent. Another bout of baking thirst intruded on my awareness, and suddenly the warm, tangy odor wasn't quite so objectionable. At least it would be something hot and wet in my desiccated mouth. My eyes snapped open.

"Don't think about it," he suggested as he lifted his hands off my face and took a step back. "Just follow your instincts."

I let myself drift with the scent, barely aware of my movement as I ghosted down the incline to the narrow meadow where the stream flowed. My body shifted forward automatically into a low crouch as I hesitated at the fern-fringed edge of the trees. I could see a big bull, two dozen antler points crowning his head, at the stream's edge, and the shadow-spotted shapes of the four others heading eastward into forest at a leisurely pace.

I centered myself around the scent of the male, the hot spot in his shaggy neck where the warmth pulsed strongest. Only thirty yards—two or three bounds—between us. I tensed myself for the first leap.

But as my muscles bunched in preparation, the wind shifted, blowing stronger now, and from the south. I didn't stop to think, hurtling out of the trees in a path perpendicular to my original plan, scaring the elk into the forest, racing after a new fragrance so attractive that there wasn't a choice. It was compulsory.

The scent ruled completely. I was single-minded as I traced it, aware only of the thirst and the smell that promised to quench it. The thirst got worse, so painful now that it confused all my other thoughts and began to remind me of the burn of venom in my veins.

There was only one thing that had any chance of penetrating my focus now, an instinct more powerful, more basic than the need to quench the fire—it was the instinct to protect myself from danger. Self-preservation.

I was suddenly alert to the fact that I was being followed. The pull of the irresistible scent warred with the impulse to turn and defend my hunt. A bubble of sound built in my chest, my lips pulled back of their own accord to expose my teeth in warning. My feet slowed, the need to protect my back struggling against the desire to quench my thirst.

And then I could hear my pursuer gaining, and defense won. As I spun, the rising sound ripped its way up my throat and out.

The feral snarl, coming from my own mouth, was so unexpected that it brought me up short. It unsettled me, and it cleared my head for a second—the thirst-driven haze receded, though the thirst burned on.

The wind shifted, blowing the smell of wet earth and coming rain across my face, further freeing me from the other scent's fiery grip—a scent so delicious it could only be human.

Edward hesitated a few feet away, his arms raised as if

to embrace me—or restrain me. His face was intent and cautious as I froze, horrified.

I realized that I had been about to attack him. With a hard jerk, I straightened out of my defensive crouch. I held my breath as I refocused, fearing the power of the fragrance swirling up from the south.

He could see reason return to my face, and he took a step toward me, lowering his arms.

"I have to get away from here," I spit through my teeth, using the breath I had.

Shock crossed his face. "*Can* you leave?"

I didn't have time to ask him what he meant by that. I knew the ability to think clearly would last only as long as I could stop myself from thinking of—

I burst into a run again, a flat-out sprint straight north, concentrating solely on the uncomfortable feeling of sensory deprivation that seemed to be my body's only response to the lack of air. My one goal was to run far enough away that the scent behind me would be completely lost. Impossible to find, even if I changed my mind . . .

Once again, I was aware of being followed, but I was sane this time. I fought the instinct to breathe—to use the flavors in the air to be sure it was Edward. I didn't have to fight long; though I was running faster than I ever had before, shooting like a comet through the straightest path I could find in the trees; Edward caught up with me after a short minute.

A new thought occurred to me, and I stopped dead, my feet planted. I was sure it must be safe here, but I held my breath just in case.

Edward blew past me, surprised by my sudden freeze.

He wheeled around and was at my side in a second. He put his hands on my shoulders and stared into my eyes, shock still the dominant emotion on his face.

"How did you do that?" he demanded.

"You let me beat you before, didn't you?" I demanded back, ignoring his question. And I'd thought I'd been doing so well!

When I opened my mouth, I could taste the air—it was unpolluted now, with no trace of the compelling perfume to torment my thirst. I took a cautious breath.

He shrugged and shook his head, refusing to be deflected. "Bella, how did you do it?"

"Run away? I held my breath."

"But how did you stop hunting?"

"When you came up behind me . . . I'm so sorry about that."

"Why are you apologizing to *me*? I'm the one who was horribly careless. I assumed no one would be so far from the trails, but I should have checked first. Such a stupid mistake! *You* have nothing to apologize for."

"But I growled at you!" I was still horrified that I was physically capable of such blasphemy.

"Of course you did. That's only natural. But I can't understand how you ran away."

"What else could I do?" I asked. His attitude confused me—what did he *want* to have happened? "It might have been someone I know!"

He startled me, suddenly bursting into a spasm of loud laughter, throwing his head back and letting the sound echo off the trees.

"Why are you laughing at me?"

He stopped at once, and I could see he was wary again.

Keep it under control, I thought to myself. I had to watch my temper. Just like I was a young werewolf rather than a vampire.

"I'm not laughing at you, Bella. I'm laughing because I am in shock. And I am in shock because I am completely amazed."

"Why?"

"You shouldn't be able to do any of this. You shouldn't be so . . . so rational. You shouldn't be able to stand here discussing this with me calmly and coolly. And, much more than any of that, you should *not* have been able to break off mid-hunt with the scent of human blood in the air. Even mature vampires have difficulty with that—we're always very careful of where we hunt so as not to put ourselves in the path of temptation. Bella, you're behaving like you're decades rather than days old."

"Oh." But I'd known it was going to be hard. That was why I'd been so on guard. I'd been expecting it to be difficult.

He put his hands on my face again, and his eyes were full of wonder. "What wouldn't I give to be able to see into your mind for just this one moment."

Such powerful emotions. I'd been prepared for the thirst part, but not this. I'd been so sure it wouldn't be the same when he touched me. Well, truthfully, it wasn't the same.

It was stronger.

I reached up to trace the planes of his face; my fingers lingered on his lips.

"I thought I wouldn't feel this way for a long time?" My

uncertainty made the words a question. "But I still *want* you."

He blinked in shock. "How can you even concentrate on that? Aren't you unbearably thirsty?"

Of course I was *now*, now that he'd brought it up again!

I tried to swallow and then sighed, closing my eyes like I had before to help me concentrate. I let my senses range out around me, tensed this time in case of another onslaught of the delicious taboo scent.

Edward dropped his hands, not even breathing while I listened farther and farther out into the web of green life, sifting through the scents and sounds for something not totally repellant to my thirst. There was a hint of something different, a faint trail to the east. . . .

My eyes flashed open, but my focus was still on sharper senses as I turned and darted silently eastward. The ground sloped steeply upward almost at once, and I ran in a hunting crouch, close to the ground, taking to the trees when that was easier. I sensed rather than heard Edward with me, flowing quietly through the woods, letting me lead.

The vegetation thinned as we climbed higher; the scent of pitch and resin grew more powerful, as did the trail I followed—it was a warm scent, sharper than the smell of the elk and more appealing. A few seconds more and I could hear the muted padding of immense feet, so much subtler than the crunch of hooves. The sound was up—in the branches rather than on the ground. Automatically I darted into the boughs as well, gaining the strategic higher position, halfway up a towering silver fir.

The soft thud of paws continued stealthily beneath me

now; the rich scent was very close. My eyes pinpointed the movement linked with the sound, and I saw the tawny hide of the great cat slinking along the wide branch of a spruce just down and to the left of my perch. He was big—easily four times my mass. His eyes were intent on the ground beneath; the cat hunted, too. I caught the smell of something smaller, bland next to the aroma of my prey, cowering in brush below the tree. The lion's tail twitched spasmodically as he prepared to spring.

With a light bound, I sailed through the air and landed on the lion's branch. He felt the shiver of the wood and whirled, shrieking surprise and defiance. He clawed the space between us, his eyes bright with fury. Half-crazed with thirst, I ignored the exposed fangs and the hooked claws and launched myself at him, knocking us both to the forest floor.

It wasn't much of a fight.

His raking claws could have been caressing fingers for all the impact they had on my skin. His teeth could find no purchase against my shoulder or my throat. His weight was nothing. My teeth unerringly sought his throat, and his instinctive resistance was pitifully feeble against my strength. My jaws locked easily over the precise point where the heat flow concentrated.

It was effortless as biting into butter. My teeth were steel razors; they cut through the fur and fat and sinews like they weren't there.

The flavor was wrong, but the blood was hot and wet and it soothed the ragged, itching thirst as I drank in an eager rush. The cat's struggles grew more and more feeble, and his screams choked off with a gurgle. The warmth of the blood radiated throughout my whole body, heating even my fingertips and toes.

The lion was finished before I was. The thirst flared again when he ran dry, and I shoved his carcass off my body in disgust. How could I still be thirsty after all that?

I wrenched myself erect in one quick move. Standing, I realized I was a bit of a mess. I wiped my face off on the back of my arm and tried to fix the dress. The claws that had been so ineffectual against my skin had had more success with the thin satin.

"Hmm," Edward said. I looked up to see him leaning casually against a tree trunk, watching me with a thoughtful look on his face.

"I guess I could have done that better." I was covered in dirt, my hair knotted, my dress bloodstained and hanging in tatters. Edward didn't come home from hunting trips looking like this.

"You did perfectly fine," he assured me. "It's just that . . . it was much more difficult for me to watch than it should have been."

I raised my eyebrows, confused.

"It goes against the grain," he explained, "letting you wrestle with lions. I was having an anxiety attack the whole time."

"Silly."

"I know. Old habits die hard. I like the improvements to your dress, though."

If I could have blushed, I would have. I changed the subject. "Why am I still thirsty?"

"Because you're young."

I sighed. "And I don't suppose there are any other mountain lions nearby."

"Plenty of deer, though."

I made a face. "They don't smell as good."

"Herbivores. The meat-eaters smell more like humans," he explained.

"Not that much like humans," I disagreed, trying not to remember.

"We could go back," he said solemnly, but there was a teasing light in his eye. "Whoever it was out there, if they were men, they probably wouldn't even mind death if you were the one delivering it." His gaze ran over my ravaged dress again. "In fact, they would think they were already dead and gone to heaven the moment they saw you."

I rolled my eyes and snorted. "Let's go hunt some stinking herbivores."

We found a large herd of mule deer as we ran back toward home. He hunted with me this time, now that I'd gotten the hang of it. I brought down a large buck, making nearly as much of a mess as I had with the lion. He'd finished with two before I was done with the first, not a hair ruffled, not a spot on his white shirt. We chased the scattered and terrified herd, but instead of feeding again, this time I watched carefully to see how he was able to hunt so neatly.

All the times that I had wished that Edward would not have to leave me behind when he hunted, I had secretly been just a little relieved. Because I was sure that seeing this would be frightening. Horrifying. That seeing him hunt would finally make him look like a vampire to me.

Of course, it was much different from this perspective, as a vampire myself. But I doubted that even my human eyes would have missed the beauty here.

It was a surprisingly sensual experience to observe Edward hunting. His smooth spring was like the sinuous strike of a snake; his hands were so sure, so strong, so completely inescapable; his full lips were perfect as they parted gracefully over his gleaming teeth. He was glorious. I felt a sudden jolt of both pride and desire. He was *mine*. Nothing could ever separate him from me now. I was too strong to be torn from his side.

He was very quick. He turned to me and gazed curiously at my gloating expression.

"No longer thirsty?" he asked.

I shrugged. "You distracted me. You're much better at it than I am."

"Centuries of practice." He smiled. His eyes were a disconcertingly lovely shade of honey gold now.

"Just one," I corrected him.

He laughed. "Are you done for today? Or did you want to continue?"

"Done, I think." I felt very full, sort of sloshy, even. I wasn't sure how much more liquid would fit into my body. But the burn in my throat was only muted. Then again, I'd known that thirst was just an inescapable part of this life.

And worth it.

I felt in control. Perhaps my sense of security was false, but I did feel pretty good about not killing anyone today. If I could resist totally human strangers, wouldn't I be able to handle the werewolf and a half-vampire child that I loved?

"I want to see Renesmee," I said. Now that my thirst

was tamed (if nothing close to erased), my earlier worries were hard to forget. I wanted to reconcile the stranger who was my daughter with the creature I'd loved three days ago. It was so odd, so wrong not to have her inside me still. Abruptly, I felt empty and uneasy.

He held out his hand to me. I took it, and his skin felt warmer than before. His cheek was faintly flushed, the shadows under his eyes all but vanished.

I was unable to resist stroking his face again. And again.

I sort of forgot that I was waiting for a response to my request as I stared into his shimmering gold eyes.

It was almost as hard as it had been to turn away from the scent of human blood, but I somehow kept the need to be careful firmly in my head as I stretched up on my toes and wrapped my arms around him. Gently.

He was not so hesitant in his movements; his arms locked around my waist and pulled me tight against his body. His lips crushed down on mine, but they felt soft. My lips no longer shaped themselves around his; they held their own.

Like before, it was as if the touch of his skin, his lips, his hands, was sinking right through my smooth, hard skin and into my new bones. To the very core of my body. I hadn't imagined that I could love him more than I had.

My old mind hadn't been capable of holding this much love. My old heart had not been strong enough to bear it.

Maybe this was the part of me that I'd brought forward to be intensified in my new life. Like Carlisle's compassion and Esme's devotion. I would probably never be able to do anything interesting or special like Edward, Alice, and

Jasper could do. Maybe I would just love Edward more than anyone in the history of the world had ever loved anyone else.

I could live with that.

I remembered parts of this—twisting my fingers in his hair, tracing the planes of his chest—but other parts were so new. He was new. It was an entirely different experience with Edward kissing me so fearlessly, so forcefully. I responded to his intensity, and then suddenly we were falling.

"Oops," I said, and he laughed underneath me. "I didn't mean to tackle you like that. Are you okay?"

He stroked my face. "Slightly better than *okay*." And then a perplexed expression crossed his face. "Renesmee?" he asked uncertainly, trying to ascertain what I wanted most in this moment. A very difficult question to answer, because I wanted so many things at the same time.

I could tell that he wasn't exactly averse to procrastinating our return trip, and it was hard to think about much besides his skin on mine—there really wasn't that much left of the dress. But my memory of Renesmee, before and after her birth, was becoming more and more dreamlike to me. More unlikely. All my memories of her were human memories; an aura of artificiality clung to them. Nothing seemed real that I hadn't seen with these eyes, touched with these hands.

Every minute, the reality of that little stranger slipped further away.

"Renesmee," I agreed, rueful, and I whipped back up onto my feet, pulling him with me.

22. PROMISED

Thinking of Renesmee brought her to that center-stage place in my strange, new, and roomy but distractible mind. So many questions.

"Tell me about her," I insisted as he took my hand. Being linked barely slowed us.

"She's like nothing else in the world," he told me, and the sound of an almost religious devotion was there again in his voice.

I felt a sharp pang of jealousy over this stranger. He knew her and I did not. It wasn't fair.

"How much is she like you? How much like me? Or like I was, anyway."

"It seems a fairly even divide."

"She was warm-blooded," I remembered.

"Yes. She has a heartbeat, though it runs a little bit faster than a human's. Her temperature is a little bit hotter than usual, too. She sleeps."

"Really?"

"Quite well for a newborn. The only parents in the world who don't need sleep, and our child already sleeps through the night." He chuckled.

I liked the way he said *our child*. The words made her more real.

"She has exactly your color eyes—so that didn't get lost, after all." He smiled at me. "They're so beautiful."

"And the vampire parts?" I asked.

"Her skin seems about as impenetrable as ours. Not that anyone would dream of testing that."

I blinked at him, a little shocked.

"Of course no one would," he assured me again. "Her diet . . . well, she prefers to drink blood. Carlisle continues to try to persuade her to drink some baby formula, too, but she doesn't have much patience with it. Can't say that I blame her—nasty-smelling stuff, even for human food."

I gaped openly at him now. He made it sound like they were having conversations. "Persuade her?"

"She's intelligent, shockingly so, and progressing at an immense pace. Though she doesn't speak—yet—she communicates quite effectively."

"Doesn't. Speak. *Yet.*"

He slowed our pace further, letting me absorb this.

"What do you mean, she communicates effectively?" I demanded.

"I think it will be easier for you to . . . see for yourself. It's rather difficult to describe."

I considered that. I knew there was a lot that I needed to see for myself before it would be real. I wasn't sure how much more I was ready for, so I changed the subject.

"Why is Jacob still here?" I asked. "How can he stand it? Why should he?" My ringing voice trembled a little. "Why should he have to suffer more?"

"Jacob isn't suffering," he said in a strange new tone. "Though I might be willing to change his condition," Edward added through his teeth.

"Edward!" I hissed, yanking him to a stop (and feeling a little thrill of smugness that I was able to do it). "How can you say that? Jacob has given up *everything* to protect us! What I've put him through—!" I cringed at the dim memory of shame and guilt. It seemed odd now that I had needed him so much then. That sense of absence without him near had vanished; it must have been a human weakness.

"You'll see exactly how I can say that," Edward muttered. "I promised him that I would let him explain, but I doubt you'll see it much differently than I do. Of course, I'm often wrong about your thoughts, aren't I?" He pursed his lips and eyed me.

"Explain what?"

Edward shook his head. "I promised. Though I don't know if I really owe him anything at all anymore. . . ." His teeth ground together.

"Edward, I don't understand." Frustration and indignation took over my head.

He stroked my cheek and then smiled gently when

my face smoothed out in response, desire momentarily overruling annoyance. "It's harder than you make it look, I know. I remember."

"I don't like feeling confused."

"I know. And so let's get you home, so that you can see it all for yourself." His eyes ran over the remains of my dress as he spoke of going home, and he frowned. "Hmm." After a half second of thought, he unbuttoned his white shirt and held it out for me to put my arms through.

"That bad?"

He grinned.

I slipped my arms into his sleeves and then buttoned it swiftly over my ragged bodice. Of course, that left him without a shirt, and it was impossible not to find that distracting.

"I'll race you," I said, and then cautioned, "no throwing the game this time!"

He dropped my hand and grinned. "On your mark . . ."

Finding my way to my new home was simpler than walking down Charlie's street to my old one. Our scent left a clear and easy trail to follow, even running as fast as I could.

Edward had me beat till we hit the river. I took a chance and made my leap early, trying to use my extra strength to win.

"Ha!" I exulted when I heard my feet touch the grass first.

Listening for his landing, I heard something I did not expect. Something loud and much too close. A thudding heart.

Edward was beside me in the same second, his hands clamped down hard on the tops of my arms.

"Don't breathe," he cautioned me urgently.

I tried not to panic as I froze mid-breath. My eyes were the only things that moved, wheeling instinctively to find the source of the sound.

Jacob stood at the line where the forest touched the Cullens' lawn, his arms folded across his body, his jaw clenched tight. Invisible in the woods behind him, I heard now two larger hearts, and the faint crush of bracken under huge, pacing paws.

"Carefully, Jacob," Edward said. A snarl from the forest echoed the concern in his voice. "Maybe this isn't the best way—"

"You think it would be better to let her near the baby first?" Jacob interrupted. "It's safer to see how Bella does with me. I heal fast."

This was a test? To see if I could not kill Jacob before I tried to not kill Renesmee? I felt sick in the strangest way— it had nothing to do with my stomach, only my mind. Was this Edward's idea?

I glanced at his face anxiously; Edward seemed to deliberate for a moment, and then his expression twisted from concern into something else. He shrugged, and there was an undercurrent of hostility in his voice when he said, "It's your neck, I guess."

The growl from the forest was furious this time; Leah, I had no doubt.

What was with Edward? After all that we'd been through, shouldn't he have been able to feel some kindness for my best friend? I'd thought—maybe foolishly—that Edward was sort of Jacob's friend now, too. I must have misread them.

But what was Jacob doing? Why would he offer himself as a test to protect Renesmee?

It didn't make any sense to me. Even if our friendship had survived . . .

And as my eyes met Jacob's now, I thought that maybe it had. He still looked like my best friend. But he wasn't the one who had changed. What did I look like to him?

Then he smiled his familiar smile, the smile of a kindred spirit, and I was sure our friendship was intact. It was just like before, when we were hanging out in his homemade garage, just two friends killing time. Easy and *normal*. Again, I noticed that the strange need I'd felt for him before I'd changed was completely gone. He was just my friend, the way it was supposed to be.

It still made no sense what he was doing now, though. Was he really so selfless that he would try to protect me— with his own life—from doing something in an uncontrolled split second that I would regret in agony forever? That went way beyond simply tolerating what I had become, or miraculously managing to stay my friend. Jacob was one of the best people I knew, but this seemed like too much to accept from anyone.

His grin widened, and he shuddered slightly. "I gotta say it, Bells. You're a freak show."

I grinned back, falling easily into the old pattern. This was a side of him I understood.

Edward growled. "Watch yourself, mongrel."

The wind blew from behind me and I quickly filled my lungs with the safe air so I could speak. "No, he's right. The eyes are really something, aren't they?"

"Super-creepy. But it's not as bad as I thought it would be."

"Gee—thanks for the amazing compliment!"

He rolled his eyes. "You know what I mean. You still look like you—sort of. Maybe it's not the look so much as . . . you *are* Bella. I didn't think it would feel like you were still here." He smiled at me again without a trace of bitterness or resentment anywhere in his face. Then he chuckled and said, "Anyway, I guess I'll get used to the eyes soon enough."

"You will?" I asked, confused. It was wonderful that we were still friends, but it wasn't like we'd be spending much time together.

The strangest look crossed his face, erasing the smile. It was almost . . . guilty? Then his eyes shifted to Edward.

"Thanks," he said. "I didn't know if you'd be able to keep it from her, promise or not. Usually, you just give her everything she wants."

"Maybe I'm hoping she'll get irritated and rip your head off," Edward suggested.

Jacob snorted.

"What's going on? Are you two keeping secrets from me?" I demanded, incredulous.

"I'll explain later," Jacob said self-consciously—like he didn't really plan on it. Then he changed the subject. "First, let's get this show on the road." His grin was a challenge now as he started slowly forward.

There was a whine of protest behind him, and then Leah's gray body slid out of the trees behind him. The taller, sandy-colored Seth was right behind her.

"Cool it, guys," Jacob said. "Stay out of this."

I was glad they didn't listen to him but only followed after him a little more slowly.

The wind was still now; it wouldn't blow his scent away from me.

He got close enough that I could feel the heat of his body in the air between us. My throat burned in response.

"C'mon, Bells. Do your worst."

Leah hissed.

I didn't want to breathe. It wasn't right to take such dangerous advantage of Jacob, no matter if he was the one offering. But I couldn't get away from the logic. How else could I be sure that I wouldn't hurt Renesmee?

"I'm getting older here, Bella," Jacob taunted. "Okay, not technically, but you get the idea. Go on, take a whiff."

"Hold on to me," I said to Edward, cringing back into his chest.

His hands tightened on my arms.

I locked my muscles in place, hoping I could keep them frozen. I resolved that I would do at least as well as I had on the hunt. Worst-case scenario, I would stop breathing and run for it. Nervously, I took a tiny breath in through my nose, braced for anything.

It hurt a little, but my throat was already burning dully anyway. Jacob didn't smell that much more human than the mountain lion. There was an animal edge to his blood that instantly repelled. Though the loud, wet sound of his heart was appealing, the scent that went with it made my nose wrinkle. It was actually *easier* with the smell to temper my reaction to the sound and heat of his pulsing blood.

I took another breath and relaxed. "Huh. I can see what everyone's been going on about. You stink, Jacob."

Edward burst into laughter; his hands slipped from my shoulders to wrap around my waist. Seth barked a low chortle in harmony with Edward; he came a little closer while Leah retreated several paces. And then I was aware of another audience when I heard Emmett's low, distinct guffaw, muffled a little by the glass wall between us.

"Look who's talking," Jacob said, theatrically plugging his nose. His face didn't pucker at all while Edward embraced me, not even when Edward composed himself and whispered "I love you" in my ear. Jacob just kept grinning. This made me feel hopeful that things were going to be right between us, the way they hadn't been for so long now. Maybe now I could truly be his friend, since I disgusted him enough physically that he couldn't love me the same way as before. Maybe that was all that was needed.

"Okay, so I passed, right?" I said. "Now are you going to tell me what this big secret is?"

Jacob's expression became very nervous. "It's nothing you need to worry about this second. . . ."

I heard Emmett chuckle again—a sound of anticipation.

I would have pressed my point, but as I listened to Emmett, I heard other sounds, too. Seven people breathing. One set of lungs moving more rapidly than the others. Only one heart fluttering like a bird's wings, light and quick.

I was totally diverted. My daughter was just on the

other side of that thin wall of glass. I couldn't see her—the light bounced off the reflective windows like a mirror. I could only see myself, looking very strange—so white and still—compared to Jacob. Or, compared to Edward, looking exactly right.

"Renesmee," I whispered. Stress made me a statue again. Renesmee wasn't going to smell like an animal. Would I put her in danger?

"Come and see," Edward murmured. "I know you can handle this."

"You'll help me?" I whispered through motionless lips.

"Of course I will."

"And Emmett and Jasper—just in case?"

"We'll take care of you, Bella. Don't worry, we'll be ready. None of us would risk Renesmee. I think you'll be surprised at how entirely she's already wrapped us all around her little fingers. She'll be perfectly safe, no matter what."

My yearning to see her, to understand the worship in his voice, broke my frozen pose. I took a step forward.

And then Jacob was in my way, his face a mask of worry.

"Are you *sure*, bloodsucker?" he demanded of Edward, his voice almost pleading. I'd never heard him speak to Edward that way. "I don't like this. Maybe she should wait—"

"You had your test, Jacob."

It was Jacob's test?

"But—," Jacob began.

"But nothing," Edward said, suddenly exasperated. "Bella needs to see *our* daughter. Get out of her way."

Jacob shot me an odd, frantic look and then turned and nearly sprinted into the house ahead of us.

Edward growled.

I couldn't make sense of their confrontation, and I couldn't concentrate on it, either. I could only think about the blurred child in my memory and struggle against the haziness, trying to remember her face exactly.

"Shall we?" Edward said, his voice gentle again.

I nodded nervously.

He took my hand tightly in his and led the way into the house.

They waited for me in a smiling line that was both welcoming and defensive. Rosalie was several paces behind the rest of them, near the front door. She was alone until Jacob joined her and then stood in front of her, closer than was normal. There was no sense of comfort in that closeness; both of them seemed to cringe from the proximity.

Someone very small was leaning forward out of Rosalie's arms, peering around Jacob. Immediately, she had my absolute attention, my every thought, the way nothing else had owned them since the moment I'd opened my eyes.

"I was out just two days?" I gasped, disbelieving.

The stranger-child in Rosalie's arms had to be weeks, if not months, old. She was maybe twice the size of the baby in my dim memory, and she seemed to be supporting her own torso easily as she stretched toward me. Her shiny bronze-colored hair fell in ringlets past her shoulders. Her chocolate brown eyes examined me with an interest that was not at all childlike; it was adult, aware and intelligent. She raised one hand, reaching in my direction for a moment, and then reached back to touch Rosalie's throat.

If her face had not been astonishing in its beauty and

perfection, I wouldn't have believed it was the same child. My child.

But Edward *was* there in her features, and I was there in the color of her eyes and cheeks. Even Charlie had a place in her thick curls, though their color matched Edward's. She must be ours. Impossible, but still true.

Seeing this unanticipated little person did not make her more real, though. It only made her more fantastic.

Rosalie patted the hand against her neck and murmured, "Yes, that's her."

Renesmee's eyes stayed locked on mine. Then, as she had just seconds after her violent birth, she smiled at me. A brilliant flash of tiny, perfect white teeth.

Reeling inside, I took a hesitant step toward her.

Everyone moved very fast.

Emmett and Jasper were right in front of me, shoulder to shoulder, hands ready. Edward gripped me from behind, fingers tight again on the tops of my arms. Even Carlisle and Esme moved to get Emmett's and Jasper's flanks, while Rosalie backed to the door, her arms clutching at Renesmee. Jacob moved, too, keeping his protective stance in front of them.

Alice was the only one who held her place.

"Oh, give her some credit," she chided them. "She wasn't going to do anything. You'd want a closer look, too."

Alice was right. I was in control of myself. I'd been braced for anything—for a scent as impossibly insistent as the human smell in the woods. The temptation here was really not comparable. Renesmee's fragrance was perfectly balanced right on the line between the scent of the most beautiful perfume and the scent of the most delicious food. There was enough of the sweet vampire smell to keep the human part from being overwhelming.

I could handle it. I was sure.

"I'm okay," I promised, patting Edward's hand on my arm. Then I hesitated and added, "Keep close, though, just in case."

Jasper's eyes were tight, focused. I knew he was taking in my emotional climate, and I worked on settling into a steady calm. I felt Edward free my arms as he read Jasper's assessment. But, though Jasper was getting it firsthand, he didn't seem as certain.

When she heard my voice, the too-aware child struggled in Rosalie's arms, reaching toward me. Somehow, her expression managed to look impatient.

"Jazz, Em, let us through. Bella's got this."

"Edward, the risk—," Jasper said.

"Minimal. Listen, Jasper—on the hunt she caught the scent of some hikers who were in the wrong place at the wrong time. . . ."

I heard Carlisle suck in a shocked breath. Esme's face was suddenly full of concern mingled with compassion. Jasper's eyes widened, but he nodded just a tiny bit, as if Edward's words answered some question in his head. Jacob's mouth screwed up into a disgusted grimace. Emmett shrugged. Rosalie seemed even less concerned than Emmett as she tried to hold on to the struggling child in her arms.

Alice's expression told me that she was not fooled. Her narrowed eyes, focused with burning intensity on my borrowed shirt, seemed more worried about what I'd done to my dress than anything else.

"Edward!" Carlisle chastened. "How could you be so irresponsible?"

"I know, Carlisle, I know. I was just plain stupid. I should have taken the time to make sure we were in a safe zone before I set her loose."

"Edward," I mumbled, embarrassed by the way they stared at me. It was like they were trying to see a brighter red in my eyes.

"He's absolutely right to rebuke me, Bella," Edward said with a grin. "I made a huge mistake. The fact that you are stronger than anyone I've ever known doesn't change that."

Alice rolled her eyes. "Tasteful joke, Edward."

"I wasn't making a joke. I was explaining to Jasper why I know Bella can handle this. It's not my fault everyone jumped to conclusions."

"Wait," Jasper gasped. "She didn't hunt the humans?"

"She started to," Edward said, clearly enjoying himself. My teeth ground together. "She was entirely focused on the hunt."

"What happened?" Carlisle interjected. His eyes were suddenly bright, an amazed smile beginning to form on his face. It reminded me of before, when he'd wanted the details on my transformation experience. The thrill of new information.

Edward leaned toward him, animated. "She heard me behind her and reacted defensively. As soon as my pursuit broke into her concentration, she snapped right out of it. I've never seen anything to equal her. She realized at once what was happening, and then . . . *she held her breath and ran away.*"

"Whoa," Emmett murmured. "Seriously?"

"He's not telling it right," I muttered, more embarrassed than before. "He left out the part where I growled at him."

"Did ya get in a couple of good swipes?" Emmett asked eagerly.

"No! Of course not."

"No, not really? You really didn't attack him?"

"Emmett!" I protested.

"Aw, what a waste," Emmett groaned. "And here you're probably the one person who could take him—since he can't get in your head to cheat—and you had a perfect excuse, too." He sighed. "I've been *dying* to see how he'd do without that advantage."

I glared at him frostily. "I would never."

Jasper's frown caught my attention; he seemed even more disturbed than before.

Edward touched his fist lightly to Jasper's shoulder in a mock punch. "You see what I mean?"

"It's not natural," Jasper muttered.

"She could have turned on you—she's only hours old!" Esme scolded, putting her hand against her heart. "Oh, we should have gone with you."

I wasn't paying so much attention, now that Edward was past the punch line of his joke. I was staring at the gorgeous child by the door, who was still staring at me. Her little dimpled hands reached out toward me like she knew exactly who I was. Automatically, my hand lifted to mimic hers.

"Edward," I said, leaning around Jasper to see her better. "Please?"

Jasper's teeth were set; he didn't move.

"Jazz, this isn't anything you've seen before," Alice said quietly. "Trust me."

Their eyes met for a short second, and then Jasper nodded. He moved out of my way, but put one hand on my shoulder and moved with me as I walked slowly forward.

I thought about every step before I took it, analyzing my mood, the burn in my throat, the position of the others around me. How strong I felt versus how well they would be able to contain me. It was a slow procession.

And then the child in Rosalie's arms, struggling and reaching all this time while her expression got more and more irritated, let out a high, ringing wail. Everyone reacted as if—like me—they'd never heard her voice before.

They swarmed around her in a second, leaving me standing alone, frozen in place. The sound of Renesmee's cry pierced right through me, spearing me to the floor. My eyes pricked in the strangest way, like they wanted to tear.

It seemed like everyone had a hand on her, patting and soothing. Everyone but me.

"What's the matter? Is she hurt? What happened?"

It was Jacob's voice that was loudest, that raised anxiously above the others. I watched in shock as he reached for Renesmee, and then in utter horror as Rosalie surrendered her to him without a fight.

"No, she's fine," Rosalie reassured him.

Rosalie was reassuring Jacob?

Renesmee went to Jacob willingly enough, pushing her tiny hand against his cheek and then squirming around to stretch toward me again.

"See?" Rosalie told him. "She just wants Bella."

"She wants me?" I whispered.

Renesmee's eyes—my eyes—stared impatiently at me.

Edward darted back to my side. He put his hands lightly on my arms and urged me forward.

"She's been waiting for you for almost three days," he told me.

We were only a few feet away from her now. Bursts of heat seemed to tremble out from her to touch me.

Or maybe it was Jacob who was trembling. I saw his hands shaking as I got closer. And yet, despite his obvious anxiety, his face was more serene than I had seen it in a long time.

"Jake—I'm fine," I told him. It made me panicky to see Renesmee in his shaking hands, but I worked to keep myself in control.

He frowned at me, eyes tight, like he was just as panicky at the thought of Renesmee in my arms.

Renesmee whimpered eagerly and stretched, her little hands grasping into fists again and again.

Something in me clicked into place at that moment. The sound of her cry, the familiarity of her eyes, the way she seemed even more impatient than I did for this reunion—all of it wove together into the most natural of patterns as she clutched the air between us. Suddenly, she was absolutely real, and *of course* I knew her. It was perfectly ordinary that I should take that last easy step and reach for her, putting my hands exactly where they would fit best as I pulled her gently toward me.

Jacob let his long arms stretch so that I could cradle her, but he didn't let go. He shuddered a little when our skin touched. His skin, always so warm to me before, felt like an open flame to me now. It was almost the same temperature as Renesmee's. Perhaps one or two degrees difference.

Renesmee seemed oblivious to the coolness of my skin, or at least very used to it.

She looked up and smiled at me again, showing her square little teeth and two dimples. Then, very deliberately, she reached for my face.

The moment she did this, all the hands on me tightened, anticipating my reaction. I barely noticed.

I was gasping, stunned and frightened by the strange, alarming image that filled my mind. It *felt* like a very strong memory—I could still see through my eyes while I watched it in my head—but it was completely unfamiliar. I stared through it to Renesmee's expectant expression, trying to understand what was happening, struggling desperately to hold on to my calm.

Besides being shocking and unfamiliar, the image was also wrong somehow—I almost recognized my own face in it, my old face, but it was off, backward. I grasped quickly that I was seeing my face as others saw it, rather than flipped in a reflection.

My memory face was twisted, ravaged, covered in sweat and blood. Despite this, my expression in the vision became an adoring smile; my brown eyes glowed over their deep circles. The image enlarged, my face came closer to the unseen vantage point, and then abruptly vanished.

Renesmee's hand dropped from my cheek. She smiled wider, dimpling again.

It was totally silent in the room but for the heartbeats.

No one but Jacob and Renesmee was so much as breathing. The silence stretched on; it seemed like they were waiting for me to say something.

"What . . . was . . . *that*?" I managed to choke out.

"What did you see?" Rosalie asked curiously, leaning around Jacob, who seemed very much in the way and out of place at the moment. "What did she show you?"

"*She* showed me that?" I whispered.

"I told you it was hard to explain," Edward murmured in my ear. "But effective as means of communications go."

"What was it?" Jacob asked.

I blinked quickly several times. "Um. Me. I think. But I looked terrible."

"It was the only memory she had of you," Edward explained. It was obvious he'd seen what she was *showing* me as she thought of it. He was still cringing, his voice rough from reliving the memory. "She's letting you know that she's made the connection, that she knows who you are."

"But *how* did she do that?"

Renesmee seemed unconcerned with my boggling eyes. She was smiling slightly and pulling on a lock of my hair.

"How do I hear thoughts? How does Alice see the future?" Edward asked rhetorically, and then shrugged. "She's gifted."

"It's an interesting twist," Carlisle said to Edward. "Like she's doing the exact opposite of what you can."

"Interesting," Edward agreed. "I wonder. . . ."

I knew they were speculating away, but I didn't care. I was staring at the most beautiful face in the world. She was hot in my arms, reminding me of the moment when the blackness had almost won, when there was nothing in the world left to hold on to. Nothing strong enough to pull me through the crushing darkness. The moment when I'd thought of Renesmee and found something I would never let go of.

"I remember you, too," I told her quietly.

It seemed very natural to lean in and press my lips to her forehead. She smelled wonderful. The scent of her skin set my throat burning, but it was easy to ignore. It didn't strip the joy from the moment. Renesmee was real and I knew her. She was the same one I'd fought for from the beginning. My little nudger, the one who loved me from the inside, too. Half Edward, perfect and lovely. And half me—which, surprisingly, made her better rather than detracting.

I'd been right all along. She was worth the fight.

"She's fine," Alice murmured, probably to Jasper. I could feel them hovering, not trusting me.

"Haven't we experimented enough for one day?" Jacob asked, his voice a slightly higher pitch with stress. "Okay, Bella's doing great, but let's not push it."

I glared at him with real irritation. Jasper shuffled uneasily next to me. We were all crowded so close that every tiny movement seemed very big.

"What is your *problem*, Jacob?" I demanded. I tugged lightly against his hold on Renesmee, and he just stepped closer to me. He was pressed right up to me, Renesmee touching both of our chests.

Edward hissed at him. "Just because I understand, it doesn't mean I won't throw you out, Jacob. Bella's doing extraordinarily well. Don't ruin the moment for her."

"I'll help him toss you, dog," Rosalie promised, her voice seething. "I owe you a good kick in the gut." Obviously, there was no change in *that* relationship, unless it had gotten worse.

I glared at Jacob's anxious half-angry expression. His eyes were locked on Renesmee's face. With everyone pressed together, he had to be touching at least six different vampires at the moment, and it didn't even seem to bug him.

Would he really go through all this just to protect me from myself? What could have happened during my transformation—my alteration into something he hated—that would soften him so much toward the reason for its necessity?

I puzzled over it, watching him stare at my daughter. Staring at her like . . . like he was a blind man seeing the sun for the very first time.

"No!" I gasped.

Jasper's teeth came together and Edward's arms wrapped around my chest like constricting boas. Jacob had Renesmee out of my arms in the same second, and I did not try to hold on to her. Because I felt it coming—the snap that they'd all been waiting for.

"Rose," I said through my teeth, very slowly and precisely. "Take Renesmee."

Rosalie held her hands out, and Jacob handed my daughter to her at once. Both of them backed away from me.

"Edward, I don't want to hurt you, so please let go of me."

He hesitated.

"Go stand in front of Renesmee," I suggested.

He deliberated, and then let me go.

I leaned into my hunting crouch and took two slow steps forward toward Jacob.

"You didn't," I snarled at him.

He backed away, palms up, trying to reason with me. "You know it's not something I can control."

"You *stupid mutt*! How *could* you? *My baby!*"

He backed out the front door now as I stalked him, half-running backward down the stairs. "It wasn't my idea, Bella!"

"I've held her all of *one* time, and already you think you have some moronic wolfy claim to her? She's *mine*."

"I can share," he said pleadingly as he retreated across the lawn.

"Pay up," I heard Emmett say behind me. A small part of my brain wondered who had bet against this outcome. I didn't waste much attention on it. I was too furious.

"How dare you *imprint* on *my* baby? Have you lost your mind?"

"It was involuntary!" he insisted, backing into the trees.

Then he wasn't alone. The two huge wolves reappeared, flanking him on either side. Leah snapped at me.

A fearsome snarl ripped through my teeth back at her. The sound disturbed me, but not enough to stop my advance.

"Bella, would you try to listen for just a second? Please?" Jacob begged. "Leah, back off," he added.

Leah curled her lip at me and didn't move.

"Why should I listen?" I hissed. Fury reigned in my head. It clouded everything else out.

"Because you're the one who told me this. Do you remember? You said we belonged in each other's lives, right? That we were family. You said that was how you and I were supposed to be. So . . . now we are. It's what you wanted."

I glared ferociously. I did dimly remember those words. But my new quick brain was two steps ahead of his nonsense.

"You think you'll be part of my family as my *son-in-law*!" I screeched. My bell voice ripped through two octaves and still came out sounding like music.

Emmett laughed.

"Stop her, Edward," Esme murmured. "She'll be unhappy if she hurts him."

But I felt no pursuit behind me.

"No!" Jacob was insisting at the same time. "How can you even look at it that way? She's just a baby, for crying out loud!"

"That's my *point*!" I yelled.

"You know I don't think of her that way! Do you think Edward would have let me live this long if I did? All I want is for her to be safe and happy—is that so bad? So different from what you want?" He was shouting right back at me.

Beyond words, I shrieked a growl at him.

"Amazing, isn't she?" I heard Edward murmur.

"She hasn't gone for his throat even once," Carlisle agreed, sounding stunned.

"Fine, you win this one," Emmett said grudgingly.

"You're going to stay away from her," I hissed up at Jacob.

"I can't do that!"

Through my teeth: "*Try*. Starting *now*."

"It's not possible. Do you remember how much you wanted me around three days ago? How hard it was to be apart from each other? That's gone for you now, isn't it?"

I glared, not sure what he was implying.

"That was her," he told me. "From the very beginning. We had to be together, even then."

I remembered, and then I understood; a tiny part of me was relieved to have the madness explained. But that relief somehow only made me angrier. Was he expecting that to be enough for me? That one little clarification would make me okay with this?

"Run away while you still can," I threatened.

"C'mon, Bells! Nessie likes me, too," he insisted.

I froze. My breathing stopped. Behind me, I heard the lack of sound that was their anxious reaction.

"*What* . . . did you call her?"

Jacob took a step farther back, managing to look sheepish. "Well," he mumbled, "that name you came up with is kind of a mouthful and—"

"You nicknamed my daughter after the *Loch Ness Monster?*" I screeched.

And then I lunged for his throat.

23. MEMORIES

"I'M SO SORRY, SETH. I SHOULD HAVE BEEN CLOSER."

Edward was *still* apologizing, and I didn't think that was either fair or appropriate. After all, *Edward* hadn't completely and inexcusably lost control of his temper. *Edward* hadn't tried to rip Jacob's head off—Jacob, who wouldn't even phase to protect himself—and then accidentally broken Seth's shoulder and collarbone when he jumped in between. *Edward* hadn't almost killed his best friend.

Not that the best friend didn't have a few things to answer for, but, obviously, nothing Jacob had done could have mitigated my behavior.

So shouldn't *I* have been the one apologizing? I tried again.

"Seth, I—"

"Don't worry about it, Bella, I'm totally fine," Seth said at the same time that Edward said, "Bella, love, no one is judging you. You're doing so well."

They hadn't let me finish a sentence yet.

It only made it worse that Edward was having a difficult time keeping the smile off his face. I knew that Jacob didn't deserve my overreaction, but Edward seemed to find something satisfying in it. Maybe he was just wishing that he had the excuse of being a newborn so that he could do something physical about his irritation with Jacob, too.

I tried to erase the anger from my system entirely, but it was hard, knowing that Jacob was outside with Renesmee right now. Keeping her safe from me, the crazed newborn.

Carlisle secured another piece of the brace to Seth's arm, and Seth winced.

"Sorry, sorry!" I mumbled, knowing I'd never get a fully articulated apology out.

"Don't freak, Bella," Seth said, patting my knee with his good hand while Edward rubbed my arm from the other side.

Seth seemed to feel no aversion to having me sit beside him on the sofa as Carlisle treated him. "I'll be back to normal in half an hour," he continued, still patting my knee as if oblivious to the cold, hard texture of it. "Anyone would have done the same, what with Jake and Ness—" He broke off mid-word and changed the subject quickly. "I mean, at least you didn't bite me or anything. That would've sucked."

I buried my face in my hands and shuddered at the

thought, at the very real possibility. It could have happened so easily. And werewolves didn't react to vampire venom the same way humans did, they'd told me only now. It was poison to them.

"I'm a bad person."

"Of course you aren't. I should have——," Edward started.

"Stop that," I sighed. I didn't want him taking the blame for this the way he always took everything on himself.

"Lucky thing Ness—Renesmee's not venomous," Seth said after a second of awkward silence. "'Cause she bites Jake all the time."

My hands dropped. "She does?"

"Sure. Whenever he and Rose don't get dinner in her mouth fast enough. Rose thinks it's pretty hilarious."

I stared at him, shocked, and also feeling guilty, because I had to admit that this pleased me a teensy bit in a petulant way.

Of course, I already knew that Renesmee wasn't venomous. I was the first person she'd bitten. I didn't make this observation aloud, as I was feigning memory loss on those recent events.

"Well, Seth," Carlisle said, straightening up and stepping away from us. "I think that's as much as I can do. Try to not move for, oh, a few hours, I guess." Carlisle chuckled. "I wish treating humans were this instantaneously gratifying." He rested his hand for a moment on Seth's black hair. "Stay still," he ordered, and then he disappeared upstairs. I heard his office door close, and I wondered if they'd already removed the evidence of my time there.

"I can probably manage sitting still for a while," Seth

agreed after Carlisle was already gone, and then he yawned hugely. Carefully, making sure not to tweak his shoulder, Seth leaned his head against the sofa's back and closed his eyes. Seconds later, his mouth fell slack.

I frowned at his peaceful face for another minute. Like Jacob, Seth seemed to have the gift of falling asleep at will. Knowing I wouldn't be able to apologize again for a while, I got up; the motion didn't jostle the couch in the slightest. Everything physical was so easy. But the rest . . .

Edward followed me to the back windows and took my hand.

Leah was pacing along the river, stopping every now and then to look at the house. It was easy to tell when she was looking for her brother and when she was looking for me. She alternated between anxious glances and murderous glares.

I could hear Jacob and Rosalie outside on the front steps bickering quietly over whose turn it was to feed Renesmee. Their relationship was as antagonistic as ever; the only thing they agreed on now was that I should be kept away from my baby until I was one hundred percent recovered from my temper tantrum. Edward had disputed their verdict, but I'd let it go. I wanted to be sure, too. I was worried, though, that *my* one hundred percent sure and *their* one hundred percent sure might be very different things.

Other than their squabbling, Seth's slow breathing, and Leah's annoyed panting, it was very quiet. Emmett, Alice, and Esme were hunting. Jasper had stayed behind to watch me. He stood unobtrusively behind the newel post now, trying not to be obnoxious about it.

I took advantage of the calm to think of all the things

Edward and Seth had told me while Carlisle splinted Seth's arm. I'd missed a whole lot while I was burning, and this was the first real chance to catch up.

The main thing was the end of the feud with Sam's pack—which was why the others felt safe to come and go as they pleased again. The truce was stronger than ever. Or more binding, depending on your viewpoint, I imagined.

Binding, because the most absolute of all the pack's laws was that no wolf ever kill the object of another wolf's imprinting. The pain of such a thing would be intolerable for the whole pack. The fault, whether intended or accidental, could not be forgiven; the wolves involved would fight to the death—there was no other option. It had happened long ago, Seth told me, but only accidentally. No wolf would ever intentionally destroy a brother that way.

So Renesmee was untouchable because of the way Jacob now felt about her. I tried to concentrate on the relief of this fact rather than the chagrin, but it wasn't easy. My mind had enough room to feel both emotions intensely at the same time.

And Sam couldn't get mad about my transformation, either, because Jacob—speaking as the rightful Alpha— had allowed it. It rankled to realize over and over again how much I owed Jacob when I just wanted to be mad at him.

I deliberately redirected my thoughts in order to control my emotions. I considered another interesting phenomenon; though the silence between the separate packs continued, Jacob and Sam had discovered that Alphas could speak to each other while in their wolf form. It wasn't the same as before; they couldn't hear every thought the way they had prior to the split. It was more like speaking aloud, Seth had said. Sam could only hear the thoughts Jacob wanted to share, and vice versa. They found they could communicate over distance, too, now that they were talking to each other again.

They hadn't found all this out until Jacob had gone alone—over Seth's and Leah's objections—to explain to Sam about Renesmee; it was the only time he'd left Renesmee since first laying eyes on her.

Once Sam had understood how absolutely everything had changed, he'd come back with Jacob to talk to Carlisle. They'd spoken in human form (Edward had refused to leave my side to translate), and the treaty had been renewed. The friendly feeling of the relationship, however, might never be the same.

One big worry down.

But there was another that, though not as physically dangerous as an angry wolf pack, still seemed more urgent to me.

Charlie.

He'd spoken to Esme earlier this morning, but that hadn't kept him from calling again, twice, just a few minutes ago while Carlisle treated Seth. Carlisle and Edward had let the phone ring.

What would be the right thing to tell him? Were the Cullens right? Was telling him that I'd died the best, the kindest way? Would I be able to lie still in a coffin while he and my mother cried over me?

It didn't seem right to me. But putting Charlie or Renée in danger of the Volturi's obsession with secrecy was clearly out of the question.

There was still my idea—let Charlie see me, when

I was ready for that, and let him make his own wrong assumptions. Technically, the vampire rules would remain unbroken. Wouldn't it be better for Charlie if he knew that I was alive—sort of—and happy? Even if I was strange and different and probably frightening to him?

My eyes, in particular, were much too frightening right now. How long before my self-control and my eye color were ready for Charlie?

"What's the matter, Bella?" Jasper asked quietly, reading my growing tension. "No one is angry with you"—a low snarl from the riverside contradicted him, but he ignored it—"or even surprised, really. Well, I suppose we *are* surprised. Surprised that you were able to snap out of it so quickly. You did well. Better than anyone expects of you."

While he was speaking, the room became very calm. Seth's breathing slipped into a low snore. I felt more peaceful, but I didn't forget my anxieties.

"I was thinking about Charlie, actually."

Out front, the bickering cut off.

"Ah," Jasper murmured.

"We really have to leave, don't we?" I asked. "For a while, at the very least. Pretend we're in Atlanta or something."

I could feel Edward's gaze locked on my face, but I looked at Jasper. He was the one who answered me in a grave tone.

"Yes. It's the only way to protect your father."

I brooded for a moment. "I'm going to miss him so much. I'll miss everyone here."

Jacob, I thought, despite myself. Though that yearning was both vanished and defined—and I was vastly relieved that it was—he was still my friend. Someone who knew the real me and accepted her. Even as a monster.

I thought about what Jacob had said, pleading with me before I'd attacked him. *You said we belonged in each other's lives, right? That we were family. You said that was how you and I were supposed to be. So . . . now we are. It's what you wanted.*

But it didn't feel like how I'd wanted it. Not exactly. I remembered further back, to the fuzzy, weak memories of my human life. Back to the very hardest part to remember— the time without Edward, a time so dark I'd tried to bury it in my head. I couldn't get the words exactly right; I only remembered wishing that Jacob were my brother so that we could love each other without any confusion or pain. Family. But I'd never factored a daughter into the equation.

I remembered a little later—one of the many times that I'd told Jacob goodbye—wondering aloud who he would end up with, who would make his life right after what I'd done to it. I had said something about how whoever she was, she wouldn't be good enough for him.

I snorted, and Edward raised one eyebrow questioningly. I just shook my head at him.

But as much as I might miss my friend, I knew there was a bigger problem. Had Sam or Jared or Quil ever gone a whole day without seeing the objects of their fixations, Emily, Kim, and Claire? *Could* they? What would the separation from Renesmee do to Jacob? Would it cause him pain?

There was still enough petty ire in my system to make me glad, not for his pain, but for the idea of having Renesmee away from him. How was I supposed to deal with having her belong to Jacob when she only barely seemed to belong to me?

The sound of movement on the front porch interrupted my thoughts. I heard them get up, and then they were through the door. At exactly the same time, Carlisle came down the stairs with his hands full of odd things—a measuring tape, a scale. Jasper darted to my side. As if there was some signal I'd missed, even Leah sat down outside and stared through the window with an expression like she was expecting something that was both familiar and also totally uninteresting.

"Must be six," Edward said.

"So?" I asked, my eyes locked on Rosalie, Jacob, and Renesmee. They stood in the doorway, Renesmee in Rosalie's arms. Rose looked wary. Jacob looked troubled. Renesmee looked beautiful and impatient.

"Time to measure Ness—er, Renesmee," Carlisle explained.

"Oh. You do this every day?"

"Four times a day," Carlisle corrected absently as he motioned the others toward the couch. I thought I saw Renesmee sigh.

"Four times? Every day? *Why?*"

"She's still growing quickly," Edward murmured to me, his voice quiet and strained. He squeezed my hand, and his other arm wrapped securely around my waist, almost as if he needed the support.

I couldn't take my eyes off Renesmee to check his expression.

She looked perfect, absolutely healthy. Her skin glowed like backlit alabaster; the color in her cheeks was rose petals against it. There couldn't be anything wrong with such radiant beauty. Surely there could be nothing more dangerous in her life than her mother. Could there?

The difference between the child I'd given birth to and the one I'd met again an hour ago would have been obvious to anyone. The difference between Renesmee an hour ago and Renesmee now was subtler. Human eyes never would have detected it. But it was there.

Her body was slightly longer. Just a little bit slimmer. Her face wasn't quite as round; it was more oval by one minute degree. Her ringlets hung a sixteenth of an inch lower down her shoulders. She stretched out helpfully in Rosalie's arms while Carlisle ran the tape measure down the length of her and then used it to circle her head. He took no notes; perfect recall.

I was aware that Jacob's arms were crossed as tightly over his chest as Edward's arms were locked around me. His heavy brows were mashed together into one line over his deep-set eyes.

She had matured from a single cell to a normal-sized baby in the course of a few weeks. She looked well on her way to being a toddler just days after her birth. If this rate of growth held . . .

My vampire mind had no trouble with the math.

"What do we do?" I whispered, horrified.

Edward's arms tightened. He understood exactly what I was asking. "I don't know."

"It's slowing," Jacob muttered through his teeth.

"We'll need several more days of measurements to track the trend, Jacob. I can't make any promises."

"Yesterday she grew two inches. Today it's less."

"By a thirty-second of an inch, if my measurements are perfect," Carlisle said quietly.

"*Be* perfect, Doc," Jacob said, making the words almost threatening. Rosalie stiffened.

"You know I'll do my best," Carlisle assured him.

Jacob sighed. "Guess that's all I can ask."

I felt irritated again, like Jacob was stealing my lines—and delivering them all wrong.

Renesmee seemed irritated, too. She started to squirm and then reached her hand imperiously toward Rosalie. Rosalie leaned forward so that Renesmee could touch her face. After a second, Rose sighed.

"What does she want?" Jacob demanded, taking my line again.

"Bella, of course," Rosalie told him, and her words made my insides feel a little warmer. Then she looked at me. "How are you?"

"Worried," I admitted, and Edward squeezed me.

"We all are. But that's not what I meant."

"I'm in control," I promised. Thirstiness was way down the list right now. Besides, Renesmee smelled good in a very non-food way.

Jacob bit his lip but made no move to stop Rosalie as she offered Renesmee to me. Jasper and Edward hovered but allowed it. I could see how tense Rose was, and I wondered how the room felt to Jasper right now. Or was he focusing so hard on me that he couldn't feel the others?

Renesmee reached for me as I reached for her, a blinding smile lighting her face. She fit so easily in my arms, like they'd been shaped just for her. Immediately, she put her hot little hand against my cheek.

Though I was prepared, it still made me gasp to see the memory like a vision in my head. So bright and colorful but also completely transparent.

She was remembering me charging Jacob across the front lawn, remembering Seth leaping between us. She'd seen and heard it all with perfect clarity. It didn't look like *me*, this graceful predator leaping at her prey like an arrow arcing from a bow. It had to be someone else. That made me feel a very small bit less guilty as Jacob stood there defenselessly with his hands raised in front of him. His hands did not tremble.

Edward chuckled, watching Renesmee's thoughts with me. And then we both winced as we heard the crack of Seth's bones.

Renesmee smiled her brilliant smile, and her memory eyes did not leave Jacob through all the following mess. I tasted a new flavor to the memory—not exactly protective, more possessive—as she watched Jacob. I got the distinct impression that she was *glad* Seth had put himself in front of my spring. She didn't want Jacob hurt. He was *hers*.

"Oh, wonderful," I groaned. "Perfect."

"It's just because he tastes better than the rest of us," Edward assured me, voice stiff with his own annoyance.

"I told you she likes me, too," Jacob teased from across the room, his eyes on Renesmee. His joking was halfhearted; the tense angle of his eyebrows had not relaxed.

Renesmee patted my face impatiently, demanding my attention. Another memory: Rosalie pulling a brush gently through each of her curls. It felt nice.

Carlisle and his tape measure, knowing she had to stretch and be still. It was not interesting to her.

"It looks like she's going to give you a rundown of everything you missed," Edward commented in my ear.

My nose wrinkled as she dumped the next one on me. The smell coming from a strange metal cup—hard enough not to be bitten through easily—sent a flash burn through my throat. Ouch.

And then Renesmee was out of my arms, which were pinned behind my back. I didn't struggle with Jasper; I just looked at Edward's frightened face.

"What did I do?"

Edward looked at Jasper behind me, and then at me again.

"But she was remembering being thirsty," Edward muttered, his forehead pressing into lines. "She was remembering the taste of human blood."

Jasper's arms pulled mine tighter together. Part of my head noted that this wasn't particularly uncomfortable, let alone painful, as it would have been to a human. It was just annoying. I was sure I could break his hold, but I didn't fight it.

"Yes," I agreed. "And?"

Edward frowned at me for a second more, and then his expression loosened. He laughed once. "And nothing at all, it seems. The overreaction is mine this time. Jazz, let her go."

The binding hands disappeared. I reached out for Renesmee as soon as I was free. Edward handed her to me without hesitation.

"I can't understand," Jasper said. "I can't bear this."

I watched in surprise as Jasper strode out the back door. Leah moved to give him a wide margin of space as he paced to the river and then launched himself over it in one bound.

Renesmee touched my neck, repeating the scene of departure right back, like an instant replay. I could feel the question in her thought, an echo of mine.

I was already over the shock of her odd little gift. It seemed an entirely natural part of her, almost to be expected. Maybe now that I was part of the supernatural myself, I would never be a skeptic again.

But what was wrong with Jasper?

"He'll be back," Edward said, whether to me or Renesmee, I wasn't sure. "He just needs a moment alone to readjust his perspective on life." There was a grin threatening at the corners of his mouth.

Another human memory—Edward telling me that Jasper would feel better about himself if I "had a hard time adjusting" to being a vampire. This was in the context of a discussion about how many people I would kill my first newborn year.

"Is he mad at me?" I asked quietly.

Edward's eyes widened. "No. Why would he be?"

"What's the matter with him, then?"

"He's upset with himself, not you, Bella. He's worrying about . . . self-fulfilling prophecy, I suppose you could say."

"How so?" Carlisle asked before I could.

"He's wondering if the newborn madness is really as difficult as we've always thought, or if, with the right focus and attitude, anyone could do as well as Bella. Even now—perhaps he only has such difficulty because he believes it's natural and unavoidable. Maybe if he expected more of himself, he would rise to those expectations. You're making him question a lot of deep-rooted assumptions, Bella."

"But that's unfair," Carlisle said. "Everyone is different; everyone has their own challenges. Perhaps what Bella is doing goes beyond the natural. Maybe this is her gift, so to speak."

I froze with surprise. Renesmee felt the change, and touched me. She remembered the last second of time and wondered why.

"That's an interesting theory, and quite plausible," Edward said.

For a tiny space, I was disappointed. What? No magic visions, no formidable offensive abilities like, oh, shooting lightning bolts from my eyes or something? Nothing helpful or cool at all?

And then I realized what that might mean, if my "superpower" was no more than exceptional self-control.

For one thing, at least I had a gift. It could have been nothing.

But, much more than that, if Edward was right, then I could skip right over the part I'd feared the very most.

What if I didn't have to be a newborn? Not in the crazed killing-machine sense, anyway. What if I could fit right in with the Cullens from my first day? What if we didn't have to hide out somewhere remote for a year while I "grew up"? What if, like Carlisle, I never killed a single person? What if I could be a good vampire right away?

I could see Charlie.

I sighed as soon as reality filtered through hope. I couldn't see Charlie right away. The eyes, the voice, the perfected face. What could I possibly say to him; how could I even begin? I was furtively glad that I had some excuses for putting things off for a while; as much as I wanted to find some way to keep Charlie in my life, I was terrified of that first meeting. Seeing his eyes pop as he took in my new face, my new skin. Knowing that he was frightened. Wondering what dark explanation would form in his head.

I was chicken enough to wait for a year while my eyes cooled. And here I'd thought I would be so fearless when I was indestructible.

"Have you ever seen an equivalent to self-control as a talent?" Edward asked Carlisle. "Do you really think that's a gift, or just a product of all her preparation?"

Carlisle shrugged. "It's slightly similar to what Siobhan has always been able to do, though she wouldn't call it a gift."

"Siobhan, your friend in that Irish coven?" Rosalie asked. "I wasn't aware that she did anything special. I thought it was Maggie who was talented in that bunch."

"Yes, Siobhan thinks the same. But she has this way of deciding her goals and then almost . . . *willing* them into reality. She considers it good planning, but I've always wondered if it was something more. When she included Maggie, for instance. Liam was very territorial, but Siobhan wanted it to work out, and so it did."

Edward, Carlisle, and Rosalie settled into chairs as they continued with the discussion. Jacob sat next to Seth protectively, looking bored. From the way his eyelids drooped, I was sure he'd be unconscious momentarily.

I listened, but my attention was divided. Renesmee was

still telling me about her day. I held her by the window wall, my arms rocking her automatically as we stared into each other's eyes.

I realized that the others had no reason for sitting down. I was perfectly comfortable standing. It was just as restful as stretching out on a bed would be. I knew I would be able to stand like this for a week without moving and I would feel just as relaxed at the end of the seven days as I did at the beginning.

They must sit out of habit. Humans would notice someone standing for hours without ever shifting her weight to a different foot. Even now, I saw Rosalie brush her fingers against her hair and Carlisle cross his legs. Little motions to keep from being too still, too much a vampire. I would have to pay attention to what they did and start practicing.

I rolled my weight back to my left leg. It felt kind of silly.

Maybe they were just trying to give me a little alone time with my baby—as alone as was safe.

Renesmee told me about every minute happening of the day, and I got the feeling from the tenor of her little stories that she wanted me to know her every bit as much I wanted the same thing. It worried her that I had missed things— like the sparrows that had hopped closer and closer when Jacob had held her, both of them very still beside one of the big hemlocks; the birds wouldn't come close to Rosalie. Or the outrageously icky white stuff—baby formula—that Carlisle had put in her cup; it smelled like sour dirt. Or the song Edward had crooned to her that was so perfect Renesmee played it for me twice; I was surprised that I was in the background of that memory, perfectly motionless but looking fairly battered still. I shuddered, remembering that time from my own perspective. The hideous fire . . .

After almost an hour—the others were still deeply absorbed in their discussion, Seth and Jacob snoring in harmony on the couch—Renesmee's memory stories began to slow. They got slightly blurry around the edges and drifted out of focus before they came to their conclusions. I was about to interrupt Edward in a panic—was there something wrong with her?—when her eyelids fluttered and closed. She yawned, her plump pink lips stretching into a round O, and her eyes never reopened.

Her hand fell away from my face as she drifted to sleep—the backs of her eyelids were the pale lavender color of thin clouds before the sunrise. Careful not to disturb her, I lifted that hand back to my skin and held it there curiously. At first there was nothing, and then, after a few minutes, a flickering of colors like a handful of butterflies were scattering from her thoughts.

Mesmerized, I watched her dreams. There was no sense to it. Just colors and shapes and faces. I was pleased by how often my face—both of my faces, hideous human and glorious immortal—cropped up in her unconscious thoughts. More than Edward or Rosalie. I was neck and neck with Jacob; I tried not to let that get to me.

For the first time, I understood how Edward had been able to watch me sleep night after boring night, just to hear me talk in my sleep. I could watch Renesmee dream forever.

The change in Edward's tone caught my attention when he said, "Finally," and turned to gaze out the window. It was deep, purply night outside, but I could see just as far as before. Nothing was hidden in the darkness; everything had just changed colors.

Leah, still glowering, got up and slunk into the brush just as Alice came into view on the other side of the river. Alice swung back and forth from a branch like a trapeze artist, toes touching hands, before throwing her body into a graceful flat spin over the river. Esme made a more traditional leap, while Emmett charged right through the water, splashing water so far that splatters hit the back windows. To my surprise, Jasper followed after, his own efficient leap seeming understated, even subtle, after the others.

The huge grin stretching Alice's face was familiar in a dim, odd way. Everyone was suddenly smiling at me—Esme sweet, Emmett excited, Rosalie a little superior, Carlisle indulgent, and Edward expectant.

Alice skipped into the room ahead of everyone else, her hand stretched out in front of her and impatience making a nearly visible aura around her. In her palm was an everyday brass key with an oversized pink satin bow tied around it.

She held the key out for me, and I automatically gripped Renesmee more securely in my right arm so that I could open my left. Alice dropped the key into it.

"Happy birthday!" she squealed.

I rolled my eyes. "No one starts counting on the actual day of birth," I reminded her. "Your first birthday is at the year mark, Alice."

Her grin turned smug. "We're not celebrating your vampire birthday. Yet. It's September thirteenth, Bella. Happy nineteenth birthday!"

24. SURPRISE

"No. No way!" I shook my head fiercely and then shot a glance at the smug smile on my seventeen-year-old husband's face. "No, this doesn't count. I stopped aging three days ago. I am eighteen forever."

"Whatever," Alice said, dismissing my protest with a quick shrug. "We're celebrating anyway, so suck it up."

I sighed. There was rarely a point to arguing with Alice.

Her grin got impossibly wider as she read the acquiescence in my eyes.

"Are you ready to open your present?" Alice sang.

"Presents," Edward corrected, and he pulled another

key—this one longer and silver with a less gaudy blue bow—from his pocket.

I struggled to keep from rolling my eyes. I knew immediately what this key was to—the "after car." I wondered if I should feel excited. It seemed the vampire conversion hadn't given me any sudden interest in sports cars.

"Mine first," Alice said, and then stuck her tongue out, foreseeing his answer.

"Mine is closer."

"But look at how she's *dressed.*" Alice's words were almost a moan. "It's been killing me all day. That is clearly the priority."

My eyebrows pulled together as I wondered how a key could get me into new clothes. Had she gotten me a whole trunkful?

"I know—I'll play you for it," Alice suggested. "Rock, paper, scissors."

Jasper chuckled and Edward sighed.

"Why don't you just tell me who wins?" Edward said wryly.

Alice beamed. "I do. Excellent."

"It's probably better that I wait for morning, anyway." Edward smiled crookedly at me and then nodded toward Jacob and Seth, who looked like they were crashed for the night; I wonder how long they'd stayed up this time. "I think it might be more fun if Jacob was awake for the big reveal, don't you agree? So that someone there is able to express the right level of enthusiasm?"

I grinned back. He knew me well.

"Yay," Alice sang. "Bella, give Ness—Renesmee to Rosalie."

"Where does she usually sleep?"

Alice shrugged. "In Rose's arms. Or Jacob's. Or Esme's. You get the picture. She has never been set down in her entire life. She's going to be the most spoiled half-vampire in existence."

Edward laughed while Rosalie took Renesmee expertly in her arms. "She is also the most *un*spoiled half-vampire in existence," Rosalie said. "The beauty of being one of a kind."

Rosalie grinned at me, and I was glad to see that the new comradeship between us was still there in her smile. I hadn't been entirely sure it would last after Renesmee's life was no longer tied to mine. But maybe we had fought together on the same side long enough that we would always be friends now. I'd finally made the same choice she would have if she'd been in my shoes. That seemed to have washed away her resentment for all my other choices.

Alice shoved the beribboned key in my hand, then grabbed my elbow and steered me toward the back door. "Let's go, let's go," she trilled.

"Is it outside?"

"Sort of," Alice said, pushing me forward.

"Enjoy your gift," Rosalie said. "It's from all of us. Esme especially."

"Aren't you coming, too?" I realized that no one had moved.

"We'll give you a chance to appreciate it alone," Rosalie said. "You can tell us about it . . . later."

Emmett guffawed. Something about his laugh made me feel like blushing, though I wasn't sure why.

I realized that lots of things about me—like truly hating

surprises, and not liking gifts in general much more—had not changed one bit. It was a relief and revelation to discover how much of my essential core traits had come with me into this new body.

I hadn't expected to be myself. I smiled widely.

Alice tugged my elbow, and I couldn't stop smiling as I followed her into the purple night. Only Edward came with us.

"There's the enthusiasm I'm looking for," Alice murmured approvingly. Then she dropped my arm, made two lithe bounds, and leaped over the river.

"C'mon, Bella," she called from the other side.

Edward jumped at the same time I did; it was every bit as fun as it had been this afternoon. Maybe a little bit more fun because the night changed everything into new, rich colors.

Alice took off with us on her heels, heading due north. It was easier to follow the sound of her feet whispering against the ground and the fresh path of her scent than it was to keep my eyes on her through the thick vegetation.

At no sign I could see, she whirled and dashed back to where I paused.

"Don't attack me," she warned, and sprang at me.

"What are you doing?" I demanded, squirming as she scrambled onto my back and wrapped her hands around my face. I felt the urge to throw her off, but I controlled it.

"Making sure you can't see."

"I could take care of that without the theatrics," Edward offered.

"You might let her cheat. Take her hand and lead her forward."

"Alice, I—"

"Don't bother, Bella. We're doing this my way."

I felt Edward's fingers weave through mine. "Just a few seconds more, Bella. Then she'll go annoy someone else." He pulled me forward. I kept up easily. I wasn't afraid of hitting a tree; the tree would be the only one getting hurt in that scenario.

"You might be a little more appreciative," Alice chided him. "This is as much for you as it is for her."

"True. Thank you again, Alice."

"Yeah, yeah. Okay." Alice's voice suddenly shot up with excitement. "Stop there. Turn her just a little to the right. Yes, like that. Okay. Are you ready?" she squeaked.

"I'm ready." There were new scents here, piquing my interest, increasing my curiosity. Scents that didn't belong in the deep woods. Honeysuckle. Smoke. Roses. Sawdust? Something metallic, too. The richness of deep earth, dug up and exposed. I leaned toward the mystery.

Alice hopped down from my back, releasing her grip on my eyes.

I stared into the violet dark. There, nestled into a small clearing in the forest, was a tiny stone cottage, lavender gray in the light of the stars.

It belonged here so absolutely that it seemed as if it must have grown from the rock, a natural formation. Honeysuckle climbed up one wall like a lattice, winding all the way up and over the thick wooden shingles. Late summer roses bloomed in a handkerchief-sized garden under the dark, deep-set windows. There was a little path of flat stones, amethyst in the night, that led up to the quaint arched wooden door.

I curled my hand around the key I held, shocked.

"What do you think?" Alice's voice was soft now; it fit with the perfect quiet of the storybook scene.

I opened my mouth but said nothing.

"Esme thought we might like a place of our own for a while, but she didn't want us too far away," Edward murmured. "And she loves any excuse to renovate. This little place has been crumbling away out here for at least a hundred years."

I continued staring, mouth gaping like a fish.

"Don't you like it?" Alice's face fell. "I mean, I'm sure we could fix it up differently, if you want. Emmett was all for adding a few thousand square feet, a second story, columns, and a tower, but Esme thought you would like it best the way it was meant to look." Her voice started to climb, to go faster. "If she was wrong, we can get back to work. It won't take long to—"

"Shh!" I managed.

She pressed her lips together and waited. It took me a few seconds to recover.

"You're giving me a house for my birthday?" I whispered.

"Us," Edward corrected. "And it's no more than a cottage. I think the word *house* implies more legroom."

"No knocking my house," I whispered to him.

Alice beamed. "You like it."

I shook my head.

"Love it?"

I nodded.

"I can't wait to tell Esme!"

"Why didn't she come?"

Alice's smile faded a little, twisted just off what it had been, like my question was hard to answer. "Oh, you know . . . they all remember how you are about presents. They didn't want to put you under too much pressure to like it."

"But of course I love it. How could I not?"

"They'll like that." She patted my arm. "Anyhoo, your closet is stocked. Use it wisely. And . . . I guess that's everything."

"Aren't you going to come inside?"

She strolled casually a few feet back. "Edward knows his way around. I'll stop by . . . later. Call me if you can't match your clothes right." She threw me a doubtful look and then smiled. "Jazz wants to hunt. See you."

She shot off into the trees like the most graceful bullet.

"That was weird," I said when the sound of her flight had vanished completely. "Am I really *that* bad? They didn't have to stay away. Now I feel guilty. I didn't even thank her right. We should go back, tell Esme—"

"Bella, don't be silly. No one thinks you're that unreasonable."

"Then what—"

"Alone time is their other gift. Alice was trying to be subtle about it."

"Oh."

That was all it took to make the house disappear. We could have been anywhere. I didn't see the trees or the stones or the stars. It was just Edward.

"Let me show you what they've done," he said, pulling

my hand. Was he oblivious to the fact that an electric current was pulsing through my body like adrenaline-spiked blood?

Once again I felt oddly off balance, waiting for reactions my body wasn't capable of anymore. My heart should have been thundering like a steam engine about to hit us. Deafening. My cheeks should have been brilliant red.

For that matter, I ought to have been exhausted. This had been the longest day of my life.

I laughed out loud—just one quiet little laugh of shock—when I realized that this day would never end.

"Do I get to hear the joke?"

"It's not a very good one," I told him as he led the way to the little rounded door. "I was just thinking—today is the first and last day of forever. It's kind of hard to wrap my head around it. Even with all this extra room for wrapping." I laughed again.

He chuckled with me. He held his hand out toward the doorknob, waiting for me to do the honors. I stuck the key in the lock and turned it.

"You're such a natural at this, Bella; I forget how very strange this all must be for you. I wish I could *hear* it." He ducked down and yanked me up into his arms so fast that I didn't see it coming—and that was really something.

"Hey!"

"Thresholds are part of my job description," he reminded me. "But I'm curious. Tell me what you're thinking about right now."

He opened the door—it fell back with a barely audible creak—and stepped through into the little stone living room.

"Everything," I told him. "All at the same time, you know. Good things and things to worry about and things that are new. How I keep using too many superlatives in my head. Right now, I'm thinking that Esme is an artist. It's so perfect!"

The cottage room was something from a fairy tale. The floor was a crazy quilt of smooth, flat stones. The low ceiling had long exposed beams that someone as tall as Jacob would surely knock his head on. The walls were warm wood in some places, stone mosaics in others. The beehive fireplace in the corner held the remains of a slow flickering fire. It was driftwood burning there—the low flames were blue and green from the salt.

It was furnished in eclectic pieces, not one of them matching another, but harmonious just the same. One chair seemed vaguely medieval, while a low ottoman by the fire was more contemporary and the stocked book-shelf against the far window reminded me of movies set in Italy. Somehow each piece fit together with the others like a big three-dimensional puzzle. There were a few paintings on the walls that I recognized—some of my very favorites from the big house. Priceless originals, no doubt, but they seemed to belong here, too, like all the rest.

It was a place where anyone could believe magic existed. A place where you just expected Snow White to walk right in with her apple in hand, or a unicorn to stop and nibble at the rosebushes.

Edward had always thought that he belonged to the world of horror stories. Of course, I'd known he was dead wrong. It was obvious that he belonged *here*. In a fairy tale.

And now I was in the story with him.

I was about to take advantage of the fact that he hadn't gotten around to setting me back on my feet and that his wits-scramblingly beautiful face was only inches away when he said, "We're lucky Esme thought to add an extra room. No one was planning for Ness—Renesmee."

I frowned at him, my thoughts channeled down a less pleasant path.

"Not you, too," I complained.

"Sorry, love. I hear it in their thoughts all the time, you know. It's rubbing off on me."

I sighed. My baby, the sea serpent. Maybe there was no help for it. Well, *I* wasn't giving in.

"I'm sure you're dying to see the closet. Or, at least I'll *tell* Alice that you were, to make her feel good."

"Should I be afraid?"

"Terrified."

He carried me down a narrow stone hallway with tiny arches in the ceiling, like it was our own miniature castle.

"That will be Renesmee's room," he said, nodding to an empty room with a pale wooden floor. "They didn't have time to do much with it, what with the angry were-wolves. . . ."

I laughed quietly, amazed at how quickly everything had turned right when it had all had looked so nightmarish just a week ago.

Drat Jacob for making everything perfect *this* way.

"Here's our room. Esme tried to bring some of her island back here for us. She guessed that we would get attached."

The bed was huge and white, with clouds of gossamer floating down from the canopy to the floor. The pale wood floor matched the other room, and now I grasped that it was precisely the color of a pristine beach. The walls were that almost-white-blue of a brilliant sunny day, and the back wall had big glass doors that opened into a little hidden garden. Climbing roses and a small round pond, smooth as a mirror and edged with shiny stones. A tiny, calm ocean for us.

"Oh" was all I could say.

"I know," he whispered.

We stood there for a minute, remembering. Though the memories were human and clouded, they took over my mind completely.

He smiled a wide, gleaming smile and then laughed. "The closet is through those double doors. I should warn you—it's bigger than this room."

I didn't even glance at the doors. There was nothing else in the world but him again—his arms curled under me, his sweet breath on my face, his lips just inches from mine—and there was nothing that could distract me now, newborn vampire or not.

"We're going to tell Alice that I ran right to the clothes," I whispered, twisting my fingers into his hair and pulling my face closer to his. "We're going to tell her I spent hours in there playing dress-up. We're going to *lie*."

He caught up to my mood in an instant, or maybe he'd already been there, and he was just trying to let me fully appreciate my birthday present, like a gentleman. He pulled my face to his with a sudden fierceness, a low moan in his throat. The sound sent the electric current running through my body into a near-frenzy, like I couldn't get close enough to him fast enough.

I heard the fabric tearing under our hands, and I was glad *my* clothes, at least, were already destroyed. It was too late for his. It felt almost rude to ignore the pretty white bed, but we just weren't going to make it that far.

This second honeymoon wasn't like our first.

Our time on the island had been the epitome of my human life. The very best of it. I'd been so ready to string along my human time, just to hold on to what I had with him for a little while longer. Because the physical part wasn't going to be the same ever again.

I should have guessed, after a day like today, that it would be better.

I could really appreciate him now—could properly see every beautiful line of his perfect face, of his long, flawless body with my strong new eyes, every angle and every plane of him. I could taste his pure, vivid scent on my tongue and feel the unbelievable silkiness of his marble skin under my sensitive fingertips.

My skin was so sensitive under his hands, too.

He was all new, a different person as our bodies tangled gracefully into one on the sand-pale floor. No caution, no restraint. No fear—especially not that. We could love *together*—both active participants now. Finally equals.

Like our kisses before, every touch was more than I was used to. So much of himself he'd been holding back. Necessary at the time, but I couldn't believe how much I'd been missing.

I tried to keep in mind that I was stronger than he was, but it was hard to focus on anything with sensations so intense, pulling my attention to a million different places in my body every second; if I hurt him, he didn't complain.

A very, very small part of my head considered the interesting conundrum presented in this situation. I was never going to get tired, and neither was he. We didn't have to catch our breath or rest or eat or even use the bathroom; we had no more mundane human needs. He had the most beautiful, perfect body in the world and I had him all to myself, and it didn't feel like I was ever going to find a point where I would think, *Now I've had enough for one day.* I was always going to want more. And the day was never going to end. So, in such a situation, how did we ever *stop*?

It didn't bother me at all that I had no answer.

I sort of noticed when the sky began to lighten. The tiny ocean outside turned from black to gray, and a lark started to sing somewhere very close by—maybe she had a nest in the roses.

"Do you miss it?" I asked him when her song was done.

It wasn't the first time we'd spoken, but we weren't exactly keeping up a conversation, either.

"Miss what?" he murmured.

"All of it—the warmth, the soft skin, the tasty smell . . . I'm not losing anything at all, and I just wondered if it was a little bit sad for you that you were."

He laughed, low and gentle. "It would be hard to find someone *less* sad than I am now. Impossible, I'd venture. Not many people get every single thing they want, plus all the things they didn't think to ask for, in the same day."

"Are you avoiding the question?"

He pressed his hand against my face. "You *are* warm," he told me.

It was true, in a sense. To me, his hand was warm. It wasn't the same as touching Jacob's flame-hot skin, but it was more comfortable. More natural.

Then he pulled his fingers very slowly down my face, lightly tracing from my jaw to my throat and then all the way down to my waist. My eyes rolled back into my head a little.

"You *are* soft."

His fingers were like satin against my skin, so I could see what he meant.

"And as for the scent, well, I couldn't say I *missed* that. Do you remember the scent of those hikers on our hunt?"

"I've been trying very hard not to."

"Imagine kissing that."

My throat ripped into flames like pulling the cord on a hot-air balloon.

"*Oh.*"

"Precisely. So the answer is no. I am purely full of joy, because I am missing *nothing.* No one has more than I do now."

I was about to inform him of the one exception to his statement, but my lips were suddenly very busy.

When the little pool turned pearl-colored with the sunrise, I thought of another question for him.

"How long does this go on? I mean, Carlisle and Esme, Em and Rose, Alice and Jasper—they don't spend all day locked in their rooms. They're out in public, fully clothed, all the time. Does this . . . *craving* ever let up?" I twisted myself closer into him—quite an accomplishment, actually—to make it clear what I was talking about.

"That's difficult to say. Everyone is different and, well, so far you're the very most different of all. The average young vampire is too obsessed with thirst to notice much else for a while. That doesn't seem to apply to you. With the average vampire, though, after that first year, other needs make themselves known. Neither thirst nor any other desire really ever *fades*. It's simply a matter of learning to balance them, learning to prioritize and manage. . . ."

"How long?"

He smiled, wrinkling his nose a little. "Rosalie and Emmett were the worst. It took a solid decade before I could stand to be within a five-mile radius of them. Even Carlisle and Esme had a difficult time stomaching it. They kicked the happy couple out eventually. Esme built them a house, too. It was grander than this one, but then, Esme knows what Rose likes, and she knows what you like."

"So, after ten years, then?" I was pretty sure that Rosalie and Emmett had nothing on us, but it might sound cocky if I went higher than a decade. "Everybody is normal again? Like they are now?"

Edward smiled again. "Well, I'm not sure what you mean by normal. You've seen my family going about life in a fairly human way, but you've been sleeping nights." He winked at me. "There's a tremendous amount of time left over when you don't have to sleep. It makes balancing your . . . interests quite easy. There's a reason why I'm the best musician in the family, why—besides Carlisle—I've read the most books, studied the most sciences, become fluent in the most languages. . . . Emmett would have you believe that I'm such a know-it-all because of the mind reading, but the truth is that I've just had a *lot* of free time."

We laughed together, and the motion of our laughter did interesting things to the way our bodies were connected, effectively ending that conversation.

25. FAVOR

IT WAS ONLY A LITTLE WHILE LATER THAT EDWARD
reminded me of my priorities.

It took him just one word.

"Renesmee . . ."

I sighed. She would be awake soon. It must be nearly
seven in the morning. Would she be looking for me?
Abruptly, something close to panic had my body freezing
up. What would she look like today?

Edward felt the total distraction of my stress. "It's all
right, love. Get dressed, and we'll be back to the house in
two seconds."

I probably looked like a cartoon, the way I sprung up, then
looked back at him—his diamond body faintly glinting in

the diffuse light—then away to the west, where Renesmee waited, then back at him again, then back toward her, my head whipping from side to side a half dozen times in a second. Edward smiled, but didn't laugh; he was a strong man.

"It's all about balance, love. You're so good at all of this, I don't imagine it will take too long to put everything in perspective."

"And we have all night, right?"

He smiled wider. "Do you think I could bear to let you get dressed now if that weren't the case?"

That would have to be enough to get me through the daylight hours. I would balance this overwhelming, devastating desire so that I could be a good— It was hard to think the word. Though Renesmee was very real and vital in my life, it was still difficult to think of myself as a *mother*. I supposed anyone would feel the same, though, without nine months to get used to the idea. And with a child that changed by the hour.

The thought of Renesmee's speeding life had me stressed-out again in an instant. I didn't even pause at the ornately carved double doors to catch my breath before finding out what Alice had done. I just burst through, intent on wearing the first things I touched. I should have known it wouldn't be that easy.

"Which ones are mine?" I hissed. As promised, the room was bigger than our bedroom. It might have been bigger than the rest of the house put together, but I'd have to pace it off to be positive. I had a brief mental flash of Alice trying to persuade Esme to ignore classic proportions and allow this monstrosity. I wondered how Alice had won that one.

Everything was wrapped in garment bags, pristine and white, row after row after row.

"To the best of my knowledge, everything but this rack here"—he touched a bar that stretched along the half-wall to the left of the door—"is yours."

"All of this?"

He shrugged.

"Alice," we said together. He said her name like an explanation; I said it like an expletive.

"Fine," I muttered, and I pulled down the zipper on the closest bag. I growled under my breath when I saw the floor-length silk gown inside—baby pink.

Finding something normal to wear could take all day!

"Let me help," Edward offered. He sniffed carefully at the air and then followed some scent to the back of the long room. There was a built-in dresser there. He sniffed again, then opened a drawer. With a triumphant grin, he held out a pair of artfully faded blue jeans.

I flitted to his side. "How did you do that?"

"Denim has its own scent just like anything else. Now . . . stretch cotton?"

He followed his nose to a half-rack, unearthing a long-sleeved white t-shirt. He tossed it to me.

"Thanks," I said fervently. I inhaled each fabric, memorizing the scent for future searches through this madhouse. I remembered silk and satin; I would avoid those.

It only took him seconds to find his own clothes—if I hadn't seen him undressed, I would have sworn there was nothing more beautiful than Edward in his khakis and pale beige pullover—and then he took my hand. We darted through the hidden garden, leaped lightly over the stone wall, and hit the forest at a dead sprint. I pulled my hand free so that we could race back. He beat me this time.

Renesmee was awake; she was sitting up on the floor with Rose and Emmett hovering over her, playing with a little pile of twisted silverware. She had a mangled spoon in her right hand. As soon as she spied me through the glass, she chucked the spoon on the floor—where it left a divot in the wood—and pointed in my direction imperiously. Her audience laughed; Alice, Jasper, Esme, and Carlisle were sitting on the couch, watching her as if she were the most engrossing film.

I was through the door before their laughter had barely begun, bounding across the room and scooping her up from the floor in the same second. We smiled widely at each other.

She was different, but not so much. A little longer again, her proportions drifting from babyish to childlike. Her hair was longer by a quarter inch, the curls bouncing like springs with every movement. I'd let my imagination run wild on the trip back, and I'd imagined worse than this. Thanks to my overdone fears, these little changes were almost a relief. Even without Carlisle's measurements, I was sure the changes were slower than yesterday.

Renesmee patted my cheek. I winced. She was hungry again.

"How long has she been up?" I asked as Edward disappeared through the kitchen doorway. I was sure he was on his way to get her breakfast, having seen what she'd just thought as clearly as I had. I wondered if he would ever have noticed her little quirk, if he'd been the only one to know her. To him, it probably would have seemed like hearing anyone.

"Just a few minutes," Rose said. "We would have called you soon. She's been asking for you—*demanding* might be a better description. Esme sacrificed her second-best silver service to keep the little monster entertained." Rose smiled at Renesmee with so much gloating affection that the criticism was entirely weightless. "We didn't want to . . . er, bother you."

Rosalie bit her lip and looked away, trying not to laugh. I could feel Emmett's silent laughter behind me, sending vibrations through the foundations of the house.

I kept my chin high. "We'll get your room set up right away," I said to Renesmee. "You'll like the cottage. It's magic." I look up at Esme. "Thank you, Esme. So much. It's absolutely perfect."

Before Esme could respond, Emmett was laughing again—it wasn't silent this time.

"So it's still standing?" he managed to get out between his snickers. "I would've thought you two had knocked it to rubble by now. What were you doing last night? Discussing the national debt?" He howled with laughter.

I gritted my teeth and reminded myself of the negative consequences when I'd let my temper get away from me yesterday. Of course, Emmett wasn't as breakable as Seth. . . .

Thinking of Seth made me wonder. "Where're the wolves today?" I glanced out the window wall, but there had been no sign of Leah on the way in.

"Jacob took off this morning pretty early," Rosalie told

me, a little frown creasing her forehead. "Seth followed him out."

"What was he so upset about?" Edward asked as he came back into the room with Renesmee's cup. There must have been more in Rosalie's memory than I'd seen in her expression.

Without breathing, I handed Renesmee off to Rosalie. Super-self-control, maybe, but there was no way I was going to be able to feed her. Not yet.

"I don't know—or care," Rosalie grumbled, but she answered Edward's question more fully. "He was watching Nessie sleep, his mouth hanging open like the moron he is, and then he just jumped to his feet without any kind of trigger—that I noticed, anyway—and stormed out. *I* was glad to be rid of him. The more time he spends here, the less chance there is that we'll ever get the smell out."

"Rose," Esme chided gently.

Rosalie flipped her hair. "I suppose it doesn't matter. We won't be here that much longer."

"I still say we should go straight to New Hampshire and get things set up," Emmett said, obviously continuing an earlier conversation. "Bella's already registered at Dartmouth. Doesn't look like it will take her all that long to be able to handle school." He turned to look at me with a teasing grin. "I'm sure you'll ace your classes . . . apparently there's nothing interesting for you to do at night besides study."

Rosalie giggled.

Do not lose your temper, do not lose your temper, I chanted to myself. And then I was proud of myself for keeping my head.

So I was pretty surprised that Edward didn't.

He growled—an abrupt, shocking rasp of sound—and the blackest fury rolled across his expression like storm clouds.

Before any of us could respond, Alice was on her feet.

"What is he *doing*? What is that *dog* doing that has erased my schedule for the entire day? I can't see *anything*! No!" She shot me a tortured glance. "Look at you! You *need* me to show you how to use your closet."

For one second I was grateful for whatever Jacob was up to.

And then Edward's hands balled up into fists and he snarled, "He talked to Charlie. He thinks Charlie is following after him. Coming here. Today."

Alice said a word that sounded very odd in her trilling, ladylike voice, and then she blurred into motion, streaking out the back door.

"He told Charlie?" I gasped. "But—doesn't he understand? How could he do that?" Charlie *couldn't* know about me! About vampires! That would put him on a hit list that even the Cullens couldn't save him from. "No!"

Edward spoke through his teeth. "Jacob's on his way in now."

It must have started raining farther east. Jacob came through the door shaking his wet hair like a dog, flipping droplets on the carpet and the couch where they made little round gray spots on the white. His teeth glinted against his dark lips; his eyes were bright and excited. He walked with jerky movements, like he was all hyped-up about destroying my father's life.

"Hey, guys," he greeted us, grinning.

It was perfectly silent.

Leah and Seth slipped in behind him, in their human forms—for now; both of their hands were trembling with the tension in the room.

"Rose," I said, holding my arms out. Wordlessly, Rosalie handed me Renesmee. I pressed her close to my motionless heart, holding her like a talisman against rash behavior. I would keep her in my arms until I was sure my decision to kill Jacob was based entirely on rational judgment rather than fury.

She was very still, watching and listening. How much did she understand?

"Charlie'll be here soon," Jacob said to me casually. "Just a heads-up. I assume Alice is getting you sunglasses or something?"

"You assume *way* too much," I spit through my teeth. "What. Have. You. *Done?*"

Jacob's smile wavered, but he was still too wound up to answer seriously. "Blondie and Emmett woke me up this morning going on and on about you all moving cross-country. Like I could let you leave. Charlie was the biggest issue there, right? Well, problem solved."

"Do you even *realize* what you've done? The danger you've put him in?"

He snorted. "I didn't put him in danger. Except from you. But you've got some kind of supernatural self-control, right? Not as good as mind reading, if you ask me. Much less exciting."

Edward moved then, darting across the room to get in

Jacob's face. Though he was half a head shorter than Jacob, Jacob leaned away from his staggering anger as if Edward towered over him.

"That's just a *theory*, mongrel," he snarled. "You think we should test it out on *Charlie*? Did you consider the physical pain you're putting Bella through, even if she can resist? Or the emotional pain if she doesn't? I suppose what happens to Bella no longer concerns you!" He spit the last word.

Renesmee pressed her fingers anxiously to my cheek, anxiety coloring the replay in her head.

Edward's words finally cut through Jacob's strangely electric mood. His mouth dropped into a frown. "Bella will be in pain?"

"Like you've shoved a white-hot branding iron down her throat!"

I flinched, remembering the scent of pure human blood.

"I didn't know that," Jacob whispered.

"Then perhaps you should have asked first," Edward growled back through his teeth.

"You would have stopped me."

"You *should* have been stopped—"

"This isn't about me," I interrupted. I stood very still, keeping my hold on Renesmee and sanity. "This is about Charlie, Jacob. How could you put him in danger this way? Do you realize it's death or vampire life for him now, too?" My voice trembled with the tears my eyes could no longer shed.

Jacob was still troubled by Edward's accusations, but mine didn't seem to bother him. "Relax, Bella. I didn't tell him anything you weren't planning to tell him."

"But he's coming here!"

"Yeah, that's the idea. Wasn't the whole 'let him make the wrong assumptions' thing your plan? I think I provided a very nice red herring, if I do say so myself."

My fingers flexed away from Renesmee. I curled them back in securely. "Say it straight, Jacob. I don't have the patience for this."

"I didn't tell him anything about you, Bella. Not really. I told him about *me*. Well, *show* is probably a better verb."

"He phased in front of Charlie," Edward hissed.

I whispered, "You *what?*"

"He's brave. Brave as you are. Didn't pass out or throw up or anything. I gotta say, I was impressed. You should've seen his face when I started taking my clothes off, though. Priceless," Jacob chortled.

"You absolute *moron*! You could have given him a heart attack!"

"Charlie's fine. He's tough. If you'd give this just a minute, you'll see that I did you a favor here."

"You have half of that, Jacob." My voice was flat and steely. "You have thirty seconds to tell me every single word before I give Renesmee to Rosalie and rip your miserable head off. Seth won't be able to stop me this time."

"Jeez, Bells. You didn't used to be so melodramatic. Is that a vampire thing?"

"Twenty-six seconds."

Jacob rolled his eyes and flopped into the nearest chair. His little pack moved to stand on his flanks, not at all relaxed the way he seemed to be; Leah's eyes were on me, her teeth slightly bared.

"So I knocked on Charlie's door this morning and asked

him to come for a walk with me. He was confused, but when I told him it was about you and that you were back in town, he followed me out to the woods. I told him you weren't sick anymore, and that things were a little weird, but good. He was about to take off to see you, but I told him I had to show him something first. And then I phased." Jacob shrugged.

My teeth felt like a vise was pushing them together. "I want every word, you monster."

"Well, you said I only had thirty seconds—okay, okay." My expression must have convinced him that I wasn't in the mood for teasing. "Lemme see . . . I phased back and got dressed, and then after he started breathing again, I said something like, 'Charlie, you don't live in the world you thought you lived in. The good news is, nothing has changed—except that now you know. Life'll go on the same way it always has. You can go right back to pretending that you don't believe any of this.'

"It took him a minute to get his head together, and then he wanted to know what was really going on with you, with the whole rare-disease thing. I told him that you *had* been sick, but you were fine now—it was just that you'd had to change a little bit in the process of getting better. He wanted to know what I meant by 'change,' and I told him that you looked a lot more like Esme now than you looked like Renée."

Edward hissed while I stared in horror; this was headed in a dangerous direction.

"After a few minutes, he asked, real quietly, if you turned into an animal, too. And I said, 'She wishes she was that cool!'" Jacob chuckled.

Rosalie made a noise of disgust.

"I started to tell him more about werewolves, but I didn't even get the whole word out—Charlie cut me off and said he'd 'rather not know the specifics.' Then he asked if you'd known what you were getting yourself into when you married Edward, and I said, 'Sure, she's known all about this for years, since she first came to Forks.' He didn't like *that* very much. I let him rant till he got it out of his system. After he got calmed down, he just wanted two things. He wanted to see you, and I said it would be better if he gave me a head start to explain."

I inhaled deeply. "What was the other thing he wanted?"

Jacob smiled. "You'll like this. His main request is that he be told as little as possible about *all* of this. If it's not absolutely essential for him to know something, then keep it to yourself. Need to know, only."

I felt relief for the first time since Jacob had walked in. "I can handle that part."

"Other than that, he'd just like to pretend things are normal." Jacob's smile turned smug; he must suspect that I would be starting to feel the first faint stirrings of gratitude about now.

"What did you tell him about Renesmee?" I struggled to maintain the razor edge in my voice, fighting the reluctant appreciation. It was premature. There was still so much wrong with this situation. Even if Jacob's intervention had brought out a better reaction in Charlie than I'd ever hoped for . . .

"Oh yeah. So I told him that you and Edward had inherited a new little mouth to feed." He glanced at Edward.

"She's your orphaned ward—like Bruce Wayne and Dick Grayson." Jacob snorted. "I didn't think you'd mind me lying. That's all part of the game, right?" Edward didn't respond in any way, so Jacob went on. "Charlie was way past being shocked at this point, but he did ask if you were adopting her. 'Like a daughter? Like I'm sort of a grandfather?' were his exact words. I told him yes. 'Congrats, Gramps,' and all of that. He even smiled a little."

The stinging returned to my eyes, but not out of fear or anguish this time. Charlie was smiling at the idea of being a grandpa? Charlie would meet Renesmee?

"But she's changing so fast," I whispered.

"I told him that she was more special than all of us put together," Jacob said in a soft voice. He stood and walked right up to me, waving Leah and Seth off when they started to follow. Renesmee reached out to him, but I hugged her more tightly to me. "I told him, 'Trust me, you don't want to know about this. But if you can ignore all the strange parts, you're going to be amazed. She's the most wonderful person in the whole world.' And then I told him that if he could deal with that, you all would stick around for a while and he would have a chance to get to know her. But that if it was too much for him, you would leave. He said as long as no one forced too much information on him, he'd deal."

Jacob stared at me with half a smile, waiting.

"I'm not going to say thank you," I told him. "You're still putting Charlie at a huge risk."

"I *am* sorry about it hurting you. I didn't know it was like that. Bella, things are different with us now, but you'll always be my best friend, and I'll always love you. But I'll love you the right way now. There's finally a balance. We *both* have people we can't live without."

He smiled his very most Jacob-y smile. "Still friends?"

Try as hard as I could to resist, I had to smile back. Just a tiny smile.

He held out his hand: an offer.

I took a deep breath and shifted Renesmee's weight to one arm. I put my left hand in his—he didn't even flinch at the feel of my cool skin. "If I don't kill Charlie tonight, I'll consider forgiving you for this."

"*When* you don't kill Charlie tonight, you'll owe me huge."

I rolled my eyes.

He held out his other hand toward Renesmee, a request this time. "Can I?"

"I'm actually holding her so that my hands aren't free to kill you, Jacob. Maybe later."

He sighed but didn't push me on it. Wise of him.

Alice raced back through the door then, her hands full and her expression promising violence.

"You, you, and you," she snapped, glaring at the were-wolves. "If you must stay, get over in the corner and commit to being there for a while. I need to *see*. Bella, you'd better give him the baby, too. You'll need your arms free, any-way."

Jacob grinned in triumph.

Undiluted fear ripped through my stomach as the enormity of what I was about to do hit me. I was going to gamble on my iffy self-control with my pure human father as the guinea pig. Edward's earlier words crashed in my ears again.

Did you consider the physical pain you're putting Bella through, even if she can resist? Or the emotional pain if she doesn't?

I couldn't imagine the pain of failure. My breathing turned to gasps.

"Take her," I whispered, sliding Renesmee into Jacob's arms.

He nodded, concern wrinkling his forehead. He gestured to the others, and they all went to the far corner of the room. Seth and Jake slouched on the floor at once, but Leah shook her head and pursed her lips.

"Am I allowed to leave?" she griped. She looked uncomfortable in her human body, wearing the same dirty t-shirt and cotton shorts she'd worn to shriek at me the other day, her short hair sticking up in irregular tufts. Her hands were still shaking.

"Of course," Jake said.

"Stay east so you don't cross Charlie's path," Alice added.

Leah didn't look at Alice; she ducked out the back door and stomped into the bushes to phase.

Edward was back at my side, stroking my face. "You can do this. I know you can. I'll help you; we all will."

I met Edward's eyes with panic screaming from my face. Was he strong enough to stop me if I made a wrong move?

"If I didn't believe you could handle it, we'd disappear today. This very minute. But you can. And you'll be happier if you can have Charlie in your life."

I tried to slow my breathing.

Alice held out her hand. There was a small white box on her palm. "These will irritate your eyes—they won't hurt, but they'll cloud your vision. It's annoying. They also won't match your old color, but it's still better than bright red, right?"

She flipped the contact box into the air and I caught it.

"When did you——"

"Before you left on the honeymoon. I was prepared for several possible futures."

I nodded and opened the container. I'd never worn contacts before, but it couldn't be that hard. I took the little brown quarter-sphere and pressed it, concave side in, to my eye.

I blinked, and a film interrupted my sight. I could see through it, of course, but I could also see the texture of the thin screen. My eye kept focusing on the microscopic scratches and warped sections.

"I see what you mean," I murmured as I stuck the other one in. I tried to not blink this time. My eye automatically wanted to dislodge the obstruction.

"How do I look?"

Edward smiled. "Gorgeous. Of course——"

"Yes, yes, she always looks gorgeous," Alice finished his thought impatiently. "It's better than red, but that's the highest commendation I can give. Muddy brown. Your brown was much prettier. Keep in mind that those won't last forever—the venom in your eyes will dissolve them in a few hours. So if Charlie stays longer than that, you'll have to excuse yourself to replace them. Which is a good idea anyway, because humans need bathroom breaks." She shook her head. "Esme, give her a few pointers on acting human while I stock the powder room with contacts."

"How long do I have?"

"Charlie will be here in five minutes. Keep it simple."

Esme nodded once and came to take my hand. "The main thing is not to sit too still or move too fast," she told me.

"Sit down if he does," Emmett interjected. "Humans don't like to just stand there."

"Let your eyes wander every thirty seconds or so," Jasper added. "Humans don't stare at one thing for too long."

"Cross your legs for about five minutes, then switch to crossing your ankles for the next five," Rosalie said.

I nodded once at each suggestion. I'd noticed them doing some of these things yesterday. I thought I could mimic their actions.

"And blink at least three times a minute," Emmett said. He frowned, then darted to where the television remote sat on the end table. He flipped the TV on to a college football game and nodded to himself.

"Move your hands, too. Brush your hair back or pretend to scratch something," Jasper said.

"I said *Esme*," Alice complained as she returned. "You'll overwhelm her."

"No, I think I got it all," I said. "Sit, look around, blink, fidget."

"Right," Esme approved. She hugged my shoulders.

Jasper frowned. "You'll be holding your breath as much as possible, but you need to move your shoulders a little to make it *look* like you're breathing."

I inhaled once and then nodded again.

Edward hugged me on my free side. "You can do this," he repeated, murmuring the encouragement in my ear.

"Two minutes," Alice said. "Maybe you should start out

already on the couch. You've been sick, after all. That way he won't have to see you move right at first."

Alice pulled me to the sofa. I tried to move slowly, to make my limbs more clumsy. She rolled her eyes, so I must not have been doing a good job.

"Jacob, I need Renesmee," I said.

Jacob frowned, unmoving.

Alice shook her head. "Bella, that doesn't help me see."

"But I *need* her. She keeps me calm." The edge of panic in my voice was unmistakable.

"Fine," Alice groaned. "Hold her as still as you can and I'll *try* to see around her." She sighed wearily, like she'd been asked to work overtime on a holiday. Jacob sighed, too, but brought Renesmee to me, and then retreated quickly from Alice's glare.

Edward took a seat beside me and put his arms around Renesmee and me. He leaned forward and looked Renesmee very seriously in the eyes.

"Renesmee, someone special is coming to see you and your mother," he said in a solemn voice, as if he expected her to understand every word. Did she? She looked back at him with clear, grave eyes. "But he's not like us, or even like Jacob. We have to be very careful with him. You shouldn't tell him things the way you tell us."

Renesmee touched his face.

"Exactly," he said. "And he's going to make you thirsty. But you mustn't bite him. He won't heal like Jacob."

"Can she understand you?" I whispered.

"She understands. You'll be careful, won't you, Renesmee? You'll help us?"

Renesmee touched him again.

"No, I don't care if you bite Jacob. That's fine."

Jacob chuckled.

"Maybe you should leave, Jacob," Edward said coldly, glaring in his direction. Edward hadn't forgiven Jacob, because he knew that no matter what happened now, I was going to be hurting. But I'd take the burn happily if that were the worst thing I'd face tonight.

"I told Charlie I'd be here," Jacob said. "He needs the moral support."

"Moral support," Edward scoffed. "As far as Charlie knows, you're the most repulsive monster of us all."

"Repulsive?" Jake protested, and then he laughed quietly to himself.

I heard the tires turn off the highway onto the quiet, damp earth of the Cullens' drive, and my breathing spiked again. My heart ought to have been hammering. It made me anxious that my body didn't have the right reactions.

I concentrated on the steady thrumming of Renesmee's heart to calm myself. It worked pretty quickly.

"Well done, Bella," Jasper whispered in approval.

Edward tightened his arm over my shoulders.

"You're sure?" I asked him.

"Positive. You can do *anything*." He smiled and kissed me.

It wasn't precisely a peck on the lips, and my wild vampiric reactions took me off guard yet again. Edward's lips were like a shot of some addictive chemical straight into my nervous system. I was instantly craving more. It took all my concentration to remember the baby in my arms.

Jasper felt my mood change. "Er, Edward, you might

not want to distract her like that right now. She needs to be able to focus."

Edward pulled away. "Oops," he said.

I laughed. That had been *my* line from the very beginning, from the very first kiss.

"Later," I said, and anticipation curled my stomach into a ball.

"Focus, Bella," Jasper urged.

"Right." I pushed the trembly feelings away. Charlie, that was the main thing now. Keep Charlie safe today. We would have all night. . . .

"Bella."

"Sorry, Jasper."

Emmett laughed.

The sound of Charlie's cruiser got closer and closer. The second of levity passed, and everyone was still. I crossed my legs and practiced my blinks.

The car pulled in front of the house and idled for a few seconds. I wondered if Charlie was as nervous as I was. Then the engine cut off, and a door slammed. Three steps across the grass, and then eight echoing thuds against the wooden stairs. Four more echoing footsteps across the porch. Then silence. Charlie took two deep breaths.

Knock, knock, knock.

I inhaled for what might be the last time. Renesmee nestled deeper into my arms, hiding her face in my hair.

Carlisle answered the door. His stressed expression changed to one of welcome, like switching the channel on the TV.

"Hello, Charlie," he said, looking appropriately abashed.

After all, we were supposed to be in Atlanta at the Center for Disease Control. Charlie knew he'd been lied to.

"Carlisle," Charlie greeted him stiffly. "Where's Bella?"

"Right here, Dad."

Ugh! My voice was so wrong. Plus, I'd used up some of my air supply. I gulped in a quick refill, glad that Charlie's scent had not saturated the room yet.

Charlie's blank expression told me how off my voice was. His eyes zeroed in on me and widened.

I read the emotions as they scrolled across his face.

Shock. Disbelief. Pain. Loss. Fear. Anger. Suspicion. More pain.

I bit my lip. It felt funny. My new teeth were sharper against my granite skin than my human teeth had been against my soft human lips.

"Is that you, Bella?" he whispered.

"Yep." I winced at my wind-chime voice. "Hi, Dad."

He took a deep breath to steady himself.

"Hey, Charlie," Jacob greeted him from the corner. "How're things?"

Charlie glowered at Jacob once, shuddered at a memory, and then stared at me again.

Slowly, Charlie walked across the room until he was a few feet away from me. He darted an accusing glare at Edward, and then his eyes flickered back to me. The warmth of his body heat beat against me with each pulse of his heart.

"Bella?" he asked again.

I spoke in a lower voice, trying to keep the ring out of it. "It's really me."

His jaw locked.

"I'm sorry, Dad," I said.

"Are you okay?" he demanded.

"Really and truly great," I promised. "Healthy as a horse."

That was it for my oxygen.

"Jake told me this was . . . necessary. That you were dying." He said the words like he didn't believe them one bit.

I steeled myself, focused on Renesmee's warm weight, leaned into Edward for support, and took a deep breath.

Charlie's scent was a fistful of flames, punching straight down my throat. But it was so much more than pain. It was a hot stabbing of desire, too. Charlie smelled more delicious than anything I'd ever imagined. As appealing as the anonymous hikers had been on the hunt, Charlie was doubly tempting. And he was just a few feet away, leaking mouthwatering heat and moisture into the dry air.

But I wasn't hunting now. And this was my father.

Edward squeezed my shoulders sympathetically, and Jacob shot an apologetic glance at me across the room.

I tried to collect myself and ignore the pain and longing of the thirst. Charlie was waiting for my answer.

"Jacob was telling you the truth."

"That makes one of you," Charlie growled.

I hoped Charlie could see past the changes in my new face to read the remorse there.

Under my hair, Renesmee sniffed as Charlie's scent registered with her, too. I tightened my grip on her.

Charlie saw my anxious glance down and followed it. "Oh," he said, and all the anger fell off his face, leaving only shock behind. "This is her. The orphan Jacob said you're adopting."

"My niece," Edward lied smoothly. He must have decided

that the resemblance between Renesmee and him was too pronounced to be ignored. Best to claim they were related from the beginning.

"I thought you'd lost your family," Charlie said, accusation returning to his voice.

"I lost my parents. My older brother was adopted, like me. I never saw him after that. But the courts located me when he and his wife died in a car accident, leaving their only child without any other family."

Edward was so good at this. His voice was even, with just the right amount of innocence. I needed practice so that I could do that.

Renesmee peeked out from under my hair, sniffing again. She glanced shyly at Charlie from under her long lashes, then hid again.

"She's . . . she's, well, she's a beauty."

"Yes," Edward agreed.

"Kind of a big responsibility, though. You two are just getting started."

"What else could we do?" Edward brushed his fingers lightly over her cheek. I saw him touch her lips for just a moment—a reminder. "Would you have refused her?"

"Hmph. Well." He shook his head absently. "Jake says you call her Nessie?"

"No, we don't," I said, my voice too sharp and piercing. "Her name is Renesmee."

Charlie refocused on me. "How do you feel about this? Maybe Carlisle and Esme could—"

"She's mine," I interrupted. "I *want* her."

Charlie frowned. "You gonna make me a grandpa so young?"

Edward smiled. "Carlisle is a grandfather, too."

Charlie shot an incredulous glance at Carlisle, still standing by the front door; he looked like Zeus's younger, better-looking brother.

Charlie snorted and then laughed. "I guess that does sort of make me feel better." His eyes strayed back to Renesmee. "She sure is something to look at." His warm breath blew lightly across the space between us.

Renesmee leaned toward the smell, shaking off my hair and looking him full in the face for the first time. Charlie gasped.

I knew what he was seeing. My eyes—his eyes—copied exactly into her perfect face.

Charlie started hyperventilating. His lips trembled, and I could read the numbers he mouthed. He was counting backward, trying to fit nine months into one. Trying to put it together but not able to force the evidence right in front of him to make any sense.

Jacob got up and came over to pat Charlie on the back. He leaned in to whisper something in Charlie's ear; only Charlie didn't know we could all hear.

"Need to know, Charlie. It's okay. I promise."

Charlie swallowed and nodded. And then his eyes blazed as he took a step closer to Edward with his fists tightly clenched.

"I don't want to know everything, but I'm done with the lies!"

"I'm sorry," Edward said calmly, "but you need to know the public story more than you need to know the truth. If you're going to be part of this secret, the public story is the one that counts. It's to protect Bella and Renesmee as well as the rest of us. Can you go along with the lies for them?"

The room was full of statues. I crossed my ankles.

Charlie huffed once and then turned his glare on me. "You might've given me some warning, kid."

"Would it really have made this any easier?"

He frowned, and then he knelt on the floor in front of me. I could see the movement of the blood in his neck under his skin. I could feel the warm vibration of it.

So could Renesmee. She smiled and reached one pink palm out to him. I held her back. She pushed her other hand against my neck, thirst, curiosity, and Charlie's face in her thoughts. There was a subtle edge to the message that made me think that she'd understood Edward's words perfectly; she acknowledged thirst, but overrode it in the same thought.

"Whoa," Charlie gasped, his eyes on her perfect teeth. "How old is she?"

"Um . . ."

"Three months," Edward said, and then added slowly, "rather, she's the size of a three-month-old, more or less. She's younger in some ways, more mature in others."

Very deliberately, Renesmee waved at him.

Charlie blinked spastically.

Jacob elbowed him. "Told you she was special, didn't I?"

Charlie cringed away from the contact.

"Oh, c'mon, Charlie," Jacob groaned. "I'm the same person I've always been. Just pretend this afternoon didn't happen."

The reminder made Charlie's lips go white, but he

nodded once. "Just what *is* your part in all this, Jake?" he asked. "How much does Billy know? Why are you here?" He looked at Jacob's face, which was glowing as he stared at Renesmee.

"Well, I could tell you all about it—Billy knows absolutely everything—but it involves a lot of stuff about werewo—"

"Ungh!" Charlie protested, covering his ears. "Never mind."

Jacob grinned. "Everything's going to be great, Charlie. Just try to not believe anything you see."

My dad mumbled something unintelligible.

"Woo!" Emmett suddenly boomed in his deep bass. "Go Gators!"

Jacob and Charlie jumped. The rest of us froze.

Charlie recovered, then looked at Emmett over his shoulder. "Florida winning?"

"Just scored the first touchdown," Emmett confirmed. He shot a look in my direction, wagging his eyebrows like a villain in vaudeville. "'Bout time somebody scored around here."

I fought back a hiss. In front of Charlie? That was over the line.

But Charlie was beyond noticing innuendos. He took yet another deep breath, sucking the air in like he was trying to pull it down to his toes. I envied him. He lurched to his feet, stepped around Jacob, and half-fell into an open chair. "Well," he sighed, "I guess we should see if they can hold on to the lead."

26. SHINY

"I DON'T KNOW HOW MUCH WE SHOULD TELL RENÉE about this," Charlie said, hesitating with one foot out the door. He stretched, and then his stomach growled.

I nodded. "I know. I don't want to freak her out. Better to protect her. This stuff isn't for the fainthearted."

His lips twisted up to the side ruefully. "I would have tried to protect you, too, if I'd known how. But I guess you've never fit into the fainthearted category, have you?"

I smiled back, pulling a blazing breath in through my teeth.

Charlie patted his stomach absently. "I'll think of something. We've got time to discuss this, right?"

"Right," I promised him.

It had been a long day in some ways, and so short in others. Charlie was late for dinner—Sue Clearwater was cooking for him and Billy. *That* was going to be an awkward evening, but at least he'd be eating real food; I was glad someone was trying to keep him from starving due to his lack of cooking ability.

All day the tension had made the minutes pass slowly; Charlie had never relaxed the stiff set of his shoulders. But he'd been in no hurry to leave, either. He'd watched two whole games—thankfully so absorbed in his thoughts that he was totally oblivious to Emmett's suggestive jokes that got more pointed and less football-related with each aside— and the after-game commentaries, and then the news, not moving until Seth had reminded him of the time.

"You gonna stand Billy and my mom up, Charlie? C'mon. Bella and Nessie'll be here tomorrow. Let's get some grub, eh?"

It had been clear in Charlie's eyes that he hadn't trusted Seth's assessment, but he'd let Seth lead the way out. The doubt was still there as he paused now. The clouds were thinning, the rain gone. The sun might even make an appearance just in time to set.

"Jake says you guys were going to take off on me," he muttered to me now.

"I didn't want to do that if there was any way at all around it. That's why we're still here."

"He said you could stay for a while, but only if I'm tough enough, and if I can keep my mouth shut."

"Yes . . . but I can't promise that we'll never leave, Dad. It's pretty complicated. . . ."

"Need to know," he reminded me.

"Right."

"You'll visit, though, if you have to go?"

"I promise, Dad. Now that you know *just* enough, I think this can work. I'll keep as close as you want."

He chewed on his lip for half a second, then leaned slowly toward me with his arms cautiously extended. I shifted Renesmee—napping now—to my left arm, locked my teeth, held my breath, and wrapped my right arm very lightly around his warm, soft waist.

"Keep real close, Bells," he mumbled. "Real close."

"Love you, Dad," I whispered through my teeth.

He shivered and pulled away. I dropped my arm.

"Love you, too, kid. Whatever else has changed, that hasn't." He touched one finger to Renesmee's pink cheek. "She sure looks a lot like you."

I kept my expression casual, though I felt anything but. "More like Edward, I think." I hesitated, and then added, "She has your curls."

Charlie started, then snorted. "Huh. Guess she does. Huh. Grandpa." He shook his head doubtfully. "Do I ever get to hold her?"

I blinked in shock and then composed myself. After considering for a half second and judging Renesmee's appearance—she looked completely out—I decided that I might as well push my luck to the limit, since things were going so well today. . . .

"Here," I said, holding her out to him. He automatically made an awkward cradle with his arms, and I tucked Renesmee into it. His skin wasn't quite as hot as hers, but it made my throat tickle to feel the warmth flowing under the thin membrane. Where my white skin brushed him it left goose bumps. I wasn't sure if this was a reaction to my new temperature or totally psychological.

Charlie grunted quietly as he felt her weight. "She's . . . sturdy."

I frowned. She felt feather-light to me. Maybe my measure was off.

"Sturdy is good," Charlie said, seeing my expression. Then he muttered to himself, "She'll need to be tough, surrounded by all this craziness." He bounced his arms gently, swaying a little from side to side. "Prettiest baby I ever saw, including you, kid. Sorry, but it's true."

"I know it is."

"Pretty baby," he said again, but it was closer to a coo this time.

I could see it in his face—I could watch it growing there. Charlie was just as helpless against her magic as the rest of us. Two seconds in his arms, and already she owned him.

"Can I come back tomorrow?"

"Sure, Dad. Of course. We'll be here."

"You'd better be," he said sternly, but his face was soft, still gazing at Renesmee. "See you tomorrow, Nessie."

"Not you, too!"

"Huh?"

"Her name is *Renesmee*. Like Renée and Esme, put together. No variations." I struggled to calm myself without the deep breath this time. "Do you want to hear her middle name?"

"Sure."

"Carlie. With a C. Like Carlisle and Charlie put together."

Charlie's eye-creasing grin lit up his face, taking me off guard. "Thanks, Bells."

"Thank *you*, Dad. So much has changed so quickly. My head hasn't stopped spinning. If I didn't have you now, I don't know how I'd keep my grip on—on reality." I'd been about to say *my grip on who I was*. That was probably more than he needed.

Charlie's stomach growled.

"Go eat, Dad. We *will* be here." I remembered how it felt, that first uncomfortable immersion in fantasy—the sensation that everything would disappear in the light of the rising sun.

Charlie nodded and then reluctantly returned Renesmee to me. He glanced past me into the house; his eyes were a little wild for a minute as he stared around the big bright room. Everyone was still there, besides Jacob, who I could hear raiding the refrigerator in the kitchen; Alice was lounging on the bottom step of the staircase with Jasper's head in her lap; Carlisle had his head bent over a fat book in his lap; Esme was humming to herself, sketching on a notepad, while Rosalie and Emmett laid out the foundation for a monumental house of cards under the stairs; Edward had drifted to his piano and was playing very softly to himself. There was no evidence that the day was coming to a close, that it might be time to eat or shift activities in preparation for evening. Something intangible had changed in the atmosphere. The Cullens weren't trying as hard as they usually did—the human charade had slipped ever so slightly, enough for Charlie to feel the difference.

He shuddered, shook his head, and sighed. "See you

tomorrow, Bella." He frowned and then added, "I mean, it's not like you don't look . . . good. I'll get used to it."

"Thanks, Dad."

Charlie nodded and walked thoughtfully toward his car. I watched him drive away; it wasn't until I heard his tires hit the freeway that I realized I'd done it. I'd actually made it through the whole day without hurting Charlie. All by myself. I *must* have a superpower!

It seemed too good to be true. Could I really have both my new family and some of my old as well? And I'd thought that yesterday had been perfect.

"Wow," I whispered. I blinked and felt the third set of contact lenses disintegrate.

The sound of the piano cut off, and Edward's arms were around my waist, his chin resting on my shoulder.

"You took the word right out of my mouth."

"Edward, I did it!"

"You did. You were unbelievable. All that worrying over being a newborn, and then you skip it altogether." He laughed quietly.

"I'm not even sure she's really a vampire, let alone a newborn," Emmett called from under the stairs. "She's too *tame*."

All the embarrassing comments he'd made in front of *my father* sounded in my ears again, and it was probably a good thing I was holding Renesmee. Unable to help my reaction entirely, I snarled under my breath.

"Oooo, scary," Emmett laughed.

I hissed, and Renesmee stirred in my arms. She blinked a few times, then looked around, her expression confused. She sniffed, then reached for my face.

"Charlie will be back tomorrow," I assured her.

"Excellent," Emmett said. Rosalie laughed with him this time.

"Not brilliant, Emmett," Edward said scornfully, holding out his hands to take Renesmee from me. He winked when I hesitated, and so, a little confused, I gave her to him.

"What do you mean?" Emmett demanded.

"It's a little dense, don't you think, to antagonize the strongest vampire in the house?"

Emmett threw his head back and snorted. *"Please!"*

"Bella," Edward murmured to me while Emmett listened closely, "do you remember a few months ago, I asked you to do me a favor once you were immortal?"

That rang a dim bell. I sifted through the blurry human conversations. After a moment, I remembered and I gasped, "Oh!"

Alice trilled a long, pealing laugh. Jacob poked his head around the corner, his mouth stuffed with food.

"What?" Emmett growled.

"Really?" I asked Edward.

"Trust me," he said.

I took a deep breath. "Emmett, how do you feel about a little bet?"

He was on his feet at once. "Awesome. Bring it."

I bit my lip for a second. He was just so *huge*.

"Unless you're too afraid . . . ?" Emmett suggested.

I squared my shoulders. "You. Me. Arm-wrestling. Dining room table. Now."

Emmett's grin stretched across his face.

"Er, Bella," Alice said quickly, "I think Esme is fairly fond of that table. It's an antique."

"Thanks," Esme mouthed at her.

"No problem," Emmett said with a gleaming smile. "Right this way, Bella."

I followed him out the back, toward the garage; I could hear all the others trailing behind. There was a largish granite boulder standing up out of a tumble of rocks near the river, obviously Emmett's goal. Though the big rock was a little rounded and irregular, it would do the job.

Emmett placed his elbow on the rock and waved me forward.

I was nervous again as I watched the thick muscles in Emmett's arm roll, but I kept my face smooth. Edward had promised I would be stronger than anyone for a while. He seemed very confident about this, and I *felt* strong. *That strong?* I wondered, looking at Emmett's biceps. I wasn't even two days old, though, and that ought to count for something. Unless nothing was normal about me. Maybe I wasn't as strong as a normal newborn. Maybe that's why control was so easy for me.

I tried to look unconcerned as I set my elbow against the stone.

"Okay, Emmett. I win, and you cannot say one more word about my sex life to anyone, not even Rose. No allusions, no innuendos—no nothing."

His eyes narrowed. "Deal. I win, and it's going to get a *lot* worse."

He heard my breath stop and grinned evilly. There was no hint of bluff in his eyes.

"You gonna back down so easy, little sister?" Emmett taunted. "Not much wild about *you*, is there? I bet that cottage doesn't have a scratch." He laughed. "Did Edward tell you how many houses Rose and I smashed?"

I gritted my teeth and grabbed his big hand. "One, two—"

"Three," he grunted, and shoved against my hand.

Nothing happened.

Oh, I could feel the force he was exerting. My new mind seemed pretty good at all kinds of calculations, and so I could tell that if he wasn't meeting any resistance, his hand would have pounded right through the rock without difficulty. The pressure increased, and I wondered randomly if a cement truck doing forty miles an hour down a sharp decline would have similar power. Fifty miles an hour? Sixty? Probably more.

It wasn't enough to move me. His hand shoved against mine with crushing force, but it wasn't unpleasant. It felt kind of good in a weird way. I'd been so very careful since the last time I woke up, trying so hard not to break things. It was a strange relief to use my muscles. To let the strength flow rather than struggling to restrain it.

Emmett grunted; his forehead creased and his whole body strained in one rigid line toward the obstacle of my unmoving hand. I let him sweat—figuratively—for a moment while I enjoyed the sensation of the crazy force running through my arm.

A few seconds, though, and I was a little bored with it. I flexed; Emmett lost an inch.

I laughed. Emmett snarled harshly through his teeth.

"Just keep your mouth shut," I reminded him, and then I smashed his hand into the boulder. A deafening crack echoed off the trees. The rock shuddered, and a piece—

about an eighth of the mass—broke off at an invisible fault line and crashed to the ground. It fell on Emmett's foot, and I snickered. I could hear Jacob's and Edward's muffled laughter.

Emmett kicked the rock fragment across the river. It sliced a young maple in half before thudding into the base of a big fir, which swayed and then fell into another tree.

"Rematch. Tomorrow."

"It's not going to wear off that fast," I told him. "Maybe you ought to give it a month."

Emmett growled, flashing his teeth. "Tomorrow."

"Hey, whatever makes you happy, big brother."

As he turned to stalk away, Emmett punched the granite, shattering off an avalanche of shards and powder. It was kind of neat, in a childish way.

Fascinated by the undeniable proof that I was stronger than the strongest vampire I'd ever known, I placed my hand, fingers spread wide, against the rock. Then I dug my fingers slowly into the stone, crushing rather than digging; the consistency reminded me of hard cheese. I ended up with a handful of gravel.

"Cool," I mumbled.

With a grin stretching my face, I whirled in a sudden circle and karate-chopped the rock with the side of my hand. The stone shrieked and groaned and—with a big poof of dust—split in two.

I started giggling.

I didn't pay much attention to the chuckles behind me while I punched and kicked the rest of the boulder into fragments. I was having too much fun, snickering away the whole time. It wasn't until I heard a new little giggle, a high-pitched peal of bells, that I turned away from my silly game.

"Did she just laugh?"

Everyone was staring at Renesmee with the same dumbstruck expression that must have been on my face.

"Yes," Edward said.

"Who *wasn't* laughing?" Jake muttered, rolling his eyes.

"Tell me you didn't let go a bit on your first run, dog," Edward teased, no antagonism in his voice at all.

"That's different," Jacob said, and I watched in surprise as he mock-punched Edward's shoulder. "Bella's supposed to be a grown-up. Married and a mom and all that. Shouldn't there be more dignity?"

Renesmee frowned, and touched Edward's face.

"What does she want?" I asked.

"Less dignity," Edward said with a grin. "She was having almost as much fun watching you enjoy yourself as I was."

"Am I funny?" I asked Renesmee, darting back and reaching for her at the same time that she reached for me. I took her out of Edward's arms and offered her the shard of rock in my hand. "You want to try?"

She smiled her glittering smile and took the stone in both hands. She squeezed, a little dent forming between her eyebrows as she concentrated.

There was a tiny grinding sound, and a bit of dust. She frowned, and held the chunk up to me.

"I'll get it," I said, pinching the stone into sand.

She clapped and laughed; the delicious sound of it made us all join in.

The sun suddenly burst through the clouds, shooting

long beams of ruby and gold across the ten of us, and I was immediately lost in the beauty of my skin in the light of the sunset. Dazed by it.

Renesmee stroked the smooth diamond-bright facets, then laid her arm next to mine. Her skin had just a faint luminosity, subtle and mysterious. Nothing that would keep her inside on a sunny day like my glowing sparkle. She touched my face, thinking of the difference and feeling disgruntled.

"You're the prettiest," I assured her.

"I'm not sure I can agree to that," Edward said, and when I turned to answer him, the sunlight on his face stunned me into silence.

Jacob had his hand in front of his face, pretending to shield his eyes from the glare. "Freaky Bella," he commented.

"What an amazing creature she is," Edward murmured, almost in agreement, as if Jacob's comment was meant as a compliment. He was both dazzling and dazzled.

It was a strange feeling—not surprising, I supposed, since everything felt strange now—this being a natural at something. As a human, I'd never been best at anything. I was okay at dealing with Renée, but probably lots of people could have done better; Phil seemed to be holding his own. I was a good student, but never the top of the class. Obviously, I could be counted out of anything athletic. Not artistic or musical, no particular talents to brag of. Nobody ever gave away a trophy for reading books. After eighteen years of mediocrity, I was pretty used to being average. I realized now that I'd long ago given up any aspirations of shining at anything. I just did the best with what I had, never quite fitting into my world.

So this was really different. I was amazing now—to them and to myself. It was like I had been born to be a vampire. The idea made me want to laugh, but it also made me want to sing. I had found my true place in the world, the place I fit, the place I shined.

27. TRAVEL PLANS

I TOOK MYTHOLOGY A LOT MORE SERIOUSLY SINCE I'D become a vampire.

Often, when I looked back over my first three months as an immortal, I imagined how the thread of my life might look in the Fates' loom—who knew but that it actually existed? I was sure my thread must have changed color; I thought it had probably started out as a nice beige, something supportive and non-confrontational, something that would look good in the background. Now it felt like it must be bright crimson, or maybe glistening gold.

The tapestry of family and friends that wove together around me was a beautiful, glowing thing, full of their bright, complementary colors.

I was surprised by some of the threads I got to include in my life. The werewolves, with their deep, woodsy colors, were not something I'd expected; Jacob, of course, and Seth, too. But my old friends Quil and Embry became part of the fabric as they joined Jacob's pack, and even Sam and Emily were cordial. The tensions between our families eased, mostly due to Renesmee. She was easy to love.

Sue and Leah Clearwater were interlaced into our life, too—two more I had not anticipated.

Sue seemed to have taken it on herself to smooth Charlie's transition into the world of make-believe. She came with him to the Cullens' most days, though she never seemed truly comfortable here the way her son and most of Jake's pack did. She did not speak often; she just hovered protectively near Charlie. She was always the first person he looked to when Renesmee did something disturbingly advanced—which was often. In answer, Sue would eye Seth meaningfully as if to say, *Yeah, tell me about it.*

Leah was even less comfortable than Sue and was the only part of our recently extended family who was openly hostile to the merger. However, she and Jacob had a new camaraderie that kept her close to us all. I asked him about it once—hesitantly; I didn't want to pry, but the relationship was so different from the way it used to be that it made me curious. He shrugged and told me it was a pack thing. She was his second-in-command now, his "beta," as I'd called it once long ago.

"I figured as long as I was going to do this Alpha thing for real," Jacob explained, "I'd better nail down the formalities."

The new responsibility made Leah feel the need to

check in with him often, and since he was always with Renesmee . . .

Leah was not happy to be near us, but she was the exception. Happiness was the main component in my life now, the dominant pattern in the tapestry. So much so that my relationship with Jasper was now much closer than I'd ever dreamed it would be.

At first I was really annoyed, though.

"Yeesh!" I complained to Edward one night after we'd put Renesmee in her wrought-iron crib. "If I haven't killed Charlie or Sue yet, it's probably not going to happen. I wish Jasper would stop hovering all the time!"

"No one doubts you, Bella, not in the slightest," he assured me. "You know how Jasper is—he can't resist a good emotional climate. You're so happy all the time, love, he gravitates toward you without thinking."

And then Edward hugged me tightly, because nothing pleased him more than my overwhelming ecstasy in this new life.

And I was euphoric the vast majority of the time. The days were not long enough for me to get my fill of adoring my daughter; the nights did not have enough hours to satisfy my need for Edward.

There was a flipside to the joy, though. If you turned the fabric of our lives over, I imagined the design on the backside would be woven in the bleak grays of doubt and fear.

Renesmee spoke her first word when she was exactly one week old. The word was *Momma,* which would have made my day, except that I was so frightened by her progress I could barely force my frozen face to smile back at her. It didn't help that she continued from her first word to her first sentence in the same breath. "Momma, where is Grandpa?" she'd asked in a clear, high soprano, only bothering to speak aloud because I was across the room from her. She'd already asked Rosalie, using her normal (or seriously abnormal, from another point of view) means of communication. Rosalie hadn't known the answer, so Renesmee had turned to me.

When she walked for the first time, fewer than three weeks later, it was similar. She'd simply stared at Alice for a long moment, watching intently as her aunt arranged bouquets in the vases scattered around the room, dancing back and forth across the floor with her arms full of flowers. Renesmee got to her feet, not in the least bit shaky, and crossed the floor almost as gracefully.

Jacob had burst into applause, because that was clearly the response Renesmee wanted. The way he was tied to her made his own reactions secondary; his first reflex was always to give Renesmee whatever she needed. But our eyes met, and I saw all the panic in mine echoed in his. I made my hands clap together, too, trying to hide my fear from her. Edward applauded quietly at my side, and we didn't need to speak our thoughts to know they were the same.

Edward and Carlisle threw themselves into research, looking for any answers, anything to expect. There was very little to be found, and none of it verifiable.

Alice and Rosalie usually began our day with a fashion show. Renesmee never wore the same clothes twice, partly because she outgrew her clothes almost immediately and partly because Alice and Rosalie were trying to create a baby album that appeared to span years rather than weeks.

They took thousands of pictures, documenting every phase of her accelerated childhood.

At three months, Renesmee could have been a big one-year-old, or a small two-year-old. She wasn't shaped exactly like a toddler; she was leaner and more graceful, her proportions were more even, like an adult's. Her bronze ringlets hung to her waist; I couldn't bear to cut them, even if Alice would have allowed it. Renesmee could speak with flawless grammar and articulation, but she rarely bothered, preferring to simply *show* people what she wanted. She could not only walk but run and dance. She could even read.

I'd been reading Tennyson to her one night, because the flow and rhythm of his poetry seemed restful. (I had to search constantly for new material; Renesmee didn't like repetition in her bedtime stories as other children supposedly did, and she had no patience for picture books.) She reached up to touch my cheek, the image in her mind one of us, only with *her* holding the book. I gave it to her, smiling.

"'There is sweet music here,'" she read without hesitation, "'that softer falls than petals from blown roses on the grass, or night-dews on still waters between walls of shadowy granite, in a gleaming pass—'"

My hand was robotic as I took the book back.

"If you read, how will you fall asleep?" I asked in a voice that had barely escaped shaking.

By Carlisle's calculations, the growth of her body was gradually slowing; her mind continued to race on ahead. Even if the rate of decrease held steady, she'd still be an adult in no more than four years.

Four years. And an old woman by fifteen.

Just fifteen years of life.

But she was so *healthy*. Vital, bright, glowing, and happy. Her conspicuous well-being made it easy for me to be happy with her in the moment and leave the future for tomorrow.

Carlisle and Edward discussed our options for the future from every angle in low voices that I tried not to hear. They never had these discussions when Jacob was around, because there *was* one sure way to halt aging, and that wasn't something Jacob was likely to be excited about. I wasn't. *Too dangerous!* my instincts screamed at me. Jacob and Renesmee seemed alike in so many ways, both half-and-half beings, two things at the same time. And all the werewolf lore insisted that vampire venom was a death sentence rather than a course to immortality. . . .

Carlisle and Edward had exhausted the research they could do from a distance, and now we were preparing to follow old legends at their source. We were going back to Brazil, starting there. The Ticunas had legends about children like Renesmee. . . . If other children like her had ever existed, perhaps some tale of the life span of half-mortal children still lingered. . . .

The only real question left was exactly when we would go.

I was the holdup. A small part of it was that I wanted to stay near Forks until after the holidays, for Charlie's sake. But more than that, there was a different journey that I knew had to come first—that was the clear priority. Also, it had to be a solo trip.

This was the only argument that Edward and I had gotten in since I'd become a vampire. The main point of contention was the "solo" part. But the facts were what they were, and my plan was the only one that made rational sense. I had to go see the Volturi, and I had to do it absolutely alone.

Even freed from old nightmares, from any dreams at all, it was impossible to forget the Volturi. Nor did they leave us without reminders.

Until the day that Aro's present showed up, I didn't know that Alice had sent a wedding announcement to the Volturi leaders; we'd been far away on Esme's island when she'd seen a vision of Volturi soldiers—Jane and Alec, the devastatingly powerful twins, among them. Caius was planning to send a hunting party to see if I was still human, against their edict (because I knew about the secret vampire world, I either must join it or be silenced . . . permanently). So Alice had mailed the announcement, seeing that this would delay them as they deciphered the meaning behind it. But they would come eventually. That was certain.

The present itself was not overtly threatening. Extravagant, yes, almost frightening in that very extravagance. The threat was in the parting line of Aro's congratulatory note, written in black ink on a square of heavy, plain white paper in Aro's own hand:

$$\text{I so look forward to seeing the new}$$
$$\text{Mrs. Cullen in person.}$$

The gift was presented in an ornately carved, ancient wooden box inlaid with gold and mother-of-pearl, ornamented with a rainbow of gemstones. Alice said the box itself was a priceless treasure, that it would have outshone just about any piece of jewelry besides the one inside it.

"I always wondered where the crown jewels disappeared to after John of England pawned them in the thirteenth century," Carlisle said. "I suppose it doesn't surprise me that the Volturi have their share."

The necklace was simple—gold woven into a thick rope of a chain, almost scaled, like a smooth snake that would curl close around the throat. One jewel hung suspended from the rope: a white diamond the size of a golf ball.

The unsubtle reminder in Aro's note interested me more than the jewel. The Volturi needed to see that I was immortal, that the Cullens had been obedient to the Volturi's orders, and they needed to see this *soon*. They could not be allowed near Forks. There was only one way to keep our life here safe.

"You're not going alone," Edward had insisted through his teeth, his hands clenching into fists.

"They won't hurt me," I'd said as soothingly as I could manage, forcing my voice to sound sure. "They have no reason to. I'm a vampire. Case closed."

"No. Absolutely no."

"Edward, it's the only way to protect her."

And he hadn't been able to argue with that. My logic was watertight.

Even in the short time I'd known Aro, I'd been able to see that he was a collector—and his most prized treasures were his *living* pieces. He coveted beauty, talent, and rarity in his immortal followers more than any jewel locked in his vaults. It was unfortunate enough that he'd begun to covet Alice's and Edward's abilities. I would give him no more reason to be jealous of Carlisle's family. Renesmee was beautiful and gifted and unique—she was one of a kind. He could not be allowed to see her, not even through someone's thoughts.

And I was the only one whose thoughts he could not hear. Of course I would go alone.

Alice did not see any trouble with my trip, but she was worried by the indistinct quality of her visions. She said they were sometimes similarly hazy when there were outside decisions that *might* conflict but that had not been solidly resolved. This uncertainty made Edward, already hesitant, extremely opposed to what I had to do. He wanted to come with me as far as my connection in London, but I wouldn't leave Renesmee without *both* her parents. Carlisle was coming instead. It made both Edward and me a little more relaxed, knowing that Carlisle would be only a few hours away from me.

Alice kept searching for the future, but the things she found were unrelated to what she was looking for. A new trend in the stock market; a possible visit of reconciliation from Irina, though her decision was not firm; a snowstorm that wouldn't hit for another six weeks; a call from Renée (I was practicing my "rough" voice, and getting better at it every day—to Renée's knowledge, I was still sick, but mending).

We bought the tickets for Italy the day after Renesmee turned three months. I planned for it to be a very short trip, so I hadn't told Charlie about it. Jacob knew, and he took Edward's view on things. However, today the argument was about Brazil. Jacob was determined to come with us.

The three of us, Jacob, Renesmee, and I, were hunting together. The diet of animal blood wasn't Renesmee's favorite thing—and that was why Jacob was allowed to come along.

Jacob had made it a contest between them, and that made her more willing than anything else.

Renesmee was quite clear on the whole good vs. bad as it applied to hunting humans; she just thought that donated blood made a nice compromise. Human food filled her and it seemed compatible with her system, but she reacted to all varieties of solid food with the same martyred endurance I had once given cauliflower and lima beans. Animal blood was better than *that*, at least. She had a competitive nature, and the challenge of beating Jacob made her excited to hunt.

"Jacob," I said, trying to reason with him again while Renesmee danced ahead of us into the long clearing, searching for a scent she liked. "You've got obligations here. Seth, Leah—"

He snorted. "I'm not my pack's nanny. They've all got responsibilities in La Push anyway."

"Sort of like you? Are you officially dropping out of high school, then? If you're going to keep up with Renesmee, you're going to have to study a lot harder."

"It's just a sabbatical. I'll get back to school when things . . . slow down."

I lost my concentration on my side of the disagreement when he said that, and we both automatically looked at Renesmee. She was staring at the snowflakes fluttering high above her head, melting before they could stick to the yellowed grass in the long arrowhead-shaped meadow that we were standing in. Her ruffled ivory dress was just a shade darker than the snow, and her reddish-brown curls managed to shimmer, though the sun was buried deeply behind the clouds.

As we watched, she crouched for an instant and then sprang fifteen feet up into the air. Her little hands closed around a flake, and she dropped lightly to her feet.

She turned to us with her shocking smile—truly, it wasn't something you could get used to—and opened her hands to show us the perfectly formed eight-pointed ice star in her palm before it melted.

"Pretty," Jacob called to her appreciatively. "But I think you're stalling, Nessie."

She bounded back to Jacob; he held his arms out at exactly the moment she leaped into them. They had the move perfectly synchronized. She did this when she had something to say. She still preferred not to speak aloud.

Renesmee touched his face, scowling adorably as we all listened to the sound of a small herd of elk moving farther into the wood.

"*Suuuure* you're not thirsty, Nessie," Jacob answered a little sarcastically, but more indulgently than anything else. "You're just afraid I'll catch the biggest one again!"

She flipped backward out of Jacob's arms, landing lightly on her feet, and rolled her eyes—she looked so much like Edward when she did that. Then she darted off toward the trees.

"Got it," Jacob said when I leaned as if to follow. He yanked his t-shirt off as he charged after her into the forest, already trembling. "It doesn't count if you cheat," he called to Renesmee.

I smiled at the leaves they left fluttering behind them, shaking my head. Jacob was more a child than Renesmee sometimes.

I paused, giving my hunters a few minutes' head start.

It would be beyond simple to track them, and Renesmee would love to surprise me with the size of her prey. I smiled again.

The narrow meadow was very still, very empty. The fluttering snow was thinning above me, almost gone. Alice had seen that it wouldn't stick for many weeks.

Usually Edward and I came together on these hunting trips. But Edward was with Carlisle today, planning the trip to Rio, talking behind Jacob's back. . . . I frowned. When I returned, I would take Jacob's side. He *should* come with us. He had as big a stake in this as any of us—his entire life was at stake, just like mine.

While my thoughts were lost in the near future, my eyes swept the mountainside routinely, searching for prey, searching for danger. I didn't think about it; the urge was an automatic thing.

Or perhaps there *was* a reason for my scanning, some tiny trigger that my razor-sharp senses had caught before I realized it consciously.

As my eyes flitted across the edge of a distant cliff, standing out starkly blue-gray against the green-black forest, a glint of silver—or was it gold?—gripped my attention.

My gaze zeroed in on the color that shouldn't have been there, so far away in the haze that an eagle wouldn't have been able to make it out. I stared.

She stared back.

That she was a vampire was obvious. Her skin was marble white, the texture a million times smoother than human skin. Even under the clouds, she glistened ever so slightly. If her skin had not given her away, her stillness would have. Only vampires and statues could be so perfectly motionless.

Her hair was pale, pale blond, almost silver. This was the gleam that had caught my eye. It hung straight as a ruler to a blunt edge at her chin, parted evenly down the center.

She was a stranger to me. I was absolutely certain I'd never seen her before, even as a human. None of the faces in my muddy memory were the same as this one. But I knew her at once from her dark golden eyes.

Irina had decided to come after all.

For one moment I stared at her, and she stared back. I wondered if she would guess immediately who I was as well. I half-raised my hand, about to wave, but her lip twisted the tiniest bit, making her face suddenly hostile.

I heard Renesmee's cry of victory from the forest, heard Jacob's echoing howl, and saw Irina's face jerk reflexively to the sound when it echoed to her a few seconds later. Her gaze cut slightly to the right, and I knew what she was seeing. An enormous russet werewolf, perhaps the very one who had killed her Laurent. How long had she been watching us? Long enough to see our affectionate exchange before, I was sure.

Her face spasmed in pain.

Instinctually, I opened my hands in front of me in an apologetic gesture. She turned back to me, and her lip curled back over her teeth. Her jaw unlocked as she growled.

When the faint sound reached me, she had already turned and disappeared into the forest.

"Crap!" I groaned.

I sprinted into the forest after Renesmee and Jacob,

unwilling to have them out of my sight. I didn't know which direction Irina had taken, or exactly how furious she was right now. Vengeance was a common obsession for vampires, one that was not easy to suppress.

Running at full speed, it only took me two seconds to reach them.

"Mine is bigger," I heard Renesmee insist as I burst through the thick thornbushes to the small open space where they stood.

Jacob's ears flattened as he took in my expression; he crouched forward, baring his teeth—his muzzle was streaked with blood from his kill. His eyes raked the forest. I could hear the growl building in his throat.

Renesmee was every bit as alert as Jacob. Abandoning the dead stag at her feet, she leaped into my waiting arms, pressing her curious hands against my cheeks.

"I'm overreacting," I assured them quickly. "It's okay, I think. Hold on."

I pulled out my cell phone and hit the speed dial. Edward answered on the first ring. Jacob and Renesmee listened intently to my side as I filled Edward in.

"Come, bring Carlisle," I trilled so fast I wondered if Jacob could keep up. "I saw Irina, and she saw me, but then she saw Jacob and she got mad and ran away, I *think*. She hasn't shown up here—yet, anyway—but she looked pretty upset so maybe she will. If she doesn't, you and Carlisle have to go after her and talk to her. I feel so bad."

Jacob rumbled.

"We'll be there in half a minute," Edward assured me, and I could hear the whoosh of the wind his running made.

We darted back to the long meadow and then waited

silently as Jacob and I listened carefully for the sound of an approach we did not recognize.

When the sound came, though, it was very familiar. And then Edward was at my side, Carlisle a few seconds behind. I was surprised to hear the heavy pad of big paws following behind Carlisle. I supposed I shouldn't have been shocked. With Renesmee in even a hint of danger, of course Jacob would call in reinforcements.

"She was up on that ridge," I told them at once, pointing out the spot. If Irina was fleeing, she already had quite a head start. Would she stop and listen to Carlisle? Her expression before made me think not. "Maybe you should call Emmett and Jasper and have them come with you. She looked . . . really upset. She growled at me."

"What?" Edward said angrily.

Carlisle put a hand on his arm. "She's grieving. I'll go after her."

"I'm coming with you," Edward insisted.

They exchanged a long glance—perhaps Carlisle was measuring Edward's irritation with Irina against his helpfulness as a mind reader. Finally, Carlisle nodded, and they took off to find the trail without calling for Jasper or Emmett.

Jacob huffed impatiently and poked my back with his nose. He must want Renesmee back at the safety of the house, just in case. I agreed with him on that, and we hurried home with Seth and Leah running at our flanks.

Renesmee was complacent in my arms, one hand still resting on my face. Since the hunting trip had been aborted, she would just have to make do with donated blood. Her thoughts were a little smug.

28. THE FUTURE

CARLISLE AND EDWARD HAD NOT BEEN ABLE TO CATCH
up with Irina before her trail disappeared into the sound.
They'd swum to the other bank to see if her trail had picked
up in a straight line, but there was no trace of her for miles
in either direction on the eastern shore.

It was all my fault. She had come, as Alice had seen, to
make peace with the Cullens, only to be angered by my
camaraderie with Jacob. I wished I'd noticed her earlier,
before Jacob had phased. I wished we'd gone hunting
somewhere else.

There wasn't much to be done. Carlisle had called Tanya
with the disappointing news. Tanya and Kate hadn't seen

Irina since they'd decided to come to my wedding, and they were distraught that Irina had come so close and yet not returned home; it wasn't easy for them to lose their sister, however temporary the separation might be. I wondered if this brought back hard memories of losing their mother so many centuries ago.

Alice was able to catch a few glimpses of Irina's immediate future, nothing too concrete. She wasn't going back to Denali, as far as Alice could tell. The picture was hazy. All Alice could see was that Irina was visibly upset; she wandered in the snow-swathed wilderness—to the north? To the east?—with a devastated expression. She made no decisions for a new course beyond her directionless grieving.

Days passed and, though of course I forgot nothing, Irina and her pain moved to the back of my mind. There were more important things to think of now. I would leave for Italy in just a few days. When I got back, we'd all be off to South America.

Every detail had been gone over a hundred times already. We would start with the Ticunas, tracing their legends as well as we could at the source. Now that it was accepted that Jacob would come with us, he figured prominently in the plans—it was unlikely that the people who believed in vampires would speak to any of *us* about their stories. If we dead-ended with the Ticunas, there were many closely related tribes in the area to research. Carlisle had some old friends in the Amazon; if we could find them, they might have information for us, too. Or at least a suggestion as to where else we might go for answers. It was unlikely that the three Amazon vampires had anything to do with the legends of vampire hybrids themselves, as they were all female. There was no way to know how long our search would take.

I hadn't told Charlie about the longer trip yet, and I stewed about what to say to him while Edward and Carlisle's discussion went on. How to break the news to him just right?

I stared at Renesmee while I debated internally. She was curled up on the sofa now, her breathing slow with heavy sleep, her tangled curls splayed wildly around her face. Usually, Edward and I took her back to our cottage to put her to bed, but tonight we lingered with the family, he and Carlisle deep in their planning session.

Meanwhile, Emmett and Jasper were more excited about planning the hunting possibilities. The Amazon offered a change from our normal quarry. Jaguars and panthers, for example. Emmett had a whim to wrestle with an anaconda. Esme and Rosalie were planning what they would pack. Jacob was off with Sam's pack, setting things up for his own absence.

Alice moved slowly—for her—around the big room, unnecessarily tidying the already immaculate space, straightening Esme's perfectly hung garlands. She was re-centering Esme's vases on the console at the moment. I could see from the way her face fluctuated—aware, then blank, then aware again—that she was searching the future. I assumed she was trying to see through the blind spots that Jacob and Renesmee made in her visions as to what was waiting for us in South America until Jasper said, "Let it go, Alice; she's not our concern," and a cloud of serenity stole silently and invisibly through the room. Alice must have been worrying about Irina again.

She stuck her tongue out at Jasper and then lifted one crystal vase that was filled with white and red roses and turned toward the kitchen. There was just the barest hint of wilt to one of the white flowers, but Alice seemed intent on utter perfection as a distraction to her lack of vision tonight.

Staring at Renesmee again, I didn't see it when the vase slipped from Alice's fingers. I only heard the whoosh of the air whistling past the crystal, and my eyes flickered up in time to see the vase shatter into ten thousand diamond shards against the edge of the kitchen's marble floor.

We were perfectly still as the fragmented crystal bounced and skittered in every direction with an unmusical tinkling, all eyes on Alice's back.

My first illogical thought was that Alice was playing some joke on us. Because there was no way that Alice could have dropped the vase *by accident*. I could have darted across the room to catch the vase in plenty of time myself, if I hadn't assumed she would get it. And how would it fall through her fingers in the first place? Her perfectly sure fingers . . .

I had never seen a vampire drop anything by accident. Ever.

And then Alice was facing us, twisting in a move so fast it didn't exist.

Her eyes were halfway here and halfway locked on the future, wide, staring, filling her thin face till they seemed to overflow it. Looking into her eyes was like looking out of a grave from the inside; I was buried in the terror and despair and agony of her gaze.

I heard Edward gasp; it was a broken, half-choked sound.

"*What?*" Jasper growled, leaping to her side in a blurred rush of movement, crushing the broken crystal under his feet. He grabbed her shoulders and shook her sharply. She seemed to rattle silently in his hands. "*What, Alice?*"

Emmett moved into my peripheral vision, his teeth bared while his eyes darted toward the window, anticipating an attack.

There was only silence from Esme, Carlisle, and Rose, who were frozen just as I was.

Jasper shook Alice again. "What *is* it?"

"They're coming for us," Alice and Edward whispered together, perfectly synchronized. "All of them."

Silence.

For once, I was the quickest to understand—because something in their words triggered my own vision. It was only the distant memory of a dream—faint, transparent, indistinct as if I were peering through thick gauze. . . . In my head, I saw a line of black advancing on me, the ghost of my half-forgotten human nightmare. I could not see the glint of their ruby eyes in the shrouded image, or the shine of their sharp wet teeth, but I knew where the gleam should be. . . .

Stronger than the memory of the sight came the memory of the *feel*—the wrenching need to protect the precious thing behind me.

I wanted to snatch Renesmee up into my arms, to hide her behind my skin and hair, to make her invisible. But I couldn't even turn to look at her. I felt not like stone but ice. For the first time since I'd been reborn a vampire, I felt cold.

I barely heard the confirmation of my fears. I didn't need it. I already knew.

"The Volturi," Alice moaned.

"All of them," Edward groaned at the same time.

"Why?" Alice whispered to herself. "How?"

"When?" Edward whispered.

"Why?" Esme echoed.

"*When?*" Jasper repeated in a voice like splintering ice.

Alice's eyes didn't blink, but it was as if a veil covered them; they became perfectly blank. Only her mouth held on to her expression of horror.

"Not long," she and Edward said together. Then she spoke alone. "There's snow on the forest, snow on the town. Little more than a month."

"Why?" Carlisle was the one to ask this time.

Esme answered. "They must have a reason. Maybe to see . . ."

"This isn't about Bella," Alice said hollowly. "They're all coming—Aro, Caius, Marcus, every member of the guard, even the wives."

"The wives never leave the tower," Jasper contradicted her in a flat voice. "Never. Not during the southern rebellion. Not when the Romanians tried to overthrow them. Not even when they were hunting the immortal children. Never."

"They're coming now," Edward whispered.

"But *why?*" Carlisle said again. "We've done nothing! And if we had, what could we possibly do that would bring *this* down on us?"

"There are so many of us," Edward answered dully. "They must want to make sure that . . ." He didn't finish.

"That doesn't answer the crucial question! Why?"

I felt I knew the answer to Carlisle's question, and yet at the same time I didn't. Renesmee was the reason why, I was sure. Somehow I'd known from the very beginning that they would come for her. My subconscious had warned me before I'd known I was carrying her. It felt oddly expected now. As if I'd somehow always known that the Volturi would come to take my happiness from me.

But that still didn't answer the question.

"Go back, Alice," Jasper pleaded. "Look for the trigger. Search."

Alice shook her head slowly, her shoulders sagging. "It came out of nowhere, Jazz. I wasn't looking for them, or even for us. I was just looking for Irina. She wasn't where I expected her to be. . . ." Alice trailed off, her eyes drifting again. She stared at nothing for a long second.

And then her head jerked up, her eyes hard as flint. I heard Edward catch his breath.

"She decided to go to them," Alice said. "Irina decided to go to the Volturi. And then they will decide. . . . It's as if they're waiting for her. Like their decision was already made, and just waiting on her. . . ."

It was silent again as we digested this. What would Irina tell the Volturi that would result in Alice's appalling vision?

"Can we stop her?" Jasper asked.

"There's no way. She's almost there."

"What is she doing?" Carlisle was asking, but I wasn't paying attention to the discussion now. All my focus was on the picture that was painstakingly coming together in my head.

I pictured Irina poised on the cliff, watching. What had she seen? A vampire and a werewolf who were best friends. I'd been focused on that image, one that would obviously explain her reaction. But that was not all that she'd seen.

She'd also seen a child. An exquisitely beautiful child, showing off in the falling snow, clearly more than human . . .

Irina . . . the orphaned sisters . . . Carlisle had said that losing their mother to the Volturi's justice had made Tanya, Kate, and Irina purists when it came to the law.

Just half a minute ago, Jasper had said the words himself: *Not even when they were hunting the immortal children. . . .* The immortal children—the unmentionable bane, the appalling taboo . . .

With Irina's past, how could she apply any other reading to what she'd seen that day in the narrow field? She had not been close enough to hear Renesmee's heart, to feel the heat radiating from her body. Renesmee's rosy cheeks could have been a trick on our part for all she knew.

After all, the Cullens were in league with werewolves. From Irina's point of view, maybe this meant nothing was beyond us. . . .

Irina, wringing her hands in the snowy wilderness—not mourning Laurent, after all, but knowing it was her duty to turn the Cullens in, knowing what would happen to them if she did. Apparently her conscience had won out over the centuries of friendship.

And the Volturi's response to this kind of infraction was so automatic, it was already decided.

I turned and draped myself over Renesmee's sleeping

body, covering her with my hair, burying my face in her curls.

"Think of what she saw that afternoon," I said in a low voice, interrupting whatever Emmett was beginning to say. "To someone who'd lost a mother because of the immortal children, what would Renesmee look like?"

Everything was silent again as the others caught up to where I was already.

"An immortal child," Carlisle whispered.

I felt Edward kneel beside me, wrap his arms over us both.

"But she's wrong," I went on. "Renesmee isn't like those other children. They were frozen, but she grows so much every day. They were out of control, but she never hurts Charlie or Sue or even shows them things that would upset them. She *can* control herself. She's already smarter than most adults. There would be no reason. . . ."

I babbled on, waiting for someone to exhale with relief, waiting for the icy tension in the room to relax as they realized I was right. The room just seemed to get colder. Eventually my small voice trailed off into silence.

No one spoke for a long time.

Then Edward whispered into my hair. "It's not the kind of crime they hold a trial for, love," he said quietly. "Aro's seen Irina's *proof* in her thoughts. They come to destroy, not to be reasoned with."

"But they're wrong," I said stubbornly.

"They won't wait for us to show them that."

His voice was still quiet, gentle, velvet . . . and yet the pain and desolation in the sound was unavoidable. His voice was like Alice's eyes before—like the inside of a tomb.

"What can we do?" I demanded.

Renesmee was so warm and perfect in my arms, dreaming peacefully. I'd worried so much about Renesmee's speeding age—worried that she would only have little over a decade of life. . . . That terror seemed ironic now.

Little over a month . . .

Was this the limit, then? I'd had more happiness than most people ever experienced. Was there some natural law that demanded equal shares of happiness and misery in the world? Was my joy overthrowing the balance? Was four months all I could have?

It was Emmett who answered my rhetorical question.

"We fight," he said calmly.

"We can't win," Jasper growled. I could imagine how his face would look, how his body would curve protectively over Alice's.

"Well, we can't run. Not with Demetri around." Emmett made a disgusted noise, and I knew instinctively that he was not upset by the idea of the Volturi's tracker but by the idea of running away. "And I don't know that we *can't* win," he said. "There are a few options to consider. We don't have to fight alone."

My head snapped up at that. "We don't have to sentence the Quileutes to death, either, Emmett!"

"Chill, Bella." His expression was no different from when he was contemplating fighting anacondas. Even the threat of annihilation couldn't change Emmett's perspective, his ability to thrill to a challenge. "I didn't mean the pack. Be realistic, though—do you think Jacob or Sam is going to ignore an invasion? Even if it wasn't about Nessie? Not to mention that, thanks to Irina, Aro knows about our alliance with the pack now, too. But I was thinking of our other friends."

Carlisle echoed me in a whisper. "Other friends we don't have to sentence to death."

"Hey, we'll let them decide," Emmett said in a placating tone. "I'm not saying they have to fight with us." I could see the plan refining itself in his head as he spoke. "If they'd just stand beside us, just long enough to make the Volturi hesitate. Bella's right, after all. If we could force them to stop and listen. Though that might take away any reason for a fight. . . ."

There was a hint of a smile on Emmett's face now. I was surprised no one had hit him yet. I wanted to.

"Yes," Esme said eagerly. "That makes sense, Emmett. All we need is for the Volturi to pause for one moment. Just long enough to *listen*."

"We'd need quite a show of witnesses," Rosalie said harshly, her voice brittle as glass.

Esme nodded in agreement, as if she hadn't heard the sarcasm in Rosalie's tone. "We can ask that much of our friends. Just to witness."

"We'd do it for them," Emmett said.

"We'll have to ask them just right," Alice murmured. I looked to see her eyes were a dark void again. "They'll have to be shown very carefully."

"Shown?" Jasper asked.

Alice and Edward both looked down at Renesmee. Then Alice's eyes glazed over.

"Tanya's family," she said. "Siobhan's coven. Amun's. Some of the nomads—Garrett and Mary for certain. Maybe Alistair."

"What about Peter and Charlotte?" Jasper asked half fearfully, as if he hoped the answer was no, and his old brother could be spared from the coming carnage.

"Maybe."

"The Amazons?" Carlisle asked. "Kachiri, Zafrina, and Senna?"

Alice seemed too deep into her vision to answer at first; finally she shuddered, and her eyes flickered back to the present. She met Carlisle's gaze for the tiniest part of a second, and then looked down.

"I can't see."

"What was that?" Edward asked, his whisper a demand. "That part in the jungle. Are we going to look for them?"

"I can't see," Alice repeated, not meeting his eyes. A flash of confusion crossed Edward's face. "We'll have to split up and hurry—before the snow sticks to the ground. We have to round up whomever we can and get them here to show them." She zoned again. "Ask Eleazar. There is more to this than just an immortal child."

The silence was ominous for another long moment while Alice was in her trance. She blinked slowly when it was over, her eyes peculiarly opaque despite the fact that she was clearly in the present.

"There is so much. We have to hurry," she whispered.

"Alice?" Edward asked. "That was too fast—I didn't understand. What was—?"

"I can't see!" she exploded back at him. "Jacob's almost here!"

Rosalie took a step toward the front door. "I'll deal with—"

"No, let him come," Alice said quickly, her voice straining

higher with each word. She grabbed Jasper's hand and began pulling him toward the back door. "I'll see better away from Nessie, too. I need to go. I need to really concentrate. I need to see everything I can. I have to go. Come on, Jasper, there's no time to waste!"

We all could hear Jacob on the stairs. Alice yanked, impatient, on Jasper's hand. He followed quickly, confusion in his eyes just like Edward's. They darted out the door into the silver night.

"Hurry!" she called back to us. "You have to find them all!"

"Find what?" Jacob asked, shutting the front door behind himself. "Where'd Alice go?"

No one answered; we all just stared.

Jacob shook the wet from his hair and pulled his arms through the sleeves of his t-shirt, his eyes on Renesmee. "Hey, Bells! I thought you guys would've gone home by now. . . ."

He looked up to me finally, blinked, and then stared. I watched his expression as the room's atmosphere finally touched him. He glanced down, eyes wide, at the wet spot on the floor, the scattered roses, the fragments of crystal. His fingers quivered.

"What?" he asked flatly. "What happened?"

I couldn't think where to begin. No one else found the words, either.

Jacob crossed the room in three long strides and dropped to his knees beside Renesmee and me. I could feel the heat shaking off his body as tremors rolled down his arms to his shaking hands.

"Is she okay?" he demanded, touching her forehead, tilting his head as he listened to her heart. "Don't mess with me, Bella, please!"

"Nothing's wrong with Renesmee," I choked out, the words breaking in strange places.

"Then who?"

"All of us, Jacob," I whispered. And it was there in my voice, too—the sound of the inside of a grave. "It's over. We've all been sentenced to die."

29. DEFECTION

WE SAT THERE ALL NIGHT LONG, STATUES OF HORROR and grief, and Alice never came back.

We were all at our limits—frenzied into absolute still-ness. Carlisle had barely been able to move his lips to explain it all to Jacob. The retelling seemed to make it worse; even Emmett stood silent and still from then on.

It wasn't until the sun rose and I knew that Renesmee would soon be stirring under my hands that I wondered for the first time what could possibly be taking Alice so long. I'd hoped to know more before I was faced with my daughter's curiosity. To have some answers. Some tiny, tiny portion of hope so that I could smile and keep the truth from terrifying her, too.

My face felt permanently set into the fixed mask it had worn all night. I wasn't sure I had the ability to smile anymore.

Jacob was snoring in the corner, a mountain of fur on the floor, twitching anxiously in his sleep. Sam knew everything—the wolves were readying themselves for what was coming. Not that this preparation would do anything but get them killed with the rest of my family.

The sunlight broke through the back windows, sparkling on Edward's skin. My eyes had not moved from his since Alice's departure. We'd stared at each other all night, staring at what neither of us could live through losing: the other. I saw my reflection glimmer in his agonized eyes as the sun touched my own skin.

His eyebrows moved an infinitesimal bit, then his lips.

"Alice," he said.

The sound of his voice was like ice cracking as it melted. All of us fractured a little, softened a little. Moved again.

"She's been gone a long time," Rosalie murmured, surprised.

"Where could she be?" Emmett wondered, taking a step toward the door.

Esme put a hand on her arm. "We don't want to disturb . . ."

"She's never taken so long before," Edward said. New worry splintered the mask his face had become. His features were alive again, his eyes suddenly wide with fresh fear, extra panic. "Carlisle, you don't think—something preemptive? Would Alice have had time to see if they sent someone for her?"

Aro's translucent-skinned face filled my head. Aro, who

had seen into all the corners of Alice's mind, who knew everything she was capable of—

Emmett cussed loud enough that Jacob lurched to his feet with a growl. In the yard, his growl was echoed by his pack. My family was already a blur of action.

"Stay with Renesmee!" I all but shrieked at Jacob as I sprinted through the door.

I was still stronger than the rest of them, and I used that strength to push myself forward. I overtook Esme in a few bounds, and Rosalie in just a few strides more. I raced through the thick forest until I was right behind Edward and Carlisle.

"Would they have been able to surprise her?" Carlisle asked, his voice as even as if he were standing motionless rather than running at full speed.

"I don't see how," Edward answered. "But Aro knows her better than anyone else. Better than I do."

"Is this a trap?" Emmett called from behind us.

"Maybe," Edward said. "There's no scent but Alice and Jasper. Where were they going?"

Alice and Jasper's trail was curling into a wide arc; it stretched first east of the house, but headed north on the other side of the river, and then back west again after a few miles. We recrossed the river, all six jumping within a second of each other. Edward ran in the lead, his concentration total.

"Did you catch that scent?" Esme called ahead a few moments after we'd leaped the river for the second time. She was the farthest back, on the far left edge of our hunting party. She gestured to the southeast.

"Keep to the main trail—we're almost to the Quileute

border," Edward ordered tersely. "Stay together. See if they turned north or south."

I was not as familiar with the treaty line as the rest of them, but I could smell the hint of wolf in the breeze blowing from the east. Edward and Carlisle slowed a little out of habit, and I could see their heads sweep from side to side, waiting for the trail to turn.

Then the wolf smell was suddenly stronger, and Edward's head snapped up. He came to a sudden stop. The rest of us froze, too.

"Sam?" Edward asked in a flat voice. "What is this?"

Sam came through the trees a few hundred yards away, walking quickly toward us in his human form, flanked by two big wolves—Paul and Jared. It took Sam a while to reach us; his human pace made me impatient. I didn't want time to think about what was happening. I wanted to be in motion, to be doing something. I wanted to have my arms around Alice, to know beyond a doubt that she was safe.

I watched Edward's face go absolutely white as he read what Sam was thinking. Sam ignored him, looking straight at Carlisle as he stopped walking and began to speak.

"Right after midnight, Alice and Jasper came to this place and asked permission to cross our land to the ocean. I granted them that and escorted them to the coast myself. They went immediately into the water and did not return. As we journeyed, Alice told me it was of the utmost importance that I say nothing to Jacob about seeing her until I spoke to you. I was to wait here for you to come looking for her and then give you this note. She told me to obey her as if all our lives depended on it."

Sam's face was grim as he held out a folded sheet of paper, printed all over with small black text. It was a page out of a book; my sharp eyes read the printed words as Carlisle unfolded it to see the other side. The side facing me was the copyright page from *The Merchant of Venice*. A hint of my own scent blew off of it as Carlisle shook the paper flat. I realized it was a page torn from one of my books. I'd brought a few things from Charlie's house to the cottage; a few sets of normal clothes, all the letters from my mother, and my favorite books. My tattered collection of Shakespeare paperbacks had been on the bookshelf in the cottage's little living room yesterday morning. . . .

"Alice has decided to leave us," Carlisle whispered.

"What?" Rosalie cried.

Carlisle turned the page around so that we all could read.

> Don't look for us. There isn't time to waste. Remember: Tanya, Siobhan, Amun, Alistair, all the nomads you can find. We'll seek out Peter and Charlotte on our way. We're so sorry that we have to leave you this way, with no goodbyes or explanations. It's the only way for us. We love you.

We stood frozen again, the silence total but for the sound of the wolves' heartbeats, their breathing. Their thoughts must have been loud, too. Edward was first to move again, speaking in response to what he heard in Sam's head.

"Yes, things are that dangerous."

"Enough that you would abandon your family?" Sam asked out loud, censure in his tone. It was clear that he had not read the note before giving it to Carlisle. He was upset now, looking as if he regretted listening to Alice.

Edward's expression was stiff—to Sam it probably looked angry or arrogant, but I could see the shape of pain in the hard planes of his face.

"We don't know what she saw," Edward said. "Alice is neither unfeeling nor a coward. She just has more information than we do."

"*We* would not—," Sam began.

"You are bound differently than we are," Edward snapped. "*We* each still have our free will."

Sam's chin jerked up, and his eyes looked suddenly flat black.

"But you should heed the warning," Edward went on. "This is not something you want to involve yourselves in. You can still avoid what Alice saw."

Sam smiled grimly. "*We* don't run away." Behind him, Paul snorted.

"Don't get your family slaughtered for pride," Carlisle interjected quietly.

Sam looked at Carlisle with a softer expression. "As Edward pointed out, we don't have the same kind of freedom that you have. Renesmee is as much a part of our family now as she is yours. Jacob cannot abandon her, and we cannot abandon him." His eyes flickered to Alice's note, and his lips pressed into a thin line.

"You don't know her," Edward said.

"Do you?" Sam asked bluntly.

Carlisle put a hand on Edward's shoulder. "We have much to do, son. Whatever Alice's decision, we would be foolish not to follow her advice now. Let's go home and get to work."

Edward nodded, his face still rigid with pain. Behind me, I could hear Esme's quiet, tearless sobs.

I didn't know how to cry in this body; I couldn't do anything but stare. There was no feeling yet. Everything seemed unreal, like I was dreaming again after all these months. Having a nightmare.

"Thank you, Sam," Carlisle said.

"I'm sorry," Sam answered. "We shouldn't have let her through."

"You did the right thing," Carlisle told him. "Alice is free to do what she will. I wouldn't deny her that liberty."

I'd always thought of the Cullens as a whole, an indivisible unit. Suddenly, I remembered that it had not always been so. Carlisle had created Edward, Esme, Rosalie and Emmett; Edward had created me. We were physically linked by blood and venom. I never thought of Alice and Jasper as separate—as adopted into the family. But in truth, Alice *had* adopted the Cullens. She had shown up with her unconnected past, bringing Jasper with his, and fit herself into the family that was already there. Both she and Jasper had known another life outside the Cullen family. Had she really chosen to lead another new life after she'd seen that life with the Cullens was over?

We were doomed, then, weren't we? There was no hope at all. Not one ray, one flicker that might have convinced Alice she had a chance at our side.

The bright morning air seemed thicker suddenly, blacker, as if physically darkened by my despair.

"*I'm* not going down without a fight," Emmett snarled low under his breath. "Alice told us what to do. Let's get it done."

The others nodded with determined expressions, and I realized that they were banking on whatever chance Alice had given us. That they were not going to give in to hopelessness and wait to die.

Yes, we all would fight. What else was there? And apparently we would involve others, because Alice had said so before she'd left us. How could we not follow Alice's last warning? The wolves, too, would fight with us for Renesmee.

We would fight, they would fight, and we all would die.

I didn't feel the same resolve the others seemed to feel. Alice knew the odds. She was giving us the only chance she could see, but the chance was too slim for her to bet on it.

I felt already beaten as I turned my back on Sam's critical face and followed Carlisle toward home.

We ran automatically now, not the same panicked hurry as before. As we neared the river, Esme's head lifted.

"There was that other trail. It was fresh."

She nodded forward, toward where she had called Edward's attention on the way here. While we were racing to *save* Alice . . .

"It has to be from earlier in the day. It was just Alice, without Jasper," Edward said lifelessly.

Esme's face puckered, and she nodded.

I drifted to the right, falling a little behind. I was sure

Edward was right, but at the same time . . . After all, how had Alice's note ended up on a page from my book?

"Bella?" Edward asked in an emotionless voice as I hesitated.

"I want to follow the trail," I told him, smelling the light scent of Alice that led away from her earlier flight path. I was new to this, but it smelled exactly the same to me, just minus the scent of Jasper.

Edward's golden eyes were empty. "It probably just leads back to the house."

"Then I'll meet you there."

At first I thought he would let me go alone, but then, as I moved a few steps away, his blank eyes flickered to life.

"I'll come with you," he said quietly. "We'll meet you at home, Carlisle."

Carlisle nodded, and the others left. I waited until they were out of sight, and then I looked at Edward questioningly.

"I couldn't let you walk away from me," he explained in a low voice. "It hurt just to imagine it."

I understood without more explanation than that. I thought of being divided from him now and realized I would have felt the same pain, no matter how short the separation.

There was so little time left to be together.

I held my hand out to him, and he took it.

"Let's hurry," he said. "Renesmee will be awake."

I nodded, and we were running again.

It was probably a silly thing, to waste the time away from Renesmee just for curiosity's sake. But the note bothered me. Alice could have carved the note into a boulder or tree trunk if she lacked writing utensils. She could have stolen a pad of Post-its from any of the houses by the highway. Why my book? When did she get it?

Sure enough, the trail led back to the cottage by a circuitous route that stayed far clear of the Cullens' house and the wolves in the nearby woods. Edward's brows tightened in confusion as it became obvious where the trail led.

He tried to reason it out. "She left Jasper to wait for her and came here?"

We were almost to the cottage now, and I felt uneasy. I was glad to have Edward's hand in mine, but I also felt as if I should be here alone. Tearing out the page and carrying it back to Jasper was such an odd thing for Alice to do. It felt like there was a message in her action—one I didn't understand at all. But it was my book, so the message *must* be for me. If it were something she wanted Edward to know, wouldn't she have pulled a page from one of his books . . . ?

"Give me just a minute," I said, pulling my hand free as we got to the door.

His forehead creased. "Bella?"

"Please? Thirty seconds."

I didn't wait for him to answer. I darted through the door, pulling it shut behind me. I went straight to the bookshelf. Alice's scent was fresh—less than a day old. A fire that I had not set burned low but hot in the fireplace. I yanked *The Merchant of Venice* off the shelf and flipped it open to the title page.

There, next to the feathered edge left by the torn page, under the words *The Merchant of Venice by William Shakespeare*, was a note.

Destroy this.

Below that was a name and an address in Seattle.

When Edward came through the door after only thirteen seconds rather than thirty, I was watching the book burn.

"What's going on, Bella?"

"She was here. She ripped a page out of my book to write her note on."

"Why?"

"I don't know why."

"Why are you burning it?"

"I——I——" I frowned, letting all my frustration and pain show on my face. I did not know what Alice was trying to tell me, only that she'd gone to great lengths to keep it from anyone but me. The one person whose mind Edward could not read. So she must want to keep him in the dark, and it was probably for a good reason. "It seemed appropriate."

"We don't know what she's doing," he said quietly.

I stared into the flames. I was the only person in the world who could lie to Edward. Was that what Alice wanted from me? Her last request?

"When we were on the plane to Italy," I whispered——this was not a lie, except perhaps in context——"on our way to rescue you . . . she lied to Jasper so that he wouldn't come after us. She knew that if he faced the Volturi, he would die. She was willing to die herself rather than put him in danger. Willing for me to die, too. Willing for you to die."

Edward didn't answer.

"She has her priorities," I said. It made my still heart

ache to realize that my explanation did not feel like a lie in any way.

"I don't believe it," Edward said. He didn't say it like he was arguing with me—he said it like he was arguing with himself. "Maybe it was just Jasper in danger. Her plan would work for the rest of us, but he'd be lost if he stayed. Maybe . . ."

"She could have told us that. Sent him away."

"But would Jasper have gone? Maybe she's lying to him again."

"Maybe," I pretended to agree. "We should go home. There's no time."

Edward took my hand, and we ran.

Alice's note did not make me hopeful. If there were any way to avoid the coming slaughter, Alice would have stayed. I couldn't see another possibility. So it was something else she was giving me. Not a way to escape. But what else would she think that I wanted? Maybe a way to salvage *something*? Was there anything I could still save?

Carlisle and the others had not been idle in our absence. We'd been separated from them for all of five minutes, and they were already prepared to leave. In the corner, Jacob was human again, with Renesmee on his lap, both of them watching us with wide eyes.

Rosalie had traded her silk wrap dress for a sturdy-looking pair of jeans, running shoes, and a button-down shirt made of the thick weave that backpackers used for long trips. Esme was dressed similarly. There was a globe on the coffee table, but they were done looking at it, just waiting for us.

The atmosphere was more positive now than before; it felt good to them to be in action. Their hopes were pinned on Alice's instructions.

I looked at the globe and wondered where we were headed first.

"We're to stay here?" Edward asked, looking at Carlisle. He didn't sound happy.

"Alice said that we would have to show people Renesmee, and we would have to be careful about it," Carlisle said. "We'll send whomever we can find back here to you—Edward, you'll be the best at fielding that particular minefield."

Edward gave one sharp nod, still not happy. "There's a lot of ground to cover."

"We're splitting up," Emmett answered. "Rose and I are hunting for nomads."

"You'll have your hands full here," Carlisle said. "Tanya's family will be here in the morning, and they have no idea why. First, you have to persuade them not to react the way Irina did. Second, you've got to find out what Alice meant about Eleazar. Then, after all that, will they stay to witness for us? It will start again as the others come—if we can persuade anyone to come in the first place." Carlisle sighed. "Your job may well be the hardest. We'll be back to help as soon as we can."

Carlisle put his hand on Edward's shoulder for a second and then kissed my forehead. Esme hugged us both, and Emmett punched us both on the arm. Rosalie forced a hard smile for Edward and me, blew a kiss to Renesmee, and then gave Jacob a parting grimace.

"Good luck," Edward told them.

"And to you," Carlisle said. "We'll all need it."

I watched them leave, wishing I could feel whatever hope bolstered them, and wishing I could be alone with the computer for just a few seconds. I had to figure out who this J. Jenks person was and why Alice had gone to such lengths to give his name to only me.

Renesmee twisted in Jacob's arms to touch his cheek.

"I don't know if Carlisle's friends will come. I hope so. Sounds like we're a little outnumbered right now," Jacob murmured to Renesmee.

So she knew. Renesmee already understood only too clearly what was going on. The whole imprinted-werewolf-gives-the-object-of-his-imprinting-whatever-she-wants thing was getting old pretty fast. Wasn't shielding her more important than answering her questions?

I looked carefully at her face. She did not look frightened, only anxious and very serious as she conversed with Jacob in her silent way.

"No, we can't help; we've got to stay here," he went on. "People are coming to see *you*, not the scenery."

Renesmee frowned at him.

"No, I don't have to go anywhere," he said to her. Then he looked at Edward, his face stunned by the realization that he might be wrong. "Do I?"

Edward hesitated.

"Spit it out," Jacob said, his voice raw with tension. He was right at his breaking point, just like the rest of us.

"The vampires who are coming to help us are not the same as we are," Edward said. "Tanya's family is the only one besides ours with a reverence for human life, and even they don't think much of werewolves. I think it might be safer—"

"I can take care of myself," Jacob interrupted.

"Safer for Renesmee," Edward continued, "if the choice to believe our story about her is not tainted by an association with werewolves."

"Some friends. They'd turn on you just because of who you hang out with now?"

"I think they would mostly be tolerant under normal circumstances. But you need to understand—accepting Nessie will not be a simple thing for any of them. Why make it even the slightest bit harder?"

Carlisle had explained the laws about immortal children to Jacob last night. "The immortal children were really that bad?" he asked.

"You can't imagine the depth of the scars they've left in the collective vampire psyche."

"Edward . . ." It was still odd to hear Jacob use Edward's name without bitterness.

"I know, Jake. I know how hard it is to be away from her. We'll play it by ear— see how they react to her. In any case, Nessie is going to have to be incognito off and on in the next few weeks. She'll need to stay at the cottage until the right moment for us to introduce her. As long as you keep a safe distance from the main house . . ."

"I can do that. Company in the morning, huh?"

"Yes. The closest of our friends. In this particular case, it's probably better if we get things out in the open as soon as possible. You can stay here. Tanya knows about you. She's even met Seth."

"Right."

"You should tell Sam what's going on. There might be strangers in the woods soon."

"Good point. Though I owe him some silence after last night."

"Listening to Alice is usually the right thing."

Jacob's teeth ground together, and I could see that he shared Sam's feelings about what Alice and Jasper had done.

While they were talking, I wandered toward the back windows, trying to look distracted and anxious. Not a difficult thing to do. I leaned my head against the wall that curved away from the living room toward the dining room, right next to one of the computer desks. I ran my fingers against the keys while staring into the forest, trying to make it look like an absentminded thing. Did vampires ever do things absentmindedly? I didn't think anyone was paying particular attention to me, but I didn't turn to make sure. The monitor glowed to life. I stroked my fingers across the keys again. Then I drummed them very quietly on the wooden desktop, just to make it seem random. Another stroke across the keys.

I scanned the screen in my peripheral vision.

No J. Jenks, but there was a Jason Jenks. A lawyer. I brushed the keyboard, trying to keep a rhythm, like the preoccupied stroking of a cat you'd all but forgotten on your lap. Jason Jenks had a fancy website for his firm, but the address on the homepage was wrong. In Seattle, but in a different zip code. I noted the phone number and then stroked the keyboard in rhythm. This time I searched the address, but nothing at all came up, as if the address didn't exist. I wanted to look at a map, but I decided I was pushing my luck. One more brush, to delete the history. . . .

I continued staring out the window and brushed the wood a few times. I heard light footsteps crossing the floor to me, and I turned with what I hoped was the same expression as before.

Renesmee reached for me, and I held my arms open. She launched herself into them, smelling strongly of werewolf, and nestled her head against my neck.

I didn't know if I could stand this. As much as I feared for my life, for Edward's, for the rest of my family's, it was not the same as the gut-wrenching terror I felt for my daughter. There had to be a way to save her, even if that was the only thing I could do.

Suddenly, I knew that this was all I wanted anymore. The rest I would bear if I had to, but not her life being forfeited. Not that.

She was the one thing I simply *had* to save.

Would Alice have known how I would feel?

Renesmee's hand touched my cheek lightly.

She showed me my own face, Edward's, Jacob's, Rosalie's, Esme's, Carlisle's, Alice's, Jasper's, flipping through all our family's faces faster and faster. Seth and Leah. Charlie, Sue, and Billy. Over and over again. Worrying, like the rest of us were. She was only worrying, though. Jake had kept the worst from her as far as I could tell. The part about how we had no hope, how we all were going to die in a month's time.

She settled on Alice's face, longing and confused. Where was Alice?

"I don't know," I whispered. "But she's Alice. She's doing the right thing, like always."

The right thing for Alice, anyway. I hated thinking of her that way, but how else could the situation be understood?

Renesmee sighed, and the longing intensified.

"I miss her, too."

I felt my face working, trying to find the expression that went with the grief inside. My eyes felt strange and dry; they blinked against the uncomfortable feeling. I bit my lip. When I took my next breath, the air hitched in my throat, like I was choking on it.

Renesmee pulled back to look at me, and I saw my face mirrored in her thoughts and in her eyes. I looked like Esme had this morning.

So this was what it felt like to cry.

Renesmee's eyes glistened wetly as she watched my face. She stroked my face, showing me nothing, just trying to soothe me.

I'd never thought to see the mother-daughter bond reversed between us, the way it had always been for Renée and me. But I hadn't had a very clear view of the future.

A tear welled up on the edge of Renesmee's eye. I wiped it away with a kiss. She touched her eye in amazement and then looked at the wetness on her fingertip.

"Don't cry," I told her. "It's going to be okay. You're going to be fine. I will find you a way through this."

If there was nothing else I could do, I would still save my Renesmee. I was more positive than ever that this was what Alice would give me. She would know. She would have left me a way.

30. IRRESISTIBLE

THERE WAS SO MUCH TO THINK ABOUT.

How was I going to find time alone to hunt down J. Jenks, and why did Alice want me to know about him?

If Alice's clue had nothing to do with Renesmee, what could I do to save my daughter?

How were Edward and I going to explain things to Tanya's family in the morning? What if they reacted like Irina? What if it turned into a fight?

I didn't know how to fight. How was I going to learn in just a month? Was there any chance at all that I could be taught fast enough that I might be a danger to any one member of the Volturi? Or was I doomed to be totally useless? Just another easily dispatched newborn?

So many answers I needed, but I did not get the chance to ask my questions.

Wanting some normality for Renesmee, I'd insisted on taking her home to our cottage at bedtime. Jacob was more comfortable in his wolf form at the moment; the stress was easier dealt with when he felt ready for a fight. I wished that I could feel the same, could feel ready. He ran in the woods, on guard again.

After she was deeply under, I put Renesmee in her bed and then went to the front room to ask my questions of Edward. The ones I was able to ask, at any rate; one of the most difficult of problems was the idea of trying to hide anything from him, even with the advantage of my silent thoughts.

He stood with his back to me, staring into the fire.

"Edward, I—"

He spun and was across the room in what seemed like no time at all, not even the smallest part of a second. I only had time to register the ferocious expression on his face before his lips were crushing against mine and his arms were locked around me like steel girders.

I didn't think of my questions again for the rest of that night. It didn't take long for me to grasp the reason for his mood, and even less time to feel exactly the same way.

I'd been planning on needing years just to somewhat organize the overwhelming passion I felt for him physically. And then centuries after that to enjoy it. If we had only a month left together . . . Well, I didn't see how I could stand to have this end. For the moment I couldn't help but be selfish. All I wanted was to love him as much as possible in the limited time given to me.

It was hard to pull myself away from him when the sun came up, but we had our job to do, a job that might be more difficult than all the rest of our family's searches put together. As soon as I let myself think of what was coming, I was all tension; it felt like my nerves were being stretched on a rack, thinner and thinner.

"I wish there was a way to get the information we need from Eleazar before we tell them about Nessie," Edward muttered as we hurriedly dressed in the huge closet that was more reminder of Alice than I wanted at the moment. "Just in case."

"But he wouldn't understand the question to answer it," I agreed. "Do you think they'll let us explain?"

"I don't know."

I pulled Renesmee, still sleeping, from her bed and held her close so that her curls were pressed against my face; her sweet scent, so close, overpowered every other smell.

I couldn't waste one second of time today. There were answers I needed, and wasn't sure how much time Edward and I would have alone today. If all went well with Tanya's family, hopefully we would have company for an extended period.

"Edward, will you teach me how to fight?" I asked him, tensed for his reaction, as he held the door for me.

It was what I expected. He froze, and then his eyes swept over me with a deep significance, like he was looking at me for the first or last time. His eyes lingered on our daughter sleeping in my arms.

"If it comes to a fight, there won't be much any of us can do," he hedged.

I kept my voice even. "Would you leave me unable to defend myself?"

He swallowed convulsively, and the door shuddered, hinges protesting, as his hand tightened. Then he nodded. "When you put it that way . . . I suppose we should get to work as soon as we can."

I nodded, too, and we started toward the big house. We didn't hurry.

I wondered what I could do that would have any hope of making a difference. I was a tiny bit special, in my own way—if having a supernaturally thick skull could really be considered special. Was there any use that I could put that toward?

"What would you say their biggest advantage is? Do they even have a weakness?"

Edward didn't have to ask to know I meant the Volturi.

"Alec and Jane are their greatest offense," he said emotionlessly, like we were talking of a basketball team. "Their defensive players rarely see any real action."

"Because Jane can burn you where you stand—mentally at least. What does Alec do? Didn't you once say he was even more dangerous than Jane?"

"Yes. In a way, he is the antidote to Jane. She makes you feel the worst pain imaginable. Alec, on the other hand, makes you feel nothing. Absolutely nothing. Sometimes, when the Volturi are feeling kind, they have Alec anesthetize someone before he is executed. If he has surrendered or pleased them in some other way."

"Anesthetic? But how is that more dangerous than Jane?"

"Because he cuts off your senses altogether. No pain, but also no sight or sound or smell. Total sensory deprivation. You are utterly alone in the blackness. You don't even feel it when they burn you."

I shivered. Was this the best we could hope for? To not see or feel death when it came?

"That would make him only equally as dangerous as Jane," Edward went on in the same detached voice, "in that they both can incapacitate you, make you into a helpless target. The difference between them is like the difference between Aro and me. Aro hears the mind of only one person at a time. Jane can only hurt the one object of her focus. I can hear everyone at the same time."

I felt cold as I saw where he was going. "And Alec can incapacitate us all at the same time?" I whispered.

"Yes," he said. "If he uses his gift against us, we will all stand blind and deaf until they get around to killing us—maybe they'll simply burn us without bothering to tear us apart first. Oh, we could try to fight, but we'll be more likely to hurt one another than we would be to hurt one of them."

We walked in silence for a few seconds.

An idea was shaping itself in my head. Not very promising, but better than nothing.

"Do you think Alec is a very good fighter?" I asked. "Aside from what he can do, I mean. If he had to fight without his gift. I wonder if he's ever even tried. . . ."

Edward glanced at me sharply. "What are you thinking?"

I looked straight ahead. "Well, he probably can't do that to me, can he? If what he does is like Aro and Jane and you.

Maybe . . . if he's never really had to defend himself . . . and I learned a few tricks—"

"He's been with the Volturi for centuries," Edward cut me off, his voice abruptly panicked. He was probably seeing the same image in his head that I was: the Cullens standing helpless, senseless pillars on the killing field—all but me. I'd be the only one who *could* fight. "Yes, you're surely immune to his power, but you are still a newborn, Bella. I can't make you that strong a fighter in a few weeks. I'm sure he's had training."

"Maybe, maybe not. It's the one thing I can do that no one else can. Even if I can just *distract* him for a while—" Could I last long enough to give the others a chance?

"Please, Bella," Edward said through his teeth. "Let's not talk about this."

"Be reasonable."

"I will try to teach you what I can, but please don't make me think about you sacrificing yourself as a diversion—" He choked, and didn't finish.

I nodded. I would keep my plans to myself, then. First Alec and then, if I was miraculously lucky enough to win, Jane. If I could only even things out—remove the Volturi's overwhelming offensive advantage. Maybe then there was a chance. . . . My mind raced ahead. What if I *was* able to distract or even take them out? Honestly, why would either Jane or Alec ever have needed to learn battle skills? I couldn't imagine petulant little Jane surrendering her advantage, even to learn.

If I was able to kill them, what a difference that would make.

"I have to learn everything. As much as you can possibly cram into my head in the next month," I murmured.

He acted as if I hadn't spoken.

Who next, then? I might as well have my plans in order so that, if I did live past attacking Alec, there would be no hesitation in my strike. I tried to think of another situation where my thick skull would give me an advantage. I didn't know enough about what the others did. Obviously, fighters like the huge Felix were beyond me. I could only try to give Emmett his fair fight there. I didn't know much about the rest of the Volturi guard, besides Demetri. . . .

My face was perfectly smooth as I considered Demetri. Without a doubt, he would be a fighter. There was no other way he could have survived so long, always at the spear point of any attack. And he must always lead, because he was their tracker—the best tracker in the world, no doubt. If there had been one better, the Volturi would have traded up. Aro didn't surround himself with second best.

If Demetri didn't exist, then we *could* run. Whoever was left of us, in any case. My daughter, warm in my arms . . . Someone could run with her. Jacob or Rosalie, whoever was left.

And . . . if Demetri didn't exist, then Alice and Jasper could be safe forever. Is that what Alice had seen? That part of our family could continue? The two of them, at the very least.

Could I begrudge her that?

"Demetri . . . ," I said.

"Demetri is mine," Edward said in a hard, tight voice. I looked at him quickly and saw that his expression had turned violent.

"Why?" I whispered.

He didn't answer at first. We were to the river when he finally murmured, "For Alice. It's the only thanks I can give her now for the last fifty years."

So his thoughts were in line with mine.

I heard Jacob's heavy paws thudding against the frozen ground. In seconds, he was pacing beside me, his dark eyes focused on Renesmee.

I nodded to him once, then returned to my questions. There was so little time.

"Edward, why do you think Alice told us to ask Eleazar about the Volturi? Has he been in Italy recently or something? What could he know?"

"Eleazar knows everything when it comes to the Volturi. I forgot you didn't know. He used to be one of them."

I hissed involuntarily. Jacob growled beside me.

"What?" I demanded, in my head picturing the beautiful dark-haired man at our wedding wrapped in a long, ashy cloak.

Edward's face was softer now—he smiled a little. "Eleazar is a very gentle person. He wasn't entirely happy with the Volturi, but he respected the law and its need to be upheld. He felt he was working toward the greater good. He doesn't regret his time with them. But when he found Carmen, he found his place in this world. They are very similar people, both very compassionate for vampires." He smiled again. "They met Tanya and her sisters, and they never looked back. They are well suited to this lifestyle. If they'd never found Tanya, I imagine they would have eventually discovered a way to live without human blood on their own."

The pictures in my head were jarring. I couldn't make them match up. A compassionate Volturi soldier?

Edward glanced at Jacob and answered a silent question. "No, he wasn't one of their warriors, so to speak. He had a gift they found convenient."

Jacob must have asked the obvious follow-up question.

"He has an instinctive feel for the gifts of others—the extra abilities that some vampires have," Edward told him. "He could give Aro a general idea of what any given vampire was capable of just by being in proximity with him or her. This was helpful when the Volturi went into battle. He could warn them if someone in the opposing coven had a skill that might give them some trouble. That was rare; it takes quite a skill to even inconvenience the Volturi for a moment. More often, the warning would give Aro the chance to save someone who might be useful to him. Eleazar's gift works even with humans, to an extent. He has to really concentrate with humans, though, because the latent ability is so nebulous. Aro would have him test the people who wanted to join, to see if they had any potential. Aro was sorry to see him go."

"They let him go?" I asked. "Just like that?"

His smile was darker now, a little twisted. "The Volturi aren't supposed to be the villains, the way they seem to you. They are the foundation of our peace and civilization. Each member of the guard chooses to serve them. It's quite prestigious; they all are proud to be there, not forced to be there."

I scowled at the ground.

"They're only alleged to be heinous and evil by the criminals, Bella."

"We're not criminals."

Jacob huffed in agreement.

"They don't know that."

"Do you really think we can make them stop and listen?"

Edward hesitated just the tiniest moment and then shrugged. "If we find enough friends to stand beside us. Maybe."

If. I suddenly felt the urgency of what we had before us today. Edward and I both started to move faster, breaking into a run. Jacob caught up quickly.

"Tanya shouldn't be too much longer," Edward said. "We need to be ready."

How to be ready, though? We arranged and rearranged, thought and rethought. Renesmee in full view? Or hidden at first? Jacob in the room? Or outside? He'd told his pack to stay close but invisible. Should he do the same?

In the end, Renesmee, Jacob—in his human form again—and I waited around the corner from the front door in the dining room, sitting at the big polished table. Jacob let me hold Renesmee; he wanted space in case he had to phase quickly.

Though I was glad to have her in my arms, it made me feel useless. It reminded me that in a fight with mature vampires, I was no more than an easy target; I didn't need my hands free.

I tried to remember Tanya, Kate, Carmen, and Eleazar from the wedding. Their faces were murky in my ill-lit memories. I only knew they were beautiful, two blondes and two brunettes. I couldn't remember if there was any kindness in their eyes.

Edward leaned motionlessly against the back window wall, staring toward the front door. It didn't look like he was seeing the room in front of him.

We listened to the cars zooming past out on the freeway, none of them slowing.

Renesmee nestled into my neck, her hand against my cheek but no images in my head. She didn't have pictures for her feelings now.

"What if they don't like me?" she whispered, and all our eyes flashed to her face.

"Of course they'll—," Jacob started to say, but I silenced him with a look.

"They don't understand you, Renesmee, because they've never met anyone like you," I told her, not wanting to lie to her with promises that might not come true. "Getting them to understand is the problem."

She sighed, and in my head flashed pictures of all of us in one quick burst. Vampire, human, werewolf. She fit nowhere.

"You're special, that's not a bad thing."

She shook her head in disagreement. She thought of our strained faces and said, "This is my fault."

"No," Jacob, Edward, and I all said at exactly the same time, but before we could argue further, we heard the sound we'd been waiting for: the slowing of an engine on the freeway, the tires moving from pavement to soft dirt.

Edward darted around the corner to stand waiting by the door. Renesmee hid in my hair. Jacob and I stared at each other across the table, desperation on our faces.

The car moved quickly through the woods, faster than Charlie or Sue drove. We heard it pull into the meadow and stop by the front porch. Four doors opened and closed. They didn't speak as they approached the door. Edward opened it before they could knock.

"Edward!" a female voice enthused.

"Hello, Tanya. Kate, Eleazar, Carmen."

Three murmured hellos.

"Carlisle said he needed to talk to us right away," the first voice said, Tanya. I could hear that they all were still outside. I imagined Edward in the doorway, blocking their entrance. "What's the problem? Trouble with the werewolves?"

Jacob rolled his eyes.

"No," Edward said. "Our truce with the werewolves is stronger than ever."

A woman chuckled.

"Aren't you going to invite us in?" Tanya asked. And then she continued without waiting for an answer. "Where's Carlisle?"

"Carlisle had to leave."

There was a short silence.

"What's going on, Edward?" Tanya demanded.

"If you could give me the benefit of the doubt for just a few minutes," he answered. "I have something difficult to explain, and I'll need you to be open-minded until you understand."

"Is Carlisle all right?" a male voice asked anxiously. Eleazar.

"None of us is all right, Eleazar," Edward said, and then he patted something, maybe Eleazar's shoulder. "But physically, Carlisle is fine."

"Physically?" Tanya asked sharply. "What do you mean?"

"I mean that my entire family is in very grave danger. But before I explain, I ask for your promise. Listen to everything I say before you react. I am begging you to hear me out."

A longer silence greeted his request. Through the strained hush, Jacob and I stared wordlessly at each other. His russet lips paled.

"We're listening," Tanya finally said. "We will hear it all before we judge."

"Thank you, Tanya," Edward said fervently. "We wouldn't involve you in this if we had any other choice."

Edward moved. We heard four sets of footsteps walk through the doorway.

Someone sniffed. "I knew those werewolves were involved," Tanya muttered.

"Yes, and they're on our side. Again."

The reminder silenced Tanya.

"Where's your Bella?" one of the other female voices asked. "How is she?"

"She'll join us shortly. She's well, thank you. She's taken to immortality with amazing finesse."

"Tell us about the danger, Edward," Tanya said quietly. "We'll listen, and we'll be on your side, where we belong."

Edward took a deep breath. "I'd like you to witness for yourselves first. Listen—in the other room. What do you hear?"

It was quiet, and then there was movement.

"Just listen first, please," Edward said.

"A werewolf, I assume. I can hear his heart," Tanya said.

"What else?" Edward asked.

There was a pause.

"What is that thrumming?" Kate or Carmen asked. "Is that . . . some kind of a bird?"

"No, but remember what you're hearing. Now, what do you smell? Besides the werewolf."

"Is there a human here?" Eleazar whispered.

"No," Tanya disagreed. "It's not human . . . but . . . closer to human than the rest of the scents here. What is that, Edward? I don't think I've ever smelled that fragrance before."

"You most certainly have not, Tanya. Please, *please* remember that this is something entirely new to you. Throw away your preconceived notions."

"I promised you I would listen, Edward."

"All right, then. Bella? Bring out Renesmee, please."

My legs felt strangely numb, but I knew that feeling was all in my head. I forced myself not to hold back, not to move sluggishly, as I got to my feet and walked the few short feet to the corner. The heat from Jacob's body flamed close behind me as he shadowed my steps.

I took one step into the bigger room and then froze, unable to force myself farther forward. Renesmee took a deep breath and then peeped out from under my hair, her little shoulders tight, expecting a rebuff.

I thought I'd prepared myself for their reaction. For accusations, for shouting, for the motionlessness of deep stress.

Tanya skittered back four steps, her strawberry curls quivering, like a human confronted by a venomous snake. Kate jumped back all the way to the front door and braced herself against the wall there. A shocked hiss came from between her clenched teeth. Eleazar threw himself in front of Carmen in a protective crouch.

"Oh *please*," I heard Jacob complain under his breath.

Edward put his arm around Renesmee and me. "You promised to listen," he reminded them.

"Some things cannot be heard!" Tanya exclaimed. "How could you, Edward? Do you not know what this means?"

"We have to get out of here," Kate said anxiously, her hand on the doorknob.

"Edward . . ." Eleazar seemed beyond words.

"Wait," Edward said, his voice harder now. "Remember what you hear, what you smell. Renesmee is not what you think she is."

"There are no exceptions to this rule, Edward," Tanya snapped back.

"Tanya," Edward said sharply, "you can hear her heart-beat! Stop and think about what that means."

"Her heartbeat?" Carmen whispered, peering around Eleazar's shoulder.

"She's not a full vampire child," Edward answered, directing his attention toward Carmen's less hostile expression. "She is half-human."

The four vampires stared at him like he was speaking a language none of them knew.

"Hear me." Edward's voice shifted into a smooth velvet tone of persuasion. "Renesmee is one of a kind. I am her father. Not her creator—her biological father."

Tanya's head was shaking, just a tiny movement. She didn't seem aware of it.

"Edward, you can't expect us to—," Eleazar started to say.

"Tell me another explanation that fits, Eleazar. You can feel the warmth of her body in the air. Blood runs in her veins, Eleazar. You can smell it."

"How?" Kate breathed.

"Bella is her biological mother," Edward told her. "She conceived, carried, and gave birth to Renesmee while she was still human. It nearly killed her. I was hard-pressed to get enough venom into her heart to save her."

"I've never heard of such a thing," Eleazar said. His shoulders were still stiff, his expression cold.

"Physical relationships between vampires and humans are not common," Edward answered, a bit of dark humor in his tone now. "Human survivors of such trysts are even less common. Wouldn't you agree, cousins?"

Both Kate and Tanya scowled at him.

"Come now, Eleazar. Surely you can see the resemblance."

It was Carmen who responded to Edward's words. She stepped around Eleazar, ignoring his half-articulated warning, and walked carefully to stand right in front of me. She leaned down slightly, looking carefully into Renesmee's face.

"You seem to have your mother's eyes," she said in a low, calm voice, "but your father's face." And then, as if she could not help herself, she smiled at Renesmee.

Renesmee's answering smile was dazzling. She touched my face without looking away from Carmen. She imagined touching Carmen's face, wondering if that was okay.

"Do you mind if Renesmee tells you about it herself?" I asked Carmen. I was still too stressed to speak above a whisper. "She has a gift for explaining things."

Carmen was still smiling at Renesmee. "Do you speak, little one?"

"Yes," Renesmee answered in her trilling high soprano. All of Tanya's family flinched at the sound of her voice except for Carmen. "But I can show you more than I can tell you."

She placed her little dimpled hand on Carmen's cheek.

Carmen stiffened like an electric shock had run through her. Eleazar was at her side in an instant, his hands on her shoulders as if to yank her away.

"Wait," Carmen said breathlessly, her unblinking eyes locked on Renesmee's.

Renesmee "showed" Carmen her explanation for a long time. Edward's face was intent as he watched with Carmen, and I wished so much that I could hear what he heard, too. Jacob shifted his weight impatiently behind me, and I knew he was wishing the same.

"What's Nessie showing her?" he grumbled under his breath.

"Everything," Edward murmured.

Another minute passed, and Renesmee dropped her hand from Carmen's face. She smiled winningly at the stunned vampire.

"She really is your daughter, isn't she?" Carmen breathed, switching her wide topaz eyes to Edward's face. "Such a vivid gift! It could only have come from a very gifted father."

"Do you believe what she showed you?" Edward asked, his expression intense.

"Without a doubt," Carmen said simply.

Eleazar's face was rigid with distress. "Carmen!"

Carmen took his hands into her own and squeezed them. "Impossible as it seems, Edward has told you nothing but truth. Let the child show you."

Carmen nudged Eleazar closer to me and then nodded at Renesmee. "Show him, *mi querida.*"

Renesmee grinned, clearly delighted with Carmen's acceptance, and touched Eleazar lightly on the forehead.

"*Ay caray!*" he spit, and jerked away from her.

"What did she do to you?" Tanya demanded, coming closer warily. Kate crept forward, too.

"She's just trying to show you her side of the story," Carmen told him in a soothing voice.

Renesmee frowned impatiently. "Watch, please," she commanded Eleazar. She stretched her hand out to him and then left a few inches between her fingers and his face, waiting.

Eleazar eyed her suspiciously and then glanced at Carmen for help. She nodded encouragingly. Eleazar took a deep breath and then leaned closer until his forehead touched her hand again.

He shuddered when it began but held still this time, his eyes closed in concentration.

"Ahh," he sighed when his eyes reopened a few minutes later. "I see."

Renesmee smiled at him. He hesitated, then smiled a slightly unwilling smile in response.

"Eleazar?" Tanya asked.

"It's all true, Tanya. This is no immortal child. She's half-human. Come. See for yourself."

In silence, Tanya took her turn standing warily before me, and then Kate, both showing shock as that first image hit them with Renesmee's touch. But then, just like Carmen and Eleazar, they seemed completely won over as soon as it was done.

I shot a glance at Edward's smooth face, wondering if it could really be so easy. His golden eyes were clear, unshadowed. There was no deception in this, then.

"Thank you for listening," he said quietly.

"But there is the *grave danger* you warned us of," Tanya said. "Not directly from this child, I see, but surely from the Volturi, then. How did they find out about her? When are they coming?"

I was not surprised at her quick understanding. After all, what could possibly be a threat to a family as strong as mine? Only the Volturi.

"When Bella saw Irina that day in the mountains," Edward explained, "she had Renesmee with her."

Kate hissed, her eyes narrowing to slits. "*Irina* did this? To you? To Carlisle? *Irina?*"

"No," Tanya whispered. "Someone else . . ."

"Alice saw her go to them," Edward said. I wondered if the others noticed the way he winced just slightly when he spoke Alice's name.

"How could she do this thing?" Eleazar asked of no one.

"Imagine if you had seen Renesmee only from a distance. If you had not waited for our explanation."

Tanya's eyes tightened. "No matter what she thought . . . You are our family."

"There's nothing we can do about Irina's choice now. It's too late. Alice gave us a month."

Both Tanya's and Eleazar's heads cocked to one side. Kate's brow furrowed.

"So long?" Eleazar asked.

"They are all coming. That must take some preparation."

Eleazar gasped. "The entire guard?"

"Not just the guard," Edward said, his jaw straining tight. "Aro, Caius, Marcus. Even the wives."

Shock glazed over all their eyes.

"Impossible," Eleazar said blankly.

"I would have said the same two days ago," Edward said.

Eleazar scowled, and when he spoke it was nearly a growl. "But that doesn't make any sense. Why would they put themselves and the wives in danger?"

"It doesn't make sense from that angle. Alice said there was more to this than just punishment for what they think we've done. She thought you could help us."

"More than punishment? But what else is there?" Eleazar started pacing, stalking toward the door and back again as if he were alone here, his eyebrows furrowed as he stared at the floor.

"Where are the others, Edward? Carlisle and Alice and the rest?" Tanya asked.

Edward's hesitation was almost unnoticeable. He answered only part of her question. "Looking for friends who might help us."

Tanya leaned toward him, holding her hands out in front of her. "Edward, no matter how many friends you gather, we can't help you *win*. We can only die with you. You must know that. Of course, perhaps the four of us deserve that after what Irina has done now, after how we've failed you in the past—for her sake that time as well."

Edward shook his head quickly. "We're not asking you to fight and die with us, Tanya. You know Carlisle would never ask for that."

"Then what, Edward?"

"We're just looking for witnesses. If we can make them pause, just for a moment. If they would let us explain . . ." He touched Renesmee's cheek; she grabbed his hand and held it pressed against her skin. "It's difficult to doubt our story when you see it for yourself."

Tanya nodded slowly. "Do you think her past will matter to them so much?"

"Only as it foreshadows her future. The point of the restriction was to protect us from exposure, from the excesses of children who could not be tamed."

"I'm not dangerous at all," Renesmee interjected. I listened to her high, clear voice with new ears, imagining how she sounded to the others. "I never hurt Grandpa or Sue or Billy. I love humans. And wolf-people like my Jacob." She dropped Edward's hand to reach back and pat Jacob's arm.

Tanya and Kate exchanged a quick glance.

"If Irina had not come so soon," Edward mused, "we could have avoided all of this. Renesmee grows at an unprecedented rate. By the time the month is past, she'll have gained another half year of development."

"Well, that is something we can certainly witness," Carmen said in a decided tone. "We'll be able to promise that we've seen her mature ourselves. How could the Volturi ignore such evidence?"

Eleazar mumbled, "How, indeed?" but he did not look up, and he continued pacing as if he were paying no attention at all.

"Yes, we can witness for you," Tanya said. "Certainly that much. We will consider what more we might do."

"Tanya," Edward protested, hearing more in her thoughts

than there was in her words, "we don't expect you to fight with us."

"If the Volturi won't pause to listen to our witness, we cannot simply stand by," Tanya insisted. "Of course, I should only speak for myself."

Kate snorted. "Do you really doubt me so much, sister?"

Tanya smiled widely at her. "It *is* a suicide mission, after all."

Kate flashed a grin back and then shrugged nonchalantly. "I'm in."

"I, too, will do what I can to protect the child," Carmen agreed. Then, as if she couldn't resist, she held her arms out toward Renesmee. "May I hold you, *bebé linda*?"

Renesmee reached eagerly toward Carmen, delighted with her new friend. Carmen hugged her close, murmuring to her in Spanish.

It was like it had been with Charlie, and before that with all the Cullens. Renesmee was irresistible. What was it about her that drew everyone to her, that made them willing even to pledge their lives in her defense?

For a moment I thought that maybe what we were attempting might be possible. Maybe Renesmee could do the impossible and win over our enemies as she had our friends.

And then I remembered that Alice had left us, and my hope vanished as quickly as it had appeared.

31. TALENTED

"WHAT IS THE WEREWOLVES' PART IN THIS?" TANYA asked then, eyeing Jacob.

Jacob spoke before Edward could answer. "If the Volturi won't stop to listen about Nessie, I mean Renesmee," he corrected himself, remembering that Tanya would not understand his stupid nickname, "*we* will stop them."

"Very brave, child, but that would be impossible for more experienced fighters than you are."

"You don't know what we can do."

Tanya shrugged. "It is your own life, certainly, to spend as you choose."

Jacob's eyes flickered to Renesmee—still in Carmen's

arms with Kate hovering over them—and it was easy to read the longing in them.

"She is special, that little one," Tanya mused. "Hard to resist."

"A very talented family," Eleazar murmured as he paced. His tempo was increasing; he flashed from the door to Carmen and back again every second. "A mind reader for a father, a shield for a mother, and then whatever magic this extraordinary child has bewitched us with. I wonder if there is a name for what she does, or if it is the norm for a vampire hybrid. As if such a thing could ever be considered normal! A vampire hybrid, indeed!"

"Excuse me," Edward said in a stunned voice. He reached out and caught Eleazar's shoulder as he was about to turn again for the door. "What did you just call my wife?"

Eleazar looked at Edward curiously, his manic pacing forgotten for the moment. "A shield, I *think*. She's blocking me now, so I can't be sure."

I stared at Eleazar, my brows furrowing in confusion. Shield? What did he mean about my blocking him? I was standing right here beside him, not defensive in any way.

"A shield?" Edward repeated, bewildered.

"Come now, Edward! If I can't get a read on her, I doubt you can, either. Can you hear her thoughts right now?" Eleazar asked.

"No," Edward murmured. "But I've never been able to do that. Even when she was human."

"Never?" Eleazar blinked. "Interesting. That would indicate a rather powerful latent talent, if it was manifesting so clearly even before the transformation. I can't feel a way through her shield to get a sense of it at all. Yet she must be raw still—she's only a few months old." The look he gave Edward now was almost exasperated. "And apparently completely unaware of what she's doing. Totally unconscious. Ironic. Aro sent me all over the world searching for such anomalies, and you simply stumble across it by accident and don't even realize what you have." Eleazar shook his head in disbelief.

I frowned. "What are you talking about? How can I be a *shield*? What does that even mean?" All I could picture in my head was a ridiculous medieval suit of armor.

Eleazar leaned his head to one side as he examined me. "I suppose we were overly formal about it in the guard. In truth, categorizing talents is a subjective, haphazard business; every talent is unique, never exactly the same thing twice. But you, Bella, are fairly easy to classify. Talents that are purely defensive, that protect some aspect of the bearer, are always called *shields*. Have you ever tested your abilities? Blocked anyone besides me and your mate?"

It took me a few seconds, despite how quickly my new brain worked, to organize my answer.

"It only works with certain things," I told him. "My head is sort of . . . private. But it doesn't stop Jasper from being able to mess with my mood or Alice from seeing my future."

"Purely a mental defense." Eleazar nodded to himself. "Limited, but strong."

"Aro couldn't hear her," Edward interjected. "Though she was human when they met."

Eleazar's eyes widened.

"Jane tried to hurt me, but she couldn't," I said. "Edward

thinks Demetri can't find me, and that Alec can't bother me, either. Is that good?"

Eleazar, still gaping, nodded. "Quite."

"A shield!" Edward said, deep satisfaction saturating his tone. "I never thought of it that way. The only one I've ever met before was Renata, and what she did was so different."

Eleazar had recovered slightly. "Yes, no talent ever manifests in precisely the same way, because no one ever *thinks* in exactly the same way."

"Who's Renata? What does she do?" I asked. Renesmee was interested, too, leaning away from Carmen so that she could see around Kate.

"Renata is Aro's personal bodyguard," Eleazar told me. "A very practical kind of shield, and a very strong one."

I vaguely remembered a small crowd of vampires hovering close to Aro in his macabre tower, some male, some female. I couldn't remember the women's faces in the uncomfortable, terrifying memory. One must have been Renata.

"I wonder . . . ," Eleazar mused. "You see, Renata is a powerful shield against a physical attack. If someone approaches her—or Aro, as she is always close beside him in a hostile situation—they find themselves . . . diverted. There's a force around her that repels, though it's almost unnoticeable. You simply find yourself going a different direction than you planned, with a confused memory as to why you wanted to go that other way in the first place. She can project her shield several meters out from herself. She also protects Caius and Marcus, too, when they have a need, but Aro is her priority.

"What she does isn't actually physical, though. Like the vast majority of our gifts, it takes place inside the mind.

If she tried to keep *you* back, I wonder who would win?" He shook his head. "I've never heard of Aro's or Jane's gifts being thwarted."

"Momma, you're special," Renesmee told me without any surprise, like she was commenting on the color of my clothes.

I felt disoriented. Didn't I already know my gift? I had my super-self-control that had allowed me to skip right over the horrifying newborn year. Vampires only had one extra ability at most, right?

Or had Edward been correct in the beginning? Before Carlisle had suggested that my self-control could be something beyond the natural, Edward had thought my restraint was just a product of good preparation—*focus and attitude*, he'd declared.

Which one had been right? Was there *more* I could do? A name and a category for what I was?

"Can you project?" Kate asked interestedly.

"Project?" I asked.

"Push it out from yourself," Kate explained. "Shield someone besides yourself."

"I don't know. I've never tried. I didn't know I should do that."

"Oh, you might not be able to," Kate said quickly. "Heavens knows I've been working on it for centuries and the best I can do is run a current over my skin."

I stared at her, mystified.

"Kate's got an offensive skill," Edward said. "Sort of like Jane."

I flinched away from Kate automatically, and she laughed.

"I'm not sadistic about it," she assured me. "It's just something that comes in handy during a fight."

Kate's words were sinking in, beginning to make connections in my mind. *Shield someone besides yourself,* she'd said. As if there were some way for me to include another person in my strange, quirky silent head.

I remembered Edward cringing on the ancient stones of the Volturi castle turret. Though this was a human memory, it was sharper, more painful than most of the others—like it had been branded into the tissues of my brain.

What if I could stop that from happening ever again? What if I could protect him? Protect Renesmee? What if there was even the faintest glimmer of a possibility that I could shield them, too?

"You have to teach me what to do!" I insisted, unthinkingly grabbing Kate's arm. "You have to show me how!"

Kate winced at my grip. "Maybe—if you stop trying to crush my radius."

"Oops! Sorry!"

"You're shielding, all right," Kate said. "That move should have about shocked your arm off. You didn't feel anything just now?"

"That wasn't really necessary, Kate. She didn't mean any harm," Edward muttered under his breath. Neither of us paid attention to him.

"No, I didn't feel anything. Were you doing your electric-current thing?"

"I was. Hmm. I've never met anyone who couldn't feel it, immortal or otherwise."

"You said you project it? On your skin?"

Kate nodded. "It used to be just in my palms. Kind of like Aro."

"Or Renesmee," Edward interjected.

"But after a lot of practice, I can radiate the current all over my body. It's a good defense. Anyone who tries to touch me drops like a human that's been Tasered. It only downs him for a second, but that's long enough."

I was only half-listening to Kate, my thoughts racing around the idea that I might be able to protect my little family if I could just learn *fast* enough. I wished fervently that I might be good at this projecting thing, too, like I was somehow mysteriously good at all the other aspects of being a vampire. My human life had not prepared me for things that came naturally, and I couldn't make myself trust this aptitude to last.

It felt like I had never wanted anything so badly before this: to be able to protect what I loved.

Because I was so preoccupied, I didn't notice the silent exchange going on between Edward and Eleazar until it became a spoken conversation.

"Can you think of even one exception, though?" Edward asked.

I looked over to make sense of his comment and realized that everyone else was already staring at the two men. They were leaning toward each other intently, Edward's expression tight with suspicion, Eleazar's unhappy and reluctant.

"I don't want to think of them that way," Eleazar said through his teeth. I was surprised at the sudden change in the atmosphere.

"If you're right——," Eleazar began again.

Edward cut him off. "The thought was yours, not mine."

"If *I'm* right . . . I can't even grasp what that would mean. It would change everything about the world we've created. It would change the meaning of my life. What I have been a part of."

"Your intentions were always the best, Eleazar."

"Would that even matter? What have I done? How many lives . . ."

Tanya put her hand on Eleazar's shoulder in a comforting gesture. "What did we miss, my friend? I want to know so that I can argue with these thoughts. You've never done anything worth castigating yourself this way."

"Oh, haven't I?" Eleazar muttered. Then he shrugged out from under her hand and began his pacing again, faster even than before.

Tanya watched him for half a second and then focused on Edward. "Explain."

Edward nodded, his tense eyes following Eleazar as he spoke. "He was trying to understand why so many of the Volturi would come to punish us. It's not the way they do things. Certainly, we are the biggest mature coven they've dealt with, but in the past other covens have joined to protect themselves, and they never presented much of a challenge despite their numbers. We are more closely bonded, and that's a factor, but not a huge one.

"He was remembering other times that covens have been punished, for one thing or the other, and a pattern occurred to him. It was a pattern that the rest of the guard would never have noticed, since Eleazar was the one passing the pertinent intelligence privately to Aro. A pattern that only repeated every other century or so."

"What was this pattern?" Carmen asked, watching Eleazar as Edward was.

"Aro does not often personally attend a punishing expedition," Edward said. "But in the past, when Aro wanted something in particular, it was never long before evidence turned up proving that this coven or that coven had committed some unpardonable crime. The ancients would decide to go along to watch the guard administer justice. And then, once the coven was all but destroyed, Aro would grant a pardon to one member whose thoughts, he would claim, were particularly repentant. Always, it would turn out that this vampire had the gift Aro had admired. Always, this person was given a place with the guard. The gifted vampire was won over quickly, always so grateful for the honor. There were no exceptions."

"It must be a heady thing to be chosen," Kate suggested.

"Ha!" Eleazar snarled, still in motion.

"There is one among the guard," Edward said, explaining Eleazar's angry reaction. "Her name is Chelsea. She has influence over the emotional ties between people. She can both loosen and secure these ties. She could make someone feel bonded to the Volturi, to want to belong, to want to *please* them. . . ."

Eleazar came to an abrupt halt. "We all understood why Chelsea was important. In a fight, if we could separate allegiances between allied covens, we could defeat them that much more easily. If we could distance the innocent members of a coven emotionally from the guilty, justice could be done without unnecessary brutality—the guilty could be punished without interference, and the innocent could be spared. Otherwise, it was impossible to keep the coven from fighting as a whole. So Chelsea would break the ties that bound them together. It seemed a great kindness to me, evidence of Aro's mercy. I did suspect that Chelsea kept our own band more tightly knit, but that, too, was a good thing. It made us more effective. It helped us coexist more easily."

This clarified old memories for me. It had not made sense to me before how the guard obeyed their masters so gladly, with almost lover-like devotion.

"How strong is her gift?" Tanya asked with an edge to her voice. Her gaze quickly touched on each member of her family.

Eleazar shrugged. "I was able to leave with Carmen." And then he shook his head. "But anything weaker than the bond between partners is in danger. In a normal coven, at least. Those are weaker bonds than those in our family, though. Abstaining from human blood makes us more civilized—lets us form true bonds of love. I doubt she could turn our allegiances, Tanya."

Tanya nodded, seeming reassured, while Eleazar continued with his analysis.

"I could only think that the reason Aro had decided to come himself, to bring so many with him, is because his goal is not punishment but acquisition," Eleazar said. "He needs to be there to control the situation. But he needs the entire guard for protection from such a large, gifted coven. On the other hand, that leaves the other ancients unprotected in Volterra. Too risky—someone might try to take advantage. So they all come together. How else could he be sure to preserve the gifts that he wants? He must want them very badly," Eleazar mused.

Edward's voice was low as a breath. "From what I saw of his thoughts last spring, Aro's never wanted anything more than he wants Alice."

I felt my mouth fall open, remembering the nightmarish pictures I had imagined long ago: Edward and Alice in black cloaks with bloodred eyes, their faces cold and remote as they stood close as shadows, Aro's hands on theirs. . . . Had Alice seen this more recently? Had she seen Chelsea trying to strip away her love for us, to bind her to Aro and Caius and Marcus?

"Is that why Alice left?" I asked, my voice breaking on her name.

Edward put his hand against my cheek. "I think it must be. To keep Aro from gaining the thing he wants most of all. To keep her power out of his hands."

I heard Tanya and Kate murmuring in disturbed voices and remembered that they hadn't known about Alice.

"He wants you, too," I whispered.

Edward shrugged, his face suddenly a little too composed. "Not nearly as much. I can't really give him anything more than he already has. And of course that's dependent on his finding a way to force me to do his will. He knows me, and he knows how unlikely that is." He raised one eyebrow sardonically.

Eleazar frowned at Edward's nonchalance. "He also knows your weaknesses," Eleazar pointed out, and then he looked at me.

"It's nothing we need to discuss now," Edward said quickly.

Eleazar ignored the hint and continued. "He probably wants your mate, too, regardless. He must have been intrigued by a talent that could defy him in its human incarnation."

Edward was uncomfortable with this topic. I didn't like it, either. If Aro wanted me to do something—anything—all he had to do was threaten Edward and I would comply. And vice versa.

Was death the lesser concern? Was it really capture we should fear?

Edward changed the subject. "I think the Volturi were waiting for this—for some pretext. They couldn't know what form their excuse would come in, but the plan was already in place for when it did come. That's why Alice saw their decision before Irina triggered it. The decision was already made, just waiting for the pretense of a justification."

"If the Volturi are abusing the trust all immortals have placed in them . . . ," Carmen murmured.

"Does it matter?" Eleazar asked. "Who would believe it? And even if others could be convinced that the Volturi are exploiting their power, how would it make any difference? No one can stand against them."

"Though some of us are apparently insane enough to try," Kate muttered.

Edward shook his head. "You're only here to witness, Kate. Whatever Aro's goal, I don't think he's ready to tarnish the Volturi's reputation for it. If we can take away his argument against us, he'll be forced to leave us in peace."

"Of course," Tanya murmured.

No one looked convinced. For a few long minutes, nobody said anything.

Then I heard the sound of tires turning off the highway pavement onto the Cullens' dirt drive.

"Oh crap, Charlie," I muttered. "Maybe the Denalis could hang out upstairs until—"

"No," Edward said in a distant voice. His eyes were far away, staring blankly at the door. "It's not your father." His gaze focused on me. "Alice sent Peter and Charlotte, after all. Time to get ready for the next round."

32. COMPANY

The Cullens' enormous house was more crowded with guests than anyone would assume could possibly be comfortable. It only worked out because none of the visitors slept. Mealtimes were dicey, though. Our company cooperated as best they could. They gave Forks and La Push a wide berth, only hunting out of state; Edward was a gracious host, lending out his cars as needed without so much as a wince. The compromise made me very uncomfortable, though I tried to tell myself that they'd all be hunting somewhere in the world, regardless.

Jacob was even more upset. The werewolves existed to prevent the loss of human life, and here was rampant murder being condoned barely outside the packs' borders.

But under these circumstances, with Renesmee in acute danger, he kept his mouth shut and glared at the floor rather than the vampires.

I was amazed at the easy acceptance the visiting vampires had for Jacob; the problems Edward had anticipated had never materialized. Jacob seemed more or less invisible to them, not quite a person, but also not food, either. They treated him the way people who are not animal-lovers treat the pets of their friends.

Leah, Seth, Quil, and Embry were assigned to run with Sam for now, and Jacob would have happily joined them, except that he couldn't stand to be away from Renesmee, and Renesmee was busy fascinating the strange collection of Carlisle's friends.

We'd replayed the scene of Renesmee's introduction to the Denali coven a half dozen times. First for Peter and Charlotte, whom Alice and Jasper had sent our way without giving them any explanation at all; like most people who knew Alice, they trusted her instructions despite the lack of information. Alice had told them nothing about which direction she and Jasper were heading. She'd made no promise to ever see them again in the future.

Neither Peter nor Charlotte had ever seen an immortal child. Though they knew the rule, their negative reaction was not as powerful as the Denali vampires' had been at first. Curiosity had driven them to allow Renesmee's "explanation." And that was it. Now they were as committed to witnessing as Tanya's family.

Carlisle had sent friends from Ireland and Egypt.

The Irish clan arrived first, and they were surprisingly easy to convince. Siobhan—a woman of immense presence whose huge body was both beautiful and mesmerizing as it moved in smooth undulations—was the leader, but she and her hard-faced mate, Liam, were long used to trusting the judgment of their newest coven member. Little Maggie, with her bouncy red curls, was not physically imposing like the other two, but she had a gift for knowing when she was being lied to, and her verdicts were never contested. Maggie declared that Edward spoke the truth, and so Siobhan and Liam accepted our story absolutely before even touching Renesmee.

Amun and the other Egyptian vampires were another story. Even after two younger members of his coven, Benjamin and Tia, had been convinced by Renesmee's explanation, Amun refused to touch her and ordered his coven to leave. Benjamin—an oddly cheerful vampire who looked barely older than a boy and seemed both utterly confident and utterly careless at the same time—persuaded Amun to stay with a few subtle threats about disbanding their alliance. Amun stayed, but continued to refuse to touch Renesmee, and would not allow his mate, Kebi, to touch her, either. It seemed an unlikely grouping—though the Egyptians all looked so alike, with their midnight hair and olive-toned pallor, that they easily could have passed for a biological family. Amun was the senior member and the outspoken leader. Kebi never strayed farther away from Amun than his shadow, and I never heard her speak a single word. Tia, Benjamin's mate, was a quiet woman as well, though when she did speak there was great insight and gravity to everything she said. Still, it was Benjamin whom they all seemed to revolve around, as if he had some invisible magnetism the others depended upon for their balance. I saw Eleazar staring at the boy with wide eyes and assumed Benjamin had a talent that drew the others to him.

"It's not that," Edward told me when we were alone that night. "His gift is so singular that Amun is terrified of losing him. Much like we had planned to keep Renesmee from Aro's knowledge"—he sighed—"Amun has been keeping Benjamin from Aro's attention. Amun created Benjamin, knowing he would be special."

"What can he do?"

"Something Eleazar's never seen before. Something I've never heard of. Something that even your shield would do nothing against." He grinned his crooked smile at me. "He can actually influence the elements—earth, wind, water, and fire. True physical manipulation, no illusion of the mind. Benjamin's still experimenting with it, and Amun tries to mold him into a weapon. But you see how independent Benjamin is. He won't be used."

"You like him," I surmised from the tone of his voice.

"He has a very clear sense of right and wrong. I like his attitude."

Amun's attitude was something else, and he and Kebi kept to themselves, though Benjamin and Tia were well on their way to being fast friends with both the Denali and the Irish covens. We hoped that Carlisle's return would ease the remaining tension with Amun.

Emmett and Rose sent individuals—any nomad friends of Carlisle's that they could track down.

Garrett came first—a tall, rangy vampire with eager ruby eyes and long sandy hair he kept tied back with a leather thong—and it was apparent immediately that he was an adventurer. I imagined that we could have presented him with any challenge and he would have accepted, just to test himself. He fell in quickly with the Denali sisters, asking endless questions about their unusual lifestyle. I wondered if vegetarianism was another challenge he would try, just to see if he could do it.

Mary and Randall also came—friends already, though they did not travel together. They listened to Renesmee's story and stayed to witness like the others. Like the Denalis, they considered what they would do if the Volturi did not pause for explanations. All three of the nomads toyed with the idea of standing with us.

Of course, Jacob got more surly with each new addition. He kept his distance when he could, and when he couldn't he grumbled to Renesmee that someone was going to have to provide an index if anyone expected him to keep all the new bloodsuckers' names straight.*

Carlisle and Esme returned a week after they had gone, Emmett and Rosalie just a few days later, and all of us felt better when they were home. Carlisle brought one more friend home with him, though *friend* might have been the wrong term. Alistair was a misanthropic English vampire who counted Carlisle as his closest acquaintance, though he could hardly stand a visit more than once a century. Alistair very much preferred to wander alone, and Carlisle had called in a lot of favors to get him here. He shunned all company, and it was clear he didn't have any admirers in the gathered covens.

The brooding dark-haired vampire took Carlisle at his word about Renesmee's origins, refusing, like Amun, to

---

* *See page 756.*

touch her. Edward told Carlisle, Esme, and me that Alistair was afraid to be here, but more afraid of not knowing the outcome. He was deeply suspicious of all authority, and therefore naturally suspicious of the Volturi. What was happening now seemed to confirm all his fears.

"Of course, now they'll know I was here," we heard him grumble to himself in the attic—his preferred spot to sulk. "No way to keep it from Aro at this point. Centuries on the run, that's what this will mean. Everyone Carlisle's talked to in the last decade will be on their list. I can't believe I got myself sucked into this mess. What a fine way to treat your friends."

But if he was right about having to run from the Volturi, at least he had more hope of doing that than the rest of us. Alistair was a tracker, though not nearly as precise and efficient as Demetri. Alistair just felt an elusive pull toward whatever he was seeking. But that pull would be enough to tell him which direction to run—the opposite direction from Demetri.

And then another pair of unexpected friends arrived—unexpected, because neither Carlisle nor Rosalie had been able to contact the Amazons.

"Carlisle," the taller of the two very tall ferine women greeted him when they arrived. Both of them seemed as if they'd been stretched—long arms and legs, long fingers, long black braids, and long faces with long noses. They wore nothing but animal skins—hide vests and tight-fitting pants that laced on the sides with leather ties. It wasn't just their eccentric clothes that made them seem wild but everything about them, from their restless crimson eyes to their sudden, darting movements. I'd never met any vampires less civilized.

But Alice had sent them, and that was interesting news, to put it mildly. Why was Alice in South America? Just because she'd seen that no one else would be able to get in touch with the Amazons?

"Zafrina and Senna! But where's Kachiri?" Carlisle asked. "I've never seen you three apart."

"Alice told us we needed to separate," Zafrina answered in the rough, deep voice that matched her wild appearance. "It's uncomfortable to be away from each other, but Alice assured us that you needed us here, while she very much needed Kachiri somewhere else. That's all she would tell us, except that there was a great hurry . . . ?" Zafrina's statement trailed off into a question, and—with the tremor of nerves that never went away no matter how often I did this—I brought Renesmee out to meet them.

Despite their fierce appearance, they listened very calmly to our story, and then allowed Renesmee to prove the point. They were every bit as taken with Renesmee as any of the other vampires, but I couldn't help worrying as I watched their swift, jerky movements so close beside her. Senna was always near Zafrina, never speaking, but it wasn't the same as Amun and Kebi. Kebi's manner seemed obedient; Senna and Zafrina were more like two limbs of one organism— Zafrina just happened to be the mouthpiece.

The news about Alice was oddly comforting. Clearly, she was on some obscure mission of her own as she avoided whatever Aro had planned for her.

Edward was thrilled to have the Amazons with us,

because Zafrina was enormously talented; her gift could make a very dangerous offensive weapon. Not that Edward was asking for Zafrina to side with us in the battle, but if the Volturi did not pause when they saw our witnesses, perhaps they would pause for a different kind of scene.

"It's a very straightforward illusion," Edward explained when it turned out that I couldn't see anything, as usual. Zafrina was intrigued and amused by my immunity— something she'd never encountered before—and she hovered restlessly while Edward described what I was missing. Edward's eyes unfocused slightly as he continued. "She can make most people see whatever she wants them to see— see that, and nothing else. For example, right now I would appear to be alone in the middle of a rain forest. It's so clear I might possibly believe it, except for the fact that I can still feel you in my arms."

Zafrina's lips twitched into her hard version of a smile. A second later, Edward's eyes focused again, and he grinned back.

"Impressive," he said.

Renesmee was fascinated with the conversation, and she reached out fearlessly toward Zafrina.

"Can I see?" she asked.

"What would you like to see?" Zafrina asked.

"What you showed Daddy."

Zafrina nodded, and I watched anxiously as Renesmee's eyes stared blankly into space. A second later, Renesmee's dazzling smile lit up her face.

"More," she commanded.

After that, it was hard to keep Renesmee away from

Zafrina and her *pretty pictures*. I worried, because I was quite sure that Zafrina was able to create images that were not pretty at all. But through Renesmee's thoughts I could see Zafrina's visions for myself—they were as clear as any of Renesmee's own memories, like they were real—and thus judge for myself whether they were appropriate or not.

Though I didn't give her up easily, I had to admit it was a good thing Zafrina was keeping Renesmee entertained. I needed my hands. I had so much to learn, both physically and mentally, and the time was so short.

My first attempt at learning to fight did not go well.

Edward had me pinned in about two seconds. But instead of letting me wrestle my way free—which I absolutely could have—he'd leaped up and away from me. I knew immediately that something was wrong; he was still as stone, staring across the meadow we were practicing in.

"I'm sorry, Bella," he said.

"No, I'm fine," I said. "Let's go again."

"I can't."

"What do you mean, you can't? We just started."

He didn't answer.

"Look, I know I'm no good at this, but I can't get better if you don't help me."

He said nothing. Playfully, I sprang at him. He made no defense at all, and we both fell to the ground. He was motionless as I pressed my lips to his jugular.

"I win," I announced.

His eyes narrowed, but he said nothing.

"Edward? What's wrong? Why won't you teach me?"

A full minute passed before he spoke again.

"I just can't . . . bear it. Emmett and Rosalie know as much as I do. Tanya and Eleazar probably know more. Ask someone else."

"That's not fair! You're *good* at this. You helped Jasper before—you fought with him and all the others, too. Why not me? What did I do wrong?"

He sighed, exasperated. His eyes were dark, barely any gold to lighten the black.

"Looking at you that way, analyzing you as a target. Seeing all the ways I can kill you . . ." He flinched. "It just makes it too real for me. We don't have so much time that it will really make a difference who your teacher is. Anyone can teach you the fundamentals."

I scowled.

He touched my pouting lower lip and smiled. "Besides, it's unnecessary. The Volturi will stop. They will be made to understand."

"But if they don't! I *need* to learn this."

"Find another teacher."

That was not our last conversation on the subject, but I never swayed him an inch from his decision.

Emmett was more than willing to help, though his teaching felt to me a lot like revenge for all the lost arm-wrestling matches. If I could still bruise, I would have been purple from head to toe. Rose, Tanya, and Eleazar all were patient and supportive. Their lessons reminded me of Jasper's fighting instructions to the others last June, though those memories were fuzzy and indistinct. Some of the visitors found my education entertaining, and some even offered assistance. The nomad Garrett took a few turns—he was a surprisingly good teacher; he interacted so easily with others in general that I wondered how he'd never found a coven. I even fought once with Zafrina while Renesmee watched from Jacob's arms. I learned several tricks, but I never asked for her help again. In truth, though I liked Zafrina very much and I knew she wouldn't really hurt me, the wild woman scared me to death.

I learned many things from my teachers, but I had the sense that my knowledge was still impossibly basic. I had no idea how many seconds I would last against Alec and Jane. I only prayed that it would be long enough to help.

Every minute of the day that I wasn't with Renesmee or learning to fight, I was in the backyard working with Kate, trying to push my internal shield outside of my own brain to protect someone else. Edward encouraged me in this training. I knew he hoped I would find a way of contributing that satisfied me while also keeping me out of the line of fire.

It was just so hard. There was nothing to get a hold of, nothing solid to work with. I had only my raging desire to be of use, to be able to keep Edward, Renesmee, and as much of my family as possible safe with me. Over and over I tried to force the nebulous shield outside of myself, with only faint, sporadic success. It felt like I was wrestling to stretch an invisible rubber band—a band that would change from concrete tangibility into insubstantial smoke at any random moment.

Only Edward was willing to be our guinea pig—to receive shock after shock from Kate while I grappled incompetently with the insides of my head. We worked for hours at a time, and I felt like I should be covered in sweat from the exertion, but of course my perfect body didn't betray me that way. My weariness was all mental.

It killed me that it was Edward who had to suffer, my arms wrapped uselessly around him while he winced over and over from Kate's "low" setting. I tried as hard as I could to push my shield around us both; every now and then I would get it, and then it would slip away again.

I hated this practice, and I wished that Zafrina would help instead of Kate. Then all Edward would have to do was look at Zafrina's illusions until I could stop him from seeing them. But Kate insisted that I needed better motivation— by which she meant my hatred of watching Edward's pain. I was beginning to doubt her assertion from the first day we'd met—that she wasn't sadistic about the use of her gift. She seemed to be enjoying herself to me.

"Hey," Edward said cheerfully, trying to hide any evidence of distress in his voice. Anything to keep me from fighting practice. "That one barely stung. Good job, Bella."

I took a deep breath, trying to grasp exactly what I'd done right. I tested the elastic band, struggling to force it to remain solid as I stretched it away from me.

"Again, Kate," I grunted through my clenched teeth.

Kate pressed her palm to Edward's shoulder.

He sighed in relief. "Nothing that time."

She raised an eyebrow. "That wasn't low, either."

"Good," I huffed.

"Get ready," she told me, and reached out to Edward again.

This time he shuddered, and a low breath hissed between his teeth.

"Sorry! Sorry! Sorry!" I chanted, biting my lip. Why couldn't I get this right?

"You're doing an amazing job, Bella," Edward said, pulling me tight against him. "You've really only been working at this for a few days and you're already projecting sporadically. Kate, tell her how well she's doing."

Kate pursed her lips. "I don't know. She's obviously got tremendous ability, and we're only beginning to touch it. She can do better, I'm sure. She's just lacking incentive."

I stared at her in disbelief, my lips automatically curling back from my teeth. How could she think I lacked motivation with her shocking Edward right here in front of me?

I heard murmurs from the audience that had grown steadily as I practiced—only Eleazar, Carmen, and Tanya at first, but then Garrett had wandered over, then Benjamin and Tia, Siobhan and Maggie, and now even Alistair was peering down from a window on the third story. The spectators agreed with Edward; they thought I was already doing well.

"Kate . . . ," Edward said in a warning voice as some new course of action occurred to her, but she was already in motion. She darted along the curve of the river to where Zafrina, Senna, and Renesmee were walking slowly, Renesmee's hand in Zafrina's as they traded pictures back and forth. Jacob shadowed them from a few feet behind.

"Nessie," Kate said—the newcomers had quickly picked up the irritating nickname, "would you like to come help your mother?"

"No," I half-snarled.

Edward hugged me reassuringly. I shook him off just as Renesmee flitted across the yard to me, with Kate, Zafrina, and Senna right behind her.

"Absolutely not, Kate," I hissed.

Renesmee reached for me, and I opened my arms automatically. She curled into me, pressing her head into the hollow beneath my shoulder.

"But Momma, I *want* to help," she said in a determined voice. Her hand rested against my neck, reinforcing her desire with images of the two of us together, a team.

"No," I said, quickly backing away. Kate had taken a deliberate step in my direction, her hand stretched toward us.

"Stay away from us, Kate," I warned her.

"No." She began stalking forward. She smiled like a hunter cornering her prey.

I shifted Renesmee so that she was clinging to my back, still backing away at a pace that matched Kate's. Now my hands were free, and if Kate wanted to keep *her* hands attached to her wrists, she'd better keep her distance.

Kate probably didn't understand, never having known for herself the passion of a mother for her child. She must not have realized just how far past *too far* she'd already gone. I was so furious that my vision took on a strange reddish tint, and my tongue tasted like burning metal. The strength I usually worked to keep restrained flowed through my muscles, and I knew I could crush her into diamond-hard rubble if she pushed me to it.

The rage brought every aspect of my being into sharper focus. I could even feel the elasticity of my shield more exactly now—feel that it was not a band so much as a layer, a thin film that covered me from head to toe. With the anger rippling through my body, I had a better sense of it, a tighter hold on it. I stretched it around myself, out from myself, swaddling Renesmee completely inside it, just in case Kate got past my guard.

Kate took another calculated step forward, and a vicious snarl ripped up my throat and through my clenched teeth.

"Be careful, Kate," Edward cautioned.

Kate took another step, and then made a mistake even someone as inexpert as I could recognize. Just a short leap away from me, she looked away, turning her attention from me to Edward.

Renesmee was secure on my back; I coiled to spring.

"Can you hear anything from Nessie?" Kate asked him, her voice calm and easy.

Edward darted into the space between us, blocking my line to Kate.

"No, nothing at all," he answered. "Now give Bella some space to calm down, Kate. You shouldn't goad her like that. I know she doesn't seem her age, but she's only a few months old."

"We don't have time to do this gently, Edward. We're going to have to push her. We only have a few weeks, and she's got the potential to—"

"Back off for a minute, Kate."

Kate frowned but took Edward's warning more seriously than she'd taken mine.

Renesmee's hand was on my neck; she was remembering Kate's attack, showing me that no harm was meant, that Daddy was in on it. . . .

This did not pacify me. The spectrum of light I saw still seemed tainted with crimson. But I was in better control of myself, and I could see the wisdom of Kate's words. The anger helped me. I would learn faster under pressure.

That didn't mean I liked it.

"Kate," I growled. I rested my hand on the small of Edward's back. I could still feel my shield like a strong, flexible sheet around Renesmee and me. I pushed it farther, forcing it around Edward. There was no sign of a flaw in the stretchy fabric, no threat of a tear. I panted with the effort, and my words came out sounding breathless rather than furious. "Again," I said to Kate. "Edward only."

She rolled her eyes but flitted forward and pressed her palm to Edward's shoulder.

"Nothing," Edward said. I heard the smile in his voice.

"And now?" Kate asked.

"Still nothing."

"And now?" This time, there was the sound of strain in her voice.

"Nothing at all."

Kate grunted and stepped away.

"Can you see this?" Zafrina asked in her deep, wild voice, staring intently at the three of us. Her English was strangely accented, her words pulling up in unexpected places.

"I don't see anything I shouldn't," Edward said.

"And you, Renesmee?" Zafrina asked.

Renesmee smiled at Zafrina and shook her head.

My fury had almost entirely ebbed, and I clenched my teeth together, panting faster as I pushed out against the elastic shield; it felt like it was getting heavier the longer I held it. It pulled back, dragging inward.

"No one panic," Zafrina warned the little group watching me. "I want to see how far she can extend."

There was a shocked gasp from everyone there—Eleazar, Carmen, Tanya, Garrett, Benjamin, Tia, Siobhan, Maggie—everyone but Senna, who seemed prepared for whatever Zafrina was doing. The others' eyes were blank, their expressions anxious.

"Raise your hand when you get your sight back," Zafrina instructed. "Now, Bella. See how many you can shield."

My breath came out in a huff. Kate was the closest person to me besides Edward and Renesmee, but even she was about ten feet away. I locked my jaw and shoved, trying to heave the resisting, resilient safeguard farther from myself. Inch by inch I drove it toward Kate, fighting the reaction that fought back with every fraction that I gained. I only watched Kate's anxious expression while I worked, and I groaned quietly with relief when her eyes blinked and focused. She raised her hand.

"Fascinating!" Edward murmured under his breath. "It's like one-way glass. I can read everything they're thinking, but they can't reach me behind it. And I can hear Renesmee, though I couldn't when I was on the outside. I'll bet Kate could shock me now, because she's underneath the umbrella. I still can't hear you . . . hmmm. How does that work? I wonder if . . ."

He continued to mumble to himself, but I couldn't listen to the words. I ground my teeth together, struggling to force the shield out to Garrett, who was closest to Kate. His hand came up.

"Very good," Zafrina complimented me. "Now—"

But she'd spoken too soon; with a sharp gasp, I felt my shield recoil like a rubber band stretched too far, snapping back into its original shape. Renesmee, experiencing for the first time the blindness Zafrina had conjured for the others, trembled against my back. Wearily, I fought back against the elastic pull, forcing the shield to include her again.

"Can I have a minute?" I panted. Since I'd become a vampire, I hadn't felt the need to rest even once before this moment. It was unnerving to feel so drained and yet so strong at the same time.

"Of course," Zafrina said, and the spectators relaxed as she let them see again.

"Kate," Garrett called as the others murmured and drifted slightly away, disturbed by the moment of blindness; vampires were not used to feeling vulnerable. The tall, sandy-haired Garrett was the only non-gifted immortal who seemed drawn to my practice sessions. I wondered what the lure was for the adventurer.

"I wouldn't, Garrett," Edward cautioned.

Garrett continued toward Kate despite the warning, his lips pursed in speculation. "They say you can put a vampire flat on his back."

"Yes," she agreed. Then, with a sly smile, she wiggled her fingers playfully at him. "Curious?"

Garrett shrugged. "That's something I've never seen. Seems like it might be a bit of an exaggeration. . . ."

"Maybe," Kate said, her face suddenly serious. "Maybe it only works on the weak or the young. I'm not sure. You look strong, though. Perhaps you could withstand my gift." She stretched her hand out to him, palm up—a clear invitation. Her lips twitched, and I was pretty sure her grave expression was an attempt to hustle him.

Garrett grinned at the challenge. Very confidently, he touched her palm with his index finger.

And then, with a loud gasp, his knees buckled and he keeled over backward. His head hit a piece of granite with a sharp cracking noise. It was shocking to watch. My instincts recoiled against seeing an immortal incapacitated that way; it was profoundly wrong.

"I told you so," Edward muttered.

Garrett's eyelids trembled for a few seconds, and then his eyes opened wide. He stared up at the smirking Kate, and a wondering smile lit his face.

"Wow," he said.

"Did you enjoy that?" she asked skeptically.

"I'm not crazy," he laughed, shaking his head as he got slowly to his knees, "but that was sure something!"

"That's what I hear."

Edward rolled his eyes.

And then there was a low commotion from the front yard. I heard Carlisle speaking over a babble of surprised voices.

"Did Alice send you?" he asked someone, his voice unsure, slightly upset.

Another unexpected guest?

Edward darted into the house and most of the others imitated him. I followed more slowly, Renesmee still perched on my back. I would give Carlisle a moment. Let him warm up the new guest, prepare him or her or them for the idea of what was coming.

I pulled Renesmee into my arms as I walked cautiously around the house to enter through the kitchen door, listening to what I couldn't see.

"No one sent us," a deep whispery voice answered Carlisle's question. I was immediately reminded of the ancient voices of Aro and Caius, and I froze just inside the kitchen.

I knew the front room was crowded—almost everyone had gone in to see the newest visitors—but there was barely any noise. Shallow breathing, that was all.

Carlisle's voice was wary as he responded. "Then what brings you here now?"

"Word travels," a different voice answered, just as feathery as the first. "We heard hints that Volturi were moving against you. There were whispers that you would not stand alone. Obviously, the whispers were true. This is an impressive gathering."

"We are not challenging the Volturi," Carlisle answered in a strained tone. "There has been a misunderstanding, that is all. A very serious misunderstanding, to be sure, but one we're hoping to clear up. What you see are witnesses. We just need the Volturi to listen. We didn't—"

"We don't care what they say you did," the first voice interrupted. "And we don't care if you broke the law."

"No matter how egregiously," the second inserted.

"We've been waiting a millennium and a half for the Italian scum to be challenged," said the first. "If there is any chance they will fall, we will be here to see it."

"Or even to help defeat them," the second added. They spoke in a smooth tandem, their voices so similar that less sensitive ears would assume there was only one speaker. "If we think you have a chance of success."

"Bella?" Edward called to me in a hard voice. "Bring Renesmee here, please. Maybe we should test our Romanian visitors' claims."

It helped to know that probably half of the vampires

in the other room would come to Renesmee's defense if these Romanians were upset by her. I didn't like the sound of their voices, or the dark menace in their words. As I walked into the room, I could see that I was not alone in that assessment. Most of the motionless vampires glared with hostile eyes, and a few—Carmen, Tanya, Zafrina, and Senna—repositioned themselves subtly into defensive poses between the newcomers and Renesmee.

The vampires at the door were both slight and short, one dark-haired and the other with hair so ashy blond that it looked pale gray. They had the same powdery look to their skin as the Volturi, though I thought it was not so pronounced. I couldn't be sure about that, as I had never seen the Volturi except with human eyes; I could not make a perfect comparison. Their sharp, narrow eyes were dark burgundy, with no milky film. They wore very simple black clothes that could pass as modern but hinted at older designs.

The dark one grinned when I came into view. "Well, well, Carlisle. You *have* been naughty, haven't you?"

"She's not what you think, Stefan."

"And we don't care either way," the blonde responded. "As we said before."

"Then you're welcome to observe, Vladimir, but it is definitely not our plan to challenge the Volturi, as *we* said before."

"Then we'll just cross our fingers," Stefan began.

"And hope we get lucky," finished Vladimir.

In the end, we had pulled together seventeen witnesses— the Irish, Siobhan, Liam, and Maggie; the Egyptians,

Amun, Kebi, Benjamin, and Tia; the Amazons, Zafrina and Senna; the Romanians, Vladimir and Stefan; and the nomads, Charlotte and Peter, Garrett, Alistair, Mary, and Randall—to supplement our family of eleven. Tanya, Kate, Eleazar, and Carmen insisted on being counted as part of our family.

Aside from the Volturi, it was probably the largest friendly gathering of mature vampires in immortal history.

We all were beginning to be a little bit hopeful. Even I couldn't help it. Renesmee had won over so many in such a brief time. The Volturi only had to listen for just the tiniest second. . . .

The last two surviving Romanians—focused only on their bitter resentment of the ones who had overthrown their empire fifteen hundred years earlier—took everything in stride. They would not touch Renesmee, but they showed no aversion to her. They seemed mysteriously delighted by our alliance with the werewolves. They watched me practice my shield with Zafrina and Kate, watched Edward answer unspoken questions, watched Benjamin pull geysers of water from the river or sharp gusts of wind from the still air with just his mind, and their eyes glowed with their fierce hope that the Volturi had finally met their match.

We did not hope for the same things, but we all hoped.

33. FORGERY

"CHARLIE, WE'VE STILL GOT THAT STRICTLY NEED-TO-know company situation going. I know it's been more than a week since you saw Renesmee, but a visit is just not a good idea right now. How about I bring Renesmee over to see you?"

Charlie was quiet for so long that I wondered if he heard the strain beneath my façade.

But then he muttered, "Need to know, *ugh*," and I realized it was just his wariness of the supernatural that made him slow to respond.

"Okay, kid," Charlie said. "Can you bring her over this morning? Sue's bringing me lunch. She's just as horrified by my cooking as you were when you first showed up."

Charlie laughed and then sighed for the old days.

"This morning will be perfect." The sooner the better. I'd already put this off too long.

"Is Jake coming with you guys?"

Though Charlie didn't know anything about werewolf imprinting, no one could be oblivious to the attachment between Jacob and Renesmee.

"Probably." There was no way Jacob would voluntarily miss an afternoon with Renesmee sans bloodsuckers.

"Maybe I should invite Billy, too," Charlie mused. "But . . . hmm. Maybe another time."

I was only half paying attention to Charlie—enough to notice the strange reluctance in his voice when he spoke of Billy, but not enough to worry what *that* was about. Charlie and Billy were grown-ups; if there was something going on between them, they could figure it out for themselves. I had too many more important things to obsess over.

"See you in a few," I told him, and hung up.

This trip was about more than protecting my father from the twenty-seven oddly matched vampires—who all had sworn not to kill anyone in a three-hundred-mile radius, but still . . . Obviously, no human being should get any-where near this group. This was the excuse I'd given Edward: I was taking Renesmee to Charlie so that he wouldn't decide to come here. It was a good reason for leaving the house, but not my real reason at all.

"Why can't we take your Ferrari?" Jacob complained when he met me in the garage. I was already in Edward's Volvo with Renesmee.

Edward had gotten around to revealing my *after* car; as he'd suspected, I had not been capable of showing the appropriate enthusiasm. Sure, it was pretty and fast, but I liked to *run*.

"Too conspicuous," I answered. "We could go on foot, but that would freak Charlie out."

Jacob grumbled but got into the front seat. Renesmee climbed from my lap to his.

"How are you?" I asked him as I pulled out of the garage.

"How do you think?" Jacob asked bitingly. "I'm sick of all these reeking bloodsuckers." He saw my expression and spoke before I could answer. "Yeah, I know, I know. They're the good guys, they're here to help, they're going to save us all. Etcetera, etcetera. Say what you want, I still think Dracula One and Dracula Two are creep-tacular."

I had to smile. The Romanians weren't my favorite guests, either. "I don't disagree with you there."

Renesmee shook her head but said nothing; unlike the rest of us, she found the Romanians strangely fascinating. She'd made the effort to speak to them aloud since they would not let her touch them. Her question was about their unusual skin and, though I was afraid they might be offended, I was kind of glad she'd asked. I was curious, too.

They hadn't seemed upset by her interest. Maybe a little rueful.

"We sat still for a very long time, child," Vladimir had answered, with Stefan nodding along but not continuing Vladimir's sentences as he often did. "Contemplating our own divinity. It was a sign of our power that everything came to us. Prey, diplomats, those seeking our favor. We sat on our thrones and thought ourselves gods. We didn't notice for a long time that we were changing—almost petrifying.

I suppose the Volturi did us one favor when they burned our castles. Stefan and I, at least, did not continue to petrify. Now the Volturi's eyes are filmed with dusty scum, but ours are bright. I imagine that will give us an advantage when we gouge theirs from their sockets."

I tried to keep Renesmee away from them after that.

"How long do we get to hang out with Charlie?" Jacob asked, interrupting my thoughts. He was visibly relaxing as we pulled away from the house and all its new inmates. It made me happy that I didn't really count as a vampire to him. I was still just Bella.

"For quite a while, actually."

The tone of my voice caught his attention.

"Is something going on here besides visiting your dad?"

"Jake, you know how you're pretty good at controlling your thoughts around Edward?"

He raised one thick black brow. "Yeah?"

I just nodded, cutting my eyes to Renesmee. She was looking out the window, and I couldn't tell how interested she was in our conversation, but I decided not to risk going any further.

Jacob waited for me to add something else, and then his lower lip pushed out while he thought about what little I'd said.

As we drove in silence, I squinted through the annoying contacts into the cold rain; it wasn't quite cold enough for snow. My eyes were not as ghoulish as they had been in the beginning—definitely closer to a dull reddish orange than to bright crimson. Soon they'd be amber enough for me to quit the contacts. I hoped the change wouldn't upset Charlie too much.

Jacob was still chewing over our truncated conversation when we got to Charlie's. We didn't talk as we walked at a quick human pace through the falling rain. My dad was waiting for us; he had the door open before I could knock.

"Hey, guys! It seems like it's been years! Look at you, Nessie! Come to Grampa! I swear you've grown half a foot. And you look skinny, Ness." He glared at me. "Aren't they feeding you up there?"

"It's just the growth spurt," I muttered. "Hey, Sue," I called over his shoulder. The smell of chicken, tomato, garlic, and cheese issued from the kitchen; it probably smelled good to everyone else. I could also smell fresh pine and packing dust.

Renesmee flashed her dimples. She never spoke in front of Charlie.

"Well, come on in out of the cold, kids. Where's my son-in-law?"

"Entertaining friends," Jacob said, and then snorted. "You're *so* lucky you're out of the loop, Charlie. That's all I'm going to say."

I punched Jacob lightly in the kidney while Charlie cringed.

"Ow," Jacob complained under his breath; well, I'd *thought* I'd punched lightly.

"Actually, Charlie, I have some errands to run."

Jacob shot a glance at me but said nothing.

"Behind on your Christmas shopping, Bells? You only have a few days, you know."

"Yeah, Christmas shopping," I said lamely. That explained the packing dust. Charlie must have put the old decorations up.

"Don't worry, Nessie," he whispered in her ear. "I got you covered if your mom drops the ball."

I rolled my eyes at him, but in truth, I hadn't thought about the holidays at all.

"Lunch's on the table," Sue called from the kitchen. "C'mon, guys."

"See you later, Dad," I said, and exchanged a quick look with Jacob. Even if he couldn't help but think about this near Edward, at least there wasn't much for him to share. He had no idea what I was up to.

Of course, I thought to myself as I got into the car, it wasn't like I had much idea, either.

The roads were slick and dark, but driving didn't intimidate me anymore. My reflexes were well up to the job, and I barely paid attention to the road. The problem was keeping my speed from attracting attention when I had company. I wanted to be done with today's mission, to have the mystery sorted out so that I could get back to the vital task of learning. Learning to protect some, learning to kill others.

I was getting better and better with my shield. Kate didn't feel the need to motivate me anymore—it wasn't hard to find reasons to feel angry, now that I knew that was the key—and so I mostly worked with Zafrina. She was pleased with my extension; I was able to cover almost a ten-foot area for more than a minute, though it exhausted me. This morning she'd been trying to find out if I could push the shield away from my mind altogether. I didn't see what the use of that would be, but Zafrina thought it would help strengthen me, like exercising muscles in the stomach and back rather than just the arms. Eventually, you could lift more weight when all the muscles were stronger.

I wasn't very good at it. I had only gotten one glimpse of the jungle river she was trying to show me.

But there were different ways to prepare for what was coming, and with only two weeks left, I worried that I might be neglecting the most important. Today I would rectify that oversight.

I'd memorized the appropriate maps, and I had no problem finding my way to the address that didn't exist online, the one for J. Jenks. My next step would be Jason Jenks at the other address, the one Alice had not given me.

To say that it wasn't a nice neighborhood would be an understatement. The most nondescript of all the Cullens' cars was still outrageous on this street. My old Chevy would have looked healthy here. During my human years, I would have locked the doors and driven away as fast as I dared. As it was, I was a little fascinated. I tried to imagine Alice in this place for any reason, and failed.

The buildings—all three stories, all narrow, all leaning slightly as if bowed by the pounding rain—were mostly old houses divided up into multiple apartments. It was hard to tell what color the peeling paint was supposed to be. Everything had faded to shades of gray. A few of the buildings had businesses on the first floor: a dirty bar with the windows painted black, a psychic's supply store with neon hands and tarot cards glowing fitfully on the door, a tattoo parlor, and a daycare with duct tape holding the broken front window together. There were no lamps on inside any of the rooms, though it was grim enough outside that the humans should have needed the light. I could hear the low mumbling of voices in the distance; it sounded like TV.

There were a few people about, two shuffling through the rain in opposite directions and one sitting on the shallow porch of a boarded-up cut-rate law office, reading a wet newspaper and whistling. The sound was much too cheerful for the setting.

I was so bemused by the carefree whistler, I didn't realize at first that the abandoned building was right where the address I was looking for should exist. There were no numbers on the dilapidated place, but the tattoo parlor beside it was just two numbers off.

I pulled up to the curb and idled for a second. I was getting into that dump one way or another, but how to do so without the whistler noticing me? I could park the next street over and come through the back. . . . There might be more witnesses on that side. Maybe the rooftops? Was it dark enough for that kind of thing?

"Hey, lady," the whistler called to me.

I rolled the passenger window down as if I couldn't hear him.

The man laid his paper aside, and his clothes surprised me, now that I could see them. Under his long ragged duster, he was a little too well dressed. There was no breeze to give me the scent, but the sheen on his dark red shirt looked like silk. His crinkly black hair was tangled and wild, but his dark skin was smooth and perfect, his teeth white and straight. A contradiction.

"Maybe you shouldn't park that car there, lady," he said. "It might not be here when you get back."

"Thanks for the warning," I said.

I shut off the engine and got out. Perhaps my whistling friend could give me the answers I needed faster than breaking and entering. I opened my big gray umbrella—not that I cared, really, about protecting the long cashmere sweaterdress I wore. It was what a human would do.

The man squinted through the rain at my face, and then his eyes widened. He swallowed, and I heard his heart accelerate as I approached.

"I'm looking for someone," I began.

"I'm someone," he offered with a smile. "What can I do for you, beautiful?"

"Are you J. Jenks?" I asked.

"Oh," he said, and his expression changed from anticipation to understanding. He got to his feet and examined me with narrowed eyes. "Why're you looking for J?"

"That's my business." Besides, I didn't have a clue. "Are you J?"

"No."

We faced each other for a long moment while his sharp eyes ran up and down the fitted pearl gray sheath I wore. His gaze finally made it to my face. "You don't look like the usual customer."

"I'm probably not the usual," I admitted. "But I do need to see him as soon as possible."

"I'm not sure what to do," he admitted.

"Why don't you tell me your name?"

He grinned. "Max."

"Nice to meet you, Max. Now, why don't you tell me what you do for *the usual*?"

His grin became a frown. "Well, J's usual clients don't

look a thing like you. Your kind doesn't bother with the downtown office. You just go straight up to his fancy office in the skyscraper."

I repeated the other address I had, making the list of numbers a question.

"Yeah, that's the place," he said, suspicious again. "How come you didn't go there?"

"This was the address I was given—by a very dependable source."

"If you were up to any good, you wouldn't be here."

I pursed my lips. I'd never been much good at bluffing, but Alice hadn't left me a lot of alternatives. "Maybe I'm not up to any good."

Max's face turned apologetic. "Look, lady—"

"Bella."

"Right. Bella. See, I need this job. J pays me pretty good to mostly just hang out here all day. I want to help you, I do, but—and of course I'm speaking hypothetically, right? Or off the record, or whatever works for you—but if I pass somebody through that could get him in trouble, I'm out of work. Do you see my problem?"

I thought for a minute, chewing on my lip. "You've never seen anyone like me here before? Well, *sort of* like me. My sister is a lot shorter than me, and she has dark spiky black hair."

"J knows your sister?"

"I think so."

Max pondered this for a moment. I smiled at him, and his breathing stuttered. "Tell you what I'll do. I'll give J a call and describe you to him. Let him make the decision."

What did J. Jenks know? Would my description mean something to him? That was a troubling thought.

"My last name is Cullen," I told Max, wondering if that was too much information. I was starting to get irritated with Alice. Did I really have to be quite this blind? She could have given me one or two more words. . . .

"Cullen, got it."

I watched as he dialed, easily picking out the number. Well, I could call J. Jenks myself if this didn't work.

"Hey J, it's Max. I know I'm never supposed to call you at this number except in an emergency. . . ."

Is there an emergency? I heard faintly from the other end.

"Well, not exactly. It's this girl who wants to see you. . . ."

I fail to see the emergency in that. Why didn't you follow normal procedure?

"I didn't follow normal procedure 'cause she don't look like any kind of normal—"

Is she a badge?!

"No—"

You can't be sure about that. Does she look like one of Kubarev's—?

"No—let me talk, okay? She says you know her sister or something."

Not likely. What does she look like?

"She looks like . . ." His eyes ran from my face to my shoes appreciatively. "Well, she looks like a freaking super-model, that's what she looks like." I smiled and he winked at me, then went on. "Rocking body, pale as a sheet, dark brown hair almost to her waist, needs a good night's sleep—any of this sounding familiar?"

No, it doesn't. I'm not happy that you let your weakness for pretty women interrupt—

"Yeah, so I'm a sucker for the pretty ones, what's wrong with that? I'm sorry I bothered you, man. Just forget it."

"Name," I whispered.

"Oh right. Wait," Max said. "She says her name is Bella Cullen. That help?"

There was a beat of dead silence, and then the voice on the other end was abruptly screaming, using a lot of words you didn't often hear outside of truck stops. Max's whole expression changed; all the joking vanished and his lips went pale.

"Because you didn't ask!" Max yelled back, panicked.

There was another pause while J collected himself.

Beautiful and pale? J asked, a tiny bit calmer.

"I said that, didn't I?"

Beautiful and pale? What did this man know about vampires? Was he one of us himself? I wasn't prepared for that kind of confrontation. I gritted my teeth. What had Alice gotten me into?

Max waited for a minute through another volley of shouted insults and instructions and then glanced at me with eyes that were almost frightened. "But you only meet downtown clients on Thursdays—okay, okay! On it." He slid his phone shut.

"He wants to see me?" I asked brightly.

Max glowered. "You could have told me you were a priority client."

"I didn't know I was."

"I thought you might be a cop," he admitted. "I mean, you don't look like a cop. But you act kind of weird, beautiful."

I shrugged.

"Drug cartel?" he guessed.

"Who, me?" I asked.

"Yeah. Or your boyfriend or whatever."

"Nope, sorry. I'm not really a fan of drugs, and neither is my husband. *Just say no* and all that."

Max cussed under his breath. "Married. Can't catch a break."

I smiled.

"Mafia?"

"Nope."

"Diamond smuggling?"

"Please! Is that the kind of people you usually deal with, Max? Maybe you need a new job."

I had to admit, I was enjoying myself a little. I hadn't interacted with humans much besides Charlie and Sue. It was entertaining to watch him flounder. I was also pleased at how easy it was not to kill him.

"You've got to be involved in something big. *And* bad," he mused.

"It's not really like that."

"That's what they all say. But who else needs papers? Or can afford to pay J's prices for them, I should say. None of my business, anyway," he said, and then muttered the word *married* again.

He gave me an entirely new address with basic directions, and then watched me drive away with suspicious, regretful eyes.

At this point, I was ready for almost anything—some

kind of James Bond villain's high-tech lair seemed appropriate. So I thought Max must have given me the wrong address as a test. Or maybe the lair was subterranean, underneath this very commonplace strip mall nestled up against a wooded hill in a nice family neighborhood.

I pulled into an open spot and looked up at a tastefully subtle sign that read JASON SCOTT, ATTORNEY AT LAW.

The office inside was beige with celery green accents, inoffensive and unremarkable. There was no scent of vampire here, and that helped me relax. Nothing but unfamiliar human. A fish tank was set into the wall, and a blandly pretty blond receptionist sat behind the desk.

"Hello," she greeted me. "How can I help you?"

"I'm here to see Mr. Scott."

"Do you have an appointment?"

"Not exactly."

She smirked a little. "It could be a while, then. Why don't you have a seat while I—"

April! a man's demanding voice squawked from the phone on her desk. *I'm expecting a Ms. Cullen shortly.*

I smiled and pointed to myself.

Send her in immediately. Do you understand? I don't care what it's interrupting.

I could hear something else in his voice besides impatience. Stress. Nerves.

"She's just arrived," April said as soon as she could speak.

What? Send her in! What are you waiting for?

"Right away, Mr. Scott!" She got to her feet, fluttering her hands as she led the way down a short hallway, offering me coffee or tea or anything else I might have wanted.

"Here you are," she said as she ushered me through the door into a power office, complete with heavy wooden desk and vanity wall.

"Close the door behind you," a raspy tenor voice ordered.

I examined the man behind the desk while April made a hasty retreat. He was short and balding, probably around fifty-five, with a paunch. He wore a red silk tie with a blue-and-white-striped shirt, and his navy blazer hung over the back of his chair. He was also trembling, blanched to a sickly paste color, with sweat beading on his forehead; I imagined an ulcer churning away under the spare tire.

J recovered himself and rose unsteadily from his chair. He reached his hand across the desk.

"Ms. Cullen. What an absolute delight."

I crossed to him and shook his hand quickly once. He cringed slightly at my cold skin but did not seem particularly surprised by it.

"Mr. Jenks. Or do you prefer Scott?"

He winced again. "Whatever you wish, of course."

"How about you call me Bella, and I'll call you J?"

"Like old friends," he agreed, mopping a silk handkerchief across his forehead. He gestured for me to have a seat and took his own. "I must ask, am I finally meeting Mr. Jasper's lovely wife?"

I weighed that for a second. So this man knew Jasper, not Alice. Knew him, and seemed afraid of him, too. "His sister-in-law, actually."

He pursed his lips, as if he were grasping for meanings just as desperately as I was.

"I trust Mr. Jasper is in good health?" he asked carefully.

"I'm sure he is in excellent health. He's on an extended vacation at the moment."

This seemed to clear up some of J's confusion. He nodded to himself and templed his fingers. "Just so. You should have come to the main office. My assistants there would have put you straight through to me—no need to go through less hospitable channels."

I just nodded. I wasn't sure why Alice had given me the ghetto address.

"Ah, well, you're here now. What can I do for you?"

"Papers," I said, trying to make my voice sound like I knew what I was talking about.

"Certainly," J agreed at once. "Are we talking birth certificates, death certificates, drivers' licenses, passports, social security cards . . . ?"

I took a deep breath and smiled. I owed Max big time.

And then my smile faded. Alice had sent me here for a reason, and I was sure it was to protect Renesmee. Her last gift to me. The one thing she would know I needed.

The only reason Renesmee would need a forger was if she was running. And the only reason Renesmee would be running was if we had lost.

If Edward and I were running with her, she wouldn't need these documents right away. I was sure IDs were something Edward knew how to get his hands on or make himself, and I was sure he knew ways to escape without them. We could run with her for thousands of miles. We could swim with her across an ocean.

If we were around to save her.

And all the secrecy to keep this out of Edward's head. Because there was a good chance that everything he knew,

Aro would know. If we lost, Aro would certainly get the information he craved before he destroyed Edward.

It was as I had suspected. We couldn't win. But we must have a good shot at killing Demetri before we lost, giving Renesmee the chance to run.

My still heart felt like a boulder in my chest—a crushing weight. All my hope faded like fog in the sunshine. My eyes pricked.

Who would I put this on? Charlie? But he was so defenselessly human. And how would I get Renesmee to him? He was not going to be anywhere close to that fight. So that left one person. There really had never been anyone else.

I'd thought this through so quickly that J didn't notice my pause.

"Two birth certificates, two passports, one driver's license," I said in a low, strained tone.

If he noticed the change in my expression, he pretended otherwise.

"The names?"

"Jacob . . . Wolfe. And . . . Vanessa Wolfe." Nessie seemed like an okay nickname for Vanessa. Jacob would get a kick out of the Wolfe thing.

His pen scratched swiftly across a legal pad. "Middle names?"

"Just put something generic in."

"If you prefer. Ages?"

"Twenty-seven for the man, five for the girl." Jacob could pull it off. He was a beast. And at the rate Renesmee was growing, I'd better estimate high. He could be her step-father. . . .

"I'll need pictures if you prefer finished documents," J said, interrupting my thoughts. "Mr. Jasper usually liked to finish them himself."

Well, that explained why J didn't know what Alice looked like.

"Hold on," I said.

This was luck. I had several family pictures shoved in my wallet, and the perfect one—Jacob holding Renesmee on the front porch steps—was only a month old. Alice had given it to me just a few days before . . . Oh. Maybe there wasn't that much luck involved after all. Alice knew I had this picture. Maybe she'd even had some dim flash that I would need it before she gave it to me.

"Here you go."

J examined the picture for a moment. "Your daughter is very like you."

I tensed. "She's more like her father."

"Who is not this man." He touched Jacob's face.

My eyes narrowed, and new sweat beads popped out on J's shiny head.

"No. That is a very close friend of the family."

"Forgive me," he mumbled, and the pen began scratching again. "How soon will you need the documents?"

"Can I get them in a week?"

"That's a rush order. It will cost twice as—but forgive me. I forgot with whom I was speaking."

Clearly, he knew Jasper.

"Just give me a number."

He seemed hesitant to say it aloud, though I was sure, having dealt with Jasper, he must have known that price wasn't really an object. Not even taking into consideration the bloated accounts that existed all over the world with the Cullens' various names on them, there was enough cash stashed all over the house to keep a small country afloat for a decade; it reminded me of the way there were always a hundred fishhooks in the back of any drawer at Charlie's house. I doubted anyone would even notice the small stack I'd removed in preparation for today.

J wrote the price down on the bottom of the legal pad.

I nodded calmly. I had more than that with me. I unclasped my bag again and counted out the right amount—I had it all paper-clipped into five-thousand-dollar increments, so it took no time at all.

"There."

"Ah, Bella, you don't really have to give me the entire sum now. It's customary for you to save half to ensure delivery."

I smiled wanly at the nervous man. "But I trust you, J. Besides, I'll give you a bonus—the same again when I get the documents."

"That's not necessary, I assure you."

"Don't worry about it." It wasn't like I could take it with me. "So I'll meet you here next week at the same time?"

He gave me a pained look. "Actually, I prefer to make such transactions in places unrelated to my various businesses."

"Of course. I'm sure I'm not doing this the way you expect."

"I'm used to having no expectations when it comes to the Cullen family." He grimaced and then quickly composed his face again. "Shall we meet at eight o'clock a week from tonight at The Pacifico? It's on Union Lake, and the food is exquisite."

"Perfect." Not that I would be joining him for dinner. He actually wouldn't like it much if I did.

I rose and shook his hand again. This time he didn't flinch. But he did seem to have some new worry on his mind. His mouth was pinched up, his back tense.

"Will you have trouble with that deadline?" I asked.

"What?" He looked up, taken off guard by my question. "The deadline? Oh, no. No worries at all. I will certainly have your documents done on time."

It would have been nice to have Edward here, so that I would know what J's real worries were. I sighed. Keeping secrets from Edward was bad enough; having to be away from him was almost too much.

"Then I'll see you in one week."

34. DECLARED

I HEARD THE MUSIC BEFORE I WAS OUT OF THE CAR. Edward hadn't touched his piano since the night Alice left. Now, as I shut the car door, I heard the song morph through a bridge and change into my lullaby. Edward was welcoming me home.

I moved slowly as I pulled Renesmee—fast asleep; we'd been gone all day—from the car. We'd left Jacob at Charlie's—he'd said he was going to catch a ride home with Sue. I wondered if he was trying to fill his head with enough trivia to crowd out the image of the way my face had looked when I'd walked through Charlie's door.

As I walked slowly to the Cullen house now, I recognized that the hope and uplift that seemed almost a visible aura around the big white house had been mine this morning, too. It felt alien to me now.

I wanted to cry again, hearing Edward play for me. But I pulled it together. I didn't want him to be suspicious. I would leave no clues in his mind for Aro if I could help it.

Edward turned his head and smiled when I came in the door, but kept playing.

"Welcome home," he said, as if this was just any normal day. As if there weren't twelve other vampires in the room involved in various pursuits, and a dozen more scattered around somewhere. "Did you have a good time with Charlie today?"

"Yes. Sorry I was gone so long. I stepped out to do a little Christmas shopping for Renesmee. I know it won't be much of an event, but . . ." I shrugged.

Edward's lips turned down. He quit playing and spun around on the bench so that his whole body was facing me. He put one hand on my waist and pulled me closer. "I hadn't thought much about it. If you *want* to make an event of it—"

"No," I interrupted him. I flinched internally at the idea of trying to fake more enthusiasm than the bare minimum. "I just didn't want to let it pass without giving her something."

"Do I get to see?"

"If you want. It's only a little thing."

Renesmee was completely unconscious, snoring delicately against my neck. I envied her. It would have been nice to escape reality, even for just a few hours.

Carefully, I fished the little velvet jewelry bag from my clutch without opening the purse enough for Edward to see the cash I was still carrying.

"It caught my eye from the window of an antique store while I was driving by."

I shook the little golden locket into his palm. It was round with a slender vine border carved around the outside edge of the circle. Edward popped the tiny catch and looked inside. There was space for a small picture and, on the opposite side, an inscription in French.

"Do you know what this says?" he asked in a different tone, more subdued than before.

"The shopkeeper told me it said something along the lines of *'more than my own life.'* Is that right?"

"Yes, he had it right."

He looked up at me, his topaz eyes probing. I met his gaze for a moment, then pretended to be distracted by the television.

"I hope she likes it," I muttered.

"Of course she will," he said lightly, casually, and I was sure in that second that he knew I was keeping something from him. I was also sure that he had no idea of the specifics.

"Let's take her home," he suggested, standing and putting his arm around my shoulders.

I hesitated.

"What?" he demanded.

"I wanted to practice with Emmett a little. . . ." I'd lost the whole day to my vital errand; it made me feel behind.

Emmett—on the sofa with Rose and holding the remote, of course—looked up and grinned in anticipation. "Excellent. The forest needs thinning."

Edward frowned at Emmett and then at me.

"There's plenty of time for that tomorrow," he said.

"Don't be ridiculous," I complained. "There's no such

thing as *plenty of time* anymore. That concept does not exist. I have a lot to learn and—"

He cut me off. "Tomorrow."

And his expression was such that not even Emmett argued.

I was surprised at how hard it was to go back to a routine that was, after all, brand new. But stripping away even that little bit of hope I'd been fostering made everything seem impossible.

I tried to focus on the positives. There was a good chance that my daughter was going to survive what was coming, and Jacob, too. If they had a future, then that was a kind of victory, wasn't it? Our little band must be going to hold their own if Jacob and Renesmee were going to have the opportunity to run in the first place. Yes, Alice's strategy only made sense if we were going to put up a really good fight. So, a kind of victory there, too, considering that the Volturi had never been seriously challenged in millennia.

It was not going to be the end of the world. Just the end of the Cullens. The end of Edward, the end of me.

I preferred it that way—the last part anyway. I would not live without Edward again; if he was leaving this world, then I would be right behind him.

I wondered idly now and then if there would be anything for us on the other side. I knew Edward didn't really believe so, but Carlisle did. I couldn't imagine it myself. On the other hand, I couldn't imagine Edward not existing somehow, somewhere. If we could be together in any place, then that was a happy ending.

And so the pattern of my days continued, just that much harder than before.

We went to see Charlie on Christmas Day, Edward, Renesmee, Jacob, and I. All of Jacob's pack were there, plus Sam, Emily, and Sue. It was a big help to have them there in Charlie's little rooms, their huge, warm bodies wedged into corners around his sparsely decorated tree—you could see exactly where he'd gotten bored and quit—and overflowing his furniture. You could always count on werewolves to be buzzed about a coming fight, no matter how suicidal. The electricity of their excitement provided a nice current that disguised my utter lack of spirit. Edward was, as always, a better actor than I was.

Renesmee wore the locket I'd given her at dawn, and in her jacket pocket was the MP3 player Edward had given her—a tiny thing that held five thousand songs, already filled with Edward's favorites. On her wrist was an intricately braided Quileute version of a promise ring. Edward had gritted his teeth over that one, but it didn't bother me.

Soon, so soon, I would be giving her to Jacob for safekeeping. How could I be bothered by any symbol of the commitment I was so relying on?

Edward had saved the day by ordering a gift for Charlie, too. It had shown up yesterday—priority overnight shipping—and Charlie spent all morning reading the thick instruction manual to his new fishing sonar system.

From the way the werewolves ate, Sue's lunch spread must have been good. I wondered how the gathering would have looked to an outsider. Did we play our parts well enough? Would a stranger have thought us a happy circle of friends, enjoying the holiday with casual cheer?

I think Edward and Jacob both were as relieved as I was when it was time to go. It felt odd to spend energy on the human façade when there were so many more important things to be doing. I had a hard time concentrating. At the same time, this was perhaps the last time I would see Charlie. Maybe it was a good thing that I was too numb to really register that.

I hadn't seen my mother since the wedding, but I found I could only be glad for the gradual distancing that had begun two years ago. She was too fragile for my world. I didn't want her to have any part of this. Charlie was stronger.

Maybe even strong enough for a goodbye now, but I wasn't.

It was very quiet in the car; outside, the rain was just a mist, hovering on the edge between liquid and ice. Renesmee sat on my lap, playing with her locket, opening and closing it. I watched her and imagined the things I would say to Jacob right now if I didn't have to keep my words out of Edward's head.

If it's ever safe again, take her to Charlie. Tell him the whole story someday. Tell him how much I loved him, how I couldn't bear to leave him even when my human life was over. Tell him he was the best father. Tell him to pass my love on to Renée, all my hopes that she will be happy and well. . . .

I would have to give Jacob the documents before it was too late. I would give him a note for Charlie, too. And a letter for Renesmee. Something for her to read when I couldn't tell her I loved her anymore.

There was nothing unusual about the outside of the Cullen house as we pulled into the meadow, but I could hear some kind of subtle uproar inside. Many low voices murmured and growled. It sounded intense, and it sounded like an argument. I could pick out Carlisle's voice and Amun's more often than the others.

Edward parked in front of the house rather than going around to the garage. We exchanged one wary glance before we got out of the car.

Jacob's stance changed; his face turned serious and careful. I guessed that he was in Alpha mode now. Obviously, something had happened, and he was going to get the information he and Sam would need.

"Alistair is gone," Edward murmured as we darted up the steps.

Inside the front room, the main confrontation was physically apparent. Lining the walls was a ring of spectators, every vampire who had joined us, except for Alistair and the three involved in the quarrel. Esme, Kebi, and Tia were the closest to the three vampires in the center; in the middle of the room, Amun was hissing at Carlisle and Benjamin.

Edward's jaw tightened and he moved quickly to Esme's side, towing me by the hand. I clutched Renesmee tightly to my chest.

"Amun, if you want to go, no one is forcing you to stay," Carlisle said calmly.

"You're stealing half my coven, Carlisle!" Amun shrieked, stabbing one finger at Benjamin. "Is that why you called me here? To *steal* from me?"

Carlisle sighed, and Benjamin rolled his eyes.

"Yes, Carlisle picked a fight with the Volturi, endangered his whole family, just to lure me here to my death," Benjamin said sarcastically. "Be reasonable, Amun. I'm committed to do the right thing here—I'm not joining any other coven.

You can do whatever you want, of course, as Carlisle has pointed out."

"This won't end well," Amun growled. "Alistair was the only sane one here. We should all be running."

"Think of who you're calling sane," Tia murmured in a quiet aside.

"We're all going to be slaughtered!"

"It's not going to come to a fight," Carlisle said in a firm voice.

"You say!"

"If it does, you can always switch sides, Amun. I'm sure the Volturi will appreciate your help."

Amun sneered at him. "Perhaps that *is* the answer."

Carlisle's answer was soft and sincere. "I wouldn't hold that against you, Amun. We have been friends for a long time, but I would never ask you to die for me."

Amun's voice was more controlled, too. "But you're taking my Benjamin down with you."

Carlisle put his hand on Amun's shoulder; Amun shook it off.

"I'll stay, Carlisle, but it might be to your detriment. I *will* join them if that's the road to survival. You're all fools to think that you can defy the Volturi." He scowled, then sighed, glanced at Renesmee and me, and added in an exasperated tone, "I will witness that the child has grown. That's nothing but the truth. Anyone would see that."

"That's all we've ever asked."

Amun grimaced, "But not all that you are getting, it seems." He turned on Benjamin. "I gave you life. You're wasting it."

Benjamin's face looked colder than I'd ever seen it; the

expression contrasted oddly with his boyish features. "It's a pity you couldn't replace my will with your own in the process; perhaps then you would have been satisfied with me."

Amun's eyes narrowed. He gestured abruptly to Kebi, and they stalked past us out the front door.

"He's not leaving," Edward said quietly to me, "but he'll be keeping his distance even more from now on. He wasn't bluffing when he spoke of joining the Volturi."

"Why did Alistair go?" I whispered.

"No one can be positive; he didn't leave a note. From his mutters, it's been clear that he thinks a fight is inevitable. Despite his demeanor, he actually does care too much for Carlisle to stand with the Volturi. I suppose he decided the danger was too much." Edward shrugged.

Though our conversation was clearly just between the two of us, of course everyone could hear it. Eleazar answered Edward's comment like it had been meant for all.

"From the sound of his mumblings, it was a bit more than that. We haven't spoken much of the Volturi agenda, but Alistair worried that no matter how decisively we can prove your innocence, the Volturi will not listen. He thinks they will find an excuse to achieve their goals here."

The vampires glanced uneasily at one another. The idea that the Volturi would manipulate their own sacrosanct law for gain was not a popular idea. Only the Romanians were composed, their small half-smiles ironic. They seemed amused at how the others wanted to think well of their ancient enemies.

Many low discussions began at the same time, but it was the Romanians I listened to. Maybe because the fair-haired Vladimir kept shooting glances in my direction.

"I do so hope Alistair was right about this," Stefan murmured to Vladimir. "No matter the outcome, word will spread. It's time our world saw the Volturi for what they've become. They'll never fall if everyone believes this nonsense about them protecting our way of life."

"At least when we ruled, we were honest about what we were," Vladimir replied.

Stefan nodded. "We never put on white hats and called ourselves saints."

"I'm thinking the time has come to fight," Vladimir said. "How can you imagine we'll ever find a better force to stand with? Another chance this good?"

"Nothing is impossible. Maybe someday—"

"We've been waiting for *fifteen hundred years*, Stefan. And they've only gotten stronger with the years." Vladimir paused and looked at me again. He showed no surprise when he saw that I was watching him, too. "If the Volturi win this conflict, they will leave with more power than they came with. With every conquest they add to their strengths. Think of what that newborn alone could give them"—he jerked his chin toward me—"and she is barely discovering her gifts. And the earth-mover." Vladimir nodded toward Benjamin, who stiffened. Almost everyone was eavesdropping on the Romanians now, like me. "With their witch twins they have no need of the illusionist or the fire touch." His eyes moved to Zafrina, then Kate.

Stefan looked at Edward. "Nor is the mind reader exactly necessary. But I see your point. Indeed, they will gain much if they win."

"More than we can afford to have them gain, wouldn't you agree?"

Stefan sighed. "I think I must agree. And that means . . . "

"That we must stand against them while there is still hope."

"If we can just cripple them, even, expose them . . ."

"Then, someday, others will finish the job."

"And our long vendetta will be repaid. At last."

They locked eyes for a moment and then murmured in unison. "It seems the only way."

"So we fight," Stefan said.

Though I could see that they were torn, self-preservation warring with revenge, the smile they exchanged was full of anticipation.

"We fight," Vladimir agreed.

I suppose it was a good thing; like Alistair, I was sure the battle was impossible to avoid. In that case, two more vampires fighting on our side could only help. But the Romanians' decision still made me shudder.

"We will fight, too," Tia said, her usually grave voice more solemn than ever. "We believe the Volturi will overstep their authority. We have no wish to belong to them." Her eyes lingered on her mate.

Benjamin grinned and threw an impish glance toward the Romanians. "Apparently, I'm a hot commodity. It appears I have to win the right to be free."

"This won't be the first time I've fought to keep myself from a king's rule," Garrett said in a teasing tone. He walked over and clapped Benjamin on the back. "Here's to freedom from oppression."

"We stand with Carlisle," Tanya said. "And we fight with him."

The Romanians' pronouncement seemed to have made the others feel the need to declare themselves as well.

"We have not decided," Peter said. He looked down at his tiny companion; Charlotte's lips were set in dissatisfaction. It looked like she'd made her decision. I wondered what it was.

"The same goes for me," Randall said.

"And me," Mary added.

"The packs will fight with the Cullens," Jacob said suddenly. "We're not afraid of vampires," he added with a smirk.

"Children," Peter muttered.

"Infants," Randall corrected.

Jacob grinned tauntingly.

"Well, I'm in, too," Maggie said, shrugging out from under Siobhan's restraining hand. "I know truth is on Carlisle's side. I can't ignore that."

Siobhan stared at the junior member of her coven with worried eyes. "Carlisle," she said as if they were alone, ignoring the suddenly formal feel of the gathering, the unexpected outburst of declarations, "I don't want this to come to a fight."

"Nor do I, Siobhan. You know that's the last thing I want." He half-smiled. "Perhaps you should concentrate on keeping it peaceful."

"You know that won't help," she said.

I remembered Rose and Carlisle's discussion of the Irish leader; Carlisle believed that Siobhan had some subtle but powerful gift to make things go her way—and yet Siobhan didn't believe it herself.

"It couldn't hurt," Carlisle said.

Siobhan rolled her eyes. "Shall I visualize the outcome I desire?" she asked sarcastically.

Carlisle was openly grinning now. "If you don't mind."

"Then there is no need for my coven to declare itself, is there?" she retorted. "Since there is no possibility of a fight." She put her hand back on Maggie's shoulder, pulling the girl closer to her. Siobhan's mate, Liam, stood silent and expressionless.

Almost everyone else in the room looked mystified by Carlisle and Siobhan's clearly joking exchange, but they didn't explain themselves.

That was the end of the dramatic speeches for the night. The group slowly dispersed, some off to hunt, some to while away the time with Carlisle's books or televisions or computers.

Edward, Renesmee, and I went to hunt. Jacob tagged along.

"Stupid leeches," he muttered to himself when we got outside. "Think they're so superior." He snorted.

"They'll be shocked when the *infants* save their superior lives, won't they?" Edward said.

Jake smiled and punched his shoulder. "Hell yeah, they will."

This wasn't our last hunting trip. We all would hunt again nearer to the time we expected the Volturi. As the deadline was not exact, we were planning to stay a few nights out in the big baseball clearing Alice had seen, just in case. All we knew was that they would come the day that the snow stuck to the ground. We didn't want the Volturi too close to town, and Demetri would lead them to wherever we were. I wondered who he would track in, and guessed that it would be Edward since he couldn't track me.

I thought about Demetri while I hunted, paying little attention to my prey or the drifting snowflakes that had finally appeared but were melting before they touched the rocky soil. Would Demetri realize that he couldn't track me? What would he make of that? What would Aro? Or was Edward wrong? There were those little exceptions to what I could withstand, those ways around my shield. Everything that was outside my mind was vulnerable—open to the things Jasper, Alice, and Benjamin could do. Maybe Demetri's talent worked a little differently, too.

And then I had a thought that brought me up short. The half-drained elk dropped from my hands to the stony ground. Snowflakes vaporized a few inches from the warm body with tiny sizzling sounds. I stared blankly at my bloody hands.

Edward saw my reaction and hurried to my side, leaving his own kill undrained.

"What's wrong?" he asked in a low voice, his eyes sweeping the forest around us, looking for whatever had triggered my behavior.

"Renesmee," I choked.

"She's just through those trees," he reassured me. "I can hear both her thoughts and Jacob's. She's fine."

"That's not what I meant," I said. "I was thinking about my shield—you really think it's worth something, that it will help somehow. I know the others are hoping that I'll be able to shield Zafrina and Benjamin, even if I can only keep it up for a few seconds at a time. What if that's a mistake? What if your trust in me is the reason that we fail?"

My voice was edging toward hysteria, though I had enough control to keep it low. I didn't want to upset Renesmee.

"Bella, what brought this on? Of course, it's wonderful that you can protect yourself, but you're not responsible for saving anyone. Don't distress yourself needlessly."

"But what if I can't protect anything?" I whispered in gasps. "This thing I do, it's faulty, it's erratic! There's no rhyme or reason to it. Maybe it will do nothing against Alec at all."

"Shh," he hushed me. "Don't panic. And don't worry about Alec. What he does is no different than what Jane or Zafrina does. It's just an illusion—he can't get inside your head any more than I can."

"But Renesmee does!" I hissed frantically through my teeth. "It seemed so natural, I never questioned it before. It's always been just part of who she is. But she puts her thoughts right into my head just like she does with everyone else. My shield has holes, Edward!"

I stared at him desperately, waiting for him to acknowledge my terrible revelation. His lips were pursed, as if he was trying to decide how to phrase something. His expression was perfectly relaxed.

"You thought of this a long time ago, didn't you?" I demanded, feeling like an idiot for my months of overlooking the obvious.

He nodded, a faint smile pulling up one corner of his mouth. "The first time she touched you."

I sighed at my own stupidity, but his calm had mellowed me some. "And this doesn't bother you? You don't see it as a problem?"

"I have two theories, one more likely than the other."

"Give me the least likely first."

"Well, she's your daughter," he pointed out. "Genetically half you. I used to tease you about how your mind was on a different frequency than the rest of ours. Perhaps she runs on the same."

This didn't work for me. "But you hear her mind just fine. *Everyone* hears her mind. And what if Alec runs on a different frequency? What if——?"

He put a finger to my lips. "I've considered that. Which is why I think this next theory is much more likely."

I gritted my teeth and waited.

"Do you remember what Carlisle said to me about her, right after she showed you that first memory?"

Of course I remembered. "He said, 'It's an interesting twist. Like she's doing the exact opposite of what you can.'"

"Yes. And so I wondered. Maybe she took your talent and flipped it, too."

I considered that.

"You keep everyone out," he began.

"And no one keeps her out?" I finished hesitantly.

"That's my theory," he said. "And if she can get into your head, I doubt there's a shield on the planet who could keep her at bay. That will help. From what we've seen, no one can doubt the truth of her thoughts once they've allowed her to show them. And I think no one can keep her from showing them, if she gets close enough. If Aro allows her to explain. . . ."

I shuddered to think of Renesmee so close to Aro's greedy, milky eyes.

"Well," he said, rubbing my tight shoulders. "At least there's nothing that can stop him from seeing the truth."

"But is the truth enough to stop him?" I murmured.

For that, Edward had no answer.

35. DEADLINE

"HEADED OUT?" EDWARD ASKED, HIS TONE NONCHALANT. There was a sort of forced composure about his expression. He hugged Renesmee just a little bit tighter to his chest.

"Yes, a few last-minute things . . . ," I responded just as casually.

He smiled my favorite smile. "Hurry back to me."

"Always."

I took his Volvo again, wondering if he'd read the odometer after my last errand. How much had he pieced together? That I had a secret, absolutely. Would he have deduced the reason why I didn't confide in him? Did he guess that Aro might soon know everything he knew? I thought Edward could have come to that conclusion, which explained why he had demanded no reasons from me. I guessed he was trying not to speculate too much, trying to keep my behavior off his mind. Had he put this together with my odd performance the morning after Alice left, burning my book in the fire? I didn't know if he could have made that leap.

It was a dreary afternoon, already dark as dusk. I sped through the gloom, my eyes on the heavy clouds. Would it snow tonight? Enough to layer the ground and create the scene from Alice's vision? Edward estimated that we had about two more days. Then we would set ourselves in the clearing, drawing the Volturi to our chosen place.

As I headed through the darkening forest, I considered my last trip to Seattle. I thought I knew Alice's purpose in sending me to the dilapidated drop point where J. Jenks referred his shadier clients. If I'd gone to one of his other, more legitimate offices, would I have ever known what to ask for? If I'd met him as Jason Jenks or Jason Scott, legitimate lawyer, would I ever have unearthed J. Jenks, purveyor of illegal documents? I'd had to go the route that made it clear I was up to no good. That was my clue.

It was black when I pulled into the parking lot of the restaurant a few minutes early, ignoring the eager valets by the entrance. I popped in my contacts and then went to wait for J inside the restaurant. Though I was in a hurry to be done with this depressing necessity and back with my family, J seemed careful to keep himself untainted by his baser associations; I had a feeling a handoff in the dark parking lot would offend his sensibilities.

I gave the name *Jenks* at the podium, and the obsequious maître d' led me upstairs to a small private room with a fire crackling in a stone hearth. He took the calf-length ivory trench coat I'd worn to disguise the fact that I was wearing Alice's idea of appropriate attire, and gasped quietly at my oyster satin cocktail dress. I couldn't help being a little flattered; I still wasn't used to being beautiful to everyone rather than just Edward. The maître d' stuttered half-formed compliments as he backed unsteadily from the room.

I stood by the fire to wait, holding my fingers close to the flame to warm them a little before the inevitable handshake. Not that J wasn't obviously aware that there was something up with the Cullens, but it was still a good habit to practice.

For one half second, I wondered what it would feel like to put my hand in the fire. What it would feel like when I burned. . . .

J's entrance distracted my morbidity. The maître d' took his coat, too, and it was evident that I was not the only one who had dressed up for this meeting.

"I'm so sorry I'm late," J said as soon as we were alone.

"No, you're exactly on time."

He held out his hand, and as we shook I could feel that his fingers were still quite noticeably warmer than mine. It didn't seem to bother him.

"You look stunning, if I may be so bold, Mrs. Cullen."

"Thank you, J. Please, call me Bella."

"I must say, it's a different experience working with you than it is with Mr. Jasper. Much less . . . unsettling." He smiled hesitantly.

"Really? I've always found Jasper to have a very soothing presence."

His eyebrows pulled together. "Is that so?" he murmured politely while clearly still in disagreement. How odd. What had Jasper done to this man?

"Have you known Jasper long?"

He sighed, looking uncomfortable. "I've been working with Mr. Jasper for more than twenty years, and my old partner knew him for fifteen years before that. . . . He never changes." J cringed delicately.

"Yeah, Jasper's kind of funny that way."

J shook his head as if he could shake away the disturbing thoughts. "Won't you have a seat, Bella?"

"Actually, I'm in a bit of a hurry. I've got a long drive home." As I spoke, I took the thick white envelope with his bonus from my bag and handed it to him.

"Oh," he said, a little catch of disappointment in his voice. He tucked the envelope into an inside pocket of his jacket without bothering to check the amount. "I was hoping we could speak for just a moment."

"About?" I asked curiously.

"Well, let me get you your items first. I want to make sure you're satisfied."

He turned, placed his briefcase on the table, and popped the latches. He took out a legal-sized manila envelope.

Though I had no idea what I should be looking for, I opened the envelope and gave the contents a cursory glance. J had flipped Jacob's picture and changed the coloring so that it wasn't immediately evident that it was the same picture on both his passport and driver's license. Both looked perfectly sound to me, but that meant little. I glanced at the picture on Vanessa Wolfe's passport for a fraction of a second, and then looked away quickly, a lump rising in my throat.

"Thank you," I told him.

His eyes narrowed slightly, and I felt he was disappointed that my examination was not more thorough. "I can assure you every piece is perfect. All will pass the most rigorous scrutiny by experts."

"I'm sure they are. I truly appreciate what you've done for me, J."

"It's been my pleasure, Bella. In the future, feel free to come to me for anything the Cullen family needs." He didn't even hint at it really, but this sounded like an invitation for me to take over Jasper's place as liaison.

"There was something you wanted to discuss?"

"Er, yes. It's a bit delicate. . . ." He gestured to the stone hearth with a questioning expression. I sat on the edge of the stone, and he sat beside me. Sweat was dewing up on his forehead again, and he pulled a blue silk handkerchief from his pocket and began mopping.

"You are the sister of Mr. Jasper's wife? Or married to his brother?" he asked.

"Married to his brother," I clarified, wondering where this was leading.

"You would be Mr. Edward's bride, then?"

"Yes."

He smiled apologetically. "I've seen all the names many times, you see. My belated congratulations. It's nice that Mr. Edward has found such a lovely partner after all this time."

"Thank you very much."

He paused, dabbing at the sweat. "Over the years, you might imagine that I've developed a very healthy level of respect for Mr. Jasper and the entire family."

I nodded cautiously.

He took a deep breath and then exhaled without speaking.

"J, please just say whatever you need to."

He took another breath and then mumbled quickly, slurring the words together.

"If you could just assure me that you are not planning to kidnap the little girl from her father, I would sleep better tonight."

"Oh," I said, stunned. It took me a minute to understand the erroneous conclusion he'd drawn. "Oh no. It's nothing like that at all." I smiled weakly, trying to reassure him. "I'm simply preparing a safe place for her in case something were to happen to my husband and me."

His eyes narrowed. "Are you expecting something to happen?" He blushed, then apologized. "Not that it's any of my business."

I watched the red flush spread behind the delicate membrane of his skin and was glad—as I often was—that I was not the average newborn. J seemed a nice enough man, criminal behavior aside, and it would have been a shame to kill him.

"You never know." I sighed.

He frowned. "May I wish you the best of luck, then. And please don't be put out with me, my dear, but . . . if Mr. Jasper should come to me and ask what names I put on these documents . . ."

"Of course you should tell him immediately. I'd like nothing better than to have Mr. Jasper fully aware of our entire transaction."

My transparent sincerity seemed to ease a bit of his tension.

"Very good," he said. "And I can't prevail upon you to stay for dinner?"

"I'm sorry, J. I'm short on time at present."

"Then, again, my best wishes for your health and happiness. Anything at all the Cullen family needs, please don't hesitate to call on me, Bella."

"Thank you, J."

I left with my contraband, glancing back to see that J was staring after me, his expression a mixture of anxiety and regret.

The return trip took me less time. The night was black, and so I turned off my headlights and floored it. When I got back to the house, most of the cars, including Alice's Porsche and my Ferrari, were missing. The traditional vampires were going as far away as possible to satiate their thirst. I tried not to think of their hunting in the night, cringing at the mental picture of their victims.

Only Kate and Garrett were in the front room, arguing playfully about the nutritional value of animal blood. I inferred that Garrett had attempted a hunting trip vegetarian-style and found it difficult.

Edward must have taken Renesmee home to sleep. Jacob, no doubt, was in the woods close by the cottage. The rest of my family must have been hunting as well. Perhaps they were out with the other Denalis.

Which basically gave me the house to myself, and I was quick to take advantage.

I could smell that I was the first one to enter Alice and Jasper's room in a long while, maybe the first since the night they'd left us. I rooted silently through their huge closet until I found the right sort of bag. It must have been Alice's;

it was a small black leather backpack, the kind that was usually used as a purse, little enough that even Renesmee could carry it without looking out of place. Then I raided their petty cash, taking about twice the yearly income for the average American household. I guessed my theft would be less noticeable here than anywhere else in the house, since this room made everyone sad. The envelope with the fake passports and IDs went into the bag on top of the money. Then I sat on the edge of Alice and Jasper's bed and looked at the pitifully insignificant package that was all I could give my daughter and my best friend to help save their lives. I slumped against the bedpost, feeling helpless.

But what else could I do?

I sat there for several minutes with my head bowed before the inkling of a good idea came to me.

If . . .

If I was to assume that Jacob and Renesmee were going to escape, then that included the assumption that Demetri would be dead. That gave any survivors a little breathing room, Alice and Jasper included.

So why couldn't Alice and Jasper help Jacob and Renesmee? If they were reunited, Renesmee would have the best protection imaginable. There was no reason why this couldn't happen, except for the fact that Jake and Renesmee both were blind spots for Alice. How would she begin to look for them?

I deliberated for a moment, then left the room, crossing the hall to Carlisle and Esme's suite. As usual, Esme's desk was stacked with plans and blueprints, everything neatly laid out in tall piles. The desk had a slew of pigeonholes above the work surface; in one was a box of stationery. I took a fresh sheet of paper and a pen.

Then I stared at the blank ivory page for a full five minutes, concentrating on my decision. Alice might not be able to see Jacob or Renesmee, but she could see me. I visualized her seeing this moment, hoping desperately that she wasn't too busy to pay attention.

Slowly, deliberately, I wrote the words *RIO DE JANEIRO* in all caps across the page.

Rio seemed the best place to send them: It was far away from here, Alice and Jasper were already in South America at last report, and it wasn't like our old problems had ceased to exist just because we had worse problems now. There was still the mystery of Renesmee's future, the terror of her racing age. We'd been headed south anyway. Now it would be Jacob's, and hopefully Alice's, job to search for the legends.

I bowed my head again against a sudden urge to sob, clenching my teeth together. It was better that Renesmee go on without me. But I already missed her so much I could barely stand it.

I took a deep breath and put the note at the bottom of the duffel bag, where Jacob would find it soon enough.

I crossed my fingers that—since it was unlikely that his high school offered Portuguese—Jake had at least taken Spanish as his language elective.

There was nothing left now but waiting.

For two days, Edward and Carlisle stayed in the clearing where Alice had seen the Volturi arrive. It was the same killing field where Victoria's newborns had attacked last summer. I wondered if it felt repetitive to Carlisle, like déjà vu. For me, it would be all new. This time Edward and I would stand with our family.

We could only imagine that the Volturi would be tracking either Edward or Carlisle. I wondered if it would surprise them that their prey didn't run. Would that make them wary? I couldn't imagine the Volturi ever feeling a need for caution.

Though I was—hopefully—invisible to Demetri, I stayed with Edward. Of course. We only had a few hours left to be together.

Edward and I had not had a last grand scene of farewell, nor did I plan one. To speak the word was to make it final. It would be the same as typing the words *The End* on the last page of a manuscript. So we did not say our goodbyes, and we stayed very close to each other, always touching. Whatever end found us, it would not find us separated.

We set up a tent for Renesmee a few yards back into the protective forest, and then there was more déjà vu as we found ourselves camping in the cold again with Jacob. It was almost impossible to believe how much things had changed since last June. Seven months ago, our triangular relationship seemed impossible, three different kinds of heartbreak that could not be avoided. Now everything was in perfect balance. It seemed hideously ironic that the puzzle pieces would fit together just in time for all of them to be destroyed.

It started to snow again the night before New Year's Eve. This time, the tiny flakes did not dissolve into the stony ground of the clearing. While Renesmee and Jacob slept—

Jacob snoring so loudly I wondered how Renesmee didn't wake—the snow made first a thin icing over the earth, then built into thicker drifts. By the time the sun rose, the scene from Alice's vision was complete. Edward and I held hands as we stared across the glittering white field, and neither of us spoke.

Through the early morning, the others gathered, their eyes bearing mute evidence of their preparations—some light gold, some rich crimson. Soon after we all were together, we could hear the wolves moving in the woods. Jacob emerged from the tent, leaving Renesmee still sleeping, to join them.

Edward and Carlisle were arraying the others into a loose formation, our witnesses to the sides like galleries.

I watched from a distance, waiting by the tent for Renesmee to wake. When she did, I helped her dress in the clothes I'd carefully picked out two days before. Clothes that looked frilly and feminine but that were actually sturdy enough to not show any wear—even if a person wore them while riding a giant werewolf through a couple of states. Over her jacket I put on the black leather backpack with the documents, the money, the clue, and my love notes for her and Jacob, Charlie and Renée. She was strong enough that it was no burden to her.

Her eyes were huge as she read the agony on my face. But she had guessed enough not to ask me what I was doing.

"I love you," I told her. "More than anything."

"I love you, too, Momma," she answered. She touched the locket at her neck, which now held a tiny photo of her, Edward, and me. "We'll always be together."

"In our hearts we'll always be together," I corrected in

a whisper as quiet as a breath. "But when the time comes today, you have to leave me."

Her eyes widened, and she touched her hand to my cheek. The silent *no* was louder than if she'd shouted it.

I fought to swallow; my throat felt swollen. "Will you do it for me? Please?"

She pressed her fingers harder to my face. *Why?*

"I can't tell you," I whispered. "But you'll understand soon. I promise."

In my head, I saw Jacob's face.

I nodded, then pulled her fingers away. "Don't think of it," I breathed into her ear. "Don't tell Jacob until I tell you to run, okay?"

This she understood. She nodded, too.

I took from my pocket one last detail.

While packing Renesmee's things, an unexpected sparkle of color had caught my eye. A chance ray of sun through the skylight had hit the jewels on the ancient precious box stuffed high overhead on a shelf in an untouched corner. I considered it for a moment and then shrugged. After putting together Alice's clues, I couldn't hope that the coming confrontation would be resolved peacefully. But why not try to start things out as friendly as possible? I asked myself. What could it hurt? So I guess I must have had some hope left after all—blind, senseless hope—because I'd scaled the shelves and retrieved Aro's wedding present to me.

Now I fastened the thick gold rope around my neck and felt the weight of the enormous diamond nestle into the hollow of my throat.

"Pretty," Renesmee whispered. Then she wrapped her arms like a vise around my neck. I squeezed her against my chest. Interlocked this way, I carried her out of the tent and to the clearing.

Edward cocked one eyebrow as I approached, but otherwise did not remark on my accessory or Renesmee's. He just put his arms tight around us both for one long moment and then, with a deep sigh, let us go. I couldn't see a goodbye anywhere in his eyes. Maybe he had more hope for something after this life than he'd let on.

We took our place, Renesmee climbing agilely onto my back to leave my hands free. I stood a few feet behind the front line made up by Carlisle, Edward, Emmett, Rosalie, Tanya, Kate, and Eleazar. Close beside me were Benjamin and Zafrina; it was my job to protect them as long as I was able. They were our best offensive weapons. If the Volturi were the ones who could not see, even for a few moments, that would change everything.

Zafrina was rigid and fierce, with Senna almost a mirror image at her side. Benjamin sat on the ground, his palms pressed to the dirt, and muttered quietly about fault lines. Last night, he'd strewn piles of boulders in natural-looking, now snow-covered heaps all along the back of the meadow. They weren't enough to injure a vampire, but hopefully enough to distract one.

The witnesses clustered to our left and right, some nearer than others—those who had declared themselves were the closest. I noticed Siobhan rubbing her temples, her eyes closed in concentration; was she humoring Carlisle? Trying to visualize a diplomatic resolution?

In the woods behind us, the invisible wolves were still and ready; we could only hear their heavy panting, their beating hearts.

The clouds rolled in, diffusing the light so that it could have been morning or afternoon. Edward's eyes tightened as he scrutinized the view, and I was sure he was seeing this exact scene for the second time—the first time being Alice's vision. It would look just the same when the Volturi arrived. We only had minutes or seconds left now.

All our family and allies braced themselves.

From the forest, the huge russet Alpha wolf came forward to stand at my side; it must have been too hard for him to keep his distance from Renesmee when she was in such immediate danger.

Renesmee reached out to twine her fingers in the fur over his massive shoulder, and her body relaxed a little bit. She was calmer with Jacob close. I felt a tiny bit better, too. As long as Jacob was with Renesmee, she would be all right.

Without risking a glance behind, Edward reached back to me. I stretched my arm forward so that I could grip his hand. He squeezed my fingers.

Another minute ticked by, and I found myself straining to hear some sound of approach.

And then Edward stiffened and hissed low between his clenched teeth. His eyes focused on the forest due north of where we stood.

We stared where he did, and waited as the last seconds passed.

36. BLOODLUST

THEY CAME WITH PAGEANTRY, WITH A KIND OF BEAUTY.

They came in a rigid, formal formation. They moved together, but it was not a march; they flowed in perfect synchronicity from the trees—a dark, unbroken shape that seemed to hover a few inches above the white snow, so smooth was the advance.

The outer perimeter was gray; the color darkened with each line of bodies until the heart of the formation was deepest black. Every face was cowled, shadowed. The faint brushing sound of their feet was so regular it was like music, a complicated beat that never faltered.

At some sign I did not see—or perhaps there was no sign, only millennia of practice—the configuration folded outward. The motion was too stiff, too square to resemble the opening of a flower, though the color suggested that; it was the opening of a fan, graceful but very angular. The gray-cloaked figures spread to the flanks while the darker forms surged precisely forward in the center, each movement closely controlled.

Their progress was slow but deliberate, with no hurry, no tension, no anxiety. It was the pace of the invincible.

This was almost my old nightmare. The only thing lacking was the gloating desire I'd seen on the faces in my dream—the smiles of vindictive joy. Thus far, the Volturi were too disciplined to show any emotion at all. They also showed no surprise or dismay at the collection of vampires that waited for them here—a collection that looked suddenly disorganized and unprepared in comparison. They showed no surprise at the giant wolf that stood in our midst.

I couldn't help counting. There were thirty-two of them. Even if you did not count the two drifting, waifish black-cloaked figures in the very back, who I took to be the wives—their protected position suggesting that they would not be involved in the attack—we were still outnumbered. There were just nineteen of us who would fight, and then seven more to watch as we were destroyed. Even counting the ten wolves, they had us.

"The redcoats are coming, the redcoats are coming," Garrett muttered mysteriously to himself and then chuckled once. He slid one step closer to Kate.

"They did come," Vladimir whispered to Stefan.

"The wives," Stefan hissed back. "The entire guard. All of them together. It's well we didn't try Volterra."

And then, as if their numbers were not enough, while

the Volturi slowly and majestically advanced, more vampires began entering the clearing behind them.

The faces in this seemingly endless influx of vampires were the antithesis to the Volturi's expressionless discipline—they wore a kaleidoscope of emotions. At first there was the shock and even some anxiety as they saw the unexpected force awaiting them. But that concern passed quickly; they were secure in their overwhelming numbers, secure in their position behind the unstoppable Volturi force. Their features returned to the expression they'd worn before we'd surprised them.

It was easy enough to understand their mindset—the faces were that explicit. This was an angry mob, whipped to a frenzy and slavering for justice. I did not fully realize the vampire world's feeling toward the immortal children before I read these faces.

It was clear that this motley, disorganized horde—more than forty vampires altogether—was the Volturi's own kind of witness. When we were dead, they would spread the word that the criminals had been eradicated, that the Volturi had acted with nothing but impartiality. Most looked like they hoped for more than just an opportunity to witness—they wanted to help tear and burn.

We didn't have a prayer. Even if we could somehow neutralize the Volturi's advantages, they could still bury us in bodies. Even if we killed Demetri, Jacob would not be able to outrun this.

I could feel it as the same comprehension sunk in around me. Despair weighted the air, pushing me down with more pressure than before.

One vampire in the opposing force did not seem to

belong to either party; I recognized Irina as she hesitated in between the two companies, her expression unique among the others. Irina's horrified gaze was locked on Tanya's position in the front line. Edward snarled, a very low but fervent sound.

"Alistair was right," he murmured to Carlisle.

I watched Carlisle glance at Edward questioningly.

"Alistair was right?" Tanya whispered.

"They—Caius and Aro—come to destroy and acquire," Edward breathed almost silently back; only our side could hear. "They have many layers of strategy already in place. If Irina's accusation had somehow proven to be false, they were committed to find another reason to take offense. But they can see Renesmee now, so they are perfectly sanguine about their course. We could still attempt to defend against their other contrived charges, but first they have to stop, to hear the truth about Renesmee." Then, even lower. "Which they have no intention of doing."

Jacob gave a strange little huff.

And then, unexpectedly, two seconds later, the procession *did* halt. The low music of perfectly synchronized movements turned to silence. The flawless discipline remained unbroken; the Volturi froze into absolute stillness as one. They stood about a hundred yards away from us.

Behind me, to the sides, I heard the beating of large hearts, closer than before. I risked glances to the left and the right from the corners of my eyes to see what had stopped the Volturi advance.

The wolves had joined us.

On either side of our uneven line, the wolves branched out in long, bordering arms. I only spared a fraction of a second to note that there were more than ten wolves, to recognize the wolves I knew and the ones I'd never seen before. There were sixteen of them spaced evenly around us—seventeen total, counting Jacob. It was clear from their heights and oversized paws that the newcomers all were very, very young. I supposed I should have foreseen this. With so many vampires encamped in the neighborhood, a werewolf population explosion was inevitable.

More children dying. I wondered why Sam had allowed this, and then I realized he had no other choice. If any of the wolves stood with us, the Volturi would be sure to search out the rest. They had gambled their entire species on this stand.

And we were going to lose.

Abruptly, I was furious. Beyond furious, I was murderously enraged. My hopeless despair vanished entirely. A faint reddish glow highlighted the dark figures in front of me, and all I wanted in that moment was the chance to sink my teeth into them, to rip their limbs from their bodies and pile them for burning. I was so maddened I could have danced around the pyre where they roasted alive; I would have laughed while their ashes smoldered. My lips curved back automatically, and a low, fierce snarl tore up my throat from the pit of my stomach. I realized the corners of my mouth were turned up in a smile.

Beside me, Zafrina and Senna echoed my hushed growl. Edward squeezed the hand he still held, cautioning me.

The shadowed Volturi faces were still expressionless for the most part. Only two sets of eyes betrayed any emotion at all. In the very center, touching hands, Aro and Caius had paused to evaluate, and the entire guard had paused with them, waiting for the order to kill. The two did not look at each other, but it was obvious that they were communicating. Marcus, though touching Aro's other hand, did not seem part of the conversation. His expression was not as mindless as the guards', but it was nearly as blank. Like the one other time I'd seen him, he appeared to be utterly bored.

The bodies of the Volturi's witnesses leaned toward us, their eyes fixed furiously on Renesmee and me, but they stayed near the fringe of the forest, leaving a wide berth between themselves and the Volturi soldiers. Only Irina hovered close behind the Volturi, just a few paces away from the ancient females—both fair-haired with powdery skin and filmed eyes—and their two massive bodyguards.

There was a woman in one of the darker gray cloaks just behind Aro. I couldn't be sure, but it looked like she might actually be touching his back. Was this the other shield, Renata? I wondered, as Eleazar had, if she would be able to repel *me*.

But I would not waste my life trying to get to Caius or Aro. I had more vital targets.

I searched the line for them now and had no difficulty picking out the two petite, deep gray cloaks near the heart of the arrangement. Alec and Jane, easily the smallest members of the guard, stood just to Marcus's side, flanked by Demetri on the other. Their lovely faces were smooth, giving nothing away; they wore the darkest cloaks beside the pure black of the ancients. The witch twins, Vladimir had called them. Their powers were the cornerstone of the Volturi offensive. The jewels in Aro's collection.

My muscles flexed, and venom welled in my mouth.

Aro's and Caius's clouded red eyes flickered across our

line. I read disappointment in Aro's face as his gaze roved over our faces again and again, looking for one that was missing. Chagrin tightened his lips.

In that moment, I was nothing but grateful that Alice had run.

As the pause lengthened, I heard Edward's breath speed.

"Edward?" Carlisle asked, low and anxious.

"They're not sure how to proceed. They're weighing options, choosing key targets—me, of course, you, Eleazar, Tanya. Marcus is reading the strength of our ties to each other, looking for weak points. The Romanians' presence irritates them. They're worried about the faces they don't recognize—Zafrina and Senna in particular—and the wolves, naturally. They've never been outnumbered before. That's what stopped them."

"Outnumbered?" Tanya whispered incredulously.

"They don't count their witnesses," Edward breathed. "They are nonentities, meaningless to the guard. Aro just enjoys an audience."

"Should I speak?" Carlisle asked.

Edward hesitated, then nodded. "This is the only chance you'll get."

Carlisle squared his shoulders and paced several steps ahead of our defensive line. I hated to see him alone, unprotected.

He spread his arms, holding his palms up as if in greeting. "Aro, my old friend. It's been centuries."

The white clearing was dead silent for a long moment. I could feel the tension rolling off Edward as he listened to Aro's assessment of Carlisle's words. The strain mounted as the seconds ticked by.

And then Aro stepped forward out of the center of the Volturi formation. The shield, Renata, moved with him as if the tips of her fingers were sewn to his robe. For the first time, the Volturi ranks reacted. A muttered grumble rolled through the line, eyebrows lowered into scowls, lips curled back from teeth. A few of the guard leaned forward into a crouch.

Aro held one hand up toward them. "Peace."

He walked just a few paces more, then cocked his head to one side. His milky eyes glinted with curiosity.

"Fair words, Carlisle," he breathed in his thin, wispy voice. "They seem out of place, considering the army you've assembled to kill me, and to kill my dear ones."

Carlisle shook his head and stretched his right hand forward as if there were not still almost a hundred yards between them. "You have but to touch my hand to know that was never my intent."

Aro's shrewd eyes narrowed. "But how can your intent possibly matter, dear Carlisle, in the face of what you have done?" He frowned, and a shadow of sadness crossed his features—whether it was genuine or not, I could not tell.

"I have not committed the crime you are here to punish me for."

"Then step aside and let us punish those responsible. Truly, Carlisle, nothing would please me more than to preserve your life today."

"No one has broken the law, Aro. Let me explain." Again, Carlisle offered his hand.

Before Aro could answer, Caius drifted swiftly forward to Aro's side.

"So many pointless rules, so many unnecessary laws you

create for yourself, Carlisle," the white-haired ancient hissed. "How is it possible that you defend the breaking of one that truly matters?"

"The law is not broken. If you would listen—"

"We see the child, Carlisle," Caius snarled. "Do not treat us as fools."

"She is *not* an immortal. She is not a vampire. I can easily prove this with just a few moments—"

Caius cut him off. "If she is not one of the forbidden, then why have you massed a battalion to protect her?"

"Witnesses, Caius, just as you have brought." Carlisle gestured to the angry horde at the edge of the woods; some of them growled in response. "Any one of these friends can tell you the truth about the child. Or you could just look at her, Caius. See the flush of human blood in her cheeks."

"Artifice!" Caius snapped. "Where is the informer? Let her come forward!" He craned his neck around until he spotted Irina lingering behind the wives. "You! Come!"

Irina stared at him uncomprehendingly, her face like that of someone who has not entirely awakened from a hideous nightmare. Impatiently, Caius snapped his fingers. One of the wives' huge bodyguards moved to Irina's side and prodded her roughly in the back. Irina blinked twice and then walked slowly toward Caius in a daze. She stopped several yards short, her eyes still on her sisters.

Caius closed the distance between them and slapped her across the face.

It couldn't have hurt, but there was something terribly degrading about the action. It was like watching someone kick a dog. Tanya and Kate hissed in synchronization.

Irina's body went rigid and her eyes finally focused on

Caius. He pointed one clawed finger at Renesmee, where she clung to my back, her fingers still tangled in Jacob's fur. Caius turned entirely red in my furious view. A growl rumbled through Jacob's chest.

"This is the child you saw?" Caius demanded. "The one that was obviously more than human?"

Irina peered at us, examining Renesmee for the first time since entering the clearing. Her head tilted to the side, confusion crossed her features.

"Well?" Caius snarled.

"I . . . I'm not sure," she said, her tone perplexed.

Caius's hand twitched as if he wanted to slap her again. "What do you mean?" he said in a steely whisper.

"She's not the same, but I think it's the same child. What I mean is, she's changed. This child is bigger than the one I saw, but—"

Caius's furious gasp crackled through his suddenly bared teeth, and Irina broke off without finishing. Aro flitted to Caius's side and put a restraining hand on his shoulder.

"Be composed, brother. We have time to sort this out. No need to be hasty."

With a sullen expression, Caius turned his back on Irina.

"Now, sweetling," Aro said in a warm, sugary murmur. "Show me what you're trying to say." He held his hand out to the bewildered vampire.

Uncertainly, Irina took his hand. He held hers for only five seconds.

"You see, Caius?" he said. "It's a simple matter to get what we need."

Caius didn't answer him. From the corner of his eye,

Aro glanced once at his audience, his mob, and then turned back to Carlisle.

"And so we have a mystery on our hands, it seems. It would appear the child has grown. Yet Irina's first memory was clearly that of an immortal child. Curious."

"That's exactly what I'm trying to explain," Carlisle said, and from the change in his voice, I could guess at his relief. This was the pause we had pinned all our nebulous hopes on.

I felt no relief. I waited, almost numb with rage, for the layers of strategy Edward had promised.

Carlisle held out his hand again.

Aro hesitated for a moment. "I would rather have the explanation from someone more central to the story, my friend. Am I wrong to assume that this breach was not of your making?"

"There was no breach."

"Be that as it may, I *will* have every facet of the truth." Aro's feathery voice hardened. "And the best way to get that is to have the evidence directly from your talented son." He inclined his head in Edward's direction. "As the child clings to his newborn mate, I'm assuming Edward is involved."

Of course he wanted Edward. Once he could see into Edward's mind, he would know *all* our thoughts. Except mine.

Edward turned to quickly kiss my forehead and Renesmee's, not meeting my eyes. Then he strode across the snowy field, clapping Carlisle on the shoulder as he passed. I heard a low whimper from behind me—Esme's terror breaking through.

The red haze I saw around the Volturi army flamed

brighter than before. I could not bear to watch Edward cross the empty white space alone—but I also could not endure to have Renesmee one step closer to our adversaries. The opposing needs tore at me; I was frozen so tightly it felt like my bones might shatter from the pressure of it.

I saw Jane smile as Edward crossed the midpoint in the distance between us, when he was closer to them than he was to us.

That smug little smile did it. My fury peaked, higher even than the raging bloodlust I'd felt the moment the wolves had committed to this doomed fight. I could taste madness on my tongue—I felt it flow through me like a tidal wave of pure power. My muscles tightened, and I acted automatically. I threw my shield with all the force in my mind, flung it across the impossible expanse of the field—ten times my best distance—like a javelin. My breath rushed out in a huff with the exertion.

The shield blew out from me in a bubble of sheer energy, a mushroom cloud of liquid steel. It pulsed like a living thing—I could *feel* it, from the apex to the edges.

There was no recoil to the elastic fabric now; in that instant of raw force, I saw that the backlash I'd felt before was of my own making—I had been clinging to that invisible part of me in self-defense, subconsciously unwilling to let it go. Now I set it free, and my shield exploded a good fifty yards out from me effortlessly, taking only a fraction of my concentration. I could feel it flex like just another muscle, obedient to my will. I pushed it, shaped it to a long, pointed oval. Everything underneath the flexible iron shield was suddenly a part of me—I could feel the life force of everything it covered like points of bright heat, dazzling sparks of light surrounding me. I thrust the shield forward the length of the clearing, and exhaled in relief when I felt Edward's brilliant light within my protection. I held there, contracting this new muscle so that it closely surrounded Edward, a thin but unbreakable sheet between his body and our enemies.

Barely a second had passed. Edward was still walking to Aro. Everything had changed absolutely, but no one had noticed the explosion except for me. A startled laugh burst through my lips. I felt the others glancing at me and saw Jacob's big black eye roll down to stare at me like I'd lost my mind.

Edward stopped a few steps away from Aro, and I realized with some chagrin that though I certainly could, I *should* not prevent this exchange from happening. This was the point of all our preparations: getting Aro to hear our side of the story. It was almost physically painful to do it, but reluctantly I pulled my shield back and left Edward exposed again. The laughing mood had vanished. I focused totally on Edward, ready to shield him instantly if something went wrong.

Edward's chin came up arrogantly, and he held his hand out to Aro as if he were conferring a great honor. Aro seemed only delighted with his attitude, but his delight was not universal. Renata fluttered nervously in Aro's shadow. Caius's scowl was so deep it looked like his papery, translucent skin would crease permanently. Little Jane showed her teeth, and beside her Alec's eyes narrowed in concentration. I guessed that he was ready, like me, to act at a second's notice.

Aro closed the distance without pause—and really, what did he have to fear? The hulking shadows of the lighter gray cloaks—the brawny fighters like Felix—were but a few yards away. Jane and her burning gift could throw Edward on the ground, writhing in agony. Alec could blind and deafen him before he could take a step in Aro's direction. No one knew that I had the power to stop them, not even Edward.

With an untroubled smile, Aro took Edward's hand. His eyes snapped shut at once, and then his shoulders hunched under the onslaught of information.

Every secret thought, every strategy, every insight—everything Edward had heard in the minds around him during the last month—was now Aro's. And further back—every vision of Alice's, every quiet moment with our family, every picture in Renesmee's head, every kiss, every touch between Edward and me . . . All of that was Aro's now, too.

I hissed with frustration, and the shield roiled with my irritation, shifting its shape and contracting around our side.

"Easy, Bella," Zafrina whispered to me.

I clenched my teeth together.

Aro continued to concentrate on Edward's memories. Edward's head bowed, too, the muscles in his neck locking tight as he read back again everything that Aro took from him, and Aro's response to it all.

This two-way but unequal conversation continued long enough that even the guard grew uneasy. Low murmurs ran through the line until Caius barked a sharp order for silence. Jane was edging forward like she couldn't help herself, and Renata's face was rigid with distress. For a moment, I ex-amined this powerful shield that seemed so panicky and weak; though she was useful to Aro, I could tell she was no warrior. It was not her job to fight but to protect. There was no bloodlust in her. Raw as I was, I knew that if this were between her and me, I would obliterate her.

I refocused as Aro straightened, his eyes flashing open, their expression awed and wary. He did not release Edward's hand.

Edward's muscles loosened ever so slightly.

"You see?" Edward asked, his velvet voice calm.

"Yes, I see, indeed," Aro agreed, and amazingly, he sounded almost amused. "I doubt whether any two among gods or mortals have ever seen quite so clearly."

The disciplined faces of the guard showed the same disbelief I felt.

"You have given me much to ponder, young friend," Aro continued. "Much more than I expected." Still he did not release Edward's hand, and Edward's tense stance was that of one who listens.

Edward didn't answer.

"May I meet her?" Aro asked—almost pleaded—with sudden eager interest. "I never dreamed of the existence of such a thing in all my centuries. What an addition to our histories!"

"What is this about, Aro?" Caius snapped before Edward could answer. Just the question had me pulling Renesmee around into my arms, cradling her protectively against my chest.

"Something you've never dreamed of, my practical friend. Take a moment to ponder, for the justice we intended to deliver no longer applies."

Caius hissed in surprise at his words.

"Peace, brother," Aro cautioned soothingly.

This should have been good news—these were the words we'd been hoping for, the reprieve we'd never really thought possible. Aro had listened to the truth. Aro had admitted that the law had not been broken.

But my eyes were riveted on Edward, and I saw the muscles in his back tighten. I replayed in my head Aro's instruction for Caius to *ponder*, and heard the double meaning.

"Will you introduce me to your daughter?" Aro asked Edward again.

Caius was not the only one who hissed at this new revelation.

Edward nodded reluctantly. And yet, Renesmee had won over so many others. Aro always seemed the leader of the ancients. If he were on her side, could the others act against us?

Aro still gripped Edward's hand, and he now answered a question that the rest of us had not heard.

"I think a compromise on this one point is certainly acceptable, under the circumstance. We will meet in the middle."

Aro released his hand. Edward turned back toward us, and Aro joined him, throwing one arm casually over Edward's shoulder like they were the best of friends—all the while maintaining contact with Edward's skin. They began to cross the field back to our side.

The entire guard fell into step behind them. Aro raised a hand negligently without looking at them.

"Hold, my dear ones. Truly, they mean us no harm if we are peaceable."

The guard reacted to this more openly than before, with

snarls and hisses of protest, but held their position. Renata, clinging closer to Aro than ever, whimpered in anxiety.

"Master," she whispered.

"Don't fret, my love," he responded. "All is well."

"Perhaps you should bring a few members of your guard with us," Edward suggested. "It will make them more comfortable."

Aro nodded as if this was a wise observation he should have thought of himself. He snapped his fingers twice. "Felix, Demetri."

The two vampires were at his side instantaneously, looking precisely the same as the last time I'd met them. Both were tall and dark-haired, Demetri hard and lean as the blade of a sword, Felix hulking and menacing as an iron-spiked cudgel.

The five of them stopped in the middle of the snowy field.

"Bella," Edward called. "Bring Renesmee . . . and a few friends."

I took a deep breath. My body was tight with opposition. The idea of taking Renesmee into the center of the conflict . . . But I trusted Edward. He would know if Aro was planning any treachery at this point.

Aro had three protectors on his side of the summit, so I would bring two with me. It took me only a second to decide.

"Jacob? Emmett?" I asked quietly. Emmett, because he would be dying to go. Jacob, because he wouldn't be able to bear being left behind.

Both nodded. Emmett grinned.

I crossed the field with them flanking me. I heard another

rumble from the guard as they saw my choices—clearly, they did not trust the werewolf. Aro lifted his hand, waving away their protest again.

"Interesting company you keep," Demetri murmured to Edward.

Edward didn't respond, but a low growl slipped through Jacob's teeth.

We stopped a few yards from Aro. Edward ducked under Aro's arm and quickly joined us, taking my hand.

For a moment we faced each other in silence. Then Felix greeted me in a low aside.

"Hello again, Bella." He grinned cockily while still tracking Jacob's every twitch with his peripheral vision.

I smiled wryly at the mountainous vampire. "Hey, Felix."

Felix chuckled. "You look good. Immortality suits you."

"Thanks so much."

"You're welcome. It's too bad . . ."

He let his comment trail off into silence, but I didn't need Edward's gift to imagine the end. *It's too bad we're going to kill you in a sec.*

"Yes, too bad, isn't it?" I murmured.

Felix winked.

Aro paid no attention to our exchange. He leaned his head to one side, fascinated. "I hear her strange heart," he murmured with an almost musical lilt to his words. "I smell her strange scent." Then his hazy eyes shifted to me. "In truth, young Bella, immortality does become you most extraordinarily," he said. "It is as if you were designed for this life."

I nodded once in acknowledgment of his flattery.

"You liked my gift?" he asked, eyeing the pendant I wore.

"It's beautiful, and very, very generous of you. Thank you. I probably should have sent a note."

Aro laughed delightedly. "It's just a little something I had lying around. I thought it might complement your new face, and so it does."

I heard a little hiss from the center of the Volturi line. I glanced over Aro's shoulder.

Hmm. It seemed Jane wasn't happy about the fact that Aro had given me a present.

Aro cleared his throat to reclaim my attention. "May I greet your daughter, lovely Bella?" he asked sweetly.

This was what we'd hoped for, I reminded myself. Fighting the urge to take Renesmee and run for it, I walked two slow steps forward. My shield rippled out behind me like a cape, protecting the rest of my family while Renesmee was left exposed. It felt wrong, horrible.

Aro met us, his face beaming.

"But she's exquisite," he murmured. "So like you and Edward." And then louder, "Hello, Renesmee."

Renesmee looked at me quickly. I nodded.

"Hello, Aro," she answered formally in her high, ringing voice.

Aro's eyes were bemused.

"What is it?" Caius hissed from behind. He seemed infuriated by the need to ask.

"Half mortal, half immortal," Aro announced to him and the rest of the guard without turning his enthralled gaze from Renesmee. "Conceived so, and carried by this newborn while she was still human."

"Impossible," Caius scoffed.

"Do you think they've fooled me, then, brother?" Aro's expression was greatly amused, but Caius flinched. "Is the heartbeat you hear a trickery as well?"

Caius scowled, looking as chagrined as if Aro's gentle questions had been blows.

"Calmly and carefully, brother," Aro cautioned, still smiling at Renesmee. "I know well how you love your justice, but there is no justice in acting against this unique little one for her parentage. And so much to learn, so much to learn! I know you don't have my enthusiasm for collecting histories, but be tolerant with me, brother, as I add a chapter that stuns me with its improbability. We came expecting only justice and the sadness of false friends, but look what we have gained instead! A new, bright knowledge of ourselves, our possibilities."

He held out his hand to Renesmee in invitation. But this was not what she wanted. She leaned away from me, stretching upward, to touch her fingertips to Aro's face.

Aro did not react with shock as almost everyone else had reacted to this performance from Renesmee; he was as used to the flow of thought and memory from other minds as Edward was.

His smile widened, and he sighed in satisfaction. "Brilliant," he whispered.

Renesmee relaxed back into my arms, her little face very serious.

"Please?" she asked him.

His smile turned gentle. "Of course I have no desire to harm your loved ones, precious Renesmee."

Aro's voice was so comforting and affectionate, it took

me in for a second. And then I heard Edward's teeth grind together and, far behind us, Maggie's outraged hiss at the lie.

"I wonder," Aro said thoughtfully, seeming unaware of the reaction to his previous words. His eyes moved unexpectedly to Jacob, and instead of the disgust the other Volturi viewed the giant wolf with, Aro's eyes were filled with a longing that I did not comprehend.

"It doesn't work that way," Edward said, the careful neutrality gone from his suddenly harsh tone.

"Just an errant thought," Aro said, appraising Jacob openly, and then his eyes moved slowly across the two lines of werewolves behind us. Whatever Renesmee had shown him, it made the wolves suddenly interesting to him.

"They don't *belong* to us, Aro. They don't follow our commands that way. They're here because they want to be."

Jacob growled menacingly.

"They seem quite attached to you, though," Aro said. "And your young mate and your . . . family. *Loyal.*" His voice caressed the word softly.

"They're committed to protecting human life, Aro. That makes them able to coexist with us, but hardly with you. Unless you're rethinking your lifestyle."

Aro laughed merrily. "Just an errant thought," he repeated. "You well know how that is. We none of us can entirely control our subconscious desires."

Edward grimaced. "I do know how that is. And I also know the difference between that kind of thought and the kind with a purpose behind it. It could never work, Aro."

Jacob's vast head turned in Edward's direction, and a faint whine slipped from between his teeth.

"He's intrigued with the idea of . . . guard dogs," Edward murmured back.

There was one second of dead silence, and then the sound of the furious snarls ripping from the entire pack filled the giant clearing.

There was a sharp bark of command—from Sam, I guessed, though I didn't turn to look—and the complaint broke off into ominous quiet.

"I suppose that answers that question," Aro said, laughing again. "*This* lot has picked its side."

Edward hissed and leaned forward. I clutched at his arm, wondering what could be in Aro's thoughts that would make him react so violently, while Felix and Demetri slipped into crouches in synchronization. Aro waved them off again. They all returned to their former posture, Edward included.

"So much to discuss," Aro said, his tone suddenly that of an inundated businessman. "So much to decide. If you and your furry protector will excuse me, my dear Cullens, I must confer with my brothers."

37. CONTRIVANCES

ARO DID NOT REJOIN HIS ANXIOUS GUARD WAITING ON
the north side of the clearing; instead, he waved them
forward.

Edward started backing up immediately, pulling my
arm and Emmett's. We hurried backward, keeping our eyes
on the advancing threat. Jacob retreated slowest, the fur on
his shoulders standing straight up as he bared his fangs at
Aro. Renesmee grabbed the end of his tail as we retreated;
she held it like a leash, forcing him to stay with us. We
reached our family at the same time that the dark cloaks
surrounded Aro again.

Now there were only fifty yards between them and us—a
distance any of us could leap in just a fraction of a second.

Caius began arguing with Aro at once.

"How can you abide this infamy? Why do we stand here impotently in the face of such an outrageous crime, covered by such a ridiculous deception?" He held his arms rigidly at his sides, his hands curled into claws. I wondered why he did not just touch Aro to share his opinion. Were we seeing a division in their ranks already? Could we be that lucky?

"Because it's all true," Aro told him calmly. "Every word of it. See how many witnesses stand ready to give evidence that they have seen this miraculous child grow and mature in just the short time they've known her. That they have felt the warmth of the blood that pulses in her veins." Aro's gesture swept from Amun on one side across to Siobhan on the other.

Caius reacted oddly to Aro's soothing words, starting ever so slightly at the mention of *witnesses*. The anger drained from his features, replaced by a cold calculation. He glanced at the Volturi witnesses with an expression that looked vaguely . . . nervous.

I glanced at the angry mob, too, and saw immediately that the description no longer applied. The frenzy for action had turned to confusion. Whispered conversations seethed through the crowd as they tried to make sense of what had happened.

Caius was frowning, deep in thought. His speculative expression stoked the flames of my smoldering anger at the same time that it worried me. What if the guard acted again on some invisible signal, as they had in their march? Anxiously, I inspected my shield; it felt just as impenetrable as before. I flexed it now into a low, wide dome that arced over our company.

I could feel the sharp plumes of light where my family and friends stood—each one an individual flavor that I thought I would be able to recognize with practice. I already knew Edward's—his was the very brightest of them all. The extra empty space around the shining spots bothered me; there was no physical barrier to the shield, and if any of the talented Volturi got *under* it, it would protect no one but me. I felt my forehead crease as I pulled the elastic armor very carefully closer. Carlisle was the farthest forward; I sucked the shield back inch by inch, trying to wrap it as exactly to his body as I could.

My shield seemed to want to cooperate. It hugged his shape; when Carlisle shifted to the side to stand nearer to Tanya, the elastic stretched with him, drawn to his spark.

Fascinated, I tugged in more threads of the fabric, pulling it around each glimmering shape that was a friend or ally. The shield clung to them willingly, moving as they moved.

Only a second had passed; Caius was still deliberating.

"The werewolves," he murmured at last.

With sudden panic, I realized that most of the werewolves were unprotected. I was about to reach out to them when I realized that, strangely, I could still feel their sparks. Curious, I drew the shield tighter in, until Amun and Kebi—the farthest edge of our group—were outside with the wolves. Once they were on the other side, their lights vanished. They no longer existed to that new sense. But the wolves were still bright flames—or rather, half of them were. Hmm . . . I edged outward again, and as soon as Sam was under cover, all the wolves were brilliant sparks again.

Their minds must have been more interconnected than

I'd imagined. If the Alpha was inside my shield, the rest of their minds were every bit as protected as his.

"Ah, brother . . . ," Aro answered Caius's statement with a pained look.

"Will you defend that alliance, too, Aro?" Caius demanded. "The Children of the Moon have been our bitter enemies from the dawn of time. We have hunted them to near extinction in Europe and Asia. Yet Carlisle encourages a familiar relationship with this enormous infestation—no doubt in an attempt to overthrow us. The better to protect his warped lifestyle."

Edward cleared his throat loudly and Caius glared at him. Aro placed one thin, delicate hand over his own face as if he was embarrassed for the other ancient.

"Caius, it's the middle of the day," Edward pointed out. He gestured to Jacob. "These are not Children of the Moon, clearly. They bear no relation to your enemies on the other side of the world."

"You breed mutants here," Caius spit back at him.

Edward's jaw clenched and unclenched, then he answered evenly, "They aren't even werewolves. Aro can tell you all about it if you don't believe me."

Not werewolves? I shot a mystified look at Jacob. He lifted his huge shoulders and let them drop—a shrug. He didn't know what Edward was talking about, either.

"Dear Caius, I would have warned you not to press this point if you had told me your thoughts," Aro murmured. "Though the creatures think of themselves as werewolves, they are not. The more accurate name for them would be shape-shifters. The choice of a wolf form was purely chance. It could have been a bear or a hawk or a panther when the first change was made. These creatures truly have nothing to do with the Children of the Moon. They have merely inherited this skill from their fathers. It's genetic—they do not continue their species by infecting others the way true werewolves do."

Caius glared at Aro with irritation and something more—an accusation of betrayal, maybe.

"They know our secret," he said flatly.

Edward looked about to answer this accusation, but Aro spoke faster. "They are creatures of our supernatural world, brother. Perhaps even more dependant upon secrecy than we are; they can hardly expose us. Carefully, Caius. Specious allegations get us nowhere."

Caius took a deep breath and nodded. They exchanged a long, significant glance.

I thought I understood the instruction behind Aro's careful wording. False charges weren't helping convince the watching witnesses on either side; Aro was cautioning Caius to move on to the next strategy. I wondered if the reason behind the apparent strain between the two ancients— Caius's unwillingness to share his thoughts with a touch— was that Caius didn't care about the show as much as Aro did. If the coming slaughter was so much more essential to Caius than an untarnished reputation.

"I want to talk to the informant," Caius announced abruptly, and turned his glare on Irina.

Irina wasn't paying attention to Caius and Aro's conversation; her face was twisted in agony, her eyes locked on her sisters, lined up to die. It was clear on her face that she knew now her accusation had been totally false.

"Irina," Caius barked, unhappy to have to address her.

She looked up, startled and instantly afraid.

Caius snapped his fingers.

Hesitantly, she moved from the fringes of the Volturi formation to stand in front of Caius again.

"So you appear to have been quite mistaken in your allegations," Caius began.

Tanya and Kate leaned forward anxiously.

"I'm sorry," Irina whispered. "I should have made sure of what I was seeing. But I had no idea. . . ." She gestured helplessly in our direction.

"Dear Caius, could you expect her to have guessed in an instant something so strange and impossible?" Aro asked. "Any of us would have made the same assumption."

Caius flicked his fingers at Aro to silence him.

"We all know you made a mistake," he said brusquely. "I meant to speak of your motivations."

Irina waited nervously for him to continue, and then repeated, "My motivations?"

"Yes, for coming to spy on them in the first place."

Irina flinched at the word *spy*.

"You were unhappy with the Cullens, were you not?"

She turned her miserable eyes to Carlisle's face. "I was," she admitted.

"Because . . . ?" Caius prompted.

"Because the werewolves killed my friend," she whispered. "And the Cullens wouldn't stand aside to let me avenge him."

"The shape-shifters," Aro corrected quietly.

"So the Cullens sided with the *shape-shifters* against our own kind—against the friend of a friend, even," Caius summarized.

I heard Edward make a disgusted sound under his breath.

Caius was ticking down his list, looking for an accusation that would stick.

Irina's shoulders stiffened. "That's how I saw it."

Caius waited again and then prompted, "If you'd like to make a formal complaint against the shape-shifters—and the Cullens for supporting their actions—now would be the time." He smiled a tiny cruel smile, waiting for Irina to give him his next excuse.

Maybe Caius didn't understand real families— relationships based on love rather than just the love of power. Maybe he overestimated the potency of vengeance.

Irina's jaw jerked up, her shoulders squared.

"No, I have no complaint against the wolves, or the Cullens. You came here today to destroy an immortal child. No immortal child exists. This was my mistake, and I take full responsibility for it. But the Cullens are innocent, and you have no reason to still be here. I'm so sorry," she said to us, and then she turned her face toward the Volturi witnesses. "There was no crime. There's no valid reason for you to continue here."

Caius raised his hand as she spoke, and in it was a strange metal object, carved and ornate.

This was a signal. The response was so fast that we all stared in stunned disbelief while it happened. Before there was time to react, it was over.

Three of the Volturi soldiers leaped forward, and Irina was completely obscured by their gray cloaks. In the same instant, a horrible metallic screeching ripped through the clearing. Caius slithered into the center of the gray melee, and the shocking squealing sound exploded into a startling upward shower of sparks and tongues of flame. The soldiers leaped back from the sudden inferno, immediately retaking their places in the guard's perfectly straight line.

Caius stood alone beside the blazing remains of Irina, the metal object in his hand still throwing a thick jet of flame into the pyre.

With a small clicking sound, the fire shooting from Caius's hand disappeared. A gasp rippled through the mass of witnesses behind the Volturi.

We were too aghast to make any noise at all. It was one thing to know that death was coming with fierce, unstoppable speed; it was another thing to watch it happen.

Caius smiled coldly. "*Now* she has taken full responsibility for her actions."

His eyes flashed to our front line, touching swiftly on Tanya's and Kate's frozen forms.

In that second I understood that Caius had never underestimated the ties of a true family. *This* was the ploy. He had not wanted Irina's complaint; he had wanted her defiance. His excuse to destroy her, to ignite the violence that filled the air like a thick, combustible mist. He had thrown a match.

The strained peace of this summit already teetered more precariously than an elephant on a tightrope. Once the fight began, there would be no way to stop it. It would only escalate until one side was entirely extinct. Our side. Caius knew this.

So did Edward.

"Stop them!" Edward cried out, jumping to grab Tanya's arm as she lurched forward toward the smiling Caius with a maddened cry of pure rage. She couldn't shake Edward off before Carlisle had his arms locked around her waist.

"It's too late to help her," he reasoned urgently as she struggled. "Don't give him what he wants!"

Kate was harder to contain. Shrieking wordlessly like Tanya, she broke into the first stride of the attack that would end with everyone's death. Rosalie was closest to her, but before Rose could clinch her in a headlock, Kate shocked her so violently that Rose crumpled to the ground. Emmett caught Kate's arm and threw her down, then staggered back, his knees giving out. Kate rolled to her feet, and it looked like no one could stop her.

Garrett flung himself at her, knocking her to the ground again. He bound his arms around hers, locking his hands around his own wrists. I saw his body spasm as she shocked him. His eyes rolled back in his head, but his hold did not break.

"Zafrina," Edward shouted.

Kate's eyes went blank and her screams turned to moans. Tanya stopped struggling.

"Give me my sight back," Tanya hissed.

Desperately, but with all the delicacy I could manage, I pulled my shield even tighter against the sparks of my friends, peeling it back carefully from Kate while trying to keep it around Garrett, making it a thin skin between them.

And then Garrett was in command of himself again, holding Kate to the snow.

"If I let you up, will you knock me down again, Katie?" he whispered.

She snarled in response, still thrashing blindly.

"Listen to me, Tanya, Kate," Carlisle said in a low but intense whisper. "Vengeance doesn't help her now. Irina wouldn't want you to waste your lives this way. Think about what you're doing. If you attack them, we all die."

Tanya's shoulders hunched with grief, and she leaned into Carlisle for support. Kate was finally still. Carlisle and Garrett continued to console the sisters with words too urgent to sound like comfort.

And my attention returned to the weight of the stares that pressed down on our moment of chaos. From the corners of my eyes, I could see that Edward and everyone else besides Carlisle and Garrett were on their guard again as well.

The heaviest glare came from Caius, staring with enraged disbelief at Kate and Garrett in the snow. Aro was watching the same two, incredulity the strongest emotion on his face. He knew what Kate could do. He had felt her potency through Edward's memories.

Did he understand what was happening now—did he see that my shield had grown in strength and subtlety far beyond what Edward knew me to be capable of? Or did he think Garrett had learned his own form of immunity?

The Volturi guard no longer stood at disciplined attention—they were crouched forward, waiting to spring the counterstrike the moment we attacked.

Behind them, forty-three witnesses watched with very different expressions than the ones they'd worn entering the clearing. Confusion had turned to suspicion. The lightning-fast destruction of Irina had shaken them all. What had been her crime?

Without the immediate attack that Caius had counted on to distract from his rash act, the Volturi witnesses were left questioning exactly what was going on here. Aro glanced back swiftly while I watched, his face betraying him with one flash of vexation. His need for an audience had backfired badly.

I heard Stefan and Vladimir murmur to each other in quiet glee at Aro's discomfort.

Aro was obviously concerned with keeping his white hat, as the Romanians had put it. But I didn't believe that the Volturi would leave us in peace just to save their reputation. After they finished with us, surely they would slaughter their witnesses for that purpose. I felt a strange, sudden pity for the mass of the strangers the Volturi had brought to watch us die. Demetri would hunt them until they were extinct, too.

For Jacob and Renesmee, for Alice and Jasper, for Alistair, and for these strangers who had not known what today would cost them, Demetri had to die.

Aro touched Caius's shoulder lightly. "Irina has been punished for bearing false witness against this child." So that was to be their excuse. He went on. "Perhaps we should return to the matter at hand?"

Caius straightened, and his expression hardened into unreadability. He stared forward, seeing nothing. His face reminded me, oddly, of a person who'd just learned he'd been demoted.

Aro drifted forward, Renata, Felix, and Demetri automatically moving with him.

"Just to be thorough," he said, "I'd like to speak with a few of your witnesses. Procedure, you know." He waved a hand dismissively.

Two things happened at once. Caius's eyes focused on Aro, and the tiny cruel smile came back. And Edward hissed, his hands balling up in fists so tight it looked like the bones in his knuckles would split through his diamond-hard skin.

I was desperate to ask him what was going on, but Aro was close enough to hear even the quietest breath. I saw Carlisle glance anxiously at Edward's face, and then his own face hardened.

While Caius had blundered through useless accusations and injudicious attempts to trigger the fight, Aro must have been coming up with a more effective strategy.

Aro ghosted across the snow to the far western end of our line, stopping about ten yards from Amun and Kebi. The nearby wolves bristled angrily but held their positions.

"Ah, Amun, my southern neighbor!" Aro said warmly. "It has been so long since you've visited me."

Amun was motionless with anxiety, Kebi a statue at his side. "Time means little; I never notice its passing," Amun said through unmoving lips.

"So true," Aro agreed. "But maybe you had another reason to stay away?"

Amun said nothing.

"It can be terribly time-consuming to organize newcomers into a coven. I know that well! I'm grateful I have others to deal with the tedium. I'm glad your new additions have fit in so well. I would have loved to have been introduced. I'm sure you were meaning to come to see me soon."

"Of course," Amun said, his tone so emotionless that it was impossible to tell if there was any fear or sarcasm in his assent.

"Oh well, we're all together now! Isn't it lovely?"

Amun nodded, his face blank.

"But the reason for your presence here is not as pleasant, unfortunately. Carlisle called on you to witness?"

"Yes."

"And what did you witness for him?"

Amun spoke with the same cold lack of emotion. "I've observed the child in question. It was evident almost immediately that she was not an immortal child—"

"Perhaps we should define our terminology," Aro interrupted, "now that there seem to be new classifications. By immortal child, you mean of course a human child who had been bitten and thus transformed into a vampire."

"Yes, that's what I meant."

"What else did you observe about the child?"

"The same things that you surely saw in Edward's mind. That the child is his biologically. That she grows. That she learns."

"Yes, yes," Aro said, a hint of impatience in his otherwise amiable tone. "But specifically in your few weeks here, what did you see?"

Amun's brow furrowed. "That she grows . . . quickly."

Aro smiled. "And do you believe that she should be allowed to live?"

A hiss escaped my lips, and I was not alone. Half the vampires in our line echoed my protest. The sound was a low sizzle of fury hanging in the air. Across the meadow, a few of the Volturi witnesses made the same noise. Edward stepped back and wrapped a restraining hand around my wrist.

Aro did not turn to the noise, but Amun glanced around uneasily.

"I did not come to make judgments," he equivocated.

Aro laughed lightly. "Just your opinion."

Amun's chin lifted. "I see no danger in the child. She learns even more swiftly than she grows."

Aro nodded, considering. After a moment, he turned away.

"Aro?" Amun called.

Aro whirled back. "Yes, friend?"

"I gave my witness. I have no more business here. My mate and I would like to take our leave now."

Aro smiled warmly. "Of course. I'm so glad we were able to chat for a bit. And I'm sure we'll see each other again soon."

Amun's lips were a tight line as he inclined his head once, acknowledging the barely concealed threat. He touched Kebi's arm, and then the two of them ran quickly to the southern edge of the meadow and disappeared into the trees. I knew they wouldn't stop running for a very long time.

Aro was gliding back along the length of our line to the east, his guards hovering tensely. He stopped when he was in front of Siobhan's massive form.

"Hello, dear Siobhan. You are as lovely as ever."

Siobhan inclined her head, waiting.

"And you?" he asked. "Would you answer my questions the same way Amun has?"

"I would," Siobhan said. "But I would perhaps add a little more. Renesmee understands the limitations. She's no danger to humans—she blends in better than we do. She poses no threat of exposure."

"Can you think of none?" Aro asked soberly.

Edward growled, a low ripping sound deep in his throat.

Caius's cloudy crimson eyes brightened.

Renata reached out protectively toward her master.

And Garrett freed Kate to take a step forward, ignoring Kate's hand as she tried to caution him this time.

Siobhan answered slowly, "I don't think I follow you."

Aro drifted lightly back, casually, but toward the rest of his guard. Renata, Felix, and Demetri were closer than his shadow.

"There is no broken law," Aro said in a placating voice, but every one of us could hear that a qualification was coming. I fought back the rage that tried to claw its way up my throat and snarl out my defiance. I hurled the fury into my shield, thickening it, making sure everyone was protected.

"No broken law," Aro repeated. "However, does it follow then that there is no danger? No." He shook his head gently. "That is a separate issue."

The only response was the tightening of already stretched nerves, and Maggie, at the fringes of our band of fighters, shaking her head with slow anger.

Aro paced thoughtfully, looking as if he floated rather than touched the ground with his feet. I noticed every pass took him closer to the protection of his guard.

"She is unique . . . utterly, impossibly unique. Such a waste it would be, to destroy something so lovely. Especially when we could learn so much . . ." He sighed, as if unwilling to go on. "But there *is* danger, danger that cannot simply be ignored."

No one answered his assertion. It was dead silent as he continued in a monologue that sounded as if he spoke it for himself only.

"How ironic it is that as the humans advance, as their

faith in science grows and controls their world, the more free we are from discovery. Yet, as we become ever more uninhibited by their disbelief in the supernatural, they become strong enough in their technologies that, if they wished, they could actually pose a threat to us, even destroy some of us.

"For thousands and thousands of years, our secrecy has been more a matter of convenience, of ease, than of actual safety. This last raw, angry century has given birth to weapons of such power that they endanger even immortals. Now our status as mere myth in truth protects us from these weak creatures we hunt.

"This amazing child"—he lifted his hand palm down as if to rest it on Renesmee, though he was forty yards from her now, almost within the Volturi formation again—"if we could but know her potential—know with *absolute certainty* that she could always remain shrouded within the obscurity that protects us. But we know nothing of what she will become! Her own parents are plagued by fears of her future. We *cannot* know what she will grow to be." He paused, looking first at our witnesses, and then, meaningfully, at his own. His voice gave a good imitation of sounding torn by his words.

Still looking at his own witnesses, he spoke again. "Only the known is safe. Only the known is tolerable. The unknown is . . . a vulnerability."

Caius's smile widened viciously.

"You're reaching, Aro," Carlisle said in a bleak voice.

"Peace, friend." Aro smiled, his face as kind, his voice as gentle, as ever. "Let us not be hasty. Let us look at this from every side."

"May I offer a side to be considered?" Garrett petitioned in a level tone, taking another step forward.

"Nomad," Aro said, nodding in permission.

Garrett's chin lifted. His eyes focused on the huddled mass at the end of the meadow, and he spoke directly to the Volturi witnesses.

"I came here at Carlisle's request, as the others, to witness," he said. "That is certainly no longer necessary, with regard to the child. We all see what she is.

"I stayed to witness something else. You." He jabbed his finger toward the wary vampires. "Two of you I know— Makenna, Charles—and I can see that many of you others are also wanderers, roamers like myself. Answering to none. Think carefully on what I tell you now.

"These ancient ones did *not* come here for justice as they told you. We suspected as much, and now it has been proved. They came, misled, but with a valid excuse for their action. Witness now as they seek flimsy excuses to continue their true mission. Witness them struggle to find a justification for their true purpose—to destroy this family here." He gestured toward Carlisle and Tanya.

"The Volturi come to erase what they perceive as the competition. Perhaps, like me, you look at this clan's golden eyes and marvel. They are difficult to understand, it's true. But the ancient ones look and see something besides their strange choice. They see *power*.

"I have witnessed the bonds within this family—I say *family* and not *coven*. These strange golden-eyed ones deny their very natures. But in return have they found something worth even more, perhaps, than mere gratification of desire? I've made a little study of them in my time here, and it seems to me that intrinsic to this intense family binding—that which makes them possible at all—is the peaceful character of this life of sacrifice. There is no aggression here like we all saw in the large southern clans that grew and diminished so quickly in their wild feuds. There is no thought for domination. And Aro knows this better than I do."

I watched Aro's face as Garrett's words condemned him, waiting tensely for some response. But Aro's face was only politely amused, as if waiting for a tantrum-throwing child to realize that no one was paying attention to his histrionics.

"Carlisle assured us all, when he told us what was coming, that he did not call us here to fight. These witnesses"—Garrett pointed to Siobhan and Liam—"agreed to give evidence, to slow the Volturi advance with their presence so that Carlisle would get the chance to present his case.

"But some of us wondered"—his eyes flashed to Eleazar's face—"if Carlisle having truth on his side would be enough to stop the so-called justice. Are the Volturi here to protect the safety of our secrecy, or to protect their own power? Did they come to destroy an illegal creation, or a way of life? Could they be satisfied when the danger turned out to be no more than a misunderstanding? Or would they push the issue without the excuse of justice?

"We have the answer to all these questions. We heard it in Aro's lying words—we have one with a gift of knowing such things for certain—and we see it now in Caius's eager smile. Their guard is just a mindless weapon, a tool in their masters' quest for domination.

"So now there are more questions, questions that *you* must answer. Who rules you, nomads? Do you answer to someone's will besides your own? Are you free to choose your path, or will the Volturi decide how you will live?

"I came to witness. I stay to fight. The Volturi care nothing for the death of the child. They seek the death of our free will."

He turned, then, to face the ancients. "So come, I say! Let's hear no more lying rationalizations. Be honest in your intents as we will be honest in ours. We will defend our freedom. You will or will not attack it. Choose now, and let these witnesses see the true issue debated here."

Once more he looked to the Volturi witnesses, his eyes probing each face. The power of his words was evident in their expressions. "You might consider joining us. If you think the Volturi will let you live to tell *this* tale, you are mistaken. We may all be destroyed"—he shrugged—"but then again, maybe not. Perhaps we are on more equal footing than they know. Perhaps the Volturi have finally met their match. I promise you this, though—if we fall, so do you."

He ended his heated speech by stepping back to Kate's side and then sliding forward in a half-crouch, prepared for the onslaught.

Aro smiled. "A very pretty speech, my revolutionary friend."

Garrett remained poised for attack. "Revolutionary?" he growled. "Who am I revolting against, might I ask? Are you my king? Do you wish me to call you *master*, too, like your sycophantic guard?"

"Peace, Garrett," Aro said tolerantly. "I meant only to refer to your time of birth. Still a patriot, I see."

Garrett glared back furiously.

"Let us ask our witnesses," Aro suggested. "Let us hear their thoughts before we make our decision. Tell us, friends"—and he turned his back casually on us, moving a few yards toward his mass of nervous observers hovering even closer now to the edge of the forest—"what do you think of all this? I can assure you the child is not what we feared. Do we take the risk and let the child live? Do we put our world in jeopardy to preserve their family intact? Or does earnest Garrett have the right of it? Will you join them in a fight against our sudden quest for dominion?"

The witnesses met his gaze with careful faces. One, a small black-haired woman, looked briefly at the dark blond male at her side.

"Are those our only choices?" she asked suddenly, gaze flashing back to Aro. "Agree with you, or fight against you?"

"Of course not, most charming Makenna," Aro said, appearing horrified that anyone could come to that conclusion. "You may go in peace, of course, as Amun did, even if you disagree with the council's decision."

Makenna looked at her mate's face again, and he nodded minutely.

"We did not come here for a fight." She paused, exhaled, then said, "We came here to witness. And our witness is that this condemned family is innocent. Everything that Garrett claimed is the truth."

"Ah," Aro said sadly. "I'm sorry you see us in that way. But such is the nature of our work."

"It is not what I see, but what I feel," Makenna's maize-haired mate spoke in a high, nervous voice. He glanced at Garrett. "Garrett said they have ways of knowing lies. I, too, know when I am hearing the truth, and when I am not." With frightened eyes he moved closer to his mate, waiting for Aro's reaction.

"Do not fear us, friend Charles. No doubt the patriot truly believes what he says," Aro chuckled lightly, and Charles's eyes narrowed.

"That is our witness," Makenna said. "We're leaving now."

She and Charles backed away slowly, not turning before they were lost from view in the trees. One other stranger began to retreat the same way, then three more darted after him.

I evaluated the thirty-seven vampires that stayed. A few of them appeared just too confused to make the decision. But the majority of them seemed only too aware of the direction this confrontation had taken. I guessed that they were giving up a head start in favor of knowing exactly who would be chasing after them.

I was sure Aro saw the same thing I did. He turned away, walking back to his guard with a measured pace. He stopped in front of them and addressed them in a clear voice.

"We are outnumbered, dearest ones," he said. "We can expect no outside help. Should we leave this question undecided to save ourselves?"

"No, master," they whispered in unison.

"Is the protection of our world worth perhaps the loss of some of our number?"

"Yes," they breathed. "We are not afraid."

Aro smiled and turned to his black-clad companions.

"Brothers," Aro said somberly, "there is much to consider here."

"Let us counsel," Caius said eagerly.

"Let us counsel," Marcus repeated in an uninterested tone.

Aro turned his back to us again, facing the other ancients. They joined hands to form a black-shrouded triangle.

As soon as Aro's attention was engaged in the silent counsel, two more of their witnesses disappeared silently into the forest. I hoped, for their sakes, that they were fast.

This was it. Carefully, I loosened Renesmee's arms from my neck.

"You remember what I told you?"

Tears welled in her eyes, but she nodded. "I love you," she whispered.

Edward was watching us now, his topaz eyes wide. Jacob stared at us from the corner of his big dark eye.

"I love you, too," I said, and then I touched her locket. "More than my own life." I kissed her forehead.

Jacob whined uneasily.

I stretched up on my toes and whispered into his ear. "Wait until they're totally distracted, then run with her. Get as far from this place as you possibly can. When you've gone as far as you can on foot, she has what you need to get you in the air."

Edward's and Jacob's faces were almost identical masks of horror, despite the fact that one of them was an animal.

Renesmee reached for Edward, and he took her in his arms. They hugged each other tightly.

"This is what you kept from me?" he whispered over her head.

"From Aro," I breathed.

"Alice?"

I nodded.

His face twisted with understanding and pain. Had that been the expression on my face when I'd finally put together Alice's clues?

Jacob was growling quietly, a low rasp that was as even and unbroken as a purr. His hackles were stiff and his teeth exposed.

Edward kissed Renesmee's forehead and both her cheeks, then he lifted her to Jacob's shoulder. She scrambled agilely onto his back, pulling herself into place with handfuls of his fur, and fit herself easily into the dip between his massive shoulder blades.

Jacob turned to me, his expressive eyes full of agony, the rumbling growl still grating through his chest.

"You're the only one we could ever trust her with," I murmured to him. "If you didn't love her so much, I could never bear this. I know you can protect her, Jacob."

He whined again, and dipped his head to butt it against my shoulder.

"I know," I whispered. "I love you, too, Jake. You'll always be my best man."

A tear the size of a baseball rolled into the russet fur beneath his eye.

Edward leaned his head against the same shoulder where he'd placed Renesmee. "Goodbye, Jacob, my brother . . . my son."

The others were not oblivious to the farewell scene. Their eyes were locked on the silent black triangle, but I could tell they were listening.

"Is there no hope, then?" Carlisle whispered. There was no fear in his voice. Just determination and acceptance.

"There is absolutely hope," I murmured back. *It could be true,* I told myself. "I only know my own fate."

Edward took my hand. He knew that he was included. When I said *my fate*, there was no question that I meant the two of us. We were just halves of the whole.

Esme's breath was ragged behind me. She moved past us, touching our faces as she passed, to stand beside Carlisle and hold his hand.

Suddenly, we were surrounded by murmured goodbyes and I love you's.

"If we live through this," Garrett whispered to Kate, "I'll follow you anywhere, woman."

"Now he tells me," she muttered.

Rosalie and Emmett kissed quickly but passionately.

Tia caressed Benjamin's face. He smiled back cheerfully, catching her hand and holding it against his cheek.

I didn't see all the expressions of love and pain. I was distracted by a sudden fluttering pressure against the outside of my shield. I couldn't tell where it came from, but it felt like it was directed at the edges of our group, Siobhan and Liam particularly. The pressure did no damage, and then it was gone.

There was no change in the silent, still forms of the counseling ancients. But perhaps there was some signal I'd missed.

"Get ready," I whispered to the others. "It's starting."

38. POWER

"CHELSEA IS TRYING TO BREAK OUR BINDINGS," EDWARD whispered. "But she can't find them. She can't feel us here. . . ." His eyes cut to me. "Are you doing that?"

I smiled grimly at him. "I am *all* over this."

Edward lurched away from me suddenly, his hand reaching out toward Carlisle. At the same time, I felt a much sharper jab against the shield where it wrapped protectively around Carlisle's light. It wasn't painful, but it wasn't pleasant, either.

"Carlisle? Are you all right?" Edward gasped frantically.

"Yes. Why?"

"Jane," Edward answered.

The moment that he said her name, a dozen pointed attacks hit in a second, stabbing all over the elastic shield, aimed at twelve different bright spots. I flexed, making sure the shield was undamaged. It didn't seem like Jane had been able to pierce it. I glanced around quickly; everyone was fine.

"Incredible," Edward said.

"Why aren't they waiting for the decision?" Tanya hissed.

"Normal procedure," Edward answered brusquely. "They usually incapacitate those on trial so they can't escape."

I looked across at Jane, who was staring at our group with furious disbelief. I was pretty sure that, besides me, she'd never seen anyone remain standing through her fiery assault.

It probably wasn't very mature. But I figured it would take Aro about half a second to guess—if he hadn't already—that my shield was more powerful than Edward had known; I already had a big target on my forehead and there was really no point in trying to keep the extent of what I could do a secret. So I grinned a huge, smug smile right at Jane.

Her eyes narrowed, and I felt another stab of pressure, this time directed at me.

I pulled my lips wider, showing my teeth.

Jane let out a high-pitched scream of a snarl. Everyone jumped, even the disciplined guard. Everyone but the ancients, who didn't so much as look up from their conference. Her twin caught her arm as she crouched to spring.

The Romanians started chuckling with dark anticipation.

"I told you this was our time," Vladimir said to Stefan.

"Just look at the witch's face," Stefan chortled.

Alec patted his sister's shoulder soothingly, then tucked her under his arm. He turned his face to us, perfectly smooth, completely angelic.

I waited for some pressure, some sign of his attack, but I felt nothing. He continued to stare in our direction, his pretty face composed. Was he attacking? Was he getting through my shield? Was I the only one who could still see him? I clutched at Edward's hand.

"Are you okay?" I choked out.

"Yes," he whispered.

"Is Alec trying?"

Edward nodded. "His gift is slower than Jane's. It creeps. It will touch us in a few seconds."

I saw it then, when I had a clue of what to look for.

A strange clear haze was oozing across the snow, nearly invisible against the white. It reminded me of a mirage—a slight warping of the view, a hint of a shimmer. I pushed my shield out from Carlisle and the rest of the front line, afraid to have the slinking mist too close when it hit. What if it stole right through my intangible protection? Should we run?

A low rumbling murmured through the ground under our feet, and a gust of wind blew the snow into sudden flurries between our position and the Volturi's. Benjamin had seen the creeping threat, too, and now he tried to blow the mist away from us. The snow made it easy to see where he threw the wind, but the mist didn't react in any way. It was like air blowing harmlessly through a shadow; the shadow was immune.

The triangular formation of the ancients finally broke apart when, with a racking groan, a deep, narrow fissure opened in a long zigzag across the middle of the clearing. The earth rocked under my feet for a moment. The drifts of snow plummeted into the hole, but the mist skipped right across it, as untouched by gravity as it had been by wind.

Aro and Caius watched the opening earth with wide eyes. Marcus looked in the same direction without emotion.

They didn't speak; they waited, too, as the mist approached us. The wind shrieked louder but didn't change the course of the mist. Jane was smiling now.

And then the mist hit a wall.

I could taste it as soon as it touched my shield—it had a dense, sweet, cloying flavor. It made me remember dimly the numbness of Novocain on my tongue.

The mist curled upward, seeking a breach, a weakness. It found none. The fingers of searching haze twisted upward and around, trying to find a way in, and in the process illustrating the astonishing size of the protective screen.

There were gasps on both sides of Benjamin's gorge.

"Well done, Bella!" Benjamin cheered in a low voice.

My smile returned.

I could see Alec's narrowed eyes, doubt on his face for the first time as his mist swirled harmlessly around the edges of my shield.

And then I knew that I could do this. Obviously, I would be the number-one priority, the first one to die, but as long as I held, we were on more than equal footing with the Volturi. We still had Benjamin and Zafrina; they had no supernatural help at all. As long as I held.

"I'm going to have to concentrate," I whispered to

Edward. "When it comes to hand to hand, it's going to be harder to keep the shield around the right people."

"I'll keep them off you."

"No. You *have* to get to Demetri. Zafrina will keep them away from me."

Zafrina nodded solemnly. "No one will touch this young one," she promised Edward.

"I'd go after Jane and Alec myself, but I can do more good here."

"Jane's mine," Kate hissed. "She needs a taste of her own medicine."

"And Alec owes me many lives, but I will settle for his," Vladimir growled from the other side. "He's mine."

"I just want Caius," Tanya said evenly.

The others started divvying up opponents, too, but they were quickly interrupted.

Aro, staring calmly at Alec's ineffective mist, finally spoke.

"Before we vote," he began.

I shook my head angrily. I was tired of this charade. The bloodlust was igniting in me again, and I was sorry that I would help the others more by standing still. I *wanted* to fight.

"Let me remind you," Aro continued, "whatever the council's decision, there need be no violence here."

Edward snarled out a dark laugh.

Aro stared at him sadly. "It will be a regrettable waste to our kind to lose any of you. But you especially, young Edward, and your newborn mate. The Volturi would be glad to welcome many of you into our ranks. Bella, Benjamin, Zafrina, Kate. There are many choices before you. Consider them."

Chelsea's attempt to sway us fluttered impotently against my shield. Aro's gaze swept across our hard eyes, looking for any indication of hesitation. From his expression, he found none.

I knew he was desperate to keep Edward and me, to imprison us the way he had hoped to enslave Alice. But this fight was too big. He would not win if I lived. I was fiercely glad to be so powerful that I left him no way *not* to kill me.

"Let us vote, then," he said with apparent reluctance.

Caius spoke with eager haste. "The child is an unknown quantity. There is no reason to allow such a risk to exist. It must be destroyed, along with all who protect it." He smiled in expectation.

I fought back a shriek of defiance to answer his cruel smirk.

Marcus lifted his uncaring eyes, seeming to look through us as he voted.

"I see no immediate danger. The child is safe enough for now. We can always reevaluate later. Let us leave in peace." His voice was even fainter than his brothers' feathery sighs.

None of the guard relaxed their ready positions at his disagreeing words. Caius's anticipatory grin did not falter. It was as if Marcus hadn't spoken at all.

"I must make the deciding vote, it seems," Aro mused.

Suddenly, Edward stiffened at my side. "Yes!" he hissed.

I risked a glance at him. His face glowed with an expression of triumph that I didn't understand—it was the expression an angel of destruction might wear while the world burned. Beautiful and terrifying.

There was a low reaction from the guard, an uneasy murmur.

"Aro?" Edward called, nearly shouted, undisguised victory in his voice.

Aro hesitated for a second, assessing this new mood warily before he answered. "Yes, Edward? You have something further . . . ?"

"Perhaps," Edward said pleasantly, controlling his unexplained excitement. "First, if I could clarify one point?"

"Certainly," Aro said, raising his eyebrows, nothing now but polite interest in his tone. My teeth ground together; Aro was never more dangerous than when he was gracious.

"The danger you foresee from my daughter—this stems entirely from our inability to guess how she will develop? That is the crux of the matter?"

"Yes, friend Edward," Aro agreed. "If we could but be positive . . . be *sure* that, as she grows, she will be able to stay concealed from the human world—not endanger the safety of our obscurity . . ." He trailed off, shrugging.

"So, if we could only know for sure," Edward suggested, "exactly what she will become . . . then there would be no need for a council at all?"

"If there was some way to be *absolutely* sure," Aro agreed, his feathery voice slightly more shrill. He couldn't see where Edward was leading him. Neither could I. "Then, yes, there would be no question to debate."

"And we would part in peace, good friends once again?" Edward asked with a hint of irony.

Even more shrill. "Of course, my young friend. Nothing would please me more."

Edward chuckled exultantly. "Then I do have something more to offer."

Aro's eyes narrowed. "She is absolutely unique. Her future can only be guessed at."

"Not absolutely unique," Edward disagreed. "Rare, certainly, but not one of a kind."

I fought the shock, the sudden hope springing to life, as it threatened to distract me. The sickly-looking mist still swirled around the edges of my shield. And, as I struggled to focus, I felt again the sharp, stabbing pressure against my protective hold.

"Aro, would you ask Jane to stop attacking my wife?" Edward asked courteously. "We are still discussing evidence."

Aro raised one hand. "Peace, dear ones. Let us hear him out."

The pressure disappeared. Jane bared her teeth at me; I couldn't help grinning back at her.

"Why don't you join us, Alice?" Edward called loudly.

"Alice," Esme whispered in shock.

Alice!

Alice, Alice, Alice!

"Alice!" "Alice!" other voices murmured around me.

"Alice," Aro breathed.

Relief and violent joy surged through me. It took all my will to keep the shield where it was. Alec's mist still tested, seeking a weakness—Jane would see if I left any holes.

And then I heard them running through the forest, flying, closing the distance as quickly as they could with no slowing effort at silence.

Both sides were motionless in expectation. The Volturi witnesses scowled in fresh confusion.

Then Alice danced into the clearing from the southwest, and I felt like the bliss of seeing her face again might knock me off my feet. Jasper was only inches behind her, his sharp eyes fierce. Close after them ran three strangers; the first was a tall, muscular female with wild dark hair—obviously Kachiri. She had the same elongated limbs and features as the other Amazons, even more pronounced in her case.

The next was a small olive-toned female vampire with a long braid of black hair bobbing against her back. Her deep burgundy eyes flitted nervously around the confrontation before her.

And the last was a young man . . . not quite as fast nor quite as fluid in his run. His skin was an impossible rich, dark brown. His wary eyes flashed across the gathering, and they were the color of warm teak. His hair was black and braided, too, like the woman's, though not as long. He was beautiful.

As he neared us, a new sound sent shock waves through the watching crowd—the sound of another heartbeat, accelerated with exertion.

Alice leaped lightly over the edges of the dissipating mist that lapped at my shield and came to a sinuous stop at Edward's side. I reached out to touch her arm, and so did Edward, Esme, Carlisle. There wasn't time for any other welcome. Jasper and the others followed her through the shield.

All the guard watched, speculation in their eyes, as the latecomers crossed the invisible border without difficulty. The brawny ones, Felix and the others like him, focused their suddenly hopeful eyes on me. They had not been sure of what my shield repelled, but it was clear now that it would not stop a physical attack. As soon as Aro gave the order, the blitz would ensue, me the only object. I wondered how many Zafrina would be able to blind, and how much that would slow them. Long enough for Kate and Vladimir to take Jane and Alec out of the equation? That was all I could ask for.

Edward, despite his absorption in the coup he was directing, stiffened furiously in response to their thoughts. He controlled himself and spoke to Aro again.

"Alice has been searching for her own witnesses these last weeks," he said to the ancient. "And she does not come back empty-handed. Alice, why don't you introduce the witnesses you've brought?"

Caius snarled. "The time for witnesses is past! Cast your vote, Aro!"

Aro raised one finger to silence his brother, his eyes glued to Alice's face.

Alice stepped forward lightly and introduced the strangers. "This is Huilen and her nephew, Nahuel."

Hearing her voice . . . it was like she'd never left.

Caius's eyes tightened as Alice named the relationship between the newcomers. The Volturi witnesses hissed amongst themselves. The vampire world was changing, and everyone could feel it.

"Speak, Huilen," Aro commanded. "Give us the witness you were brought to bear."

The slight woman looked to Alice nervously. Alice nodded in encouragement, and Kachiri put her long hand on the little vampire's shoulder.

"I am Huilen," the woman announced in clear but strangely accented English. As she continued, it was apparent she had prepared herself to tell this story, that she had practiced. It flowed like a well-known nursery rhyme. "A century and a half ago, I lived with my people, the Mapuche. My sister was Pire. Our parents named her after the snow on the mountains because of her fair skin. And she was very beautiful—too beautiful. She came to me one day in secret and told me of the angel that found her in the woods, that visited her by night. I warned her." Huilen shook her head mournfully. "As if the bruises on her skin were not warning enough. I knew it was the Libishomen of our legends, but she would not listen. She was bewitched.

"She told me when she was sure her dark angel's child was growing inside her. I didn't try to discourage her from her plan to run away—I knew even our father and mother would agree that the child must be destroyed, Pire with it. I went with her into the deepest parts of the forest. She searched for her demon angel but found nothing. I cared for her, hunted for her when her strength failed. She ate the animals raw, drinking their blood. I needed no more confirmation of what she carried in her womb. I hoped to save her life before I killed the monster.

"But she loved the child inside her. She called him Nahuel, after the jungle cat, when he grew strong and broke her bones—and loved him still.

"I could not save her. The child ripped his way free of her, and she died quickly, begging all the while that I would care for her Nahuel. Her dying wish—and I agreed.

"He bit me, though, when I tried to lift him from her

body. I crawled away into the jungle to die. I didn't get far—the pain was too much. But he found me; the newborn child struggled through the underbrush to my side and waited for me. When the pain ended, he was curled against my side, sleeping.

"I cared for him until he was able to hunt for himself. We hunted the villages around our forest, staying to ourselves. We have never come so far from our home, but Nahuel wished to see the child here."

Huilen bowed her head when she was finished and moved back so she was partially hidden behind Kachiri.

Aro's lips were pursed. He stared at the dark-skinned youth.

"Nahuel, you are one hundred and fifty years old?" he questioned.

"Give or take a decade," he answered in a clear, beautifully warm voice. His accent was barely noticeable. "We don't keep track."

"And you reached maturity at what age?"

"About seven years after my birth, more or less, I was full grown."

"You have not changed since then?"

Nahuel shrugged. "Not that I've noticed."

I felt a shudder tremble through Jacob's body. I didn't want to think about this yet. I would wait till the danger was past and I could concentrate.

"And your diet?" Aro pressed, seeming interested in spite of himself.

"Mostly blood, but some human food, too. I can survive on either."

"You were able to create an immortal?" As Aro gestured to Huilen, his voice was abruptly intense. I refocused on my shield; perhaps he was seeking a new excuse.

"Yes, but none of the rest can."

A shocked murmur ran through all three groups.

Aro's eyebrows shot up. "The rest?"

"My sisters." Nahuel shrugged again.

Aro stared wildly for a moment before composing his face.

"Perhaps you would tell us the rest of your story, for there seems to be more."

Nahuel frowned.

"My father came looking for me a few years after my mother's death." His handsome face distorted slightly. "He was pleased to find me." Nahuel's tone suggested the feeling was not mutual. "He had two daughters, but no sons. He expected me to join him, as my sisters had.

"He was surprised I was not alone. My sisters are not venomous, but whether that's due to gender or a random chance . . . who knows? I already had my family with Huilen, and I was not *interested*"—he twisted the word— "in making a change. I see him from time to time. I have a new sister; she reached maturity about ten years back."

"Your father's name?" Caius asked through gritted teeth.

"Joham," Nahuel answered. "He considers himself a scientist. He thinks he's creating a new super-race." He made no attempt to disguise the disgust in his tone.

Caius looked at me. "Your daughter, is she venomous?" he demanded harshly.

"No," I responded. Nahuel's head snapped up at Aro's question, and his teak eyes turned to bore into my face.

Caius looked to Aro for confirmation, but Aro was absorbed in his own thoughts. He pursed his lips and stared at Carlisle, and then Edward, and at last his eyes rested on me.

Caius growled. "We take care of the aberration here, and then follow it south," he urged Aro.

Aro stared into my eyes for a long, tense moment. I had no idea what he was searching for, or what he found, but after he had measured me for that moment, something in his face changed, a faint shift in the set of his mouth and eyes, and I knew that Aro had made his decision.

"Brother," he said softly to Caius. "There appears to be no danger. This is an unusual development, but I see no threat. These half-vampire children are much like us, it appears."

"Is that your vote?" Caius demanded.

"It is."

Caius scowled. "And this Joham? This immortal so fond of experimentation?"

"Perhaps we *should* speak with him," Aro agreed.

"Stop Joham if you will," Nahuel said flatly. "But leave my sisters be. They are innocent."

Aro nodded, his expression solemn. And then he turned back to his guard with a warm smile.

"Dear ones," he called. "We do not fight today."

The guard nodded in unison and straightened out of their ready positions. The mist dissipated swiftly, but I held my shield in place. Maybe this was *another* trick.

I analyzed their expressions as Aro turned back to us. His face was as benign as ever, but unlike before, I sensed a strange blankness behind the façade. As if his scheming was over. Caius was clearly incensed, but his rage was turned inward now; he was resigned. Marcus looked . . . bored; there really was no other word for it. The guard was impassive and disciplined again; there were no individuals among them, just the whole. They were in formation, ready to depart. The Volturi witnesses were still wary; one after another, they departed, scattering into the woods. As their numbers dwindled, the remaining sped up. Soon they were all gone.

Aro held his hands out to us, almost apologetic. Behind him, the larger part of the guard, along with Caius, Marcus, and the silent, mysterious wives, were already drifting quickly away, their formation precise once again. Only the three that seemed to be his personal guardians lingered with him.

"I'm so glad this could be resolved without violence," he said sweetly. "My friend, Carlisle—how pleased I am to call you friend again! I hope there are no hard feelings. I know you understand the strict burden that our duty places on our shoulders."

"Leave in peace, Aro," Carlisle said stiffly. "Please remember that we still have our anonymity to protect here, and keep your guard from hunting in this region."

"Of course, Carlisle," Aro assured him. "I am sorry to earn your disapproval, my dear friend. Perhaps, in time, you will forgive me."

"Perhaps, in time, if you prove a friend to us again."

Aro bowed his head, the picture of remorse, and drifted backward for a moment before he turned around. We watched in silence as the last four Volturi disappeared into the trees.

It was very quiet. I did not drop my shield.

"Is it really over?" I whispered to Edward.

His smile was huge. "Yes. They've given up. Like all bullies, they're cowards underneath the swagger." He chuckled.

Alice laughed with him. "Seriously, people. They're not coming back. Everybody can relax now."

There was another beat of silence.

"Of all the rotten luck," Stefan muttered.

And then it hit.

Cheers erupted. Deafening howls filled the clearing. Maggie pounded Siobhan on the back. Rosalie and Emmett kissed again—longer and more ardently than before. Benjamin and Tia were locked in each other's arms, as were Carmen and Eleazar. Esme held Alice and Jasper in a tight embrace. Carlisle was warmly thanking the South American newcomers who had saved us all. Kachiri stood very close to Zafrina and Senna, their fingertips interlocked. Garrett picked Kate up off the ground and swung her around in a circle.

Stefan spit on the snow. Vladimir ground his teeth together with a sour expression.

And I half-climbed the giant russet wolf to rip my daughter off his back and then crushed her to my chest. Edward's arms were around us in the same second.

"Nessie, Nessie, Nessie," I crooned.

Jacob laughed his big, barky laugh and poked the back of my head with his nose.

"Shut up," I mumbled.

"I get to stay with you?" Nessie demanded.

"Forever," I promised her.

We had forever. And Nessie was going to be fine and healthy and strong. Like the half-human Nahuel, in a hundred and fifty years she would still be young. And we would all be together.

Happiness expanded like an explosion inside me—so extreme, so violent that I wasn't sure I'd survive it.

"Forever," Edward echoed in my ear.

I couldn't speak anymore. I lifted my head and kissed him with a passion that might possibly set the forest on fire.

I wouldn't have noticed.

39. THE HAPPILY EVER AFTER

"So it was a combination of things there at the end, but what it really boiled down to was . . . Bella," Edward was explaining. Our family and our two remaining guests sat in the Cullens' great room while the forest turned black outside the tall windows.

Vladimir and Stefan had vanished before we'd stopped celebrating. They were extremely disappointed in the way things had turned out, but Edward said that they'd enjoyed the Volturi's cowardice almost enough to make up for their frustration.

Benjamin and Tia were quick to follow after Amun and Kebi, anxious to let them know the outcome of the conflict; I was sure we would see them again—Benjamin and Tia, at least. None of the nomads lingered. Peter and Charlotte had a short conversation with Jasper, and then they were gone, too.

The reunited Amazons had been anxious to return home as well—they had a difficult time being away from their beloved rain forest—though they were more reluctant to leave than some of the others.

"You must bring the child to see me," Zafrina had insisted. "Promise me, young one."

Nessie had pressed her hand to my neck, pleading as well.

"Of course, Zafrina," I'd agreed.

"We shall be great friends, my Nessie," the wild woman had declared before leaving with her sisters.

The Irish coven continued the exodus.

"Well done, Siobhan," Carlisle complimented her as they said goodbye.

"Ah, the power of wishful thinking," she answered sarcastically, rolling her eyes. And then she was serious. "Of course, this isn't over. The Volturi won't forgive what happened here."

Edward was the one to answer that. "They've been seriously shaken; their confidence is shattered. But, yes, I'm sure they'll recover from the blow someday. And then . . ." His eyes tightened. "I imagine they'll try to pick us off separately."

"Alice will warn us when they intend to strike," Siobhan said in a sure voice. "And we'll gather again. Perhaps the time will come when our world is ready to be free of the Volturi altogether."

"That time may come," Carlisle replied. "If it does, we'll stand together."

"Yes, my friend, we will," Siobhan agreed. "And how can

we fail, when *I* will it otherwise?" She let out a great peal of laughter.

"Exactly," Carlisle said. He and Siobhan embraced, and then he shook Liam's hand. "Try to find Alistair and tell him what happened. I'd hate to think of him hiding under a rock for the next decade."

Siobhan laughed again. Maggie hugged both Nessie and me, and then the Irish coven was gone.

The Denalis were the last to leave, Garrett with them—as he would be from now on, I was fairly sure. The atmosphere of celebration was too much for Tanya and Kate. They needed time to grieve for their lost sister.

Huilen and Nahuel were the ones who stayed, though I had expected those last two to go back with the Amazons. Carlisle was deep in fascinated conversation with Huilen; Nahuel sat close beside her, listening while Edward told the rest of us the story of the conflict as only he knew it.

"Alice gave Aro the excuse he needed to get out of the fight. If he hadn't been so terrified of Bella, he probably would have gone ahead with their original plan."

"Terrified?" I said skeptically. "Of *me*?"

He smiled at me with a look I didn't entirely recognize—it was tender, but also awed and even exasperated. "When will you ever see yourself clearly?" he said softly. Then he spoke louder, to the others as well as to me. "The Volturi haven't fought a fair fight in about twenty-five hundred years. And they've never, never fought one where they were at a disadvantage. Especially since they gained Jane and Alec, they've only been involved with unopposed slaughterings.

"You should have seen how we looked to them! Usually, Alec cuts off all sense and feeling from their victims while they go through the charade of a counsel. That way, no one can run when the verdict is given. But there we stood, ready, waiting, outnumbering them, with gifts of our own while their gifts were rendered useless by Bella. Aro knew that with Zafrina on our side, they would be the blind ones when the battle commenced. I'm sure our numbers would have been pretty severely decimated, but *they* were sure that theirs would be, too. There was even a good possibility that they would lose. They've never dealt with that possibility before. They didn't deal with it well today."

"Hard to feel confident when you're surrounded by horse-sized wolves," Emmett laughed, poking Jacob's arm.

Jacob flashed a grin at him.

"It was the wolves that stopped them in the first place," I said.

"Sure was," Jacob agreed.

"Absolutely," Edward agreed. "That was another sight they've never seen. The true Children of the Moon rarely move in packs, and they are never much in control of themselves. Sixteen enormous regimented wolves was a surprise they weren't prepared for. Caius is actually terrified of werewolves. He almost lost a fight with one a few thousand years ago and never got over it."

"So there are *real* werewolves?" I asked. "With the full moon and silver bullets and all that?"

Jacob snorted. "*Real.* Does that make me imaginary?"

"You know what I mean."

"Full moon, yes," Edward said. "Silver bullets, no—that was just another one of those myths to make humans feel like they had a sporting chance. There aren't very many of them left. Caius has had them hunted into near extinction."

"And you never mentioned this because . . . ?"

"It never came up."

I rolled my eyes, and Alice laughed, leaning forward— she was tucked under Edward's other arm—to wink at me.

I glared back.

I loved her insanely, of course. But now that I'd had a chance to realize that she was really home, that her defection was only a ruse because Edward had to believe that she'd abandoned us, I was beginning to feel pretty irritated with her. Alice had some explaining to do.

Alice sighed. "Just get it off your chest, Bella."

"How could you do that to me, Alice?"

"It was necessary."

"Necessary!" I exploded. "You had me totally convinced that we were all going to die! I've been a wreck for weeks."

"It might have gone that way," she said calmly. "In which case you needed to be prepared to save Nessie."

Instinctively, I held Nessie—asleep now on my lap— tighter in my arms.

"But you knew there were other ways, too," I accused. "You knew there was hope. Did it ever occur to you that you could have told me everything? I know Edward had to think we were at a dead end for Aro's sake, but you could have told *me*."

She looked at me speculatively for a moment. "I don't think so," she said. "You're just not that good an actress."

"This was about my *acting skills*?"

"Oh, take it down an octave, Bella. Do you have any idea how *complicated* this was to set up? I couldn't even be sure that someone like Nahuel existed—all I knew was that I would be looking for something I couldn't see! Try to imagine searching for a blind spot—not the easiest thing I've ever done. Plus we had to send back the key witnesses, like we weren't in enough of a hurry. And then keeping my eyes open all the time in case you decided to throw me any more instructions. At some point you're going to have to tell me what exactly is in Rio. Before any of *that*, I had to try to see every trick the Volturi might come in with and give you what few clues I could so you would be ready for their strategy, and I only had just a few hours to trace out all the possibilities. Most of all, I had to make sure you'd all believe that I was ditching out on you, because Aro had to be positive that you had nothing left up your sleeves or he never would have committed to an out the way he did. And if you think I didn't feel like a schmuck—"

"Okay, okay!" I interrupted. "Sorry! I know it was rough for you, too. It's just that . . . well, I missed you like crazy, Alice. Don't do that to me again."

Alice's trilling laugh rang through the room, and we all smiled to hear that music once more. "I missed you, too, Bella. So forgive me, and try to be satisfied with being the superhero of the day."

Everyone else laughed now, and I ducked my face into Nessie's hair, embarrassed.

Edward went back to analyzing every shift of intention and control that had happened in the meadow today, declaring that it was my shield that had made the Volturi run away with their tails between their legs. The way everyone looked at me made me uncomfortable. Even Edward. It was like I had grown a hundred feet during the course of the morning. I tried to ignore the impressed looks, mostly keeping my eyes on Nessie's sleeping face and Jacob's unchanged expression. I would always be just Bella to him, and that was a relief.

The hardest stare to ignore was also the most confusing one.

It wasn't like this half-human, half-vampire Nahuel was used to thinking of me in a certain way. For all he knew, I went around routing attacking vampires every day and the scene in the meadow had been nothing unusual at all. But the boy never took his eyes off me. Or maybe he was looking at Nessie. That made me uncomfortable, too.

He couldn't be oblivious to the fact that Nessie was the only female of his kind that wasn't his half-sister.

I didn't think this idea had occurred to Jacob yet. I kind of hoped it wouldn't soon. I'd had enough fighting to last me for a while.

Eventually, the others ran out of questions for Edward, and the discussion dissolved into a bunch of smaller conversations.

I felt oddly tired. Not sleepy, of course, but just like the day had been long enough. I wanted some peace, some normality. I wanted Nessie in her own bed; I wanted the walls of my own little home around me.

I looked at Edward and felt for a moment like I could read *his* mind. I could see he felt exactly the same way. Ready for some peace.

"Should we take Nessie . . ."

"That's probably a good idea," he agreed quickly. "I'm sure she didn't sleep soundly last night, what with all the snoring."

He grinned at Jacob.

Jacob rolled his eyes and then yawned. "It's been a while

since I slept in a bed. I bet my dad would get a kick out of having me under his roof again."

I touched his cheek. "Thank you, Jacob."

"Anytime, Bella. But you already know that."

He got up, stretched, kissed the top of Nessie's head, and then the top of mine. Finally, he punched Edward's shoulder. "See you guys tomorrow. I guess things are going to be kind of boring now, aren't they?"

"I fervently hope so," Edward said.

We got up when he was gone; I shifted my weight carefully so that Nessie was never jostled. I was deeply grateful to see her getting a sound sleep. So much weight had been on her tiny shoulders. It was time she got to be a child again—protected and secure. A few more years of childhood.

The idea of peace and security reminded me of someone who didn't have those feelings all the time.

"Oh, Jasper?" I asked as we turned for the door.

Jasper was sandwiched tight in between Alice and Esme, somehow seeming more central to the family picture than usual. "Yes, Bella?"

"I'm curious—why is J. Jenks scared stiff by just the sound of your name?"

Jasper chuckled. "It's just been my experience that some kinds of working relationships are better motivated by fear than by monetary gain."

I frowned, promising myself that I would take over that working relationship from now on and spare J the heart attack that was surely on the way.

We were kissed and hugged and wished a good night to our family. The only off note was Nahuel again, who looked intently after us, as if he wished he could follow.

Once we were across the river, we walked barely faster than human speed, in no hurry, holding hands. I was sick of being under a deadline, and I just wanted to take my time. Edward must have felt the same.

"I have to say, I'm thoroughly impressed with Jacob right now," Edward told me.

"The wolves make quite an impact, don't they?"

"That's not what I mean. Not once today did he think about the fact that, according to Nahuel, Nessie will be fully matured in just six and a half years."

I considered that for a minute. "He doesn't see her that way. He's not in a hurry for her to grow up. He just wants her to be happy."

"I know. Like I said, impressive. It goes against the grain to say so, but she could do worse."

I frowned. "I'm not going to think about that for approximately six and a half more years."

Edward laughed and then sighed. "Of course, it looks like he'll have some competition to worry about when the time comes."

My frown deepened. "I noticed. I'm grateful to Nahuel for today, but all the staring was a little weird. I don't care if she is the only half-vampire he's not related to."

"Oh, he wasn't staring at her—he was staring at you."

That's what it had seemed like . . . but that didn't make any sense. "Why would he do that?"

"Because you're alive," he said quietly.

"You lost me."

"All his life," he explained, "—and he's fifty years older than I am—"

"Decrepit," I interjected.

He ignored me. "He's always thought of himself as an evil creation, a murderer by nature. His sisters all killed their mothers as well, but they thought nothing of it. Joham raised them to think of the humans as animals, while they were gods. But Nahuel was taught by Huilen, and Huilen loved her sister more than anyone else. It shaped his whole perspective. And, in some ways, he truly hated himself."

"That's so sad," I murmured.

"And then he saw the three of us—and realized for the first time that just because he is half immortal, it doesn't mean he is inherently evil. He looks at me and sees . . . what his father should have been."

"You *are* fairly ideal in every way," I agreed.

He snorted and then was serious again. "He looks at you and sees the life his mother should have had."

"Poor Nahuel," I murmured, and then sighed because I knew I would never be able to think badly of him after this, no matter how uncomfortable his stare made me.

"Don't be sad for him. He's happy now. Today, he's finally begun to forgive himself."

I smiled for Nahuel's happiness and then thought that today belonged to happiness. Though Irina's sacrifice was a dark shadow against the white light, keeping the moment from perfection, the joy was impossible to deny. The life I'd fought for was safe again. My family was reunited. My daughter had a beautiful future stretching out endlessly in front of her. Tomorrow I would go see my father; he would see that the fear in my eyes had been replaced with joy, and he would be happy, too. Suddenly, I was sure that I wouldn't find him there alone. I hadn't been as observant as I might have been in the last few weeks, but in this moment it was like I'd known all along. Sue would be with Charlie—the werewolves' mom with the vampire's dad—and he wouldn't be alone anymore. I smiled widely at this new insight.

But most significant in this tidal wave of happiness was the surest fact of all: I was with Edward. Forever.

Not that I'd want to repeat the last several weeks, but I had to admit they'd made me appreciate what I had more than ever.

The cottage was a place of perfect peace in the silver-blue night. We carried Nessie to her bed and gently tucked her in. She smiled as she slept.

I took Aro's gift from around my neck and tossed it lightly into the corner of her room. She could play with it if she wished; she liked sparkly things.

Edward and I walked slowly to our room, swinging our arms between us.

"A night for celebrations," he murmured, and he put his hand under my chin to lift my lips to his.

"Wait," I hesitated, pulling away.

He looked at me in confusion. As a general rule, I didn't pull away. Okay, it was more than a general rule. This was a first.

"I want to try something," I informed him, smiling slightly at his bewildered expression.

I put my hands on both sides of his face and closed my eyes in concentration.

I hadn't done very well with this when Zafrina had tried to teach me before, but I knew my shield better now. I understood the part that fought against separation from me, the automatic instinct to preserve self above all else.

It still wasn't anywhere near as easy as shielding other

people along with myself. I felt the elastic recoil again as my shield fought to protect me. I had to strain to push it entirely away from me; it took all of my focus.

"Bella!" Edward whispered in shock.

I knew it was working then, so I concentrated even harder, dredging up the specific memories I'd saved for this moment, letting them flood my mind, and hopefully his as well.

Some of the memories were not clear—dim human memories, seen through weak eyes and heard through weak ears: the first time I'd seen his face . . . the way it felt when he'd held me in the meadow . . . the sound of his voice through the darkness of my faltering consciousness when he'd saved me from James . . . his face as he waited under a canopy of flowers to marry me . . . every precious moment from the island . . . his cold hands touching our baby through my skin . . .

And the sharp memories, perfectly recalled: his face when I'd opened my eyes to my new life, to the endless dawn of immortality . . . that first kiss . . . that first night . . .

His lips, suddenly fierce against mine, broke my concentration.

With a gasp, I lost my grip on the struggling weight I was holding away from myself. It snapped back like stressed elastic, protecting my thoughts once again.

"Oops, lost it!" I sighed.

"I *heard* you," he breathed. "How? How did you do that?"

"Zafrina's idea. We practiced with it a few times."

He was dazed. He blinked twice and shook his head.

"Now you know," I said lightly, and shrugged. "No one's ever loved anyone as much as I love you."

"You're almost right." He smiled, his eyes still a little wider than usual. "I know of just one exception."

"Liar."

He started to kiss me again, but then stopped abruptly.

"Can you do it again?" he wondered.

I grimaced. "It's very difficult."

He waited, his expression eager.

"I can't keep it up if I'm even the slightest bit distracted," I warned him.

"I'll be good," he promised.

I pursed my lips, my eyes narrowing. Then I smiled.

I pressed my hands to his face again, hefted the shield right out of my mind, and then started in where I'd left off—with the crystal-clear memory of the first night of my new life . . . lingering on the details.

I laughed breathlessly when his urgent kiss interrupted my efforts again.

"Damn it," he growled, kissing hungrily down the edge of my jaw.

"We have plenty of time to work on it," I reminded him.

"Forever and forever and forever," he murmured.

"That sounds exactly right to me."

And then we continued blissfully into this small but perfect piece of our forever.

the end

VAMPIRE INDEX

Alphabetically by coven

⤛ ⤜

*   vampire possesses a quantifiable supernatural talent
   —   bonded pair (oldest listed first)
~~struck~~   deceased before beginning of this novel

THE AMAZON COVEN
Kachiri
Senna
Zafrina*

THE DENALI COVEN
Eleazar* – Carmen
Irina – ~~Laurent~~
Kate*
~~Sasha~~
Tanya
~~Vasilii~~

THE EGYPTIAN COVEN
Amun – Kebi
Benjamin* – Tia

THE IRISH COVEN
Maggie*
Siobhan* – Liam

THE OLYMPIC COVEN
Carlisle – Esme
Edward* – Bella*
Jasper* – Alice*
Renesmee*
Rosalie – Emmett

THE ROMANIAN COVEN
Stefan
Vladimir

THE VOLTURI COVEN
Aro* – Sulpicia
Caius – Athenodora
Marcus* – ~~Didyme~~*

THE VOLTURI GUARD (PARTIAL)
Alec*
Chelsea* – Afton*
Corin*
Demetri*
Felix
Heidi*
Jane*
Renata*
Santiago

THE AMERICAN NOMADS (PARTIAL)
Garrett
~~James~~* – ~~Victoria~~*
Mary
Peter – Charlotte
Randall

THE EUROPEAN NOMADS (PARTIAL)
Alistair*
Charles* – Makenna

Acknowledgments

✦ ✦

As always, an ocean of thanks to:

My awesome family, for all their incomparable love and support.

My talented and hawt publicist, Elizabeth Eulberg,
for creating STEPHENIE MEYER out of the raw clay
that was once just a mousy Steph.

The whole team at Little, Brown Books for Young Readers
for five years of enthusiasm, faith, support, and incredibly hard work.

All the amazing site creators and administrators in the Twilight Saga
online fandom; you people astound me with your coolness.

My brilliant, beautiful fans, with your unparalleled good taste in books,
music, and movies, for continuing to love me more than I deserve.

The bookstores who have made this series a hit
with their recommendations; all authors are indebted to you
for your love of and passion for literature.

The many bands and musicians that keep me motivated;
did I mention Muse already? I did? Too bad.
Muse, Muse, Muse . . .

New gratitude to:

The best band-that-never-was: Nic and the Jens, featuring Shelly C.
(Nicole Driggs, Jennifer Hancock, Jennifer Longman, and Shelly
Colvin). Thanks for taking me under your collective wing, guys.
I would be a shut-in without you.

My long-distance pals and fonts of sanity,
Cool Meghan Hibbett and Kimberly "Shazzer" Suchy.

My peer support, Shannon Hale, for understanding *everything,*
and for feeding my love of zombie humor.

Makenna Jewell Lewis for the use of her name, and her mother,
Heather, for her support of the Arizona Ballet.

The new guys on my "writing inspiration" playlist:
Interpol, Motion City Soundtrack, and Spoon.

breaking dawn concert series

An edited interview with Stephenie Meyer and Tami Heide at Royce Hall, University of California, Los Angeles, on August 7, 2008

TAMI: You have talked about the difference between being a writer and a storyteller, and I really liked what you had to say about that, because you get compared to other writers and this and that. But a good story is a good story is a good story, and so I really appreciate your storytelling.

STEPHENIE: Oh, thank you. Yeah, I'm still perfecting that writing thing, but I've been doing the storytelling thing forever. And it's someplace I feel really comfortable.

TAMI: Well, then, we need to get started with some storytelling. Your fans have texted questions in to iClips.net from I think around the globe. I've got the questions here: "What are your intentions with the Twilight universe?"

STEPHENIE: At this point in time I'm not exactly sure what I'm going to do. I've been writing about vampires for a long time now, and there are a lot of other characters that I have waiting. They're just kind of sitting back there in the wings like, "Is it our turn yet?" I want to give them their turn. So that's something that we'll see. I don't know that I'm done with the Cullens' universe. We'll have to wait and see how that works out.

TAMI: "Can you tell us the difference between *Breaking Dawn* and *Forever Dawn*?"

STEPHENIE: I thought that was a really cool question, because I've seen some speculation on that, and the basic storyline: Bella and Edward get married, Renesmee, imprinting, and then the final scene with the Volturi—is very much the same as *Forever Dawn*. All of those things were in place with the story by fall of 2003. So for a really long time I knew where this was going and the little differences are things like, without *Eclipse* and *New Moon*, Jacob really hasn't developed as a character, so his development happens in *Forever Dawn*. And it's a little bit sketchier. You don't get to know him. Leah's not as big a part of the story in *Forever Dawn*, and I missed that. So it's just the little pieces of the characters that are really more fleshed out earlier in *Forever Dawn*, but other than that *Forever Dawn* and *Breaking Dawn* are very close.

TAMI: "How does Edward feel about himself now? Does he still see himself as a monster?"

STEPHENIE: I really love that question, because, no, there's this great evolution for him. He's kind of a pessimist. He's really always waiting for the worst thing to happen and then it doesn't. And I think his worst fear throughout this entire situation was that he would give in, he would change Bella and she would hate him for it, that she would regret what had happened. And that doesn't happen. And you can see at the end he's just changed so much. That even with this horrible impending doom he has faith in their future. He doesn't believe that anything can stop them now. And I was really happy to see that happiness in him and that evolution to where he's a believer now, and I really like that.

TAMI: "What is your favorite Bella-Edward moment?"

STEPHENIE: The last two pages of *Breaking Dawn*—that scene for me was the culmination of over two thousand pages of getting there. So really that for me was the moment. I mean, they finally see eye to eye and really know each other. And wow, that was really worth two thousand pages to get to.

TAMI: Actually I'm a little surprised because I was a big fan of that rush of new love. But that's great.

STEPHENIE: Well, you know, new love is really fantastic, but love realized is even better.

TAMI: "For *Twilight* and *New Moon*, you posted outtakes and extra stuff online. Will there be outtakes or extras for *Breaking Dawn*?"

STEPHENIE: Okay, so, as I've gotten a little bit better with the writing thing, I don't have to cut as much. The bad news is, like with *Eclipse*—there really aren't any outtakes. I did do a few extras there, and probably there's more coming. With *Breaking Dawn* there weren't a lot of major cuts or interesting cuts. Everything that went—it was a good thing. But I do think that I'll probably get around to posting little bits of *Forever Dawn* just so you can see how different it was. And some of the scenes when they take place in a totally different time and a different way but at the same time it's the same effect being achieved. So there's a possibility that there will be little pieces of *Forever Dawn* out there someday.

TAMI: "Why didn't we see Bella's pregnancy through Bella's point of view?"

STEPHENIE: All right, so, this is one of the differences from *Forever Dawn*. In *Forever Dawn* I wrote the whole pregnancy from Bella's point of view. It was actually quite a bit longer. And I notice as I'm reading through this that there is this significant lag time where Bella is stuck in the house and everything that's happening is on the outside. All the action is somewhere else. And there's all these things she's missing because she wouldn't know about them. And I always felt with that rough draft that it really needed an overhaul to make that section more interesting. And so when I started playing around with the idea of letting Jacob take over the narration, because he was the one that was seeing all the exciting stuff, it really grew on me. Then I started writing it, and it was such an awesome experience. All this time, all through *New Moon* and *Eclipse*, I'm hearing all of the snarky comments in Jacob's head that nobody else gets to hear because he's not saying them out loud. And finally, finally Jacob gets to be all snarky in his head and you get to hear it. I had a really great time with that and it really did move the story along a lot faster with a lot more action. So I think it was the right thing to do.

TAMI: Well, I'm glad we got to enjoy the snark because I love the snark. All right, next question: "Do the cover and title of *Breaking Dawn* have a meaning, and what part in the book goes with 'My Never'?" And then they say, "Love the book. Sorry it ended." So first part, do the cover and title have a meaning?

STEPHENIE: Right, so, the cover. For me this cover was extremely meaningful. I was really happy with how it turned out. This cover is not just for *Breaking Dawn*. This cover is for all four books. It shows Bella's progression from being the pawn to being the most powerful player on the board. And I was excited to show that visually. So that's why it looks like that.

So with the title, *Forever Dawn* was always way way way too cheesy, and I wanted a sense of disaster as well. This is a new awakening and a new day, but there's also a lot of problems inherent in it, so *Breaking Dawn* was the right way to go there.

Oh, there was one more part of that with "My Never," which you guys haven't heard yet because it's not out. This is one of the really cool things about touring with a rock star. You get to hear new stuff, and you're going to hear "My Never" a little bit later. And I did tell people in New York that I'd tell you which page in *Breaking Dawn* it applies to, and it's 345. It's in chapter seventeen, the four paragraphs beginning, "When I stared into her eyes, I saw everything that I'd been looking for in the park." So now you know.

TAMI: "Seeing Edward and the other Cullens through

Jacob's eyes was fascinating. If you could tell *Breaking Dawn* from another character's point of view, what character's point of view would it be?"

STEPHENIE: With Jacob's perspective, getting to see Edward, especially Jacob's evolution when he kind of has to finally admit that he was wrong about Edward all along—that was really fascinating to watch—how Bella and Edward look to someone else. I enjoyed that. But I do think that if you're looking at it from a storytelling perspective, really the only other option is Alice because she has another adventure that we don't get to see. But the book was getting really long. Sometimes you just have to draw the line at almost eight hundred pages.

TAMI: "Since Renesmee will live forever, does that mean Jacob will be immortal as well since the vampires are always going to be around?"

STEPHENIE: Actually once the whole trigger of vampires being around is over, Jacob can continue to be the same age as he is now as long as he keeps turning into a werewolf every now and then, which is really not very hard for him. So luckily for them, they're both set up for immortality, which is nice.

TAMI: "What was the phone conversation between Rosalie and Bella like?"

STEPHENIE: I actually talked to someone today who had a reaction to that that I never expected. She thought that

Rosalie and Bella were going to take off and run away, and it was kind of a cool interpretation—I can see that. But it went something like, Bella said to Rosalie, "Obviously you've heard," and Rosalie's like, "Yeah." "I don't have a lot of time," Bella says. Rosalie is very sullen at this point because here's Bella, getting what she wants again, and then Bella says, "You have to help me. And you have to help me keep this child alive." And that was when Rosalie's whole perspective on Bella changed, and they made a very fast agreement. And when Bella and Edward got home, Rosalie was ready. She took over from there. It was a very short conversation, but it changed a lot about their relationship.

TAMI: So is that what Bella said to get Rosalie on her side, "I need your help"? She reached out to her?

STEPHENIE: Yes, and she just told her the truth of the situation, and that was enough to change her mind.

TAMI: "Is Bella's 'before' car in *Breaking Dawn* a real car?"

STEPHENIE: It's not. This is the first non-real car in the Twilight series. There actually is a Mercedes Guard which is very close to the Guardian. I just wanted it one step more. I wanted more missile-proof armor. So it is a little bit different from the reality.

TAMI: Well, she'd need a safe car because she's a little accident-prone. "Why did Edward call Jacob 'son' in *Breaking Dawn*?"

STEPHENIE: That was a really odd writing moment for me. Every now and then, when I'm writing, one of my characters' voices is so loud with a line I'm not expecting and just takes me off guard. It happened in *New Moon* at the end. And in this moment I realized that Edward had completely accepted Renesmee's future and that Jake was going to be a part of it and there was no resentment. Everything was gone. Their happiness was in that moment the most important thing. And it's totally cheesy but when I heard that as I'm typing, I burst into tears. It was very odd. I do that every now and then. It scares people.

TAMI: I was going to say, I bet you've cried before.

STEPHENIE: I have.

TAMI: "What was going on between Billy and Charlie?"

STEPHENIE: Right. There was this whole romance thing going on between Charlie and Sue that Bella only barely caught the fringes of. You know Billy always kind of thought that, after a while, he'd move in there. Sue's a nice-looking woman and they have a lot in common. But she and Charlie just bonded. Billy I don't think is talking to him right now.

TAMI: So not a lot is going on then.

STEPHENIE: No. They're not speaking but I'm sure they'll get over it.

TAMI: I hope so. You would know. "Why did you have Bella envision having a son rather than a daughter?"

STEPHENIE: Renesmee was always Renesmee. She just is such a strong character to me that I always knew that was going to happen. But then I was getting into Bella's head and looking at it from her perspective. You know, she has a few issues with herself that she learned to get over. But at the time she can't imagine anything more beautiful than Edward. So it seemed to her that his son would be the most beautiful thing possible, and the most amazing thing, because she always sees him in that light. But you know Renesmee's even more than she had hoped for. So she was surprised, but happily.

TAMI: And through the series Bella's also been told, "You do not see yourself clearly." So maybe that's why she wouldn't envision a daughter as being the most beautiful. "What happened to Leah?"

STEPHENIE: Okay, Leah. So there's a lot of story there, and when we're not with Jacob we don't get her anymore. She is second-in-command of that pack, which is something that she's very pleased with, and she's so much happier than she was before, so she's in a better place. But if I were to go ahead with the series, in some other form in ten, twenty years, her story would definitely be more that I would want to follow because I'm interested in her future.

TAMI: "Has Gianna been turned into a vampire, and did she join the Volturi?"

STEPHENIE: I'm sorry to say, Gianna did not make the cut. Gianna's not with us anymore. That's one of the problems with working for the Volturi. It's a hazardous job.

TAMI: "You never explained why Heidi's eyes are purple."

STEPHENIE: Actually, I did. I pulled that one out, because it does say that the color of her eyes was something that might be achieved with blue contacts on the top of red irises. So that's why they're purple, because red and blue make purple.

TAMI: "What made you decide to do the pregnancy storyline? It seems kind of far from where the characters seem to be heading."

STEPHENIE: I have heard that, and let me tell you, in *New Moon* and *Eclipse*, with one exception, every plotline, every single moment of the story, is heading toward what happens in *Breaking Dawn*. I knew exactly where it was going, and all the hints are actually in there. You kind of have to dig for them, but everything that happens happens for this reason. The one exception was actually the back story of the Quileutes. I came up with an alternate ending—I kind of got a kick out of it. It was a little different. I don't think anyone else would have liked it. My mom hates it. But the Quileute back story indirectly leads into that alternate ending. So that's really the only part that wasn't focused on this ending and *Breaking Dawn*.

TAMI: "How early in the series did you decide that Jacob would imprint on Nessie?"

STEPHENIE: That's another one—those kind of fit together. That was part of the story from the very beginning. With *Twilight*, I wrote without knowing what I was going to do. But as soon as I was finished, I wrote a couple of epilogues and I'm like, Okay, I want to live in this world for a little while longer. That was immediately part of what was going to happen. So it was always, always the future.

TAMI: "Have you seen the movie, and if so, are you happy with it?"

STEPHENIE: I am thrilled. The only problem was that I had to pack to come on tour and I could only watch it once and I was really really upset about that. If I had gone to the theater to see that, I would have turned around, gone outside, bought another ticket and gone back in, because I am so ready to watch it again.

TAMI: The next person asks, "I love that in the end Bella was the one protecting those she loved. Did you always know that Bella would end up being so strong?"

STEPHENIE: I knew that Bella was going to be the star at the end. That she was going to make the difference. That it was all going to be about the mental strength that she'd had all along. And over the past couple of years, when people are talking about Bella being this weak human who's just getting rescued again and again, it was a little bit frustrating because I knew that this is all part of one big story arc, and each of these books is just a piece of the fabric and you can't really cut them apart. And Bella was going to end up totally kicking butt and it kind of was frustrating that I couldn't say that.

TAMI: Cause it's like, no, it's just gonna happen.

STEPHENIE: It's gonna happen. You've got to let her completely develop.

TAMI: We've come to the last question. "Do you feel sad that Bella's perspective is over now?"

STEPHENIE: Not yet. I'm not feeling sad yet. It's all so funny and weird to have created this world and live in it so much and to think about it being over. I don't know if that's ever really going to sink in and what I'll do when it does. So I don't know yet.

TAMI: Well, I think like you sort of said, it's a continuum, and this fabric can weave in and out. So it doesn't really ever end. But thank you so much, Stephenie.

STEPHENIE: Thank you.

breaking dawn concert series
Songbook

Songs performed by Blue October's Justin Furstenfeld at the
Nokia Center in New York City, on August 1, 2008

"BALANCE BEAM"
FEATURED ON THE ALBUM
CONSENT TO TREATMENT BY BLUE OCTOBER

I haven't been quite the same
So sure the story of my life would never change
In a bright eyed way
Rinsed out the soap in my eyes and wrote a song that I'm about to sing
It's about a girl that I hardly even know
It's not another love song
Just a list of things that I should know
Every man should know that...

One: You've got to take it kind of slowly
Two: You've got to hurry up and make your move
Three: You've got to tell her that she's pretty
Four: You've got to be the perfect gentleman
When you shake the walls, you've got to make 'em bend
Yeah, you've got to show her that she's the balance beam
And I keep falling all around her fairy tale.

We took a walk in the rain
My suggestion, she requested
The park nearby to cast the shade
Stay cool but I'm giddy like a schoolboy

You've got to handle with care, this is not a toy
Gradually we touched
Although our clothes were wet
We sat and smiled
I'd never thought I'd smile so much
The first kiss always says the most

One: You've got to take it kind of slowly
Two: You've got to hurry up and make your move
Three: You've got to tell her that she's pretty
Four: You've got to be the perfect gentleman
When you shake the walls, you've got to make 'em bend
Yeah, you've got to show her that she's the balance beam
And I keep falling all around her fairy tale.

Everyone should know that

One: You've got to take it kind of slowly
Two: You've got to hurry up and make your move
Three: You've got to tell her that she's pretty
Four: You've got to be the perfect gentleman
When you shake the walls, you've got to make 'em bend
Yeah, you've got to show her that she's pretty
She's so pretty
You're the balance beam
And I keep falling all around this fairy tale
OO this fairy tale OO this fairy tale
Some kind of fairy tale. Some kind of fairy tale.

Everyone should know that.

"UGLY SIDE"

FEATURED ON THE ALBUM
HISTORY FOR SALE BY BLUE OCTOBER

I must have sneezed
On knees I freeze
I mean, I just choked up
But somehow I slept
I dream, I mean
I dreamt of nothing

I'm able to breathe
A sweet relief
Now that you're here for me
A northern degree
Dove into me
Now I'm recovering

I only want you to see
My favorite part of me,
And not my ugly side
Not my ugly side

So hook up a C.B. wave
A way for conversation flow
I'm shown to your cage, to wage this rage
Don't let me go

A kick and a scream
Is all that seems to mean a lot, thus far
Yeah, I won't let you on my stage, my page
You can't know, but you have to know

That I only want you to see
My favorite part of me
And not my ugly side
And not my ugly side

So calm...you're so calm
And now it's dark
I look for you to light my heart
I'm between the moon and where you are
I know I can't be far

"BLUE SKIES"

FEATURED ON THE ALBUM
APPROACHING NORMAL BY BLUE OCTOBER

I bend to both knees
raise my hands up to the sky forgive me.
Is something out there
far beyond the clouds?
I'm asking help me,
help me to see the world
through baby eyes
and hold them closely.
I need a fresh start
on this rollercoaster made for coasting.
It's time to wake up,
time to make up,
time to shake these memories.
It's time to leave the past in the past,
lace up a new set of shoestrings.
I want the world to know
I got your back
through the up and down see
so we can sit together
side by side through amazing

Blue skies.
Calling on blue skies.
Don't take them away boys.
Don't take them away.
Cause I'll never stop, loving mine

I've broken every bone
and fought through
what felt never ending.
I thought my head was made of sadness,
my heart is mending.
I scream at sunsets
give applause to
what I can't control
then somehow laugh
at how the moon divides an ocean's soul.
I wanna be that ocean.
I wanna shine like that.
I wanna smile so big
my daughter jumps into my lap.
I wanna tell her daddy's fine
and always plans to be
then hold her in my arms
and this is what we'll always see.

Blue skies.
Calling on blue skies.
Don't take them away boys.
Don't take them away.
Cause I'll never stop, loving mine

Blue skies.
Calling on blue skies.
Don't take them away boys.
Don't take them away.
Cause I'll never stop…

So when I'm gone
I won't go screaming in the end.
I'll give you everything
my life amounts to so raise this
life up with me and baby
let's go dancing

Blue skies.
Calling on blue skies.
Don't take them away boys.
Don't take them away.

"HATE ME"

FEATURED ON THE ALBUM
FOILED BY BLUE OCTOBER

I have to block out thoughts of you
so I don't lose my head
They crawl in like a cockroach
leaving babies in my bed

Dropping little reels of tape
to remind me that I'm alone
Playing movies in my head
They do not feel like home

There's a burning in my pride
a nervous bleeding in my brain
An ounce of peace is all I want for you
will you never call again

And will you never say that you loved me
just to put it in my face
And will you never try to reach me
it is I that wanted space

Hate me today
Hate me tomorrow
Hate me for all the things I didn't do for you

Hate me in ways
Ways hard to swallow
Hate me so you can finally see what's good for you

I'm sober now for three whole months
It's one accomplishment that you helped me with
The one thing that always tore us apart is the one thing I won't
touch again

In my sick way I want to thank you
for holding my head up late at night
While I was busy waging wars on myself
you were trying to stop the fight
You never doubted my warped opinions
on things like suicidal hate
You made me compliment myself
when it was way too hard to take

So I'll drive so far away
That I never cross your mind
And do whatever it takes in your heart
to leave me behind

Hate me today
Hate me tomorrow
Hate me for all the things I didn't do for you

Hate me in ways
Ways hard to swallow
Hate me so you can finally see what's good for you

And with a sad heart I say bye to you and wave
Now I'm kicking shadows on the street for every mistake that I
had made

And like a baby boy I never was a man
Until I saw your blue eyes cry and I held your face in my hand

And then I fell down yelling make it go away
Just make her smile come back and shine just like it used to be
And then she whispered how can you do this to me

Hate me today
Hate me tomorrow
Hate me for all the things I didn't do for you

Hate me in ways
Ways hard to swallow
Hate me so you can finally see what's good for you for you for you…
This is all for you

"OVERWEIGHT" EXCERPT

FEATURED ON THE ALBUM
FOILED BY BLUE OCTOBER

I've grown up, I owned up do you remember me?
I showed up and so what if I'm the used to be
I'm here to tell you that I'm sorry I was sorry
But I'm happy that you're happy this is no longer about me
Trade roles, switch sides for your beautiful eyes
Let him be there through your beautiful cries
Let him hold you up so you can touch all four of your skies
And live your life without the pain of goodbyes
Goodbye

"MY NEVER"

FEATURED ON THE ALBUM
APPROACHING NORMAL BY BLUE OCTOBER

Will you think of me...in time?
It's never my luck
so nevermind...

I wanna say your name
but the pain starts again.
It's never my luck
so nevermind...

I had a dream that you were with me
it wasn't my fault.
You rolled me over,
flipped me over like a summersault.
That doesn't happen to me.
I've never been here before.
I saw forever in my never
and I stood outside her heaven.

Will you wait for me...in time?
It's never my luck
so nevermind...
I've lost a lot of what I don't expect to ever return.
I tend to push them till the pushing
has turned from hurt into burn.
I always take them to that place
I thought they wanted to go
then end up dancing round.
This clown commands applause at his show.

I had a dream that you were with me
it wasn't my fault.
You rolled me over,
flipped me over, a summersault.
That doesn't happen to me.
I've never been here before.
I saw forever in my never
and I stood outside her heaven.
Heaven.

I can only dream of you
and sleep and I'd never see sunlight again.
I can try to be with you
but somehow I'll end up just losing a friend.
I can only reach for you, relate to you.
I'm losing my friend.
Where did she go? Where?

I had a dream that you were with me
it wasn't my fault.
You rolled me over,
flipped me over, a summersault.
That doesn't happen to me.
I've never been here before.
I saw forever in my never
and I stood outside her...heaven.

Would you let me into your heaven?
I wanna live inside your heaven

"SOUND OF PULLING HEAVEN DOWN"

FEATURED ON THE ALBUM
FOILED BY BLUE OCTOBER

Somewhere far away from here
I saw stars, stars that I could reach
It was a midnight silent twilight
that fell down…beyond the ocean beach

I assemble all the sand that cover wedding beaches
to build a castle so your mom would have a place to stay
Behind the waterslide and down the hill where heaven
reaches land and time is left to float away

So rest assured I have the key to every opening
to every wishing well that's deep enough to dream
I want to show you just how fascinating kissing is
when earth collides with all the space between

I'm reaching farther than I ever have before
leaving all who broke your heart upon the shore
I may be some sort of crazy
We may be some sort of crazy
but I swear on everything I have and more

So never look behind you spooky people bring you down
the world is ending…but there's a party by the bay
I'll wear my suit and tie we're eye to eye and toasting to
the way you put that smile upon my face

Fill up the air balloon and ride with me
when hell is jealous of the rain
Make love like time and space is ending while befriending
fates alluring way of putting us to shame

I'm reaching farther than I ever have before
Leaving all who broke your heart upon the shore
I may be some sort of crazy
We may be some sort of crazy
but I swear on everything I have and more...

That you make the sound of pulling heaven down
You brought the rain's romantic pour
You make the sound...you make the sound
of pulling heaven down

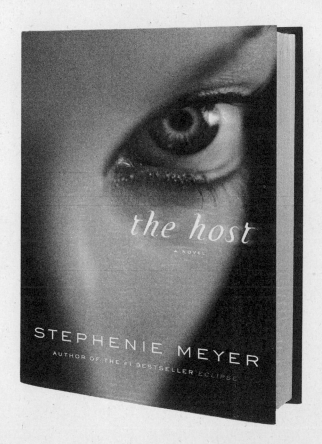